"TROUBLE! AMBUSH! SAAM AND NAKUM ARE TRYING TO FIGHT FREE!"

Nakum? Ambushed? Impossible for him and Saam to fall into a trap! But there was no time to think it through. Doyce pushed Khar flat against the platform and kicked Lokka into a gallop, swinging her sword clear of her saddle scabbard.

It seemed like only a moment passed before she spied the clash ahead, the welter of bodies dim in the falling twilight, some mounted, some afoot. An enraged ghatt's scream punctured the air. N'oor, she thought.

Straining to pick out friends, she glimpsed a raised arm, and saw Khar slash and connect. A shadowy figure grabbed for Lokka's bridle, and the mare screamed and reared, pawing through a press of bodies gathered by a broad tree overhanging the road.

Khar rasped and growled. **"Above!"** The weight crushed, a knee slamming between Doyce's shoulder blades, and Khar eeled free as Doyce crumpled against the pommel platform and was dragged from the saddle by grasping hands. . . .

Be sure to read all three novels in this
magnificent new DAW fantasy series
from
GAYLE GREENO

THE GHATTI'S TALE:
FINDERS-SEEKERS (Book One)
MINDSPEAKERS' CALL (Book Two)
EXILES' RETURN (Book Three)

Mind-Speakers' Call

Book Two of The Ghatti's Tale

Gayle Greeno

DAW BOOKS, INC.
DONALD A. WOLLHEIM, FOUNDER
375 Hudson Street. New York, NY 10014

**ELIZABETH R. WOLLHEIM
SHEILA E. GILBERT
PUBLISHERS**

First Printing, May 1994
5 6 7 8 9

DAW TRADEMARK REGISTERED
U.S. PAT. OFF. AND FOREIGN COUNTRIES
—MARCA REGISTRADA
HECHO EN U.S.A.

Printed in the U. S. A.

Writing a trilogy is a daunting—and long term—task. I would never have progressed as far as I have (midway) without the caring support of the following people: Betty Anne Crawford, who said "Of course you can!" and generously read an embryonic Book One; Sherri Zolt and Marilyn Abel, who kept the faith for over seven years; the "geographic" cheerleaders: Linda Pettit (Maine), Susan C. Wofford and Betty Devereux (Colorado), Ben and Marge Bronstein (Texas), and Mary Jane Hahn (upstate New York); the "home team": Beth Eller, Laura Shatzkin, and Stala Georgiades; the "last" NAL Education Department: Victoria Friedman, Tom Flynn, Joe Tura, Maria Barbieri, and Elizabeth Halpern; my agents Sue Herner and Sue Yuen (moral support par excellence); and of course, Sheila Gilbert, a superlatively sensitive editor who reads rather slowly but always thoroughly.

My thanks and my love to all of you.

"He telleth the number of the stars:
and calleth them all by their names."
                        —1662 Prayer Book, 147:1

✤

PART ONE

✤

The door slammed hard, heavy oak planking shuddering against the frame, lead edging of the stained-glass diamond panels buzzing as the glass vibrated under the impact. Even the latch protested, metal rattling against metal in the lock plate.

A large cat, tiger-striped in black and gray-brown with white chest and feet, rushed down the stairs, all dignity abandoned as she launched herself toward the landing, flinging herself over the last three stairs, twisting in midair to angle toward the door. A powerful thrust of hind leg muscles catapulted her into the center of the room and she alighted on a throw rug, gaily patterned with deep burgundy and royal blue swirls. The rug took off across the highly polished floor and the cat's ears tilted back, a look of disgust on her face as she and the carpet skidded like a sledding child on a snowy slope. She flexed her claws, sank them deep into the pile to hold her place, refusing to be spun off. Besides, the rug was gliding in the direction she wished to go—the door.

As the rug lost momentum, she gathered herself to resume her flight, a disdainful kick tossing the carpet behind her. She raced toward the door, stretched on hind legs and desperately began to work the knob. She was a large cat, far larger than average, and the knob was within easy reach, still vibrating faintly from the recent abusive slamming. She could feel the vibrations, hear the now nearly-silent chime of metal. Working at the knob, trying to grasp it with her paws, claws extended, she coaxed and cajoled the heavy cast-iron knob, embossed with a floral-wreath pattern worn and blurred from hard use. The knob refused to budge, so she turned her attention to the latch mechanism itself, pressing against the plate, letting it spring back, head cocked for the telltale click, waiting to see if it would spring free. But it was no use, and the giant cat suddenly sat, dismay clear in her amber eyes. She sat and stared as if sheer willpower alone could open the door, then·sprang toward a bow window indented in the wall and surrounded on three sides by leaded lozenges of glass, some clear, some of a thicker distorted glass, still lovely in its imperfections, and a few, scattered panels tinted pale amethyst or aquamarine. She leaped up and began to bat at the window, balancing on the window seat's cushioned backrest to reach the latching handle.

As she did so, she caught a glimpse of movement outside, the swirl of a short purple cloak, the flash of its red lining disappearing around the corner of the stable. She stared hard at the wall and its skirting of melting, dirty snow, a fresh line of earth edging between building and snow, warming in the reflected heat from the whitewashed walls, tiny shards of new green blind-fingering through the soil. Nothing else moved.

"Gone, gone," the cat moaned in dismay and gave the latch a final, vicious slap, claws screeching across the glass. It held firm. Now what could she do? Doyce was gone, out of her reach, who knew where? The thought galled, left her treading down the cushions, striving for yet another glimpse of the woman who meant everything to her, everything and nothing for now since the woman refused to let her enter her thoughts, refused the mindlink that let them share their innermost feelings, the intimacy that Khar so desperately, desolately missed. How much longer could she stand being so near, yet so far from the mindsharing?

With a distracted lick at her paw, Khar rubbed her ear and tried to marshal her thoughts. The stables—Lokka? If Doyce planned on riding the little sorrel mare, Khar could at least keep track of her movements through Lokka. She concentrated hard and touched the mare's mind as she dozed in her stall, startled her awake with a clatter of hooves as Khar's mindvoice tickled her. But Lokka's worried response offered no reassurance. Doyce had not entered the stables; Lokka hadn't even realized she was nearby. Her frustrated stamping echoed through the mindlink. Lokka felt as anxious and as alone as Khar, equally bereft for all that she was a mere horse and not one of the ghatti, giant cats gifted with the power of mindspeech.

With a sigh and a flicker of whiskers, the ghatta set herself to think, to be calm. How to get out? The obvious way to attract attention to herself and her plight was to mind-speak Damaris, but the thought drew her up short in dismay at how far she'd nearly fallen, how desperate she'd become. A ghatt or ghatta did not use mindspeech except with his or her Bondmate or other Seeker Veritas members; it was impolite, rude, a violation of the mind of an "other" to hold converse with an outsider. A violation of the code she held sacred. Not that Damaris wouldn't understand, being the mother of a Seeker, Jenret Wycherley. And then the most fleeting of ghatti smiles crossed her face as she let out a yowl, beginning a complaint that ranged up and down the scale and back again, a plaint that said everything to anyone who knew those pleasant but lesser beings called cats. A plaint that announced, "Hello, hello, I am on the wrong side of the door and I desperately wish to be on the other side. If I am not released soon, I shall expire from misery." She sprang into the middle of the floor and paraded in a circle, tail lashing as she sang her song of woe.

A large-boned man clad in a flowing topaz velour over-robe hurried into the room, uncertainty and confusion plain on his bland face. Though perhaps sixty, his face was as unlined and open as a child's, the faded blue eyes otherworldly and innocent, empty of coherent thought. With the cautious, stiff gait of an infant just learning to walk, he tottered forward and ran a few steps to regain his balance, only to hit the same throw rug that Khar had coasted across the room. His arms spun in circles as he sought his balance, but a smile of wonder crossed his face, brightening his eyes. Somehow he managed to retain his footing and stepped carefully off the rug toward the ghatta.

Mortified, Khar paced forward to greet him, giving him his due as master of the house, Damaris's husband and Jenret's father. She craned her head to meet the uncertain, seeking hand, palm down, fingers splayed. If she had known, had had any idea, she chided herself, that Jadrian Wycherley wandered free and unattended downstairs, she would never, *never* have yowled like that. She raised her head higher, meeting the seeking hand and the tentative palm stroke, curious at the warmth and sleek softness of the furred head.

Jadrian Wycherley reigned as titular master of the house, but he had no mind, had lacked a cognizant brain for years, ever since he tried to do what he believed was right, to rid his house of the taint of a Gleaner, a mindstealer. And the Gleaner had been his elder son, Jared. He had succeeded in killing the boy, but not before his mind had been swept clean and empty, blank as a slate on which no chalk would ever scrawl another thought.

"Mmwer?" he queried, fingers rough about the ghatta ear that wore the garnet rose earring at its tip. "Mmwa, mmwa, wha?" he asked. "Puur Khar?"

She sprang on the window seat and swatted at the panes, then dashed back to twine around his ankles, careful not to set him off balance. She hated herself for doing this to him, to Damaris, but she would follow Doyce no matter what. He reached again, awkward fingers tweaking the gold hoop in her left ear, and she held back a hiss of annoyance, struck at his hand with sharp impatience but not a claw unsheathed, and dashed toward the door. She gazed back, trying to judge his reaction, his comprehension of her command. **"Out, out!"** she mindspoke, almost screaming her thoughts, though she knew he wouldn't understand. **"Jadrian, you lackwit, let me out! Doyce is out there! My Doyce!"** If she did not cry, it was only because the ghatti lacked the capacity.

Damaris Wycherley swept into the room, keys jangling at her waist, apron flecked with flour. Supervising always seemed to lure her into helping, but the fresh dough had been irresistible, especially compared to the other duties awaiting her. And now this ruckus. She shook her head and pressed both hands to weary temples, pushed wisps of dark hair spun with silver away from her face and assessed the situation at a glance. She stopped long enough to give her husband a consoling pat as he held his hand to his lips, whimpering, and Khar shuddered with guilt; apparently at least one claw hadn't been sheathed.

"Hush, Jadrian, hush, love, we'll fix it, won't we?" she soothed as she advanced toward the ghatta and stooped to look her in the eyes. "Khar, whatever possessed you?" And stopped short. "Khar, did Doyce go out?"

The ghatta bowed to hide her shame and threw herself at the door, stretched up against its smooth oak planking, staring yearningly over her shoulder.

"Oh, Lady save us, and today of all days! Khar, go find her, bring her back if you can. You know Jenret and the others are due today. She's not supposed to be out alone!"

The ghatta made a moue of embarrassment and acknowledgment.

"I know, I know. She can still outwit us if she puts her mind to it. I suppose it should be a good sign, but I don't like it, no more than you do." She reached for the doorknob, tried it once, then wiped floury palms on her apron and turned it with both hands. "Quick, out you go. Find her and bring her back. Or if you can't, don't fret, just stay with her. Rawn will be here soon with Jenret. Still, it would be nice to have her back of her own volition."

Khar paused long enough to brush against Damaris's skirts in silent thanks.

The carriage rested on the eastern branch of the crossroads, outer wheels scraping against the receding snowbank; mud spattered the coach sides, partially obscuring the emblem on the door—a dark frame outlining a lighter gray rectangle with a jagged, green lightning bolt of a line running through it. Thick mud, the beginnings of the spring thaw, plopped from the wheel spokes, landing with a sharp protest as if angry at its reunion with the sea of mud spanning the road. The coachman leaned over, spoke into the window. "Best I should cover the horses if we're to wait much longer. We set a brisk pace out of the capital as ye asked, and they're all steamed up. Going on won't hurt them, but the waiting will—just seems like spring on account a what we had before."

At a muffled affirmative from inside he looped the reins around the brake handle and began to clamber down, hindered by the bundle of blankets under his arm. A stoutish woman heaved herself half out the window, craning to see down the northern crossroad. She gave a whoop of relief, shouted a "hello" that she knew couldn't be heard, and tried to extract herself from the window, her tabard snagging on the rolled leather window shade. "I told you she'd join us. If she said 'wait,' we wait, because Mahafny keeps her word." Hands struggled to untangle her, pull her back inside the carriage. She couldn't help grinning in relief at what she'd seen, her eyes suspiciously watery.

The brick red ghatt curled beside her on the seat yawned in mock reproach. **"Told you she'd make it. I'd think you**

didn't believe me if I didn't know that you just don't listen sometimes."

She straightened her grin into an expression of calm forbearance as she tugged her tabard into place, straightened the twisted sash. *"I know,"* she mindspoke. *"You're right, as usual. But I have had a few things on my mind lately, not to mention being worried about Mahafny and what she knows."*

"But you'd rather know the truth, wouldn't you?"

Merry blue eyes turned serious and somber. *"That I would, but I wish Mahafny didn't have to be the one to find the answers. You know people don't always distinguish between the message and the messenger. She* has *to find the answers, and if I have to answer alone, I don't think I can handle it. I wasn't exactly forthcoming with the High Conciliators because I hoped Mahafny would be there in time. Oh, I know enough—too much—but not everything Mahafny knows, that she's found out since I last saw her."*

But her inner fears did nothing to detract from her capable, confident exterior, the veneer developed from years holding the highest rank of Seeker General of the Seekers Veritas. Swan gave a nod to the middle-aged man sitting across from her, assessing him as she would a stranger, because, despite their close contact over the last few octants, in many ways he still felt a stranger to her. But then power—his, not hers—isolated the holder. At first glance he appeared nondescript in a country-cut suit of moderate quality, unofficial-looking compared to the silent young man sitting beside him and wearing a governmental uniform topped by the Seeker Veritas dress tabard. Yet despite his punctilious turnout, the younger man almost blended into the upholstery, as if his own thoughts and concerns were meaningless when weighed against the concerns of the person he served. The striped ghatta tucked behind his legs seemed self-effacing as well, ready to meld into the woodwork if necessary.

The sounds of two horses picking their way through the mud came closer, followed by the coachman's soothing sounds as he took their reins, allowing a rider to dismount. The carriage door swung open, and a mud-spattered, angular yet elegant woman grasped the door frame's leather grip straps and heaved herself inward. Still half-crouched, she tried to turn and scrape the mud from her boots, muttering as she concentrated on the task.

The older man grasped her arm and tugged her fully inside, ignoring a response that sounded like a half-checked snappish remark at his literal high-handedness. "Can't be helped at this season." His tone was reasonable but did not bear trifling with. "As much inside as out. Nothing to do but wait till it dries and brush it off." He settled Mahafny in his vacated seat and stood hunched in the middle of the carriage. With a quick murmur the younger, uniformed man rose, gesturing toward his seat while he perched at the edge of the opposite bench, sharing the space with the brick red ghatt, who slitted his eyes and stretched his legs against the intrusion before reluctantly making room.

Swan Maclough, Seeker General, reached across and grasped her cousin's cold hands. She didn't want to say the words, didn't mean to say them, but couldn't contain herself. "You're late," she chided, "we were worried sick. And where's Harrap?"

The disengagement of hands was more gentle than might have been expected, especially given the tension etched on the other woman's face. "Van Beieven, I don't suppose you've any brandy on you?" she asked, chafing her hands together. But the younger man proffered a silver flask almost before she could finish the sentence. Swan knew it for a distraction, a ploy to gain time, but she held her peace, though her forehead knotted with a frown. "It's all right, cousin, truly." Mahafny's wry smile flashed above the flask. "Have you ever noticed that babies choose the most inopportune times to be born?"

"Just like spring lambing, eh?" A deep chuckle of appreciation came from the older man. "And in the most inaccessible location as well, I'll wager."

Mahafny Annendahl nodded, let her head recline against the cushions. "And Harrap is fine, except for a pressing need to refresh his soul by visiting the Bethel in the capital. He begs your pardon, Swan, and hopes it won't be seen as a dereliction of duty."

"Sometimes I don't know what I'm going to do with him," Swan muttered, trying to look disgusted.

"Why, cherish him, of course, for his uniqueness." Van Beieven still stood, cramped under the carriage's low roof, not bothering to take the vacated seat. "Still, enough chit-chat, now that we know you're both fine. We've much to discuss and little time before our dinner tonight. There'll be time afterward, but I'd like to nail down the basics now, if we might."

Mahafny Annendahl said nothing, but cocked her chin ever so slightly in the direction of the younger man, who saw the subtle gesture and reddened. "I . . . I think it might be easier, less crowded, if I were to ride Eumedico Annendahl's horse . . . if she wouldn't mind, that is." The tiger ghatta, almost hidden in the shadows on the floor, gave a little mewl of dismay. "Oh, N'oor! I didn't forget . . . oh, dear. . . ." He spun back, abashed. "Sir, you wouldn't mind if N'oor rode along with you, would you?" he appealed.

As van Beieven started to say, "But, Aelbert, of course you and N'oor can stay," Mahafny interjected, "The ghatta can ride with you, she'll be happier that way." The Monitor made a little shrugging motion in Aelbert's direction as if to say the young man was welcome to stay or to go.

Looking as if she'd found the solution to a distasteful problem, Mahafny continued, "I brought Harrap's horse with me. He and Parm caught a wagon into the capital, said he'd spare the horse his weight in this mud. Obviously he has a pommel platform for Parm, so there's no reason that you and . . ." she pronounced the name with the discomfort she always felt in dealing with any of the ghatti, "N'oor can't ride in comfort. Together."

The exchange was made from carriage to horse, the young man scooping the ghatta into his arms so she wouldn't have to trudge through the mud, the others making themselves comfortable as van Beieven shouted instructions for the coachman to start. This time there was no preamble, no politeness to his comment. "Well?"

"Well what?" Mahafny took a final sip of brandy, screwed home the stopper. "You want to know. Well, I want to know as well. What have the High Conciliators decided?"

Van Beieven rubbed strong fingers along the sides of his skull, held them there tightly as if to anchor his thoughts.

Decided? He rubbed, small circular motions at his temples, overwhelmed by his problems, not wanting to put them in words for fear his rancor and anger at having to deal with the impossible would show. Patience! Even the eight apostle moons were allowed to wax and wane! Did she think *any* of this was easy? Hadn't the problems with Marchmont been tricky enough, convincing the High Conciliators that potentially damaging and dangerous as the situation was, no major retributive action should be taken yet? Well, at least he'd convinced them to table the motion to exact punitive damages from Marchmont—and the open-ended phrase "in whatever manner seems fitting" had left him with an ominous chill—and instead send a Special Envoy to explore the situation. And if it hadn't been for Aelbert, he doubted he'd have thought to suggest the compromise. Bless the young man for his quick head!

When they'd both ridden nearly to the border to Harleton in the dead of winter to interview Aaron Rossmeer about his sudden and unceremonious ejection from Marchmont, the poor Consul had been speaking gibberish, the result of a series of strokes suffered when he and his staff had tried to cross the border for home in a raging blizzard that left them wandering lost and helpless. Only luck had led them to stumble on a small Guardian outpost.

What little they'd learned about the surprise order to cut off diplomatic relations and depart immediately had come from Rossmeer's five staff members, especially his secretary Elkington, limping on a crutch to protect his frostbitten toes, his face patchy white and dead looking in spots from exposure to the cold. Now the poor man was trying to serve the Consul's physical needs as well as organize his papers. "They gave us the afternoon to pack and leave, even though they knew a blizzard was brewing." Elkington had blown on his fingers as if they were still cold. "Dark when we left, too, but we had no choice. Prince Maurice and some of his household guard escorted us out of town," Elkington had complained as he handed over the final reports. "The last report was never put on paper," he'd admitted. "After his last meeting with the Steward, Consul said he didn't trust having it written down, too sensitive."

Hoping against hope for a hint of what had gone wrong, they'd sat alone with Rossmeer, the right side of his mouth drooping, eyelid slack, whole side paralyzed, the final report locked within his mind by the cruel trick of the strokes. Rossmeer's eyes had lighted up when he'd seen N'oor, and he'd begun to babble. "Gotta ghatti!" he mumbled. "Gitty ghatti!" And then, "Constantly Willy!" Thrashing his left hand against the bedclothes, he'd tried again, angry at not being understood. "Will he ghatti!" he'd enunciated painfully and slumped back, energy spent, clutching the Monitor's hand as if to impress the importance of the words.

"Poor man. Whatever he's trying to say means something to him, if only we knew what it was, I suppose." Aelbert had wiped a thread of drool from the side of Rossmeer's mouth, curiously gentle and finicky. "I . . ." he'd hesitated, "I could go to Marchmont and try to determine what's happening. If that should meet with your approval, of course."

And it had, but he'd felt that Aelbert shouldn't bear all the responsibility, although he'd kept that to himself. The aide was always so good-natured about extra work, and sending him with some others, perhaps Seekers if Swan would agree, would free the young man from some of the burden, give him some companionship of his own kind. The Monitor felt guilty sometimes that Aelbert seemed to spend all his time with him, never seemed to socialize, have fun. But he'd been dutiful ever since he was lad.

So that, at least was settled, although Aelbert didn't yet know that he wasn't traveling alone—that was to be a surprise for him.

Well, he'd brought the High Conciliators around to his point of view on Marchmont after a tedious series of meetings and debates, and when the motion had been accepted, he'd asked for "New Business" with an inward sigh of relief. Had it only been four days ago?

A hand had shot up and he'd nodded his recognition. "Henry Waterston of Pennington Province requests permission to open debate on the matter of the Gleaners amongst us." The beginning was a pro forma identification for the Recorder, but the unexpected subject made the Monitor's jaw drop. He'd spent octs, octants, on private meetings with each High Conciliator, apprising him or her of the situation they'd found at the Hospice, had called *in camera* sessions for discussions with those who'd witnessed the situation firsthand—Seeker General Swan Maclough, Guardian Sergeant Balthazar Lamb—as well as with eumedicos who had any expertise in the problem, though not Mahafny Annendahl, for she had been spending all her time at the Research Hospice. He'd worked the hallways, the meeting rooms, generally pleaded and politicked to keep the subject off the main discussion floor. Good reason for that: the main discussion chamber was open to the public with galleries seating any who came and chose to listen. All citizens of Canderis had the right to hear for themselves what their High Conciliators and Monitor discussed, debated, and passed into law.

To his everlasting shame and shock, at least thirteen of the twenty-four High Conciliators had added their voices in support of Waterston. "Approve the debate." "Approved." "Approved."

He'd gaveled for order, gaveled again, had all he could do to maintain some semblance of control, and wondered if anarchy had broken out in the highest legislative chamber in the land. Desperate, he'd tried to damp the flames of outrageous rumor and rhetoric that had made him believe for the first time in spontaneous combustion that consumed every rational voice in its path even after all his painstaking efforts to avoid unreasoning panic and mayhem in the country he loved. And the galleries had been full, far fuller than he'd remembered from the morning session, a multitude of faces staring down at them, some perplexed, all too many fearful, a few grinning as broadly as if they watched a frenzied flock of hysterical, squawking guinea fowl.

Accusations and counteraccusations had been thrown in all directions until his head had spun. Tossed at anyone they'd thought an accusation might stick to if thrown hard and often enough. "Hundreds of them!" he'd heard one voice shout. "No, thousands at least!" a woman's voice had shrilled. "Why can't the eumedicos or the Seekers stop?. . ." "Quarantine them!" He'd pounded for order, pounded in vain, frustration making the veins in his temples bulge.

"Sergeants at arms!" he'd bellowed, hoping they stood close enough to hear and obey. There was no response, so he'd risen, gesturing wildly to catch their attention, and they'd swung into position in front of the dais. The crisp sound of drawn swords had a way of penetrating any din, the sharp rasp slicing through the clamor, causing frozen poses and open but silent mouths.

It was mass hysteria, mass frenzy, and even the High Conciliators, highest elected officials had been swept up in it, but then they began to take their seats shamefacedly, looking unsure as to what had happened.

One man had remained standing, patient, square-jawed face eminently sane looking. The Monitor had debated whether to recognize him or not. The man was new to his position, with perhaps only half a year's service, but the little the Monitor had seen of him he'd liked. "Yes, please." A chance, but he'd grasped at it, desperate.

"Darl Allgood of Wexler Province. I find myself a bit confused, overwhelmed." His voice had sounded good-humored but obviously concerned. "Thousands of Gleaners, you say?" He'd turned to the woman who had shrieked that statement. "Is it truly possible? Thousands of them? Should I look to the esteemed member on my right, look to my left, and assume that perhaps one of us must be a Gleaner? Are we truly knee-deep in them?" He'd leaned his weight against the top of his chair, studied his hands before glancing around again, eyes openly searching each and every person on the floor, the Monitor included. "Well, *are* you?" he looked leftward, then rightward, "Or *you?*" Some faces went stiff with embarrassment, but a ragged smattering of applause broke out on the floor, followed by a larger hand from the galleries.

Allgood had tilted his head to find the source of the sound, grinned. "Of course, everyone up there applauding is probably a Gleaner."

"Right-o!" a cheeky voice had shouted back.

"We've gotten pretty silly, haven't we? What's gotten into us all? We have a problem, but the problem's more us than it is the Gleaners. We can cope with the situation if we use our heads, figure out the dimensions of the problem, just as we did regarding Marchmont. This isn't how High Conciliators should determine what's best for Canderis, this know-nothing panicking. If we've Gleaners in Wexler Province, so be it. None of them have caused us problems. I move that this meeting be adjourned."

"Second the motion," had come from the High Conciliator from Morgaine Province, and the Monitor had slumped back into his seat, almost too shaken with relief to ask for a vote and to gavel the meeting closed.

He came back to the present, realized they were waiting for him to speak. "Did you think it was going to be easy to have them come to any consensus over what to do about the Gleaners?"

"Did you think it was going to be easy," she mimicked

him, "to determine how the Gleaners's powers work, if we can control them, what we can do with them, to them? Dear, sweet, blessed Lady, as Harrap would say," she half-exploded off the seat. "It all takes time, dammit, time, and that's the one thing we may not have! How much rumor and gossip and innuendo is out there, building, boiling, ready to blow the lid off the kettle? Is all of it negative, is any of it positive?"

"We're trying, Mahafny, we're trying," Swan pleaded, raising her hands to restrain her cousin. "The Seekers are being run ragged tracking down rumors, stamping them out, trying to keep things contained, under control. Every town has a tale—the story of a story told by a friend of a friend of my mother's uncle's cousin. In some places it's not too serious, it's being shrugged off. In other places . . ." her voice trailed away, then exploded in anger. "Do you know what nearly happened in Cheswick?" At the blank, guarded looks she launched into her report.

"We don't normally visit villages of Cheswick's size; they know full well where the Seek-points are and when the Seekers are scheduled on the circuit. But lately I've been sending the Seekers into towns and villages they don't normally visit, to reinforce their presence, make folk conscious of the fact that Seekers are available, that there is always truth." She made an imperious gesture toward the brandy flask, but never halted her recitation. Somehow holding the small silver flask conferred comfort.

"Bless the Lady that I ordered Parcellus Rudyard and Per'la to swing through Cheswick on their last circuit. He rode into the village square and discovered a man brandishing a butcher knife and chasing his mother-in-law around the village well. There must have been at least twenty other villagers there, watching, doing nothing, just muttering under their breath. And to top it off, the man had an iron kettle jammed so low over his head he could barely see where he was going, half-blind and half-drunk together, no less.

"When Parse managed to intervene—and that took drubbing the man's kettle helmet with his staff until it rang like the holy Bethel chimes at high noon—he discovered the man was convinced his mother-in-law was a Gleaner who'd been trying to steal his brain ever since he'd married her daughter. Well, Parse held a Seeking on the spot, with the villagers as witnesses, and he and Per'la proved the truth of the matter.

Gossip monger the woman might be, but no Gleaner." The Seeker General slowed for a moment, realized she had been twisting the flask's stopper on and off, shut it with a decisive twist. "And that damn kettle was jammed tight on the man's head—wouldn't come free for love nor money."

Van Beieven jammed the tip of his finger against his upper lip, but nodded in sympathy, refusing to meet Mahafny's eyes, now intent on the carriage roof. Without noticing their expressions, the Seeker General continued, bitter at the memory. "It took a blacksmith, the village midwife, a soap maker, plus a Seeker to free him, not to mention the comments and cautions of half the village.

"And if that weren't enough, Parse's love for puzzles and predicaments made him try the exact same stunt himself before he left town." Van Beieven now had his entire index finger pressed hard between his nose and lip, a tear seeping from his left eye. A muffled snort erupted from Mahafny before she fell dead silent. "It took ..." and despite herself Swan began to realize the absurdity of this part of the report. "It took ... at least the same number of helpers and the same tactics to free him." Half-dissolved with laughter, half-irritable, she kicked across the aisle at the man, now doubled over, holding his sides, and commanded his attention.

He managed to straighten, tears rolling down his face as he sputtered, "Sorry! By the Heaven's blest, I needed that, the relief. So little has been funny lately." He shook his head in mute apology.

"Yes, it's funny enough now. But the outcome could have been so different, so tragic—and I don't mean that damned kettle!" She straightened, the dead seriousness of command settling and firming her shoulders. "So savor that as one of the few times we may be able to find humor in the situation. Just remember, the only way either of you are buying any time is because of us, because of the Seekers Veritas, and our reputation for speaking the truth without fear or favor. But even we can push the truth just so far when even we don't know ... aren't sure.... Please, for the love of the Lady, have *either* of you come to any conclusions or decisions on what we are going to have to do about the hidden Gleaners in our midst?"

❧

Snow patches crunched icy and crystalline under her paw pads, prickly sharp, and Khar ignored the icy stabs, concentrating on the overpowering odor of spring, the rich patches of freshly-freed earth, the tang of tentative-reaching greenery, and the elusive yet pervasive scent of Doyce that she followed. Still, she was no tracker, and her ability to scent was not her strongest gift, not now.

Letting her mind clear, she reached out, standing stock-still, ignoring the discomfort of paws too long on moist snow. Whether Doyce would 'speak her or no, her brain pattern was etched deep with the ghatta, as familiar and reassuring as Khar's own thoughts. To mistake it or miss it would be tantamount to being struck senseless. She spared the time to soothe Lokka, sorry she'd needlessly worried the mare, and moved on, great amber eyes showing the faintest line of vertical black pupil, slitted against the sun's reflection on the snow.

She pressed around the stable corner, trying to pick the clearest, driest path, only to give up and plow ahead, disregarding the dampness, the mud clinging to her pads.

Still, the fact that Doyce had ventured out alone was something to wonder at. She'd left her voluntary prison a few times with the Erakwan lad Nakum when he and Saam came to visit, but that had been all. He had spent patience and arrows aplenty teaching her to cloud-shoot, an archery skill that involved lofting arrows far and high through the sky toward the distant target of a gaily colored rag affixed to a stake. The main contest was played against one's self and the elements, the errant breeze, the bright squintingness of the sun, the distortion of distance, not to mention the numbing necessity of holding oneself poised at full bow extension, ready to loose yet holding, holding for the perfect moment of centered stillness, a quietude within and without.

Had Doyce gone cloud-shooting alone? Khar wondered as she trotted along the bank of the brook that began in the high meadow and ran down through the pasturage and beyond the stable. A few panes of delicate ice-frost rimed some of the bank's deeper indentations, still water beyond the reach of the tumbling brook that flumed over rocks, sparkles of pale ice-green and blue, the lacy white of breaking caplets, the clear yellow-brown tint of deeper water reflecting a sunken trunk, haven for trout. Long, supple shoots of willow and poplar rattled gray and cold fingerlings but exhibited an explosion of yellow-green growth at tips and joints; a few fuzzed catkins peering out of reddening bud tips. A chickercap fluttered from branch to branch, twisting its head to watch from one eye and then the other, mocking with a saucy "chick-chipper-dee." Khar nearly lost herself in the smell of renewal, but it was not enough to override her mental awareness of Doyce somewhere ahead. The ghatta with the gray-brown bull's-eye stripings on her sides wove through the low-hanging willows, knowing she was right, feeling the pull of her Bondmate, seeing the puddled indentations where booted feet had walked not long before.

As if nature wished to reassure one of its own, a shaft of afternoon sunlight broke through the undergrowth, and Khar glimpsed what she'd so frantically sought. Sunlight reflected off a cap of brown, curly hair, tinged it with red fire in the light of the sun, glanced off the copper trim of the quiver, the copper and leather hand wrap of the unslung bow over her shoulder. With a tiny trill of relief, Khar quickened her pace, oblivious to the fact her precious white feet and white ruff were becoming damp and soggy, bedraggled with mud.

At last the woman broke for open ground, angling up and away from the brook toward the high meadows, where sheep and cows were grazed during summer. It was clear from the drag of her feet, her less-than-careful placement of steps, that she was tired, and the pallor of her face, dark shadows under her eyes standing out like smudges, showed she had been ill for some time. Anyone seeing the oval face would have noted the subtle honing of features that illness had accomplished, as if an artist had stripped away all superfluous detail to purposely accentuate the delicate strength of the long neck, the well-set cheekbones, the firm, narrow jaw. It was a face familiar yet unfamiliar to the ghatta, and the pain it set jangling inside her seemed almost an old friend. Doyce but not Doyce, not Doyce the Seeker Bondmate that Khar cleaved to as to no other, but the Doyce she had seen in Doyce's memories before, lost, afraid, alone. And how, Khar wailed to herself, could Doyce be alone when she had been gifted with Khar? But the Doyce she had Bonded with now refused to share her thoughts, and the ghatta would not, could not pry. Dared not, if the Bond were to remain intact and whole. She had sworn to wait, but it was so long, so hard.

Stripping off leathern mitts, the woman unslung her

quiver and rummaged in it for a shaft with a bright scarlet pennon anchored just below its fletching. She stuck the shaft into a tussock of dead grass, turned and marched off, quiver dangling from one hand as she counted paces across the meadow's broad flank. At a hundred paces she stopped to check, shook her head in negation and forced herself another fifty strides beyond. The scarlet flag bobbed and whipped in the breeze, standing straight out from the shaft, then dropping limp as the wind fell.

Belly low, Khar slunk closer, seeking the safety of a sheltered tumble of rocks piled near the stone retaining wall. Snow, wind, the expansion of winter ice had pried some of the stones free, and they had been stacked here to await repairs. She picked a sun-warmed one a bit lower than its mates and leaped on it, crouching low and wrapping her tail around her feet, her markings mingling with the rocks. Nothing to do now but watch and wait . . . and be near, whether Doyce realized it or not.

It took two tries to string the short, tough Erakwa bow, three-quarters the size of the standard, the length that stripling teens practiced with until they acquired the strength and expertise to draw a full-sized weapon. This one had been Nakum's; he had been gifted with the full-sized hunter's bow just two octants ago and had bequeathed his old one to Doyce to lure her outside her sickroom at the Wycherleys, to cajole her into momentarily concentrating on something, anything, beyond the terrible blankness of mind and spirit that had enveloped her over the past few octants. Khar wrinkled her nose and sneezed; thinking of the musky, smoky, but entirely pleasant smell of the Erakwan boy did that to her. Still, she liked him—more to the point, so did Saam, the steel-gray ghatt, Bondmate of Oriel Faltran, Doyce's friend and lover, now dead. Few ghatti found any pressing reason to outlive their Bondmates, and the few who did invariably returned to the wilds. First he had survived to honor his Bond-promise to protect Doyce and Khar, but later, without Nakum to give Saam a reason for staying, she knew it was unlikely that he would have remained amongst them.

Eyes narrowed, Khar recounted to herself the strange paths that had brought them all together last autumn on the trail of Vesey Bell, though none had realized then, least of all Khar, to her eternal shame, that that was the danger they hunted. Vesey Bell, Doyce's stepson, long believed dead,

immolated in the same fire that had taken the lives of his fa
ther and his infant half sister, Doyce and Varon's baby Bri
ony, more than ten years ago. But that had seemed con
signed to the far past, of no moment in their search for the
killers of Doyce's lover Oriel and the mental crippling of hi
Bondmate Saam. And so they had searched for the truth, and
found truth and danger stalking them, a danger almost sur
passing their comprehension and their abilities: Vesey'
"resurrection" as a Gleaner, the full-formed, perverted skill
of a mindstealer. The ghatta shivered at the memories and
sent a fleeting prayer of thanks in the direction of the Elder
for their strange help, although it had not seemed like help
at the time. Now she knew better.

The arrows sssh'ed through the air, some quavered in
their flight, flew wide. Khar stretched her whiskers to the
fullest to test the breeze and understood why. Most fell shor
but stood in line with the elusive scrap of scarlet; a few
overshot beyond the flag. Those few pleased Khar. She
hadn't thought Doyce had strength enough for the effort
Back and forth the woman trudged, retrieving arrows, mark
ing their flight, returning to her assigned spot, before turn
ing, left arm extended straight to hold the bow, palm
cradling the grip, much of the force cupped against the heel
of her palm and thumb. Concentrating as her right arm
cocked, elbow at ear-level, arrow nocked, ready, ready,
ready to release at that single frozen moment in time, cen
tered in perfect synchrony of heart and mind and eye.

"Peace, we've arrived," a mindvoice tickled her, and the
ghatta shifted eyes fractionally leftward, downslope toward
the setting sun. A russet ghatt picked his way across the
soggy grasses, dexterously avoiding the snow patches left in
the hummocked shadows. She looked west over the wall to
ward the human figures she had expected: two women both
in late middle age, one admittedly stout and stocky, hair a
short helm of white, Swan Maclough, Seeker General of the
Seekers Veritas. **"Mindwalk if ye will,"** Koom offered the
age-old invocation and invitation that gave permission for
the ghatti to share mind-converse with a Seeker outside the
Bond-pair. **"They're very anxious to know how she fares."**

"Ah, thank you, but later, perhaps." She rose and bow-
stretched to greet the distant figures, hidden from Doyce in
the fringe of trees behind her as she held her stance, nocked
her arrow, then released. The shorter woman nodded and re-

turned the greeting, but the other woman—tall, elegant, yet now a bit stoop-shouldered, her hair wrapped in a silvery-white chignon—darted a glance from archer to ghatta, then waved fractionally, hesitantly, wanting yet not wanting to acknowledge the greeting. Khar offered her the same stretch-bow of respect, careful not to meet her eyes, to intrude in any way. Mahafny, Mahafny Annendahl, Staff Senior, who'd been Doyce's onetime mentor in the eumedicos before Doyce was stripped of her rank and expelled from that group. Now Mahafny was in charge of the Research Hospice high in the Tetonords where she could tend to the demands of new danger-laden eumedico research and to the grave of her daughter Evelien, slain at the same moment as Doyce's stepson Vesey had died. They had both been Gleaners, both with a perverted sense of their own powers that had led them to think they could conquer the world, until Doyce had halted them, and nearly lost her mind in the attempt, only saved from that fate thanks to the efforts of Khar and their ghatti companions.

Khar and the russet ghatt Koom greet-sniffed with delicate nose wrinklings beside each other's cheeks, until the big male shouldered her, forcing her to sit upright so he could share the rock. **"Feet cold,"** he muttered in apology. **"You feel like ice."**

Khar twitched her skin, setting a ripple of motion through her fur. **"Doesn't matter. She's here."** She stretched her neck in Doyce's direction.

"Aye." Koom paused and began to groom, concentrating on an ice ball between his toes, sucking and licking, cocked an eye at the ghatta. **"Any better?"** he asked, making the question sound offhand, polite converse. He swallowed hard, only that action revealing his pressing need to know.

"You see. You see her. A few octs ago, not even this. Yes, better." But her tone sounded as if she were trying to convince herself.

"Yes, better." Koom reached over and licked with slow sympathy down the side of Khar's chin. **"But ... but, does she 'speak you?"**

The ghatta shuddered, fought it down. **"No! No, Koom! And until she does—if she does—I am not whole! I promised her I would wait forever, but these past octants seem longer than forever!"**

"Peace, peace, she will 'speak you. I can feel it, Swa▮
believes it, Mahafny believes it. If not now, later!"

Doyce nocked the last arrow, fought to steady her arm
"Weak, so very weak!" She muttered the words in a monotone, cadenced them through her brain, a rhythmic goading
or her usual silent plea for help? One final chance for a perfect shot. Her tight smile twisted into an uncontrollable grimace. Well, with a chant like that, what did she expect?
Still, she'd consider anything within a body-length of the
scarlet flag a perfect shot. Ah, Lady Bright, no concentration, no strength! So empty! The thought made her waver on
hr feet, the once-steady arrow wobbling and bobbing, etch-
ing the air with symbols of cowardice. She tensed, brought
it under control, concentrated on relaxing cramped muscles,
zeroed in on the elusive distant target that she could barely
see. And for a fleeting moment everything harmonized, so
right that despite herself she hurried her release before the
moment faded. Somehow she maintained her follow-through
position, refusing to waver until the shot landed.

The arrow severed the air, glowing like a bolt from the
Lady in the near dusk as it soared past the faint ghost-
shadows of the Lady's moons creeping over the horizon. It
sliced up and up and up through the sky as if to join the
Lady herself, then began its downward descent, silent-sure
and perfect. And just as it did . . .

. . . A rolapin skittered in panic, darted across the
meadow, away, away from the heart-stopping discovery of
two humans, silent by its bolt-hole in the stone wall, their
lurking presence shattering its little world. It flung itself
across the field, long ears streaming raggedly behind it,
stubby scut semaphoring its fear, its winter-white coat showing streaky patches of brown-gray near the legs and stomach
as it began its seasonal protective coloration change. It
sprang, veered as the flapping red rag on the stick spooked
it further . . . and the arrow sliced downward, deadly metal
point aimed toward its mark.

Transfixed, pinned through its soft underbelly skin, the
rolapin writhed and spun on its obscene spindle, paws scor-
ing the ground, digging at the shaft that nailed it to the earth

when all it wanted was to flee, hide deep and safe in its burrow.

She saw the explosion, the flurry of movement and began to run toward the target, feet stumbling, bumbling as she cursed herself, the Lady, everyone and everything, but most of all, herself. Throwing herself to her knees, she saw the rolapin twitching, flailing against the arrow that pinned it like a butterfly to a mounting board, and began to cry. No, no! No more pain, no more suffering, she couldn't bear it. Not pain that she had inflicted. No! No more!

Blindly she reached down and pressed the frantic rolapin flat, arrow protruding between her middle and ring fingers. It froze when she touched it, the only thing noticeable the abrupt panting heaves of its sides. With a sharp motion she brought her right hand to bear on the shaft, snapped it clean through, though it cost her hands, then lifted the transfixed rolapin free, pulling it straight up and off the shaft. It kicked broke loose, and ran for the underbrush.

Doyce rested her head on her knee and sobbed, beating at the earth with her bloodied hands. Cloud-shoot! Such an innocent sound to it, pretty arrows soaring like a child arching through the air on a swing, toes brushing the sky. Oh, by the Lady, what a terrible name! How could she not have considered it before? Lost, nearly lost, a blameless creature who meant her no harm, not like the other one, the ghost-white ghatt with the carnelian eyes, Cloud! The perverted Bond of her equally perverted stepson Vesey. And she sobbed for what had been, what might have been, what could have been.

Uneasy, the short, stouter woman tugged at the other's arm. "Should we go to her, do you think? What should we do?"

Tears etched glistening silver lines down Mahafny's face in the deepening dusk. "No, Swan. Wait, let her have her cry. I think it's the first one she's had since . . ." her voice stumbled, then firmed, "since then. Let her mourn by herself without us hovering."

"Are you sure?"

"No. No, I don't know." A sharp, bitter shrug proved that. "But I have to trust my instinct on this. There is no formal etiquette or etiology for grieving in our eumedico books or any others. Not even Harrap's." And she was too old, too much an agnostic to consider that a betrayal, just a fact, the truth as she knew it.

Khar wriggled, shoved the broad wedge of her striped head beneath Doyce's elbow as the woman huddled on one knee in the dirty slush, head buried in her arms, sobs shaking her. Shoved again, harder, almost overthrowing Doyce's precarious balance.

"Here," she insisted. **"Here, love, I'm here."**

For a tantalizing moment the mindlink sparkled, threatening to flare into life, and Khar's spine hairs prickled in anticipation. But as quickly as the contact had come, it dissipated. The woman stared in blind wonder at the sinking sun, scrubbing at her face with a fisted hand. A smear of dirt and rolapin blood dappled her pale cheek. She reached down and stroked the ghatta absently, then halted, as if not trusting herself with even the physical contact.

"So, they're here." Her voice knotted, tight with tears. "All of them, I suppose." Khar wondered how she knew, hadn't believed she had paid any attention to the table talk around her on the rare occasions she'd eaten dinner outside her room. Doyce stood, swung her cloak into place, stooped for the discarded bow beside her, planted it beside her right instep, and bent her left knee into it until it flexed enough so that she could unstring it. She began an unsteady walk back to where she had dropped the quiver. The ghatta sat still, wondering, waiting for a sign.

Doyce glared over her shoulder at the ghatta, slapped her thigh, a sharp sound that cracked with impatience. "Come on, hurry up." She continued walking and did not look back again. The tone set the ghatta on edge; it was the voice that humans used with pets, domesticated animals, not the speech of one Bondmate to another. Head low and dejected, she started to follow, only to rebel and choose her own path down toward the streambed.

"I am ghatti," she told herself, projecting her mindvoice as if Doyce could, would hear her. **"I do not trot at human heels like a capering dog begging for affection. I am ghatti, I am Khar'pern."**

Doyce caught up with her on the path, barely aware the ghatta stood waiting with feigned nonchalance. "I knew they'd be here soon, any day now. Damaris said as much. Wouldn't say precisely who was coming, mayhap she didn't know herself." The words were low, almost conversational in tone, but directed at no one, least of all Khar. "More poking and prodding, more guarded questioning, more curiosity, more stares, more pity, more everything . . . except what I want, what I *need*, to be alone, to not have to think or feel or love or want anything . . . or anyone.

"Oh, I *knew*. I saw the spark of gold from the tabard braid, caught the faintest whiff of disinfectant—eumedico 'perfume,' we used to call it." Her voice rose, bitter and biting. "I could feel Swan and Mahafny were there, watching me." She turned in the midst of her hurried walk and rounded on the startled ghatta. "Just as I knew *you* were there. None of you can leave me alone!"

The ghatta stopped short and sat with neck bowed, amber eyes wary and filled with hurt. A dried blade of last year's grass rustled against her side and she pinned it with a lightning-stroke paw, smashed it into the damp ground, anything to deflect the anger, the anxiety, the excess energy welling inside her.

For a moment their eyes met, hazel eyes locking with slanted amber ones. A hectic flush of anger marked Doyce's face, emphasizing her cheekbones, but the lips were pale, tinged blue with the increasing cold as the sun disappeared. The eyes were filled with hurt, haunted. "Oh, Khar, what have I done to you . . . to them . . . to me?" she choked out and began to run.

The ghatta hurried to catch up, but not another word was spoken as they journeyed back to the house, windows already ablaze with light, with activity, with people, with unspoken thoughts and questions and concerns, most of them about Doyce Marbon, Seeker Veritas, still on sick leave but soon—if rumors were right—to be back on duty, like it or not, ready or not. It sounded cruel, and it was, perhaps, but there was no other choice—not for Doyce, not for Khar, and not for their Bond if it was to survive. The time was ripe.

❧

"No!" Her voice boomed louder than intended and she winced at the expression on the serving girl's face. Doyce paid sudden attention to stripping off her boot. She grasped at heel and sole and felt her hands slide, finding no purchase in the slick black muck she had tracked inside the immaculate house. She mocked herself with the imagery of a dark, muddy soul. Not caring, she wiped her hands on her pantaloons and tried again, changing her leverage. "I am . . . oomph . . . *not* going down to dinner tonight, so there is absolutely no need to change." Tossing the boot in the corner, she tackled the other one.

The serving girl was young but not bashful; every person in the Wycherley household and mercantile was taught his or her place at an early stage—and how to stand up for that position, to be treated courteously and fairly, regardless of station. Used to dealing with recalcitrant younger siblings before she had entered service, she drew a deep breath and tried again. "Mistress Damaris asked that ye change and join them for dinner tonight. And we were instructed *not* to bring a tray should ye refuse." She grabbed the second boot before it could be tossed to join its mate and retrieved the one already thrown, holding it as far from her pristine apron as possible to avoid the mud. Back straight, she marched across the room and squared both boots outside the door. "That's where they belong in that state as well ye know. By rights they should ha been left in the mudroom. Bathwater's hot. Now, will ye bathe and change or no?" One foot tapped its impatience, but nothing else in her demeanor displayed her temper.

"Aye, I'll bathe, but no, I'll not change and join them for dinner." She stood and began to strip. Khar, curled in a tight ball at the foot of the bed, lifted her head to meet the serving maid's eyes. **"Patience,"** she 'spoke to no one in particular, **"patience."**

"Very well, Seeker Doyce. I'll so inform the mistress that ye won't be joining them." With a level yet reproving look she began to scoop discarded clothes off the floor, shaking them out, hanging the cloak and shirt, bundling the pantaloons beneath her arm for washing. "Seems to me a Seeker's duty is to serve, just as mine is." She left.

Testing the water in the large copper bathing tub in front of the fire, Doyce eased a foot in, then the other, and sat with slow deliberation. The warm water swirled against sore back, arm and shoulder muscles, tense from the afternoon's cloud-shoot and a multitude of less physical strains. She shifted, making uneasy settling movements in the tub, one foot breaking the surface of the water, startling her at the comparative coolness of the air. As far away as she was, Khar drew back in automatic distaste at the flurry of water droplets; some hit the fire irons, hissing and evaporating.

Unfair to deny Damaris anything, Doyce thought ruefully as she lathered the washrag and began to scrub her neck. But not tonight, not now, not with all of *them* present. She could cope with an intimate dinner in the small dining alcove just off the kitchen—perhaps just Damaris, Jadrian, their daughter Jacobia, tense and angry with herself and her youth now that she had finished her Tierce and still didn't know what to make of herself, what to be, what to do. Her silent anger and frustration—lodged in a heart-shaped face framed with midnight-dark hair the color of Jenret's and Damaris's but with a pair of amethyst eyes entirely her own, not inherited from either Jadrian or Damaris—hit Doyce like a searchlight every time she encountered the girl-woman, but even that she could cope with. In small doses, anyway. Funny, she hadn't even counted Holbein's presence at a small, family meal, Holbein, Damaris's nephew, solid, blond, reliable in the day-to-day running of the Wycherley cloth merchanting business, located on the eastern outskirts of Gaernett. Indispensable and totally unobtrusive except for the wistful looks he cast at Jacobia. That she could cope with as well, but, by the Lady, no, not the others from her past who were gathering here tonight.

Standing, she began to scrub savagely at her legs, resoaped the cloth and did under her arms, between her legs, dipped herself for a quick rinse, and began to swirl the cloth through the water to remove the soapy residue. Not with Jenret there, Mahafny, Swan Maclough, and who knew who else. "I can't face them yet, can't face myself, can't, can't, can't! You can't make something whole that wasn't whole to begin with!" Air rasped shakily in her throat and she fought for a deep, controlling breath, but failed, panting. "Can't . . . don't even dare . . . mindwalk with Khar. . . ." The ghatta pricked her ears at the sound of her name. ". . . Be . . . because she knows me better than I know myself . . . don't dare see her try to hide her disgust at what she finds in me!"

She balled the cloth in her hands, mashing it harder and tighter, eyes screwed shut. Her mouth opened to voice a silent scream of anguish. "I killed . . . killed them! A Seeker must not judge, a Seeker is not the Conciliator! We are the

scales of justice, not its sword! A Seeker finds Truth! A
Seeker does not kill! Does not kill! Dis . . . I . . . dis . . . honored . . . Oriel's memory!"

The knocking at the door came gentle but persistent, but
Doyce heard nothing, clutching the washcloth tightly to her
mouth, moaning into it. Taking in the scene with rigid fasci-
nation, Khar shook herself and leaped from the bed, padded
to the door and bounced against it twice. The worn latch
slipped its catch, and the ghatta wriggled her head, then
her shoulders into the widening gap. Damaris stood there, a
long, velvety gown of moss green hue spread across her
arms.

Khar eased back to let her enter, and the woman understood at a glance. Doyce was still standing stiffly in the tub,
seeing nothing beyond her. Laying the gown down on the
bed with a sigh, Damaris tossed a robe over her shoulder and
plucked a towel from the drying rack in front of the
fire. Expertly wrapping the younger woman in the towel's
warmth, she took her elbow and guided Doyce from the tub,
making sure the wet feet negotiated the two steps.

"Doyce," her voice came crisp and penetrating, "Doyce,
you haven't much time to get dressed. Everyone is waiting."

Dazed, Doyce looked down as Damaris dried her legs.
"Oh, by the Lady, I've done it again, haven't I?" She
sounded weary. "How much did you hear this time?" She
grabbed the towel with impatient hands and began where
Damaris had left off, glad of the excuse to bend over and
hide her face.

"You're reasonably consistent in your compulsions, you
know." A wry smile touched the older woman's face, the image of Jenret's, down to the startling blue eyes with their
long, curled, dark lashes. Her trim figure and upright carriage belied the fact that she'd borne three children—and
still mourned the death of the one who had destroyed her
family and her life so many years ago.

"I can't go down to dinner tonight, I really can't."
Damaris would shield her, must shield her as she had before.
"I can't face them, not yet, please!"

"Oh, you can face them, Doyce, and you will. Even if I
have to drag you down there myself. And I think I can manage that." Ignoring the stunned look of appeal, she turned
and hung the damp towel back on the warming rack, careful
to keep it clear of the dry towels. Frowning, she smoothed

a crease, checked that the towel hung evenly, and continued speaking. "It's yourself you're having trouble facing, and the sooner you come to grips with that, the better we'll all be, including you. You've shied away from facing yourself—even in a mirror—all the time you've been here. But you must understand that tonight you'll see yourself reflected in everyone's eyes, the Doyce they love and know better than you know yourself right now. They love you for your strengths . . . and your weaknesses. And each reflection will give you a clue as to who you really and truly are inside, despite what you may picture in your mind."

"You'll be there, won't you? You won't let . . ." She trembled as she snugged the robe around her.

"No, I won't let . . . whatever." Damaris sighed inwardly. The word "whatever" encompassed such a multitude of intangible fears. Like promising a child there was nothing in the dark to hurt, and it had been dark for Doyce for so long. "I brought you a gown, one of Jacobia's. It won't be a perfect fit, you've lost too much weight, not to mention that you two will never be built the same. I thought you might not want to wear your Seeker garb tonight."

Doyce flashed her a tiny smile of comprehension and gratitude. That had been an aspect she hadn't even consciously realized, of course. The Seeker garb, including the dress tabard with its gold trim, was a mark of distinction, of being "Chosen." To wear it now would make her feel a pretender dressed in stolen finery, false honor.

She held the moss green dress against herself with a certain nostalgia. How long since she'd worn a gown? Years of antiseptic white coats with the eumedicos, years of the dress Seeker Veritas uniform on high halidays or ceremonies, or the more casual dailyware of riding pantaloons and the heavy sheepskin pelt, the working tabard of a Seeker. A hand at the waist of the dress, she swished the soft fullness of the long, gathered skirt. And for a moment Damaris forgot she looked at a grown woman, a woman in her late thirties, and envisioned someone as young, as unsure, and frightened as her daughter, Jacobia. But no more lighthearted. Lady help her if she could figure out what to do with either of them, woman or woman-child!

"Don't forget to brush Khar before you put on that dress. She looks distinctly scruffy—shedding already." The ghatta's nose pinked with excitement as Damaris shared a conspiratorial wink and left.

Stripes glistening in the lamplight, Khar dipped her tongue down her flank, gave a critical look, and licked again. If Damaris had any other suggestions, Khar thought sourly, she hoped the woman would keep them to herself. Khar had been brushed every which way, including against the grain of the fur itself before Doyce finally smoothed the hairs back, bristles scraping dangerously close to sensitive skin. An errant cluster of loose ghatta hairs whirled in the warm air currents in front of the fireplace.

Doyce struggled with the back closing of the moss green gown, twisting and tugging until reluctant fingers at last remembered the complex latticework fastenings. Without thinking, she grabbed Khar's brush and raised it to do her hair, made a face, and hunted out her own. Her unruly, coppery-highlighted hair had grown from its usual boyishly short cropping. Damaris had trimmed it, evening it once when she had been too ill to protest, and she realized now that she could feel it swing when she moved her head sharply. Still, it barely extended beyond her earlobes. She touched the garnet rose in her right ear, Oriel's posthumous gift of love to her and Khar.

Watching the ghatta out of the corner of her eye, this time she anticipated the knock before it happened and faced the door, waiting. Despite the enforced silence, she was still too attuned to the ghatta's expressions and body language to miss Khar's uplifted head and expectant look. She essayed a smile, a small one, to be sure. How like Damaris to come back and check, even if only ostensibly to see if she needed help dressing. Clear where Jenret had inherited his stubbornness, though Damaris's manner was far more loving and diplomatic than her son's. The knock sounded, and she squared her shoulders, settled the dress around her. It made her feel almost good, almost right, as if the dress shielded her from her fears. She knew her face reflected her satisfaction. Bless Damaris for thinking of it! "Come in."

And immediately wished she hadn't as the door swung open to reveal Mahafny Annendahl and Swan Maclough. For a wonder of wonders they both, like Doyce, wore

gowns; Swan's a lustrous black satin topped by her formal
Seeker tabard, edged in purple and gold to denote her rank,
and a crimson sash wrapped around it. More than a touch
plump, no-nonsensical, the Seeker General held palms up in
appeasement and shrugged.

"Didn't know if it still fit. One becomes desk-bound and
the avoirdupois does multiply." Seeing her cousin transfixed
beside the door, Swan grasped Mahafny's wine-red, velvet-
clad elbow and eased her inside. The eumedico seemed unable to take her eyes from Doyce's face, and Doyce felt
unable to tear her own gaze away. Mahafny looked posi-
tively regal in that dress, silvered hair swept off the slender
neck in a figure-eight chignon held by a silver clip.

Realizing no help was forthcoming from her cousin, Swan
propelled Mahafny into the room and shut the door. "And
Mahafny does nothing but complain that this 'thing,' " she
indicated the dress with a bob of her head, "has no pockets,
and how is she to cope without pockets? Eumedicos are all
alike: they somehow think what's stored in their pockets is
more important than the medical knowledge stored in their
heads."

Mind reeling, retreating until the edge of the bed knifed
the back of her knees, Doyce sat, the silence growing louder
than her heartbeats. "Greetings," she offered at last, looking
around for Khar. Since this was her room, it was her duty to
utter the traditional phrase that would open everyone to
Khar's mindspeech. "Mindwalk ... if ye will." The necessary words tasted sour in her mouth, while Khar stared with
grave expectancy at the Seeker General. Mahafny, Doyce
knew, would never allow herself to be touched by ghatti
mindspeech and the ghatti respected her reserve. Just as
Khar now respected her own reserve against the intimacies
of mindspeech.

"I thank you, but not now, I think, much as I'd enjoy chatting with Khar'pern. She looks a bit peaky to me, Doyce.
Have you been taking proper care of her?" With a whoosh
of spread skirts and flounced petticoats, the Seeker General
landed in crackling disorder in the low easy chair, tilted her
chin in the direction of the remaining chair, and sent
Mahafny sleepwalking toward it. "Khar, Koom's waiting below with the others. Why not go down and greet them?
They've missed you."

With a smug ghatti grin, Khar jumped off the bed,

stretched forward and backward, taking her time, and strolled sedately to the door, bounced it open and left. Her tail waved farewell in an S-curve as she slid around the door casing.

Abruptly, Mahafny reclaimed her voice, though her long, patrician fingers remained clamped tightly around each other. "Oh, Doyce, why? Why are you fighting forgiveness? I, who had as much to lose as anyone, knew that Evelien's death was the only way to redeem her, and you, and all of us. The fire killed them both, not you. If I can forgive you, it must be clear that everyone else has."

Swan made a tsking sound and slapped the chair arm for emphasis. "But she hasn't forgiven herself yet, cousin. It's patently clear, isn't it, Doyce? Were the Lady herself to ride down on the beams of her eight Apostle moons, you'd be stubborn enough to refuse absolution, wouldn't you?" She rose with effort, the gown hindering her until she found the flow of it as she began a brisk pacing. "Well, Doyce, forgiven or not, unshriven or no, we've a task for you."

Doyce shook her head in weary negation as Mahafny exclaimed, "No, Swan! You promised, you promised you'd wait and assess her condition, consult with me! She isn't ready yet, you can see that! Look at her, she's not ready in mind or body."

The Seeker General swung around with hands on hips and glared at both women. "Doyce Marbon, I command your fidelity to the Seeker Veritas oath of service."

The command jerked her upright as if controlled by strings, manipulating and constraining her unless she could find the knife to sever them. Doyce rose to attention, hands clenched by her sides. "Aye, Swan Maclough. I serve, willing or no, hale or not. Whom do ye want me to kill this time?"

"Doyce!" Mahafny exclaimed, but nothing deterred the Seeker General. Before the cry could echo and die, she reached Doyce's side in two sharp steps and slapped her face.

"Aye, I had that retort coming, or so you think."

She wanted to cradle her stinging cheek, but fisted her hands at her sides, not daring to set them free. "You knew, you knew!" Adamant anger buoyed Doyce's words, high and rapid and anguished. "You *knew* what the outcome had to be, there was no choice once you set me on that path. A 'catalyst' you called me once. You *knew*, but you never let on that there was no other ordained outcome. You nocked me in the string of your bow and sent me straight for their hearts—my stepson Vesey, Mahafny's daughter Evelien! Those other poor lost souls! Why did they have to die, why did I have to be responsible?"

"Vesey died when he chose to leap into the fire to rescue his medallion; Evelien was struck down by one of the random fire bolts shooting out as he was immolated." Now Mahafny stood beside her as well. "I accepted their fates then, I accept it now. There was no other way to stop them. You did not kill them, but you kept them from killing you and Jenret and Harrap and myself, the ghatti, and who knows how many other innocent victims? Would you bear that burden as well, the lives lost if Vesey and Evelien had been allowed to continue with their vileness, their perversion of eumedico ways, of their own unique mindgifts, of the Seeker mindlink? Ultimately, would anyone in Canderis have been safe?"

Swan spoke again, voice gentle, all anger extinguished. "Call Khar back if you like, Doyce. On my honor of the Truth you were not sent to kill, though the end result was death, even if not by your own hand. Have her look into my mind and heart, let her judge if I lied before. If I lie about the task ahead of you. Trust her judgment, if not your own. Her knowledge of the Truth was the only thing that allowed you to withstand Vesey."

"I . . . I can't." Staring straight ahead in her humiliation, she acknowledged the truth. "We . . . we haven't 'linked since . . . since . . . I can't." She swallowed the lump in her throat, shame burning at her, as searing as Vesey's final pyre.

"Then come down to dinner," Swan interjected. "Listen, think, judge the tale behind the new task I've set you, if you're willing to hear of it later. Besides, others are eager to see you again, and you've new people to meet. If nothing else, let this evening take your mind off this incessant brooding, this self-flagellation. There's always tomorrow if you wish to refuse or insult me again."

Unresisting, she allowed herself to be led from the chamber, head erect, but eyes threatening to spill unshed tears. Act or be acted upon? she wondered, or be the catalyst to spark actions amongst others? And what was she now? She stumbled and momentarily lost her train of thought, dropping the shield she had wrapped around herself for so very, very long.

"A fool of the first water, I'd say." The contralto mindlink came with acerbic intensity, irritation mingling with jubilation.

"Oh, Khar!" she responded silently. The striped ghatta was nowhere in sight. *"I've made a hash of things, haven't I?"*

"Mmph. My grumpy bear." A pet name between them. **"So very, very long since you've 'spoken. I thought I would go mad. To know how Saam felt when Oriel died, the nothingness without you."**

"Oh, my love, my Khar'pern, I'm so very sorry."

The murmurous cadence of congenial company, the ringching of crystal on silver serving salvers, spangles of rainbow prisms from wall sconces and the central chandelier, but most of all the giddy vibrancy of colors assailed Doyce, threatened to overwhelm her, send her fleeing to her safe, darkened room. This sudden siege of normality on her senses made her realize how bleak and gray—but safely circumscribed—the past few octants had been. Had she really lost almost half a year, from autumn to early spring? The nursing, the cosseting, even the continual suppressed air of expectant waiting had conspired with her own fears to imprison her in that safe, solitary cell of a room.

She paused outside the door, reached to stroke Khar's head, traced the sleek line along the spine, and massaged the point where tail joined spine. Ecstatic at the touch, Khar's eyes slitted, her purr rumbled as she arched against Doyce's forearm, catching her attention. Doyce stood abruptly, managed a smile for the ghatta.

"Courage. They love you, won't hurt you."

"I know." But her lips tightened to hide the trembling. *"It's just that it's been so long."*

"Too long," the ghatta agreed, and padded ahead into the room, each slow step dignified, head high to let the garnet rose in her right ear tip, golden hoop at the base of her left ear catch the light. Fingering her own matching set, Oriel's gift, Doyce stepped forward, striving to emulate Khar, and heard conversation cease.

The group separated, forming an aisle for Doyce to walk through, walled with human faces, ghatti faces at knee level. Without willing it, she remembered the gauntlet the Erakwa had planned to make Jenret and Harrap run before ... she swallowed hard ... before Vesey had appeared and taken them prisoner. *Vesey,* she repeated the name to herself without flinching.

Eyes darting, she saw Mahafny and Swan first since they'd entered the dining salon just ahead of her, gifting her with a few precious solitary moments to regain her composure. Mahafny stood aloof, pale with nerves, while Swan's blunt fingers toyed with the stem of her wine glass, expression assessing but not directly challenging.

And from the far end of the room a burly, tonsured figure in an incongruous, mismatched outfit of monk's robe and Seeker's tabard came charging toward her, roaring with delight as he half-tripped over a ghatt with an outrageous motley of orange and black and white splotches.

Harrap, former Shepherd at the Lady's Bethel in Cyanberry, and now a Seeker after Parm's unprecedented second Bonding, swept her off her feet in an all-embracing hug, tears rolling down his cheeks. "Ah, Doyce!" he sobbed.

"So good, so good ... oh, bother, I forgot, sorry, sorry!" Parm gamboled at her feet. **"Didn't mean to pry! Harrap, ask if I may mindwalk?"**

From within the sustaining circle of Harrap's arms, Doyce took a long, hard breath, exhaled slowly, and tried for all the casualness she could muster, "Greetings, Parm. Mindwalk if ye will, and all ye others as well."

Khar's mindvoice thrummed its pleasure. **"Oh, well done, my Bondmate, my love,"** she projected on the intimate mode. **"I won't let them overwhelm you, I am here."**

Faces flashed and flickered in her vision as she patted shoulders, clasped hands, kissed—Rolf and Chak, the twins Bard and Byrta with M'wa and P'wa, and miraculously she knew which ghatti was which without a struggle. Beautiful, gilt-haired Sarrett and the equally striking T'ss with his sapphirine eyes and black stripes against white. Parcellus and the ebullient Per'la with her usual frenzied affection, the creamy plume of her tail high and crooked. Other faces she didn't know, but looking pleasant and noncommittal.

Against the far wall she spied the Erakwan woman
Addawanna and her grandson Nakum, and beside him, detached yet content to mark her progress, the steel-gray ghatt
Saam, her lover Oriel's Bondmate. She cast a welcome in
his direction and his ringless ears perked.

"Peace, Doyce. I see thee well."

"We've much to speak of later," she 'spoke back at him.
"I feared once we'd never speak again."

"As did I, but for different reasons."

The one face she'd been searching for ever since she'd
entered the room, though she hadn't realized or acknowledged it to herself, appeared: Jenret Wycherley, his lean, elegant form flanked by his coal-black Bondmate Rawn. Some
called Wycherley a rake, others judged him supercilious and
affected, arrogant; she had called him all these things and
worse once, not so long ago. But no one, herself included,
had ever denied he was a thoroughly effective, indeed, tena-
cious Seeker who worked as hard as he reveled. She had reason to know the measure of his dedication during his
self-imposed mission to salvage the Seekers' good name
when he joined her quest to discover Oriel's killer. And that
search—hers officially sanctioned by the Seekers, his en-
dorsed by the sheer force of his personality and the almost
overwhelming private demons that drove him—had united
them, uneasy allies taunting and goading each other out of
their private pain and had led them to the Gleaners ... to
Vesey and Evelien. Her earlier self-control had been short-
lived; this time she recoiled at the names.

He stood impassive except for a faint shiver of lace at his
throat, as if his heart pounded too fast. And attired in, she
caught her breath in surprise, not his normal, impeccable
black, but in pleated gray woolen dress trousers and a velvet
short-waisted jacket of midnight blue darker than his gentian
blue eyes, those eyes, fringed with long dark lashes any
woman would envy. She had before, she would again. Ivory
lace frothed at his collar and cuffs, no hint of Seeker garb
tonight. Rawn sat ebony statuelike at his feet, only the agitated twitch of tail tip showing his excitement.

She moved forward with slow ceremony and held out her
hand, cringed as his remained by his sides until good manners asserted themselves and both hands reached to grip
hers. The corner of his mouth crooked in a smile, but it
never reached his eyes, and she pulled back in dismay, only

to halt at the sudden possessiveness of his grip, so at odds with the studied, cool expression. Lady above, what ailed the man? And why should she care?

"Doyce, well met. You are . . ." and his eyes looked her over consideringly, assessing each change in her, measuring it, judging it for better or for worse. ". . . improved, I see," he concluded, in that light, clear tenor of his. His hands slackened with no warning and released hers.

She matched his cool formality. "Yes, thank you for your concern. Your mother and everyone here have been wonderful. Had you but stopped by, you would have seen." Why had she thrown his absence in his face like that? she wondered, but couldn't for the life of her decide why. As if on cue, Damaris, looking so much like her son, yet more temperate, more compassionate, appeared and linked arms with them, glancing from one face to the other, each schooled to reveal nothing.

"Doyce, the Seeker General has some guests she'd like you to meet, much as she's sorry to intrude on a gathering of friends and family." And with a gentle pressure of her arm she turned Doyce away from Jenret, away from the devouring intensity that craved something of her though she knew not what. As if released from a spell, Doyce turned without a backward glance, nothing in her carriage revealing the rippling waves of tension flowing through her body, the frustration of something dangerously throttled in her greeting of Jenret. She didn't hear Jenret's strangled exclamation as his mother's hand clamped vise-hard around his wrist.

"Jenret, I swear, don't taunt her, don't tease her—she's not ready for it yet, not from you."

"Mother, I swear by the Lady I did no such thing; Rawn can vouch for me!" He laced his hand through his mother's, the same limber fingers but browner, more callused, outdoor versus indoor hands. "Besides, you . . . heard, you had to have heard." He swallowed hard to regain composure and the ghatt at his feet did too, so in tune were they with each other's feelings. "She doesn't remember in the least how many times I've been here before, while she stayed locked senseless within her mind or screamed through daylight nightmares. How many times I soothed her, sang to her, forced her out of bed, walked her around and around the room, talked to her, told her anything and everything. Everything!" he repeated with emphasis. "I swear our heartbeats matched, we were so close! Damn it, I shared her pain! I lived it with her, relived it! Relived my own!"

"It takes two to share, Jenret, whether it's pain, or love, or hate. I thought you would have realized that by now." And Jenret knew that his mother's thoughts no longer rested on him, but strained across the room toward Jadrian, his father, flanked by Jacobia and Holbein as the older man dubiously touched a canape on the tray a servant offered, then plunged his finger into the middle of the creamy delicacy and raised it to his lips to taste. His eyes reflected the unfocused look of a person adrift in his own private dream world, and indeed he was; none of them knew what solace or pain he found in the empty, vast wasteland of his mind. That, Jenret knew, was the fate Doyce had so narrowly escaped.

"I do, Mother, oh, I do." He wrestled with bitterness, suppressed it in favor of the childhood love he remembered for the vital, opinionated being who had been, was still, his father, for better or worse. Still his mother's husband, still the head of Wycherley Merchanters, though both in name only. "She wouldn't ... couldn't remember. It's just that we shared so much together before ... and after."

"She remembers some of the before. And she may remember the rest—if she chooses to. Still, you have a foundation to build on, to aid her in remembering. Let that be enough." She patted his arm, still staring across the room, lost in her own memories before she forced her mind back to the present. "We've guests to attend to, Jenret."

He bent slightly, kissed the crown of her head. "And a Wycherley guest wants for nothing, or you'll know the reason why. Let's just hope no one ever asks for one of the Lady's moons, though I'd love to see you try to fulfill that request."

Her laughter rang genuine, the image of Jacobia's before she had gone all broody and angry and resentful this past year. He still didn't understand the changes in the little sister he loved. "Well, Jenret, if you're going to invite a Shepherd into the house, perhaps we'll have a direct link to the Lady's ear. And if that fails, no doubt Parm would fumble his way to glorious success even better than his new found Bondmate!"

❧

The table was long and glossy, Sunderlies ebony with a narrow center insert of jade-black marble edged by a white marble border inlaid with petaled florets of lapis and carnelian, stem swirls and curving leaves carved out of the same seemingly unrelenting green marble. It sat the eighteen guests with ease.

Doyce found herself seated midway down and felt grateful when Rolf, placed on her left, took her hand under the table and gave it a heartening surreptitious squeeze. Swan was seated directly across from her, and Doyce concentrated on her cutlery, shooting sidelong glances at the man to her right rather than meet Swan's eyes. She'd been introduced but hadn't caught his name because of Parse's sudden raillery at the twins. Laughter had muffled the Seeker General's introduction, and she'd felt too awkward to admit she hadn't heard.

But just as she tried to whisper to Rolf to ask the stranger's name, the stranger turned and spoke to her, some courteous banality, and she forced herself to listen politely while studying him covertly. Late forties, she suspected, but she might be underestimating. He reminded her a bit of her sister-in-law's husband Lytton, the same heartily weathered skin and solid build of a farmer out in all elements and through equally long days and nights if crops peaked for harvesting or sheep proved ready to drop their lambs. His hands and nails were well-cared for as if he hadn't done manual labor for some time, and the fine sprinkling of crow's-feet or laugh lines around his shrewd blue eyes made him look pleasant. He dressed well but not ostentatiously— nor totally stylishly, for that matter. The mustard-colored serge jacket with its overly full sleeves and tightly belted waist had been out of fashion for a number of years, at least an octad.

"An interesting gathering tonight, don't you think?" His sandy eyebrows cocked in inquiry told her more than his deceptively mild voice. Obediently she took a quick look at the others seated around them.

Either a perfectly normal question or a leading one, depending on her response. "I hadn't really thought about it. Practically everyone here tonight is an old friend or colleague." The water goblet felt precariously heavy as she raised it to moisten her lips, winning a few precious moments to think how to continue. Conversation was still an effort. "Rolf Cardamon, the gentleman on my left, helped train me when I entered Seeker Veritas service."

"So the few unknown quantities tonight are myself, my aide—the young man to Swan Maclough's right and across from Seeker Cardamon—and the gentleman to the Seeker General's other side, though perhaps you've noticed him here consulting with Mistress Wycherley on business on other occasions." It was matter-of-fact, no query in his voice, simply a man who liked to lay out the facts of the matter at the beginning.

Well, if matter-of-factness pleased him, then she had best admit her ignorance. "More unknown than you may realize. I regret to confess I didn't catch your name or your aide's during the introductions."

He laughed and edged his elbow onto the table, unselfconsciously disarranging the silverware. "Ah, because of the commotion the young man caused? The one with the fly away carroty hair? Does he always bait his friends so sharply, or aren't they friends?"

She smiled at the thought. "Parcellus is attracted to trouble the way a bee seeks honey."

"More like a moth to a flame, I should think." And Doyce's hand shook, water goblet sloshing at his words. Flames . . . singed moths . . . Vesey. Would she ever stop reacting? Would it never leave her alone? The firm touch of his fingers stabilized the goblet, and she let him take it from her hand. "My apologies if I've inadvertently upset you. And my apologies for the waylaid introduction. I'm Kyril van Beieven, and my aide who, as you can see, is also a Seeker, is Aelbert Orsborne."

The world lurched to a momentary stop with Doyce caught at its still, silent center. She opened her mouth, closed it, then tried again, while the laugh lines around his eyes crinkled deep at this more understandable discomfiture. "The Monitor?" Her voice squeaked, and incredulous, she tried it again. "The Monitor, Kyril van Beieven?"

The Monitor served as Canderis's highest elected authority, named in honor of the middle-level technicians, those ancestral space-age pioneers, who had watched and correlated information on their monitors, the data that told them what was happening with the Plumbs, analyzing their data, assessing it—and ultimately sounding the alarm, trying to chart the safe lands from the danger zones when the Periodic

Linear Ultra-Mensuration Beamers began to self-destruct
and explode. They were the highest-level technicians who
remained behind when the scientists, the engineers, the elite
commanders had cobbled together three of their disabled
spacecraft to leave the exploding planet—whether in search
of help or simply to escape was still a hotly-contested question. Cowards or lost heroes? So Kryil van Beieven was the
current duly-elected Monitor, now completing the seventh
year of his octad-long term of service.

"Khar, why didn't you say something?" She mindspoke
the ghatta, seated with neat decorum to the left of her chair.

**"Thought you heard. Assumed you'd ask if you hadn't.
Besides, didn't you recognize him?"**

*"Obviously not, but then I've only seen him at a distance
during ceremonies, not up close. You'd think you'd seen him
up close."*

Rewrapping her tail around white toes, the ghatta examined the tip with interest, clearly abashed. **"Have. A ghatti
may look at a Monitor. Part of the tradition when we
were in training, Novies. Everyone did it at least once,
slipped out and entered Monitor's Hall unseen, caught a
glimpse of the Monitor. I've seen two new—the previous
one and this one when I guided a group of younglings
through. He'd just begun then."**

"I'm ashamed of you, Khar, that's spying!" Then a worse
thought struck her. *"Khar, you didn't 'read him, did you?"*

"Of course not! It was just to see."

As if realizing that she hadn't been struck dumb but was
conversing privately with the ghatta, van Beieven picked up
the conversational thread. "Yes, the one and only until the
election next year. Is your Bondmate telling you about the
little expeditions the youngsters have?"

"You know?" she asked, incredulous. "Or do you read
minds as well?"

The skin around his eyes tightened for a moment, then relaxed. "No, neither a Gleaner nor a Seeker am I." And
Doyce shivered at hearing the word used with such casual
familiarity, no flinching, no hint of a warding sign, and the
Monitor continued unperturbed. "But it's hard for a man of
my background, years spent watching nature and her creatures, not to sense when other eyes are on me. Ask your
Khar'pern if sometimes the explorers didn't find a bowl of

milk in their path. I knew they meant no harm, just curiosity, and I never sensed them trying to read me."

Scooting beneath Doyce's chair, Khar popped up next to the Monitor and strained her neck, chin angled in the air. He scratched it with pleasure. "Lucky the man or woman to have one of the ghatti as boon friend and companion. I've always envied Aelbert that, not that I envy him much else since he suffers me all the time." Across the table Aelbert dipped his head and blushed.

Two servants arrived bearing the first course, poached salmon heady with the scent of white wine and fresh dill from the indoor herbaria. A collective sigh escaped the assembled ghatti. As each diner received a plate, a smaller, empty plate was positioned to the right of those who were part of a Bond-pair. Aelbert examined it with perplexity, then seemed to be in conversation with his Bondmate, a ghatta that Doyce hadn't had any real chance to meet either.

When his look of puzzlement didn't clear, she caught his attention and whispered, "For your ghatta. Mistress Wycherley knows our Bonds' secrets when it comes to food, especially fish. Jenret and Rawn visit often enough to make it a necessity." And, as the guests were served, each Seeker portioned a smaller piece on the companion dish and set it on the floor, Aelbert watching and following suit only fractionally late, gave her a tiny smile of thanks. A satisfied hum rose from floor level.

Prodding a bone to the plate's rim with a finicky move, the Monitor chuckled. "It's always amazed me how they can manage to purr and eat at the same time."

The flaky delicacy of the fish preoccupied everyone for some moments, halting conversation, and she used the time to further scan the guests. Somehow, something about the seating arrangement struck her as odd. Still, she'd frequented few formal dinners in private homes; she had attended haliday and ceremonial banquets at Seeker headquarters or degree investitures during her old days of training as a eumedico, before she had been stripped of her rank and expelled for her refusal to perpetuate the lie about the eumedicos' ability to mindtrance with their patients. She looked across at Mahafny, seated with the other unknown man on her right and Harrap at her left. Mahafny, too, was casting strained looks at her neighbors while the Monitor engaged Addawanna in conversation on the other side.

Mahafny gave a little shake of her head, then pursed her mouth, caught Doyce watching her, and managed a reluctant smile as she continued rearranging her food on her plate. The servants began to remove the first course, and Doyce followed their movement to the other end of the table where Damaris sat, Bard on her left next to Byrta and Parse, Sarrett on her right next to Holbein and Jacobia. Jadrian had been present at the beginning, during the easy mingling before dinner, but a servant had escorted him to his rooms shortly thereafter. She could sympathize with the reasoning behind it: the poor man became restive at long, drawn-out affairs and at best was likely to pat experimentally at his food, caress and squeeze it, drape his napkin over his head, or sing mindless nonsense syllables while filching tidbits off others' plates. No one within the family thought anything of it, but outsiders tended to be somewhat nonplussed by his behavior, although the reason for it showed clearly in his gentle, vacant expression.

What was wrong with the seating? She concentrated again, and then it struck her—guests of honor. Kyril van Beieven, the Monitor, should be seated at Damaris's right as ranking guest, perhaps Harrap at her left to balance church and state. Then Swan at Jenret's right and perhaps Addawanna as a foreign visitor, at his other side. There was absolutely no reason for the Monitor to be seated beside Doyce. Yet somehow all the power, if that was the word she wanted, ran along the table from her right to Jenret at the other end, although the merchant and Addawanna's grandson Nakum seemed unknown quantities in the equation.

"Excellent salmon," the Monitor announced to the group at large, "though increasingly rare these days. 'Tis said the best salmon comes from the icy rivers of Marchmont."

"Aye, that's true enough." The merchant to Swan's left spoke. His name popped into her head, an unexpected relief—Syndar Saffron. She'd noticed him coming and going from Damaris's offices on several occasions. A textile merchant as well, a competitor but sometimes a partner in far-flung trading ventures with Wycherley House to share expenses and provide greater volume in certain textiles or furnish complementary but noncompetitive fabrics to meet a broader range of demands. That much, and his name, she'd gathered from overhearing the servants. He was one of the ugliest men she'd ever seen, broad of chest with practically no neck and a bullet head devoid of all but the faintest fringes of dark hair. His features looked as if they'd been pummeled by numerous fists during a rough and tumble youth; his generous nose was splayed to one side and a scar flashed across his cheekbone and through the bristly, black brow.

Saffron scrutinized her as well but directed his words to the Monitor. "The best salmon does come from Marchmont, and precious little we've gotten of that or any other trade good or gold recently, as well you know, van Beieven." His eyes glinted with striking violet sparks, totally incongruous with his brawler's build and scarred face. A shock of recognition flowed through her—those eyes, exactly the same shape and shade as Jacobia's, Jenret's sister. She spun toward Jenret and saw him gauging her reaction. He raised his wine glass in a sketchy salute to her powers of observation and motioned to a servant to pour more wine around the table.

Was it possible? Head spinning, she swung toward Damaris, sure that the sight of her would reassure her of the falsity of the sudden insight she'd had and didn't want to believe. Damaris? Syndar Saffron? No, the Damaris she knew was totally, completely loyal to Jadrian, incapable of having an affair.

But Damaris was listening with indulgent amusement as Parse spun some sort of nonsense tale, hands as mobile as his mouth. Only her profile showed as she rested chin on hand and concentrated on Parse, a dimple flashing as she smiled. And if she had had an affair with Syndar Saffron, if Saffron were Jacobia's father? Doyce scolded herself for her prudery. Yet Damaris's loyalty to Jadrian had appeared unquestionable, an unbreakable bond.

Khar broke into her confusion. **"And how long has Jadrian not been Jadrian?"**

The main course arrived, crown roasts of beef, one at each end of the table. Khar stopped her tail-flickering pattern as the servers began to apportion glazed carrots, mounds of steaming, fluffy potatoes, rosy-hued, hot-spiced beets, and Jenret and Damaris simultaneously carved the roasts.

Doyce did some quick calculations in her head before she responded. *"About twenty-five years? At least that."*

"Then think before you judge. Seekers never judge. Think what those long, lonely years cost her."

The weight of the burden, the loss, overwhelmed her as she considered Khar's reproach. Here was suffering with which she could identify. A son dead, a husband no longer a husband but a child, and another child still taut with grief and the burning knowledge that his own life would have been forfeit had his father been able to contrive it, plus a business to run under the pretense that Jadrian had become reclusive but still maintained control. Practically no one except close friends and family knew of Jadrian's mindlessness.

"You found Oriel after Varon's death. Do you blame Damaris for finally turning to someone else for comfort during those long, lonely years? It was less a betrayal than a need for survival, for sanity."

Tears barely held in check, Doyce shook her head. Longer than she had suffered, and Damaris seemed the stronger for it, not weaker. "No. No, I don't." And realized she had spoken aloud. She froze, afraid someone had heard, had noticed.

Only the merchant's violet eyes met hers, and she lowered hers in embarrassment and concentrated on her food. For the rest of the dinner she directed a flood of desperate conversation at Rolf, catching up on old news, old friends, but every time she looked around the table, she caught someone's eyes on her—Mahafny, Jenret, Swan, Aelbert's reserved glance, the Monitor's considering looks, Damaris, and always, always, the bright, intent violet eyes of Syndar Saffron.

Bed. Her whole body craved it, nerves ajangle from the long evening and the strain of socializing with so many. Still, not a bad feeling, merely a tired one. I've been more ready for this than I realized, she admitted to herself with mounting surprise. Except now no one will let me retreat into my cocoon of indifference again. But it's still up to me to set the pace, not them. My life, mine and Khar's, not theirs. And I won't have Khar dragging me as a dead weight, a burden, so she must still be patient, poor love.

She stood saying good night to the Ambwasali twin-pairs, Bard and Byrta and their Bonds, M'wa and P'wa. She no longer had trouble telling who would start or finish a sentence, though this was less a time for conversation than for companionship. Nakum, the Erakwan lad, no, she corrected herself, a man now, according to his people, hovered at her right, for all the world like a fretful chaperon. He had shot up; now he stood a head taller than she, and taller than most of his people, perhaps the heritage of his grandfather, the trader Addawanna had met and loved so long ago in Marchmont.

And that, for some reason, brought her tired thoughts full circle to salmon and Marchmont, and Syndar Saffron's mention of the trade problems there. The Monitor had been noncommittal, to say the least, as if it were the last thing on his mind. All through the evening she had sensed him wrestling with problems far deeper than the conversations he carried on.

Four of the ghatti, Khar, P'wa, M'wa, and Saam, sat in a half-circle, eyes partially closed in contentment, their stillness broken by an occasional rumbling purr from one or another. P'wa raised her right foreleg, the one with the long white stocking, and gave it a look and a lick. M'wa mimicked the action, raising his left foreleg with the matching white stocking, and the two cast an amused whisker-flicker at each other and at Doyce.

"Doesn't work now," began P'wa, **"does it?"** finished M'wa. **"You can tell,"** they finished together.

"No, it doesn't, silly tricksters." She shook a warning finger at them, made them freeze in mock alarm. *"And you didn't enjoy it either when I couldn't tell you apart. Though if I ever catch your reflections in a mirror, I'm liable to be confused."*

Saam's deeper purr trailed into a flurry of inaudible falanese laughter. **"Now that's a trick they should try on Parse."**

Damaris, trailed by Holbein and Sarrett, Parse and Jacobia, joined them at the doorway, Parse chattering with Jacobia, and for once the girl appeared animated, not sulky. Holbein acted bemused and slightly jealous, but Sarrett paid them no mind as she asked him a shrewd question about the recent dip in the price of wool. Doyce had a feeling Sarrett had invested her Seeker wages in a number of mercantile investments, a nest egg against the future. And if she were to marry Parse, which seemed likely, someone would have to keep shrewd watch over the family finances or Parse would fritter everything away on the latest puzzle-toys.

"It's been a delight having you all here," Damaris's pleasant voice embraced them. "Jenret seldom brings friends home, so I'm doubly pleased to have had the chance to meet you at last and for you to have the opportunity to judge for yourselves how well Doyce now fares."

Crossing his wrists and bringing them to his chest, Bard bowed with graceful formality, the gesture a vestige of his Sunderlies heritage, clearly foreign yet appropriate to the evening. "All honor to the house of Wycherley and the gracious lady who heads it."

"Your hospitality enhances the occasion of our reunion with old friends," Byrta bowed as well, "and we thank you for it."

Parse quivered with unreleased laughter until Sarrett gave his arm an unobtrusive pinch that brought him to sober self-control.

"And I am delighted to have a houseful of visitors, now friends. May you all sleep well." Damaris clasped hands with her visitors, then turned to Doyce. "Come join me in the parlor for a cup of cha. Nakum, your grandmother's there, waiting for you."

"May I come as well, Mother?" Jacobia strove to sound affable, not whining, Doyce could tell, but it didn't come out that way, the tinge of "but I *want* it" all too obvious.

Damaris's lips tightened until she schooled her face to patience. "No, dear, off to bed with you. You have to be up early tomorrow if you're going to help Holbein tally the outgoing shipment. And you did promise you would."

"Yes, I know I did, but it's just that . . . I wanted. . . ." She rushed the next sentence, "And besides, Holbein can do it faster and more accurately alone. We *all* know that."

Making inarticulate noises of protest, Holbein's fair face crimsoned in dismay, but Damaris overrode him. "Yes, but if you truly plan to take an interest in the business, you have to start somewhere, and the inventory tally is as good a place as any."

"And I don't mind . . . would be delighted to have you there," Holbein stammered, hand raking fine blond hair across his eyes as if to hide himself.

With a snap of her skirts, Jacobia turned and stalked out the door, stopped long enough to spin back, skirts swirling in the opposite direction, her color high and angry. "Ah, poor Holbein," and the word "poor" dripped with sarcasm. "Wouldn't it have been easier if you'd been born me instead of only a poor nephew, and I could have been born as anything, anyone else? Oh!" Frightened, she clasped her hands over her mouth as if to push the words back in, disavow them. She sped down the hall without looking back, only the sound of her running feet echoing her self-reproach.

"Never mind, Holbein, it's not you she's mad at," Damaris soothed.

Shoulders slumped, head down, he walked away. "I know, it's everyone and everything, but most of all herself. Doesn't she know, doesn't she understand . . . ?" But his lament faded unfinished as he continued out the door.

And with a look that brooked no further words, Damaris turned down the hall toward the parlor, Doyce and Nakum, Saam and Khar falling into step behind her. No one said anything.

The intimate little family gathering for cha that Doyce had visualized was hardly that, she realized with a sinking heart as she entered the parlor. Tricked again, and she wrestled with the sinking suspicion that she wouldn't much like whatever was due to happen. The room was too small for this many people, and Jenret, Kyril van Beieven, and Syndar Saffron stood crowded together near the fire, Jenret leaning with insolent grace against the mantel. Each of the three held a short glass of celvassy, a potent after-dinner drink.

Settling into the chair Damaris indicated, Doyce took in her surroundings as Nakum wove through the room and sank down by his grandmother's feet where she sat on a settee with Swan. Damaris sat on the opposite settee next to Aelbert Orsborne, who had withdrawn into himself, pulled as far against the arm as he could, his unobtrusive Bondmate N'oor pressed against his leg, peeking out from her sanctuary. Jenret moved to the drinks tray and picked up a glass, cocking an eyebrow in Doyce's direction.

She shook her head, a bare negative, and forced herself back into her chair, though with no sense of relaxation. A barking cough, hastily stifled, told her Chak was there, and she searched for Rolf, discovering his narrow form jackknifed on a ridiculously small footstool, fingers picking at the needlepoint cover. A flurry of scratches at the window caught everyone's attention, and Rolf, closest to it, unfolded himself and threw up the sash.

"More company?" He scooped a delicately-boned white and gray cat to his chest and lifted her into the room. The

cat leaped from his arms, stalked a circuit of the room, stiff
and formal as she assayed the unfamiliar ghatti, then rubbed
familiarly at Rawn, the black ghatt towering over her. With
regal disdain she jumped into Damaris's lap, turned three
times and curled up, eyes bright with excitement.

"Oh, Bess, curiosity killed the cat," Damaris scolded as
she stroked her.

"And information brought it back," Doyce finished, despite her resolve to remain silent. "And information, I'll wager, is why we're here." All too obvious, contrived, this
convenient gathering of the powerful with the ability to
command and demand. Why hadn't she gone to bed when
she had the chance? They had no right to do this to her, not
after what she'd been through. Well, she'd listen, but that
was all they'd get from her if she could help it. Khar stirred
beside her, uneasy over her thoughts or over what was brewing in the room, she wasn't sure which.

A flurry of softly ironic applause from Saffron. "Well,
shall we get on with it, Monitor?" The emphasis on "Monitor" was heavy. "The lady has the right to know."

Van Beieven stirred, an awkward shifting of shoulders and
arms, and again she read the discomfort of an outdoors man
trapped within a confining space, filled with finicky, too-
delicate, uncomfortable women's furniture and knickknacks
that identified it as Damaris's uniquely private place of solace. Despite his greater bulk, Saffron appeared totally comfortable and at ease, as if he'd been here many times before.
The Monitor took a step forward and, as if at a signal,
Aelbert sprang to his feet, clutching a leather tube in front of
him. He twisted it until it separated in half, pulled out a
map, and began to unroll it on the low table between the settees, pinning the curling corners with whatever came to
hand, a discarded celvassy glass, a convoluted pink shell, a
pewter owl figurine.

Craning her neck, half-rising from her chair, Doyce identified the ragged outlines of Princept, the continent that contained both Canderis and Marchmont. A thick crease showed
that the map had been folded, the southernmost continent,
the Sunderlies, bent unregarded beneath the rest. And so, for
the most part, had it always been with the Sunderlies—good
for the raw materials of trade, but little else. The half-
forgotten shapes and outlines of Princept came back to her
slowly and with effort. The small geographies, the intimate

boundaries of her Circuits she recognized with ease, as did every Seeker Veritas, aided by his or her map book, but that was for viewing the individual pieces in detail, not the whole. Here, most of the fine details of streams, meadows, hill regions, and marshes were lost in the overwhelming major features of the continent.

Strange, with it spread before her like this, she was amazed anew that so much of the boundary between Canderis and Marchmont was a watery one. Only on the farthermost western and eastern reaches did a broken line march across land masses, and in the west it was simply a formality, for neither country had had the people to populate those unexplored, unsettled western reaches. Unless, she thought, the Erakwa had settled there to escape our intrusions. Addawanna was certainly examining the map with interest, twisting in her seat, murmuring under her breath. Still, perhaps she had never seen a map before, had never realized the full immensity of the land in which she lived and roamed.

But it was water that divided the two nations for close to half the continent, watery shapings that created boundaries across the map. She ticked them off on her fingers, recited the names under her breath: the three Balaenas—Perebal, Merebal, and Pettibal—giant inland seas, or more accurately, inland lakes, shaped like cavorting whales—large, medium, and small—in a line, nose to tail with each other. And from the mouth of the smallest, most easterly "whale" flowed a wide, twisting river called The Spray, for indeed, it looked as if the baby "whale" had sent a jetting flume of water from its blowhole in play. The Spray arched up and away, then fell through Canderis, where on its lowest reaches it branched into the Taglias as it reached out to the sea.

The Balaenas were divided across their middles with the boundary line, and The Spray itself served as boundary until it reached the peak of its upward rise. As it flowed south, the land on both sides belonged to Canderis's Pennington Province, known for its rolling grazing hills, wheat fields, and fruit orchards. The boundary line continued across this eastern land just below the Marchmontian Massif, a wide swath of mounded, worn mountains, far gentler and older than the other two towering ranges that hemmed in Marchmont on the west, the Stratocum and Cumulonim Ranges. She had forgotten that the Tetonords were, in truth, the "toe" of the boot of the Stratocum Range, the only part that jutted into Canderis, while the Pettibal flooded over the ankle of the "boot" itself.

She shook herself, gave up her covert study of the map as she realized that the Monitor had begun to speak, indeed, had been speaking for how long now she wasn't sure. His body posture still seemed ill at ease, but his voice came confident and commanding, almost hypnotizing in his relentless recitation. Again she realized how badly she wanted to sleep. What, how much had she had missed? She widened her eyes, tried hard to listen.

"Marchmont has always been a safe, albeit standoffish, neighbor to our northern boundaries. Or at least they were until Queen Wilhelmina's death not quite a year ago. She left no children, no obvious heirs. The information we have is scanty, to say the least, but someone named Constant Minor is serving as Steward until an heir is chosen. At the moment none of us here is sure who is in the running although rumors are rife, and I'm not sure we can wait for a decision. For the first time since that mistaken, and thankfully abortive attack on our capital nearly one hundred years ago, our boundaries have been breached. As yet it's only brief sorties, seemingly exploratory, but our Guardian forces patrolling the borders can't seem to catch them or even confront them."

Scanning the faces around him as they listened to his superior, Aelbert saw curiosity, boredom, incomprehension. Well, he'd warned the Monitor to come right to the point. He stroked N'oor's head for comfort, needing it as much as she did. For her sake he tried to hide his exasperation even more deeply, though no one but he was aware of it. It was always that way. Still, didn't they—especially the Monitor, his idol, so wise in so many other ways—have any clue, any inkling at the connection of their problems? He might have been ejected from the earlier meeting in the coach today, but he was no fool when it came to tracing and linking a chain of seemingly unrelated events. Nor was Doyce Marbon, so he'd been told, if she still retained that ability. From what he'd observed of her tonight, he doubted it. She looked ready to start at a shadow. He pressed his leg against N'oor, felt her trembling, but was too preoccupied to wonder why she was so upset. After all, it wasn't his place to advance his

ideas, or if he did, he made sure the Monitor received cred
for them.

"We've no idea, no evidence whether these sorties ar
sanctioned—officially or unofficially—by their governmen
or whether some faction is attempting to stir up dissensio
during this vacuum of power. It's equally possible the
could be brigands, taking advantage of the situation for thei
own gain. Whoever they are, they slide in and out with im
punity, particularly on the eastern borders, and that I canno
have because I don't know if and when it may escalate.

"You should also be aware they summarily expelled ou
Consul, Aaron Rossmeer, and his staff two octants ago, an
because of that I've had no choice but to reciprocate by ex
pelling their Consul from Gaernett. Madame LaRoche wa
as bewildered and surprised as we were. Most of the infor
mation we were able to put together came from Rossmeer'
staff, because Rossmeer suffered a series of small stroke
when they became lost during a blizzard as they crosse
back into Canderis."

Saffron broke in, eyes hard beneath his corrugated brow
"Aye, and now it's about time you concentrated on the busi
ness of business. You and the High Conciliators have bee
too preoccupied of late, haring off after who knows what sil
liness, closed sessions with preposterous rumors slipping ou
about invasions by Gleaners." He bowed with hard-won pa
tience to Damaris and Doyce. "Forgive me, ladies, for men
tioning something that has touched you both so intimately
but we all know that Gleaners are few and far between an
hardly likely to organize or be more than a random, individ
ual threat. Don't you agree, Eumedico Annendahl?" But h
wasted no time in waiting for Mahafny's response, who sub
sided with a look of relief.

"Those sorties, as ye call them, van Beieven, are ba
enough. But they've abrogated our trade agreements withou
any direct word, costing us merchanters thousands of gold
ens. There's scarce a mercantile house that hasn't been hi
regardless of what it trades—wine ships pirated on th
Baelenas, foodstuffs by the bridge-way, anything and every
thing stopped, turned back, or seized outright. And if it cost
us thousands," he shot a rancorous look at the Monitor, "i
costs you and our government goldens as well, no trade, les
tax to be paid. And that's only the beginning. Any chil
knows Canderis serves as the trade hub between Marchmon

nd the Sunderlies, so the trade losses will eventually pinch
s there as well."

"Jenret, I don't know if your mother's told you, but we've
ad five joint trade caravans turned back. Three at
slebridge," he stabbed his finger at the map where The
Spray reached its northernmost course, "and two of our
quick-riggers sailing across Pettibal for Gavotte. Worse, they
confiscated the sixth caravan, trussed the men, escorted them
back to our side of the bridge, and kept the wagons and
goods. Loaded, I might add, with the choicest bolts of fine-
weave woolens, the kind that only the Houses of Wycherley
and Saffron can produce. In brief, Jenret, your mother and I
are parlously short of ready cash. Too much of our trade depends on Marchmont because we have always made a specialty of it."

Jenret cursed under his breath as he knelt at his mother's
side. "Why didn't you send word, Mother? I'd have come
sooner."

She patted his hand. "And what good would it have done?
You've no more power than we have to open the borders
again."

"I could have asked for a leave of absence, ridden with
the next caravan, done something. I've my savings, my
inheritance from granther. Bribes, we could have tried
bribes—that's what Jadrian would have done." He threw his
father's name at Syndar Saffron with a certain ring of defiance and challenge.

The sharpest of smiles knifed Saffron's face. "I thought of
that already and tried it, Jenret—your father taught me well,
though he wasn't a man who enjoyed employing guile or
dishonesty. My man came back horseless, breechless, and
shaven-headed in shame. Can't say the money came back."

Jenret paced, Rawn following with worried intensity. Khar
stretched to plant her chin on Doyce's knee, waiting to be
noticed. **"Interesting. But what does this have to do with
us? Seekers aren't politicians, aren't merchanters."**

*"I don't know either, but I've a feeling this is a prelude to
something,"* she responded. *"How upset is Jenret? Rawn
looks miserable."*

**"Too much emotion in this house sometimes—Jenret,
Jacobia, even Damaris. It gnaws Rawn's stomach when
he's here too long."**

"And what do the Erakwa know of this, Addawanna?"

Swan Maclough's question sounded commonsensical, ex
actly what they needed.

"Mebbe much, mebbe liddle. Depend on what you mea
by dat." Addawanna shifted, uncomfortable on the settee, re
arranged the clinging folds of foreign fabric imprisoning he
limbs, and subsided with a disgusted grunt. Nakum patte
her arm in a steadying rhythm, but she brushed the han
away as she would a bothersome fly. "Erakwa go where de
wanna go, when dey wanna go. Hunt, fish, explore. Liddl
trade here, liddle there. No go much to Marchmont now, n
for long time. Try stay clear all you. You all bein' too bus
wid silly rules. Make line here, lines dere, lines nobody se
but you say are dere." Her finger darted at the dotted line
that divided the lands, jabbing as if she could blot them ou
as she chose.

Van Beieven hurried to smooth over the situatior
"Boundaries are an integral part of any society that calls it
self civilized. Each country must determine where it begin
and ends to protect its people, provide services, assess an
collect taxes . . ."

"Are you saying we are not civilized?" Nakum had sprun
to his feet, his coppery body slim and straight, glinting lik
a blade in the firelight, arms fisted at his sides. Perhaps
was only a reflection, but the faintest crackling blue aura en
veloped him, vibrating with his anger. "Are you saying tha
Erakwa had no need of boundaries and all the idiotic thing
they impose because we aren't civilized? The land belonge
to itself before you came, before you arbitrarily decide
there should be a Canderis, a Marchmont, a Sunderlies. Yo
do not try to own the sunlight, the air, the water—how dar
you try to claim the land?"

With swift, sinuous grace he confronted the larger, mor
solid man, glaring into his face, though the Monitor was
full head taller than he. He started to raise one hand, a smal
leather pouch clutched tightly between his fingers. Doyc
could feel the barely controlled fury, and knew that Saar
felt it too as the blue-gray ghatt gathered himself on the bac
of the settee, poised to spring, tail tip quivering. He seeme
to crackle with static, hair fluffing up, tingling, but he ig
nored it, intent on the movements around him.

She blinked and realized that the unobtrusive Aelbert nov
stood beside the two, hadn't a notion of when he had maneu
vered to protect the Monitor, so caught up had she been i

the conflict. He deftly insinuated himself with diffident politeness between the Monitor and the young Erakwan, back vulnerable to Nakum in a show of trust, and facing his superior, van Beieven. N'oor had also positioned herself to intercept Saam's leap if it proved necessary.

"Prideful," Khar observed, eyes wide and neck weaving snakelike as she concentrated on N'oor and Saam, alert for the faintest muscle twitch or eye flicker indicating attack.

Doyce found herself striving to control nervous laughter. She rubbed a hand across the lower half of her face to muffle the sound, then thought hard. *"Which one?"* she asked, uncertain.

"All three."

"All three? You mean Saam as well?"

Khar flicked her tail once and it audibly thumped against the wooden floor, but all thoughts were turned on the frozen tableau. **"All four if you want, then. The Monitor, Nakum, Saam, and Aelbert. Though not N'oor."**

"Aelbert?" Well, no reason he shouldn't take pride in his duties.

"Aye, though he camouflages it. Can't you feel it?"

A sharp bark of laughter split the air. Syndar Saffron threw his head back and laughed long and heartily, applauding the motionless tableau in front of him, giving the figures an excuse to turn, disengage from the contest of wills. Addawanna, with a rustle and an audible "umph" of effort, hoisted herself free and stood commandingly. The elderly Erawkan woman was not ungraceful, but the deeply upholstered settees were uncomfortable, alien to one who preferred to sit on the ground.

"Nakum." Reluctantly he turned, unable or unwilling to face his grandmother, but dropped his hand, loosened his fingers instinctively on the pouch so that it swung back around his waist. "Dis house of Wycherley—Dam'ris, Jenret, friends. Food, drink, shelter, friendship, dey gib us. No Erakwan disgrace dat. Not while I be here."

"Nor while I'm here," Saffron added. "Van Beieven, sit down and have another celvassy." The big merchanter approached them with easy command, and it was only out of the corner of her eye that Doyce noticed Aelbert's tactful withdrawal. He had sat back down as if nothing out of the ordinary had happened, except for his nervous fingers play-

ing with a tiny cha pot lid from a child's dolly china set. The
cha pot itself sat on the shelf under the map table.

Damaris joined Syndar in handing out glasses of celvassy
to everyone, as if they had worked as a pair many times before, displaying an easy familiarity born of long together-
ness. "Your grandson's right, madam." Saffron handed the
tiny glass of potent alcohol to Addawanna. "But you've the
righter of it. Not in this house, surely, are arguments necessary amongst friends."

Without a knock or announcement, Harrap burst into the
room, Parm bounding at his side, nearly tweaking his tail in
the closing door as he spun around.

"There was a marriage ceremony to be performed,"
Harrap declared, waving his hands and beaming in expansive delight. "Jacobia . . ."

Damaris blundered to her feet, the color draining from her
face. "Jacobia married?" She glanced around the room in
blind appeal, sliding by Syndar Saffron's face, curiously
blank and still, only his eyes glowing bright with suppressed
emotion.

Oblivious to the startled reaction he'd caused, Harrap
plowed on with his tale. "Oh, yes, of course. Or I mean, no,
of course not. Jacobia told me in confidence about one of
your maids and one of your apprentice weavers who fell in
love without the benefit of the Bethel. Still, it's rectified
now, and our Lady never turns her eye from anyone who
loves her, but sends her Shepherds looking for strays. Oh,
celvassy?"

Doyce gave a soft, irritated whistle of dismay. Parm's
scatterbrained ways were rubbing off on Harrap, no doubt
about it.

As if released from a trance, Jenret poured a glass for the
Shepherd, his face studiously turned away from his mother's
and ignoring Syndar Saffron's.

Overshadowed by the Shepherd's interruption, Nakum
still stood frozen, momentarily ignored except by Doyce as
she accepted the unwanted drink thrust at her. For all that he

was now a full-fledged hunter, a full-grown man, he hovered nearer still to boyhood, and the anger, pride, and hurt made his hazel eyes glisten fiercely with unshed tears. Unbearable to retreat to his grandmother's side like a chided child, and he didn't know where else to go, what to do.

"Khar, have Saam ask him to come sit beside me, say I've a private question for him."

The striped ghatta concentrated, and Doyce wondered yet again if Khar and Saam didn't share yet a third intensely private language beyond their mindspeech or their normal falanese converse. Whatever it was, it worked, for none of the other ghatti—Koom, Rawn, Chak, or N'oor—turned a hair, but Saam blinked once and then, as if a bowstring had snapped, Nakum rushed to her side, ungainly with desperation.

"I do *not* esteem that man!" His whisper intense, a tiny gust of air puffing the hair near her ear. "He may know Canderis, but he knows *nothing* of us, of the Erakwa! How could my grandmother . . .?"

"Don't judge from one unthinking statement. And don't you judge your grandmother either. Do you Erakwa play politics?"

Nakum's face went still, as if listening inside himself. "I hear your people use the word, but I do not know what it means, really," he confessed. "It seems to indicate a . . . a sort of competition over silly things, or things that could be decided in other, better, easier ways. Am I not right?"

Now she had gotten herself into it. Explain politics? She mindspoke Khar for help, but the ghatta craned her neck to examine the ceiling for invisible birds, then tucked in her chin with a smug little gesture. **"Ghatti don't have politics. Are we uncivilized?"**

Saam's tail flickered with appreciation at the ghatta's words as he joined them. Voices rang and counterpointed against each other across the room, weaving a curtain of sound that nagged at Doyce's concentration but at least hid her stumbling explanation from other ears.

"When the Monitor said 'civilized,' he chose the wrong word. 'Complex' or 'sophisticated' might have been better, but it's not right either. Your people are complex in ways unlike ours. We are complex in some of the things we've organized, quantified, codified—the way we govern, for instance." She hesitated, unsure where she was headed, not certain she'd recognize her destination, let alone whether the young Erakwan could follow.

"We have rules that govern our people." Nakum's lower lip jutted forward with scorn. "Mayhap not as many as yours, but we don't need as many. Every child learns them at the knees of the lore-masters through the tales they tell. So it goes for each generation."

She tried again. "Well, the more rules or laws you have, or we have, the more gray areas they create. The more you define something, the more definition it takes to cover every exception. And when a society exhibits that kind of complexity, there's always room for politics—for playing one side against the other, for bargaining and balancing so that the majority is satisfied and the minority not too dissatisfied because it knows it's protected and that at some point in time it may become the majority."

"Then politics is more like trading? As when we trade our garnets or gold or furs for something else?" Nakum's posture loosened with relief. "And sometimes you decide to give a little more because you know that next time you may receive a little more of what you desire in return?"

"Sort of, but sometimes the other person doesn't give a little more back, but just keeps taking and taking more than he deserves. It's not always good, and sometimes people get hurt."

"Killed?"

"No, well, yes . . . sometimes, when you have wars. Where two countries or factions decide to force each other further and further over something, and innocent people who have no reason to be angry at people they don't even know find themselves fighting each other."

Nakum nodded shrewdly. "As the Monitor fears for Canderis and Marchmont?"

Now it was Doyce's turn to be startled, transfixed by the enormity of the idea. Not possible—was it? From what she had absorbed of the Monitor's speech she hadn't taken it to those extremes, no matter how clear the danger signals rang in retrospect. But Nakum in his innocence had made the transition with no trouble. War? In Canderis? Had things gone that far, could they go that far? The inexplicable stoppage in trade, the border incursions, the apparent lack of decisive rule in Marchmont—were these the beginning moves, a disintegration that left once stable things vulnerable to challenge? But why, why after all these years?

Scratching Saam's ears, Nakum shared a comradely wink. Her thoughts and fears tumbling, she tried to concentrate on his words. "Then I think we Erakwa are much wiser than your people. So are ghatti. Neither of us sees the need for wars."

"War is for children. The pouncing mock-battles of ghatten, no one hurt." Saam's eyes half-closed in delight at the ear-rub but his narrowed look was deeply aware and concerned. **"Seekers and Bondmates fight if they must to survive, but war?"**

"Hush, Saam, no one's going to die," Nakum rubbed harder to comfort the ghatt.

"Oriel died." The two words carried a weight of finality and sorrow.

Stricken, the two humans looked at each other. Doyce flinched at the hurt and surprise flooding Nakum's face and dared not think what he read on hers. Oriel, dead, dead and gone so long now.

Khar chimed in, **"But you have Nakum now."**

But the steel-blue ghatt pursued his train of thought relentlessly, hunting the hurt as if it were prey. **"But Nakum isn't Oriel."**

"No, Nakum isn't Oriel. But Oriel wasn't Nakum either. All ghatti revel in diversity, no one ghatt can replace another, no human can replace another. Nakum's difference is good. He cannot replace Oriel, but he can be in addition to Oriel."

"And whom do I have in addition to Oriel?" Doyce mindspoke diffidently, afraid there was no answer but compelled to ask all the same.

Khar came upright, limbered her spine, sitting taller and taller, delaying her answer, considering. Doyce held her breath, heart frozen, unwarmed by the activity and voices around her in the room.

"Was Oriel Varon? No. But you knew Oriel stood in addition to Varon. Who will be in addition to Oriel for you, I don't know. It depends on how many rooms you have in your heart." She rubbed silky-smooth against Doyce's skirted leg and the static electricity crackled between them, blurring Khar's final words. Without warning, the ghatta detached herself from the tight circle of loneliness

and loss and love, padding briskly across the room, her tail
an S-curve of curiosity. **"Rawn calls,"** she sent back over
her shoulder. **"But you have me. Always."**

Doyce let her go, the jaunty curve of Khar's tail with its
bands of gray-tan and black waving farewell, and found herself looking beyond Khar and Rawn to Rawn's Bondmate,
Jenret, pensive, still, and equally alone.

Tiny glass cupped in huge hands, Harrap loomed over
Doyce's chair, expression benevolent, rich baritone capturing the room's attention even though he attempted to whisper. "And have you decided when you're going to leave for
Marchmont, my dear? The sooner, the better, according to
the Seeker General, and Mahafny's anxious to get back
to the Research Hospice. As am I. I think I've found my
home there—even a broom closet-sized chapel I never expected. And those poor, tortured souls, afraid of themselves,
afraid of us. We all need each other so much now. Of course,
you probably don't remember much of that, do you?" he
confided, only to catch the stony, set expressions of the
roomful of people around him.

"Oh, by the Lady, I've done it, haven't I?" he murmured
to no one in particular. Parm gave a wriggle of glee. With a
sketchy bow in Swan's direction, the Shepherd stood silent
but resolute, waiting for reprimand. Impetuous he might be
at times, and innocent, but never a fool.

"You're just a little ahead of yourself, Seeker Harrap."
Swan's dry emphasis on his title of Seeker rather than Shepherd warned Harrap of his blunder. "And of everyone else in
the room," she concluded.

Jenret threw a consoling arm over Harrap's shoulders. "I
think you've just brought things back on track, my friend.
And for that I thank you. I, for one, have no idea where this
conversation is leading, though I've my own suppositions."
The celvassy had flushed his face, two hectic spots of crimson patched his cheekbones, and his eyes gleamed, fervent
and intent. Doyce shivered; she knew too well the extremes
he was capable of when he wore that look.

"Aye, don't keep us in suspense." Syndar directed his
words to Swan Maclough but his violet eyes challenged the
Monitor.

"Are you agreed, Seeker General, that it's time?" Swan dipped her head toward the Monitor and he continued. "We've concluded that we must send a Special Envoy to Marchmont, someone to assess the situation firsthand, resolve any immediate territorial and trade problems, and collect information, make recommendations on the larger issues that will need to be debated amongst the Conciliators and myself. If relations haven't completely deteriorated between our two countries, my seal should allow a small group diplomatic immunity." He ignored Saffron's low gibe, "Make sure they pack extra breeches." "And I emphasize 'small' because it's crucial that our actions don't appear provocative in any way to Marchmont and its leaders, given the strange instabilities we've witnessed."

"Will there be danger?" Damaris's query surprised them all.

"Possibly, yes," van Beieven admitted with reluctance, "although I think, I hope, it will be minimal. Still, as you well know, Madame, any caravan traveling to Marchmont faces a certain amount of danger just from the terrain and the weather. Nothing is completely safe no matter how hard we try. We've no idea what these sorties and raids across the border indicate. No sense in damning Marchmont outright if it's something beyond their control. I hope they'll respect our flag, but if not, I want a small, self-reliant group capable of slipping to safety unobserved."

"Hear you league away, way you people tromp de woods." The Erakwan matriarch sniffed in contempt.

The Monitor bowed in her direction. "And that is why, Addawanna, I've asked you here, to request permission for your grandson Nakum to serve as scout for our Envoy and his group. He knows much of the wilderness toward Marchmont, and you yourself have knowledge of some of the farther reaches of the trek that you could share with him. Will you?" Clearly the Monitor was uncomfortable about asking this favor, about involving the Erakwa, but it was equally clear that he felt he had no choice.

"Who else be wid him?"

Van Beieven surveyed the room as if still considering. "As I noted, the group will be small."

"And how small is small?" Doyce wondered to Khar, while she warily kept watch on Jenret, ready to jump forward and volunteer to lead the group. He radiated hope, the

desire for action, and for a chance to teach the March-montians a lesson for having disrupted Wycherley House trading. Action offered an anodyne to his thoughts and fears, and she suspected there was something beyond the trading problems he yearned to numb as well, although she couldn't surmise what.

"Very small," Khar responded. **"You know N'oor is blocking? Koom noticed right away. He is very sensitive to slights about his bond with the Seeker General. In truth, it's an insult, not a slight."**

"Why? Why the mystery? I thought this was an open meeting of minds. Oh, not in our sense, since not everyone here is a Seeker, but generally speaking."

"N'oor is also blocking the Monitor, as if any of us would be ill-bred enough to try to read any non-Seeker. A bit overzealous as to her duty, I'd say, just as her Aelbert is. I don't think the Monitor asked to be shielded."

Startled, Doyce concentrated on the Monitor instead of on Jenret, waiting for van Beieven's next words, wondering what secrets inside him required such zealous and insidious protection, whether he realized it or not.

"While those chosen must have Canderis's best interests at heart, I've striven to select people known for their strict impartiality, their dedication to seeking the truth, even when the truth is painful to hear. If we've wronged Marchmont—advertently or inadvertently—I want to know so it can be rectified. With these thoughts in mind, I turned to the Seeker General for advice, for it's known to all in Canderis—and I hope in Marchmont as well—that the honor of the Seekers Veritas is above reproach. Neither politics nor passions can sway them from discovering the truth. Were that not so, Canderis might never have come to be as we know it.

"I have selected Rolf Cardamon as my Special Envoy, as Canderis's Envoy with every vested power and authority. Since he has no formal training in the politics of diplomacy, I appoint Aelbert Orsborne as his aide. Aelbert knows the ways of Seekers and the ways of politicians. To accompany them, Jenret Wycherley as special trade consultant, and Doyce Marbon as transcriber and recorder. That means five ghatti and five humans, including Nakum with Saam as scouts."

"Not enough!" Rolf's and Jenret's simultaneous expostulations clashed for attention, but the Monitor deferred to Rolf.

Rolf cleared his throat, tugged at his goatee, his expression thoughtful as he marshaled his response. "When we originally discussed this mission, I suggested we set up message outposts along the way. I hope you've had time to give further thought to that. Way stations where we can depend on the quick transmission of mindmessages, something separate from the formal post-relays of the Guardian sites close to the border. Distasteful as it may be to consider, we've no idea if some of their number may have been suborned, given their isolation and proximity to the border. The Guardians have always been unstinting in their devotion to and defense of Canderis, but remember, it takes only one disaffected or misguided man to betray us. If the Seeker General can spare additional help, the way stations will offer us extra security."

Swan nodded, "I've mulled it over since you first suggested it, Rolf, and I'm willing, if the Monitor approves."

"The thought of betrayal galls me, but I applaud Seeker Cardamon's caution and foresight." Van Beieven spoke as if a burden had been shifted off his shoulders.

"Aelbert looks dismayed." Khar's thought nudged Doyce before the most fleeting wrinkling of disappointment on Aelbert's modest face smoothed itself into its usually equable but politely interested expression.

At the Monitor's terse nod of agreement, Swan continued. "Whom would you suggest, Rolf, as if I didn't have any inkling?"

Rolf's goatee wiggled as he controlled a reminiscent smile. "Why, the Ambwasali twins with P'wa and M'wa, Sarrett Brueckner and T'ss, and Parcellus Rudyard and Per'la. They'll ride with us part of the way and set up individual camps at intervals as we come closer to the border. We know too well that the farther north we travel, the more difficult it can be for the ghatti to transmit messages. The Marchmontian mountain ranges create too many echoes, ghost voices, too much static, or so Chak tells me. Their communal mindnet may be disrupted, reverberate in the wrong directions." A faint smile finally broke across Rolf's pale, tired face. "And if we don't let Parse and Sarrett come along, we both know what's likely to happen. The Monitor will be forced to incarcerate them, or they'll set off on their own to help as they did the last time."

Jenret's protest echoed loud and clear. "But we'll be cutting our strength just when we may need it the most!"

Rolf confronted him. "The Monitor wants a small group, Jenret. A group of five doesn't feel intimidating, although I've no idea how the Marchmontians feel about ghatti."

"Well disposed, I trust," Chak rumbled. **"I will not bide at a way station while you ride on without me."** The gentle reproof reached every Seeker, and even those who were not seemed to sense what had been said from Chak's possessive paw on Rolf's knee.

"Ah, de no mind big khatts." Addawanna gave Chak a rough caress and the gentlemanly gray cat startled as if shocked, then settled his fur and permitted himself a tiny purr. "De jes don' tink de anyt'ing more dan big khatts. Nakum find dat out laz new double-moon when out 'sploring."

Attention fixed on him, Nakum gulped audibly but responded. "Saam and I journeyed northward while I was tuning my earth-bond." He patted his pouch as if no further explanation were necessary—or likely to be forthcoming. "We ran into two scouts from Marchmont. They weren't very difficult to locate, not the way they stumbled and fumbled about." He laughed, waving arms miming protection against lashing branches, exaggerated high-stepping over minor obstacles. "Oh, not badly for someone who isn't Erakwa, but to an Erakwan their presence was unmistakable. They were curious about Saam, but simply because he was with me, that we seemed to be partners. Saam thought they treated him as if he were the equivalent of a hunting dog, strange but something they could cope with under those terms.

"I don't think having the ghatti along represents any problem, Seeker Cardamon," Nakum affirmed. "But I differ with both your idea and Jenret's. The smaller the party, the less likely it is to attract attention until it's too late to turn us back. Still, I'd rather have more help available than less. I'd recommend sending the others ahead, one by one over different routes, to set up individual base camps. Let them quietly establish their routines before we arrive on the scene. It may help draw attention from us."

Rolf and Jenret spoke in an undertone, Jenret angry at being balked. Not an argument, exactly, for Rolf remained controlled, reserved, as if conserving his energy, but Jenret was voluble.

Aelbert Orsborne broke the impasse. "I agree with the Erakwan lad." Despite herself, Doyce pulled a face at the condescending use of the word "lad," hoped that Nakum hadn't caught it. Strange, Aelbert didn't strike her as the condescending sort, or was she being as oversensitive to Nakum's youth as he sometimes was? Aelbert had undoubtedly been oblivious to his choice of words, more concerned with the issue at hand. "If he's to be scout, the one leading us into Marchmont, we should trust his judgment. He's in charge until we arrive and set to work. Still, I'd like to know your precise location when you met the two Marchmont scouts. Did you report it to anyone?" He balanced a small notebook against his bent knee, pencil poised, ready to impale the information with lead-pointed facts. "Well? Can you place it on the map?"

Nakum's hand hovered, finger swinging in tightening circles, conning the map's shrunken two dimensions. His finger arrowed down. "About two days' run north-northeast of the Hospice, at the edge of the Tetonords near Two Bears Mound. You know, where the rock heaves skyward like two bears balancing on their hind legs and wrestling each other."

"That's more than two days' march." The Monitor considered the distance in his mind, shook his head. "Much more, as I recall."

"Two days' run for my people, more for yours," Nakum corrected. "There weren't any Guardians to tell, and they were doing no harm. But Saam spread the word to any ghatti in the area; three Seeker-Bond pairs were working circuits in the region, though none very near. He asked the ghatti to keep their eyes and ears open."

With a brisk rub of his hands, van Beieven spoke. "Are we agreed, then? Five as a group, those five to follow the advance parties as they set up individual relay stations along the way? We'll map it in the morning, draw up the schedule, discuss supplies and victualing." He looked relieved to have settled things with such neat economy, although Aelbert still made rapid, tiny notations in his notebook. "To bed now, I think. . . ."

"A moment, please." Doyce spoke with deceptive mildness, or so she hoped, but couldn't quite bury the underlying edge of sharp anger she felt at being moved, unconsulted, like a pawn sent scurrying across the board. "I don't remember anyone asking me if I'd go, nor do I remember saying I accepted the assignment." She walked with deliberate slowness across the room until the Monitor framed her left, Swan Maclough her right. "I am *not* baggage to be packed up and brought along willy-nilly. In fact, I see no reason why this expedition needs me at all. Unless there's something you've both conveniently neglected to mention? Is this therapy of some sort?" She flung the next words as a challenge, amazed that she could say them with apparent casual scorn. "Or are Gleaners striving to take over Marchmont? Or is it something else altogether?"

"There are a number of reasons." Sententious, that's how Swan's voice sounded to Doyce, and she gritted her teeth as she concentrated on the Seeker General's words, waiting, waiting to jump in and demolish her arguments. "Firstly, you're . . ."

Koom's rich mindvoice cut in. **"Peace, Swan, peace. Don't prevaricate. You know you're a failure at it, especially when we ghatti are in the room. It's up to Khar to explain."**

Khar? What did Khar have to do with this? But Doyce knew the ghatta and her moods too well not to perceive when Khar was hiding something from her. The downcast amber eyes examining the cracks in the floor with scrupulous care, the nervous tongue licking along her chops, the anxious swish of the tail told her that.

"I asked them to make you go!" The words came in a rush. **"I said that if they didn't make you go that you might fade away, and if you faded away, so would I! You hadn't spoken in so long . . ."** Khar concluded, body miserable and tight with guilt.

Scooping the ghatta into her arms, Doyce inhaled the talc-like scent of warm ghatta, lips brushing the downy, cinnamon-colored fur behind an ear. Ah, the pain she'd so unwittingly inflicted on the poor ghatta. She didn't want to go, wasn't sure she could muster the strength, but it was time to return some of the love she'd received—or as much as she was able. "So we go, then, don't we? If a Seeker can't make her Bondmate happy, what good is anything in life? And after all, we know that the ghatti never lie, so I wouldn't want to prove you a liar."

"And learning diplomacy never hurts either," Swan added with a sage shake of her head.

"Oh, cousin!" Mahafny exploded in laughter, only to be joined by the rest as she continued. "Are you admitting that she couldn't have learned it from you?"

Laughing, Doyce whirled around, skirts flying, Khar still cradled in her arms, wide-eyed with excitement at the bobbing dance.

"To Marchmont!" she cried, giving the ghatta a little toss into the air. **"To Marchmont!"** the ghatta sang back.

"To Marchmont!" the others echoed.

Jenret slipped behind Doyce and trapped her elbows, matching his steps to hers, letting her lead while he echoed her steps, his face hidden. He bent close, his breath warm on the back of her neck, spice-scented with the celvassy. Without realizing it she let herself yield against him, into the comfort he offered, letting him bear her along. Then—perversely—she pulled away from the warmth of his body, uneasy, determined to stand alone. "It's not a picnic, you know," he whispered in her ear. "But I'm very glad you'll go with us."

※

The late night quiet enveloped the darkened reception rooms, the unlit bedrooms, the dim corridors of the Wycherley household, cradling the house in silence, secure and peaceful against the night. But that was misperception, for pockets of light and activity still unsettled various parts of the house and grounds, keeping the crumb-seeking mice on edge, amplifying their nervous skitterings, startling them with the creaking of beams that normally sounded as an old friend to them. . . .

A candle flame cast its flickering, haloed reflection against the terrace doors of one of the master bedrooms in the west, or family wing, as Damaris sat beside Jadrian's bed, watching him sleep. The indistinct light flattered him, made him look young and strong, peaceful in slumber, the semblance of the once vital man she had loved and married. Sighing, she stood, tucked the covers around him where he'd tossed them free, put a hand on the placid, guileless brow, and bent to kiss him farewell. Then she retrieved the candle and started for the door. She caught her ghostly reflection in the mirror and muttered "hypocrite" at herself, but the word no longer carried any sting. She had come to terms with it, she thought wryly as she exited the door and locked it behind her. . . .

Mahafny sat tailor-style on the foot of Swan's bed, once-supple fingers fumbling as she shuffled and reshuffled the deck for another game of Tally-Ho. "Deal or concede I've beaten you," Swan crowed, letting the coppers pour through her cupped hands, a metallic, chiming shower of coins.

Beginning to deal, Mahafny remonstrated, "But only because I'm distracted. I think, perhaps, you were right about Doyce, but I'm still not sure. You know she's capable of putting on a facade, of making believe everything is fine."

The Seeker General made a face at the words she'd heard as she fanned the new hand she'd been dealt. "You can't be her shadow, can't be there to pick up the pieces and put them together again. She has to learn to do that herself."

"But aren't we doing that in a sense?" was her cousin's worried rejoinder. "You yourself suggested it might be best to move Doyce and Jenret and the others out of harm's way until the Gleaner issue is settled. If that day ever comes in our lifetimes. You can't hide them away forever because of their involvement, of what they know, of what people might learn."

Ignoring her, Swan discarded a card, then wished she'd considered her move more carefully. But it was too late to pull back now. In some games it was a discard, in others a trump, and sometimes she had no idea at all which game she was being forced to play, or what rules held. . . .

It couldn't be true! It mustn't be true! She was a Wycherley, everyone knew that. Jacobia curled tighter into the curved arm of the library sofa, clutched a pillow to her chest as a shield, used it to smother a sob. She'd almost blurted out her fears without meaning to earlier, and wished the words buried in the depths of the sea, mortified at how she'd behaved in front of everyone.

Her fears had exploded, expanded in her mind ever since that snowy day when she'd watched the front desk for Holbein while he went in search of some files to prepare for a visit from an out-of-town merchanter. The man had come early, brazenly looking her up and down like a bolt of cloth while he pounded snow and ice from his clothes, stamped his feet. How dare he say that her eyes were the exact match to Syndar Saffron's? And then to have given her that lewd, knowing wink when she'd protested she was a Wycherley, through and through. What was it he'd said? "Aye, your mother's looks through and through. And if you've her looks, mayhap you've her temperament too when it comes to having a good time." She'd slapped him as his hand reached across the counter, slipped up her neck, fingers sliding into her hair. She'd fled without a backward glance.

Was it true? It couldn't be! She couldn't even face her mother with that story, beg her to say it was all a lie, let alone acknowledge why she didn't want to help Holbein anymore. Worst of all, she couldn't bear to be near Syndar Saffron since then, had avoided him for at least three octants until tonight, afraid that meeting his eyes would be like looking in a mirror. But her mother wouldn't invite Syndar Saffron to dine with them if it were true, would she? Jacobia sniffled, tried to work it out in her mind.

She didn't know, she wasn't sure of anything anymore. Tears began to fall. Lady bless, how she craved reassurance. Once a Wycherley, always a Wycherley. Jenret? He'd tell her the truth, tease her gently about how wrong she was to even suspect such a thing, but he'd been so preoccupied lately. Could she talk to him tonight? Perhaps after their silly meeting she could find him. . . .

Chin propped on folded arm, Doyce dragged a blank sheet of paper across the desk and picked up the pen. Cramped writing in this position, but she was too tired to lift her head. How many sheets had she destroyed through the days and octs past? If the maid had reported the mysterious dwindling of writing paper to Damaris, the lady of the house had had no comment other than to order the stock replenished. Most of what she'd written, she'd burned, ashamed that the printed words rambled as mindlessly as she did. Still, the effort of forming a coherent sentence or paragraph forced her mind to work, to focus, and a few grew good enough to be fresh-copied into her record book, in the final section where she kept her random jottings. They served as reminders, mostly bleak ones, of the sine curve of her life. Pressing pen point against paper, she watched the divided nib spread to

distribute the ink, the blue ink sinking into the paper just as
it absorbed her thoughts, and began:

> I am more whole than before, but I am not yet "Me;" I
> am not yet well. I am trying, Lady knows, to compen-
> sate, to give what I can. Better, but not enough—for me,
> for Khar. And does the world go on beyond our two
> polarities—Khar and myself? It must, it must, for we are
> not the be-all and end-all of our world, no matter how
> sweet the seeming seems.

She risked a tentative mental caress at the ghatta sitting on
the corner of the desk, absorbed in her own musings. The
ghatta yawned pinkly at her, jaws snapping shut with a little
click. **"You are back, you are my Bondmate, my love."**
"Yes, love. As best I can, as much as I can, I am yours."
"Will you sleep easy tonight at last?"
Doyce produced a sleepy smile, vulnerable and childlike.
"Yes. Yes, I think so." Raising her arms above her head and
arching her back, she stretched, felt tired muscles relax. She
stood, crumpled the message, and tossed it into the fire. Perhaps someday she should consider putting these musings
into bottles and casting them adrift into the sea to discover
where they lapped ashore on the tide, snug in a safe harbor.
Or tie them to arrows, shoot them to the Lady's Havens. The
whimsy amused her, amused the ghatta who shared her
thoughts.
"Bottle-bobbing? Sky-writing?" the ghatta murmured,
then returned to her earlier question. **"If you will sleep now,
I will depart for a little while, if you don't mind?"**
I don't suppose you can undo this fastening, can you?"
Struggling and twisting, Doyce began to unhook the dress.
No easier getting out than in, she decided. *"No, of course
you can't. Have a good ramble. I'll seek you in my
dreams. . . ."*

Syndar Saffron prowled the halls, checking doors and
windows, snuffing unneeded lamps and candles, for all the
world like the master of the house. A gentle spill of lamplight from under the library's closed door attracted him, and
he stopped, hand on the knob, wondering if he should interrupt and whom he would interrupt if he entered. Most likely
that little tailcoat grabber Aelbert Orsborne shuffling his pa-

pers, he decided, as he turned the knob, clearing his throat
to announce himself as he pushed open the door. But the
eyes that swept in fright to meet his were identical to his
own, and his words came with a strangled harshness that he
didn't mean. "Go up now, Jacobia. Everyone's to bed except
you. I'll see to the lamps." And she hurtled by him in a
flash, but not before he marked the tears on her face. . . .

Ghatti sat on the steps of the broad, curving stairs, peering
between the banisters, gem-eyes suffused by moonlight-
sparkle. The Lady's second Apostle moon would soon peak
in its fullness, the first beginning to wane, the third beginning to wax. They spoke little, communing in silence. P'wa
and M'wa hunkered together on the third step from the top,
just below Per'la whose long, feathery tail swung like the
slow stretching of pale toffee. It tickled M'wa's nose, made
him screw up his muzzle, and his sisterling P'wa hooked the
tail away with a considerate paw. Above Per'la Saam leaned
his head against a spindled banister column, rubbing the
edge of his jaw, while Parm and T'ss curled on the treads
just below the twins, jester and juvenile chuckling at some
private joke. The ghatti's shadowed, compact forms harmonized, their positions almost akin to musical notes on a staff.
Rawn sat on the landing, a lone bass note emphasizing the
ghatti melody above.

N'oor's surreptitious entry into the group jarred, a discordant sharp, as if a willing but unskilled fingering had strayed
in plucking the melody. An inaudible humming vibration
from the others smoothed her entry into the group as she
flinched, then relaxed at the solidarity shared with her, not
against her. Her racing heart at last steadied to match the
others' rhythm, enfolding her—at least for a time—without
judging, simply weighing her need to belong, to be a part.
She was ghatti, after all.

Khar found them on the stairs, basking in the moonlight,
gilded grays, silvery whites, damasked blacks, flashing eyes.
Padding down the steps she greeted each by name, even
stopping to exchange a word with the trembling N'oor, who
looked ready to flee, half on one step, half on the other. Her
tail stroked Rawn's chest as she moved by him, intent on
finding her way outside. Saam 'spoke her at last. **"Nakum's
and Addawanna's room is empty, the window open.**

Bounce hard, then pause and twice more soft usually pops it open."

"Thank you." She flowed back up the stairs. **"Will anyone join me outside?"** No one accepted, just as she knew they would not, just as they knew why she wanted to be outside for a time alone. There was communion—and there was communion. Some might be higher on the Spirals of Knowledge than she, and some lower, but all knew the need to sometimes commune with the Elders, the ghatti past and present, the wisest of the wise.

Stars. Stars clustered and sparking the night sky, some trace pale, some steady signal beacons with a strong ruddy or bluish throb to their light. Stretching against a tree, Khar sank her claws into the outer bark, conquered her desire for a soothing scratch, and sprang onto a low-hanging branch where the broad limb offered a perch. Stars. She tilted her neck, chin pointed skyward as she surveyed the pinpricks of light. Funny how humans insisted on connecting one star to another, drawing false patterns to outline imaginary creatures—fish, hunters, scorpions, rockets. Didn't they see the one overriding pattern that was not a pattern so much as a turning, wheeling connection of each to all? No matter how you looked, no matter where you started, it was there, the constant of all the constellations, making them whole.

She had been remiss of late, had ignored the debt of thanks owed to the Elders. Working her claws, she rested her chin on her paws, allowed her mind to float up and outward, into the first spiral of connection and communion and through it into the next, reveling in the effortless slipstream of power that circled her higher and higher, into the third turning, where she had lingered so long, unable to gain or accept the wisdom needed to raise her higher, closer to perfection. The wisdom had been hard-won, but she had at last attained the fourth spiraling, had grown to deserve it. She took the fourth spiral with lazy assurance, knowing she would not be halted until she reached its end.

"Will you answer me tonight? I come not to demand or ask, but to thank you." The night sky continued its stately waltz, the heavens shifting with it. Mindvoices from beyond reverberated, tinkled like icicles wind-chimed by an errant breeze under the eaves. The echo of otherworldly coolness prickled her fur before she shivered and forced it flat.

"**A bit tardy but always welcome.**" Mr'rhah's rich mindvoice touched her. Mr'rhah, so old, so wise, stretched paper-thin between bodily being and nonbeing, and thus still identifiable as a unique voice.

Khar took the chiding in good stead, glad to hear the familiar, revered voice. "**I did not show proper gratitude at the time of my elevation, I know, but my heart was heavy, sore with other concerns. You know we swing like pendulums from patience to not-patience, and I have swung back and forth so many times of late that I have been sore dizzy with it. Your help was true, was right, though I did not always hear as clearly as I should have.**" Here she was, talking with the Elders, and rambling worse than a ghatten. She tried to organize her thoughts, but the Elder beat her to it with a question.

"**And how is she, your Bondmate?**"

Khar considered her answer, did not want to complain but to thank. "**We are one again in the sharing of minds, like sweet water after a long, parching thirst. Still, my thirst is so great.**"

Throaty chuckles came and went, soft and loud, high and low. Not laughter at, but rueful laughter with, savoring the joy with the pain. "**Then . . . do not . . .**" the voices faded momentarily, until Mr'rhah's came back, distant but clear. "**Do not . . . drink too fast . . . or too deeply then, despite your thirst. Thirst is one thing, but you are partners . . . relearning the dance, relearning the rhythm and flow. Lead and follow, follow and lead, each of you must learn both until the balance is reached.**"

Khar bowed her head. "**I know. I have not yet risen so high on the spiral that there are not further turnings, further levels of knowledge. But I thank you for what I have, both within myself and with her again at last. My thanks, O Elders.**"

"**Good . . . journey then . . . however . . . wherever . . . you . . . travel. Travel . . . broadens . . . so humans . . . say.**"

And the ghatta knew the audience was over, had felt herself delicately turned around, sliding down the turnings, the old, familiar ways, until she was where she was again. The smell of shredded bark greeted her nose; she realized she'd been clawing the tree in her excitement. But then the smell that was not a smell, but a summoning, the thirst for the sweet water of sharing drew her back toward the darkened house, summoned by Doyce's dreams that drew her gently home.

❧

Nakum moth-touched his grandmother's arm, pointed to the shadow-striped figure of Khar trotting toward the house, jaunty, tail high in anticipation. They waited until she reached the trellised entryway and climbed up through the ivy stems, gained the roof, and from there the ledge beneath their window. The exact route, in reverse, that they had taken in climbing down, wanting to be outside the confining walls unobserved. "You t'ink I no notice?" Addawanna chided. "No be born yes'erday like some I know." She gave the pouch at his waist a playful tug to remind him precisely how long he'd had his earth-bond and how much longer she'd had hers. "Liddle Pern khatt be happy 'gain. Good."

Sinking into a cross-legged position, Nakum surveyed his grandmother, waited for her to speak again, but she seemed lost in thought. "Would you prefer to sleep outside? I could go back for blankets, our bedrolls." He half-rose, ready to turn words into deeds.

"Nah, nah." Addawanna rolled her shoulders, sighed with relief. "I be gettin' soft, I t'ink, wid ol' age. Be likin' what they call it? 'Luck'ry?' Or sometime, an'way," she amended.

Nakum grinned. His grandmother's adaptive ways never ceased to amaze him, yet no matter how much she changed, grew, the core of strong sameness always remained. "Luxury . . . lux . . . ur . . . y," he enunciated, shocked by how much his vocabulary had expanded since his visits to the Wycherleys; he now far surpassed the teachings his grandmother had given him in this other strange tongue. He shivered, wondering how much he had changed in other ways, how much they might be drawn apart by this and other things he couldn't even begin to name. Part of him was frightened, part of him proud. It had all happened so quickly, in just two seasons: the gifting of his earth-bond before he'd even reached official manhood, the testings, and the tribe's decision to award him his man-sized bow. And, of course, Saam, as wondrous in his own way as his earth-bond.

As if his grandmother had read his thoughts, she answered him. "Yah, dif'ent but same inside, long as dat what you want. Dat why I be sittin' out here, ol' bones on col' ground, remind you. Od'er t'ings I got tell you. Where you goin', where you been."

"About the route to Marchmont, you mean?" He knew he had much to learn, things to commit to memory about the forthcoming journey. And now to be chosen as scout, deferred to as leader for the trip to Marchmont. He licked his lip, suddenly overwhelmed by it all, wanting nothing more than Addawanna's sheltering arms.

"Ob course dat. But od'er t'ings, too, t'ings 'bout us, 'bout our people long afore when worl' dif'ent place ... afore dem. Sometimes, 'fore us." Her words had taken on a strange intensity, her face tilted skyward, illuminated by the moonlight, the stars.

He protested. Some things he was sure he knew, even if other things seemed impossibly different. "I know the old tales, the rules, the ways. You and the lore-masters made sure of that."

"You know, but you not know *dat* much." She gave a scornful flick of her braid at him, as she had so many times before when he was growing up, motherless, fatherless. The flick that said as loudly as words, "Not now, you ask too many questions." But now, with patience, he might find out the answers. An answering grin plumped her cheekbones. "Is lux ... ur ... y," she stretched the word out, caressing its syllables, "ob de ol' to lecture de young. You listen."

Nakum nodded. This he knew how to do. And through the long night he sat spellbound, listening to tale after new tale unfold, tales that he strove to commit to memory as they fell fast and breathless from the lips of a woman who was more than a woman, more than a grandmother ... a tale-teller of epic proportions.

PART
TWO

He tottered from window to window in the tiny solarium, the location above the library forgotten by almost everyone now living. Easing his face between the dusty and crumbling draperies, he scanned and rescanned the horizon. He stumbled several times, chided himself, "Eyes on your feet, not on the stars, you're still not steady yet. A fall will do you no good at all!" Head thrown back, he laughed. "Paltry poetry, too!" It felt so good to be free, walking, searching the sky, but it was so limited compared to where he had been, how he had tapped into the search before.

Nice to leave the draperies wide open, candles and lamps a pallid contrast to the glories in the heavens above, but the light from his windows caused needless worry, uneasiness for the populace. He knew that, had already sensed and heard the whispers about his unseemly lack of need for sleep. No sense starting rumors because, after all, rumors always had a tangible, though very remote, basis in fact. What if he left the draperies wide open but all the lights out, simply basked in the moonlight, the starlight, the wheeling pattern of the constellations swinging on their distant pole star? Possible, certainly. A clear view, a few tiny pinpricks of light from the city below, the sleepless, the early risers, scant competition for the stars' brilliant splendor.

"Oh, Carrick!" he breathed to himself. "Where are you out there? Where? I remember things I'm not supposed to remember, the shock of the severing of the umbilical cord, but that was nothing compared to the shock when our link was severed." With hasty steps he began to snuff the candles, the lamps, smashed hard against a table in the semi-darkness. He put his hand against his belly, fumbled against his robes until his fingers discerned the steady hum, the minute vibrations that told him that he lived, almost as he had once before, so long ago. His free hand pushed the wisps of hair off his forehead, sticky with sweat at the near calamity. With a growl he kicked off his sandals, more secure in his movements with the stone against his bare soles.

Drape after drape swept back with a muffled rush across the rods. He stood, arms outstretched, pressed against the window casing. "Carrick, have you seen anything more? Anything similar to what I saw, oh, near four octants ago? That corona of flame, like a solar flare-up? And then the explosions of light, golden petals of fire surrounding those faces? Some were faces I knew, others I didn't; and of the ones I knew, some were from a past so long ago that I almost didn't remember them, almost didn't remember my own face. But I remembered yours when I saw you there. How could I not?" He bowed his head, eyes squinted shut. "I don't know what it is, Carrick, but there's power out there, someone with powers greater than anything we ever imagined. It's still raw, unformed, I think. I've been calling out to it, trying to bring it near. And maybe that's not right, maybe all that is gone, dead and buried, and I should bend my attention to the problems here. But I can't *not* try, Carrick. It's for you that I'm trying. With power like that I could track you to the stars, find you, and reunite us again."

His arms dropped to his sides, too heavy to hold up, any other words lost as mere muttering sounds, a child's night whimpers while asleep. At length he roused himself and, shoulders slumped and weary, left the window. "Sleep," he said wistfully, and tottered to the long, low platform molded to his body conformation. He lay down, pulled the lid over himself. It wasn't the same anymore, not since the disconnection, but it would do, it would have to do.

Overcast gray as a mouse's belly, mist sleek and moistly sweet, early spring enveloped everything and each figure with a delicate tenacity. Moisture clung to creases of clothes, muffled the deeper creaks of leather, amplified the errant squeaks; faces and eyebrows glowed, radiant damp with tiny droplets of water-gilded tracery where highlighted by the pale dawn.

"It'll burn off," Khar prophesied.

Doyce heaved her saddlebags over Lokka's back and checked the struts on the pommel platform where the ghatta would ride. Lokka swung round to nose her, anticipating a treat, and Doyce dug for a sugar nugget, munched one herself. *"Weather forecasting now?"* She swiped at her face with her sleeve, leaving a swath of cheek smooth and dry, the rest still slicked with moisture.

The ghatta examined a foot preparatory to licking it, decided no additional moisture was necessary and began to scrub energetically behind her right ear. Her head tilted, twisted sideways to make the reaching easier. **"No."** The washing paw slid across an eye and down her muzzle, whiskers pinned tight. **"Byrta said the same to P'wa, weather was like this a few days ago when they left. Said her leg'd tell her otherwise."**

"Byrta's broken leg hasn't been healed long enough for her to know what every weather change feels like."

"Mmph, no." The ghatta started work on the other ear, making the golden hoop gyrate back and forth. **"But she knew what it didn't feel like. She healed during the winter, knows how snow makes her leg ache."**

"All right, you win." Throwing her arms across the saddle, Doyce sagged against Lokka, and the little sorrel mare blew contentedly.

"Always do." Nothing beat the smugness of a ghatta; the thought always made Doyce laugh.

"No, you don't, I just let you think you do."

The easy jocularity of their private mindspeech left them as self-contained as if they stood alone in the courtyard, rider, horse, and ghatta, but in truth the yard bustled with activity. Seven other horses stood saddled and ready while packhorses were being loaded. Nakum swooped by, seemingly everywhere at once, soaring and darting like a chimney swift after an insect. Voices rose in brief clamor, raucous yet invisible as the nearby crows she could hear but not see, only to stop, dampered off. Nakum had won his argument, and now he ran by to see to the lashings of another pack beast.

Jenret's form loomed like a mist-shadow, wading through mist tatters that wisped about him, water-webs spun by raindrop spiders. He thrust a bulky, paper-wrapped bundle into her hands and she recoiled at its soggy texture, the heavy, pulpy smell. "What is it?" Turning the package round and about, another aroma gradually reached her nose—the smell of fine-cured leather.

"You owe me three golden, six silver plus delivery charges, personal hand delivery, as you may have noticed."

"Mintor?" She was sure now, it was the boots, it had to be the boots of fine green leather that Mintor had coerced her into buying before she left on that final, fatal circuit to find the reason behind Oriel's death. She had never returned to the capital to pick them up, a reminder she didn't want, even now.

"About ready to go?"

Tugging a flap free, she stowed the package in her saddle-bag, then nodded, beset without warning with an aching desire for her solitary bed, alone, unaware, unchallenged. She shook herself as if it could dislodge the seductive ghosts of uncaring. The old burdens of the last few octants still clung to her although she'd made a determined effort to throw them off. She nodded more forcefully, more for herself than for Jenret's benefit. "Aye. Just waiting for Nakum to give the signal."

Innocent as they were, she sensed the words' sting as soon as they left her mouth. Jenret was still coming to grips with their respective assignments—Nakum in charge of their welfare during the journey, with Rolf responsible for their negotiations once they reached Marchmont. Jenret was not in charge, was merely a trade adviser. She tried to think of something heartening to add, then stopped. No, she'd not cozen him. He was full-grown and able to take disappointment in his stride, wasn't he? Besides, amending her statement would only make it worse, show him she knew how much it rankled. Always on tiptoe with him around, he always on tiptoe near her to avoid piercing each other's carefully constructed shell or revealing new and untested feelings. They had learned, grudgingly, how to work around each other on their previous journey, how to work as a team yet preserve their separateness, but still, the wariness remained. And something more she couldn't quite put her finger on. That night of the banquet . . . his touch. She shivered, stiffened.

Rawn glided over, nosed Khar into a pretend jump of startlement though she full-well knew the ghatt was near.

Amused by their mock antics, Doyce forced herself back to Jenret, standing with unexpected patience, waiting as if for her to speak again. She asked the question that had been

uppermost in her mind for days. "Do you think the others
are well on their way? No problems?"

Sarrett, Bard, Byrta, and Parse had ridden toward
Marchmont at two-day intervals, beginning with Sarrett's
leave-taking an oct earlier and with Parse's only two days
ago. Sarrett had the farthest to travel with orders to locate
herself as close to Marchmont's borders as she could without
arousing suspicion. As she approached the border she would
assume the guise of an itinerant peddler, tabard and all other
evidence of Seeker garb packed away, and with T'ss, her
pale-hued Bondmate with black striping, staying out of
sight, ghosting along side streets or overgrown side trails, in
constant mental contact but invisible to the casual eye.
Sarrett was the one free-moving piece of the four back-
ups, with discretion to cross the border or fall back as
needed. Risky, that, both the fact that T'ss wouldn't be riding with her at the end and the fact that she could not claim
Seeker immunity while in disguise. They, at least, had never
been harassed near the border.

Bard, Byrta, and Parse had instructions to hold normal
Seeker circuits, hearing cases as they traveled from one
small town or hamlet to another until relieved by replace-
ments. Their spacing had been calculated to span the maximum ghatti communication distance should problems arise.
As usual, the gap between Bard and Byrta was greater than
that between any of the others: their twinship and the ghatti's twinship endowed their mindspeech with a potency and
distance that no other Seeker Bond-pairing could match.

Jenret stood as though lost in thought, or listening to
Rawn. He started, then fixed his gaze on Doyce, again captivating her with his long, dark lashes, but the speculative
urgency of his glance clawed at her. For a dawning moment
she almost understood why he looked at her thus, but her
subconscious smothered the intuition before it began.

Khar's tail twitched at Rawn's elaborate, nonchalant indifference to Saam's approach. There was still no love lost between the midnight-hued and the steel-gray ghatts. They
weren't enemies, but they were both overly strong-willed,
each testing his dominance. Chak would serve as buffer, of
course, on their journey. And how the demure, dainty ghatta
N'oor would fit in, Khar had no idea. Nearly as self-effacing
as her Bondmate Aelbert Orsborne, always circling just beyond the sphere of their communal mindsharing, like a land

bird driven out to sea by a storm, yearning for the safe shore
of their minds. Khar sneezed. Irritation at the mist, she told
herself, and swallowed her faint misgivings much as Doyce
had controlled hers.

More shapes visible in the patchy mist now, more people
scurrying about, Wycherley household servants, Damari
moving grave and quiet toward her son, but with Synda
Saffron protective at her elbow, and Jacobia in her own hesitant approach to her elder brother, magnetically drawn
nearer and nearer yet pretending indifference. The first
swelling notes of the Lady's sunrise chant echoed from
Harrap's expansive lungs as he joined them, arms linked
with Mahafny and Rolf. A weak beam of sunlight glanced
off his medallion and she realized that the mist was dissipat-
ing, the sun steadily burning through.

He materialized at her elbow, inconspicuous as a creeping
ground fog. Aelbert's diffident throat-clearing startled her,
brought her away from Lokka's comforting side as quickly
as she could move. N'oor sat a calculated distance from
Khar, who cast one sidelong glance in her direction and
sighed as she dipped her head in greeting.

"Sleek-footed," Khar whispered, then held her peace.

"Where did you learn to move so silently?" Doyce asked
him.

Clearly gratified at being noticed and addressed, a fleeting
expression of pleasure illuminated the younger man's face. It
was not an unpleasant face, she had to admit, the remnant of
an uptilted smile made it seem tentative, hesitant, young—
yet as wary as the oldest and canniest of forest creatures.
The face of a survivor, able to blend into its surroundings,
efface itself at the most subtle scent of danger. But she
posed no danger to Aelbert, obviously a young man on the
rise with his dual status of Seeker and aide to the Monitor.
Young for it, too, about twenty-three at most. Unusual to attain this dual position, admittedly mostly a ceremonial one,
while he still wore the silver edging on his tabard, the mark
of a junior, not a seasoned Senior Seeker.

"It's nothing I practice, I assure you. Disconcerts people
at times, though I don't mean to. The Monitor has threatened
to bell me so he'll know when I'm around." His hands made
the motion of jangling a bell at his neck. Then, as if appalled
by the implications of what he'd said, his hands dropped and
he stammered, "Not . . . not, of course . . . that the Monitor's

a mouse. I . . . I never meant . . . not, no . . . not in the least
that he's . . . or that I'm . . . well, you know what I
mean. . . ."

Taking pity, she tried to change the subject. "Wouldn't it
be more comfortable to wear something else while we're
traveling?" She gestured at the trim, tightly cut uniform of
the Monitor's Hall, its high, gold-braided collar constraining
as a stockade, forcing him to look straight ahead although
his eyes rolled whitely as if seeking cover. The question
only made him more ill at ease.

His hands tugged at the Seeker's tabard he wore over his
uniform, rolling it, twisting its hem. "No," he managed with
distinct effort, articulating each word. "No, really, it's fine,
and uniforms are the only clothes I own. It's always work,
you see, no time for play." Pride and panic in his statement, as if he hid behind the dark navy uniform and its gold
braid and red facings, behind the Seeker's dress black tabard, not even the standard issue heavy sheepskin tabard they
all wore while on the road. As if without these garments, he
was nothing.

Nervously, he continued, "I'm sorry that your friends,
Eumedico Annendahl and Shepherd Harrap, will only ride
with us for a few leagues. I know it hurts to part with friends
so soon, but we haven't time to detour to the Research Hospice, too. . . ." Consternation clouded his face. "Oh, I
shouldn't have mentioned the Hospice. He explicitly told me
. . . said I wasn't to bring it up . . ." and with that he fled,
jostling Jacobia as he sped away, surprising in a young man
as surefooted as he. N'oor peered after him.

Striding forward, Doyce steadied Jacobia. The girl stood
shaking and close to tears, but not from the jostling, she suspected. *"Khar, do you know what the problem is?"*

"Yes, youth," the answer shot back at her.

"I was hoping for something more specific than that."
Doyce enveloped Jacobia in an impulsive hug, then set her
back a pace so she could see the girl's face. The wondrous
eyes, the image of shy violets on a secluded, shade-dappled
bank, cried a wordless appeal to her innermost soul.

But the sudden, arrogant lift of her chin destroyed her
fragile, lost look, no matter how Doyce tried to convince
herself it was a gesture of self-defense. "Doyce, *please,* I
want to go with you. Please, I want to ride to Marchmont
with you all. I can be useful, I can help. I *need,* I've *got* to

get away, to prove myself, to prove to them. . . ." Her words landslided over each other, pitching and tumbling. "I *can* do it, I *know* I can. You'll let me go with you, won't you? You *know* what it's like, you have to!"

Youth. Khar had been right. Reining in her annoyance along with her smile, Doyce gave Jacobia the slightest shake to focus her attention. "Have you asked your mother or Jenret about your idea? I think they have more right to make the decision than I do."

"But if you say something, Jenret will listen, I know he will! So will Mother. Please, Doyce, say yes. Ask them if you must, but let me go with you." He tone wheedled, cajoled, the sound of a child trying to stay up just a little later.

"And I asked if you'd asked your mother or Jenret. Have you?"

"Doyce, mount up! We're ready. Hurry and say your good-byes." Nakum's shout caught her unprepared, and she fought the compulsion to obey without finishing the task in front of her.

"You did, didn't you? And they said no, I presume?" Exasperated, Doyce gave the younger woman a harder shake. "And now you want me to intervene to convince them otherwise, am I correct? That's *not* the way to do it, Jacobia, playing one person against another, testing to see who'll give you the response you want." The girl looked woebegone but hardly chastened.

"Wanting to go along isn't a good enough reason, not on this trip. It isn't a party picnic, we've serious work to do. Do you have something to contribute, some skill or special knowledge we need, something that you alone can offer beyond the simple desire to go? If so, inform the Monitor, convince him, and let him convince your mother." She scrutinized the girl, trying to read her, and at last was rewarded with the least little negative shake of her head, violet eyes avoiding hers.

"No . . . but I thought you'd . . . . Jenret won't listen to me, either!" Abruptly, she spun on her heel and marched off, making a wide detour around her mother and Jenret to stand beside Holbein, obviously befuddled by her sudden rapproachment with him. She kept her back turned to her brother as if refusing to wish him farewell.

"*As spoiled and obstinate as Jenret,*" Doyce fumed at Khar.

With a neat jump, the ghatta beat her in mounting Lokka. She turned three times on the narrow pommel platform and sat, wrapping her tail around her. **"As obstinate as someone else I know."**

Doyce feigned surprise. *"Who, me?"*

"No, Harrap," and Khar slanted her eyes sarcastically.

"Then Lady protect Jacobia if she ever takes it into her head to argue theology with the Shepherd. Or anything else, for that matter." Doyce swung up on Lokka and brought her around.

The others sat mounted and ready, Jenret and Rolf leading, with a space held open behind them for Doyce. Then Mahafny and Harrap who would travel with them for a half-day before branching toward the Hospice, and lastly, Aelbert, holding the leads for the packhorses. Standing aloof, untouched by their urgency, Nakum waited to give the signal to be off.

At a wave of his arm, they broke into motion, Nakum running ahead to guide the group, faster and more tireless than any horses as his Erakwa training took hold, transported him into another realm of being, senses keener than any forest creature's, and with a swift, noiseless pace as relentless as the wind. Saam sprang beside him, matching him stride for stride, a blue-gray threading of color.

Without any prompting Lokka surged ahead, and Doyce wobbled in surprise before clenching her knees and settling into the rhythm. How long had it been since she'd ridden? She turned to wave at those left behind: Damaris, Addawanna, who stood apart near a shelter of trees at meadow's edge, Jacobia beside Holbein, Syndar Saffron, standing four-square in the middle of the yard, hands planted on hips, legs splayed, motionless yet vaguely foreboding in the quiescently massed power his pose symbolized.

It was that image she was to hold with her as she rode along, off at last on a new journey that was supposed to finish her healing, make her whole. I will try, will give the best I can without being asked for it, she pledged to herself, in her own heart. But don't let them ask more than I can give, please. Even I can't chart the depths yet.

❖

"Come on, Twink, let's scan the bridge while it's still light."
Scribbling a few final notes on his topographical map,
Faeralleyn Thomas, Faertom to his fellow Transitors, stuck
his pencil in the holder on the scribing board affixed to
Twink's broad back, and drummed his heels against the
mare's gray sides. Tail swishing, Twink began to amble
down the road, high speed for her. That was why some of
the Transitors groaned when assigned Twink for survey
work: "Miss Twinkletoes, Slower Than Death Warmed
Over," they gibed. Faertom didn't agree, indeed, was pleased
to draw her name. Slow the old mare might be, but eminently steady, wouldn't have jarred a baby, and he could
sketch directly on the accordion-folded map for each route,
noting the washouts, potholes, obstructions, brush overhangs
in precise scale so that work crews could locate and repair
any problems.

He refolded the route map to its last page, pulled the
bridge diagram from the folder's flap, and fingered the pencil supply in his leather pocket holder. Check the bridge for
winter damage, make sure the supports hadn't been ice-
damaged, and he'd be set for his next assignment. Shoving
shaggy bangs away from his eyes, he puffed round cheeks
and blew, still astonished that at only nineteen he'd been
made a full-fledged surveyor. Not everyone had his second
sight, so they said, for spotting structural defects almost hidden to the naked eye. The compliment of "second sight"
made him nervous, because it was a little too close to the
truth.

Being a Transitor suited Faertom, allowed him out in the
world but not too near it, most of his work done alone. Solitary was safe, that he knew, because Faeralleyn Thomas
was a Gleaner, taught from birth that secrecy wasn't mere
necessity, but life or death itself. He'd had it drummed into
him by his parents and older brothers, reclusive folk who
built and sold narrow-prowed guideboats prized for their
ability to carry three people and their gear, yet light enough
for one-man portage with a specially carved shoulder yoke.
But no boat buyers, indeed, no strangers ever set foot on
Thomas's Island on Aries Lake; only Faertom's father or his
uncle transacted orders, met with customers at the little boat-
house across from the island on the lakefront.

As a child the island had been a small paradise, but as he
grew older, the constraints and the cautions mounted, even

though he understood why they lived as they did. Play with
stranger children who waved from a passing boat? Never.
Visit town with his eldest brother for supplies? Out of the
question. There was a whole world out there, and Faertom
wanted to taste at least part of it, ever mindful of his own
limitations, of the Gleaner heritage that bound his family to
the island. His family had been adamantly opposed, but at
sixteen Faertom declared he was leaving home, unable to
bear the island's isolation; protected from almost every human contact, the loneliness was unbearable.

His father had countered by offering to let him move to
his maternal uncle's sheep stead in Pennington Province, but
that was equally isolated: rolling hills instead of the wave-
swept lake, placid sheep instead of shrieking gulls and cavorting water animals. No, he'd seen the Transitors from
afar, inspecting the canal linking Aries Lake with the River
Kuelper, knew they had something to do with roads and
bridges as well. Being a Transitor meant exploring, seeing
the world, but with far fewer chances of revealing himself
than a town job would offer.

Twink's steady gait brought them closer to the bridge, and
Faertom's mind reeled back to his stop in Gaernett two octs
ago to pick up the bridge renderings. Dangerous to think of
things like that; wandering thoughts had a way of finding
other homes, his father had always warned. "Trust only
those you know," was his motto. Usually Faertom kept his
visits to the Transitor offices brief, rarely stayed over, never
lingered for more than one ale, and that only to appear
friendly with any fellow workers who might be in town. Not
that he didn't want friendship, but it wasn't wise with outsiders. For some reason or another he'd allowed himself to
be talked into touring the High Conciliation Chambers, seeing government at work. Something exotic to tell his folks
about when he took leave.

But the topic that day had left him near paralyzed with
fear, round face sheened with sweat as he heard them debate
his fate and the fate of his parents, other relatives, and
Gleaners he'd never even met. And not simply debate, but
nearly froth and foam at the mouth about innocent people
they didn't even know, let alone understand! After so many
years of care, to have it come to this! And all because of
those renegades at the Research Hospice in the Tetonords,
jeopardizing innocent folk, promising them who knew

what—"normality," power, whatever. There'd been few sorrowers amongst Gleaners scattered throughout Canderis when Vesey Bell had met his match. And if outsiders could conquer Vesey, what would they do to the rest of the Gleaner communities?

Despite his terror, despite trying to keep up an amused chatter with his friend in the galleries, what had awed Faertom and given him faint reassurance was hearing Darl Allgood speak, and Faertom had experienced a fresher shock, one of recognition. He knew, though he didn't know how, that Darl Allgood was a Gleaner, he'd stake his life on it! A Gleaner as a High Conciliator! Not living in life's half-shadows, not fearfully skirting the daily contacts that most people took for granted. Amazing!

He'd not followed up on his intuition about Darl Allgood. Perilous if he were wrong. Besides, he'd remembered his father's dictum about identifying Gleaners: "Sometimes it's best not to know—who or what you don't know, you can't betray." But he'd think on it, decide what it meant, that one of his own, even if a stranger, could live in the bright light of regular life. Oh, not openly yet, but more openly than he and his family had ever dared, or their parents before them. With a start, he realized Twink had halted, patient, head digging to crop at some new grass. The bridge loomed ahead of him, waiting for inspection. Well, inspection it would be, and no more introspection until later. Carelessness, mind-wandering like that could get one caught. Still, if he could send a message to his family....

Lady bless, she'd forgotten the boredom of traveling as part of a group, especially as a follower, not a leader. Not that she had any desire to lead, not with its chimerical illusion of power overbalanced by the responsibilities that went with it. Doyce sniffed in exasperation as she reined in, pulled up short at Nakum's peremptory signal while he glided ahead to scout their route. They'd been riding for four days now, four days nearer the Marchmont border but not near enough by far. She hoped that Mahafny and Harrap had reached the Hospice in good time. The return to a self-appointed task was far better than the anticipation of it, and she prayed that both would succeed at restructuring a noble idea—a Research Hospice—warped from its original goals by Vesey, Evelien, and Gleaner compatriots. And most of all she knew the shame Mahafny lodged in her heart: eumedicos led astray by visions of discovering that the mindtrance, the direct reading of one mind by another, might be within their grasp instead of continuing to carry out the charade upon which they'd based their reputations, their lives, and the lives of their patients. The living lie that she had been unable to accept, that had caused her expulsion from the eumedicos, betrayal by those she loved and revered. Not the first betrayal, nor the last in her life, and she was beginning to come to grips with that fact.

She let her prayers for success float in their direction, despite the distance. But there was something nearer to hand, a puzzle that Mahafny had set for her, things said and unsaid with more meanings than she'd realized. Before they'd separated that first afternoon, Mahafny had ridden beside her, more from the need for companionship than a desire to talk, Doyce had decided. She'd respected that need, immersed in her own thoughts, and had been totally startled at words that seemed to come out of the blue. "Wyn and Dwyna Bannerjee. I assume they're still there, but who knows? I met them during the half-year's training I took in Marchmont. Should you need help, I think you'll find it with them."

"Eumedicos, then?" She hadn't wanted to make any assumptions, but given the rigors of training, meeting outsiders was unlikely. So, for that matter, was training in Marchmont.

"Yes." A strange hesitation about the answer, so unlike the straightforward Mahafny. "Yes. An ... unusual pair ... to say the least." And said nothing further until it was time for farewells, when she struggled against some inner restraint that wouldn't allow her to repeat the names. "Give them my regards when—" she broke off, corrected herself, "*if* you see them."

Why Mahafny had been so elusive, almost coy, she still couldn't decide three days later, so she forced herself to concentrate on matters closer at hand. If the days had been exhausting, the evenings had been equally wearing as Rolf lectured them, no other word for it, on Marchmont past and present. She'd never realized his penchant for the past, and Aelbert chimed in whenever Rolf paused or hesitated over a fact. Despite Jenret's grins, she'd taken copious notes, just to keep from falling asleep. And there were always ways,

tricks, to memorize unwieldy or boring data, she'd learned
that from her eumedico training. During the riding each day
she'd fitted facts into jingles, discovered them winding
through her brain when she least expected, like some maud-
lin tavern love song one finds oneself humming at odd moments. Well, then, drill time.

Lesson One had become:

> Domain Lords of Four there be,
> Hereditary rule with dignity,
> Lordlings of the Sud and of the Nord,
> Will honor us with rare accord,
> Lord of the Levant and Lord of the Ouest,
> Pray welcome us as honored guests.
> Mercilot and Clairvaux,
> Are relatives but act like foe,
> Vannevar and Napier,
> One is weak, the other sneers.

Aelbert had provided those details from notes he'd taken
during interviews with Consul Aaron Rossmeer's staff.
Pausing for breath, she tried to tick off the Ministration
Lords, all seven of them. No rhymes served. She almost had
the positions committed to memory but who held what position hadn't sorted itself out yet. Taking a deep breath, she recited, "*I*n *A*ll *E*veryday *A*ffairs (*I*nternal *A*ffairs, *E*xternal
*A*ffairs), *E*mbark *D*ynamically (*E*xchequer and *D*efense),
*P*roceed *W*isely (*P*ublic *W*eal), *C*onclude *J*oyously (*C*om-
merce and *J*ustice)." The seven offices were named!

Khar stared down her nose. **"Is it fair to use affairs in a
memory sentence when it's part of what you're remembering?"**

"*I'm not sure,*" Doyce confessed. "*In fact, I think reciting
that senseless sentence is worse than remembering the Ministration Lords. It's not,*" she considered, "*exactly a saying
worthy of embroidering on a pillow. And a large pillow at
that.*"

**"Duly appointed by the Lords of Domain, Serving at
the monarch's pleasure while he reigns. . ."** the ghatta
ground to a halt, shocked. **"Now I'm doing it! No fair!"**

The next night's lecture, Lesson Two, concerned the
founding of Marchmont and its rulers, past and present, a
fairy tale of sorts that buoyed Rolf with animation as he es-

corted them down the paths of yesteryear. "Both similar and dissimilar to our ways and customs, Marchmont was settled by some of our original ancestor-explorers, men and women left behind when the Plumbs began to randomly explode. They trekked north because fewer Plumbs were sited there, less likely to cause havoc, and because they scorned those passive enough to huddle together, helpless, waiting for the next explosion, the end. They wanted the open, pristine territory that Marchmont offered, a rich wilderness only the Erakwa knew.

"And they wanted one other thing, something incomprehensible to most of the expedition members, those left behind when three of the original spacer ships managed to take to the air, escaping the exploding planet: they wanted not an elected head of state, not a Monitor," he made a self-deprecating gesture in Aelbert's direction, "but an absolute ruler, a monarch, one person with total life authority to make the decisions that would insure their survival. They found that man in Venable Constant, or Constant I, as he came to be called." Rolf seemed to wander in his thoughts. "Perhaps they were right, at least initially—they *were* better organized because of that leadership, while we were in disarray, still coping with the Plumbs and with our inadvertent exile, unable to rebuild a civilization. So much responsibility . . . so much power concentrated in one person . . . I wonder what. . . ." And at a throat-clearing from Aelbert, he brought himself back on track.

"Constant was both genius and maverick, a stellar physicist credited with advanced discoveries in his field but who hated being subordinate to anyone. To his way of thinking, he had no peers. And because of this disdain for any authority other than his own, despite his scientific training, his natural genius, he chose to become a sculptor. Gifted, too, that much is obvious or he wouldn't have been selected for the first settlement flight to Methuen. But he possessed yet another gift, an intangible one he kept under careful wraps—the charisma to convince others that he, and he alone, knew best in any given situation. Some say he became worse, more dictatorial, after the three spacers left, whether out of blatant cowardice or in hopes of seeking rescue for those left behind, we'll never know. Constant's twin brother, Carrick, escaped on one of the spacers, and some say Constant never recovered from the separation, the desertion." Rolf paused, gestured to Aelbert to refill his cha mug, took a small sip, patted his lips with his handkerchief.

"In his own way, Constant wasn't a bad ruler, and neither were his descendants. Canderis and Marchmont observed a strict neutrality, respected each other's boundaries and laws, and entered into trade agreements as necessary. Immigration from Canderis to Marchmont and vice versa occurred but wasn't encouraged, and neither country ever gave sanctuary to the other's lawbreakers or criminals."

The lesson wound on, personalizing the various kings and queens succeeding Constant I, and though she'd tried not to doze, she suspected she had, because suddenly she'd heard, "Constant's last direct descendant through the first-born rulers, Wilhelmina, died without issue, without naming an heir."

Aelbert had interjected, "And that may be part of the problem we face. A Steward has been appointed until the rightful heir is determined, but whether in the interim—or interregnum, more precisely—he's trusted, has power, is unclear."

And if that genealogical saga hadn't been enough to make her head spin, last night Rolf had invited Jenret to discuss trade. She'd suspected but hadn't appreciated how much Jenret knew about trade in general, beyond his own family's concerns.

Jenret had gradually warmed to the task, fielding questions from Nakum and Rolf. Trade, he'd explained, was legally sanctioned in only a few designated sites—the Marchmontian capital of Sidonie, Gavotte, Islebridge, and Mirabelle, farthest east. Most merchants had main offices at these sites, or sent their agents to bid when a Canderisian caravan or ship was due. With the exception of Sidonie, located inland, the other sites were on the border. To Nakum's question of why, Jenret complained, "It's as if they don't want us to penetrate far into Marchmont itself. Only a few of our most trusted merchanters are given leave to deliver goods directly to the buyer's warehouse or shop. Father was one of those so trusted." His pride was unmistakable. Doyce had cleared her throat, started to ask Syndar Saffron's status, but decided against it. "Oh, a few small traders or peddlers wander the border without much hindrance. Peddling trifles is almost impossible to regulate. That's why we assume Sarrett's disguise as a peddler will work, if necessary."

Jenret then waxed expansive about Marchmont's exports: fish, both fresh and smoked, furs, precious metals and superior iron, and strangely enough, what he referred to as "dainties" of various sorts. "Do you remember Mother's dining room table, with all its inlays? That's from Marchmont. They're justly famed for their carved and inlaid furniture, incredibly intricate and highly prized. I suspect that's what they trade with the Sunderlies, but no one knows for sure. We handle their transhipping because we've more ocean-going vessels capable of carrying cargo, but we've never been entirely sure what they trade in down there. They provide us with seaworthy, sealed containers, and the bills of lading are in a locked box for the ship's captain to turn over to the Sunderlies buyers when the ship docks."

What tonight's lesson was going to be, she had no idea, but it was sure to fill up pages of her notebook. As usual, Jenret and Aelbert were bickering over something or other; she'd halted too far away to hear and had no desire to press closer. Actually, to be more accurate, Jenret was bickering with Aelbert, while the young aide maintained an uncomfortable, deferential silence except for one mild remonstrance. The silence, more than the rebuke, stimulated Jenret to further flights of argumentation, his whole body twisted with pent-up anger, arms hacking the air for emphasis.

"Doesn't do much good, does it?" Rolf's thin face crinkled in amusement. "Or perhaps it does a great deal, depending on whose point of view you're considering?"

"Not from Jenret's." Doyce gave a reluctant chuckle. It felt good to have Rolf with her again, although she wished he didn't look so perpetually tired and drawn. "But what's Aelbert's point, what's his game?"

Chak lazily opened an eye, then closed it, bundling himself tighter on Rolf's pommel platform. **"Checking to see where the prickle pig doesn't have spines? In other words, searching for a soft, vulnerable underbelly. When he's ready, all he has to do is roll him over and expose it."** But his final remark sounded deadly serious. **"He wouldn't dare try it with Rolf. I am here."**

"Not exactly that, old friend." Rolf laid a restraining hand on the white-toed paw. "Van Beieven made it clear to him that I'm in command, nominal as that may be, when we reach Marchmont. There's time enough then to test me, if he feels the need, though I've tried to convince him how much

I'm depending on his expertise in diplomatic niceties. I've little enough, regardless of their decision to send me. If they wanted a Seeker as well as a bureaucrat, they could have had both in Aelbert."

She started to ask why he'd been chosen for such a strenuous yet delicate task as this, why Swan had excused him from the Tribune, but Rolf interrupted. "Look! There's Nakum and Saam! What a picture!"

And it was, she had to agree. Where no one had been in sight moments before, two slim, arrow-fast figures wove their way with such speed yet economy of movement that the very air seemed ignorant of their intrusion. At first scarcely visible, they gained ground, grew steadily larger, the steel-blue ghatt and the Erakwan man-boy, clad in leather leggings, breechclout, and a tiny leather vest, arms and chest bare despite the spring chill of the forest. The pouch with his earth-bond swung from his waist.

"But what will he do when he is older?" The sorrow in Chak's voice, along with the envy, was unmistakable.

"They will grow older together, slower in body, perhaps, but always quick with the sharing of minds." Rolf mused aloud, caressing the gray ghatt's broad head, its muzzle beginning to whiten with age.

But Chak refused to be comforted. **"But the Erakwa do not age the same as . . . others do."** The thought choked him with pain. **"Saam cannot run like that forever. I know."**

"Peace, Chak, peace." And Rolf scooped the ghatt into an awkward embrace, as if the ghatt were too heavy to cradle except for the strength of his love.

Too old, her heart cried, too old and ailing for this expedition. Oh, dear Lady, why did the Monitor agree to this madness? How could Swan have approved it? And yet, Rolf wasn't that terribly old, not as old as Swan, though the last few years had etched their own long calendar of travails on his face, the once trim body now cadaverously thin, the skin so pale and drawn. Was it Chak who was the most frail, the most aged? Or was it Rolf?

"They will do what they have to do, that is why they are here," Khar consoled, but her brow stripes furrowed with worry.

❧

Jenret spurred Ophar forward to meet Nakum and Saam, though it was unnecessary, given the rapidity of their approach. Still, he could muster no better excuse for leaving Aelbert behind, and he desperately needed an excuse before they came to blows. Even in his anger, he meticulously corrected himself. Before *I* come to blows. Why do I let him goad me like that? And he knows full well that I'm no patient ox, to take the goading, gee or haw as he directs.

Shaking his head, he reined in Ophar, the stallion trembling with nerves at the anger transmitted through the tense legs, the roughly handled reins. He rubbed the stallion's neck, whispered apologies. Rawn leaped from his platform without a backward glance; he, too, was miffed by the confrontation, Jenret knew, but didn't dare ask whom he was miffed at—indeed, suspected he already knew the answer. Rawn read him all too well. Pensively, he patted Ophar again, watching Rawn's swift run to intersect the path of Saam and the Erakwan lad.

Black ghatt danced on hind legs to strike at the steel-blue ghatt, both of them rearing and cuffing, mock ferocious snarls, corkscrewing into the air, landing, striking, dodging and spinning like two oversized ghatten, all their adult differences and reserve forgotten. A spring so heady, even in this woods with its shadowed snowbanks, that no one, animal or human, could resist the urge toward youth and playfulness, renewal that for a moment held time and age at bay.

"But my tussle with Saam is different from your argument with Aelbert." Rawn trotted up, Saam a half-length behind, and the coal black ghatt lolled on the ground, flanks heaving slightly, while Saam sat and began to groom.

His response came gruffer than he'd intended. *"Aren't I allowed a spring tonic, too?"*

"It isn't that. You know it." Rawn sprawled, spine wriggling, shoulder blades digging into the earth, errant new grass stems poking through tussocks bleached pale by the winter's snow and ice. The bruised greenery released a scent heady as fine wine. **"There's nothing to pin on him, he's scrupulously correct at every turn, just as a Monitor's aide should be. And he takes orders more readily than some I could name."**

Biting back a retort, Jenret clenched his lips as he considered the justice of Rawn's words. Outwardly correct—

Aelbert Orsborne was certainly that. But it amazed him what that unremarkable face could express—the faintest feathering of a raised eyebrow to indicate skepticism, the fractional curl of his lip, the interrogative rise to the deferential voice that implied "Are you really sure?" Aelbert Orsborne did more with less than anyone he'd ever experienced. A maximum effect with minimal effort.

"Short of your mother Damaris."

"Ah, but mothers are allowed that, that's how they cow unruly youngsters. I'm living proof it works." Rawn made a muffled snort of protest as Jenret continued. *"It even works on Jacobia, but the effects don't last as long. She has a much thicker skin and a much harder head."* Good humor partially restored, he watched Nakum make a final circuit before advancing toward horse and rider. His walk, his gait, were now nothing more than normal, with no indication of the incredible endurance, the stamina and speed bred into the very sinews and muscles and heart of the Erakwa. Little or no hint of that strange power showed itself when Nakum or his grandmother Addawanna stayed with the Wycherleys—as if the very walls of the house drained it from them until they acted like ordinary human beings.

Nakum gave a half-salute and dropped down beside the ghatti, arms thrust behind him for support, and sniffed at the air with deep appreciation. Saam sprawled across his legs, eyes slitted as he waited to see if a toe might wriggle in a moccasin, require chastisement. "I think it's manageable," he paused. "If you so wish it? It isn't necessary—we've made good time, and the plan was to cross at Islebridge. While I agree that gaining a day or two might mean we're less likely to be noticed, I'm still not sure it's the best choice. For one thing we'll be out of sequence with the others by veering west, then north, and that's not wise if we need to relay messages." Perplexity furrowed his brow as he played the arguments over in his mind. "And it *is* my decision," he stated finally. He wasn't used to making decisions like this, of being in charge, but he was. His earth-bond did nothing to lighten his responsibilities.

Jenret considered his response with care, more care than he'd used with Aelbert. He liked and, most of all, trusted Nakum, had no desire to antagonize the Erakwan. His hands tightened on the reins. The real enemy lurked across the border in Marchmont, disrupting Wycherley House trade, slinking across the border, scouting for Lady knew what. Potential danger, and he'd be ready for it, no matter what form it might take. His fist slammed the pommel platform, making Rawn jump. **"Harder to mindlink if we go that way."**

He ignored the ghatt, had had that argument before, but perhaps he could win with Nakum. "Yes, it's your decision. You're in charge, but I hope you'll take my suggestion. Let's be a little unexpected, unpredictable. And Islebridge is utterly predictable—it's the major crossing point. It's the logical place to turn us back, make a public spectacle of refusing us entry. There are too many people there— merchanter offices, weighing stations, customs officials, a posting of our Guardians, a troop of their armed forces. We can regain contact with the others soon enough. And if anyone *is* shadowing us, I want them to truly believe we're alone, not allied with Parse and the others. The more strangers they see, the more they may wonder."

"But I would know if anyone watched us, followed us." It wasn't a protest, simply a statement of fact. With incredible speed the Erakwan's hand shot out, and an early beetle, small, quirky, and spry, found his trundling journey across the mountain of Nakum's moccasin rudely interrupted. Nakum snapped the beetle with his finger, sending it spinning in its shell, legs contracted in fear. But because he couldn't bear untruth, although indirection was another matter, Nakum amended his previous statement. "I would know if anyone following us presented any danger." And felt better, for in truth they *were* being followed, and he was in a quandary about what to do. Still, in this instance, it was none of his business, and he had taken pains to ensure that the follower could trail them without difficulty, was never in any danger.

Saam sniffed at the curled beetle, batted it like a skittle in Nakum's direction. **"He won't be well-pleased when he finds out."**

Nakum 'spoke back, *"Well, be that as it may, it's not my place to interfere in a family dispute."*

"It is if it affects the group's goal. Little Miss Gets-Her-Own-Way should have been sat on as a child."

Nakum shook his head warningly at the ghatt to remind him that neither Erakwa nor ghatti could fathom the ways of outsiders. And both of them knew that Jacobia rode a half-day behind, following them to Marchmont.

"Well?" Jenret had run shy on patience. "We should go, regardless of which path we take."

"Then we will try your way this time and see how it goes." Nakum sprang up, Saam caught off-guard and embarrassed as he twisted in midair to right himself. He shot a look of reproach at Nakum, and nosed the beetle a final time, hoping it might wriggle.

"Just for that I'll make sure she has no trouble following us when we branch onto that overgrown trail."

"That was the idea, my friend."

Cold. It wasn't supposed to be this cold, not in the spring. Where were the gentle zephyr breezes, green-perfumed air, redolent of rising sap and new growth, shoots exposing tender heads, fresh earth turnings from small, burrowing animals? Instead, it felt as if every bit of moisture from the earth had been sucked into a clinging gray dampness, chilling Doyce's bones. Almost cold and raw enough to snow. Condensation dripped from branches, bark black with moisture, greenery weeping in the dampness, dripping on her head, her back, sliding down her collar in a rivulet. Grumbling, she belatedly tugged the collar tighter around her throat, squirmed as a droplet raced down her spine. And the moisture would increase before it lessened, Nakum had promised that. They had entered the water gap at the "mouth" of the Pettibal, with the Tetonords indistinct to the south and west behind her and the Stratocums rearing somewhere grim and invisible north of them. The nearer they came to The Shrouds with its roaring flume of water, higher than the Lady's Bethel in Gaernett, the damper it would be, its mists enveloping everything nearby in perpetual glistening moisture, thousands of tiny rainbows gleaming when the sun hung high and unobscured by clouds.

Once the sight of such a natural wonder would have thrilled her; now she wasn't so sure. For The Shrouds were Jenret's shortcut, an old route now seldom used, and with good reason, but it offered their quickest entry into Marchmont. And that preyed at her mind, worried her as much as the clammy damp, the coldness that had turned Rolf trembling and pale, lips tinged with blue, dark crescents of weariness smeared under his sunken eyes as he sat his horse beside her, hands wrapped in blanket strips fumbling to draw Chak tight to his chest. The elderly ghatt was quivering so hard she feared he might break, an occasional snort of sound wheezing from his nose. By the Lady, she felt cold and soggy, but nothing to compare to these two. At least if they were moving, were riding, they'd gain some warmth from the horses, from the movement, but no, they had stopped again. Nakum's cautious ways galled her, gnawed at her as she watched her old friends suffering far more patiently than she did.

Khar flicked her ear, hunched pitifully as a droplet of water trickled from Doyce's hat brim and hit the ghatta square in the middle of her striped head.

"Sorry." Doyce swept off her hat and shook it, sending a spray of water in Rolf's direction. A weak smile of commiseration wavered across his face, but Chak's eyes remained tightly closed, ears limp, bedraggled body shuddering.

Khar fluffed, fur clumped in wet spikes, and settled more tightly against Doyce, her eyes slitted with worry. **"Scarf?"**

Oh, how the ghatti hated wetness, she thought, still absorbed by the misery beside her. *"Of course, love, if you're that cold."* With guilty fingers she began to unwind the sodden wool around her neck.

"Not me," Khar shrugged her impatience. **"Chak. He's not well. He'll shake himself to death."**

Edging Lokka closer, Doyce handed over the scarf. Rolf took longer than she liked to come out of himself, from wherever he'd banked his hidden fires, and he looked at her with perplexity, then with a touch of anger, his pride wounded.

"Doyce, dear, thank you, but you're chilled as well. Keep it, please, I'm fine. Once we get started again, I'll warm up."

She pushed past his rejecting arm and draped the scarf over Chak. "Not for you, dear, but for Chak. Wrap it round him. It's damp, but even damp wool helps hold the warmth. He needs it, and I don't think he's too proud to admit it."

With shaking fingers, Rolf wrapped the scarf as best as he could without disturbing Chak, pulled him close again. "Gift wrapped," he managed with weak humor. Chak opened one eye and wrinkled his muzzle in thanks at Doyce and Khar.

Jenret and Aelbert rode into view, Nakum walking between them, Saam at his side, fur blotched with dampness, head high and questing. His golden eyes locked with Khar's and he broke into a trot, springing up beside Khar on the pommel platform as the ghatta shifted to make room.

Doyce stroked him, but he shrugged it off, intent on Chak, on the little of him visible through the folds of the red knit wool with its absurdly jaunty tassels. With a chin rub across Khar's ear, Saam turned and jumped down; Doyce barely had warning to counterbalance her weight on Lokka.

Nakum viewed it all, impassive except for the clenching of his teeth on his lower lip before turning back to the two men. "We'll camp here for the rest of the afternoon and the night. The rain's not going to let up, it's likely to snow, and we'd best face the falls when the weather breaks. We couldn't see our way across like this. Let's get a fire going, Aelbert, hot cha to hearten us all."

Not well pleased, Jenret opened his mouth but shut it without a word. He'd not argue with Nakum in front of Aelbert, though it exasperated him not to push on. What guarantee did Nakum have that the weather would improve in another day or two? Reluctantly, he laughed at himself. If an Erakwan didn't know, then who did? Not he, certainly. Besides, why not reinforce Nakum's command, order Aelbert around himself? The thought warmed him more than cha could, and he searched for a suitably hearty, haughty tone.

"Come on, Aelbert, set up camp. Rolf and I'll go collect some firewood. Start Doyce on the cha. And some dinner, if you dare. Her cooking's worse than mine . . . but better than yours." As usual, his insult lofted over Aelbert, gaining no response. But a glimmer of hurt washed over Doyce's face and he cursed himself for it. Anything he said or did, the most innocent things, flayed her vulnerabilities, made her shield herself, ignore him.

"Dismount, then," Nakum clapped his hands. Startled at the sound, Rolf and Doyce obeyed, Rolf cautiously dragging Chak off the platform after he'd dismounted.

The usual flurry of activity accompanied the setting up of camp—horses to be unsaddled and wiped down, blanketed; Aelbert constructed a rock ring to encompass and protect the fire, sheltering the feeble flame with his body, teasing it along with twigs. Jenret busied himself, stringing tarps, stowing gear, cursing as every branch he touched showered him with moisture; Doyce rummaged for the makings of dinner once Aelbert had retrieved a kettle of water for cha.

Only Rolf stood stock-still in the midst of the bustle, clutching Chak to his chest. Nakum glided from camp, hunting bow in hand, Saam at his side.

"Rolf, come on! Firewood, hey?" Jenret strode by, slapping Rolf on the back. The older man took a stumbling step to regain his balance, and Doyce tried to mask her dismay at his awkwardness, the exhaustion blurring his face.

"Jenret, I'll go," she protested, frustrated at his insensitivity. Hard enough lately to protect herself from his moods without having to protect Rolf as well, she thought, still stung by his earlier careless remark. Couldn't he see how tired Rolf was? "Leave Rolf and Chak by the fire, let them toast a bit. And Rolf cooks a better meal than I do. If you want to eat hearty tonight, it's the safest course." Taking Rolf by the elbow, she guided him toward the crackling fire, which popped and snapped as the moisture in the branches heated and exploded, puffs of steam mingling with the smoke.

Like a mechanical man, Rolf took a faltering step or two, mentally shook himself and halted. "No, Doyce, no, thank you. If I sit now, I'll be permanently locked in that position by morning. Best to limber a few kinks before I relax." His eyebrows twisted with concentration, as if the words were foreign, hard to come by, though his sense of chivalry remained intact. Then he realized what he still clutched to his chest. "Could you, do you think you might hold Chak a little while? He's cold and tired, but once he warms up, he'll be fine."

Tongue clamped between her teeth to quell her protest, she scooped the limp ghatt from Rolf's shaking arms. And what frightened her no end as she hugged the ghatt was that Chak radiated heat, waves of it rippling from his quaking body, burning against her chest. Hadn't Rolf noticed? Rolf gave a half-salute in thanks and tottered after Jenret.

"Come, if we can stop his quivering, he'll be warmer. Using up too much energy like that." Amber eyes wide, Khar pushed against her knee as Doyce deposited the ghatt on her lap.

Without replying, she scrubbed vigorously at the old ghatt, as if every stroke could peel days, octs, octants, years away from him. When she hesitated for a moment, she could feel the fragile, thready pumping of his heart, and the labored, whistling breathing wheezing from lungs that seemed to bubble.

Khar set to work licking and licking at Chak's face, hard and patient and thorough until the ghatt squeezed open an eye, hastily shut it to avoid the rasping tongue, for all the world like a ghatten weary of maternal ablutions but with no hope of escape. **"Rolf doesn't know,"** she confided on the intimate mode. **"Suspects but doesn't want to see. Chak knows."**

"Haven't lost him yet," she whispered with fierce determination. "Don't plan to." And was startled when hands pushed hers away from the ghatt's sides and began with gentle persistence to strip off the sodden red scarf. "No, don't!" she protested to Aelbert. "Not yet, not now! We can't uncover him!"

But his capable spatulate fingers replaced the scarf with a frayed wool sweater, nearly shapeless from age and heavy wear, inexpert darns scattered through the ugly but serviceable green-gray wool, frayed and near raveling at the cuffs. "Hush, it's drier than the scarf. Had it well to the bottom of my pack."

She sat back to give him room for his fussy tucking and reached into her waist pouch for a shred of fever bark to force between Chak's clenched jaws. Her fingers pushed the jaw joint, forced it open a crack.

"Will it do any good?" he asked with interest. "Is there anything better? Something?"

"Don't know. Can't harm him, I hope. Mayhap it'll bring the fever down. Thank you for the sweater."

Startled, he pulled away, crossing his arms over his chest, tucking his hands under his armpits as if to hide them or warm them. At a loss for words, he dragged N'oor closer, pushing her into a crouch against Chak's flank. The little ghatta acted almost paralyzed with fear, eyes wide and staring. He stroked her and she began to relax, though she still directed a look of terror at Chak. Khar rapped her on the nose, claws sheathed, and she gave an apologetic bob in Khar's direction, licking at Chak, working her way down his neck until her tongue rasped the sweater's edge.

A thought seemed to strike Aelbert. "Just . . . just so I get the sweater back. It means . . . I mean, well, it's handy to have, never know when you'll need another layer." He rose, a restraining hand on N'oor to keep her in place. "Water's boiling for cha."

As he busied himself around the campfire, she was left considering why a ragged old sweater meant so much to him. It looked small, too small for him, knitted for a stripling boy in his teens, and knitted none too well, that she could see. Dropped stitches, twisted seams. Plenty of hard wear, plenty of hard use. And she wondered about the boy-Aelbert who'd worn it, the man-Aelbert who'd sworn he had nothing casual to wear, only his uniforms. But the man kept it, brought it along, freely shared it when it was needed.

The prick of claws against her knee brought her back to the present. Chak opened rheumy eyes, flexed his dainty white paw against her leg.

"Thanks be for old friends," he whisper-spoke, mind-voice flat but clear. **"Not so cold now, cursed shivering's stopped. Hard to be hot and cold at once."**

Khar gave him an affectionate lick. **"Like being silly and wise together?"**

He wheezed what could have passed for a laugh, coughed, swallowed hard. **"Ghatti, never. Humans, yes."** And he and Khar looked as if they shared the greatest joke in the world, enveloped in a falanese mind-set that Doyce could not pierce. Even N'oor seemed to share in the humor. With a sigh, Chak pillowed his head on N'oor's back, exhaustion reclaiming him. **"Wonderful times,"** he mumbled in drowsy contentment, **"wondrous friends,"** and slept the sleep of the exhausted, as if he had completed a long and arduous race, finish line crossed at last.

With fierce tenderness, Doyce willed time to halt, and for long moments it seemed to have obeyed while she sat still as a stalked rolapin, paralyzed until the death-hawk's swooping sky-shadow passed over it. A prayer arrowed from her mind to strike death down. The only sounds she heard were not the beating wings of death, but the faint, murmurous exhalations from three sleepy ghatti, the crackling of the fire, water rolling slowly off the tarp in fat plops. A few fleece-white flakes floated, danced with limpid ease. *Not while I hold you safe in my keeping will I let anyone, anything harm you, let them try! I will hold the world at bay single-handedly if I must!* Her protective mood continued when Jenret and Rolf returned, Rolf weary, sliding down beside her, his shoulder sagging against hers companionably, his eyes tired but with

Rolf behind them, not emptiness. Safe within her compass. Safe, safe for now, weary but safe, she crooned to herself, willing her lullaby to make it so. Rolf's eyelids flickered shut, snapped open again, slid closed, and he slept.

Abruptly her serenity was shattered by a dark figure looming on the far side of the firelight. She bolted upright, heart pounding, gasping in fright. It stood, legs spread apart, hands on hips, menacing in the shadows. For some reason she was reminded of Syndar Saffron's pose the day they had left. The power, the hidden force of the man. Of course, that was absurd, but no more absurd than what she had taken the figure to be, the death she'd pledged to fight.

"I'm tired, and hungry, and chilled to the bone!" The voice complained, husky with cold but definitely feminine. "My lucifers are all wet, I'm nearly out of food, and it's snowing. I just can't bear any more!"

She knew the voice, recognized the whine, as if everything that had happened were someone else's fault, never her own. Jacobia! Jacobia, Jenret's sister, had somehow trailed them here in the midst of the forest, a day-and-a-half's ride from The Shrouds, nigh onto Marchmont territory.

With a muffled curse, Doyce eased the sweater-wrapped bundle of Chak onto Rolf's lap and edged away, settling Rolf against the saddle, still blessedly sound asleep.

Drier and at least marginally content, Jacobia sat cross-legged by the fire, engulfed in a blanket, cup of cha clasped in grubby hands. Wet boots steamed, as close to the warm rock rim as they dared set them. Her amethyst eyes darted in wide-eyed curiosity, voice pitched high and excited as she recounted her adventures, the center of attention, waiting for the accolades due her.

Doyce sat across the fire, clasping her knees to her chest. Jacobia wasn't impossible to deal with, simply not easy to deal with, she decided, but suspected her new found charitability would be short-lived. Half-woman, half-child, Jacobia's sulkiness and whining was directed as much at the lapses within herself as it was at the world around her. From Jenret's stiff-legged pacing, the sharp turns and knotted fists, *he* was going to be the one impossible to deal with, or so Doyce called the situation. It was most emphatically not going to be a pleasant evening. She started to speak, then subsided, unsure whether interrupting Jacobia in mid-flight of fancy over her tribulations had any more merit than letting her continue.

"Botheration," she muttered to no one in particular.

Concentrating on the simmering stew while Nakum added chunks of partridge, Aelbert rested the spoon on the kettle's lip. "Brotheration, you mean," but his tone reflected a hint of admiration.

Doyce gave a derisive snort. "That, too. What think you, Nakum?" And was left waiting for an answer, the young Erakwan's coppery face turning redder by the moment, she would swear. And Saam's too, if a ghatt were capable of blushing. Nakum was never a chatterer, but she'd never seen him struck dumb before.

". . . and I swore that if I were going to prove myself to everyone . . . to you, to Mother, and all the rest, there ought to be one more Wycherley on this trip." The blanket had slipped from her shoulders, her drying hair a darkly wavy mass around her face. She glowed with the innocent exultation of a child on a quest to discover the ends of the world, complete with supplies of two hard-boiled eggs, a meat pie, and a purloined cookie wrapped tightly in a kerchief, and with the ear-ringing admonition to be back in time for cha. "I need to be tested, to prove that I'm as good as anyone, and then," she concluded triumphantly, "there'll be another Wycherley accounted a leader amongst the merchanters!"

"You stupid featherhead! Less brains than a tree-tapper addled from rapping too many tin roofs!" Jenret jerked her to her feet, cha mug bouncing and rolling, blanket abandoned. He shook her with brisk efficiency, her head wobbling in helpless shock, more at the indignity of the treatment than the actual physical force. "Did you *ever* think how Mother's going to feel? Did you? Did you *ever* think she'll be worried sick wondering where you've gone?" With a final shake he let her drop, only to resume his strained pacing along the firelight's perimeter. He threw the final words over his shoulder. "Not that she'd worry any less if she knew you were with us." A few giant snowflakes drifted against his chest and shoulders, festive ice jewels emphasizing the grim black of his clothes and his mood. "What am I going to do with you!"

She answered back, all wounded and self-righteous dignity. "But I left word, really I did. Not so Mother'd receive it right away, or she'd have sent someone to stop me, but I sent a note to Syndar Saffron's factor with instructions to deliver it a half-oct hence. I hope he remembered." Her violet eyes were dark pools of amethyst indignation.

"*Syndar Saffron!*" Doyce breathed in Khar's direction. "*Bad enough before, but she's done it now.*"

"And with the best intentions in the world." The ghatta's ears swiveled and dipped, contradictory emotions at work. **"Syndar Saffron. Oh, dear, she's done it now."** Simultaneously they looked to gauge the black ghatt's reaction, but Rawn sat, mute and immobile as an ebony statue, green eyes tracking his Bondmate's increased agitation and throttled response to the name.

With a muffled oath about feckless, foolish women, Jenret Wycherley flung a dismissive gesture in Jacobia's direction as if to cast her off, and strode into the night, Rawn a flowing curl of black at his heels.

"Now *what* have I done? I thought it was *perfectly* sensible!" Jacobia wailed at his receding back.

"Nothing, dear, it's already done, and a part of it long before you were born. Never mind." Pushing a startled Aelbert aside, Doyce began ladling broth, leaving the meat to stew a bit longer. "Never mind him for now, but you'd better think, we'd all better think," and she cast an assessing look at Aelbert and, especially, Nakum, "what we're going to do about you."

They had settled for the night, Aelbert and Nakum sharing one tarp, Jacobia minnowed beside the still-sleeping Rolf, as Doyce sat, a mug of cha in hand, and the comforting warmth of a half-full pot still brewing by the embers. She'd been scribbling in her day log or, more accurately, putting down a word or two, worrying at the pencil with her teeth. Picking over and discarding words. Mayhap she should toss the log in the air, pages flapping, let the wheat separate from the chaff. Siblings. . . . It wasn't the same as her own relationship with her sister Francie, but there were eerie similarities of love and hate. . . .

"Coming," Khar remarked. **"Hungry and grumpy."**

"*Rawn or Jenret?*"

"Both. Rawn tried to talk some sense into him, but it didn't do much good."

She began to dish out the remaining stew, cooked together

into an indistinguishable mush, but still fragrant with last season's wild onions and the early cress Nakum had found near the stream. "Here," she offered, reaching behind her with the bowl.

Jenret took it without questioning how she knew he was there. He shoveled in a spoonful, then panted, vivid blue eyes wide with pain, as the heat burned his tongue. Plunging the spoon around in the bowl, he tried to cool it. "You heard her, you heard what she said."

"Yes, and she doesn't know why that turned out to be the final straw, why it upset you so much. To her, Syndar Saffron is a neighbor, a friend, a competitor, whatever. She's too egocentric right now to analyze a situation she's taken for granted all her life, to see the nuances of that relationship through adult eyes. Would she judge Damaris harshly or view it as a hopelessly romantic idyll—and do you want her locking on either of those choices here and now?"

"I think she does know, or at least suspects. Something's been bothering her lately. But I'm afraid I'd run in the opposite direction if she brought it up. I don't want to cope with it." He gloomily poked at the stew, scooped up a spoonful and dribbled it into the bowl. Finally he levered a small spoonful into his mouth and muttered, "'S good," almost in surprise, then compensated, "a little overcooked."

"And whose fault is that? As to the fact it's good, Aelbert and Nakum did the cooking." She wouldn't let him rile her, let him deflect his frustration and anger onto her. No easy out for Jenret Wycherley tonight if she could help it. Let him face the facts, and if he couldn't face the facts, how could he expect Jacobia to do so?

The spoon clattered against the empty bowl. "'S'plains it." One lock of dark hair sprang over his forehead, an old familiar friend to her. After a lengthening pause he hazarded a grudging question. "So what are we going to do?"

It was tempting, too tempting to respond, *"About the fact that Syndar Saffron's her father?"* Khar had caught her thought and shifted from one front paw to the other in mute disapproval.

She poured a cup of overbrewed cha, strong enough to tan shoe leather, but warm and homey nonetheless. "Do I have a say in it?" She picked her words with deliberation. "It's a family matter, isn't it?"

He thrust the curl back, pinned it in place with the heel of his hand. "Small-scale, yes. Large-scale, no, and you know that full well, Doyce. Small-scale it's family disobedience that I have to deal with, but large-scale it's the mission we're on. I don't have the right," he swallowed hard, "and Jacobia doesn't have the right to jeopardize that."

"Then it's a decision we should reach by consensus, all of us—Rolf and Chak, Aelbert and N'oor, Nakum and Saam, Rawn and Khar, as well as you and me."

The roll call of names left him melancholy. As if in sympathy, a nightbird crooned a descending three-note mournful trill. Jenret stared hard into his cup, face studiously tilted downward, long lashes shielding his eyes. "Still, I'd welcome your opinion first. And the others must be consulted as well."

"Then I'd say I doubt she could find her way home alone. I've a suspicion Nakum knows more than he's telling about how she was able to follow us this far." Khar concurred, a small nod of agreement, but kept her own counsel. "I doubt she realizes how easy he made it for her to track us, though why he didn't let us know. . . ." She left the sentence unfinished, the answer all too obvious to anyone who had ever suffered the pangs of that first bashful, inarticulate love. Jenret sat erect, scowling, assessing her words, those spoken, those not. She continued. "So if she goes back, who's going to take her?"

"And if we *don't,* Mother won't know that she's all right. It's too much for her to bear."

Rawn wedged his head against Jenret's hand, began to gnaw at his knuckles until his ears were rubbed. **"We can send word, work the links in the mindmeld. The others can pass word along."**

Relief lightened Jenret's face, then faded. "But who's going to receive it? You know Mother doesn't like to be 'spoken."

"A messenger ghatt can carry written word for the final transmittal. Dinner?"

Disconcerted by the change in topic, Jenret looked puzzled. With a chuckle, Doyce rummaged in her saddlebags for the sack of ghatti trail mix. Ever optimistic, Khar nudged her elbow and jarred a few nuggets loose for herself.

Jenret chuckled. "A more immediate reality. My apologies, old friend. Now we owe Khar a dinner. But perhaps to make up for it, we might offer dessert?" He searched his own baggage, excavating a crumpled wrapping paper, its oiled surface still miraculously dry. Nestled within were four well-traveled cookies, brown, hard, studded with raisins, resembling nothing so much as little rocks. "Last of them, and not the freshest. Still, they revive if you dip them in cha."

Gingerly easing the cookie into her mug, Doyce followed his advice and nibbled at the edge, expecting a tooth to break. To her surprise it was chewy, pleasantly redolent of molasses and spices. She dunked it again before she spoke. "How much will she hamper us if she comes along?"

Jenret rebuilt the fire, hands busy as he thought it through. "Some, perhaps quite a lot. Depends on how tight a rein I keep on her—and I propose to keep it very tight. Assuming you all approve of her coming along," he amended.

"And if there's trouble, more than we've bargained for?"

"I don't like that thought. But she'll have to face it, just as the rest of us must. She might as well learn that bad times pair with good, having with not having. It's a risk I have to take, that she'll cope. After all, she does come from strong scrappy stock—on both sides of the family."

Doyce rose. "So be it, then. I'm for bed."

Jenret sat back, stretched his long legs, expression pensive. "I'll stay up a bit longer. Some things to think out, things to work through."

Nodding her understanding, she walked toward the tarp where Rolf and Jacobia slept. He gestured toward his own tarp. "I won't be . . ." a diffident invitation, but she put a hand down to forestall him.

"I'll ask the others in the morning, see if they approve about Jacobia, if you like," she said over her shoulder.

A lonely smile crept across his face. "I'll thank you for that. And for the stew you kept warm. Sleep well."

Rawn sat, watching Jenret doze, chin slumped on chest, cha mug still clutched on his lap. At last he raised his head, little circlings in the air, and mindspoke. **"Your pardon, Saam, but I wish your help."** The request gave him no pleasure, but he was not as stubborn as Jenret, and while need was there, he would ask. His Bondmate came first, not his own desires.

Saam slipped free from the tarp, sniffed at the dampness,

stretched one hind leg, then the other, dug claws into the earth, tossing little gouts behind him. Rawn held his tongue, waiting. **"Sorry, deep asleep. Dreaming of summer and sun, the baking warmth of the plaza stones outside Headquarters ..."** He whisker-flicked repentance, a wry apology in falanese. **"How may I serve?"**

Rawn's chin worked back and forth, as if he would ask, but hated to ask, the favor needed. **"It is needful that I send a message to ease my Bondmate's heart."** A head jut toward the tarp where Doyce, Rolf, and Jacobia slept. **"About that young scamp of a ghatten-child. But the distance is too great for me alone. I warned Jenret of the difficulties if we took his route, but still he felt ..."** he trailed off, not wishing to criticize his Bond, but stymied, all the same.

"Ah, Jacobia." Saam settled close to the warm rock rim, basking in the radiated heat. **"But no decision has been reached about whether she'll stay or return, or at least no formal decision."** He shrugged, wrinkled his face. **"Ah, but you're right, it doesn't matter. We know the outcome. Best to put the dam's heart at ease. I am pleased to aid you, you honor me with the asking, but ..."** he looked more apologetic than before, **"but sometimes I am erratic with the sendings. There is still so much I am re-learning. Strange, but it helps when Nakum and his earth-bond are nearby."**

And Rawn knew that he alluded to his loss of mind-speech, destroyed almost beyond redemption when Oriel had died. The yellow ghatt Mem'now had striven to retrain Saam, repattern his mind, and it had worked, but not perfectly. Rawn had suspected, but hadn't known for sure until now, and however he might feel about Saam, the shared knowledge made him ache with sympathy.

With a head nudge, Saam reclaimed Rawn's attention. **"So we ask Khar to join us, add her mindvoice to ours. If you can admit to needing help, I can as well."** Before Rawn could object, Khar had slipped over by the fire.

"Took you long enough," she grumped, wriggling between the two ghatts, sharing the warmth.

They began, Rawn's mindvoice soaring, conscious of the strong bass solidity Saam would need. And Saam wove his way through the links, breathing steadily, concentrating, extending beyond Rawn, working himself farther, searching, seeking for a kindred receptive voice out there. Khar light-footed into the meld, balancing Saam between herself and Rawn, allowing him the stability to push himself farther. Their voices spun through the night, sweeping the skies, buffeted by a constant, low rumbling that human ears could not yet perceive, strange flashes of energy that tossed them sideways, up and down, off course when they were not careful. **"It's no use!"** Khar gasped. **"I've been trying for M'wa and P'wa—T'ss is probably off course since we shifted westward. I can't sense anyone's presence!"**

Rawn took a deep breath, exhaled, pushed harder and harder, supporting the weight of their minds, base to the pyramid of voices. He'd rupture something if he kept on like this, not mentally, he decided, but something deep within his gut. And just as he thought he might cave in, crumple, he heard Khar vocalize her delight aloud, but he didn't dare the distraction. **"Got them! Got through! Message sent! All well there!"** Rawn collapsed, sprawled on the ground, weak and panting as relief flooded through him.

But Khar had rounded on something, someone, hissing, a stinging broadside of a paw swipe. N'oor tumbled head over tail, whimpering, pulling away. **"Don't you *ever*, don't you *ever* join a mindmeld again without announcing yourself!"** Khar snarled. **"Look what you did to poor Rawn, no wonder he almost couldn't bear the weight. He had no idea you were joining in!"**

He saw N'oor cowering, timid, not sure whether to flee or stay, baffled as to why her help was being rejected. There was something about the large, multi-toed feet that touched his heart, made him feel protective, as if she were a ghatten who hadn't caught up with its growth yet. **"Peace, Khar, peace. Phew. I'll be fine. And we couldn't have done it without her."**

Saam nose-touched N'oor. **"But in the future, little ghatta, do knock before you enter."** With a sniff of disgust, Khar marched back to her tarp. **"Ghatts!"** she snapped to no one in particular.

❖

Dawn greeted them, air still damp but without yesterday's greedy heaviness. The temperature had risen, leaving a forlorn ridging of snow in dark shadows: the moisture had dissipated enough so that water no longer beaded and condensed on everything in sight. Tolerable, more than tolerable, Doyce decided. A few odd patches of clothing still hadn't completely dried: the inward turned toe of one sock, her left coat sleeve. Her flesh goose-bumped at the clammy contact. She stamped her foot, wriggled her toes, and told them they'd warm.

They'd decided that Jacobia should accompany them. Only Rolf was opposed, protesting at first, too gallant for his own good, concern plain in the nervous hunching of his shoulders. Even he had had to accede that the alternative was equally unpalatable, forced to admit their mission took precedence. Aelbert had weighed the pros and cons, head tilted to one side, eyes considering and bright, and nodded agreement, tractable as always.

But Nakum had tried to physically divorce himself from the discussion, edging away, separate. "It's nothing to do with me, I'm the scout," he'd protested, palms extended to ward off the decision. Doyce took amused note of his guilty innocence and decided to have a little talk with Nakum later.

Allowed to sleep through the discussion, Jacobia was roused as they broke camp, allotted scant time to dash the sleep from her eyes, drink a hasty mug of cha and munch a biscuit. She acted surprisingly subdued, and Doyce hoped that was a good omen.

Despite the fact that both Aelbert and Nakum hovered, alert to her needs, Jacobia flashed a gamine grin at them. "I made it this far without anyone to help, so there's no reason I can't keep it up." A note of pride echoed in her voice, showed in her carriage. Aelbert and Nakum backed away, began to busy themselves elsewhere.

Campsite neatened, fire extinguished, the last odds and ends packed and strapped, everyone mounted, ready. Rolf slapped his pommel platform to bring Chak springing up beside him. His face hinted at a bare hue of color this morning, though he moved with lingering discomfort. Hind legs wavering, Chak marched to the horse's side, gathered himself and sprang—and fell short, scrabbling claws raking the gelding's shoulder as the ghatt fought for leverage. He tumbled to the ground, huddled in a forlorn, shrunken mound as the horse shied in protest, jumping forward until Rolf reined him in.

Head low, ears wilted with dejection, Chak quivered with humiliation. Then, forcing himself upright, he stared up, up t his friend, his Bond, and with halting determination gathred himself for a second attempt. His hind legs wobbled, played outward, barely supporting him. But Nakum foretalled him, scooping the gray ghatt into the air and passing im to an anxious Rolf, trying to kick free of his stirrups and ismount.

"Still a little stiff from last night." He gave Chak's ears a ough, affectionate scrubbing and moved on before Rolf ould voice his thanks. With an arm motion he brought aam to his side and the two took the lead, the rest falling 1, trying to spare Rolf and Chak embarrassment.

They rode all day at a steady, easy pace, making good me once they angled onto a wide, well-packed trail, easily road enough to take a fully-loaded trade wagon. From the eaching, overgrown branches it didn't appear that many agons had passed through recently; not since the past summer at the latest. The land rose and fell in easy swells, gradally becoming steeper, Doyce realized when she glanced ack to check on Rolf. Jenret had ridden beside Jacobia for nost of the morning, hand on her reins, talking intently with is sister. She had stayed as far back as possible to give nem privacy, although the scattered words she caught, and ne tone, made it clear that Jenret was giving his sister a ood tongue-lashing.

"Easier to talk than to listen," Khar remarked, tangling paw in Lokka's mane.

"Meaning that not much is sinking in?" Doyce laughed. *'Well, let's hope something is."*

Khar's ears pricked, garnet rose flashing, ear hoop quivring, as she strained toward the distant voices. **"I believe he part about spanking in public might have. Oh, poor Rawn, burdened with two such willful humans. I only ave to suffer one."**

"And perhaps Jenret was right. A public spanking might e a good idea," she answered.

"For you?" Bewildered, Khar snapped her head around, veighing Doyce's seriousness.

"No, dear, for you!" And took inordinate delight in Khar's chagrin.

As the day wore on, Doyce found herself rubbing her ears, ressing first one then the other to create a momentary sucion, the way she had as a child with water lodged in her ars from swimming or diving too deeply. Her whole head

throbbed, making her tired and edgy, a low-grade hum ju
beyond her perception echoing in her head. She caught he
self massaging her temples again, and forced herself to sto
shaking her head to clear it. Nothing seemed to work. Dam
all! Mayhap this was where the expression "to have a bee i
your bonnet" came from, and a whole hive's worth at tha

Khar might know what the problem was, but she hated
expose her weakness to the ghatta, wondered if her min
were playing tricks the way it had sometimes during tho
long, empty octants barricaded in Damaris's guest roon
She'd stared into the fire one night and the normal crack
lings had howled at her, turning into screams, Vesey
screams, both the long-ago screams from the first fire whe
he was a child and his final, more recent pyre. There ha
been other instances as well, but usually visual tricks not a
ral ones. The thought of some subtle incapacitation no
blossoming forth terrified her. Lock it in? Let it burst forth

In her distraction and worry she hadn't noticed until no
that Khar was batting at her own ears, flicking them as if
dislodge swarming midges. *"Khar, love, what's happenin*
what's the matter?"

"Phew! We heard it in the distance last night, an
Rawn warned me it would grow worse, but ..."

Aelbert reined in beside them, interrupting. "You kno
what it is, don't you?"

She shook her head, half negative response, half a vain a
tempt to clear her head and ease her fears. What her expre
sion betrayed she couldn't judge, but she prayed for th
same noncommittal aspect that Aelbert usually wore.

"It's a well-documented fact. Haven't you ever read abo
it?"

"Read about what?" His pedantic tone irked her. Was h
type of insanity so common that it had been written up b
the eumedicos, familiar even to the general populace?

He swung his arms wide in wonder, then hugged himse
hard, embracing his excitement. "The falls, the falls,
course. You can hear The Shrouds already! I've read o
Tavistock's *Journey to Marchmont,* and he swore you cou
sense them half-a-league or more before you arrived. An
it's true!" He squinted, thinking, recapturing the words fro
memory. " 'And the sound came subtly, like the lowe
string on a bass, vibrating, vibrating, just below the level
conscious hearing. And as we approached closer, I feare

hat I had been struck dumb from the increasing rush of
ound, as if all the daemonic spirits of the deep earth wailed
heir inchoate lament for me to hear.' Isn't it marvelous?"
His face glowed at the sudden sharing, himself as instructor,
he his student.

"You mean we're that close?" Doyce picked the most
pragmatic fact from Aelbert's flight of fancy. No, not mad at
all, not she, and she sagged with relief, though Aelbert
looked almost manic with rapture.

"Oh, yes, I thought you realized, assumed Jenret mentioned it to you last night. He came this way once years ago.
Nakum told me how close we were some time ago."

She bit off each word, sharp and distinct, to make herself
heard, voice her complaint. "Word didn't get passed all the
way down."

"I'm sorry." The glory evaporated from his face, dimming
him into the Aelbert she knew. "I told Jacobia, and she said
he'd drop back and let you know."

Doyce nodded ahead at Jenret and Jacobia. "I think she's
had other things on her mind."

With a shamefaced grin that made him look about eleven,
Aelbert shrugged. "So it appears. And I was so excited, I
didn't even realize she hadn't. Amends are in order. I'll tell
you what else Nakum told me. He said that by the time we
reach the hem of The Shroud, it'll be too late to cross today.
The cliff shadows fall fast and deep there this early in the
season, so we'd best wait until morning."

"Our last night in Canderis, then." Doyce's fingers tugged
at a cuff button, worried and twisted it, though her voice
stayed level. "It begins tomorrow. Marchmont, the cautions,
the questions, the negotiations. It's up to you and Rolf from
now on, you're the Envoys."

He spent considerable time examining N'oor's sleek head,
the tilt of her ears, her earrings, as if he'd never really studied them before. Finally he responded. "Rolf's the Envoy,
I'm the aide, just the aide. The Monitor knows my . . .
worth," the last word so softly mouthed she almost missed
it.

"Well, I've seen some of your worth, and it's considerable. The hardest thing in the world is to be the second, the
line that uncomplainingly spans from the anchor to the ship.
Rolf's going to need your support and knowledge, he's
thankful for your presence. Don't belittle yourself, Aelbert,

because there's more to you than meets the eye." Kir
words never hurt, and somehow she sensed his hunger f
them right now, a craving unassuaged for too long.

Khar rubbed at her ear. **"There's more there than mee
the eye. I'm still not fond of him, or his precious N'oor**

*"What is it about her that rubs you the wrong way? Y
aren't jealous because Rawn likes her?"*

"Rawn—and Saam—can like anyone they want."

Unfair of her to tease the ghatta like that, put it down
jealousy when Khar was usually right in her assessment
The ghatti senses, so much sharper than a human's, so mu
more aware, caught nuances beyond the obvious. Had Kh
been reading Aelbert? she wondered, but thought not, it w
too impolite, not without a real reason, a definite nee
They'd both know the truth then, but without it all they h
were their perceptions.

"No, of course not," her tone disgruntled, Khar conti
ued. **"You know I wouldn't. And besides, N'oor's sti
shielding, even Rawn's noticed."**

"Why?" She nearly spoke aloud, she was so shocke
*"Surely there's no need, no reason to shield? What mak
her or him, I guess, so distrustful? It's unseemly behavior f
a Seeker."*

**"Which makes me wonder what she's shielding an
why it seems such habit. What is it about Aelbert tha
makes him so secretive?"**

And Doyce found no rejoinder to that, just a different pe
spective, as if a lens had been changed, throwing som
things out of focus, and clarifying new and strange image
and ideas.

The humming rose stronger now, truly as if daemonic er
gines steadily churned beneath the surface of the eartl
chewing, growling, snarling as they gnawed in never-endin
ceaseless hunger. Tavistock's *Journey to Marchmont*? A ra
book, a very rare book. No more than three copies extant,
memory served: one in the Master Libris of Gaernett in th
Closed Room, considered too fragile except for the most s
nior scholars to consult; one in Sidonie, the capital c
Marchmont, their destination; and the final copy in th
hands of a private collector or antiquariatt, and his cop
along with other rare works relating to the early settleme
days of Canderis and Marchmont, had been stolen som
years ago. *That* was why she had remembered the title, be

cause she had felt a pang at the news of the robbery, any ledger or transcriber would, anyone whose job involved the detailed, accurate recording and saving of information for future generations. A piece of early settler history vanished no one knew where.

The trail swept along the top of a broad cliff, and gasping, Doyce drew Lokka up short. Not daring to trust her eyes, she sidestepped the little mare closer to the edge. And there it was, roaring, raging, an incredible majestic flume of water falling at least seventy meters, crashing white on the river rocks below. Mist-filtered sunlight cast rainbows in every direction, a prodigality of tiny prisms shimmering, coruscating, breaking, re-forming in the late afternoon sun. She watched, watched as if she could never see enough of the primeval sight, marginally aware that the others had pulled up beside her, mouths ajar in wonderment, awe, and fear. And how, Lady Bright, did Nakum propose they were to cross that? Fly? Swim? A shudder ran the length of her spine. Too much to hope for a nice, normal, mundane bridge just out of sight.

At last, one by one, they turned without speaking and began setting up the night's camp on a site that had obviously known previous visitors. Commonplace actions seemed meaningless next to the sheer power of The Shrouds, dwarfing everything with its mind-numbing presence, its overwhelming intensity. Rolf remained staring the longest, at last wheeling his horse toward the sheltered dip where they would spend the night.

He dismounted in jerky moves, leaned against his gelding, and reached to lift Chak. Doyce hurried to spread her saddle blanket, and he laid the elderly ghatt down. Aelbert stopped his work and circled the blanket, face worried as he squatted for a closer inspection. Chak sighed, eyes closed, his head falling limply.

"Both still a bit tired," Rolf confessed as he returned to strip his horse. But Jacobia had already begun, flipping up the stirrups and loosening the girth, hauling off the heavier Seeker saddle with its pommel platform. "Here, no need for that," he protested.

Struggling with the saddle, Jacobia smiled. "Earning my keep. That's the way Jenret put it. You're doing me a favor by letting me, or else I'll have to answer to him." A meaningful nod in Jenret's direction made it clear to whom she referred. "The phrase 'chief cook and bottle washer' was mentioned, too, but I reminded him about my cooking. If you'd advise in that, sir, we may all live long and prosper, which is more than I can say if I cook."

With a grateful sigh, Rolf collapsed by the campfire. "Cookery's an art, child, though you should learn it well enough to at least call it a craft. Come here when you're done and let me instruct you. Favor for favor, so to speak."

And soon, gray and dark-haired heads bent over the pot, whispering, commenting, bits of conversation ebbing and flowing with the wisps of cook fire smoke. "Seasonings . . . definitely . . . but first, there's basic cookery . . ." "But why sear . . .? How big should the pieces be?"

"Reformed already?" Jenret inquired as he came by after staking the horses.

Busy unrolling her bedding, Doyce smiled in their direction. "It's rather charming, don't you think?"

Catching a corner of her blanket, he helped her shake it out. "Depending on how long it lasts."

"Perhaps Rolf is just the sort of person she needs. Sooner or later everyone strives to rise to his level of courtesy."

"Now, keep stirring . . . no, don't beat it, gently and evenly as I showed you, that's right . . . until I get back." Rolf passed them, limping slightly. "A pleasant child, though a bit strong-minded," he murmured to Jenret as he continued toward Chak, stretched on his side on the blanket.

"Here, Chak, look lively," Rolf mindspoke as he forced himself down on one knee. No response, but he didn't think anything of it. Chak had grown a bit hard of hearing, and it seemed to have touched his mindspeech as well. *"Come on, old chap, let's snooze by the fire and keep an eye on things, shall we?"* His hand reached to touch the gray side, and then held itself arrested. A trick of the failing light, the deepening shadow surely, he told himself, his heart beginning a convulsive hammering, beating at his breastbone. No movement, no slight rise and fall to the gray-furred side, none whatsoever.

His hand dropped hard, harder than he'd intended, and he promised himself to apologize, make amends for the rude awakening. But nothing happened. He stroked the fur absently, rubbed the ears, ran a tender finger along the muzzle flecked with random white hairs, whiskers rasping against his skin. *"Ah, Chak,"* his heart cried, as if the ghatt could still hear him. *"Ah, Chak, oh dearest heart unto my own. Not now! Oh, dear Lady, not now, when there's still a task to be done. We've never, ever shirked before."* A single tear landed softly on the gray fur, glimmered for an instant, a badge of love.

He arose, knees stiff, and began rummaging in his saddlebags, knowing it was there, way at the bottom. After all, he'd written it in the Seeker General's presence and had shown her and the Monitor its contents. Had convinced them of the unlikelihood that it would be needed, but better to be safe than sorry. His fingers touched it at last, a leather case, and inside, a waxsealed letter bearing his crest. An affectation, he knew, but he was proud of it, the ring had journeyed with his ancestor on that first exploratory flight to Methuen and had remained in his family ever since. That made him stop and think for a moment, and he slipped the dull gold ring from his left hand, pulled paper and pencil from his breast pocket, scribbled a few words and screwed the slip of paper through the ring. He left both the leather case and the ring on the top of the saddlebags and returned to Chak's side.

With a lurching apprehension, Doyce realized the ghatti had gone dead silent, no murmurous comments, no purring, not a muscle moving. Each had frozen, neck stretched in the direction Rolf had taken. Turning to see what had caught their attention, she spied Rolf walking with painful deliberation toward the cliff's edge, climbing the footpath that culminated in nothingness, a sharp drop overlooking The Shrouds and the aggressive river below. He cradled a blanket-wrapped bundle in his arms.

As one, Khar, Saam, and Rawn rose and began to trot after, maintaining a respectful distance behind Rolf. But N'oor let out a plaintive mewl of dread and, belly low, slunk away in the opposite direction. Rolf glanced back once, his silvered beard and hair shining in the final moments of the setting sun, making his face glow ruddy and full of health, his hair gleam coppery red. She thought he smiled, but wasn't sure; it might have been a trick of the light.

"Jenret!" Her voice scalded her throat, hot with foreboding, not of the unknown but of the known. She'd seen the death-hawk swooping but had willed herself blind. The black-clad form of Jenret swung around, his stance inquiring. "Jenret, it's Chak! Chak's dead, Rolf is going to bury him. Lady bright, what do we do?"

He took a step toward her, reached out as if to stop her in her tracks, but halted, hand dropping to his side. "Nothing." And tried again, sick at heart, hating to admit the truth. "Nothing we can do, it's his right, his duty, to dispose of the remains." The word sounded harsh, callous in her ears, remains? Chak, remains?

Without volition, she found herself running up the path, Jacobia pounding along after her, exclaiming, "What's wrong, what is it?" her tone first fretful, finally frantic at the lack of response.

The last paring of orange-red sun haloed the thin body, bent with its burden. He reached the lip, balanced. The Shrouds boomed, thundered, Doyce's final shout dying in her throat. She couldn't outshout it, make herself heard. The silhouette straightened, head erect, shoulders back. He took one final step into thin air . . . and was gone, falling arrow-straight and proud. The Shrouds still roared in her ears as if welcoming the sacrifice, leaving her numb.

The ghatti began their chant. **"May you see with eyes of light in ever-dark, may your mind walk free and unfettered amongst all, touching wisely and well. May you go in peace."**

Panicked, Aelbert thrust through the underbrush, felt it snag on his uniform, refused to care. *"N'oor, love, N'oor, darling, where are you?"* he mindspoke desperately. Whether anyone would notice his absence or remark on it left him unmoved. He had to find her. Besides, if they thought it natural for him to withdraw, grapple with Rolf's and Chak's deaths in solitude, perhaps that's why they'd think N'oor had fled. *"N'oor, where are you? What is it, what's wrong?"*

A branch slapped him in the face and the tears started in his eyes. All wrong! It wasn't meant to be like this. *"N'oor, please, 'speak me."* The tears had stopped, locked inside, the way he always kept them, but he collapsed on the damp leaves, holding himself tight, rocking back and forth. *"N'oor, it was all a misunderstanding, believe me!"*

The familiar, loved mindvoice spiraled from the top of a nearby oak. **"What did you give Chak? I saw you, I saw you."** Never had her 'speech sounded so accusing.

With shaking hands, he pulled the jeweled pillbox from his pocket and cracked it open. Another of his little garnerings, the absentminded collecting of things that didn't belong to him, "rescuing" them, to his mind. He'd tried to control the habit; N'oor knew of it and did not approve. The pills within had been "rescued" as well; liberated during his final visit to the Hospice because they resembled little unpolished gems and he needed something for his pillbox to hold. For a moment he wondered where the little china cha pot lid was, but it didn't matter. *"I thought . . ."* he sniffled once. *"thought it might help Chak. The pill was the same color and shape as the ones Rolf takes . . . took. He . . . always tried to be secretive about it, but the Monitor told me he had angina."* With a deep breath, he continued, *"N'oor, believe me, I thought if they helped Rolf, they might be good for Chak. I don't know, maybe I was wrong, maybe I didn't give him what I should have, but I didn't mean to hurt him!"*

"Honestly?" The branches quivered above his head; he could just make out one of the absurdly large feet, claws sunk into the bark. **"You were jealous of Rolf. You know the truth of that. You must have known what losing Chak would do to him!"**

He bowed his head at the truth. *"Yes, but I wouldn't . . . I didn't. For all my faults, I'm not that!"* The pillbox was still clutched in his hand, the raised jewels indenting his flesh. Inspiration struck, or perhaps desperation, he wasn't sure. *"You have to know I speak the truth, you know my mind unlike anyone else alive."* And that was true, because Evelien was dead. *"But I'll prove it to you; I don't know what kind of pills I have in here, I've forgotten, but I'll take them, swallow every one."* He raised the pillbox to his mouth. *"Take my chances, just as I took a chance with Chak, trying to help! If I fail again, so be it!"*

"No!" N'oor came slithering backward down the tree, multi-toed feet doing too good a job of holding her back. Halfway down she turned and sprang desperately for his chest, knocking the pillbox aside. **"No, no, no! I know, I know it was an accident, but why, why didn't you ask me before you did it? Human medicine isn't always good for us ghatti."** He held her tight, wiping his eyes on her fur, and N'oor wondered yet again how it was possible to be loved so deeply and love so deeply and still feel that something was desperately amiss. Was it possible her love hurt him and his love her?

"You won't tell, will you?"

"No, beloved, no, that's what Bonds are for, this secret sharing."

❧

Nakum and Saam stood watch while the others slept, more drained by grief and loss than from the day's hard ride. Nakum didn't feel tired; he needed less and less sleep now that he had tasted of the earth. He touched his pouch ruminatively, fingering the lump inside. So it was true, the gift gave strength at need; he had sensed it before when he had first been gifted with it, but he was still learning, pressing the boundaries. He could see Doyce asleep with her arm wrapped around Khar, protective, holding her close. Aelbert and Jenret slept in similar poses, Jenret with one arm outflung to ward off danger, the other enveloping Rawn, pressing him to the curve of his waist. Back from wherever they'd been in the woods, Aelbert now barricaded N'oor beneath his blankets, crushing her against his chest. Only Jacobia lacked a Bond to comfort her, lacking the firsthand knowledge of the overwhelming sense of pain and loss that had driven Rolf to jump—the severing of a Bond. Still, death, unexpected, had struck her hard. It was her first—of many things—he suspected. His first, too, of other things equally impossible to comprehend. With a little whimper, she burrowed against Doyce's back, taking comfort in contact.

A shooting star scored the heavens, the Lady and her Disciples secure in their quadrant. The night was velvet dark, wrapped in the continuous battening of sound from The Shrouds. Saam leaned against his knees, alone in his grief. *"Is it customary, then, when a Bondmate dies . . . for this to happen?"* He phrased the question with care, but Saam remained aloof. *"There is so much I do not know about the Seekers, about you . . . and your ways. Sometimes I think I know, but I make assumptions and then am proved wrong. I do not wish to cause pain, but I wish to know."*

"No."

"Ah, I am sorry. I should not intrude." The Erakwan kept his apology formal and brief.

"No. It was the answer to your question." Saam's back was to Nakum, and he did not turn. "No, generally when ghatti Bonds die, the human Bonds live on. They are not as sensitive."

"Rolf was, I think, an exceptional man."

"He was. Had he died first, Chak would not have cared for life without him, not without the link. Rolf felt much the same."

The conversation circled close, closer, and closer to something Nakum desperately desired to know but dared not ask.

"So it was with me ... and the other, my Bondmate. That was what you wished to ask, was it not?" Twisting his head around, Saam regarded him until Nakum dropped his eyes.

"Yes," he whispered. *"But you lived. Why?"*

"Because others forced me to, gave me a reason, and then I forced myself to keep on living. Doyce and Khar shared my pain when I had no way to cry out, my voice silent, locked inside. And I had promised ... him," the steel-blue ghatt could not bring himself to utter the name, "that I would always watch over her and the little Khar'pern."

He wanted with desperate urgency to touch the sleek shoulder, even if only with a tracing finger, but he stilled his hand. "And will you stay?" He barely breathed the words.

"Yes ... since I have you. Oriel rests in peace. He will find his way. So must I."

His thin brown hand, middle fingers callused from the bowstring, essayed a tentative stroke against the supple line from neck down along the spine. *"Chak was very old ... and ill."*

"Aye, he was. But ask yourself what he died from. And if you find the answer, tell me."

"But surely it was to be expected."

Saam's eyes burned, reflecting Lady-light. "Something is ... fishy."

Nakum tried and failed to stifle a giggle. Sputtered, wiped the moisture from his upper lip. *"Fishy? What is ... 'fishy?' I do not know the meaning you give it."*

"An old word." The ghatt's impatience was clear. "Something that is not right, that stinks to high heaven. Know you what I mean?" His nose wrinkled, upper lip curling back as he inhaled an imaginary but clearly unsavory scent.

Nakum digested the idea. *"I think I know what you mean,"* he ventured at last. *"But why, who, what?"*

"Wait and see." A tongue burred against his knee. **"Now sleep. Take it while you can. You have your ways, but sleep should always be taken when there is time. All ghatti know the wisdom of this. I will watch."**

Wary of disturbing Doyce, Jacobia rose, untangling the blankets, tucking them back around the Seeker. Khar opened an eye and blinked at her before burrowing deep against the breathing warmth of her Bond.

What was it like to have a link with them, to speak with them more intimately than the secret sounds of mother and child, the secret language of lovers? For that was how she imagined the language they must have. What was it like? For years when she'd been little she'd tried to get Rawn to 'speak her, but the ophidian ghatt obeyed her whims in everything but that. Suffered tail pulls, the pummelings of child-sized fists, the too-tight ribbon bows, the love and crooning, special tidbits stolen from the kitchens, but uttered nothing beyond the meows of regular cats.

She arched her back, stretched, feeling rested and at ease. Nakum sat a little distance away, asleep, head pillowed on arms folded on knees. She had never met anyone before with his remote handsomeness, the vibrant coloring so unlike that of the pallid Holbein. And Aelbert, deferential and dashing in his uniform. The morning sun shone soft, testing, but there was no question it would rise, strong and bright above the mountain ranges she could barely glimpse in the north. The roar of The Shrouds rumbled as a similar constant in this land between Canderis and Marchmont. She felt so alive, at the border of so many things, not just the geography of the land but of her very soul.

Hungry? She considered it, but the need to relieve herself proved more pressing. She pulled on boots, hopping on one foot, then the other, then shrugged on her outer jacket. Without warning, the memory hit her, doubling her over in pain.

He was dead. Rolf Cardamon, that nice old man and that precious gray ghatt who looked so wise yet so concerned about his dainty white feet, his face dappled white with age—dead!

She dashed tears from eyes, hands scrubbing like an anxious, small animal. Dead? Why, why? That sweet old ghatt and the man. He had reminded her of Syndar Saffron, though she didn't know why; no two people could be less alike externally. But she'd sensed a caring in Rolf, the same she'd always sensed in Syndar Saffron, more than her own father, poor purblind fool, had ever given her. At least Jenret had that from the past, from before. She'd never had a taste of fatherly love and the emptiness hurt. Without volition her thoughts circled round to Syndar Suffron again—how could he care, why should he? It wasn't true! Better poor Jadrian Wycherley than Syndar Saffron!

Lashes bright with tears she marched into the scrub, returned, hitching her pants in place around her tiny waist, narrow hips. With a longing sigh, she stoked the fire and put water on for cha. Either too weak or too strong. Stewed, or Lady knew what else you could do to cha. You couldn't burn it, could you? Why hadn't he stayed longer? She needed more cookery lessons. The tears flowed in earnest now, and she realized what else could harm cha—salting it.

Doyce touched Jacobia's arm and thrust a handkerchief at her, a handkerchief so capacious and snowy-white she realized she'd borrowed it from Rolf the day before. She'd seen him loan them to Parse often enough, locked in a chain of allergic sneezes, inopportune as always. She had no mothering left for the girl this morning, craved the comforting all too badly herself. The dual loss left her hollow, eyes stinging fiercely, mouth striving to twist into an angry, involuntary wail.

Oh Rolf, I miss you so already! So patient yet so exacting, always so circumspect yet so concerned for your friends, Seeker and ghatti alike. If you strove to stem those emotions, it was only because they welled so deep within. And Chak, an elder statesman even in ghattenhood, I suspect, face pursed in query, natty white feet and jabot. You both helped in our training, mine and Khar'pern's, over ten years past when I joined the Seekers Veritas. You meted out the lessons, the drills, repetition after weary repetition with a polite "and again, please," exercise gradations until we melded into a wholeness, a Seeker-Bond partnership. Oriel and Saam helped, bless them, generous with emotional support, but it was you and Chak who transformed us. I hope, I pray, you were proud of your work."

"They were proud. Rolf 'slipped' once; I think on purpose, wanted to share what he couldn't say aloud." Khar's head slid against her knee, a circular rubbing with chin and cheek. With a fine sense of impartiality, she rubbed against Jacobia, still snuffling into the handkerchief. Lost in thought, Doyce reached by her to caress Khar, Jacobia managing a tentative, watery-eyed smile at the ghatta. Khar's amber eyes squinted and a purr rumbled as she pressed harder against the girl's leg.

"You rub me, and I rub her. She needs some comfort." A raised-eye apology in Doyce's direction.

"So do we all this morning."

Jacobia froze, worried she'd missed something of importance. "So do we all *what?*"

"Need comfort, as Khar reminded me. And breakfast, as I'm sure she was about to mention. None of us had much stomach for dinner last night."

A dreamy expression flittered across Jacobia's face. "Poached eggs, brown sugar-glazed ham, butter biscuits dripping with comb honey, hot chocolate. . . ." With a sigh and a guilty conscience she was earthbound again and twice as hungry.

Doyce swallowed in sympathy but kept a straight face. "I'm afraid it's going to be boiling water and the ever-faithful oatmeal bag."

"Oatmeal?" Jacobia pouted. Khar managed a pitiful face. "The way I cook it, no one will eat it, lumpy, bumpy, probably a black-crust bottom."

Doyce dropped her voice to a conspiratorial whisper. "Then I'll share a secret with you . . . no, two. First, keep it well away from the heat and stir constantly. And secondly, add raisins or dried apricots or nuts—disguises the lumps. As one mediocre cook to another, those are the secrets. Rolf taught them to me."

Good humor partially restored, Jacobia began readying the kettle while Doyce walked to where Aelbert and Jenret now stood, bodies tensely angry, faces red. She hadn't noticed they'd gotten up, and wondered what else she'd missed.

They fell silent as she approached, eyes downcast to look at Rolf's gear, neat, tidy, and now utterly abandoned.

"What's the fuss?" Neither seemed to want to speak first. Then both spoke simultaneously, trying to outshout each other.

"I've a right to see if . . ." "Absolutely not, it's not your place to rummage . . ." Aelbert's voice overrode Jenret's. "But I *am* in charge now. I am the Envoy." Triumph shone on his face, in his very stance. "Rolf's death makes *me* Envoy, that was why I was seconded to him in the first place. That was why the Monitor agreed I should go—precisely because of such a possibility. Anyone could see Rolf was too frail for this task."

Spinning on his heel, Jenret thrust a leather case at her, jammed something that crackled into his pocket with his other hand. "Well, it's not clear to me that that's the case," he snarled. "You've no written authorization to supersede Rolf, none that I've seen, and those of us here have a right to decide who's in charge now. Perhaps you're right, but I wouldn't count on it." Then, resentment restrained, "Doyce, Rolf left this for you. I don't know what it's about, it's sealed inside. I, for one, know to turn over things not addressed to me. You'd have had that opened if I hadn't stopped you."

She backed away from their hostility, half-sheltered the case and removed the envelope. Fingers stroked the wax seal with its rampant leopard crest. The last she'd ever see of that design, the old ring gone with its owner. No choice but to crack the seal, splinters of red wax littering the ground, the leopard destroyed, gone forever except in memory.

My Dear Doyce,

While I pray the Lady never lets you read this, the fact that I write it indicates the real probability that you shall. I must be honest with myself and you. Chak, dearest unto my heart, is not well, nor am I for that matter—the angina worsens and Twylla warns against exertion. We are both striving to survive—for our own sakes, for Canderis's and Marchmont's, and for the continued pleasure both you and Khar have given us. A selfish reason, but true.

I hesitate to burden you (yes, that is a plural, Khar'pern, for well we know your powers of mindspeech), but should Chak or I fail, I doubt the other will have the strength or the will to persevere. You must accept this appointment as Special Envoy, charged with all the powers that were vested in me. The Monitor grants full approval as denoted by his signature below. The Seeker General also agrees that it is right, fitting, and proper. This is what you have been called to do, and you will do it well. Chak and I had the training of you both, and we know.

Would that there were another way. Neither Chak nor I abandon a task lightly, but where one goes, the other must follow. That is the way of it. Honor our wishes, and do well.

Affectionately yours,
Rolf and Chak

P.S. We love you both, daughters that you never were. We hope that our actions spoke, as words could not, of our love.

A blunter, much more forceful hand had penned additional lines below Rolf's postscript.

Seen and approved this Sixday of Mars, 233 AL. Should anything unforeseen happen to Rolf Cardamon in pursuit of his duties as Special Envoy to Marchmont, I hereby charge Seeker Veritas Doyce Marbon to continue this mission and vest in her the full powers of Special Envoy to negotiate in Canderis's best interests.

Kyril van Beieven, Monitor
Swan Maclough, Seeker General (witness)

Laughter, dismay, anger, tears. . . . She tried them all in rapid succession, tried combinations, and finally concluded with a weak wash of laughter, mirth bordering on hysteria, as she well knew. Rolf, who had always looked askance on Parse's practical jokes, had just played one of cosmic proportions on her, although he hadn't meant it that way. Special Envoy? She? The note dropped unregarded from lax fingers.

Oh, Rolf, so meticulous, so careful to plan for every contingency. You always had too much faith in me. She hugged herself, gripped her arms harder to subdue the shaking, aware of Jenret's and Aelbert's confusion and concern. Hysterical women, they're probably thinking. Oh, Rolf, dammit all, why me? I'm over and done with growing, stretching to meet your expectations. You didn't have to die to try to make me whole, give me a purpose in life. I'm finding a purpose as I go along.

How long she stood there shivering, she had no idea, until, with rising awareness, she sensed that Jenret and Nakum held her upright, securing her in the here-and-now. Why was Jenret always grabbing at her? He'd almost done it yesterday when she ran after Rolf—was he afraid she was going to bolt over the edge of the cliff after him, do something else equally mad? Jenret's strained countenance said more than words, and she flinched. Heavenly Lady, he *did* believe she was going mad again! Shaking herself free, she managed to touch Nakum's shoulder, reassure him and herself that she was in control, and sighing with relief, the Erakwan lad moved away as silently as he'd arrived. She didn't bother to comfort Jenret, let him think as he would if he didn't know better.

Khar's mindvoice cast a sane-sounding lifeline to rescue her. **"And who's going to inform Aelbert he's not Envoy?"** Despite her concern, Khar's query held a touch of relish. The ghatta batted at the letter, paw-pinned it by its fluttering edge.

Attention diverted, Jenret rescued the creamy sheet of paper, sharing a worried look with Khar.

"You'd better read it, Jenret, Aelbert. No, wait! Give it here first." She retrieved the letter, refolded it so that only the last third showed, the section containing the Monitor's note and sprawling signature and the neat, tight script of the Seeker General. The first part was hers alone, hers and Khar's. Wordlessly, she handed it back, Jenret and Aelbert jostling shoulder to shoulder to read it. And rereading it, as if the short paragraph concealed secrets decipherable only through repeated scannings. With a murmur of dissent, Aelbert snared the letter from Jenret, perused it a final time, and returned it to Doyce, his hand trembling.

"The note hit Aelbert hard—pulse racing, breathing shallow, pupils dilated. Jenret's radiating jealousy, but he'll get over it."

"And what am I radiating?"

"Jumbled, indecisive, frightened. Not what an Envoy is

supposed to radiate. And you're holding your breath. I think they're allowed to breathe as well."

She breathed in, hearing the hoarse sound as she sucked air between her teeth. *"And what is an Envoy supposed to radiate?"*

"Why, tact and diplomacy, of course."

Playing for time, she bent to smooth Chak's blanket, her fingers catching on something smooth hidden in a fold. A tiny lid for an equally tiny china cha pot, dollhouse-sized. How odd. She took another deep breath, less noisy this time, expelled it, and bounced the little lid in her hand as she rose.

"Aelbert, Jenret, I trust that this satisfactorily answers the discussion you were engaged in earlier." The two stood stiff, uncomfortable, sharing sidelong glances of mutual dislike as well as the mutual knowledge, fast sinking in, that they'd both been passed over. "Whether I like it or not, whether you like it or not, I've been designated Envoy. And just as Rolf did, I need you both, your expertise and knowledge to complete this mission. I hope you'll willingly offer them."

Jenret smiled, almost a real one, until his whole body began to relax. "My pleasure to be sure, Madame Envoy." She flinched, hearing the slightest mocking note to the title he gave her, but knew it was directed at Aelbert, not herself.

Aelbert stood rigid, jaw locked, middling brown eyes flat and unreadable. The silence lengthened, threatening embarrassment or worse, disobedience and disloyalty. His jaw shifted from side to side, muscles bulging, but no words emerged.

N'oor broke the silence as she stepped forward, bowstretched formally, worried green eyes examining Doyce. "We hope you will accept our aid and support. It will be not only our duty but our pleasure to assist you."

"I wanted ..." Aelbert's face twisted, one hand rose, paused at his brow, fingers and thumb dragging down as if he could remold his face into submission. He moved his jaw, forced his face smooth, and tried again. "I want you to know, Madame Envoy ... that N'oor and I will do everything in our power to ensure the success of our mission."

Not to help me, but to ensure the success of the mission. She measured his choice of words, weighed them as lacking, too noncommittal about her and her elevation to Envoy. But she could expect no more from him right now, his dreams cracked beyond repair. The pain ran deep, she was sure of that, no matter how he tried to hide it. What went on behind that usually smooth brow? What was it he sought, was seeking? Perhaps she'd find out . . . in Marchmont. Marchmont.

She pivoted on her heel. "Gentleman, shall we inform the others and have breakfast? We cross into Marchmont today." Wonderful! She sounded as if she commanded a force of hundreds. The sound of The Shrouds echoed like distant, rumbling applause, ironic clapping for her first performance as Envoy.

It wasn't *that* narrow, it *couldn't* be *that* narrow, she muttered and refused to look again, edging along the moisture-slicked stone path, feet scuffling as if they alone had been gifted with vision. She planted her left shoulder against the sheer wall, examined the paler to darker striations of sand-tan red to darker red-brown cliffs above. A wedge of bottle-green plushy moss caught her attention, a dried twig poking out like a desolate lightning-struck tree, tilted and blasted by the elements.

Nakum trotted ahead, leading a pair of packhorses, their eyes bandaged to prevent them from glimpsing the sheer drop and churning water to their right. She stifled a shout as Jacobia dropped the lead reins of her pair and pushed beside the two lead horses, nothing separating her from the void but air, mist, and a rainbow fragment. Well, if it was wide enough for two burdened beasts and a human, then what was her problem? She took a firmer grip on Lokka's reins and those of Rolf's mount and forced herself forward another step, yet another, and a third. A dark form plummeted through the air, then swooped high and looped, a bird of some sort, she guessed, darting in and out of the spray, aerial acrobatics letting it shower in mid-flight. She thrust her shoulder against the wall for reassurance and marched ahead. Hut! Two, three, four! And still the damnable thundering and rumbling kept on, distorting her very equilibrium, as did the sight of the rolling waters below, until she lost all sense of up from down, top from bottom.

"**You're ruining your jacket, scrunching like that,**" came Khar the-ever-helpful's advice. "**Don't look if you don't want to.**"

She didn't bother to look at the ghatta riding, comfortable and dry-footed on Lokka's back. *"And miss the nightmare of a lifetime, the chance to see myself meet my own doom?"*

"We could blindfold you the way we've done the horses. But it's a pity to miss a view like this. Ooh ... look! Over there, where the water races and boils in a circle and then pours out!"

Involuntarily, Doyce gulped and obeyed. With a weak bleat of protest, she slitted her eyes, concentrating on the smooth, worn path of black basalt in front of her feet. It seemed to grow darker the closer they came to the actual falls and its majestical down-pouring.

"Well, of course it's darker. We're entering deeper into the mouth of this ... what do you call this, Doyce? The sun's shielded by the sides of the ..."

"Will you stop nattering!"

Khar continued the ride in long-suffering silence, every hair and whisker rigid with indignant forbearance. Doyce concentrated on the fact that generations of heavily burdened merchanters had traversed this route for well over 150 years, at least according to Jenret. It was scant comfort except that traders didn't needlessly risk their wares—or their profits.

"The next time we take one of the other routes, even if it is longer," she informed no one in particular. "I didn't become Envoy to see the scenery, to view the natural wonders of the world, no, I did not."

Nakum waited ahead, Jacobia standing between her two packhorses, a hand on each bridle, while the Erakwan draped his arms across the offside horse, his back exposed to the open drop behind him, oblivious to the air currents tugging at his hair, stirring the leather fringes of his leggings. Aelbert and Jenret brought their mounts and packhorses in closer behind Doyce. Eyes uncovered and rolling ceaselessly, white showing at the rims, Jenret's black stallion Ophar walked rock steady, deliberately placing each hoof, instilling confidence in the blinkered packhorses tethered behind him.

With a shouted hallo, Nakum sprang onto the lead packhorse and faced them, Saam matching his movements on the other pack beast.

"We'll be under The Shrouds shortly. It's a wondrous sight, something you'll never forget, almost sacred, as if the spirits of the oldest parts of the earth were there to greet you. Or so our legends say."

"Or the spirits of the poor unfortunates who didn't cross safely." Jenret the boy might have bragged about his one previous crossing nearly fifteen years ago, but the mature Jenret sounded dubious, and the realization buoyed Doyce's spirits long enough for her to crane her neck and look up . . . and up. . . .

The sun hung suspended over the apex of the falls, a steady, burning orb like the flame at the tip of an incredibly long, tapering white candle, sides running and reshaping themselves, replenishing, diminishing, replenishing at the base as water flowed like melting wax, pooled and splattered, exploded, crashing and running free. A candle that never diminished, showed no signs of guttering, never leaving the world in darkness and in peace.

Reluctantly they stepped forward, coaxing the horses along, the line stringing out. An errant stream of water struck with unexpected force against a rocky outcrop, spattering high and raining down on them. As the spray struck, Doyce pulled back in dismay, half-hunched, shoulder rising. Jenret and Jacobia echoed her pose, Jacobia with arm outflung, but Aelbert strode ahead, head thrown back, eyes wide with wonder and an unhearable cry of delight splitting his rapt face. She felt shamed, almost voyeuristic about spying on his personal moment of ecstasy, so needful after his disappointments.

A few more paces around the trail's curve and they slipped behind a curtain of water, uncertain translucence of light and unremitting motion on their right, gray gloom to their left. The sharp, flinty smell of wet stone assaulted their nostrils, the odor trapped by the cavern's dripping roof. The unceasing roar abated somewhat, casting itself outward rather than inward, and Doyce cringed at the unexpected clarity of sound as an unwary shod hoof struck stone, a minute ripple of echoes following in its wake. And then, wonder of wonders, the ringing plink of a single droplet striking a puddle, like the plink of a pebble cast into a pool. It shook her to her very core to be able to hear and distinguish one tiny droplet, unique from its falling brethren.

Reaching the crescent curve's midpoint, she stared at the ragged window of light and air suddenly gaping before her, framing edges of cascading water that ceaselessly altered their dimensions. Reluctant yet intrigued, she edged closer, straining to see through it. A rib of ceiling rock thrust itself out, shunting the downflow to each side the way a finger pressed against a streaming window redirects the water, leaving a brief clear space. Straining to peer out, she discovered she was staring straight down, vertigo nearly claiming her as she fought it, fought against the urge to overbalance as if a giant magnet drew her toward and through the curtain "window." She fell back gasping, but the compulsion to look again was too strong to deny.

The calm at the center of the storm. The water beat down and the river seemed to swallow it whole, shivering and writhing, uneasy with digesting such force, like the shudders of a snake swallowing a small beast. The river twisted and flowed with an explosion of motion as the rapids revealed themselves in the distance.

Lokka bumped Doyce with her shoulder, uneasy at the press of other bodies building behind her. With a final look, Doyce wrenched herself free, stroked Lokka's neck, and went on, shortening the leads until the horses followed the familiar tug. The sunlight grew stronger as she forged ahead, and she quickened her pace, eager to escape the curtain wall, to abandon the sudden shifts and seductions, the naked force of the water behind her. But the forgetting of the experience was beyond her.

Subdued, exhausted and, though she hated to admit it, touched with a hint of the same exhilaration that had gripped Aelbert, she climbed the slope, murmuring encouragement to the horses. The trail pitched upward and outward, widening at last, the footing more sure ascending than it had been descending on the other side. Pressing closer and closer to the heels of Jacobia's horses, driving her tighter to Nakum's pack beasts, Doyce marked the sharp line of clifftop dark against the sky. Nearly there, nearly close enough to mount and gallop forth—she swallowed hard, fingers clenching spasmodically on the reins, expression frozen—to Marchmont.

They were in Marchmont now, had entered undetected, unannounced, and she was the Special Envoy, Canderis's Envoy, the burden now hers. Not a burden she had chosen, but hers all the same. Better than some she had shouldered, no need of emotional involvement in this; it was a job, an appointment, nothing more.

❖

PART
THREE

❖

PART
THREE

Hmmph, midmorning by the slanting window light. She'd forgotten to pay any heed, so engrossed was she in the trials. Not everyone, as Harrap had more than once reminded her, enjoyed commencing these exercises at the crack of dawn. Nor did she, for that matter, but since she was awake, the others might as well be, too. Something positive ought to come out of the pain in her hands, the sensation that red-hot wires inhabited her fingers, unceasing claw-bent agony unless she strained to flex and straighten them. So lack of sleep simply meant more time to experiment, to discard false hypotheses, and perhaps, perhaps, find an answer. She screwed up her face as the "chinking" sound came; count five and it would again, and again, and again.

Resting her hands along the smooth, narrow arms of the straight-backed rocker, Mahafny allowed her fingers to mold around the armrest's curve, the chair's one decorative touch. She believed, to a certain extent, the reports the eumedicos had compiled at the Research Hospice, details of years of experiments, from their first halting, disbelieving reports on Vesey's Gleaner powers to the later, more precise accounts prepared under her daughter Evelien's supervision. Some of the reports, so precise, so clinically detailed, almost obscured their horrors beneath the weight of neutral scientific terms. But the phantom cries unwritten on paper had haunted her day and night at what her peers had perpetuated in the name of expanding medical horizons. That was why she required the reassurance of her own tests, avoiding pain and invasive cruelty if she could possibly help it. And her own tests of Gleaner abilities were showing results, even if not always what she hoped. So slow! Knowing what they could do still left her clueless as to how those Gleaner powers might be modulated, moderated, trained, or controlled.

With a mental shudder, she drew her attention back to the

testing. Davvy was due another partner now, and she nodded, directing them to bring in the next one while Davvy stuck out his lower lip, blew a gusty "phew" upward and almost crossed his eyes trying to seeing if his bangs lifted. Experimenting on children, twelve-year-old boys, no less, rousting them from innocent slumber at first light to do this. "Two more partners, Davvy, and then we'll break, I promise," she offered by way of consolation.

"Sweet rolls?" he pleaded, rubbing at his stomach, pantomiming hunger. "Watch how fast I can run the sequence then!"

Two Seekers escorted a man in late middle age into the room and seated him to her right. His shoulders hunched almost under his ears, as if to protect him from a blow. "Mr. Farnham, please," she instructed, knowing she should, she must reassure the man, but tired of it. "It's the exact same drill as before, just different partners, nothing to fear." His mouth worked in fitful movements, and at last he licked his lips, tried to smile. He did manage a genuine smile for the boy, invisible behind the partition.

"Come on, Farnie, it's fine," the boy wheedled. "Soon's I get through you and one more, it's sweet rolls for me! For us all!" He inhaled deeply, nose in the air. "Bet you could smell them as you came down the hall, couldn't you, now?"

Eyes brightening, Farnham gave a head-bob, one emphatic jerk, even though the boy couldn't see him, and readied himself. A eumedico placed two bowls in front of Farnham while another set a narrow-necked jug in front of Davvy. With a glance at Mahafny, a third eumedico called "Begin!"

The wooden partition separating Davvy and Farnham didn't block Mahafny's view because she sat to the side, the partition no more hindrance than a vertical line on a chalkboard. Her position allowed her to view both participants. Davvy plunged his hand into the jug, fingers rattling the contents until he pulled his hand out, opened his fist and glanced at the marble, dropped it down a narrow tube that projected below the desk. Eyes screwed tight in concentration, he paused, began the procedure anew when he heard an answering swoosh and chink from the other side.

Mahafny reviewed the safeguards again. The "Sender," or so she termed Davvy in her mind, was given a jug containing fifty marbles, randomly mixed between black and white. Each test had a different ratio of black to white; it might be one black and forty-nine white, twenty-five of each, or anything in between. The mouth of the jug was too narrow for Davvy to see in advance what color he would pull out. After extracting a marble, the "Sender" would examine it and "project" to his partner, the "Receiver," the color selected. Each marble was dropped, in sequence, into a tube, so that the selections piled up one on top of the other as the test continued.

The "Receiver" had two bowls of marbles in front of him, one containing fifty white, the other fifty black. It was up to him to select one color or the other to match his partner's selection, and drop his choice into a similar tube. At the end, the order of black and white marbles in each tube would be aligned against the other to determine how often the sequence matched.

On devising the test, Mahafny had posited four basic permutations to it, but now she wasn't as confident. Something more subtle was happening. She had paired "Normal" with "Normal," people with no Gleaner abilities, and the results were as expected: a few random matches, the same that chance would afford. Using a Normal as "Sender" and a Gleaner as "Receiver" increased the matches to an average of fifty percent, some higher, some lower, depending on the Normal's powers of concentration. A cold, worry, sleeplessness, all seemed to lower the odds.

Using a Gleaner as "Sender" and a Normal as "Receiver" came out to roughly a fifty percent match as well, but that average was misleading, skewed by incredible highs and lows in the scores. And the high scores left the Normals agitated, exhausted, brows furrowed with a phantom pain that they couldn't even begin to describe except to say that no, it wasn't really a headache, but yet it was. . . . Only two Gleaners seemed to cause that effect in the "Receiver," and something about them, a hint of gloating, left her uneasy. She had instructed the ghatti to keep very close mind-tabs on those two.

But, of course, the best matches, line upon line of marbles stacked identically, came from the trials with Gleaner projecting to Gleaner. Hardly unexpected, she knew. But within that were misses, a string of three or four marbles that didn't correspond, then a run of matches, a few more random mismatches. What she was coming to realize was that not all Gleaners were equal, did not share the same powers in the same proportions. Indeed, it seemed likely that some were perfect Receivers while others were perfect Senders, and one talent did not automatically indicate the other. Now she was winnowing through who possessed which traits and in what degree, a time-consuming process: select one Gleaner as "Sender" and there were nineteen other Gleaners who must receive from him, without even worrying how many trials each pairing should undertake. Time-consuming, tedious, and utterly necessary. And if and when she determined who excelled at what, could they be trained to enhance the weaker skill?

"Fifty!" Davvy sang out, drumming fists on the table. "Come on, Farnie, we're done! One more and it's sweet rolls! You did fine, I can feel it. More to you than meets the eye!" And the older man's shoulders thrust back for a moment, as if they'd been unlatched from his ears. The toothless smile was one of gratitude. "Now, Farnie, don't warm the chair forever," the boy warned with mock severity. "I've still work to do." And the man scuttled from his seat and out the door without a backward look, too used to obeying to object to dismissal by a mere boy rather than by Mahafny.

"Davvy, not too eager now, are we?" she chided. How a boy like that had ever come to be here astounded Mahafny. Sheer random chance, and was there such thing as random chance? From what she could gather, there had been a knock at the door one dark, stormy night (and was there any other kind in a tale like this? Mahafny had snorted) and Cook had opened the door, only to have a day-old baby thrust into her arms by a young woman. She'd started to protest, but the baby had protested louder, and in her confused efforts to dandle the baby, quiet him, the woman had escaped without a trace. The cook, Mrs. Cook, to be precise, name and occupation a serendipitous match, had kept the baby, resisting eumedico suggestions that he be placed with a younger family or sent to an orphanage. Now Davvy was the pet of the place, beloved of Gleaners and eumedicos alike, and the discovery that he had Gleaner potentials had surprised everyone, though Mahafny strongly suspected that was why he'd been left here in the first place.

Yulyn Biddlecomb was now seated across the partition from Davvy, watching with patience for the boy to cease his antics and settle himself. Eyes the color of copper pennies opened wide in commiseration with Mahafny at the delay.

She had hopes for the young woman, the closest she had to an acknowledged ally amongst the Gleaners. "Ready? Who's there? You didn't announce yourself!" the boy shouted out, dragging his chair back to the table.

"And it's not necessary for you to know whom you're projecting to, Davvy, that's part of the experiment." Mahafny yearned for the break as well. Perhaps wrapping her hands around a hot cup of cha would ease the pain. "That's why the partition is there, and you're not meant to peer over it or try to peek around it." The boy jolted back into the seat as if slapped, an incongruous expression of surprise on his face.

"How'd you know? You aren't supposed to be able to read minds? Are you cheating on us?"

Mahafny waited for his sputtering indignation to die down. "Because it's something any boy would try, Gleaner or not, so don't pride yourself on being so different from all the rest. Now," she gestured to one of the other eumedicos at the side table, "are the marbles set?"

They began, like mirror images of each other. The rattle of the marble jug, the pause, the swoosh, and chink-ching as the marbles piled up one on top of another in the tube. Harrap and Parm slipped into the room and stood behind Mahafny's chair, watching. "Nana Cookie's bringing the sweet rolls up the stairs," Harrap whispered in Mahafny's ear, and she could smell sugar-cinnamon on his breath, meaning that he'd lightened Nana Cookie's tray for her as he'd passed by. She felt him pull away, preoccupied by something else, and then his urgent whisper made her sit straight, intent, watching the scene in front of her. "Parm says he's cheating!" "But how?" she whispered back.

And without a word being spoken, the boy swiveled around, "Am not! I'm not cheating! I just changed the rules! I got . . . bored! Silly to have to do so many times! I'm hungry and I've had enough of this!" He was standing now, stamping his foot, daring someone, anyone to object, to contradict him. "Mayhap you can work all day, but I can't. I'm a . . ." he searched for the phrase, clearly one he wouldn't use to describe himself but which he thought carried weight, "growing boy!"

"Shades of Nana Cookie!" Yulyn stepped around the partition, marble tube in hand. "Well, Davvy, shall we show them how smart you are, how cleverly you've tricked me?"

The words weren't mean-spirited, but they brought the boy back to the present and what he had done. "We've not finished, but I think we've enough to compare. Bring your tube over and let the eumedico empty it into the trough." Complying, Davvy handed his tube to the eumedico, let her pour the marbles into the lower of two narrow troughs that allowed comparison of the matches. Yulyn handed over her tube as well, the marbles spilling out while Davvy turned to Mahafny, not even bothering to compare the lines of marbles.

"See! Exact opposites! Two white, black, white, three blacks, white, black. And she's got two blacks, white, black, three whites, black, white! I projected the exact opposite of what I had!"

Yulyn rested her hands on Davvy's shoulders, spinning him to face the slate-topped trestle table. "Oh, really? Did you now?" The two rows of marbles aligned perfectly, matched color by color.

"But how'd you guess? I've worked it on others. Oh, not often, but just for fun, just when I was bored."

"Just because Bert taught you sleight of hand on his last visit doesn't mean you have the right to turn it into sleight of mind." Yulyn slumped as if the burden carried were far too heavy for her. "You must never, *never* try to tamper with someone else's abilities like that!"

"But Vesey always said . . ." he whined, struggling to pull free from the hands gripping his shoulders.

"You don't know half of what Vesey did or didn't do. And be thankful you don't!" She caught Mahafny's eye, where she sat frozen in the chair, the eumedico aware that things had spun out of control before she had even had time to realize it. "I think I hear them setting up the cha things in the hallway. May we go?"

Numb, Mahafny nodded assent. "Yulyn . . ." her voice trailed off into a croak, but she cleared her throat and tried again. "Yulyn." Yes, that was right, authority and polite command in her voice. "We must talk . . . later."

"Of course. I promised you I had nothing to hide," she hesitated, "but sometimes even I don't know what you should ask." And she left. Yulyn wanted to make things right for everyone, Gleaner and Normal alike. Naive? Mahafny smothered a sigh. If so, then so was she for thinking she could solve anything.

❖

They lounged on new grass shoots, leaning against the bank with sighs, but mostly with silences. The quiet soothed like balm, the grinding falls distant enough that they could convince themselves it echoed only in their memories, not in reality. With one accord they had mounted and galloped away after cresting the far side of The Shroud. No looking back toward Canderis, though in her heart Doyce had bade a final farewell to Rolf and Chak.

Jacobia lay wriggling on her back, legs waving as she planted one boot against the heel of the other and levered it off. The boot yielded, and with an enthusiastic toss of her leg, she sent it flying. Unlikely missile though it was, it arched through the air, landing smack in the middle of Jenret's stomach. With a nervous giggle, Jacobia shielded her eyes against the sun while Doyce waited for Jenret's explosion. Instead, he grumbled and tossed it back in a high, easy curve. Aelbert sprang to intercept it, holding it high in triumph while Jacobia reached to reclaim it. Instead, impulsively, he tossed it to Nakum.

Hands crossed behind her head, Doyce watched the impromptu game as Aelbert and Nakum lobbed the boot back and forth, Jacobia rushing in one direction, waving her arms to block, then dashing back. Khar's chin rested on Doyce's thigh while her amber eyes tracked the boot's progress, its capricious curves and dives.

"Want me to bring it down?" The ghatta fought the urge to bat at the flying object.

Doyce allowed herself a lazy yawn, mouth uncovered. *"Why spoil their fun? They'll stop when they're tired of it."*

Jacobia's yells grew shrill, frustrated, her feints and dashes more erratic, awkward with exhaustion, trying too hard and failing more badly with each lunge. Her face simmered redly, dark brows lowering over narrowed eyes, ready to tear at any moment. Jenret lay still, purposely oblivious to what he'd started.

"Push her too hard and you don't know how she'll react, other than most likely childishly. Worth it or not? She's been on her best behavior so far, trying hard."

"Then let it be Jenret's problem, she's his sister." Doyce

laid a warning hand on Khar's back. *"Besides, it never hurts to let her learn what is and isn't a game."*

Face clenched tight as a fist, Jacobia grunted and sprang to block Aelbert's toss. Missing, she landed with a yelp and began to dance on one foot, stockinged foot cradled in her hands. With a moan, she collapsed on the grass, still clasping her foot, massaging it, head low, dark mane of hair curtaining her face.

Nakum and Aelbert approached from opposite directions, hesitant, hovering but unsure what to do. Finally Aelbert, still clutching the boot, squatted beside her, normally expressionless face raw with concern.

"Here," he offered, thrusting her boot at her, staring as if mesmerized by the narrow, stockinged foot, stained with grass and dirt.

Jacobia snatched the boot and lofted it in the air, threatening Aelbert's bowed head. But with slow unwillingness, she pulled her arm back, clutching the boot to her chest. "It was *just* a game," her voice choked, "but enough is enough." Her glare swept them impartially. "You just *don't* know when to stop, when it *isn't* funny any longer, do you?"

Nakum's hazel eyes filled with consternation, his mouth downturned as he took a deep breath. "Sometimes the boundary between fun and not fun is not as clear as the boundary between Canderis and Marchmont. I . . ." he glanced at Aelbert for support, ". . . we . . . are sorry."

Wincing, Jacobia jammed her foot into her boot, stamped on it gingerly. "I think I started it, though Jenret helped." She nodded in Jenret's direction, but Jenret, hat tipped over his face, seemed sound asleep. "Oh, by the Lady, do I need a sip of water." And both Aelbert and Nakum dashed to fetch waterskins.

"Charming," murmured Khar with grave deliberation.

"Absolutely. She'll have them both on her string before they know it." Doyce copied Jenret's action and tilted her hat over her eyes. *"Of course, if you angle it, you can see everything that's going on. I wonder what Jenret thought of it all?"*

Khar considered responding, then curled up, chin pillowed on hind paw, half-dozing. Still, she saw enough of the tableau of the three younglings sharing water to smile with falanese amusement.

❖

"Carrots!" He snorted, disgust commingled with worry. "Carrots." The last of the winter storage, shrunken, gnarled, and hairy with questing rootlets, fine and wispy white as an elder's beard. Carrots—the only thing the villagers showed willingness to trade. Oh, they'd looked at the silver in silent covetousness; he'd been wily enough not to flash the gold he'd secreted about him. They hadn't appeared ill-fed; they'd looked as if they could easily spare better, especially given the price offered. But they'd held themselves with an aloof, wary regard, unwilling to trust strangers this close to the border. He wondered who else had passed through recently and what they had offered—or threatened.

The gelding was dead, left leg splintered just above the fetlock, his belt knife clean but still warm from the farewell blooding. Too bad, he'd been a fine horse. He'd never grown overattached to his horses or dogs the way some did, but he respected a good animal and treated it well. How could it serve one competently if mistreated? The horse had given his best and he regretted he hadn't been able to ease its suffering more quickly.

Syndar Saffron stood, arms akimbo, fists on his hips, staring down the road and squinting defiance at the setting sun. Nothing for it but to walk, and walk through the dark at that. No choice, he had to make good time and without the horse that was near impossible.

He would find Jacobia, *must* find her, Lady bless or damn him to the Beyond and back with his ancestors in space if he didn't. He'd do anything to find her, and if an unwary traveler happened by, well, he'd have another mount whether the traveler yielded it willingly or not.

For a moment he wished his friend Jadrian Wycherley were by his side, jesting, teasing, yet rock solid reliable as he had been in so many earlier trading ventures and competitions. But that wasn't possible, and if it were, things would be changed beyond measure and meaning—for he would be the stalwart friend aiding the father's search for the daughter, his goddaughter.

No, he wouldn't, he struck the thought down viciously, couldn't change a thing. His daughter, not Jadrian's, his travail . . . for Damaris, and most of all for himself, an acknowl-

edgment of the daughter he was not allowed to acknowl
edge.

Syndar Saffron stroked the cooling body of his horse i
farewell, threw his saddle over one shoulder, the saddlebag
over the other, hefted the burlap sack, light on carrots, an
strode on.

❧

Hooves click-clopped along the road, its surface a myria
of hexagonal paving stones, saucer-sized, each snug-fitte
like outsized pieces in a leagues-long game. Most wer
black or gray with the occasional relief of a white hexago
or two, markers of some sort, Doyce suspected, more com
plex clusters denoting distance or fording signs, since th
road paralleled the river. Wide and swift, with only an occa
sional tumble to break and whiten the current, the river di
not here reveal itself as the source of the falls they'd crosse
under, guarding its secret. The mountains reared up higher i
front of them the farther they rode.

She cantered beside Jenret, Jacobia and Aelbert followin
with the packhorse string. Sometimes the hilly forest nudge
the road toward the river; in other spots it wandered awa
from its liquid companion. Late afternoon, shadows stretch
ing long, ready to fade into dusk. The forest began to thin
replaced by rolling hummocks and hills, fields ridged wit
freshly plowed earth. Two white specks, oxen, she judged,
human by their side tramping homeward, beyond hailing dis
tance.

The aroma of the fresh-turned loam left the ghatti twitch
with anticipation. Random mindvoice twitters floate
through her mind. **"Sooo much . . .!"** **"Oooh . . .!"** **"Coul
we . . .?"** **"Dream come true . . .!"**

"Jenret, I think we need a brief halt." She raised an eye
brow at the tilled earth. "We can catch up with Nakun
later."

"What? Why?" By then Rawn caught Jenret's attention
urgent, requesting permission, offering enlightenment. "Oh."

Within moments, the three ghatti were racing across th
field, furiously digging here and there, inspecting anothe
site, even a third, enraptured by the multiplicity of choices
all so soft, so rewardingly workable. Squatting, sounds o
pleasurable relief.

"It seems strange we haven't seen anyone else on the road," she hazarded, politely averting her eyes from the frantic activity in the field.

He shrugged, twisted at the waist to stretch. "I know, perhaps it's a sort of no-man's-land this close to the border. That Customs Station we passed had been deserted for a long time, not just closed for the winter. It's . . . odd." Shading his eyes, he stared into the distance where Nakum and Saam ranged ahead, scouting as they went. "Rawn said Saam hasn't reported anything of interest, but he was a mite distracted." He managed a straight face, "Mayhap there's nothing worth discovering, only depositing."

Kicking the stirrup free, she swung her leg over Lokka's head, nearly brushing the horse's ears, and crossed her ankle over her left thigh. "Phew, not as easy as it used to be," she admitted and Jenret treated her to a sidelong grin. "Still, if Marchmont is so concerned about its border, it just doesn't make sense that they haven't detected us. We're intruding, and it should make them damn curious, don't you think? Aelbert's displaying the pennant announcing our diplomatic status; you'd think someone would respond to it. Two oxen and a Marchmontian farmer three fields distant hardly constitute a welcoming committee."

Jenret regarded her for longer than she liked, and she busied herself by swinging her leg back into the stirrup, shying from his gaze. "Perhaps it's a silent homage," he cocked his head, blue eyes intense. The ghatti came scampering back, leaping aboard with smug self-satisfaction. Without exchanging another word they started forward, but she was the one who dropped back, making up an excuse to talk with Jacobia, anything to escape the palpable yearning of those eyes that played such havoc with her heart and soul.

To her dismay, Jacobia persisted in nattering about Jenret, regaling her with stories of their childhood or rather, Jacobia's childhood and Jenret's early adulthood, as he was sixteen years her senior. Doyce half-listened, letting her mind wander, although where it wandered sent her retreating from the associations it conjured up. No, not after Oriel. Humming under her breath for distraction, she concentrated on an old ballad. "Oh, Matthias did ride with his ghatta beside as they sought for the Truth of it all . . ." She drew a blank, the words evaporating, and she da-da-da-dummed.

"Khar what comes after . . . ?" But Khar was perched

bolt-upright on the platform, straining over Lokka's neck,
pupils wide with concern, body taut. So, for that matter, was
N'oor, she realized, and when Jenret half-swung Ophan
around, as if torn between advance and retreat, it was clear
that Rawn was equally upset.

"**Saam! Trouble!**" Khar hissed, the hair on her spine
cresting. "**Ambush! Saam and Nakum are trying to fight
free!**"

Nakum? Ambushed? Impossible for him and Saam to fall
into a trap! But there was no time to think it through. Doyce
pushed Khar flat against the platform and kicked Lokka into
a gallop, swinging her sword clear of her saddle scabbard.
Aelbert matched her movements, tossing the packhorses'
leads to Jacobia who sat her mount openmouthed, unaware
of an alarm, of what prompted the sudden flurry of activity.
Nor was she armed, Doyce realized belatedly.

She shouted, caught Aelbert's attention. "Can't leave her!
Someone should guard her!"

His expression wavered, his face white, N'oor's delicate
face peering from beneath his crouching figure, eyes blaz-
ing, mouth drawn in a snarl. "You," he ordered, "get her,
guard her, follow after. I'll join with Jenret!" His gelding,
undistinguished-looking but well-bred, one of the beasts
from the Monitor's stables, surged ahead. Damn Aelbert for
stealing the initiative! Lokka protested at being reined back
beside Jacobia's mount.

"What? What's happening?" she gasped. "Where . . . ?"

Doyce grabbed Jacobia's reins and dragged her horse into
a gallop alongside Lokka, the burdened pack string stumbling but falling into place like a kite tail. Well, now she'd
have to protect Jacobia and fight as well. "Be ready to drop
their leads if I tell you." She wished she had a free hand to
pass Jacobia her staff, anything to arm the girl, but it would
have to wait.

A clash ahead, a welter of bodies dim in the falling twilight, some mounted, some afoot. An enraged ghatt's scream
punctured the air. N'oor, she thought, and a compact shape
launched itself from horseback, leaping full into the face of
an enemy. The next scream, all too human, was unsurpris-
ing. "**Well done!**" Khar growled.

She drummed her heels against Lokka, Jacobia's mount
matching the pace. "Through the middle," she ordered.
"When I yell 'now,' drop their leads! Keep riding. Veer at

the first deep cover, burrow in and wait!" She pounded Jacobia's arm, made her acknowledge the command.

With a shove and a kick, she sent Jacobia's mount angling to the right while she kneed Lokka leftward. "Now!" she whooped and slapped the flat of her sword on the gelding's rump for emphasis. The spooked animal shot ahead and Jacobia dropped the leads, whether in fright or obedience Doyce didn't know or care.

Diversion, confusion, that was her strategy, and at first it worked perfectly, the pack beasts shooting through the middle of the melee, confused and panicky horses rammed through in all directions, some of the milling, riderless steeds following after them. Straining to pick out her friends, she glimpsed a raised arm and saw Khar slash and connect. But in the midst of this distraction a shadowy figure grabbed for Lokka's bridle, and the mare screamed and reared, pawing through a press of bodies gathered by a broad tree overhanging the road.

Khar rasped and growled. **"Above!"** The weight crushed, a knee slamming between her shoulder blades, and Khar eeled free as Doyce crumpled against the pommel platform, felt herself dragged from the saddle by grasping hands.

A packhorse staggered through, reared to avoid trampling her shoulder as Doyce slammed facedown on the ground. The earth trembled with the horses' hooves, and eager hands rolled her over, pinned her flat. A trickle of blood from her nose slid across her cheek, rolled into her hair. She struggled, gasping for air, and tried to tear loose, but the pinioning hands held iron-firm.

"Ease up!" Khar commanded, fidgeting sideways, abristle, and a man nudged her away with the side of his boot. She spat at the insult but yielded with marginal grace, leaping clear to land beside a large dog, black with a white muzzle and chest, long and lean of leg and body, its loppy ears framing an elongated snout. With calculated disdain, Khar dipped her head to lick her soft underbelly, flaunting her vulnerable neck to those long jaws with their deadly pointed teeth. The dog regarded the ghatta with interest, enthusiastic panting, tongue lolling in a doggy grin. **"Ease up,"** Khar instructed Doyce again. **"Ease up and so will they."**

Doyce relaxed, stopped struggling, and immediately some

of the hands released her. *What's going on? What happened?"* she 'spoke to Khar.

Khar danced at her side, ignoring the long-limbed dog so tauntingly close. Overcome with curiosity he stretched his long snout toward the ghatta who sidestepped with ease, hissing a comment that set the dog pulling back in confusion. **"Ugh! Slobber tongue! Welcoming committee, though not exactly the most welcoming I've ever met. You wanted to meet Marchmontians, now you've met them."**

She thrust her arms behind her to sit up; immediately two men helped raise her, one supplying a muscled thigh and knee as a backrest. Another face loomed close, onionybreathed, blotted at her cheek and nose; she gratefully pressed the damp cloth against her throbbing nose to staunch the flow. Baffled at the unexpected violence, the equally unexpected kindness, and judging Khar's actions as a bellwether indicating little potential danger, she remained silent, groping to read the situation.

She spotted Nakum and Jenret held on the far side of the roadway, arms loose-bound and a man on each side restraining them. Rawn paced, hackles raised, uneasy but not alarmed, while Saam sat stock-still at Nakum's feet, yellow eyes noting everything. A flicker and then the sudden unshuttered beam of a lantern at the road's center spotlighted Aelbert. She could just hear a volley of words, muted and placating, as he expostulated, defying a man half again his size as he waved his pennant on its whiplike mount. At the stranger's gesture, hands hoisted her to her feet and walked her over; the familiar word "envoy" separated itself from Aelbert's rapid commentary.

"I've been telling them and telling them that we're on a diplomatic mission," he whispered, voice urgent.

"Then they're not brigands?" Doyce's question brought a hearty laugh from the larger man. After all, didn't brigands wear barbaric, colorful garb? Or had she read too many swashbuckling adventures as a child? Gaudy it might be, but it did constitute a uniform of sorts: a black shirt with flowing crimson-slashed sleeves, a heavy red-leather vest topping it, tight pants of Prussian blue with a red seam stripe, and a yellow sashing around his waist. Four gold bars marked each epaulet, and pinned over his heart was a lavender and white cockade edged in black. His dark hair and luxuriant mustache matched the pirate portraits of her girlhood dreams.

"Brigands? We thought *you* were," his rhythm and cadence made her strain to decipher familiar words, accented on different syllables. "We saw the hoofprints at the old Customs Shed. Brigands, invaders, it matters not, it's our duty to stop them."

Nose muffled by the wet rag, she snapped, "Didn't you see the pennant? Doesn't that proclaim our diplomatic status? Or are such things not honored in Marchmont? Do you ambush everyone and ask questions afterward?" She waved the cloth in his face. "Well, I'm sorry this can't serve as a flag of truce, but it's all bloody now, isn't it? I'm waiting for an apology. By insulting me, you have insulted all of Canderis."

Aelbert's face went ashen, and the larger man was obviously stung by her tone. "We ambush or, as we might more precisely put it, repel or capture all who cross our boundaries unheralded and uninvited. As to the pennant," he hurled a sharp query at his followers, voice hard. "Who was on watch?"

A spindly youth clad in a black shirt with yellow-slashed sleeves seemingly fuller than his narrow chest, was pushed forward. As questions were hurled, he began to wilt as if wishing he could withdraw and hide within the showy, over-sized shirt. A final barked command elicited a convulsive salute before he pivoted on his heel and marched to his post.

The commander shook his head in disgust. "They assign the youngest, the newest as lookout, and do not even bother to find out who he is, how do you say, short of the sight?"

She puzzled it through until it finally dawned on her. "Shortsighted, nearsighted?"

He waved an eloquent hand. "Exactly so. Without doubt poor Tienyard thought it your laundry blowing in the breeze. For that I apologize. Still, I have no other reason to believe you, other than your pennant. If you would be so kind . . ." he let the words linger and waited expectantly.

She goggled, distracted by new yells of glee echoing from the roadway ahead, beyond her sight. Aelbert jogged her elbow, prompting, his voice a thready hiss. "The papers, Doyce. The papers of passage the Monitor gave Rolf."

She nodded, still distracted, still straining for the cause of the commotion as she fumbled inside her jacket. Jovial laughter, followed by a curse and a yelp of pain, a string of curses peppered the air. The commander listened and then shouted, wheeled back smiling as Jacobia was hauled into view, struggling. "Your final companion has been collected as well, though it appears the little honey bee has a sting my men did not watch for."

Relief and dismay flooded Doyce. How could she have forgotten Jacobia, pounding along alone, terrified? Still, she looked to have come to no great grief, though she swore, dragging her heels and fighting like a little wildcat. Jenret's call broke through her terror and she pulled free and ran to him, flinging her arms around his waist. He kissed the top of her head, shushing her.

Dark eyes continued their level inspection, unperturbed, waiting to regain her attention. Well, now that he knew that both Jacobia and she could sting, she could afford to be polite, diplomatic. "Papers, I believe you said," and handed the packet to him. "I trust the papers of passage will prove sufficient since the sealed message is directed to your new ruler, whomever is in charge since her Gracious Majesty Wilhelmina's death. I apologize for the lack of superscription, but as you must be aware, communications have parlously broken down between us in recent octants."

Unfolding the papers in the lantern light, he noted the official watermark woven into the paper, examined the seal with the Monitor's crest. "It appears official enough to assure passage into Sidonie, though with an escort, as you may well expect. And if you are the Envoy," he laid apologetic emphasis on the "if," "we owe you that courtesy as penance for our rough welcome. Still, we Marchmontians are an unpolished people, good-hearted but prone to forget the niceties of life." He whetted his words with a hint of her own sarcasm; she sensed how little slipped by this man.

"Such as introductions?" she prompted.

"Such as introductions." White teeth flashed against the magnificent mustache.

"Well, then, I believe my aide, Aelbert Orsborne, has given you my name, but if I may repeat it? I am Doyce Marbon, and this is my Bondmate Khar'pern. The tall man in black is Jenret Wycherley, accompanied by his Bond Rawn and his sister Jacobia. Our scout is Nakum of the Erakwa people with his," she hesitated over the proper word, "companion Saam. Orsborne's Bond is N'oor."

"And I am Arras Muscadeine." His mustache wriggled alarmingly, whether from perplexity or an attempt to disguise a smile, she couldn't judge. "I am the Captain of this squad that you have met so abruptly tonight." Again the mustache squirmed as he pursed his mouth and whistled. The lanky dog raised its head and trotted to his side, ears flapping, long muzzle upthrust into the cupped hand. The dog's shoulder reached Doyce's waist. It looked at her, nostrils flaring as it sought to capture her scent and its head bobbed closer, only to pull back at a sharp tongue click from Muscadeine. "This is my compatriot Felix, though we do not generally bother to introduce our animals."

"Of course not, ill-bred, ignorant dogs," Khar sputtered and continued in the same vein, expanding Doyce's vocabulary with a breadth and depth of derogatory terms she'd thought impossible. Felix, too, seemed to sense his dignity impugned, even if he couldn't understand the words. His lips curled, exposing the long canines, and a monotone growl rumbled deep in his chest.

Muscadeine quieted him with a good-natured cuff. "Hush, Felix! Never have dog and cat been friends. And never have Felix and I seen cats so . . . so amply big as these of yours, so grandly large, so grossly giant." One bold, dark eye winked at her, the quickest flicker, testing her reaction to his hyperbole.

Khar was not amused, but Doyce tuned out her cries of outrage.

With grave reciprocity she studied Felix, taking her time, admired the luster of his thick coat, complimented the nobility of his broad brow, the length and sharpness of his teeth, and most of all, his size, the length of the long, slim legs with their speckled featherings, his elegant plumed tail. She omitted nothing, giving him his due.

Muscadeine nodded, chest thrown forward, enjoying the game. "And nearly big enough to ride. For you he would be, eh?"

Doyce could feel Aelbert's dismay and simmering outrage at her sheer foolishness, the burning knowledge of his clear superiority as an Envoy, his skills in negotiations. She treated him to a cool smile, then turned its force on Muscadeine.

"But enough diplomacy for this evening, Captain. I believe you mentioned escorting us to the capital? Shouldn't we be riding?"

His eyes sparkled. "So. We go. Let us gather your horses and let us reclaim ours. Most will be abed when we reach Sidonie, but I would not deprive myself of the treat of waking the world to announce your presence, the Special Envoy of Canderis."

❧

They rode in full dark now, Doyce and her companions at the squad's core, jostled by Marchmontian soldiers. Their colorful uniforms made them appear foppish at first, but beneath the gaudery they wore an alert, hard-bitten look, poised for violence, unlike Canderis's Guardians, as if battle were their daily fare. Who made the better soldier, a peace-loving man fighting on rare occasions for what he holds sacred, or seasoned professionals like Arras Muscadeine and his men? And whom or what had they been fighting, for no word had leaked to Canderis. The odd white paving stones she'd remarked on earlier glowed luminescent along the highway's shoulders, guiding them.

"Were all boundaries this clear, humans would know when they trespassed."

"It doesn't do much good to build walls, physical barriers between countries. They tried that thousands of years ago on Olde Earth in a place called China, but even those walls were breached," she whispered back, still struck by the ghostly beauty of the glowing marker stones. *"I wonder what makes them do that?"*

"Makes humans want to build walls?"

"No, makes them glow. The stones, that is."

"Like our eyes." The shiver rippled through Khar. **"They wouldn't dare extract that...."**

Muscadeine pulled closer, hand lingering on her arm to attract her attention. "Now listen, be ready," he commanded. "Few from Canderis have had the privilege to hear."

She strained her ears, waiting. As a darker blackness reared from the darkness ahead, she momentarily distinguished a building perched high above the roadway, pillars lofting it skyward. Then a strident sundering of the air, a sound so blaring she almost lost her seat as Lokka jerked and trembled. A horn, a deep bass note sped them along and, as if in answer, a pinprick light flared about a half-league ahead, a tiny, beckoning glimmer.

The horn's long, lonesome note hung in the air as they reached the light source, and she saw she was correct: a compact watchtower stilted on wooden pilings beside the highway, affording an unhindered view in all directions. The light came from a tripod signal blazer. A new horn sounded, a richer vibrato than the first, its after-chill shivering her spine. And so it continued, light after light, bass note after bass note as they advanced. Some notes sounded rich and true, perfectly pitched to carry, others produced only a strenuous blat of sound.

"We choose them for their strong lungs, not their musical ability," Muscadeine quipped as Doyce twisted away, wishing she could blot out a particularly tooth-clenching sound. Behind them Jacobia yelped, clapping hands over ears while Nakum, Aelbert, and Jenret rode stoically; Nakum ill-at-ease on horseback but with no other choice because he'd been denied permission to run afoot.

Gradually the highway began showing signs of habitation: high-peaked log houses, timbers cunningly notched and fitted into elaborate corner facades. Some boasted lower levels of stone topped with dressed timber on the second and third stories.

"Do not forget our early heritage, the materials we had at hand." Muscadeine gestured toward the houses. "Timber aplenty to shelter new settlers facing a long, hard mountain winter." Architecture did not appear on her mental list of discussion topics, she thought sourly.

Muscadeine laughed, head thrown back. "Much on your mind, eh? And not always easy to find the words to follow a conversation beyond the one in your mind." He continued without waiting for an answer. "Still, a lesson in early history is not a hindrance but a help, background. Everything must have background, eh?" Hadn't she absorbed enough history from Rolf? The loss ached anew because she'd hear no more. "Now only the truly rich can afford such timbered housing, what was once common is now an extravagance, an affectation, to relive our founding fathers' way of life. Still, we have always revered our past, esteeming the memory of our founder-king, Venable Constant."

This turn in the conversation she could cope with—whatever more she could learn about Marchmont's early governance might well help explain why its current inhabitants acted as they did. "Then the royal family still commands the respect and loyalty of your people?"

The muscles in Muscadeine's face tightened, his eyes hooded and sad. If only the luxuriant mustache would evaporate so she could read his expression more easily.

"Even with nothing left to command loyalty, old habits die hard. And our rulers were not figureheads, they governed us, cared for us, put our needs ahead of their own. Now we have only a Steward, and if we do not elevate one of the blood royale soon . . ." his lower lip jutted. "Some are too forward, too eager for anointment. But you will hear of that soon enough, so wait. Besides, we come soon to the main way."

"What's a steward?" Restless, Khar shifted and half-rose only to resettle on her platform. **"Is it good?"**

"I don't know if it's good or not. A steward is a person put in charge of another's affairs. Whether it's good or bad depends on the steward. What I'm more concerned with is what he meant by elevating someone of the blood royale, and he's implied that there's more than one candidate. . . ."

"Then not just anyone can be king?" Ghatti had never worried about royalty or the fine points of inheritance, legitimacy, or rank.

"Or queen," Doyce added. *"In Marchmont the firstborn inherits, whether the child is male or female. The eldest rules."*

"Mmph." Khar shook herself with excitement. **"And Wilhelmina had no children. Rolf said so."**

"Precisely."

"Then who's her next closet relative?"

Doyce shook her head. *"That, my precious, appears to be the problem, but is that what's affecting Marchmont's relations with Canderis?"* And now she could feel a city looming ahead of her, its smells, its muted sounds, its late-night lights.

A three-note trumpet blast shattered the dark as they approached Sidonie, the outer walls surrounding the city's heart—and its castle—one and the same, perhaps. "Better musicianship, no?" Arras pointed toward one of the rounded guard towers. "But these fight as well as play. Much endurance for fighting. Lungs strong enough to blow these horns, arms strong enough to hold such instruments, mean greater strength in battle."

She shivered despite herself. "You talk," she hesitated, "you talk as if fighting . . . as if war," such a short, ugly word, "were commonplace, something you were used to." She rushed on. "You've spoken of men's ability to fight as calmly as we speak of the weather!"

Puzzled by her outburst, he folded a hand over hers on the reins. Instead of comforting, it made her want to pull free, frightened by the careless strength of someone who fought, controlled others. "But of course," he agreed. "Men must fight—whether against the cowardice that lurks within, or against the hostile elements, or sometimes, oftentimes, against each other. How can you not understand that?"

"But battles? Wars? You have that?"

His voice dropped, left her straining to hear. "Yes, we have lived through them in recent years, and some of us will live through more. And no, they are not grand or glorious. They are dirty, nasty, and brutal, too often waged unjustly and for no clear cause. Now, let us forget about war so that I may welcome you to Sidonie."

Walls of sheer dressed stone, joined almost without crack or seam, blocked her vision. They rose six times her height; she craned to see their tops, found them surmounted by equally tall iron columns, each boasting a base circumference larger than her embrace. The columns were tight-fitted at the base, no space between the next and its neighbor, but as they soared she could distinguish chinks of light, as if they grew narrower the higher they rose. And without knowing why, "grew" seemed apt to describe them.

"I didn't realize Marchmont mined that much easily workable ore." Her eyes kept tracing up the dark smooth sides until she viewed the stars.

"Ore? What?" The Capitain followed her gaze. "Ah, ore. Yes, we have much, a richness of ore, though not the capability to cast columns of such magnitude. The weight alone would be . . ." he shrugged. "You do not know, eh, of our arborfer? Not iron, but wood. Cut it while it is fresh and it can be shaped, trimmed, or cut as normal wood. But once the sap has dried, it hardens, becomes dense, and does not decay. Only diamond-edged drills or blades can slice it, but slowly, slowly, with much effort and dulled points. Nor can fire scorch it. Our fathers did not rush to build foundries, despite the abundance of ore; why should they with the plentitude of arborfer? Rich and poor alike built their houses from it, formed it into plowshares, swords, knives. Some of the first trees our fathers harvested still carry water, bored to form underground piping." Muscadeine fingered his own sword hilt, fingers caressing the intricate carvings that decorated the basket. "Now it is scarce. We harvested too fast, did not realize how long it took to mature."

"Is your sword arborfer?" In the midst of the attack she had never doubted it was fine-honed steel.

"But of course. A family heirloom."

Before he could say more, the heavy arborfer gates parted, their timbers incised with a row of simple yet powerful carvings, geometric shapings about the size of her palm. If only she were closer, had more light. Behind her Nakum stifled a sharp exclamation, but she had no time to wonder why as torches sprang to life around the courtyard's perimeter. The brightness dazzled, broken only as figures bestirred themselves, some, unlike the duty guards, only just roused by the commotion and still fastening final buttons and points, pulling clothes into place. Nakum and Aelbert had fanned to her left, Jacobia and Jenret on Muscadeine's right, the horses stamping with fatigue, the smell of nearby stabling, grain and water fresh in their nostrils.

Crouching like a powerful hunkering beast at the far end of a level avenue, the castle's two watchtowers peaked like alert ears, the domed roof giving the impression of a compact, powerful body. Fool's fancy, perhaps, but she couldn't resist asking if Khar saw the resemblance. *"It looks like a ghatt."* Khar sneezed surprised agreement. Dark green, clinging ivy further enhanced the illusion, rippling furlike in the breeze. From the right watchtower a light bobbed by a window slit, reappeared at the next lower level, and the next, as if someone trudged down winding stairs, lantern in hand, until a small side door creaked open.

"Now what, now what? I've *finally* gotten him to bed. . . ." The voice trembled with fatigue. A gangling man, thin and bowed as a barrel stave, popped into view, lantern held high while his other hand shielded his eyes. Grizzled red hair tufted the sides of a bald head, waxed luxuriant in a magnificent set of muttonchops, compensation for the barren expanse of scalp. Sky-blue livery showed a misbuttoned front, the right edge dangling two button notches lower than the left, and the lavender sash hung askew, one end trailing. "This had better prove urgent or I swear I'll break the soul who caused this fuss. . . ."

"Pax, Ignacio, pax." Muscadeine dismounted, nodded to Doyce to do the same, but a held hand restrained the others. His words were conciliatory, but they bore a note of command.

Arching his back in relief, the man holding the lantern rushed forward, long, thin shanks scissoring, a water bird wading through reeds of hangers-on, castle servants. "Oh, Chevalier Capitain, I did not realize it was *you.*" Doyce noted the expanded title, wondered at its significance. More than a mere Capitain, surely.

"Yes, 'tis I." Sympathetic hands repinned the cockade on the man's livery, a cockade that matched the coloring of Muscadeine's. "A hard night, old friend."

A grimace of distaste crossed Ignacio's face. "A long night, as usual. Late, as usual, late, late, late, late." The repetition seemed to wind him tighter. "He says he isn't tired, that elderly people do not require much sleep. True, I know that for a fact myself, but we all need *some.* Couldn't he at least have the courtesy to go to bed and pretend to sleep so that others may?" He cowed the small assembly with a baleful look. "And if you've disturbed him . . ." the words hung ominously.

Muscadeine mock-groaned. "You'll make us pay, eh?" he finished with a chuckle. "It may be worth it, if only for the pleasure of your apology when I tell you who I have here."

Doyce found herself propelled forward, acutely aware of her tatterdemalion appearance, dried bloodstains on her jacket and tabard, a ripped elbow and, she suspected, a crusting of blood at one nostril. She gave a hasty rub with her handkerchief. Highly unprofessional for a Seeker, and even more so for a Special Envoy. Especially with Aelbert's neat, perfect turnout to serve as a silent reproach.

Ignacio peered close, sniffed, held the lantern higher. "Arras, old friend, your taste in women has changed somewhat."

Doyce whirled on Muscadeine, anger flaring, but he made frantic shushing motions, playing up the misidentification while she seethed.

"Ignacio, Chamberlain to the Steward of us all, may I present Doyce Marbon and her party. La Marbon is Canderis's Special Envoy, though met with a somewhat unseemly welcome on our part, for which I pray she has forgiven us." He reached into his waistband and handed over her leather case with a flourish. "The papers of passage are in order, and a letter from the Monitor of Canderis is within, for the eyes of our Steward only, though you can judge enough by the outer superscription to know I speak the truth."

Handing his lantern to a servant, Ignacio held the papers at arm's length, studying the seal with obvious suspicion. At last he grudged a reply. "I know the seal, though it's been long years since formal requests were necessary to ensure a night's hospitality. But then, these are strange times."

"I should like to meet with your Steward." She overemphasized the final word, determinedly correct. "At his and, of course, your convenience. Indeed, we've all ridden for several days and would appreciate a chance to rest and refresh ourselves until a meeting can be arranged."

Ignacio slipped the packet into his pocket, buttoning it for security. "Oh, very well, very well." His grumbling sounded feigned. "Arras, I have spoken with unseemliness to you and your guest." A quick, imperative gesture brought other servants to his side in huddled conversation before they darted away. Ticking off their numbers on his fingers as if mentally assigning rooms, he finally forced himself to look down at Khar, sauntering closer and closer to his bony knees, preparatory to rubbing against them.

"Must these cats stay with them as well?" Ignacio's bushy red eyebrows rose, aggrieved at the idea of a menagerie in the castle.

Muscadeine winked at Khar. "But of course, old friend, of course. I guarantee they will be neater and of less distress to you than my dear Felix, whom you've come to esteem. Besides, they may catch us some rats while they are in residence."

"Rats?" Indignant, mouth working furiously, Ignacio jabbed a finger at Doyce. "Let me assure you, Mam'selle, Madame, that we have no rats, absolutely no rats in this castle! I have seen to that. The Chevalier Capitain jests at my expense."

"Ah, Ignacio, I never suggested that you had four-legged rats, but perhaps these wondrously large cats can trap some of the two-legged kind?"

❖

Jenret sprawled in an overstuffed easy chair, stockinged feet stretched toward a small fire, half-lost in the fireplace's over-scale grandeur, large enough to hold logs as long as he was tall, and the massive bronze fire irons gave proof against over-exaggeration. Rawn perched on the arm of his chair, grooming concluded and now comtemplating the flickering flames, paws kneading the fabric. "Don't even dare think about sharpening your claws," Jenret growled, shaking Rawn's tail tip for emphasis.

Rawn flexed his claws once more, barely missed puncturing the plush fabric. **"The world is my scratch post ... if I so choose. But I don't. Some of us aren't ruled by our emotional wants. I may want to scratch, but I don't need to do so."** Jenret didn't acknowledge his comment.

Jacobia pattered around the vast sitting room, oohing and aahing over the vibrant hangings, shades of flame from yellow, topaz, and orange through blood red to burgandy. The colors glowed against the dark oiled walnut panels with more warmth and intimacy than the fire cast. He shifted in the chair, pushed the heels of his hands against his temples, miserable; somehow comfort wasn't what he wanted right now, but he wasn't sure what he did want ... or need.

Wandering back to the table with its remains of a heartily-eaten meal, Jacobia sleeve-polished an apple, eyed it for blemishes, and tossed it toward her brother's vulnerable middle. Rawn reared, slapping it aside, so that it dropped onto the thick carpeting, rolling back toward Jacobia's feet.

He raised his head. "Damn it, Jacobia, I've warned you not to throw things. Boots, fruit, what next? And why aim at me?"

She retrieved the apple, checked it for bruising, and bit into it. "M' sorry." A spurt of juice escaped from the corner of her mouth and she wiped hastily. "Thought you'd want one. You always liked them."

Lady bless, his head ached, a tingling under the skin. Had ever since their encounter with Muscadeine and his crew. He massaged his temples again, exchanged a weary look with Rawn. "I do, but the service leaves something to be desired."

She took a silver fruit knife to a fresh apple and began to pare it, the thin, unbroken strand of peel growing longer and longer, spiraling and looping. Rawn jumped down to watch, one paw hesitating, ready to bat at it. Finished, she reeled in the long curl and deposited it on the tray, placed the peeled apple on a fresh plate and dissected it into neat segments, coring each piece.

She handed the plate over with a flourish. "Better?"

"Much, thank you. Mother will never believe you've mastered that trick." He didn't want the apple, had no desire to feel the firm white flesh crunch between his teeth. What he wanted was another ale or, better yet, something stronger. Instead he took an apple crescent, turning it over between long fingers before popping it in his mouth.

"I will *not* eat apple," Rawn warned. "Many things I'll do for you, but not that."

"*I know, and I wouldn't ask it, but could you hide some pieces while she's not looking?*"

Rawn's whiskers flexed and spread as he considered it and returned to his spot on the arm of the chair. "Mayhap."

Jacobia moved toward the fire and poked at it, while Rawn hooked an apple segment, ready to toss it behind the chair. Instead, he slammed it against his chest, crouched on it in disgust when Jacobia suddenly spun around. Jenret knew his look of reproach all too well.

"Isn't he romantic looking?" Jacobia asked, eyes dreamy with recollection.

"Who?" Nakum or Aelbert, he wondered, and rubbed at his forehead again. Mayhap another drink would ease the tension he felt, let him relax. He didn't want to talk about young love, rapture; he had enough trouble with mature love, unrequited. It was beastly and he felt beastly.

"Perhaps if you told her, you wouldn't feel so beastly." Rawn slipped the apple between the seat cushion and chair arm, making a face as he licked his paw clean.

"*And if she doesn't feel the same, and it's a near certainty she doesn't from the way she acts, I'll make the whole situation unbearable.*"

"More than it is now?"

"*We have a job to do. She has other things to concentrate on, not love—if I should be so lucky—or trying to smooth over my hurt feelings if she doesn't.*" His thoughts veered. "*You know, the worst of it is I should have saved her from Vesey, spared her such pain.*"

"Why? Because it would show you are stronger and

she is weaker, dependent on you?" Rawn asked with genuine interest. **"Do you wish power over her? How human!"**

"Just as she wields power over me—without knowing it?"
he bit at his lip, emotions surging. *"No, it's not that, Rawn.
Truly. You always want to protect those you love . . . no matter what price you pay."*

"Just as I would for you."

Oblivious to the internal dialogue, Jacobia cocked her
head. "Who? Why that Captain Muscadeine, of course.
Doesn't he look just ravishing? Those dark, brooding eyes,
that wonderful mustache. And have you seen him when he
looks at Doyce?" She sighed at the memory. "It's funny. I
wouldn't think she'd attract a man like that, but there's no
telling, is there?"

With a muffled curse, Jenret levered himself out of the
chair and poured himself a drink, not ale, but something
stronger, he had no idea what, from the decanter on the sideboard. He tossed it back, felt the flood of release, poured another. "Go to bed, child. Now." His voice was thick.

And for once, wonder of wonders, Jacobia did so, no back
talk, no whining. She rolled her eyes but headed without
complaint for her bedroom, situated off the sitting room.

"There may be hope for the child yet," Jenret muttered.

**"Perhaps, but only a fool wouldn't know when not to
take shelter. Especially when a storm threatens."** Rawn
watched Jenret heft the glass, bring it to his lips and drain
half the contents. **"How much of that are you going to
drink?"** He pulled himself up primly on the chair arm.

"Enough, old friend, enough." He emptied the glass.

"That is not enough?"

The bottle was still more than half full, a relief. *"Enough
meaning enough to do what it's meant to do, and I mean to
let it do it."* Better an alcoholic haze on the morrow than the
constant tingling throb as if something tried to crawl into his
brain.

It would not be a pleasant evening, Rawn knew.

❧

Khar winced and ducked. Close, a near-hit to the jaw,
however unintended. She debated reaching a paw, claws extended to pierce through the satin comforter in a retaliatory

poke. Instead, she scrambled toward the foot of the bed and
curled in a ball, rump in the direction of the flying foot.
Safer that way. Doyce subsided, resting flat on her back, and
Khar presumed she was concentrating, running through her
litany of calming exercises. It worked—briefly—and the
next thing Khar knew she was bouncing, heaving, and shifting in a turbulent satin sea, Doyce's legs flailing, pulling up
darting toward the foot of the bed like a borer worm. Then
peace again.

"Have you nested yet?" Khar managed bleak forbearance
as she gave her bruised rump a lick.

Doyce flipped over, thumped the pillow. "Wha? Oh, sorry,
love. Just can't seem to get comfortable."

**"I would think a bed might feel good after all those
nights of sleeping on the ground."** She paused for emphasis, **"It does to me—especially when the bed stays still,
when it doesn't rock as if a Plumb's exploded."**

A gurgle of laughter greeted her remark. "Poor, long-
suffering ghatta. Bear with me, I'll settle in yet." Piling the
pillows behind her, she sat, hugging her knees and cuddling
the comforter around her waist. Cautiously, Khar slithered
higher, moving stealthily against the satin covering until she
reached Doyce's hip. She settled near, but not too near, and
began to purr sleepily.

"So what do you make of it?" Khar would know what she
meant, so she waited, not wanting to prompt, to let the
ghatta evaluate things in her own way.

Khar rolled onto her side and stretched, toes touching. **"I
have not been Seeking, you did not ask,"** she warned but
she sounded worried. **"Should I have been?"**

Doyce gave her a reassuring stroke. *"No, no, of course
not. Not unless the person is being 'read' as part of the
Truth-Seeking ceremony, or it's a life or death situation.
Then the strictures don't apply."* She waited, Khar deep in
thought. *"Ever since I met Muscadeine and Ignacio, I feel as
if I've been straining to hear a conversation just beyond earshot. You're more sensitive than I, you must have felt something."*

**"This place is in turmoil, the very walls shout it, but
it's being kept under control, the beast still in its cage."**

Leave it to the ghatta to perplex with a gnomic phrase.
"But who or what is the beast?"

"I don't know why I said that, just that I felt it.

Ignacio is not happy, Muscadeine is not happy, their worries roil like smoke, ready to smother them." So did Jenret's for that matter, from the little Rawn had said to her, but she didn't share that with Doyce.

Doyce pondered it all. Good and bad were subjective enough to human beings, to one of the ghatti the terms were even more difficult, more a distinction of right or not-right, a harmony between the physical world and the inner mind world. Good by human standards, a person might not be whole within or in tune with the outer world, and by ghatti standards would be not-right, not-true. And that was an important distinction to the ghatti mind-set. Changing her tack, she asked, *"Are they to be trusted? Can I believe what they say?"*

"They are not dishonest, but listen to what they don't say as well as what they do. What do we know so far?" Khar prompted.

Concentrating, Doyce began to itemize, lacking the comfort of paper and pencil, beyond reach on the bureau. *"That a Steward rules Marchmont, that there appears to be no immediate or obvious heir to the throne. That the Steward is old, at least according to Ignacio, very old."* She rubbed her chin. *"Of course, that could be because only someone very old, with no desire for the throne, would be chosen for the post, someone venerable, respected by all as above the fray."* Khar let her reconsider. *"But that's an assumption, isn't it? Plausible, but only one possible answer."*

The ghatta nodded, eyes moonlight-bright, the rest of her swirls, shadows, and white patches against the comforter.

Juggling ideas, interpretations against facts, Doyce plunged ahead. *"Well, facts are scanty right now. But Marchmont's no stranger to war, to fighting anyway. Muscadeine's never said if it's been declared war, or with whom. But they know how to fight—and how to spy. They've spied on Canderis, and I can't help but wonder if they weren't spying on us, planning to snare us today until they discovered who we were. They could have been waiting for brigands; it's possible, but wasn't it a mighty big coincidence that we happened to fall into their ambush? And they're superb, because they caught Nakum and Saam unaware."*

"What else?"

Doyce replayed the night's conversations, ruminating. *"Two-legged rats,"* she offered. *"Muscadeine used the phrase, and Ignacio didn't deny it. But who's betraying whom? And whose side are Ignacio and Muscadeine on?"* She straightened her legs, slapping the mattress, but Khar was prepared and didn't flinch. *"Oh, bother, even assuming they're on the same side. Anything else I've missed?"*

Khar prompted, **"One more. Perhaps important, perhaps not. Something with emotional resonance though they don't always consciously think about it."**

The word "resonance" appealed, the mere sound of it, but that wasn't Khar's point, and she had no idea what it was. *"What, Khar? I'm not up to playing twenty questions. I'm sleepy."*

"And who was trying to sleep but kept getting disturbed?"

"Don't be sulky. I'm sorry, but give me a hint or we'll be up all night. You know how I worry things."

Relenting, Khar dangled a hint. Best to let her work it out herself, but the ghatta was tired, cool satin against fur promising garnered warmth through the night as she curled close to Doyce. **"The houses. Muscadeine's sword."**

"Old things, old ways. So? Oh . . ." Khar could feel the tumbling images reshuffled, repatterned, something Doyce did well. *"Is it . . . their heritage, their past and the objects of their past seem to mean a great deal to them? Their past and present . . . blended together. I wonder what it means, if it means anything. Maybe because of their idea of the blood royale, a kingship, a linking of the past to the present? Not enough to go on to judge, but it's interesting . . ."* She yawned and, despite herself, Khar did as well.

"Sleep now?"

Doyce plumped her pillows, jerked the bed hangings straight, and Khar, her floor twitched from beneath her, levitated, airborne, caught off-guard. "Just making my nest," Doyce apologized and burrowed in, sighing in contentment.

She fell asleep almost immediately, but Khar found herself wide awake, considering, uneasy. At last, resting her chin on her white paws, she fell into a fitful doze, dreaming of Doyce, of kings and crowns and commotions. It all came of begging smoked fish too close to bedtime, but she wouldn't have forgone it for the world.

❖

N'oor huddled on the window ledge, listening to Aelbert's breathing as it softened and evened into sleep. She so desperately wanted to be alone to think. She worked along the ledge, side pressed against the wall, shoulder aching from the blow and the rough landing after she'd leaped to Aelbert's aid during the attack.

Reaching a broader ledge where a dormer jutted at right angles, she stopped and curled beside a chimney pot radiating warmth against the coolness of the night. She licked a paw and rubbed her ear in a circular motion, flinching as saliva stung raw skin. Torn, she knew. Ripped during her unseemly roll in the dirt when she'd hit, breathless, mind screaming bloody fury. And he had said, had said ... she licked her paw again and rubbed until the pain intensified, distracted her from thoughts she didn't want to face.

How could she have been so blind, so foolishly naive? She was ghatti, able to read him inside and out, her own, her Bondmate. But he held so many contradictions, one layer of emotions overwriting and obscuring another, almost scraped clean but still faintly visible, past remnants imperfectly erased. He had always seethed with the plaint of "never good enough," the constant lament of the poor child shoving to the top of the rubbish heap, a frantic look behind at those who clawed at his heels, a desperate bowel-clenching fire driving him up and up. But he had controlled that upon becoming the Monitor's aide, had begun mastering it when the Monitor had taken him in, well before his election. She knew too well the source of his yearnings, had explored his innermost mind when she had 'Printed on him. She shivered, fastidious dismay at the shared memories: the slat-ribbed child, no more than three, scrabbling through the garbage midden, face pinched blue with cold, hands black with dirt, barely able to clutch at a crust from stiffness and chilblains. And the crust was almost invariably stolen from him, leaving him wailing with hunger. She had never known where this took place, wondered if the town had a name or if Aelbert even knew it. Indeed, if he could later recreate a name for himself, he could have named the town, she thought. But she knew she'd never journeyed there in all their travels, except in his nightmares.

The image of Chak rose unbidden, Chak at the end, shivering with cold, Aelbert massaging him, and then, that last

afternoon, Chak, alone, exhausted on the blanket. Aelbert
slipping him a treat while Rolf was away. He had promised
her, sworn, an accident, a tragic mistake, not malice. A mistake. What had he given Chak? No! She would have known,
have sensed . . . ! He didn't have it in his heart to purposely
hurt. . . .

She circled back to the shame of earlier today. Why had
he done it, let her launch herself at those men, why hadn't
he protected her as she had protected him? Why had his
warning come too late, hasty words that all was well, when
she was already in mid-jump, claws lashing to wound and
tear? Why hadn't he alerted her sooner? His sudden reassurance, too late, had made her pull back, off balance, and allowed the not-foe to strike, slamming her into an undignified
tumble, breathless with shock, defenseless. A mistake . . .
only a mistake, always a mistake.

Resting chin on paws, N'oor gave way to grief, letting it
blanket her, weigh her against the slates. Little crooning
sobs stuck deep in her chest as she gave herself over to her
anguish, her fears, her desperate suppositions. The aloneness
was piercing and bitter. I will shield him no more from the
others, she vowed, but knew that on the morrow she probably would again. He made mistakes, so did she. Who else
was there, who else was her Bond, her reason for living?

"Peace, little sister." The comforting falanese almost
made her careless; she blinked once, seeking control. The
ghatt Rawn stood before her, obsidian fur melding into the
dark of the night. He sat, curled tail around him on the ledge
and yawned hugely, pointed white teeth glowing. "You hurt,
little sister, can I help?"

Her mind urged caution. She did not truly know this black
ghatt with his impetuous Bond. "I am afraid of fighting."

"Aren't we all? But you were brave today, overzealous,
even. Jenret was angered but realized they sought to contain
us, not hurt us. I had no chance to strike a blow." His tail tip
flickered a regretful tattoo.

"But I got hurt. They hit me back!" Her throat tightened.
"It hurt!"

"It does," he sniffed her ear, licked it. It felt harsh but
good, better than she'd been able to do with her paw. "But
would you do it again to save Aelbert, even if you knew it
would hurt?"

She sighed, head bobbing. "Yes. Yes, I would."

"So would we all," he agreed and kept on with his cleansing.

❖

He'd been expecting it, hadn't known when but knew it would come. No sense in overanticipating, he'd learned that long ago. But he'd slept fitfully, waiting, watchful. Wiping the last of the shaving lather off his chin, Aelbert shrugged into his jacket, settled the tabard in place, sashing it. Secure, that's how he felt with the uniform in place. So much to prepare for today with the ceremony, the public presentation of credentials. A legitimate excuse for his dawn rising, should anyone ask.

"Someone's at the door!" N'oor warned, springing from where she'd curled on the neatly made bed.

Afraid of waking Nakum in the adjoining room, Aelbert wrenched open the door before a knock could sound, his vision eclipsed by the largest fist he'd ever seen in his life, frozen just short of his forehead. Close-cropped head brushing the top of the door casing, the man pushed his way into the room, Aelbert retreating. Coward he was not; pragmatist he was. "Don't worry, I'd have noticed the difference from the tone, if nothing else," and he mock-rapped Aelbert's head. "Come along, he wants you now," the voice came whisper-cold, mate to the ice-chill eyes above wide, flat cheekbones and mouth, narrow as a dueling scar.

"Well, better sooner than later." Make light of the summons and he could reassert some control. "Come on, N'oor," and pointed the ghatta to the door.

"Oh, I don't believe so, not that cat-thing, not this time, or so he said." N'oor jittered and arched, hissing her outrage.

Dropping to his knee, he soothed the ghatta, stroked spiked spine hairs smooth, spoke aloud for his visitor's benefit. "It's all right, love, everything will be fine. Wait for me here." But as they left, Aelbert made sure the door didn't latch. If anything went wrong, he loved her too much not to give her a chance at escape. And though he wouldn't ask it, he hoped she might follow, know that he'd told her the truth.

No point in keeping track of where they went, how they got there, best save his energy to conquer his dread—and his anticipation. How long had he waited for this? Too long—

and he was ready to seize his opportunity. At last they arrived.

The antechamber off the main sitting room was small and close, no more than a nook with heavy velvet swaggings across the opening. Protesting despite himself, Aelbert was shoved between the drapings, propelled into darkness. He stood, silent and wary, searching for his bearings. The fragrance of perfume, pungent as a hyacinth forced to full bloom in a windowless room, made him giddy, but he recognized the scent layering the alcove's tight stuffiness. Once his eyes adjusted, he spoke. "You could have met me without this early morning melodrama, the massive messenger. N'oor's frantic at being left behind. And I've a thousand things to do before the ceremony. What if the others discover I'm missing? This isn't a prudent plan."

How often had he deferentially employed that phrase with the Monitor? And, for the most part, been heeded. But the pouty face before him in the dimness was not the Monitor's, and he had experienced too much to be misled by Maurice's childlike, sulking expression. "You used to like visiting here when Evelien sent you on her silly little errands from the Hospice. Oh, you've grown since then, but still have that ordinary little face, unremarkable in the midst of a crowd. But I can recognize your wants. Still clawing and needy, aren't you, Aelbert?"

Undeterred by the lack of acknowledgment, the voice purred on. "And who did you think was behind those little gifts, the money and gold trinkets, back at the Monitor's Hall? The information, the gossip, you so eagerly hoarded, except with Madame Consul LaRoche. Innocent chatter, I suppose you thought?" He stood closer now, his scent overpowering Aelbert's nostrils, so cloyingly sweet he thought he might be ill. He'd smelled worse in his time, and cleaned it up without adding his own vomit to the floor.

He breathed through his mouth. "No, of course not, not really. But what do you have to measure my words against? After all, you can't plant spies everywhere—you lack the resources. Especially now, with the borders closed and trading stopped." He congratulated himself on pinking Maurice, not truly wounding but making him realize the danger, but avoided growing overconfident. Never underestimate anyone, an adage both he and Maurice should live by.

"Right or wrong, true or false, it doesn't matter, really.

After all, I've evidence enough to proclaim you traitor. Or if not that, I suspect you're still at your jackdaw thieving, aren't you?" Aelbert stiffened, yearned for the comfort that would come from thrusting his hand in his pocket, fondling his treasures for reassurance, but that little gesture would give him away. Instead he listened hard, refused to be distracted. "Once a street urchin, always a street urchin, despite those respectable trappings. I tried to warn Evelien of that. I assume you still have that gold and jeweled pillbox you stole from my wife. You never can give anything up, sell it or barter it, you just want to collect it, cherish it, don't you?" The voice insinuated silky smooth, coiling its way into Aelbert's brain. "And, of course, we hang thieves here. No coddling, no rehabilitation, or deportation to the Sunderlies."

He clamped down on his fears, stamped them down, ground one boot heel into the carpet, panicked that even that reflexive action revealed too much. Never plead or bluster. It didn't work, hadn't saved him from the undeserved childhood thrashings, but a rational warning might. "I won't be threatened." A little, looping gesture with his finger yoked them together. "It cuts both ways. If you want to hang me for thievery, so be it. That's my weak point. But if you name me traitor, some may ask who turned me into such." A gamble as to which vulnerability was greater, Maurice's desire to get rid of him or have him on his side, but he was ready for either. Power didn't have to flow only one way, fed from the weak to the strong; it could circle. Years of constant observation, pliant acquiescence as a protective shield left him determined to draw power to him, make it his own, or counteract its thrust. But best tread with care. Maurice's power had grown since he'd last seen him: it hammered at the edges of his awareness, seeking entry, and Aelbert denied it with polite obdurance, blank stupidity. "So what do you want of me?"

Silence hovered longer than Aelbert liked, but not as long as he'd expected. "Precisely what I wanted before, unless I inform you otherwise. Watch, wait, report back as necessary. We'll find an intermediary." Reading Maurice was no easy task, but he thought he detected a glimmer of appreciation, of grudging respect. Oh, not as equals by any stretch of the imagination; he'd not be gulled that easily. "I want to know why Seekers were sent, why your Special Envoy is really here. Why trade has been disrupted. Valeria Condorcet's highly upset, as well she should be as Ministration Lord of External Affairs. But oddly enough, Lysenko Boersma acts cheery, shrugs his shoulders, says it will all work itself out. A little more worry and hand-wringing from the Commerce Lord might be appropriate, don't you think?"

Aelbert cocked his head to one side, considering why Maurice had confided in him. Play a card, see if Maurice would trump it or allow him the trick, secure enough to wait for a richer one. Ultimately king would trump prince. "I don't know if you heard, but after Aaron Rossmeer was expelled, he suffered a stroke on his way home."

"Ah, a shame. He seemed so healthy. Terrible things, strokes, wipe your mind completely blank. . . ." He let the thought drift, heaved a sigh laden with pleasurable repletion.

Now tease out the next card. "He managed a few words when the Monitor and I visited, but they were garbled, senseless." The rising scent of Maurice's perfume told him of the man's burgeoning apprehension, of pulse points pounding. "I think the Monitor read more into Rossmeer's words than was there, but the Consul did keep mentioning ghatti."

"Ghatti . . ." Maurice's eyes focused distantly, lower lip thrusting forward in thought. "Ghatti. Well, well, perhaps I dealt with Rossmeer a little too hastily." He paced a small circle around Aelbert. Yes, power circles. "I hadn't intended this result, but yet . . . and yet . . . it just might prove an advantage, now that I have you here." Aelbert had him now, was sure of it, all he had to do was turn it to his own ends. "Yes, yes, it just might work!" Fingers pinched tight, Maurice concentrated as if something invisible were locked within his grasp. "Yes . . . now why don't you have Gregor escort you to your room? After all, you're going to be a very busy young man today, aren't you? And for many days to come."

N'oor dashed away through the halls, thankful for the head start. What was Aelbert playing at? Cat and mouse was a dangerous game for the mouse, and mice couldn't transform themselves into cats, could they? But whatever was going on, the stalker always won—sooner or later. And she was very afraid for Aelbert, her Bond, her love, but what could she do, how could she help?

❖

Doyce hovered on the periphery, shifting to avoid dashing servants, middle-level bureaucrats on self-important missions bustling by as if she didn't exist. Not that she wanted to be noticed, but it struck her as odd, distinctly odd, that so few met her eye. Come to think of it, she'd noticed the same thing last night with the servants. She twisted at her jacket to settle it, to calm her nerves. The great hall wasn't even half-full yet but the swarming, seemingly mindless activity keyed her up almost beyond bearing. Grasping Aelbert's sleeve, she swung him around to face her. "I told you we were too early," she whispered. "I don't see Jenret or Jacobia or Nakum anywhere, do you? Did you check on them before we came down?"

"There wasn't time." He flicked his sleeve free of her fingers, smoothed it. N'oor leaned against his leg, agitated by the commotion, by the furious flurries of activity, the occasional shouts and hails. Everyone backed an involuntary step as a castered platform loaded with benches rumbled into the room, wheels squeaking and protesting.

Khar patted at Doyce's knee, stared down Aelbert's reproachful "Have to brush your uniform down again," and swatted harder to attract her Bond's attention. **"Look! Over there!"**

"Who? Why didn't you just 'speak me?" Doyce scanned the moving bodies.

"When you get distracted, it's almost impossible to make you listen. And then you say 'why didn't you tell me?' when I've already told you five times. Nothing registers."

Hands on hips in mock anger, boot tip poised dangerously close to a certain tail, Doyce continued to search. *"Just the way you haven't noticed my toe is hovering over your tail right this very instant? And whom am I looking for? I haven't seen Muscadeine yet, or anyone else I recognize."*

Aelbert's pointing finger oriented her. Yes, the sky blue livery, properly pressed and buttoned, sash evenly tied, cockade pinned straight. "Ignacio! Over here!" Relief at seeing a familiar face, even if she scarcely knew him.

"Ah, there you are." He wound through the bustling crowd, giving orders, turning here and there to confer as he wove toward them, shadowed by an auburn-haired young man wearing similar livery. He was writing furiously, taking dictation as Ignacio waded along, hurried, fussy, skip-stepping from tile to tile, as if only certain ones were safe. Again she thought of a long-limbed water bird stepping among the lily pads.

"You might mention there weren't any rats last night."

"Hush!" Hand outstretched, she stepped forward to greet him.

But he forestalled her, bowing formally, the young man beside him following his lead a half-beat late, as if waiting to judge the degree of protocol required. "My apologies for the ... untidiness ... of last night's meeting. If I may be permitted to formally present myself, Madame Envoy?" She dropped her hand, nodded. "Ignacio Lauzon, royal chamberlain, at your service." The heel-click was impressive. "And if I may, my grandson, Ezequiel Dunay, in training in the royal household." Unlike his grandfather, he didn't meet her eye, but his bow was exquisite, even though Ignacio nudged his grandson's foot back until the tip of his boot barely brushed the floor.

"A pleasure, I'm sure." Starting to bow in return, she felt Aelbert gripping her coattail to make her remain upright. She contented herself with a generous nod, suspected her face shared the younger man's rueful look: both of them were receiving etiquette lessons this morning. "I trust we're not too early."

"No, no, no," gripping his grandson's shoulder he leaned backward for distance to read the list. "Yes, yes, fine. Now hurry, off with you!" and Ezequiel rushed off without a backward glance to see the look of pride flooding his grandfather's face.

"He's going to be a fine one." Her observation seemed to melt any reserve the older man might have had about her.

"Especially when he learns how to survive on less sleep without being cranky." He tugged at a muttonchop, waiting to see if she'd accept the backhanded apology. "No, you're not too early. Always wise to check the lay of the land, the siting for a ceremony. Means not making a sweeping exit into a broom closet. Happened once, you know, poor old Hebert made his petition to the Queen and ..."

"Precisely," Aelbert interrupted. "One can never be too concerned about all aspects, large and small, of a ceremony. As I've tried to instruct the Special Envoy ..."

But he, in turn, was overridden by a piercing and imperious "Yoo hoo! Ignacio!" And the three turned as one to discover an imposing woman bearing down on them, swathings of fabric billowing in her formidable wake, and two considerably smaller gentlemen bobbing behind. "Come along, Auguste! Lysenko can keep the pace, not get sidetracked by all this foo-fa-rah. You've seen enough in your time, now don't be timid!" The small man called Auguste appeared more than timid; he acted downright terrified. She swept up to Ignacio, a trailing, sea blue sleeve-paneling swinging ahead of her and wrapping itself around the chamberlain. "Has Fabienne arrived yet?"

He disengaged, a half-turn unveiling him, not the least flustered. "I haven't seen her, m'Lady."

The sandy-haired man beside her, Lysenko, tapped her arm, murmured something in her ear that erased the pout on her face. "Ignacio, am I forced to perform my own introductions?" she chided.

Ignacio's mouth opened, but before he could speak, a large, well-kept hand engulfed Doyce's. "I'm Quaintance Mercilot, Lord of the Sud. Ignacio insists it should be Lady of the Sud, but I'll lord it over anyone I want. Most days being a lady isn't what it takes." Large, even teeth flashed as she shared a companionable laugh with Ignacio, as if they'd gone through this many times before. Her head tilted back, Doyce found herself peering over a mountainous bosom to the full-moon face above, crowned with an intricate mass of braidings, interwoven with lavender, black, and white ribbons.

Quaintance Mercilot leaned a large but shapely arm on the sandy-haired man's shoulder, the gesture almost possessive, although he appeared perhaps twenty years her junior. Reaching for her hand, he gave the back of it a courtly kiss and deftly freed himself from her arm. "As you can see, Quaintance hasn't been as biddable since Maurice refused to let her bring her spaniels to the formal presentations," he remarked with a wicked grin as he legged a short, neat bow. "Lysenko Boersma, Commerce Lord, at your service. Is it true a Wycherley's with you for trade negotiations? Not the father, I suspect, he's not personally visited in years. Thought Syndar Saffron would be a more likely choice." Without waiting for an answer, he continued the introductions. "And the gentleman sheltering behind the Lord of the

Sud's ample protection is Auguste Vannevar, Lord of the Levant."

Lady Quaintance stage-whispered, "Hasn't been the same since Wilhelmina died, you know. Hit him hard, it did. And of course he misses my spaniels."

"Domain Lords of Four there be, Hereditary rule with dignity," Doyce recited under her breath and found it helped marginally to lock them in her mind. Two of the four accounted for, and "Commerce" equaled . . . equaled . . . what?

"Equals 'Conclude,' " Khar prompted, **"but not 'Conclude Joyously' because we haven't met the Justice Lord yet."**

"Well, I admitted it was a silly sentence, didn't I?" she shot back at the ghatta. Aelbert, she was sure, was encountering no problems remembering who was what, undoubtedly knew everything—including how many spaniels Lady Quaintance owned. She turned her attention on Lord Auguste, taking in the sweet-natured, intelligent face with its fringe of gray hair and sad brown eyes suffused with suffering, something she recognized all too well. He managed a creditable bow, as if his body recollected earlier, happier times and responded, but the cockade over his heart shuddered and vibrated. The colors matched the ribbons in Lady Quaintance's braids—lavender and white and black, but his edging of black was narrow, far narrower than the black on Lysenko Boersma's or Ignacio's. What did the cockades mean?

Hanging on Lady Quaintance's elbow, swinging her around with the implacable determination of a pilot boat hauling a large, oceangoing vessel into dockage, Lord Auguste's face now registered sheer terror, mouth straining in a wordless cry.

With a backward glance Lady Quaintance checked out the situation. "It'll be fine, Auguste. We'll sit on the other side, won't we, Lysenko? Or you can sit in the rear if it means so much to you to be seen as neutral. I'll understand. This shouldn't be a day for confrontations." And as she soothed, she and Lysenko were supporting Auguste, working their way with unhurried but determined footsteps out of Doyce's presence. "A pleasure meeting you. I know you and Lord Boersma will have some lovely times talking trade later."

The group cutting across the floor toward them left crowds backing and bowing, giving way. Whoever this per-

on was, he wielded power and influence, his retinue making
he Lord of the Sud look like a poor relation with her two
ompanions.

"Or the threat of power." Khar made a little hissing
ound of distaste. **"The perfume he's doused himself with
s threat enough."**

Nose wrinkling, praying she wasn't that suggestible,
Doyce looked to Ignacio and Aelbert for guidance. Ignacio's
mouth and nose muscles tightened once, a pinched disap-
proving expression before it smoothed to urbanity. But
Aelbert surprised her—eyes fever-bright and darting, breath
rapid—until the shell she knew so well encased him, and he
became the Monitor's dependable aide, her aide-de-camp.
'Who is that?" she asked, hoping someone would answer.

"Maurice, Prince of the Blood, Lord of the Nord and De-
ense Lord," Aelbert stated, never taking his eyes off the
ast-approaching group.

"But how do you know?" she whispered back. "You can't
ave met him before."

Middling brown eyes rebuked her innocence. "Because I
make it my business to learn as much as I can, however I
an. And that," he shrugged, "means paying close attention
o what servants, tailors, and other unimportant people say
r don't say, and how they say it."

With a flourish, the lord's entourage swept in front of
hem, the leaders folding to each side like petals unfurling to
eveal the rose within. Doyce suppressed a gasp; this, this
was not what she had expected. This was power—portly,
painted, and dyed? Oh, the rouging and powdering were sub-
le but there, and the sunlight on the dark hair reflected iri-
descent peacock purples and greens, sure sign the color
came from a bottle. He stood in front of her, posing, almost
preening. Emerald green long hose, rather than trousers or
pantaloons, accentuated trim and shapely legs granted by na-
ure. But nature had not been kind to the rest of him, a once
muscular body now quilted and ruched in fat, once fine fea-
ures fat-blurred and buried in the ruins of a face. He looked
gorgeous as a raddled crocus in deep yellow and purple-
lashed silks, green-stemmed legs all but too thin to support
he corpulent upper body.

A deep bray of laughter degenerated into a wheeze.
'Ignacio, last night a little bird informed me we had visitors.
How thoughtful of you not to disturb my sleep . . . or my

morning's work with the news. Such a nicety of discretio
on your part."

Ignacio bowed. "I sent messages to all Domain Lords an
all Ministration Lords when their private breakfasts we
served. I offer my most abject apologies if someone on yo
staff did not promptly deliver the message, but then, it w
hardly necessary, was it?" More than mere dislike was su
merged in Ignacio's formality, more like an abiding hatre
and she wondered if it were justified for such a pompou
painted fool as this man appeared to be. She'd met his kin
before, the ones who stood on their rank as if it were a pe
estal elevating them above the rest. Well, Marchmont w
bound to harbor fools, grandiose, self-important figures, ju
as Canderis did. Perhaps more, if it went with royalty. Us
ally a little soothing, a little syrupy politeness smoothed ru
fled feathers, and that might be prudent about now.

She widened her eyes, rounded her mouth with a sile
sigh of admiration. "Lord Maurice," she gauged the rea
tion, increased her awe another notch. "Forgive me, *Prin*
Maurice. With so many resounding titles I was in a quanda
as to which one to use first, but, of course, Prince Mauric
we seldom meet such exalted figures as yourself
Canderis." Lady help her, the man was simpering, eyes a
most buried in the folds of fat. "I am Doyce Marbon, Sp
cial Envoy from Canderis, and any aid you can spare me
learning about your country would be so deeply apprec
ated."

"Don't bring up the cockades." Khar broke in, always
jump ahead of her. **"And don't choke on the honey, or e
pect me to fight off a swarm of bees ready to carry yo
away."**

Sometimes the only thing to do was to ignore the ghatt
tune out her secondary carpings before she fixated c
Maurice as a giant beehive. But why not mention the coc
ade? His, and all his followers, was the same lavender an
white as the others, but edged in a deep purple rather tha
black. What did the ghatta know that she didn't? Well, she
find out later; there was no time now that she had Mauri
dancing attendance on her. Wishing for Jenret's eyelashe
she batted her own at Maurice as he tucked her hand into h
arm and swept her into his retinue, bending to speak to h
in confidential tones.

But Ignacio blocked their path, his skinny, slat-ribbed fi

re implacable yet polite. "Prince Maurice, the welcoming
ceremony will begin momentarily, and I believe you have a
message waiting." A gesture beckoned his grandson
Ezequiel to his side, flourishing a piece of thick, creamy paper with a beribboned wax seal.

Maurice snatched it, broke the seal and scanned the note.
"Hmph!" He did not sound well pleased. "Couldn't the Lady
Giselle wait to discuss Justice affairs later?" He released
Doyce's hand but not before raising it to his lips for a kiss.
"Duty first, eh?" His regret sounded genuine and he strode
off, his retinue caught by surprise, lizard-tailing in his wake.
One retainer held his ground, offering her a long, insolent
look. How she'd missed him before, she couldn't imagine,
unless she'd mistaken him for a pillar. He stood well over
two meters tall, with thighs like girders and upper arms bigger than her waist. His gaze lingered, as if committing her
features to memory, before he followed after the others with
long, unhurried strides.

"Phew!" Doyce wiped the back of her hand against her
forehead as she watched them arrow toward a thin, dark-
haired woman waiting on the opposite side of the hall. She
wasn't sure, but she thought Lysenko Boersma, Commerce
Lord, slipped from her side and made a hasty exit. "Aren't
we about ready to begin?" she asked in general and belatedly 'spoke Khar, *"What about the cockades? Why aren't I
supposed to mention them?"*

"**Factions,**" Khar was succinct, sometimes too succinct.
he relented. **"Two different factions. Believe it or not,
'oor shared that nugget of information with me."**

As the crowds began entering the hall from various doors,
the chamberlain started shooing them into position, creating
order. "Yes, just about," and distractedly patted his grandson
with a shaking hand. "Good work, boy, excellent initiative."
Before Doyce could wonder what he meant, Nakum, Jenret,
Jacobia, and the two ghatts entered the hall and began to
make their way to her. But Aelbert and Ezequiel were already deep in consultation, Aelbert dragging her along after
him.

❧

Late morning sun spilled crazy-quilt patches on the faded
red carpet, splintered across the marble-tiled floor. Watching

the warmed dust motes rising and dancing, Nakum wedge
himself between Jacobia and Jenret, the crowd behind ar
beside them while Doyce stood ten paces ahead, Aelbert ci
cumspect behind her right shoulder. Doyce fidgeted, shou
der blades twisting, and he mimicked her until he realize
what he was doing; the uniform, despite hasty alteration
didn't fit properly, and he empathized with her discomfo
his own as well when burdened by too many of their clothe
Rolf had been broader through the shoulder, narrow
through the chest and hips than Doyce. How had Aelbe
convinced her to wear Rolf's ceremonial gear, the high
collared, dark-green coat with its gold frogs indicating th
Monitor's service? Wasn't her Seeker Veritas uniform goo
enough? Aelbert's sleek uniform made him look the par
while Doyce resembled a child in hand-me-downs, not to h
taken seriously despite the adult garb. Or did Aelbert inten
precisely that?

Worrying at his lower lip, Nakum wondered if Aelbe
took him seriously. Did any of them now? The dark gree
coat was a tangible rebuke, a burning reminder he'd failed
escort his party intact to Marchmont. How could he tell h
grandmother that he'd lost Rolf and Chak, permitted them
die while he was in charge, their scout?

"We all die sometime." Saam's tail curled aroun
Nakum's bare ankle.

"Yes, but if I hadn't . . ." he couldn't finish, swept up b
his misery, didn't know what to accuse himself of first.

"If you hadn't what?"

His mindspeech writhed with his shame. *"I pushed them
I pushed everyone too hard to keep the pace. You know wh
my earth-bond gives me . . . gives us. If I'd thought . .
maybe my earth-bond could have helped them, given the
strength."* Vehement now, *"I would have shared, no or
could stop me! I could have slowed everything, stretche
their time!"*

**"So everything spirals around you? You hold them i
the palm of your hand, do you, able to give and take?**
The tail tip flicked against his other ankle in reprimand
**"Have you forgotten what you know? Even ghatten kno
this—we all die sometime, some sooner, others later. Na
ture reaps some, and for others, their natures cause thei
death. That is the way of things. I thought you Erakw
knew this nearly as well as we ghatti do."**

"But it was my responsibility! No one will respect me, trust me after this!"

"Chak died; that was Nature." Saam twisted slightly, wondered if Nakum remembered their previous conversation, his doubts. **"And Rolf died because of his nature. They went together, as they wished, and none of us have the right to change their decision."** The steel gray ghatt refused to speak of what it was like to keep vigil over another's dying, wishing it were the other way around, empty with loss. Time enough for Nakum to learn that, though no time was ever right. **"You did well. Wanting to do better is not wrong, but sometimes the goal is unreachable; perhaps that is your nature. Now let it be, it's done."**

He fidgeted, sighed, forced himself to take an interest in what was happening around them. A slant-eyed glance told him that Jenret wasn't holding up well; his face was a sickly mushroom white, with eyes cracked open, and beads of water flecking his temples, either the residue of his recent cold water immersion or droplets of sweat. He rocked, steadied himself, pulled his shoulders back, mouth clenched as he swallowed hard. Nakum felt exasperation rather than sympathy.

The summons for the ceremony—to be held without delay—had found Jenret drunk, out like a light. Jacobia had done what she could, then had Rawn call Saam and Nakum to help. Since Erakwa rarely drank, Nakum had been at a loss but decided a brisk application of cold water, repeated at bone-chillingly regular intervals, should have some effect. It had, though not the effect Nakum had hoped for; he fingered the bruise under his eye and prodded the swelling. After the first two pitchers of water Jenret had reared free, hair and face streaming, arms pistoning. Grabbing his waist to steady him, Nakum had blocked Jenret's elbow with his face. At that Rawn had sprung forward, tail lashing, ignoring the puddles of water, and fixed Jenret with a gimlet stare. What words were exchanged, Nakum didn't ask, but Jenret had quieted, hands over his face, body shaking, but in bare control, allowing himself to be shaved and dressed and escorted downstairs.

Nakum took a deep breath and immediately wished he hadn't; the place smelled faintly of refuse: old, congealed grease from long-past banquets, moldy rushes, smoke from torches and candles and fires improperly ventilated, and most of all sweat, not honest exertion, but the musky-perfumed stink of lazy, over-warmed bodies and, worst of all, the stink of fear. Raucous color and random movement assaulted his eyes, dizzied him with its lack of coherence: bright, clashing colors jostling and shoving, darting here and there, flurries and eddies of sound, loud laughter abruptly dampened, whispers crescendoing, scabbarded swords slap-rattling benches. His long house was never like this, and the thought constricted his throat and made him long for his grandmother. Even the Wycherleys' house, so very different, so foreign, had never affected him this way. Different, but warm and soothing once one came to know it, despite the constraints he placed on himself.

The hall curved high above his head, broad beams arching like mammoth ribs, dark with ages of soot. Weaponry hung on the walls, swords and pikes, axes and shields; faded banners crested with strange beasts and emblems, wavering in the rising heat from the bodies below. Shifting his feet, his moccasins dragging against the carpeting's worn pile, Nakum pictured himself standing on the tongue of some monstrous beast, the banners the faded remains of other less lucky captives, leftovers from the crushing, churning digestive process. He must keep his wits about him, not be swallowed whole.

First one, and then a second and third trumpet blared, startling Nakum despite his having seen them lining up from the corner of his eye. Rattled, Jacobia started to speak, but he whispered a sharp negation and she subsided, eyes large with eagerness at the pageantry. Jenret looked as if he wished he could hold his head, while Doyce and Aelbert stiffened to attention. As the final notes faded, a metallic bong iced the air, freezing everyone within hearing, and the fine hairs on Nakum's arms rose.

"All hail!" a voice commanded. "Hail!" shouted the crowd. "All hail!" "Hail!" came the obedient response. "All hail!" "All hail to he who serves as Steward of us all, father, protector, hand of guidance, hail!"

Still intent on the man in sky-blue livery leading the ex-hortations, the grumpy man they'd met last night, Nakum realized with consternation that someone now stood on the broad marble step below the empty throne. How the elderly man had gotten there, he couldn't fathom, as if he'd descended from above, spirit made flesh from the old ceiling banners. He counted quickly, just to reassure himself. Indeed, the old man's insubstantiality made Nakum suspect he viewed a spirit, and he clutched his pouch for reassurance.

"No, he's flesh and blood," Saam 'spoke. "Though not much of either."

Facing the empty throne, the old man bowed low, allowing ancient knees time to bend and straighten. He turned back to the crowd, bowed again, but from the waist only. "Shall I take the throne, my children?" he asked, his plaintive, old man's voice shaking.

"Take it, respected one, take it!"

A gesture of denial, a shrug, before he hopped up the remaining step and backed into the throne, hands on its arms to lever him onto the high seat. "Only because you insist, my children, and only to hold it until Marchmont's rightful ruler can be proclaimed."

The crowd breathed a collective sigh as if it had been holding its breath. Scattered voices throughout the room shouted "May you live a hundred, two hundred years!" But few joined in the cry, and some faces looked grim and suspicious.

The old man broke into bubbly laughter, bright and innocent as a child. "Only two hundred, my children? Only two hundred? Scant time to do all that must be done for Marchmont. And how selfish of you to command poor old Constant Minor to toil so long for you, beyond the allotted span of men. Still, you command, and I must strive to obey."

He was enjoying it, reveling in every word of it, manna to nourish spirit and body. Yet there was no derision in the tone, just straightforward pleasure, enjoying something too-long absent. Baffled, ready to dislike, to distrust, Nakum could find no concrete reason. True, the man looked as pale, waxy white as a grub under a dead log, but somehow it made him feel protective. Who and what was this man?

The old hands clapped in enjoyment and delight. "Visitors? Have we visitors before us? How thrilling, bring them closer," he commanded, and Nakum obeyed, stepping forward with the others, holding himself straight, wanting to impress, to be noticed, unsure why. But then, when one confronts a legend from the past, one must show the honor and reverence due such a figure. So his grandmother had taught him.

❖

With a shrug which served only to exacerbate the jacket's pinch under her arms and while her narrow shoulders floated free inside the padded shoulders, Doyce stepped forward. The coat still held Rolf's scent, and she blinked to halt unbidden tears. Khar marched with her, tail S-curving, ears alert, whiskers fanned wide and sampling. The old man sat, blue eyes as bright and alert as a baby viewing a new toy. With an upraised finger tapping his lips as if to silence himself, he bobbed his head; whether it was a quaver of old age or a private confirmation she couldn't determine.

Deftly deferential, Aelbert slipped by her and grazed the floor with his right knee in a sketchy bow weighed for both its timing and level of obsequiousness. Outstretched hands balanced the leather case containing the Monitor's letter, apparently Ignacio had returned it. Again she searched for Arras Muscadeine, craning her neck, fenced in by the unyielding high-necked collar.

"I, Aelbert Orsborne, take honor in presenting to Constant Minor, most puissant and wise Steward of Marchmont, Canderis's Special Envoy, Doyce Marbon, here at the behest of our most esteemed and duly-elected Monitor, Kyril van Beieven." A sonorous cadence, with no dying fall or choking rush for air at the end. "May our shared beginnings and long relationship offer common grounds for continued amity."

Collar biting the soft underside of her jaw, she inclined her head; Aelbert had warned her about this, rehearsed her time and again over their hurried breakfast and frenzied uniform refittings, aided by castle tailors. Wait. Wait in respectful silence until spoken to; it struck her as servile, but he maintained that that was protocol, Marchmontian etiquette prevailing while they stood on its soil. She waited, chin tucked in, began to count heartbeats to pace herself.

"Hullo." Seven, eight, nine . . . oh, dear Lady, he'd spoken . . . hadn't he? Did Stewards simply say "hullo" to diplomats? Confused, she searched his face for permission to respond. Risking a half-smile, she mouthed back "hullo" to see what would happen. Shaggy eyebrows nearly invisible against the paleness of his skin scooted up the high forehead, and his right eye twitched a wink, so fleeting she thought it might be a tic.

"Well, that's a start, isn't it?" He spoke as if they shared an intimate pot of early morning cha. Fumbling, he hauled a pair of spectacles from the front of his robe, amber-tinted lenses like miniature full moons in gold frames that hung from an ornate chain. The spectacles refused to balance on his nose, mainly because one earpiece was askew, thrusting up floss-white hair, and the chain became entangled in his wispy beard. With a muttered "Oh, bother," he screwed them into place. "That's an awfully big cat." And he levered himself clear of the throne, skip-stepped for balance and tottered toward Khar, bending with hand outstretched in invitation. "Here, nice kitty, come see Uncle Constant."

Khar took one unwilling step forward, then another, mortified at the form of address. Pink nose and white whiskers skimmed the old man's hand and withdrew. He used both hands to push the glasses into place. "*That* is a ghatta, is it not?" And no longer did the voice sound helpless or elderly, the tremulous giggle gone. "Well, well, and in Marchmont, in my castle, of all places."

He whirled, robe flowing and straining across his old man's paunch and spindly legs. "Who brought them here? Where did they come from?"

The beads of perspiration built under her arms, trapped, with no place to run. Aelbert paled, pivoted toward her and swayed on his feet, his consternation clear. Rawn, Saam, and N'oor threaded through the crowd until they reached Khar: black, steel-gray, tiger, muted tiger, all in a row. What was she supposed to do if Aelbert fainted.

"First loosen your collar, then loosen his." Ghatti advice was always straight to the point, but Doyce had no time to obey.

"I brought them here, sire." The voice rang from the far wall of the chamber, the crowd parting to avoid being shoved as Arras Muscadeine and twelve of his men marched centerward. His dark eyebrows winged down in a frown and his mustache bristled. "If there is an interdiction against these beasts in Marchmont, then I have unwittingly broken it, for I knew of no such rule." He pushed past the last of the shocked courtiers and took his place beside Doyce. "If my loyalty to Marchmont and the throne needs proving, then strip me of my honors, my title and rank, and let me earn them from your own hand."

"There is always that distinct possibility, Chevalier Capitain." The old man polished his glasses on the front of his robe, refitted them to his face without a fumble. "Your loyalty has never been in question ... yet." He paused, lips moving as he counted the ghatti under his breath, amber lenses flashing at four pairs of ghatti eyes examining him with frank curiosity. "But your common sense often has been. Do you truly *comprehend* what these creatures are?"

Witches, familiars of witches, mindstealers, brain stalkers, Doyce's breath crimped inside her chest as she waited for the familiar litany. To have traveled so far only to encounter ancient prejudices. And worst of all, had no one in the Monitor's Hall or among the Seekers Veritas realized the ghatti might hinder their cause? Why send Seekers in the first place? Even Aelbert had been utterly taken aback by the reaction.

Debonair in a slate-gray military jacket with red piping and a yellow sash, Muscadeine waded into the midst of the ghatti, polished black thigh-boots straddling Khar on either side. Unbothered, the ghatta shifted to allow his foot more room between her and N'oor. The gray astrakhan cap with its lavender, white, and black cockade was now over his heart. "They are large cats, ghatti as they are called in Canderis. It's said some still live wild in our forests, though I have never seen one. They catch more than vermin, or so I've heard. When asked to Seek as part of a Seeker Veritas pair, they seek and catch the truth. A good thing, is it not? Indeed, a man with your wisdom should welcome the truth if they can determine the true ruler of Marchmont."

A bead of sweat broke free, escaped, and ran down her ribs. If only she dared drag a finger inside the edge of her collar, ease it from her throat so she had room to swallow. What game was Arras Muscadeine playing, and was it working? The crowded hall stirred with murmurings, questioning exclamations, rustling like a breeze through dry, clattering autumn foliage. One spark would ignite it.

"And so you *seek* to ease my burden?" he snapped each word short and hard, misering them. "To ease my burden and restore a true ruler to Marchmont? How laudable of you, Chevalier Capitain."

"Only because of your express wish that this happen, sire.

How often have you lamented that you are but the Steward and that, through no wish or desire of your own, you serve solely until the rightful heir is designated?"

A creeping regret tinged Constant Minor's response. "My blood is too thin to rule for long. Only your entreaties, your acclamations," his arms spread to encompass the entire room, "melted my heart, warmed the blood in icy veins, made me assume this toil. And I will happily accede it when the rightful ruler comes . . ." his voice dropped, and Doyce strained to hear, his lips mouthing the words almost soundlessly, "but that may not be for a long, long time, I fear." And a final bleak whisper she sensed more than heard, or else her hearing had gone preternaturally sharp, "Unless these poor innocents from Canderis know more of the truth than we."

The silence stretched, just as an icicle imperceptibly but steadily lengthens with each minute accretion of water glazed on it. Doyce tried to swallow, failed, tried again and swore the entire assemblage could hear her gulp. The Steward faltered, swayed, and Ignacio rushed to him. The crocus yellow and purple form of Maurice sprang up the stairs, thin, green-hosed legs spry, and he began a frantic whispering in the old man's ear, jerky hands gesticulating with slashes savage as a sword's.

Arras Muscadeine stood, straddling the ghatti, his face defiant, watchful, worried. Not a man to back down, even though it might be in his best interests. *"Khar, what do we do now?"* she hissed. *"Is the Steward ill? What's happening?"*

Khar drank in the scene, ears swiveling to capture each minute sound, fascinated. **"I suppose it's impolite to seek since we haven't been asked,"** she commented, **"but it is nice to have keener ears than you humans do."**

"What are they saying? What can you hear?"

"Wait! Hush!" The ghatta craned in Muscadeine's direction a fraction ahead of Ignacio's plea, "Chevalier Capitain, the Steward requires your presence."

But before Muscadeine could respond, Prince Maurice barked, "As Defense Lord I command you, put them under guard! This audience is dismissed!" From dead silence to a babble of confused voices, the audience began to shift and sway, rustling like a flock of birds about to explode skyward in fear. A score of House Guards, all clad in sky-blue livery with navy berets sporting the purple rimmed cockade pushed through the crowd, hisses following in their wake from certain quarters. Equally implacable, Muscadeine's twelve faced them down, outnumbered until at an abrupt hand signal Ezequiel opened the far doors, admitting another thirty of the Chevalier Capitain's followers. Half fanned along the perimeters, the rest marching centerward to reinforce their beleaguered fellows. Not a weapon had been drawn on either side.

It was, she decided, a contest of wills so far. On tiptoe, weaving to see between rapidly moving figures, she caught a glimpse of the Steward, slumped on the throne, Ignacio fanning him. Apoplectic, rouged cheeks ruddier than the rest of his face, Maurice snarled at a House Guard lieutenant. Muscadeine sketched a half-bow in the Prince's direction. "You didn't mention who should guard them, your excellency, so I presumed you commanded us, true soldiers rather than the House Guard. After all, our mission in life is Marchmont's safety."

Muscadeine shifted a careful foot from between ghatti haunches and stood at attention before bowing toward the throne. Before anything further could be said, he wheeled, grasping Doyce's elbow and escorting her inexorably toward the door. His gray-uniformed compatriots formed a protective wedge around them, gathering in Nakum and Jacobia, Jenret and Aelbert, quick-marching them through the throng, forcing a path as necessary. Others of the troops began herding the audience toward the doors, the space around the throne emptying, widening, as if swept clear by a tidal wave.

"The ghatti!" she strained against his grip and Muscadeine half-turned, face suffused, dark eyes fever-hot.

"Don't worry, they're in no danger." He cast a look back over his shoulder. "They've found their own path. Now be silent, please! Time enough for talk later." More supporters gathered outside the doors and he turned her over to them, left without a backward glance.

PART FOUR

PART
FOUR

Is it safe yet to venture out?" From under the mahogany
able Khar 'spoke Saam; he held a better, though more pre-
arious vantage point, perched on a pedestal housing a
ronze bust of some past-distant Marchmontian worthy.

N'oor's mindvoice chattered with nerves, broke into
aam's response. "No, no! Stay underneath, it's safer,
much safer! The room's too small. I've been trod on
wice, everyone's pacing, distracted, whirling back and
orth without considering us!" She winced in memory,
nade sure her tail was fully withdrawn under the table.
That young woman, that sister of your Bond, Rawn, is
otally heedless, a menace!"

Rawn's tail whipped against the table leg, then stilled.
She's simply trying to be helpful, dashing after every-
ne with cha, or shortcake, or—" He broke off in mid-
entence, mindspeech forgotten as he yelped out loud, a
iercing, sharp "Raow!" and levitated off the carpet, jerking
is tail to safety. "Blasted little . . . ! Hardly exposed, just
nough for her to trample!" Sniffing at the injured mem-
er, he gave it a gingerly lick.

"Rawn!" Jenret commanded. "Enough noise, we're trying
o think." He continued pacing from window to table and
ack and then detoured along the credenza, sloshing milk
nto his cha without pausing.

Doyce dragged the heavy carved chair from the head of
he table and threw herself into it, tossing a leg over the arm.
Everyone, sit down, now! I mean it! The room's too small,
nd pacing doesn't do a bit of good anyway. Not to mention
he ill it does the ghatti when they're caught underfoot. Now,
it." They did so reluctantly, grumbling, Nakum and Aelbert
olliding as they both raced for the vacant chair beside
acobia. Both placed a proprietary hand on the chair's back,

Nakum's eyes impassive, Aelbert's lips compressed, only
simultaneously discover Jenret occupying it.

"Ample seating across the way, gentlemen," he snapp
and the two separated in opposite directions to the o
side.

Saam's alert came loud and clear. **"Best retreat out fr
under there, my friends. They may have stopped paci
but the leg-swinging and kicking will begin moment
ily."**

Khar eeled through the chair-leg maze, Rawn behind
N'oor dashing from the other side, belly-slithering into sc
hiding space beneath a heavy chest raised off the floor
ball and claw feet. She cringed from the nearest bronze f
clutching its glass ball and wailed, **"I don't think I lik
here, I feel as if an eagle is hatching me!"**

But Aelbert paid no attention to her distress, she co
feel it, his thoughts partitioning—suppressed jealousy
Nakum, eagerness toward Jacobia, dislike toward Jenret,
cautious consideration of a hunting beast deciding whet
or not to stalk when he looked at Doyce. And a jumbled
citement, almost exaltation . . . residue from that secret
early-morning visit she'd spied upon. She could read him
too well, but never well enough to be sure what he really
sired, wondered if he knew himself. The lingering scent
his uniform almost stifled her senses.

Playing hostess, Jacobia poured more cha, urged ca
and pastries on everyone around the table. She slid a pas
plate in Doyce's direction, only to have Doyce slide it b
without comment. "Sorry," she said to no one in particu
and began crumbling a piece of cake.

"Aelbert, what do you think went wrong in there?" Do
asked yet again.

He slumped in his chair. "You saw it as well as I, bet
in fact, since you were closer. Constant Minor called Khai
him, realized she wasn't a cat, and became highly agitate
The crispness of his facts belied his slouched position.

"I know that, you know that, we *all* know that. I did
ask what you knew, I asked you what you thought." C
vincing the aide to venture a personal opinion made to
extraction seem easy. "Why did the Steward react like th
Do you have any idea? You're supposed to be convers
with Marchmontian protocol. Did the ghatti's presen
breach it?"

He squared his shoulders. "Not that I'm aware of, certainly. They don't see the need for ghatti, don't view them with the same seriousness that we do, but I've never heard of any animosity. Mostly they view them as an exotic curiosity; very few have ever actually seen them or been involved in a Seeking. I had many formal and informal talks with Marchmont's last Consul, Fausta LaRoche, and with various of her visitors from Marchmont, and none objected to N'oor that I could judge, did they, N'oor?" he appealed as he bent, stretching toward the chest.

A soft little **"No,"** echoed from underneath, followed by a cautious whisker extension, until her whole head popped out. Flattening herself further, she squeezed into the open, sniffed his extended hand, and sneezed. **"They just never took me very seriously."** Why add that they hadn't taken him very seriously either, and that had bothered her. Did he know they didn't take him seriously? And if he did, why didn't he seethe with the resentment she usually sensed when he was slighted?

"What's the relationship between Prince Maurice and Aras Muscadeine?" Doyce pondered.

Aelbert came upright. "Technically, Muscadeine reports to Prince Maurice, since Maurice is Defense Lord and Muscadeine heads the army. His 'disobedience' could be construed as an act of defiance or as overzealousness to Maurice's commands. He did obey, after all, though not quite as Maurice anticipated."

"Stop quibbling and qualifying," Jenret jeered. "Just try to explain . . ."

"But I'm trying to ex—"

With a slap on the table, Doyce interrupted, "Khar, are the guards still outside?"

Before the ghatta could reply, Jenret pushed his chair back and cracked open the door with exaggerated caution. "Two," he reported and eased the door shut, "and still at full present arms, I'd say. Their backs are to me—can't tell the color of their cockades."

"They're meant to keep others out, not keep us in," Khar emended, tired of having her answers snatched away. Still, it was better than the question she knew was coming and wasn't sure how to respond to. It was building in her Bondmate's mind; Doyce suspected she might not answer it,

not from lack of knowledge but from reticence. At last th
question came.

"Khar, what were they saying—Maurice, the Steward, an
Muscadeine—when they were all gathered around th
throne?"

She inspected her white bib, down to her white feet. Trut
had many more levels than humans realized. Saam an
Rawn waited for her to speak, for they, as well as N'oor, ha
heard. **"You didn't bid me Seek during the presentation
so I didn't. Suffice it to say that what my ears heard,"** th
hoop on her left ear trembled, **"indicated no danger to us
just confusion about us."**

She played the words over in her mind but kept them t
herself. Constant had been excited and more than a littl
fearful. "Ghatti—and in our kingdom at last! Wilhelmin
was right, more right than you credited her." And Maurice'
hurried, "A pure coincidence, nothing more. In over tw
hundred years we've *never* relied on them, nor should w
now! Those foreigners are here for their precious trade, thei
borders. Don't muddy the waters, your excellency.'
Muscadeine's saturnine contribution followed. "Then poli
tics and civility demand they stay while we consider th
problems at hand, does it not?" His excitement quivere
around her, his thoughts dancing in the air, the chance the
might catalyze something he badly wanted—an answer t
the question: who should rightfully rule Marchmont?

But that she wouldn't say. **"To repeat their words woul
be gossip, ill-bred and rude unless lives were at stake.'**
What continued to puzzle her was the sound issuing from
Constant, a subtle buzzing, almost a ticking, sounds tha
shouldn't emanate from a human. The other ghatti hadn'
understood any better, had measured it in their demeanor
their imperceptible bristling of nervous curiosity at a secre
beyond their ken. The truth was there if they knew how t
read it.

It was the sort of answer Doyce had expected, thoug
she'd hoped for more. Trust the ghatti not to reveal mor
than they chose to give, and trust them to know the impor
tance of what they heard and surmised.

The knock at the door startled them all. "Come in, it's no
locked," Doyce called and nearly laughed at her automati
response. Not locked, indeed, no need with guards outside
Without fully opening the door, Arras Muscadeine slippe

in, his body blocking their view into the hall. "I trust you've enjoyed your cha? You must thank Ignacio for that," he added, hardly pausing for a reply before continuing. "I've been asked to inform you that our most esteemed Steward, Constant Minor, requests the pleasure of the Envoy's company at a small, private audience."

Aelbert rubbed his hands together, eager to begin work. "Good, good! Precisely what we need, get things out in the open, explain our position. If you'll allow me to go collect my paperwork, we can be ready in no time! Jenret, you've studied the trade figures I gave you? I hope you didn't put it off. Of course, it's too soon for more than preliminary discussions, but it pays to be prepared, start off on the right foot."

Arras interrupted. "Your enthusiasm is laudable but in advance of itself, m'ser. This is to be a very small, private meeting of your Special Envoy, the Steward, the Prince Maurice, and myself. And, of course, the beauteous ghatta Khar'pern, to make up for any ill manners displayed earlier." Khar gave a magnanimous dip of her head.

Aelbert's fingers splayed, almost clawed the air before he mastered himself. "Not going?" he whispered, half-incredulous at the thought. "But I should ... I have to ... I'm the one who ..." he lamented before mastering himself. "Yes, that's right, time enough for that later, this is merely a preliminary meeting. Time enough, time enough." Only N'oor caught the peculiar, wounded smile that flitted across his face as Doyce and Khar exited the room with Muscadeine.

Holding the candle higher, Sarrett tilted her chin and looked in the tiny mirror, then swung the length of hair over her shoulder. *Almost didn't recognize myself,* she grinned at the image. *Eyebrows ought to be darker, though.* Still, considering she'd transformed herself in a rickety outbuilding to a deserted farm, it wasn't bad, not bad at all. Lucky she'd been to find this place with its old wash tub and a few reasonably unleaky buckets, a hearth to build a fire and warm the water, if not thoroughly heat it.

"Well, what do you think?" she asked T'ss.

The ghatt jumped on the bench and began his inspection.

He sniffed in little, rapid motions, inhaled more deeply—and
sneezed. Pushing closer, he nosed at her hair, and touched an
experimental paw, threw himself backwards as he sneezed
again. **"Doesn't look like you,"** he acknowledged, **"and
most of all, doesn't smell like you."** A paroxysm of sneez-
ing convulsed him, his head tossing from side to side
"Phew!"

"Don't tell me you're allergic—like Parse?" Worry
creased her brow as she held the tail of hair to her own nose
sniffed, considering. Herbal, but overlaid with a harsher
chemical scent, not pleasant up close.

T'ss made a face, shook his head. **"Don't mistake me for
Parse just because you think about him too much."**

"That obvious?"

"As obvious as the dye job," he affirmed with a saucy
wink, **"but only to the trained eyes of the ghatti. That's
me, T'ss!"**

Ignoring him, she checked the mirror again, judging the
job she'd done dyeing her bright gilt hair to a medium
brown. Less obvious, certainly, and that was what she
needed. Tomorrow she'd set forth dressed as an itinerant
peddler, not as a Seeker. *"Are you sure you shouldn't be a
little less conspicuous? I've enough dye left to do a ghatt."*
She threatened with the bottle in T'ss's direction.

T'ss retreated along the bench, sapphire eyes fixed on the
offending object. **"Don't think it would help. Once a
ghatt, always a ghatt—white with black stripes or brown
with black doesn't really matter. I'm still going to have
to hide."** He sagged, dejected. **"Don't want to."**

She tickled his ears to restore his humor. *"You know why.
If Marchmont has spies on this side of the border, they must
know by now that Doyce and the others have crossed, or
were about to when we heard from Rawn. Seeing another
Seeker and ghatt in the vicinity might make them think
they're relaying information back to us—which they are, of
course. I just wish they'd stay in contact a little more often.
If we have to cross the border, an itinerant peddler is likely
to get farther than another Seeker."*

T'ss paused, nose in the air, ringed ears cocked, listening.
**"Hush! M'wa's sending! Bard sends greetings. Wants us
on the lookout for Syndar Saffron. Koom told him that
Syndar's searching for Jacobia?"**

"More uninvited guests . . . ?" she let the thought hang,

worried at having Saffron landing in the midst of their carefully laid plans.

"Well, if you want a bull charging over the border, Syndar Saffron's your man. Not going to be very subtle, I'm afraid."

"Do you think we can locate him, tell him Jacobia's fine?"

"Not likely, but we can try."

They ground his face into the dirt once more, a hand wrapped in his collar, another pushing against the back of his head. Syndar Saffron went limp, let them feel his muscles relax in defeat before he heaved upward with a roar, spitting pieces of gravel and dirt. He slammed one arm around a man's neck, elbow crook tightening against the vulnerable throat, crushing harder and harder before the blow hit the back of his head, leaving him viewing a galaxy of stars as he blacked out.

When he came to, he discovered his arms roped behind his back, his feet tied and drawn up to meet his hands. Trussed like a pig! Glaring out of his one unswollen eye, he snorted a grass stem from his nose. A pair of shiny black boots loomed a few centimeters from his nose. Made him want to spit, they did.

"Now let's try again. Where did you get that horse?" the boots' owner asked as if from a great height.

"Chap sold him to me." Saffron probed the corner of his mouth with his tongue; the gash stung, tasted of blood salt. "Paid twenty golden for it. Find him, check his pockets and see. Saddle's mine. Think a nag like that would boast a saddle of that quality." The thought aggrieved him somehow, as if the valiant creature he'd had to put down were being forced to share with that . . . that plug.

As if sensing their interest, the horse ambled a step or two closer, nose snuffling at Saffron's ear, a wet string of saliva dangling down. Hardly a plug, but its breeding had been undistinguished, although it looked well kept.

"How touching." The boots circled his head, one kicked to shoo the horse away. "And when and how did you cross the border?" He twisted to follow the boots, clamped down on a sigh of exasperation, fashioned it into an inadvertent exhalation of pain.

"Told you before. Went to take a leak out back of the tavern in Bidenbridge, you know, about two kilometers west of Islebridge. Met a chap trying to peddle some fish to the tavern keeper. No trade in Bidenbridge, footbridge's been burned." His tongue wedged thick in his mouth, but it seemed important to explain exactly what had happened and how. "No trade means no tavern customers, except a few spending their last coin. No customers means no need to cook for meals. No need to cook means no need to buy fish." His head ached worse than any hangover he'd ever had.

Hands rolled him onto his side and he sagged his free shoulder to relieve the pain dragging at his wrists. "We know the economics of supply and demand," the soldier informed him. An expanse of uniform above Syndar, sleeves with gaudy swirled slashes, a sash end swinging in his face, distracting, but he couldn't peer high enough to look at the face. Can't see the top of the tree when you're directly beneath it, he thought, amused despite himself. "How did you cross the border?"

He tried to marshal his thoughts, but the image of Jacobia intruded. If these ruffians had seized her . . . ! The rage cleared his head, made him realize how important it was to explain, to be released. "Chap said if I'd spend the evening helping lantern-charm fish he'd ferry me to the other side and he'd try to sell the fish there. Knew of a horse for sale when we got there. Said his brother-in-law needed ready money more than he needed a horse these days." Anger welled within him again, almost as severe as the anger he felt about Jacobia, lost, wandering alone somewhere. "Why have you stopped the trade?" He'd like to know.

No answer to that, just a new question, and he puzzled at the different tack they were taking. "Didn't you notice anything about the old saddle when you went to put your own saddle on?" Think! What did they want him to say? What were they getting at? Which was more important—crossing into Marchmont or possessing the horse? A different pair of boots nudged his face, another kicked idly at his back, just above the kidney. The next kick carried more force, left him gasping in agony. He hadn't seen it coming. "Anything identifying about the saddle that should have made you think?"

"Sort of an oak wreath?" His response elicited another kick, more an admonitory tap. Face clenched, he tried to visualize it. "Initials . . . inside. Big L in the middle, smaller I and A to each side."

"Exactly, exactly." The man squatted, hooked Syndar's chin with a thumb, making sure their eyes met. "And it isn't wise to steal . . . or purchase property stolen from the Internal Affairs Lord. Everyone knows the oak leaves signify a Ministration Lord."

Oh, have mercy, Syndar chortled to himself. It *is* the damn horse they're concerned about, not how I got here! Now who the hells was the Internal Affairs Lord these days? Found he hadn't the foggiest idea, gone from his head, except for the germ of a plan that remained. "Normally I borrow a mount from Lysenko if I need one, but I haven't been able to get in touch with him yet." He half-lidded his violet eyes to hide the glint in them. "You do know Lysenko Boersma, of course? Your Commerce Lord?" And if Lysenko had resigned or been stripped of his position, he was in even deeper trouble now.

"You're acquainted with the Commerce Lord?" The query sounded just a little too smug. "Any fool can pretend friendship, the name's hardly unknown, especially if you've merchantered either side of the border. So tell me what he looks like, something beyond his size, his hair color. Something more . . . relevant."

"Hates wine, loves beer. Writes left-handed, but fights like a righty. But beware, he's not just covering himself with his left—when you think he's delivering a right hook from the hells' shades and weave to avoid it, he'll pop a left on the bridge of your nose. . . ." It made his own nose ache with memory of that little trick. "Of course, Lysenko hasn't fought professionally in years, called himself Bedrick in the ring. Friends named him Bedtrick for his other little antics." How much more should he reveal? Boersma'd worked hard to live down those earlier days, unfair to drag it out like this. No shame to it, but he'd admitted those times made others doubt his qualifications as Commerce Lord.

"And I suppose you fought him in the ring?"

Despite himself, Saffron laughed with the sheer joy of memory. "Look at me! I outstripped him as a featherweight when I was twelve!" He wished he could wipe his eyes.

"But he flattened my nose in a tavern brawl—with a beer stein, not his fist!" And was laughing uncontrollably now.

"If you'd said you'd fought him and won, I'd have handed you over to Emeril Alighieri, Internal Affairs Lord, without a qualm, regardless of the rules. As it is, I'll remand you to the Justice Lord . . ." "Lady," Saffron interrupted, still choking on his own laughter. "Lady of Justice and let her decide if you can contact Lord Boersma."

"Thank you." He thought it was worth that much politeness.

"I'm still concerned about your entry into Marchmont, not just the possession of the horse." And he rose, returning with a canvas sack emitting a scent that made the horses prick up their ears, their nostrils widen. "Did you steal the carrots as well?"

"Carrots?" Saffron roared. "How the hell can you tell if carrots are stolen? A carrot looks like a carrot, regardless of which side of the border it grows on, you bloody fool!"

"I suppose." The soldier rummaged inside the sack. "And there's no evidence if it's been eaten, is there?" One horse after another pushed toward him, whickering, eager.

"That's my bloody dinner they're eating!"

The old man with the wispy white hair clung to Doyce's elbow, waved at the portrait, hand swooping to push his glasses up his nose yet again. "Fine family, don't ye think?" An ingratiating yet slightly wintry undercurrent in his tone added emphasis to a basically banal statement. Obedient yet baffled, she studied the oil portraiture again, an intimate family scene, its sitters relaxed, confident, self-assured. An overweight man with grizzled red hair and beard draped a confident arm over his wife's shoulder, the woman looking tired but pleasant, a snood hooding her blonde hair, fond eyes downcast at the chubby boy of about two in her lap, his expression suggesting an incipient squirm.

A boy and a girl-woman ranged around the couple, the girl perhaps twenty, a strapping blonde, buxom and rosy-cheeked, then a thin boy of about five or six, frail compared to the hardy younger lad. The boy held a book under one arm, the quirky, tremulous "V" of his smile hinting at his discomfort with the fatherly hand heavy on his shoulder. "A pleasant-looking family." What more could she say? "How long ago was it painted?"

Constant Minor chortled, poked his knuckles at her ribs. "Ye don't know who they are, do ye? Nay, no reason you should. So let me introduce you. The late King Sebastien and his lovely consort, Hortensia. To his left, Wilhelmina, our late and much revered Queen, and her two brothers, Maarten and Ludovico. No wonder Hortensia looks tired with Sebastien still such a lusty fellow so late in life. . . ." He winked, dislodged his glasses, slid them back. "Introductions are so hard to do properly, even for the dead—especially for the dead, don't you think?"

"They're all dead, then?"

"Well, of course they are—Sebastien'd be damnably near a hundred! Good stock but weak by the sixth generation. And Wilhelmina wouldn't have ruled had he still been alive." He peered over the amber lenses, mouth drawstring tight. "Oh, the brothers, that's what you mean. Dead as well, both in their twenties, and both without issue. O' course there're some tales that Ludo scattered a few by-blows, always the lusty one, he was, like his father. But that's not the issue here and now, is it?"

With monumental self-control, she refrained from asking what was as she let him nudge her toward the table, exerting more energy than expected, though he tottered against her every other step. Maurice and Arras Muscadeine sat, ignoring each other, waiting, as if they'd witnessed Constant Minor's foible of showing off royal portraits all too often. "This . . . this thing, this trouble with Canderis, none of my doing, you know. Always thought Canderis a nice enough country, good enough neighbor as long as they kept to their place and we to ours. Nice to see you come, nicer to see you go, old expression . . . don't you know? Why in the old days . . ." He plopped into the chair Doyce pulled back for him, eyes rolling and vague, whether in memory or in a sudden loss of energy, she wasn't sure.

Claiming her seat at the table, she debated how to begin. No Rolf to guide her, nor Aelbert; on her own now except for Khar. "I gather this is meant to serve as an informal meeting to air our concerns, explore our relationship?" She trailed a hand beside her chair, relieved as the soft head slipped into her cupped palm, warm and reassuring.

"Officially unofficial," Maurice confirmed, smoothing his

dyed locks, giving her the uneasy feeling he used her as his mirror. "Some things are better aired in private than at a general audience. More suitable, especially after the Chevalier Capitain's arrant misinterpretation of my orders earlier, usurping my powers."

Muscadeine made an explosive sound of denial, mustache billowing, then regained control. "Maurice, mon oncle, I have explained and apologized already. Enough!"

"Enough?" Maurice blustered. "Usurping, usurping, everyone constantly usurping, chipping away at what's right and proper. I am your superior, your commander as Defense Lord and as a Prince of the realm. You obey my orders, not interpret them to your liking as a whim! And let me remind you, 'nephew,' that we are related by marriage, not by blood." He stretched across the table toward Muscadeine, the veins on his temples bulging, the crocus yellow and purple silk ruckling, his weight pinning it against the table's edge. "The blood royale does not flow through your veins, even if some fear mine is too distant!"

A rapid drumming brought them back to themselves. Constant Minor thumped the table with a silver spoon with a shell-shaped bowl, much as a child might do to attract attention. At their deferential but strained silence, he went back to spooning up his bread and milk. " 'S good!" he slurped. "Sure no one wants some? A midday snack . . . miraculous for sharpening the brain . . . and for stopping the mouth from singing the same old sad, tired tune, is it not, Maurice?" He buried his face in the porringer, slurped again. "Mi, mi, mi, *mi*, mi, mi, mi, la-dah! Now, yes, why are we here? Why *are* we here?" A droplet of milk pearled his spectacles.

"Sometimes the very young and the very old exhibit true wisdom," Khar noted with a certain admiration.

"Holy innocents?" she asked.

"Or wholly innocents," Khar shot back, pleased at the wordplay. **"Now, start speaking while you have the floor, before it's snatched from under you again. That's why he interrupted."**

She obeyed. "First, Canderis and the Monitor, Kyril van Beieven, are concerned about our Consul's precipitous expulsion, leaving us no recourse but to take retaliatory measures. Secondly, we are dismayed by the unwarranted and secret closure of our border and the restraint of hitherto free trade. No advance discussion, let alone warning, preceded this stoppage of free movement and trade. Finally, to attack and loot our merchanters who approached the border unaware of the closure edict is a highly provocative action, as you must be well aware. We would like to know what we've done to warrant this treatment." She hoped she'd remembered the gist of Aelbert's formal complaint.

A gobbet of milk-soaked bread leaked from Constant's mouth. "Well, of course the borders are sealed, told Valeria myself I wanted 'em that way. After all, she's in charge of External Affairs, isn't she? Forgot at the time to mention the closure, Maurice," but he didn't look at all repentant. "But attacked? Looted? What is she talking about?"

She gauged the expressions around her, felt as if she played in a high stakes card game where the level of bluffing and calling were beyond her skills. A tight little frown puckered Maurice's face, but it was Muscadeine who was forced to speak. "There have been brigands about. Who they are we are not sure. At your direct command, my Lord," a tight nod in Maurice's direction, "we've tried to quell the recent skirmishes in the North Domain, but we've been stretched thin patrolling and sealing the border under the Steward's direct orders. Of course the Steward's orders take precedence over your own." He paused, had the grace to look puzzled. "But I was unaware we had seized any goods; certainly our orders directed us to escort any stranded trade parties to the capital, bypassing their usual trading venues. Lord Boersma also told us that all transactions should be completed as quickly as possible, and the merchanters escorted to their side of the border."

"Probably more of the same that you can't control in the north," Maurice added with a triumphant little smirk.

Muscadeine's chair crashed behind him as he jumped to his feet, face red, "Strange, is it not, that only your Domain suffers from these battles? And if I could find the instigators . . .!"

"I've told you it's those damn Erakwa! Put them in their place, show them who's in control!"

"Erakwa? Maurice, are you mad? Just because a few signs seem to indicate . . .!"

"Oh, sit down, sit down, both of you or we'll be here forever. Let's return to the matter at hand." Tilting his bowl, Constant scooped up the last bit of bread, held the spoon poised. "Yes, we expelled your Consul shortly after Wilhel-

mina's death. Our present problems in deciding on an he
struck me as none of Canderis's concern—housekeeping is
private affair, not a public one. I felt it wiser to dismiss yo
Consul and seal our borders to contain gossip and rumor, b
instead it seems we've only stirred up more. As you've gat
ered, we had no intention of cutting off trade or stealin
from Canderis. For that I apologize." Maurice sputtere
while Muscadeine looked partially mollified. The sudden c
gency and command to Constant Minor's voice took h
aback.

"Well, what do you propose to do about it?" she asked b
fore anyone could interrupt.

"That we'll have to think on." He disappeared beneath th
table, one sandaled foot counterbalancing in the air as h
hung over the chair arm and set his bowl on the carpe
"Here, kitty-ghatta, here, kitty-ghatta. Want nice milk?"

Off-balanced yet again by his transformation back into
doddering old man, Doyce scarely heard Khar comment, '
think some refreshment might be in order," as she prom
enaded around the table toward the bowl.

"I . . . I take it you don't dislike ghatti, then? We were u
clear about that after this morning's meeting."

Constant struggled upright, his head rising above the tab
again. "Phew! Long way down! Dislike them? Hardl
hardly. Surprised, that's all. They certainly weren't comm
when I was younger. Not much call for them in Marchmon
don't you know? We've our own ways—different heritag
We're not all equal despite our shared beginnings."

"But what about the Queen's dying words?" Muscadei
shouted. "The ghatti could be the answer to our—" Ma
rice's complaint overrode the Capitain's question. "Clearl
delusional . . . on her deathbed . . . not to be taken ser
ously!"

"Hush!" The single word silenced like the crack of a whi
and Constant continued, almost placating. "Gentlemen, th
is not the matter at hand." With a businesslike air he peere
down the table at Doyce. "Well, Envoy Marbon, we sti
have much to discuss amongst ourselves before I can dete
mine how to right certain inadvertent wrongs and clarify ou
relationship with Canderis," Constant said. "Since you an
your group are here, please stay, by all means. Indeed, I *i*
sist you stay. I'd hate to see you fall prey to those brigand

whomever they may be. You'll find much of interest in Marchmont, have you eyes to see it."

Knowing a dismissal when she heard it, she rose, made the short, formal bow she hadn't been able to make earlier. "May I be excused, then, until our next meeting?"

"Of course, of course, you are free to go." An airy hand wave knocked the spectacles on the table. "Free to leave this room, this castle, but not to venture beyond our town walls. Not all Marchmontians take kindly to outsiders. Enjoy your visit. You'll be guided and guarded as needed. And by guarded I mean protected. No, no, it wouldn't do for anything to happen to Canderis's Special Envoy, would it, gentlemen?"

❧

Servants streamed from kitchen to dining hall, circling tables, swooping by with groaning platters, extracting plates littered with the debris of hearty eating, pouring amber arcs of ale, pulsing purple burgundy and straw yellow crescents of wine. They served without any command he could hear or see, no collision or missed steps, never mistaking a request or dropping a tray, Ignacio and Ezequiel stationed at opposite ends of the hall, supervising. Nakum sat mesmerized, dizzy, almost nauseous from the unceasing, hypnotic movement and the surfeit of food, heavily seasoned and spiced, dripping with sauces. The young man to his right caught his eye, but the Erakwan ignored him, couldn't cope with another flood of words. Easier by far to focus on the head table and the man known as the Lord of the Nord and Defense Lord, tearing into each course with hearty appetite.

This, he had been informed, was an informal dinner, not as rigorously structured as the Steward's presence would require, lacking the full complement of diners, servants, courses, and toasts expected at a formal meal. A chance for influential people to casually meet the Special Envoy, or so Aelbert had explained before instructing him in the rituals and niceties of fine dining. Queasiness increasing, he scrutinized Aelbert's behavior, compared it to his own close-mouthed agitation. Outwardly convivial yet circumspect, Aelbert was busily introducing himself, eliciting conversations but withholding his own opinions.

"I'm surprised his ears don't wriggle from sorting so

many strands of conversation," Saam 'spoke from beneath Nakum's chair. **"N'oor's going to have a headache."** Then his voice gentled, concern clear as he continued, **"You should eat more, you know. It's not all rich—the bread smells good, the cheese, the baked fowl plain if you avoid the dressing. Try it."**

"I will, I will," he promised, striving for composure. How long could he remain bottled in this castle, this city, unable to roam free? What was he when he wasn't scout, waiting, forced to remain in Sidonie while they had their silly discussions? Worst of all his earth-bond kept surging unpredictably. He touched it, caressed the object shrouded by the doeskin pouch at his waist. It almost hummed, vibrating with strangeness, as if this country had released something long suppressed within it, something that could force him down strange paths, walkways, corridors, though it subsided when he protested, willed himself in control. Still, the tug was strong and he fretted he wasn't strong enough. His grandmother had never mentioned anything like this to him.

The noise ratcheted a notch higher, yet Nakum could still hear Jenret as he leaned across to Doyce, two seats down on his right. "And the condemned man ate a hearty meal." He indicated his plate, already loaded with seconds from overly zealous servants. "They're stuffing us just the way you do a goose for pate!"

She stopped with her fork half-way to her mouth, returned it to the plate. "No one's forcing you to eat it all. Look at Nakum's spartan portions. Jacobia's as well, but I surmise she's saving herself for dessert." Then, mulling it over, "As to condemned, we're certainly not that, just say that both our restraint and theirs are being put to the test."

Jenret cupped his wineglass, half-smothering his reply, but Nakum watched his lips form the words, magnified by the crystal. "Ah, but I am condemned, condemned by love." Catching Nakum's dismay, he raised his glass in salute and a servant promptly filled it. Still solitary in the midst of company, Nakum listened to conversations break and shift, reform, Doyce now speaking with the young man who sat between her and Nakum, Jenret returning to his talk with Lord Boersma.

Hating the feel of the heavy silver forks, tridents big enough for spearing fish, Nakum toyed with a slice of fowl.

"Is he truly in love with Doyce, Saam, or does he just think he is?"

The steel-gray ghatt deliberated. **"It's love, and it pains him because he's never caught it before, not like this. Rawn has intimated that he has great experience in loving but not in the emotions of it."**

The ghatt's response puzzled him, even though he heard Saam's mindspeech in his own familiar Erakwa language, no need to translate, laboriously consider the fine shadings or double meanings of foreign words. Was there someone he could ask later to explain about the emotions of loving, what they were? Not Jacobia, certainly, not and admit his ignorance, and the thought of Jacobia made him flush hot, then cold. And he still felt curious about Doyce and Jenret. *"Does Doyce love him?"*

"I think she may, although she doesn't realize it. She's learning to love herself and that comes first."

Confusing, all too confusing, this talk of love. Could he ever sort it out? Giving up on the fork, he lifted a piece of fowl to his mouth with precise fingers. Chewing at least precluded conversation with his neighbors, although it didn't hamper his continuing conversation with the ghatt. *"Would it bother you if she comes to love Jenret?"*

"Bother? Why should it bother me?" The ghatt acted genuinely amused.

"Because ... because of Oriel." He hesitated over saying it. *"That it would be disloyal to Oriel's memory to love another."*

Saam touched his bare ankle with a velvet paw. **"Then you don't know much about love either. Doyce and I both know Oriel is gone, will always miss him, but have love left to share. Else I would not be with you."** Nakum had trouble swallowing his food. The velvet paw tapped him twice, reclaimed his attention. **"If you aren't going to eat all that fowl, I'd be glad to help."**

Hurriedly, Nakum slipped a piece from his plate and passed it under his chair, the movement attracting his neighbor's attention. "A little sharing?" Embarrassed at being noticed, unsure what to talk about, Nakum tried to ignore him. "I've an old dog back home who always insists on his portion—even a bit of my rightful share if he can make me feel guilty enough. Slips right by my mother and next thing

you know he's pressing his head in your lap and sighing as
if he'd waste away from hunger."

"We share everything." Nakum meant it, though he knew
the other wouldn't understand. "Everything," he repeated
more firmly and smiled, sure of that if nothing else.

Gray eyes in an outdoors-tanned face twinkled, skin
chapped red from wind and weather. "Is that a fact? Old
Kesta draws the line at mashed turnip, just as I did. No help
there." Laugh lines bracketed his mouth as he recounted a
long-ago incident. "Though he didn't mind the stewed
prunes, lapped them up like mad and begged for more. So I
obliged, made Mother think I'd been a good lad and had
doubles without coaxing. O'course the end results were all
too clear!" And waited for Nakum's laughter.

Baffled, Nakum sat solemn, speculative about what the
young man meant, liking his friendliness, his frankness, but
suspecting he'd missed something. Was it not good to share
doubly with a friend? "Prunes?" he queried. "End results?"

With a quick and hot whisper in Nakum's ear, the young
man pulled back to gauge his comprehension, whispered
again. Despite himself, Nakum began to giggle as he poked
worriedly around his plate with the fork. "There are no
prunes in this, are there?"

"Blessed Lady, no! Though a few nicely flavor a stuffing,
but none here tonight that I've sampled, and I've sampled
most everything. No food or cooking like this where I've
been." He sagged back with a groan and patted his belly
contentedly. "I confess, your friends make me a bit edgy,
not wise to trust strangers. But you're Erakwa. I've been trying
to catch your attention all evening. Ignacio seated me here
because he thought we'd have something in common. I'm
Roland d'Arnot, one of the foremen up at the tree nursery
where we're cultivating arborfers. A number of your people
help us as well."

"My people?"

"Yes, Erakwa—distant cousins of yours, at least."

The thought electrified Nakum, his heart bounding and
leaping. His own kind around him at last! Maybe that explained his earth-bond's strange sensations, like calling out
to like. "Where in the city is this nursery for trees?"

"Not in the city, but several days' ride to the northwest.
Not enough room here for arborfers. I wouldn't offer

Canderisian dignitaries a guided tour, but you, yes. Want to venture out and see it?"

"Yes!" Nakum breathed the word with longing, then sat still. They weren't to leave, and even if he could, was it right to desert Doyce and the others in this strange land, in a strange situation? Yet wasn't his job completed until the time came to escort them home to Canderis?

Without realizing he was rising, caught in the wave of movement that had guests standing as Prince Maurice bade them good evening and left the room with a sad-faced woman on his arm, Nakum clutched at Roland, fearful he'd leave before he could answer. "Let me find if I'm needed here, if I might go. When would it be?"

"In a few days' time if you can obtain permission. We'll stay perhaps an oct, let you see the country."

Although the exit of a monarch or the Steward would have concluded the meal, the Prince's leave-taking didn't indicate formal dismissal. People drifted away in twos or threes, others reminiscing over a final glass of wine or simply content to sit, too satiated with food and fellowship to move. As Doyce strolled out with Arras Muscadeine, chatting pleasantries, Jenret shadowed them, determined to cut her away from Muscadeine, have her to himself. Certain things needed discussing, and he wouldn't wait any longer.

He could imagine the brushing and tickling of Muscadeine's mustache as he leaned close to Doyce and heard something not meant for his ears. "You have the invisible leash on him, eh? Just as my Felix knows to follow."

She stopped short and Jenret's anger carried him forward, ready to confront Muscadeine, his chest bouncing against her shoulder before he pulled back, brusque and embarrassed. "What are you talking about? He's just leaving dinner—aren't you, Jenret?—along with most other people."

With a triumphant head toss, Muscadeine hovered at her side, too intimately for Jenret's peace of mind. "No need to jerk the leash with this one, he knows his paces. I have the vision to see why. But never mind, I have someone I'd like you to meet."

Before he could avenge the insult, thrash the man, and free Doyce from his influence, Muscadeine hurried her along, his laughter carrying contempt. With a low growl, Jenret surged after them, only to discover his right foot weighted down. Rawn sat straddling it, forelegs clutching his shin, claws extended just enough to make his point. **"You will not follow. Show some pride. There will be other times, more private."**

He reached for his pride, afraid he'd buried it too deeply to find, though he'd stored it somewhere . . . or had he abandoned it because of Doyce? The effort hurt. Sullenly, *"I wasn't following her, I wanted a word with Muscadeine."*

"Better, better." Rawn shifted, eased his claws from the fabric. **"I don't believe it, but others less sensitive to the truth might. If you're done acting the fool, I'll get off."**

"You're more weighty than my conscience," Jenret grumbled, forcing himself not to track the diminishing figures with his eyes. He discovered Nakum hovering nearby, feared the Erakwan had seen his lapse, would think less of him. But Nakum was bubbling with excitement, begging for a hearing. "Fine, come along, then, and tell me all about it." He didn't want to hear, but any distraction was preferable to brooding.

Back in Jenret's suite, they'd discussed the arborfer nursery, the possibility that Nakum might be permitted to visit, and then both had gradually fallen silent in front of the fire, not exactly asleep but musing comfortably. Nakum was half-lost in the oversized chair, contented with his thoughts, curled tight like an animal in his burrow. The wine at dinner had helped erase last night's headache, and Jenret, eyes hooded, cradled a brandy snifter, deriving more comfort from holding it than from drinking from it.

He wasn't asleep, was he? He had no idea if the knocking at the door sounded in reality or in a dream, but prayed it was a dream as he found himself with his back to the door, braced hard against it to keep it shut, chest heaving, heart rising into his throat. Keep the voices at bay, he commanded himself, lock them out! But they slipped under the door, wafted through the cracks between the panels, whisper voices taunting his brain. Muscadeine shouting at him to do his duty, and he couldn't bear to face the man after their near-contretemps over Doyce earlier that evening. Nor would he give him the satisfaction of obeying, for the Chevalier Captain had no right to order him, even an order as simple as "Listen, listen, you fool!"

He wouldn't, refused to listen, glared wildly around the room as he molded his whole body against the door, heels dug in, arms thrown wide for stability. And on the foot of the bed, legs crossed tailor-style, a young boy grinned at him, mocking his fears. "Jared!" he shouted. "You're dead! Go away, you can't be here, I won't let you!" Jared, his eight-year-old brother, killed by their father to control his raw Gleaner skills, skills that had already shattered minds like panes of glass.

"Jenner, Jenner, won't you let me in?" Jared pleaded.

"But you are in!"

"That's not what I meant. . . ." Before Jared could explain any further, the voice of Constant Minor whispered from behind the door, "Begone now! He isn't ripe," and shooing everyone away in a querulous voice.

The infernal doomsday knocking resonated through his brain, and in stocking feet Jenret sprang for the door, panting, ready to confront whatever demons lurked outside, no more hiding. It was only Jacobia, looking bereft and alone. "Jenner, could we . . . could we talk? I've something I want to ask you." Clear she'd screwed her courage as tight as it would wind.

"About what?" His headache had returned, soaring to the level it had reached this morning, spikes pounding into his brain, colored flashes, echoing reverberations. But no more internal voices, Lady be blessed for that! He waved her in, indicated a bench near the door, eager to rid himself of her problems as quickly as possible.

Ceaselessly twisting a lock of hair, she met his eyes, violet locking with blue, only to glance away. "I . . . I've wanted to ask . . . but there's never been a good time!" she wailed. And this wasn't a good time, he thought ominously, for whatever it was she wanted to ask. "I . . . wanted to ask . . . about Father."

Too, too much for one night. "What about Father?"

"Is he . . . ? Was he . . . ?" she hovered over the words, finally set them free. "Is he really my father?"

His headache exploded. "Blessed Lady, Jacobia! How can you ask that with Nakum in the room?" Jacobia burst into tears and fled toward her bedroom while a startled Nakum dashed for the door like a deer fleeing wolves. Sinking on Jacobia's vacated bench, he propped his head in his hands. "What do you make of all that?" he asked Rawn bitterly as the ghatt nudged at his leg.

What Rawn made of it he wasn't sure, but he wished he knew. Jacobia had driven all of Jenret's earlier daydream from his mind, and Rawn had no desire to remind him. Jenret hadn't slumbered, of that he was sure ... oh, tired, yes ... suggestible, perhaps ... but nothing more. Sometimes words weren't enough, even the intimacies of mindspeech, so he contented himself with purring, hoping the hypnotic sound would lull like waves rolling into shore. Too many vibrations in this place. Or mayhap Nakum's presence had triggered it, Rawn decided. Saam had mentioned the strange, tingling effect of Nakum's earth-bond. Perhaps it was affecting everyone. He'd have to ask Saam about it later.

❖

Provoking either man would be strangely easy, though to what she wasn't sure; the crosscurrents of their personalities pulled her first one way, then the other, and she refused to be swept in either direction, she decided as Muscadeine escorted her down the hallway, Jenret stock-still behind them, following no further.

They journeyed through winding corridors, up and down stairs until they entered a private part of the castle, living quarters for relatives, the late Queen's Ladies in Waiting. With a flourish he rapped and swung open the door after pausing for a response, inviting Doyce to enter first.

"We all need an island of safety, and I introduce you to mine," he murmured as he secured the door. An older woman, sable hair scattershot with silver, laid her needlepoint aside, stretched her hands toward Muscadeine. Her face bore vestiges of an earlier beauty, just as a flower's fallen petals serve as a reminder of its former radiant grace.

"Arras, you found time to visit your old Tantie." She airkissed both his cheeks as he took her hands. "And you bring someone to brighten the night with stories of distant places, other lives." Both hands now reached to clasp Doyce's, though the worry-marked blue eyes scanned by her, quick-searching the room and toward the door. "Ah, and without the pretty ghatta? I would have enjoyed meeting her as well."

Caught off-guard, Doyce realized that the ghatta had wandered and desperately scrolled her mental signature, calling her name. **"You weren't listening, were you? Saam and I are walking off our dinner outside. Am I needed?"**

Relieved, Doyce returned a genuine smile to the woman. "Khar's taking an evening constitutional." After a moment's thought, she told Khar, *"No, love, enjoy the fresh air. I'll call if I need you. Stay within my mindreach."*

Giving a reproving tap to the cheek that she'd last kissed, the woman asked, "Well, Arras, are you not introducing us?"

A playful gravity overtook Muscadeine as he extended a leg, winged the air with his arm and intoned, "I am honored to present Special Envoy Doyce Marbon of Canderis to the most esteemed Lady Fabienne Marie Elizalde Clairvaux, wife of Prince Maurice Louvois Diederick Clairvaux, Lord of the Nord and Defense Lord." A devilish grin slashed under the mustache as he finished, "The honorable Lady Fabienne is more familiarly known as Tantie, at least to me!"

She allowed her fingers to be taken and kissed. "And you, Harris Emile Glendower Muscadeine, dear nephew, are entirely too familiar."

"Harris!" It burst out before Doyce could stop herself. "Harris?"

"Ah, when you say it with such disapproval, it is not my name," he gave her a saucy wink but amplified. "More commonly pronounced 'Arras' 'ere. We tend to slide over our 'h's' and I answer more quickly to 'Arras' than 'Harris,' should you care to try." A subtle invitation to familiarity if she chose to act on it, but before she could decide Fabienne drew her toward a cozy table set with a bone china cha set and various decanters.

"No need for additional sweets, I think, though I can ring for those should you still be hungry. But another cup of cha, sipped and savored, and perhaps a digestif would soothe, no?" With a swish of skirts, she allowed Arras to seat her and offer Doyce the same courtesy before he himself sat.

The room was cool and uncluttered, decorated in shades of palest sand and limpid greens, sea shoal tones with coral touches vibrant as a seabed. Done exclaiming over the etched wave and fish pattern on her tiny glass of anise-flavored liquor, Doyce became aware that Fabienne had been assessing her. She came to the point immediately. "My nephew deduces that you are a woman of conviction and perhaps great courage, concerned with the truth regardless of its advantage or disadvantage to you. Given human nature, that's a rarity, but perhaps you Seekers are different than most. Further, he wishes you to know you have his unconditional support." Her cha cup clattered as she set it back on its saucer, its rattling the only betrayal of her nerves. "I, too, respect women of courage and conviction. Our late Queen was such a woman, and what little I possess of those qualities I learned from her, serving at her side for so many years. I miss her still—as friend, confidante, and queen." With an abrupt flick of her wrist, she swirled the cha dregs against the near-translucent sides of the cup, marking the designs. "Would that we had a cha leaf reader or your ghatta here to unravel the patterns, reveal the truth."

Listening without comment, Muscadeine slouched in his chair, legs extended, arms folded across his chest. Unhurriedly he retrieved his liquor glass, sipped, and at last spoke. "While your claims regarding our recent actions against Canderis require further discussion, some of us felt you must understand our other problems to perceive if yours may interlink with ours."

Ill at ease, she let her thumb roam over the repeating wave pattern on the glass. And by participating in this clandestine meeting had she already set unknown others against her cause? Still, hadn't she and Khar pondered some of these very things last night? "I take it you mean the problem of succession? If the late Queen and her brothers left no heirs, there still must be someone, however distantly related, to claim the throne?" The longer this issue remained unresolved, the longer it would take to reconcile Canderis and Marchmont. Not an appealing thought, being thrust slowly, inexorably into the middle of conflict in which she should play no part. Did Muscadeine count on her choosing sides so easily when she didn't even know which side was which? It struck her as a betrayal on his part—so much for his "unconditional support." And why hadn't he told her directly, but allowed Fabienne to pledge for him? A witness to his intentions? An oath binding them both?

"Exactement," commented Muscadeine, gloomy behind his mustache. Lady protect her, he couldn't have read her houghts, could he? Playing with her as Vesey had? She tried o slow her racing thoughts; he'd simply responded to her poken question.

"Not precisely, Arras," Fabienne corrected. "There are—nd there aren't—distant relations. Let me explain the family istory to you. As you've gathered from the portrait—yes, I now how Constant Minor persists in showing it off—Wilhelmina had two brothers, both considerably younger han she. After years of hope, Sebastien and Hortensia con-eived Maarten fifteen years after Wilhelmina's birth, and Ludovico another four years after Maarten.

"Wilhelmina's marriage to Baron Gaultier Urban Geri-ault was not childless, but none of the children survived. Such a sadness for a healthy, strong woman such as Wilhelmina, to suffer four miscarriages, one stillbirth, and ear three beautiful infants, none of whom survived more han two years. Such effort, such tragedy, all to ensure a hild to love, an heir to succeed her. To lose a beloved child, et alone so many, might have destroyed a lesser woman. It vould have destroyed me . . . is destroying me." Eyes tear-ilmed, she sought refuge at the darkened window, questing eyond the drawn drapes and the dark, as if reliving the joy-us hopes and fearful losses of each of Wilhelmina's preg-ancies.

Her voice grew thinner, more brittle. "Still, the laws of uccession cover such an eventuality, which meant that Maarten or his offspring stood next in line for the throne. Should his line falter, Ludovico came next, and his chil-dren."

"And were there children?" Doyce prompted.

Fabienne held a restraining hand, refusing to jump ahead of her story. "You must understand that for the longest time everyone—including Maarten and Ludo—assumed Wilhel-mina would produce an heir. Indeed, with both boys so much younger, she indulged them as she would have her wn children, cossetted them, allowed them their own inter-sts with no worry about the trappings of state and the de-mands of future rule. The boys were as different from each ther as night and day. Even Arras remembers that."

"Indeed, I was but a child when they both died, but old nough to clearly picture them, especially Maarten." Arras ook over the story, leaving his Tante to pour more cha, lasp the thin-walled cup as if to chase the chill of recited

deaths. "Interesting, though, that they both enjoyed the ou
doors, but in very different ways. As I trailed after Maarte
in the woodlands and meadows, I wasn't sure he notice
anything not right under his nose. Take out his book, foc
his magnifying glass, compare a flower or a leaf to the illu
tration, make notes and meticulous little sketches, secure th
flower in his press. He never knew whether the sky was bl
or cloudy, whether danger lurked or not. Everything was d
tail, detail, detail, fascinated by his books and the minutia
life." A gentle, reminiscent chuckle. "He let me tag alo
but sometimes forgot my presence.

"He taught me much, the importance of precision, of n
ticing little differences, of believing in the importance
books but not always trusting them when the flower itse
held the real answer. But," and he wriggled in his chai
aware of its confines, "can a boy stay still, mute, concentra
all that long when he wants to run, laugh, shout, pop fro
behind trees to surprise, shy pine cones at squirrels?"

"And even now you cannot stay still," chided Fabienn
"Maarten accused you of having ants in your pants."

As if to confirm her complaint, Muscadeine slithered a
writhed before abruptly stilling himself, melodrama va
quished, somber again. "Maarten was thirty when he die
and I but twelve. He died of exposure, caught in a sudd
storm that pounded icy rain and sleet all afternoon and nig
on the scarp we'd ascended to collect some flowers growir
in a crevasse. I'd sprained my ankle skidding on wet grave
and he broke his leg trying to block my fall. No shelter
sight, and he warmed me all night with his own body. W
were rescued the next morning, but Maarten died of pne
monia two days later."

Soundless tears streaked Fabienne's cheeks. "And Maa
ten was too interested in botany and books, too shy for mo
than a bashful interest in women, though Wilhelmina ha
convinced him he must marry—and with good reason." Ag
thinned hands wrung each other, twisted at too-large ring
one on her left thumb with a large, domed stone the col
and clarity of palest honey, set round with twisted silver.

As if against his better judgment, Arras pointed to th
ring. "Should you be wearing that?"

Protective, she shielded it with her right hand. "Hus
You sound as suspicious as Maurice. It may look like it, b

this one isn't Wilhelmina's, it's mine, although I've her ring hidden safe away. She entrusted it to me to ward until the new heir was found."

Arras persisted. "Still, I wouldn't wear that in public, or in private. Despite her size the Queen had dainty hands, no larger than your own, and her ring fit her perfectly. If I notice such things, Maurice may as well."

"I know, you're right. But just for tonight, just for the tale," she pleaded. "It comforts me, whether or not you approve or understand." The impetuous, intimate exchange left Doyce full of misgivings. Was she to pretend she wasn't aware or had she been subtly included, perhaps implicated by hearing their exchange? But Fabienne smoothed over the interruption, lifting her head in Doyce's direction. "You see, Ludo, poor Ludovico, died three years earlier, and he, too, without marrying and leaving any known heirs."

Doyce's ears pricked up at that. "Known heirs?"

"Aye, that's the rub." Muscadeine's dark eyes questioned his aunt.

She nodded, one decisive bob of her head, circling the large ring around her thumb, still contemplating the twin losses. Muscadeine again picked up the story's thread. "Ludo was everything Maarten wasn't—outgoing, full of sport, footloose and fancy-free with life and with women. He loved to explore, wander the length and breadth of Marchmont, hunt, fish, visit with the Erakwa, cross into Canderis when the spirit moved him. His diary entries record money settled on at least two women for children he sired, but he encoded the names and we don't know their identity. His death was unexpected as well, mauled by a bear."

"Did anyone try tracing his movements, tracking down the women?" Doyce asked. "Question his companions from that time?"

"I blush to say that we've located more women than you'd willingly count who claim or say they claim such a liaison with Ludo. An amorous fellow by all counts, and a good thing he began early since his life was short. But that was all so long ago that the trail grows thin. Ludo's probably a grandfather by now. We think we've determined the two women, but both are dead and both left children we've been unable to trace."

She measured one solemn face against the other, searching

for a way to delicately phrase her question. "Is a . . . is . . . an . . . illegitimate offspring allowed to inherit the throne? And if not, are there any other legitimate though distantly related possibilities?"

Like a delighted fox taunting the hounds, Muscadeine uttered a sharp bark of laughter. "You wish to know if we'll crown a bastard king?" He caught the bleak, closed-off anguish on Fabienne's face, paler than the room's palest sand colors, her sanctuary. "Ah, Tantie, Tantie, forgive me my outspokenness." Arras knelt at her side in silent apology and she sat with straight, frozen dignity, neither flinching at nor denying the vulgarity.

Rising at last, he poured more cha, curiously fussy and intent, ill-at-ease over his blunder. "The issue has never arisen before," and Doyce fought the urge to giggle at the double meaning, but Arras continued without noticing, "though I suspect some of our previous rulers produced by-blows in addition to their legitimate heirs. After much discussion, our feeling—or the feelings of most of the nobility—is that illegitimate offspring have a valid claim before the throne shifts to a more distant lineage.

"As to who would rule if Ludo's heirs cannot be located, then there are other possibilities, including Tante Fabienne's husband, Maurice, and various cousins of his."

"Maurice?" she asked, surprised. She had heard him style himself a prince but hadn't realized his nearness to the throne.

"Yes, heaven knows it's not as complicated as the pedigree the kennel master drew up for my Felix, but it feels it sometimes. Wilhelmina's father Sebastien had two younger brothers and two sisters—Danielle, Lucien, Ruina, and Quintijn. Again, following the rules of primogeniture, in the absence of any living heirs of Wilhelmina, Maarten, or Ludo, the children or grandchildren of Danielle would be next in line, followed by Lucien's line, Ruina's line, and Quintijn's line. Maurice is Quintijn's youngest son, youngest of the youngest of that lineage."

The names swarmed and swirled; she wanted to bat them away, clear her brain. "If the Queen didn't name an heir, why hasn't the next lineal descendant been determined? And how did Constant Minor come to be Steward?" Dinner sat heavy in her stomach, left her slow to grasp the obvious when it remained shrouded in mystery to her. Oh, to be out walking and thinking with Khar and Saam, letting her mind digest this confusion just as her stomach digested the heavy meal. Despite herself she stifled a yawn, but it crept back without warning, nearly splitting her face.

"Let the child sleep, Arras," Fabienne urged. "There will be other days or nights to explain ourselves."

"No, Tantie, I can't agree." Muscadeine stood beside Doyce, hand on her shoulder, and she conquered an absurd desire to have him pick her up and tuck her into bed. "I will defer Constant Minor's story, indeed, a tale so strange should be told in daylight, I think, but I will finish this story of succession."

"No, Arras, you shall not, for it isn't yours to tell. I was there at the end and you were not." Fabienne joined them, thoughtfully examining Doyce's face. "First, I shall answer one obvious question: There are other first cousins ahead of Maurice, including Quaintance Mercilot, no less, but none anxious to assume the crown, only Maurice. Never have I understood . . ." she drifted off, made a visible effort to pull herself together.

"As I said, I was there at the end. It was so sudden, so unexpected that we could not even call the Bannerjees in time to save her. Wilhelmina's dying words were these: 'Choose not too quickly Marchmont's new ruler, for a ghatt shall judge the truth.' She tried to say more, her eyes desperate, lips moving, but she had not the strength. And with a last intensity of effort, 'Wait for the ghatt!'

"Thus you can imagine our surprise, our consternation, when you and your group arrived from Canderis with four ghatti. Rumors have run rife, stories blown out of proportion in only a day. Nothing could be more foreign to our ways than what you and your ghatti represent. We don't know what your coming means, whether it truly bears on our problems, or if it's sheer coincidence. Foreigners are rare in Marchmont; we don't hate you, but we do fear you, what you may represent. Our turmoil is greater than before, and all because of you. You are our fate." Her fingers made a dismissive snapping sound. "Trade problems, border disputes are nothing compared to your potential as kingmakers. And winners are always paired with losers, remember that."

Fabienne reached for Doyce's hand, staring into her eyes as if waiting, praying for an answer, then she shrugged.

"Too much, too soon, I know. And you've been ill not so long ago, I can read the signs. Have Arras walk you to your room, sleep. Think about things tomorrow. Forget for now this tangled tale, worse than a fairy story." Dropping Doyce's hand she walked to the door while Doyce shook herself awake, shook the story from her like the dregs of a half-remembered dream. But the names, the personalities still floated before her face, leaving her half-tranced, overwhelmed, unsure.

Escorting her out, Muscadeine turned to bid his aunt good night. The door hid their faces, but not the desperate clarity of their rushed words. "Arras, has there been any word, any sign at all of Eadwin?"

"None, Tantie, none at all, but we're still looking. He can't have vanished off the face of the earth. We search whenever and wherever we can, in between our other duties."

Pain warped the sigh that followed. "I know, I know, Arras. I know you've done everything in your power to locate him. But I'm so alone, so very afraid. If you," she broke off, "*when* you find him, give him this. I promise it's not Wilhelmina's and is mine to give."

"Pax, Tantie, pax. We'll find him, my pledge on that." And emerging from behind the door, he waited until a key turned in the lock, and began walking Doyce down the hall.

Her brain felt rusty, eyes bleary, tired, and she rubbed at them, wondering if she should, indeed, wanted to ask one more question. Nor was she sure it was any of her business. She risked a glance at Muscadeine's face, mustache obscuring his expression, decided to risk it. "Who's Eadwin?"

"Tante Fabienne's son," but he gave no more identification than that, not slowing his walk. Her head began to pound in tempo to his footsteps, ribbon streamers of pain flashing as they wove through. But within a few paces the pain eased, as if someone rewove the damage, making her whole again.

Only after she'd undressed, opened the window a crack for Khar's return, and crawled under the covers did his answer strike her as slightly skewed. "Tante Fabienne's son?" Why not "Tante Fabienne's and Oncle Maurice's son?" She sank into the pillows and sleep fogged her brain.

❧

Lifting each paw high to elude the offending dampness, Khar shifted from the manicured lawn to the gravel path. Saam kept pace but remained on the lawn itself. "Don't you mind the dampness?" she whisker-flicked in falanese.

His eyebrow whiskers antennaed at her fussiness. "Feels like crushed velvet."

"Soggy velvet," she contradicted.

"Herb plantings to the right." He pointed with his chin, lower jaw working in anticipation. "Want to meander that way? Tender greens, sample a nip here and there."

They ambled, idling where it suited them, senses alert but at ease in the dark. With a supple leap, each sprang to the top of the herb garden's low enclosing wall and sat, companionable shoulders bumping. Luxuriating in the smells, Saam switched to mindspeech: falanese was fine except that all his facial muscles were involuntarily flickering, registering the scents. **"Basil, rosemary, tarragon. Ah ... anise, my favorite."** He separated each distinct odor, wafting the scents across the roof of his mouth. **"Anise, mmm! So ...?"** He let it dangle, noncommittal.

The tiger-striped ghatta swiveled her head, uneasy over something, Saam judged, but he didn't intrude. He reviewed his scent inventory, the noise of a munching rolapin confirming tiny lettuce leaves, when she spoke with a rush. **"It's the sound I don't understand. You heard too—at the audience, didn't you? I heard it even more distinctly at our private meeting when Constant Minor bent and gave me the milk dish."** She hesitated, muzzle screwed tight. **"Humans don't make sounds like that."**

"You mean the faint whirring, a sort of ticking sound from his belly?" Sam considered his own chest and stomach, licked once in a downward sweep to reassure himself of his own internal sounds.

"Whirring and clicking like a child's windup toy that's running down, that's what it sounded like. But what does it mean?"

"Mayhap he needs to be wound up," San tried for a touch of humor, bothered by Khar's concern. **"He's old enough to be running down. Very old, I'd say, older than any suspect. His sounds are the sounds of the past, somehow, shades of voices in my head like long-ago echoes."** What had made him say that? he wondered, and found he had no idea where the thought had come from. **"Do we like**

him?" He nudged her. "By the Elders, I sound like a human—'liking this' or 'not liking' that. Their likes and dislikes are so irrational, not based on truth."

"He makes the fur on my spine rise and ripple, that visceral automatic reaction that keeps us alive before we have time to think," Khar admitted. "A whiff of Elder Time around him, but I don't know why. Not-being, more than being, I think, but that may be because he's so old. Still, how can that be?"

Saam bristled in sympathy at her tension, no matter how she tried to disguise it. "Have you consulted the Elders? Turned the spirals to see if they will explain? If Mem'now were here he'd probably dredge up a suitable Minor Tale that even the Ancient Ones have forgotten."

Khar's claws rasped against the stonework, her agitation increasing. "No, no, not yet. I can't even form the question. First I must understand what I understand."

Abandoning his longing for lettuce, though his front teeth nipped together once in frustration, he flowed off the wall like warm syrup, heading toward the castle. Khar would catch up to him when and if she chose to do so. "Just don't wait too long to ask," he tail-flicked his farewell. "I'm for bed, now. How about you?"

She caught up, matched him stride for stride, but lost in her thoughts. Her sleep would be thin tonight, he knew.

For the sixth time Doyce realigned her papers, harrumphed a throat-clearing sound to attract attention. As usual, it didn't work. Aelbert finished some calculations, boxed the final figure, unperturbed by the chatter around him. The fifth day of discussions and negotiations felt more like the tenth, and she could envision five days more with nothing concrete to show. So this was diplomacy, politics? Out of the clear blue she thought of Darl Allgood, former Chief Conciliator in the grape-growing region of Wexler, and recently appointed High Conciliator. Knowing his plainspoken ways, his deflating humor, she couldn't imagine him enjoying his new role.

When she finished with meetings she had Nakum's reproachful expression to bear, the Erakwan lad sulking and mournful at her refusal to let him visit the arborfer nursery.

With nothing else to do, he'd taken to shadowing Ezequiel on his rounds and was now all too ready to explain the intricate placing of fish forks in a table setting. What good that skill would do him as a scout she didn't want to contemplate. Too bad Jacobia didn't seem to absorb as much from her time with Ignacio.

She'd met with the four Domain Lords, each responsible for a quadrant of Marchmont and all temporarily residing in Sidonie until an heir was selected. She'd met with various Ministration Lords, alone and in groups, and always it seemed that whoever attended didn't want or approve of what another Lord wanted, for whatever obscure reason. It made for a colossal headache, damn near a permanent state of affairs these days, she thought, mouth bitter after too much cha. Not only that, her bladder was full. She debated pounding the flat of her hand on the table to restore order but couldn't bring herself to do it.

Khar was curled on a chaise behind the table, Rawn stretched out beside her, sound asleep. N'oor sat at the farthest end of the chaise, prim as usual. Achingly bored as well, the ghatti were hampered by the lack of a formal request for them to Seek. **"So tell them it's time for a break,"** Khar murmured. **"If a full bladder made for quick solutions, you'd have resolved matters long ago."**

"I know, but if I let them out, they'll go haring off all over the place and I'll never gather them together again." Today she'd corralled Prosper Napier, Lord of the Ouest, Lysenko Boersma, Commerce Lord, and Faribault DeSaulniers, Exchequer Lord. Since the topic was trade with Gavotte and lake trade in general, it explained Napier's presence, since his lands abutted the Balaenas, and Boersma for commerce. Why DeSaulniers was present, she wasn't sure, but thought it must involve cash flow, or the lack thereof, given the trade stoppage. Acting as trade expert, Jenret exhibited all the telltale signs that revealed patience worn thin at their discord. Whatever Boersma pressed for, Napier vetoed, and vice versa. Although he'd said little, DeSaulniers seemed amenable to anything Napier wanted. That plus his ability to send Aelbert into convoluted reforecastings of import and export duties, projected cash flows, and anything else that left the aide feverishly re-adding and subtracting. It was enough to make her feel sorry for him, but he toted through each variation without complaint.

"Don't jump," she warned Khar, *"I'm going to pound for order, see if we can agree on a recess."* Her hand hovered but halted as Ezequiel slipped in, a piece of paper clutched in his hand. Initially reserved, Ignacio's grandson had been a godsend over the past few days, smoothing and expediting things as much as they could be. He displayed the qualities of a good chamberlain, able to anticipate in advance what was required, resourceful, deferential, but with little sparks of his own personality individualizing it. He rolled his eyes in commiseration, cocked his eyebrows in Boersma's direction and she nodded her permission to approach.

Deftly, he slipped the paper in front of Boersma, blocking Napier's view as the Commerce Lord slit open the note. "Truly?" he asked Ezequiel. Whatever the message was, it had restored his good humor. He leaned toward Jenret, whispering, but the confidence did nothing to improve Jenret's humor. Instead, he scowled, bit back an expletive, and Rawn came upright on the chaise in one easy move.

"Madame Envoy," Boersma had her attention now. "Might we adjourn this meeting until another day? Something urgent has arisen that I must see to."

DeSaulniers sniffed, a derisive sound that made it clear what he thought about calling a halt. "What can be more urgent than what we're discussing? It's not as if you're overwhelmed by trade supervision, and that's the point of this meeting, I might remind you. Resumed trade means funds in our coffers, funds that pay our troops, our public welfare needs." His mouth twisted into the half-sneer that Doyce had come to recognize and dread all too well. "Not to mention little incidentals such as food, servants, and so forth—all the comforts you take for granted stop short without money."

"I'm well aware, Faribault." Boersma tried to sound contrite, concerned, but she could sense his eagerness to be off. "No one's task has been made easier since the Queen's death. But Giselle Goelet has asked for a consultation." He smiled as if he'd played a trump card. "I know it's difficult to accept, but affairs of justice can be as important as monetary affairs."

Before they could start quibbling again, Doyce slammed her hand on the table, breaking the impasse. "Then we're adjourned until . . . ?" she checked with Aelbert as he opened his agenda book, "tomorrow after lunch?"

"Done, then." Boersma was already halfway across the

room. "Wycherley, sure you don't want to come with me?" But Jenret shook his head, dark brows still knit together, pencil digging deep into his note pad, punching little holes in it.

DeSaulniers and Napier gathered their papers, talking amongst themselves while she excused herself and tried for a stately, unhurried walk to the nearest lavatory. Once outside, she scampered, giving a little hoot of anxiety.

Returning for her notes, she found Ezequiel still in the room, aligning the chairs, straightening up, noting chores to be done by servants. "A good meeting?" he asked and grinned. "Sorry, it's the polite inanity I'm supposed to ask. Always think positive, that's Grandfather's rule."

She grinned back, propped her hip on the table. "Do you people ever reach a consensus, let alone a decision on things?"

"Yes, we do. I'm sorry you have to see us like this now." He fiddled with the chair in front of him, checking the indentations the legs made on the carpet, positioning the chair exactly in its place.

Not fair to tease the boy; it wasn't his fault things weren't going well. "Ezequiel, I haven't really been outside since we arrived, and I'm about to go stir-crazy. There're some people I'd like to visit—if I knew where to find them. Perhaps you could give me directions?"

"Better yet, if I know, I'll take you there myself. I should be free until it's time to start supervising the evening meal. If Grandfather sees me leaving, I'll wave a list and tell him I'm bargaining with suppliers. He won't be fooled, but he'll pretend he is." He made a moue of mock dismay. "And give me a list that I really *will* have to attend to. Now, who is it you want to visit?"

"A couple named Wyn and Dwyna Bannerjee, eumedicos. I assume they must live at the Hospice here in the city." And wasn't prepared for the almost imperceptible tightening of his face, indeed, of his entire body. She could see him calculating, weighing his options: pretend ignorance as to knowing them and where they lived, remember a task to be done, distract her with another idea.

He relaxed, ran his tongue along his upper teeth, still thinking. "Does Jules Jampolis know you know of them?" At her negative headshake he relaxed further, came to a decision. "Then *don't* let him know you're visiting. There's no

love lost between them. You see, they used to jointly hold
the title of Public Weal Lord, the position Jampolis holds
now. They resigned right after the Queen's death and
Maurice appointed Jampolis as Acting Ministration Lord."

"Maurice? I should think that would be up to the Steward." It didn't make sense to her. Maurice was powerful,
with his double title of Domain Lord and Defense Lord, but
she hadn't realized he could appoint Ministration Lords.

Ezequiel took pity on her confusion. "Domain Lords select Ministration Lords, and three out of the four voted for
Jules Jampolis. The ruler, in this case the Steward, has the
right to veto choices. Constant Minor granted conditional
approval until a new heir is crowned."

"So, do you know where the Bannerjees live?" She was
so heartily tired of politics she thought she might scream.

"Oh, yes, of course. Everyone knows where they live.
Though I think it might be wiser if I took you there by some
side streets I know."

She didn't know why this mattered, but as long as it got
her outside and walking, she didn't care. "So shall we go?"

"Are you sure you can find your way back?" Ezequiel
queried one more time from where he stood in the street
while she paused at the top of the landing.

Not to be outdone, she asked, "Are you *sure* this is the
right place? It doesn't look like a hospice to me." But relented as far as reassuring him, reciting, "Turn left when I
leave. Cross over two streets, then right. Cross six more
streets, not seven or I'll be on Taverner's Lane. Right again
until I hit the back alley where the castle supplies are delivered." She forestalled him, "And no, you don't have to wait
and spoil your afternoon. Besides, if I forget my lefts and
rights, Khar will remind me. Now be off with you, shoo!
And don't *you* stop at Taverner's Lane."

With a wave he trotted off, long legs so like his grandfather's but without the striding, stilted gait; his were coltish-
gangly and long, hosen constantly knee-ruckled and
ankle-bagged. Front paws planted on the door sill, Khar
sniffed the door, its blue paint faded and shabby, three diamond window panes dusty. The building had been whitewashed recently enough to still look fresh, the freshest

hing in this rundown neighborhood with its dirt streets,
lingy houses and shops, and brawling, tumbling children
who considered the street their yard. Few of the adults
they'd passed on their way over had met her eyes, their
gaze sweeping across her face and taking in the ghatta,
walking in the middle of the street, or hugging close to the
buildings as if her sleeve-touch might contaminate.

"Smells like a eumedico place." Khar's pink nose wrinkled in the air. **"Wouldn't that bracket hold the three lanterns at night?"**

She considered, sniffed the air as well for the telltale scent
of disinfectant, "eumedico perfume," as they'd jokingly
called it. No eumedico, no hospice could ever completely escape the sharp, disinfectant smell, something she'd gotten
used to during her years of training. "It's too small, not
much more than a house," she protested, "not enough space
for contagion rooms, wards, labs, offices."

"Not everything has to be big to be good." Khar
wrapped herself around Doyce's knees, tried to ignore a sailing apple core that almost grazed her head. **"Now use the
knocker, please. I hate to mention it, but that's not the
first thing thrown since we've been standing here. I'd
rather not wait to see what else they've collected."**

She raised the knocker and rapped a brisk tattoo, harder
than intended as she ducked an egg smashing beside the
door, yolk rawly bright against the white wall. It made her
think of her first meeting with Maurice, dressed in his crocus yellow and purple, the stemlike green legs. Without
waiting, she thumbed the latch and put her shoulder to the
door, hoisting it open and darting inside, Khar two steps
ahead of her. A stone rattled against the door, and she
heaved it shut, fumbled in the half-light for a bolt or latch of
some sort to secure it. Raucous childish chants blurred, although she caught, "Stranger's a danger, naa, naa!"

"What's going on out there? Can't you keep the noise
down, we've sick people here." The white coat floated in the
semi-gloom as he came down the narrow stairs, the same
sort of lab coat that Mahafny wore so proudly, that she'd
once worn with the same pride. She inhaled and felt as if she
were home again. "If it's an emergency, then sing out," the
voice continued and at last she made out a face, short blond-
ish hair, a somewhat darker, almost ruddy beard, though

close cropped. Young, probably just finished training, sh
judged.

"My apologies." She stuck out her hand. "I usually wa
to be admitted, but your street children don't need addition
target practice. I'm Doyce Marbon." He shook automat
cally, a firm grip but soft, well-cared-for skin—the consta
washing, the need for unblemished, sensitive hands.

He peered through the lowest pane, something sh
couldn't accomplish even on tiptoe. Rapping on the glass, h
opened the door, stuck out his head. "Arvon, Tace, Aloi
Blanchette! Get home with you or I'll double-dose you th
next time your mother brings you in!" Back inside, he no
ticed her wincing at the noise. "Broke our own rule. I'm i
for it now. Still, those neighborhood children need a pad
dling. Now what can I . . ." he broke off, catching sight o
Khar's shadow-striped figure. "Sweet Lady, what in th
name of heaven is that beast?" He was backing clear, search
ing for something to put between himself and Khar.

Khar took one step forward, then plopped on he
haunches. "Yeeow? Merow?" **"That's my cat imitation.**
love imitating a cat. You could suggest those urchi
planned to hang me by my tail, I suppose."

"And you do it so well, love, you've convinced me yc
were a cat," Doyce 'spoke back, trying not to laugh. *"No*
behave or I'll hang you by your tail and deliver you to tho
charming children." Khar muttering about some peop
lacking humor, she answered the eumedico. "It's a ghatta,
female of the ghatti species, not terribly common in thes
parts, I understand. Perfectly harmless, though." Clearly d
bious, the eumedico did succeed in holding his ground. "I'
here to see the Bannerjees, Wyn and Dwyna Bannerjee. I u
derstand they work here?"

"Yes. Yes, they do." He'd squatted, still poised for escap
if necessary, striving for a better look while Khar sat, pree
ing at the attention. "I'd no idea they were that . . . large.
fine specimen."

"I don't like it when they use that word!" Khar dre
herself upright in insulted hauteur. For that matter Doyc
found she wasn't that fond of the word either, too mar
memories of Vesey and Evelien in it. "The Bannerjees," sh
reminded him.

He rose with reluctance, unable to take his eyes off Kha
"I'll see if one or the other is available. They're on roune

now, not the best time to visit, but perhaps they can spare a moment. Wait right here if you would." Backing until his foot hit the first step, he finally turned to climb the stairs, still looking over his shoulder. "What did you say your name was?"

"Doyce Marbon. Tell them I'm a friend of Mahafny Annendahl, if you would, please."

The wait wasn't long, the young eumedico now guiding her into a cramped office, two desks shoved together to form an "L", shelves brimming with books, scribbled reports, beakers and vials of chemical compounds, and a few containing various parts of peoples' anatomies, an appendix here, gall stones there, a solitary finger suspended, pointing accusatively. It had never bothered her when she was training, but it did now, these random, floating specimens. **"Ooh! Just like jars of pickles!"** Khar announced in wonderment. **"Look! That jar on the floor, doesn't that look like tripe at the butcher's?"**

Doyce swallowed the excess saliva flooding her mouth, prelude to a queasiness she wasn't sure she could conquer. Blast the ghatta for her literal-mindedness! A sound behind her made her spin around, glad to look in another direction. A spice colored woman, complexion a nutmeg tint with highlights of cinnamon, braided hair a lustrous black, hesitated at the threshold, fluttering, shifting, as if looking for a perch. Against the darkness of her coloring, aquamarine eyes stood out as totally incongruous. With a gentle, fluting laugh she swayed by Doyce, her white coat partially obscuring the strange garments beneath, a skirting of sheer material wrapped and gathered around her waist, midriff bare and then a matching top in the same parrot green shade. A green and red striped stole hung over the white-coated shoulders, gold tasseled ends tucked inside each elbow, a delicate chime of bangles accompanying her movements.

Having gained her desk, the woman sat, aquamarine eyes wide, little chirping laughs muffled by a hand over her mouth, a hand with a giant square-cut emerald ring. "So, you are Doyce Marbon? I am Dwyna Bannerjee. Wyn will be along shortly. How is Mahafny?"

As Doyce started to explain, a distant bell rang twice, a summoning signal. Dwyna Bannerjee floated by with a graceful, deceptive quickness that took her from the room before Doyce could even move clear. "You will excuse,

please," drifted behind her. Khar settled on the scrap of
carpet that extended just beyond the desks while Doyce
liberated a chair from its burden of papers, dragged a
pharmacopeia from the shelf.

Within a chapter she was immersed in it, reveling in the
herbal section's precise line drawings, flipping pages, reading a section, halting to admire a hand-tinted plate. **"Company,"** Khar announced as Dwyna reentered the office,
scanning shelves, dragging fingers across book spines until
locating the one she wanted. Her emerald sparkled in the
light.

Clearing her throat, Doyce rose, book held to her chest. "I
can come back another day if it's more convenient."

The figure whirled, hand to mouth in shock. "Who the
devil are you!" she blurted. "How did you get in here?"

"I . . . but you said . . ." And didn't know what else to say.
**"Humph. Remarkable likeness, remarkable, but not
one and the same."** Khar appeared to be hugely enjoying
her quandary. **"And you thought telling M'wa and P'wa
apart was difficult."**

Twins? Identical twins? She thought hard: Dwyna at the
desk, hand covering her mouth, the ring. Right hand. The
ringed hand trailing across the books just now, left hand.
And the stole this woman wore had somewhat narrower
green but wider red stripes, while the first stole had been the
reverse. "Wyn?" she tested the name, saw the aquamarine
eyes blink in surprise. "I'm Doyce Marbon, an old acquaint-
ance of Mahafny Annendahl. Dwyna left me here for a bit
while she tended to an emergency."

Wyn Bannerjee sagged against the bookshelves, striping
the arm of her white coat with dust. "Observant, aren't you?
More observant than I. Mutual apologies for startling each
other. Then I take it you haven't seen Dwyna recently?" As
if on cue, Dwyna's head popped around the door casing.

Both began to giggle, a high, soft sound like aviary birds
with reed flutes tied to their pinions, whistling and whispering through the air when they flew. At some hidden signal
the laughter ended simultaneously. Dwyna advanced, placed
herself side by side with her twin. The same startling gem-
like eyes, the same dark, braided hair, the same generous,
curvaceous build with perhaps just a touch of plumpness to
it, especially at the waist. And older than Doyce had first estimated, younger than Mahafny but older than herself, per-

haps fifty. Worst of all, Doyce wondered if her face reflected her worry as to who would begin and who would end a sentence, just as she'd worried in the past with Bard and Byrta.

"Oh, don't frown, we're easy enough to tell apart," Dwyna said, grasping her sister's arm. "Wyn's the solemn one, and I'm the silly one." She winked at her sister. "That *is* a ghatt with you, isn't it? May we examine it?"

Doyce outraced Khar's mindcry of outrage. "She is *not* about to be examined," and felt the hostility in her own voice.

Wyn stopped a neat distance from Khar, ears laid back, ready to snarl and strike. "No, no, not like that. I'm sorry. That would be interesting—but rude. Does it, she," she corrected herself, "head isn't broad enough for a male, I don't think, do you, Wyn? Does she enjoy being petted? She's so lovely!"

And in short order Dwyna and Wyn were ensconced on the floor, tickling Khar's chin, rubbing her ears, admiring her ear hoop and garnet rosette. Khar twined her tail around Wyn's wrist and the eumedico captured the tip, bent it to tickle Khar's nose. Waggling a pencil under the edge of the carpet, Dwyna tried to steal Khar's attention from her twin. This meeting wasn't going as she'd planned, Doyce decided. Not a meeting in Marchmont had so far, so why should this be different? Retrieving her book, she squeezed by the Bannerjees and sat at a desk. Both looked up, repentant, and scrambled off the floor.

"Our apologies. Seldom do we meet such captivating creatures." Wyn gave a final tickle to Khar's chin, the ghatta purring.

"Khar, don't act the fool," Doyce warned. *"You're behaving as if you'd sell your soul for a scrap of affection."*

Khar decided to wash a hind foot, obscure her face. **"There's something tantalizing about them, a potentiality, a similarity of spirit, something . . ."**

But before Khar could explore the idea any further, Dwyna spoke. "So Mahafny sent you to us. And not to catch up on old times, because she was never one for that."

Resting her chin on the heavy book, Doyce considered what to say, how to say it. What precisely had she come here for? Simply the need to get out, talk to someone new who wouldn't argue and obstruct? Inquisitiveness? Information? Aid?

The twins laughed, polite behind their hands, bracelets falling with a soft, metallic rush of sound. "So. Come tour the hospice first, think of why you're here as we go." Without waiting for further invitation, Doyce followed them.

❖

It was dark when the twins eased her out the door with fluttery little pats of affection, dove-crooning their goodbyes to Khar. "Sure you know the way now?" "Absolutely sure?" Their words bubbled and flowed over each other's until she no longer knew which was which. As the door closed behind her, she started down the steps, only to stop and sit on the lowest one, overwhelmed, determined to seek her bearings, both geographical and mental. She shook her head, wishing all the little pieces would fall in place.

"An absolute wellspring of information." Khar sat beside her, but disinclined to say anything more than **"My, my, my ..."** The ghatta was equally dazzled.

The twins had been both amazingly forthcoming and maddeningly indirect, freely dropping nuggets of information, delicately alluding to things ranging just beyond her coherent thoughts, tantalizing but evasive. At least she'd gained another perspective on some of the personalities at court, including Maurice's heavy reliance on his royal arborfer monopoly, cutting the dwindling supply, wantonly harvesting his own source of income with no concern for future arborfer growth. If so, that certainly should make him desirous of the funds a trade reconciliation would bring.

Balancing against her elbows, she decided she approved of small, community hospices, rather than an imposing giant one. The eumedicos gained closer contact with the people they served and the setting in which they lived. And although secretly relieved at no longer serving as joint Public Weal Lords, the twins clearly held no love for Jules Jampolis. But their amused reaction at her mention of Constant Minor had been puzzling and hardly helpful. Their blue eyes had locked, a multitude of thoughts exchanged within a glance. Apologetic over their exclusion, Wyn's dimple flashed on her left cheek as she suppressed a smile, "So, Constant is awake at last?"

"According to Ignacio Lauzon he's awake all the time,"

she'd shot back and wondered why they found it so divert-ing.

"**Well, mayhap you weren't talking about the same thing. There's just one thing, though ...**"

Bless the ghatta's loyalty, she thought. *"What, dear?"*

"**I really wouldn't loiter here, sitting and thinking.**" Khar jitter-pranced to entice her to follow.

The ghatta appeared eager, but not anxious, and she wasn't sure what the problem was. *"Are those little monsters sneaking up on us? Have they rearmed themselves with eggs?"*

"**No, I'm afraid it's worse than that ... oh, too late. You're so slow sometimes.**"

"Doyce!" An ebullient shout slurred through the night. "Tol' ol' Nakum we'd find you! Tol' him I could track you anywhere better'n he could." Jenret hove into view, stump-ing along, one foot in the gutter, the other on the plank side-walk, silhouette rising and falling as he negotiated each step. Nakum trailed behind, arms folded, face inscrutable.

"Didn't wanna go with Lysenko ... but woulda gone any-where with you. Anywhere! Should ... shouldn'ta left with-out telling me." The liquor almost masked his concern, but not quite. He aimed a playful punch at her shoulder. "Sort of detoured finding you, though. Marvelous street back there, abso-lute-ly mar-ve-lous! Come along with us, there's one place we haven't tried yet." Impeccable as always, dapper in black, but with that lock of dark hair springing free over his eye, as it so often did when he was in the grip of some strong emotion. His pale face glistened as if lightly misted, and from his breath she knew all too well he'd already been drinking. Rawn sat at his feet, muzzle primly screwed as he stared Jenret up and down, then looked away stolidly, as if ignoring the whole issue would make it disappear. When it did not, the ghatt motioned for Saam to follow and they crossed the street, greeted Khar nose-to-nose, and huddled in private commentary.

Dusting herself off as she rose, she wondered how to drag Jenret home without causing a commotion. Over Jenret's shoulder Nakum's eyebrows rose to eloquent new heights of self-control. Still, while Jenret was drunk, she didn't think he was *that* drunk, she had certainly seen him worse. He'd been drinking too much, had been for some time. Why? Lady knew the negotiations were frustrating, endlessly circular. But wasn't it to his advantage to remain patient, talk with as many officials as possible, discover what had gone wrong with the trade negotiations? If anything, he was using tonight's spree as a cover, pretending concern for her unexplained absence. And since when did she have to report her whereabouts to him? Well, Taverner's Lane was on the way home, and after the day she'd had, from mule-headed obduracy to verbose circumlocutions to this, a drink would be welcome.

Gruff but pleading, Rawn murmured, **"Please do anything to make him happy and head him toward bed. My patience has worn thin."**

"Meaning I shouldn't cross either of you?"

"Only at your own risk." He shook his head as Khar batted him, catching his ear hoop with her claw. **"Oow! I told you I was in a bad mood, but yes, I was overexaggerating, and you know it."**

Doyce thumped the ghatt's shoulder in sympathy, and linked her arm through Nakum's, pulling him after Jenret. Cruel, but she couldn't resist it, "Well, Nakum, have you had an interesting evening so far?"

"Not nearly as interesting as I'm sure you'll have." His honeyed tones reminded her of Ignacio and his grandson.

No need to share a table, in fact, that entire side of the room had cleared, people resettling, wedging into more crowded spots, grumbling at their presence before returning to their drinking. Hardly an elegant establishment, the Green Fir's patrons mostly appeared to be the adult counterparts of the urchin crew she'd met in the street earlier. Hardworking folk, eking out a living, overly suspicious, with no inclination to drink or talk with strangers. Strangers to them might well be anyone who lived three streets away from their tight little enclave. And since no one showed any curiosity or inclination to discuss life in distant Canderis with them, Jenret had gained her undivided attention. She'd desperately tried to include Nakum in their conversation, but he sat in mute rebellion in the corner of the booth, back to the wall, staring beyond them.

Strangely, Jenret's diction had improved with further drinks, as if his slurred speech were a reaction to something other than the liquor. How long could she nurse her ale before he noticed?

"Not long enough," Rawn grumbled. **"He'll go on all night if you let him."** The three ghatti huddled beneath the table, lost in the shadows and out of sight. A drop of ale leaked through a crack in the trestle; Saam startled as it hit square between his eyes. *"Sorry, Saam."*

As a fresh pitcher of ale appeared, Doyce glumly weighed the amount left in her mug, gave up, and downed it. How much did the pitcher hold? **"If you really want to know,"** Saam offered as Khar polished the ale off his face, **"About four of his mugs to one of yours. Nakum and I counted before. Actually,"** he confided to Doyce, **"Nakum doesn't feel very well—he drank two mugs."**

Jenret's voice wove around and through her, intimate, confiding, soothing, and she brought her attention back with a start. What was he talking about? Half-hanging across the table, head bent toward hers, breath warm on her cheek and ear, Jenret had gained possession of her hand, holding it tight, his other hand pinning her arm to the table. "Don't you agree, Doyce?" His persistence increased. "Well, don't you? It's so clear to me." His fingers stroked the back of her hand. How had she let him come so close?

"Khar!" she practically screamed out loud. *"What in the name of the merciful Lady are we discussing? Ship trade? Reciprocal trade tariffs? What? He isn't making a fool of himself, is he? Talking about ..."* she couldn't finish the sentence, *"... you know."*

"He's imparting—with great confidentiality and concern, I might add—some interesting gossip that came his way this afternoon when the meeting was adjourned." Khar paused for dramatic effect until Doyce poked her with her toe. **"He's been yearning to ask your advice about the fact that Syndar Saffron is here in Marchmont, hot on Jacobia's trail. That's what Lysenko Boersma's message concerned. You know, the one he received from the Justice Lord. I believe his last direct question to you involved what he should tell Jacobia."**

Thunderstruck as well as relieved, she realized she'd been staring with rapt eyes at Jenret all the time she listened to Khar's abridged version of the conversation. "Ah." A weak response, but the best she could manage. "I see."

"Exactly, but what am I going to do? What should I tell

her?" His fingers now intertwined with hers. "What does she know about love?"

"Nothing." Her response came quick and to the point as she retrieved her hand. "Absolutely nothing right now, because she's here—along with Aelbert and Arras Muscadeine. What did you do, hang a sign proclaiming this the tavern of choice for Canderisians away from home?" Dismayed, she waved the three over, the crowds joking and yielding as Muscadeine passed, more pleasantry than they'd shown the strangers.

If she'd hoped the new arrivals would improve the evening, she'd judged wrongly. Crammed between Nakum and Muscadeine, Doyce watched the evening degenerate, Jenret arrogant, showing off, now insisting on ordering finer and finer wines, flinging gold pieces at the bar maid when Muscadeine tried to pay. Cutting remarks knifed past Aelbert's ears, and he controlled himself, circumspect, casting little, sidelong glances that Jenret always construed as suppressed disapproval of everything he said. Each time Jenret's voice reached a new elevation, the ghatti cringed.

"Is he usually so theatrical as this?" Muscadeine tilted her head toward him so he could catch her ear. "What next?"

She watched with growing horror as Jenret rose, sure he was going to swing at Aelbert. Catching at his arm, she dragged him back. "Don't, Jenret. You're angry at things, but don't make Aelbert your target. It's not his fault," she pleaded, shamed for him if he couldn't be ashamed for himself that Muscadeine was seeing him act the fool.

"Don't ... what?" Hazy amusement in his eyes at her plea. "Rather you'd say 'do' than 'don't,' but what am I not supposed to do?"

"Don't hit him," she said between gritted teeth.

"Wasn't planning to ... yet." Sweeping up a wine bottle, he emptied it and tossed it aside, the bottle rattle-rolling across the floor, silencing the tavern. He had a full audience now. "I thought you meant don't piss! That's a relief, because if you'd meant that, I don't think I could've complied. Excuse me, please."

He'd planned his exit to be debonair but unsteady albeit for one thing: N'oor chose that instant to push her way to Aelbert's side, and Jenret went sprawling, the contents from his half-open money purse scattering, dancing goldens, silvers, and coppers, the usual odds and ends, lucifers, a pen knife, a twist of paper with something inside. "Don't worry, I'll pick it up when I get back," he declaimed grandly as Muscadeine righted him with one powerful heave.

"The jake's out back," Muscadeine pointed. "And we're leaving as soon as you return."

Aelbert crawled on his knees along with Jacobia, earnestly sweeping coins into a cluster, helping pour them back into the bag. Sliding along the bench, Doyce vaguely saw him thrust the twist of paper into his pocket. No matter, Jenret didn't need his scraps returned. At least the evening and this display were over.

Only N'oor paid any attention. **"I didn't mean to . . ."** she wailed at Saam, closest to the uproar. **"I'll make him give it back later, it's just a twist of paper."** Saam's lower jaw thrust forward, but he said nothing.

Later than she'd suspected, she thought as, arm and arm with Muscadeine, they made their somewhat unsteady way back from the tavern to the citadel. Aelbert had copied the Capitain's gesture, offering a courteous arm to Jacobia, while Nakum lagged behind, shepherding Jenret, his boots scuffing, clattering against paving stones, counterpoint to his petulant comments on a host of topics. Nakum, having nursed two small beers the entire evening, appeared the soberest of them all, but she'd noticed his usual coppery complexion was tinged green with nausea.

Only a few lights sparked in castle windows as a beacon, although Arras knew his way through the twists and turns of the streets, past shuttered shops, good-humoredly chivvying the occasional night watch they met. Lady be thanked Muscadeine had found them at the tavern. A lucky coincidence . . . or more than that?

"What do you think?" Khar asked, padding beside her. **"My guess is that it's the tenth tavern he checked after Jacobia told him Jenret had started looking for you."**

"Most likely," she agreed internally. Luckily, Arras seemed content to stroll, shortening his pace to match hers, conversing lightly on anything that caught his fancy, but demanding little in return, and for that she was grateful.

Arras Muscadeine's unexpected arrival with the others had been a Lady-sent gift of distraction, a breath of sober

sanity, although he'd matched Jenret drink for drink, emptying more flasks of wine than she'd thought possible. The relief now at being outside in the damp, fresh air, free of the
tang of smoke and beer, made her give a little skip at Arras's
side. She shivered, almost yawned, and let Muscadeine
throw his cloak around her, drawing her close. "A long day,"
he murmured, tightening her against the warmth of his side.
"The meetings start again early in the morning."

Her arm slipped around his waist, easier to balance her
stride with his. "For whatever good it does," she acknowledged with a wry smile. And then, as if apology were necessary, or at least the need to confess her own inability to
understand, "I don't know what makes him act like this
lately." She tossed her head over her shoulder to indicate
Jenret.

"You don't?" He was honestly surprised at her ignorance.
"There is none so blind as she who will not see."

Jerking her arm away, she turned into his arms, straining
up at his face in the dark. "Will not see what?"

An index finger tapped her nose and she snatched it, ag-
gravated at the reprimand. "What's in front of your face. It's
not my place to explain it to you. Ask Jenret, if you must."

With that they crossed through the citadel gates, Muscadeine returning the guards' salutes, and continued on into
the formal side garden with its marble benches and twisted
trees, its flower beds showing the early spikes of spring
flowers, a few hardy buds. "Shall we go in now? You're
ready for bed, and I still have a few things to check with
Ignacio. From the lights on, I suspect he's still up."

She stretched and yawned. "A good idea. Later, then."
And it seemed the reasonable thing to give Muscadeine a
brotherly kiss on the cheek, silent gratitude for his timely arrival tonight.

But Jenret had caught up with them, and was putting his
hand on her shoulder, pulling her around and away. "Doyce,
wait! I want to talk with you, please? Alone?"

The thought of bed was inviting, but she stifled it ill-
humoredly. "Oh, all right." Discreetly, Muscadeine waited a
few paces ahead, and Nakum and Saam joined him, the three
regarding them with an air she could only describe as reproving. At least Aelbert and Jacobia had gone inside without pausing, two less, although N'oor remained, hesitant,
torn between the evening air and the warmth of bed. "I

won't be long," she promised. "Go ahead without me." Perhaps now she could find out what was eating at Jenret, though she wished it could wait till morning. Still, that old adage about truth found in the bottom of a wineglass had a point—or more likely, that wine simply loosens the tongue, she decided.

As the others bade them good night, Jenret drew her along a tree-lined path, sat her on a polished granite bench. The cold leached into the backs of her thighs, her bottom, and she gave an involuntary shiver. His usual elegance wine-blurred, he draped his cloak over her, played with the collar around her face. It felt very unlike Muscadeine's comradely cloak-sharing a few moments past.

"Rawn and I are going to take a little stroll. He's in a gloomy mood tonight," Khar announced as she and the black ghatt trotted down the path.

She pushed his hands away, impatient over the fussing. *'Who's gloomy, Rawn or Jenret?"* she 'spoke back.

A tiny ghatti laugh reached her. **"Rawn. Oh, the burdens we ghatti have to bear from our Bondmates."** A minute pause, and then she heard, **"Oh, good evening, N'oor."** Khar sounded less than gracious, she could tell, but the great black ghatt's ears perked up. **"Yes, of course we'll join you on the wall."** Khar turned her attention back to Doyce. **"Call when you're ready to go in."**

Jenret still stood in front of her, hands balanced on her shoulders, a little too personal, too intimate, and she stiffened involuntarily, hoping he'd register her dislike for such intimacy without having to say so. "The ghatti deserve a little time on their own as well," he remarked. "We've all been too jammed together, always in groups, never any chance alone." He hesitated, swung his head in Rawn's direction and chuckled, low and familiar. "And I think Rawn has a yen for N'oor. Of course, she doesn't care a whit. I know what that's like." His thumb, seemingly unconsciously, was stroking the line of her jaw.

She jerked her head, and that was a mistake, for she was staring straight into his eyes now, and she knew she'd been trapped. His hands slid down and locked on her upper arms, lifting her off the bench and into his embrace, kissing her. "Why him, why not me? Why?" Without warning, he tumbled her down, the ground slamming her back, granite bench

grazing her head, stinging pain to counteract the den.
weight boring down on her, imprisoning her.

"Jenret!" she wedged an arm in front of her to shove hi
clear, but she was pinned, entangled in the cloak and in h
arms. Frustrated, she squirmed again, bucked, but he pe
sisted, tearing at her clothes, dragging them open. She didr
know whether to laugh in hopes of shaming him, or cry
scream. Screaming would be an embarrassment, she ought
be able to cope without bringing someone running to h
aid. "Jenret!" she tried again, hissed in his ear, "Stop it!"

But he was beyond hearing, wild with an unbridle
strength. He'd forced himself between her legs, working
the laces on his pantaloons with one free hand, the oth
hand encompassing both her wrists, pinning them above h
head. "Waited so long for this ... wanted it so badly!"
panted, almost crying. "And then you tell him 'later' whe
you don't really care for him, can't really care for him! If I
can have you, why can't I? Don't you understand? Can't ye
feel, don't you feel what I feel? Are you *immune* to fee
ings?" Gasping, she wrenched one hand free and slamme
the heel of her palm under his chin, jolting his head bac
He recaptured it with a growl of pain and continued jar
ming down his pants.

"Oooh, what *are* they doing?" N'oor asked in the midd
of her conversation with Rawn and Khar. **"Look, ov
there!"** Both Khar and Rawn whirled, Khar snarling ug
and low in her throat. **"Wouldn't it be easier if he bit t
back of her neck and took her from behind?"** N'oor co
tinued, interested, craning to see over the other two ghatt

Poised to launch herself to rescue Doyce, Khar felt Raw
shove her aside. **"The damnable fool!"** he thundered, **"Ru
ting and lusting like that!"** as he soared off the wall in
the night, guided by the pale flashes of Jenret's buttock
glowing moonlight-white.

She struggled again, the gravel grinding into her ba
through the cloak's fabric, the inexorable thrusting weight
his body trapping her. Damn all, she thought desperately,
am going to be raped! A part of her deep inside wanted
yield, have it over and done with, go on, but another part
herself refused to make it easy. Frantic, she opened h
mouth to scream, but he ground his mouth over hers, tee
crushing her lower lip.

And then the weight was gone, a curdled scream of pa

as he rolled and scrambled wildly, curling to protect his privates. "Lady Mother! Lady Bright, what have you done, Rawn?" He was shivering, pulling clear, the black ghatt stalking him like an inexorable nightmare, muzzle curling in contempt, fangs bared. Jenret's eyes leaked tears, teetering on the brink of hysterical laughter. "Oh, Lady, Lady, *what* have I done?"

"If you ever indulge yourself like that again, I will slash your butt," Rawn snarled. "You will not demean any female's honor like that, not without her willingness. Must I dose you with our 'script like a lust-sick ghatt who prowls and yowls, mounts any female in sight?" Rawn reared on his hind legs, outstretched claws flashing a warning near Jenret's face.

Half repelled, half fascinated, she gathered her clothes around her, watching the confrontation play itself through. Despite herself she winced in sympathy at the thought of Rawn's flashing claws lancing Jenret's bare buttocks. Decently clothed, she rolled upright, preparing to escape while she still could. Anger at her helplessness still boiled within her, and worst of all, anger that someone she considered a friend, someone she trusted would do this to her. Low, hiccuping giggles issued from Jenret, still sprawled on the path. She tossed his cloak toward him, wrapped her own around her more tightly to hide her dishabille, and turned to leave.

"Doyce, don't go, please, I beg you!" She stalked on, boot heels slamming and crunching on the graveled walkway, ignoring him. "Please! I know you've no reason to trust me, but I need to talk, need to explain! Just don't . . . don't leave me like this! Don't leave me alone, I beg you."

Khar swirled beside her, amber eyes luminescent with anxiety. **"I know you're angry, and rightly so, but I think . . ."** she hesitated, obviously baffled by conflicting emotions, **"that you should listen. He needs to confess. Not so much to this as to something more, something deeper. It wasn't the sex he wanted as much as the sharing, the comfort. Males are *not* socially adept,"** she sniffed. **"Nothing more will happen, not with Rawn and me to protect you."**

Still angry, unwilling, yet her interest piqued, Doyce halted, looking at the crouched figure attempting to redress himself. Rawn paced toward her, one foot directly in front of the other, both front and back, as if walking an invisible boundary, as perhaps he was. He bow-stretched in greeting. **"I convey abject apologies, most especially my own for not realizing he was in such a state, and his,"** an almost contemptuous head toss set the ghatt's hoop quivering in the moonlight, **"for being the most dissolute, despicable fool in Marchmont and Canderis combined. And I agree with his assessment,"** Rawn added parenthetically. **"But you *must* listen to him, help him, understand what makes him as he is. He needs more than I can offer him."**

Hands on hips, she glared at the ghatt, tapping her foot. *"If you think I'm going to offer consensual sex after that to pacify his bruised ego, you're absolutely wrong!"*

Rawn drew back, wounded, groomed his flank, embarrassed to meet her gaze. **"Never would I ask for that. He's not a child to be given a sweet to soothe a bruised knee. Give him the gift of your understanding, that is all I,"** he bowed his head in Khar's direction, **"we ask of you."**

Despite herself, unwilling, she retraced her footsteps, sat again, a calculated distance from Jenret, ready to flee at the slightest provocation. Khar jumped beside her, while Rawn nosed at Jenret's prostrate form. An unsteady hand ruffled the black ghatt's ears. With a pent-up sigh, Jenret rose, cocooned in his cloak, and sat at the bench's farthest end, facing away from her. He rubbed splayed fingers through his hair, pressing the heels of his hands against his eyes to blot the tears. Then he reached, blindly, aching to bridge the distance between them. "Doyce, hold my hand, please," he begged.

Anger coursed through her again. Did he think she'd be so gullible a second time? Khar leaned into her arm, warm and soft. **"All emotions are ambiguous, especially your anger."**

She elbowed the ghatta's ribs. *"Not in this case!"* she 'spoke.

Leaning harder, cajoling, the ghatta tried again. **"Be honest, see the truth. What do you truly feel?"**

How to catalog her feelings? *"Anger, rage, shame, betrayal. Rage that someone I cared about, someone I thought I might even ..."* she left the word "love" unsaid, but realized, tried to reshape her thoughts, rekindle the anger. *"That ... if things were different ... if I were different ... it might have ..."* she stumbled to a halt. *"Oh. But not like that, not like that ever!"* she finished vehemently.

His hand, white in the darkness, shook, waiting, alone. "Doyce, please let me explain," the words plaintive, almost lost in the night. She reached out hesitantly, let her fingers connect with his, felt them crushed tight, but he made no move to draw her closer. Instead, he let their entwined hands rest on the bench. The heat of her anger throbbed against the cold of his grip, the cold of the bench.

"What I did ... what I almost did just now was unconscionable. It's just that everything ... the waiting, the wondering ... about what's happening here, what's going to happen, has driven me crazy with impatience. Everything broke wide-open tonight—not knowing where you'd gone, seeing you with him. And wondering if you were ever going to notice that I love you, that I need you, that I care for you and want you so much I can hardly survive. Sometimes I think you don't even know that I'm alive, and after everything we've suffered together, that hurts most of all."

"Wanting something doesn't always mean you get it," she replied, more tartly than she'd intended. "Especially like that."

"Oh, I know, believe me, I *know*. But if I didn't reach out and grab it, I was terrified everything would desert me, everything I've yearned for. And I couldn't let that happen. I thought you'd understand when you got better, reach out to me as I'd reached out to you during all those long octants when you were half-mad with grief." He swung their locked hands back and forth, fingers woven through hers.

"I don't know what I feel about you, Jenret. Not until I know what to feel about myself. You have to let me have that first before you can even begin to hope about anything else, and even the hope may be in vain. Can you let me have that time, that space ... ? Or is my very presence going to be a burden?"

"If I know that there's hope and not a black void swallowing all the stars in the heavens, I can try. I can even try not to be jealous when Muscadeine is beside you instead of me. But it won't be easy. Just don't flaunt him in my face."

"Well, try, then. Arras Muscadeine means no more or less to me than you do."

"Chill comfort," he rasped with a touch of mock humor, "But not cold comfort at least."

It was a totally irrelevant thought, but she couldn't help asking it, despite the fact that it was personal, the sort of question perhaps best not brought up under the circumstances. "Doesn't it . . .? Doesn't it hurt to sit after that?"

He exploded with laughter. "It stings like the very devil," he admitted. "But Rawn told me that if I moved or even squirmed, I'd feel worse from him. Besides, it's mild penance for what I deserved for doing that." He shook their linked hands, pounded them gently on the stone bench for emphasis. "Now, don't you think you'd better go in for the night?" He rose and released her hand, bowing, face still averted. "I . . . think I'll stay out a bit longer. Good night."

"I've escorted them safe inside. Will you remain much longer?" Rawn asked.

"What? Oh." Elbows on knees, head in cupped hands, Jenret shook himself. Rawn pushed at his arm, crawled across his lap, felt the icy fingers slide along his fur, rhythmic stroking. He rumbled a rough purr for both their comfort, but Jenret didn't seem to notice. He huddled over the ghatt, clutching him to his chest, the cold seeping through him, chilling his heart, grief at what he'd attempted mingled with the cold night air. *"No, I need to stay a little longer— there's an old lecture I must give myself again, since Mahafny's not here to administer it."* This evening served him right, served him bloody well right, he lamented and recollected another night long ago, of almost-love, both very like and very unlike this one.

He'd been, what, sixteen? Yes, that must be right, because his mother was pregnant with Jacobia, and he knew damn well how she'd gotten that way, and who the father really was. And in the light of his own burgeoning sexuality, his own physical longings and confusions, his jealousy, frustrations and fears, he'd cajoled a serving girl into joining him in one of the deserted mercantile outbuildings that night. Stunned by his luck and with no idea what to do with it because it was his first time, he was filled with his need and his desire to strike back at the world for his problems.

A warm, slightly humid night, skin sticking to skin, the slithering down long, moist slopes, fumbling and frantic with need and no earthly idea which ribbon lacings or tabs or buttons to undo to find his goal. But the serving girl had laughed, a full-throated indulgent laugh that hadn't shamed him and his eagerness, only served to enhance it. She'd even made him wait, pulled off his boots for him so he could slide down the formfitting trousers, the ones so in vogue that year. And then he was in heaven, veritable heaven between her clasping legs, his bottom flashing in the moonlight through the window, her face and breasts beneath him milky white and silver-gilded with light. Just as he began to discover the thrusting rhythm that carried them both on and up and away into ecstasy, he'd felt the boot on his backside, the sharp sting of leather against bare flesh, sending him tumbling over the willing girl.

He'd rolled onto his back, gasping with fury, astonished at how his world of pleasure could have ground to such an abrupt halt, aching with lust. Saw his Aunt Mahafny standing there, flinty-gray eyes assessing and cool. She threw his trousers into his lap. "Cover yourself," she commanded, "And you, missy," this to the serving girl, "we'll have a little chat later about some things I hope you know but suspect you don't. Now go." The girl had scrambled up, bodice unlaced, skirts and petticoats in a tangled mass, and had hurried out without a backward, regretful glance.

He pulled on his trousers, back to Mahafny as he settled them around his hips, misbuttoning buttons, not caring, anything so that he was dressed. He whirled back, finally, hands fisted at his sides, face taut with anger and embarrassment. "How could you?" His voice cracked on the words. "I'm a man now, not a child! I have every right . . ."

But she interrupted him, "You have every right to make love to a consenting woman—and that she was, I have no doubt—but not without taking precautions."

"Precautions?" he nearly spat the word at her. "Precautions? I thought we had, were nice and private until you barged in."

Mouth narrowed, she shook her head. "I thought as much. That's not the sort of precautions I meant. What I don't want is for you to make any woman pregnant. Do you know how to have your pleasure and not do that?" She motioned him to sit on a cloth bale, and he did, stiffly, unwillingly, ego more bruised than his butt, still swollen with anger and the remains of lust. Mahafny hoisted herself onto a barrel. "I warned your mother she'd best have a talk with you, or delegate someone who could, Syndar Saffron or whomever."

"Well, they obviously don't practice what you preach!"

"Regardless. So I'm going to have that talk with you now. Jenret, you know your heritage, know it too well, know what can possibly come of it. You've no right to satisfy your urges unless you can rest assured they don't result in bringing another Jared into the world."

He hung his head at the sound of his dead brother's name, his terrifying, untrained Gleaner skills that had killed two servants, stripped their father of his mind. Chewing at his lower lip, concentrating on the pain to counteract the sudden welling of tears. "Merciful Lady, I never thought, I never . . . not that!" he trailed off, memories washing over him, leaving him spent with grief.

"What you did isn't shameful, Jenret, but it was shameful not to consider the consequences. And I doubt you did, did you? Do you know about sheaths, pessaries, about abortifacents and contraceptives?"

And that night he had learned, in numbing detail, how not to make a woman pregnant, and he . . . he had never even thought about that tonight with Doyce.

❖

Satisfied that Jenret slept the sleep of the exhausted after physical and emotional turmoil, Rawn eased through the window and onto the roof, seeking the spot where he'd comforted N'oor that first night. He settled by the chimney pot, his mindvoice reaching to call Saam, Khar, and N'oor to him. Time, way past time, to seek counsel.

Khar arrived first, followed by Saam, who sat and yawned hugely, yawned again and squinted his eyes. **"Fast asleep when you called."** A little shake, several blinks. **"Couldn't it wait, whatever it is?"**

Wedging herself between Rawn and Saam, Khar settled, saying nothing as N'oor slipped up to join them. She, too, looked drowsy, but the combined presence of the ghatti startled her awake.

Stretching his chin skyward, eyes searching for stars, Rawn wondered how to begin. **"Do you know what happened tonight?"**

Only Saam showed any puzzlement. **"Well, of course. I was the one who got ale dripped on my head. Awful stink. So that's what humans mean by a night on the town. Couldn't wait for it to end."** He smiled to himself, he'd left Nakum spread-eagled facedown on the bed, exhausted. Uneasy skin ripples from Khar alerted him to some inner distress. "**What do you mean?**" He had an uneasy intuition something was far from right.

"**Jenret ... tried ... to rape Doyce.**" Khar's mindvoice came in stacato bursts. "**Rawn brought him to his senses before he did too much harm.**"

Saam's mouth hung ajar, chin jerking angrily. Rape? All things were possible to humans, but not to Seekers, he'd thought. Oriel forgive him for not having known, not having done something to stop it!

But Rawn interrupted his thoughts. "**I have to ask, Saam. I won't lay blame where it doesn't belong, but what does Nakum's earth-bond do?**" Saam started to protest, but Khar hushed him. "**No, wait, let me explain. Remember that first formal dinner in Marchmont? Well, after dinner Nakum came back to Jenret's room to talk. After a while Jenret began hearing things,**" he corrected himself, "**hearing voices, actually. I couldn't catch much of it, but I know he wasn't dreaming. Bear in mind, Nakum was there. And tonight, all night, Nakum and Jenret were together. Could Nakum's earth-bond power be involved? Have a spillover effect on anyone near him?**"

Had Rawn lost his wits? Saam chose his words with care. "**How could it spill over?**"

Rawn pressed his point home. "**Think, Saam! You partake of Nakum's power when you're with him, we've all seen that, as if the earth-bond gives you endurance as well.**"

"**True.**" Saam shifted, uncomfortable by the turn Rawn's questioning had taken. "**Nakum's earth-bond has had more force since we've been here, enough to make every hair on my body tingle sometimes. But that's the only spill-over I've sensed. Nakum has no evil in him, nor does his earth-bond. Jenret's problems are his own.**"

Khar finally spoke. "**Rawn, what about all the headaches Jenret's been having? Doyce, too, at times. Nakum hasn't been anywhere near them when it happens. It's probably stress. Everything's strange here, distorted somehow. We couldn't even contact Bard and the others two nights ago.**"

Rawn whipped his head in N'oor's direction, had almost

forgotten her presence, so sleekly silent was she. **"What about Aelbert?"**

N'oor bristled slightly. **"What about him?"** Desperate, defensive, she fought for time. Did they know? Suspect? Poor, poor Chak! A mistake, he'd sworn it, and she'd believed him. Would they? Had they learned Aelbert had secretly met with Maurice? Did they mistrust him?

With supreme patience, Rawn nudged N'oor and brought her out of herself. **"Does Aelbert have headaches as well? Any sensation of hearing echoing, distant voices?"**

Relief almost palpable, she countered, **"He's stronger than he looks."** Pride in that statement, because he was. Strong enough to face down Maurice, despite his fears. She wanted to share her pride in Aelbert, but yearned even more to share their companionship, to be comforted until her fears fled. Would they understand how rushed their training had been, accelerated so Aelbert could serve the Monitor? What portion of herself, of Aelbert could she give to gain admittance? **"Doesn't everyone hear voices?"** She'd never stopped to wonder, assumed everyone did since Aelbert did. **"He always hears voices but he just doesn't listen to them. He says you don't have to unless you want to. I help him not to hear, he needs me for that."** Maybe she didn't have as deep a training as they did, but she could protect her Aelbert, just as they did their Bonds. **"I guard him, shield him, help him conserve his strength. Although . . ."** she considered, **"it has been much harder here, I'm constantly on guard."**

Uncomprehending, she watched as the three imperceptibly drew away from her, a united front that left her alone, outside again, no longer a part. What had she said, what had she done? Everyone heard voices. They heard the Elders, after all. Why couldn't humans hear something similar? Oh, maybe she should have listened harder, studied harder during training. What had she missed?

"I think," Rawn stretched with slow deliberation, **"that that's enough for tonight."** He dipped his head in Saam's direction. **"I apologize for suspecting Nakum. Khar's right, he's under stress, susceptible, that's all. We're in a strange land."** He padded with care down the roof's slope to the ledge. **"I thank you all, and good night."**

Without appearing to rush, Saam immediately followed after, but before Khar could depart, N'oor sidled beside her, diffident, green eyes beseeching a moment of her time. **"A favor, Khar."** Khar's tail swished, but N'oor ignored the warning. **"Have you any 'script to spare?"** Embarrassing to ask for it, admit her need, but she was coming into heat and the 'script controlled her suffering, avoided the terrible longing for mating, a distraction from her Bond. **"Aelbert keeps forgetting. He's been so busy lately. He always thinks of others before himself, but he thinks I'm a part of him, so sometimes I'm overlooked a little."** She shrugged, as if to explain and forgive his flaw. **"Rather than bother him again, I thought I'd ask you."** And what she didn't say, couldn't admit to herself, was that she no longer trusted Aelbert to give her any medicine, any 'script. Wrong, wrong, wrong, unjust! But look what had happened to Chak!

Mahafny shifted the oil lamp, twisted its reflector, but the shadow still fell across the page in front of her. Perhaps the shadow served as palpable reality of her own obscured vision, and gave a hearty snort of disgust at her suggestibility. Omens, portents, superstitions, what next? The test figures were there in black and white—and gray. Columns noting Senders, Receivers, Distance, and Results recorded during the field trials. In a variation on the Marble Test, she'd moved the Receivers farther and farther distant, first to different parts of the Hospice, and finally outside at calibrated distances. Busying herself recopying the figures, she ranked them sequentially by Highest Match/Greatest Distance. For no reason at all, she thought of Saam, and discovered her pen enscribing a ghatt on the paper's margin.

She X-ed through it, two firm strokes, the nib catching on a thread in the paper, scattering a fine spray of ink. "Well, I'll admit I wish you were here," she declared aloud, "but I doubt even you could make heads or tails of these figures." The memory of the steel-blue ghatt rubbing good-bye before he bounded after Nakum made her reach down and touch her shin. "Well, damn all, I explained why it wouldn't work. I'm too old and set in my ways." Her querulousness surprised her, but what amazed her more was conversing with a non-existent ghatt. Oh, she could rationalize it; after all, Harrap and Parm had said no one had had word of Doyce for some days now. Bard and the others were growing nervous. No wonder her thoughts fixed on Saam and the others.

Putting the papers aside with notes for one of the copy clerks, she heaved open the desk drawer, prepared for its habitual screeching protest. Nonetheless, she winced, teeth grating at the sound. If you can't figure out one puzzle, try another, she advised herself, there's bound to be an answer somewhere, somehow, sometime. But the sarcastic admonition only heightened her fear. What if there were no answers? Or worse, what if the answers were unacceptable—socially, morally, ethically? What would she tell the Monitor then, and how would he and the High Conciliators react? It wasn't just finding answers, it was what they did with those answers that assumed the gravest importance. Riders carried daily messages from Gaernett, apprising her of discussions and best-case and worst-case scenarios for coping with the unknown Gleaners they now realized were scattered throughout Canderis. How could they plan when they still didn't have all the facts!

Heartsick with the weight of her responsibility, she dragged the navy leather folder from the drawer and slapped it on the desk. Snapping at the ribbon that tied it closed, she regarded it with revulsion, forced her fingers to pick at the knot securing it. It had been knotted when she'd discovered it and she'd reknotted it after each perusal, rather than tying a simple bow. Each time she considered slicing it with a penknife, but rejected it as too easy; besides, the effort of forcing her obdurate, inflexible fingers to work at it gave her time to come to grips with what it contained.

The knot felt more stubborn this time, but she persisted, patiently teasing it loose. Inside, genealogical charts with their genesis in her own years of labor. But Evelien's boasted far more detail, and she never failed to marvel at the organized, indomitable mind responsible for searching out this additional information, although at what cost Mahafny didn't want to know. She stretched the accordion folds of one chart piece and smoothed it flat, sorted through until she located the piece of onion skin tracing paper she wanted. This was where she floundered each time. The tracing paper was decorated with stars and various other symbols, most notably scatterings of three wavy parallel lines and two inverted V's like pointed, alert ears. Generally the symbols stood alone, but in other spots one was drawn above the other, although never did all three cluster together.

She held it to the light, stretched it at arm's length and brought it closer. Top, bottom, side? Damned if she knew. What she did know was that it served as an overlay for one of these charts. The symbols' spacing was similar to the genealogy charts' spacing, but every one she'd tried so far, from the very first Spacer inhabitants to the most recent ones, never quite matched, some symbols aligning over names, others floating in the chart's empty spaces. As impossible as someone presenting her with a constellation pattern and turning her loose in a galaxy, telling her to match it. Her hands clenched the paper's edge, making it crackle, and she forced her fingers to relax, although how much more conscious volition she'd have over that, she couldn't judge. Marvelous when a eumedico couldn't heal herself.

At first she wasn't sure she heard a knock, it came so hesitantly. Harrap, without a doubt, checking up, convincing her to call it a night. "Enter," she called, prepared not to react too strongly to his scolding. Instead, a bobbed head peered around the door, low, just below the knob as if the person stooped. "Davvy, peeping through the keyhole, were you? Don't let it become a habit. Come in. What are you doing up so late? If Nana Cookie finds you're not abed, you're in for trouble."

Still hunched, one arm locked across his chest, Davvy popped inside, sticking his head back out to survey the hallway before closing the door. He made for the chair opposite her desk and slid into it, stooped at the waist, nose nearly grazing his knees. "You're not sick, are you?" She couldn't fathom why he was folded in half, unless doubled over with pain. His normally merry eyes were solemn as he raised his head high enough to see over the desk.

"Couldn't sleep," he confessed. "Figured you'd be up as well." He squirmed in the chair, shifted and clutched at his chest. "More that I thought about it, realized that I'd forgotten, the guiltier I felt. But I really did forget, honest!" He momentarily sat upright, arms still plastered across his chest, and Mahafny could glimpse the lines, the sharp corners of something tucked under his shirt. "Everything happened so fast, and not being sure if it was good or bad or if we were safe or not, that's how I forgot, even though she made me promise to never, ever forget where it was and to keep it

safe. Bert gave it to her and she thought the world of it. An
I did keep it safe! Davvy McNaught keeps his word!"

Whatever the boy meant, he was dead serious, Mahafn
had no doubt. He radiated earnestness from every pore, a
well as a grim resolve too big for a boy his age to carry. "
know you did, Davvy. It takes a big man to admit his mi:
takes, and the only mistake you made was in forgetting f
a bit."

He nodded, mouth scrunched, kept on nodding as if pe
suading himself. "It was hers, you know. She asked me t
keep it for her, said that all children have places for their se
cret treasures, so I hid it with my special things, in the sa
place where Bert stashed things when he lived here. And
was a safe place, none of you eumedicos or Seekers foun
it when you all were turning the place upside down, lookin
for things you didn't even know you were looking for."

She flinched at the accuracy of his description; it wa
true, they'd searched for anything and everything, whethe
hidden weapons or secret documents. At first Mahafn
hadn't been sure whom Davvy meant when he'd said "she,
but only because she hadn't wanted to acknowledge i
"She" was Evelien, without a doubt. Davvy was trying t
work the book through the neck of his shirt without unbut
toning it, his face growing red, the fabric straining, a corne
of the book jabbing the soft underside of his jaw.

"By the Blessed Lady, child," she lost patience. "Untucl
your shirt and drop it out. That's how you got it in there
wasn't it?"

The book retreated downward. Davvy tugged his shirt fre
from his waistband and the book fell into his lap with
plop. He handled it with reverence, offered it balanced o
his palms as if he'd present it on a tray. "Once I remembere
I had it, I thought and thought about what to do with it, an
she said keep it safe, so I figured mayhap you could do tha
better than I could." Anxious, he scanned her face to see i
he'd made the right decision. "A few others fancied it a
times, offered me oodles of things for it, but I always sai
I didn't know where it was. Finally, they believed me."

She took the book, though the weight made her wrist
ache. Now she could see why the boy had been bent doubl
hiding his heavy, unwieldy burden. "Who, lad? Who wante
it? Who else knew about it?"

Hitching himself out of the chair, he whispered tw

names, and Mahafny schooled herself not to react. In a way she wasn't surprised: one was a eumedico who'd assisted Evelien, the other, one of the Gleaners adept at creating headaches in his Receivers. "Thank you, Davvy. You've done well, very well. I'm proud of you." She hated to say it but did, although she couldn't bring herself to speak the name. "And she would be proud of you, too."

He let out a pent-up sigh of relief. "Think mayhap I can sleep now. You should try, too." With a curious formality he made her a little half-bow and left, again checking both ways before he slipped away with a murmured "Good night."

Dismayed, confused, Mahafny stared at the book, not sure what to expect. An old book, the leather dull, cracking, especially along the spine; some of the pages hung out unevenly, detached from their binding. The cover's pressed gold lettering was worn, but she ran her fingers across it, half-feeling, half-reading the words: *Journey to Marchmont* by Ian Tavistock. Wonderful, an old travelogue. Opening it, she flipped the pages at random, stopped at the flyleaf to read the faded ink names of its succession of owners. The newest inscription was fresh and clear: "To E.A.W. from A.O."

"To Evelien Annendahl Wycherley from . . . A.O." Well, Vesey at least hadn't given her the book, but who was A.O.? And what would Evelien have wanted with a historical curiosity, the story of Tavistock's visit to Marchmont shortly after its founding, or so it appeared? She flipped back and forth, scanning the headings, skimming bits of prose best described as "purple." A hyperbolic writer, to say the least, whether Ian Tavistock admired or loathed something, he employed ten adjectives or adverbs to elucidate his point. Not her idea of informative reading, nor Evelien's either, she would have guessed.

The list caught her by surprise. "This bee, to the beste of my most humble knowledge, the most complete, most accurate, and most factual liste of the pioneers who first settled this lande of Marchmont." Still chuckling over his extravagance, not to mention his extra "e's", Mahafny ran her fingers down the list, confident she already knew these Spacer names from her own research. With rising excitement she realized the list ran far longer than any other she'd seen and that, she calculated rapidly, at least one in five a revelation.

Licking her lips, excited despite herself, she perused the list again, shook her head at her eagerness. Once she'd have given almost anything for this information ... once. But what good was it now? It had no bearing on the problems at hand. Scolding herself for her eagerness, her ability to be distracted, she shut the book, cut off the old, familiar longing. "Into the drawer with you," she told it, "I've other work tonight." And thumped the book, its spine overhanging the edge of the desk while she fumbled with the drawer. A tube of paper shifted in the loose, buckled spine, slipped far enough to catch her attention.

"Well, well, was A.O. hiding notes for Evelien? Who were you, A.O., anyway?" But Davvy had said Bert had given Evelien the book, and there was no Bert at the Hospice now. Come to think of it, Davvy had mentioned him before, or more accurately, Yulyn had, and not in very complimentary terms. "Bert, Bert," she ruminated, the scrolled paper in her hands, not bothering to unroll it. "Bertram, Berthold, Berthier." Absolutely nothing. "Albert?" And the knowledge sledged her with a paralyzing certainty. "Not Albert, but Aelbert. Aelbert Orsborne!" Possible, not possible? Coincidental initials, nothing more. But tomorrow she'd have a little talk with Yulyn and Davvy about Bert.

Abstractedly she unrolled the paper, smoothed it flat with the palm of her hand, but stubborn, it still tried to recurl itself. With a muttered oath she flattened one edge with her forearm, grabbed for something to weight it. Panting at the effort, she forced *Marchmont* on it one-handed, that would do for one side, dragged an inkwell to the opposite corner, planted her elbow on the fourth corner. Yes, Evelien's handwriting, all right. Another genealogy chart. Except this one struck a little too close to home, her own name, Evelien's, Jenret's, and other family names appearing.

Without quite knowing what she did or why, Mahafny stretched her hand across the desk, snagged the edge of the onion skin tracing paper, overlaid it on the chart. No, fool, not that way, this way! Shifted it back and forth, blind panic setting in as symbol after symbol matched with a name, everything aligning generation after generation after generation, not a symbol without a name. But what did it mean? With a shaking finger she traced her own name underneath the tissue, saw three wavy lines by it. By Evelien's, the three wavy lines and underneath it a star. Moved over to her brother-in-law's line: Jared, star; Jenret, the two inverted V's and underneath it, a star; Jacobia, no markings. She moved back and forth, checking wavy lines, found that easy to decipher: eumedico. She knew her family history. And had a sinking suspicion she knew what the star meant: Gleaner. Breathing hoarse and labored, she traced and traced, almost missed the separate family tree hidden beneath her elbow: Doyce's. Confirmed the stars as Gleaner because they were with Vesey's name and his mother's, but Doyce as well as Jenret had the two inverted "V's" and the star. She'd noted without thinking about it that the "V's" reminded her of ears before—ghatti ears? But Jenret, Doyce, Gleaners? Not possible, she would have known! But her fears intensified, all the same, and she squeezed her eyes shut against the vision in front of her. "Oh, Saam, where are you when I need you?" she whispered, and felt the tears start down her cheeks.

He swung himself onto the desktop, let his feet dangle, swinging his legs. Funny how different things appeared in the dark, the High Conciliation Chamber now gloomy and quiet, a few outside street lamps and torcheres casting feeble light through the long windows above the gallery. Darl Allgood could still hear the shouts ringing in his ears during that panicked meeting nearly an octant ago, his fellow Conciliators working themselves into a frenzy over the Gleaner menace.

Menace? Hardly! He dragged thumb and forefinger up his forehead, tracing the receding hairline on each side. An old habit, and his wife swore it explained why he was balding like that, hair follicles fleeing nervous fingers. She might have a point. In the half-year he'd served, he had a feeling his fingers sought further and further before touching any hair. Oh, to be a Chief Conciliator again! Not to have these dilemmas thrust upon him and, though no one knew, he with a foot in both camps, plea-bringer and defendant at once.

They'd be removing the protective straw from the grapevines about now, hoping the new rootings had taken. If only he were back in Wexler! Hard work being Chief Conciliator, but everyone respected his judgments, said he was so accurate they practically didn't need the Seekers. But his Gleaner talent played no role in his judgments, because even his wife didn't know his secret, and mindreading didn't mean he could determine the truth the way the ghatti did. He envied them that trait. Still, being a Gleaner meant a heightened awareness, ever-alert to what others thought and whether they endangered his secret. That heightened awareness let him judge the human condition from the smallest gestures, the relaxation or tensing of facial muscles, the way people breathed, the contraction or dilation of their pupils. It wasn't infallible, but it gave him an edge in assessing who told the truth or didn't.

He continued swinging his legs, enjoying the sensation, lost in his own thoughts. The sudden rush of air, the dark shape bearing down on him caused him to jump in fright. The dark shape stumbled backward, cursed, equally startled.

"Lady bless us both, Monitor," he could tell from the stride, the bulk who it was, "if we scare each other like that again, we'll fright ourselves into the grave!"

"Allgood, is that you?" The Monitor worked his way closer, hands extended to fend off desks and chairs lurking in the dimness. "Phew, right you are! And the eumedicos swear your heart doesn't stop when you're frightened like that." He hopped onto the desk beside Allgood. "Never had a chance to really thank you for your support the other day. I'm grateful. A good part of Canderis saw the best and worst of us that day, I'm afraid."

Allgood shrugged off the thanks. Back in Wexler he wouldn't need it or expect it for doing his job. "Any word from the Hospice?"

Kyril van Beieven gave a whistling sigh. "The experiments are progressing, but not fast enough. Darl, how do we know what we're dealing with and how many? How do we make these Gleaners reveal themselves?"

Was he a traitor, a liar, not acknowledging what he was? "Would you?" he couldn't help his bitterness. "What can you promise them? How can you protect them? They've survived on their own wits, their instincts this long. Would you blame them for not trusting outsiders? Our charming citizens recently stoned a man in Ruysdael because they suspected he was a Gleaner. Lucky for him he found refuge with the local baker who refused to have any truck with such idiocy. In Batavia they burned a family's house and barn in the dead of night because of a Gleaner rumor. Thank the Lady's intervention they escaped with their lives. The Seekers have proved that none of these victims were Gleaners."

"I know, I've seen the reports. A mob takes on a life of its own, causes sane people to commit acts that would shame them if they truly thought about their actions, instead of being consumed by their emotions. But people are panicky at discovering Gleaners in their midst, penetrating society."

"They haven't exactly infiltrated, Monitor. They've been here all along, a part of us we just didn't know, didn't recognize." Darl wrestled with his frustration, his desire to "confess" and have at least one outsider understand what their lives were like. Perhaps someday, but not now. Old hatreds, older fears died hard, indeed, like a mob engendered a force, a life of their own, gave credence to the idea that "different" meant dangerous no matter how long they'd lived together amiably without knowing the truth. Was it worth it to try out his idea on the Monitor? "I hate to link the two, sir, but our trading problems with Marchmont are part of our Gleaner problem."

"How so?" van Beieven groped for the connection.

"Nobody's truly suffering from the embargo yet, but pockets are pinched, especially the trade towns. There's a ripple-down effect: when business is bad for the merchanters, it's bad for those who supply them, whether with trade goods or with the necessary goods to outfit caravans or ships. If the ship chandler can't sell the merchanter rope, the chandler can't buy his children shoes. What do you project for taxes this quarter?" and didn't wait for an answer. "What if we can't afford to pay as many Guardians or Seekers as we need, can't support the needy, repair roads?"

"Come to the point, man," the Monitor pounded his fist for emphasis, "I still don't see the connection."

Allgood took a deep breath. "The Gleaners serve as scapegoats. People can't do anything about the trade stoppage, so they vent their anger on something else, something they dislike or fear, choosing the most vulnerable, anyone who can't fight back."

"Allgood, Gleaners can certainly fight back, wipe minds clean, cause brains to explode!" Van Beieven thought of Jadrian Wycherley, adrift in his own private world, no memory of anything or anyone. Shivering, he made the sign of the eight-pointed Lady's star.

"Oh, they might strike back if you corner them, just as any frantic animal will fight to survive. But then they'd truly reveal themselves as Gleaners. Better to die from stones or fire than to expose loved ones as Gleaners, give the mob more victims." Allgood started down the aisle, walking quickly, voice shaking. "I'm sorry, but I've had about all I can stomach of this discussion for tonight. Human nature frightens me too much. Let's save it for the light of day."

And van Beieven was left alone, wondering what in the world had upset Allgood so? He hadn't believed the man so emotional.

As a walking tour of Sidonie, it left something to be desired, Doyce decided as she watched Arras Muscadeine visibly swallow his frustration at the laggards in the group. And given the group's small size, amazing that they should have so many laggards or—not exactly laggards, she told herself—but six people and four ghatti, each with very different personal agendas as to what they found interesting and uninteresting, exciting and boring, worthy of close scrutiny or being ignored. Still, it was a sharp spring day, nearly noon, the air crisp with a clearing breeze that snapped and popped banners and flags.

"Worse than children," Arras muttered.

"And you don't exactly find yourself endowed with mother hen proclivities, I gather?" she asked as Khar angled back to her, equally guilty of wandering.

His first laugh was a reluctant, polite sound, but it gradually deepened with a growing and genuine amusement. "Ah, how right you are! Short on patience to gather them close, cajole them to obey." He threw his hands wide in mock dismay. "I think to myself that they've been cloistered in meetings, always busy—except for last night's tavern visit, and you shouldn't judge our town by our taverns. So, how hospitable, how gracious of the Chevalier Capitain to escort his new-found friends through Sidonie, show to them the sights, expound on our heritage, bask in their admiration at our culture and style. But instead, instead . . ." he shrugged, spinning in a helpless half-circle to check on his charges.

Doyce leaned against a shop's sun-drenched wall and

folded her arms, content to wait. Jenret lagged a good two blocks behind, squatting to inspect a drain, asking intently about heavy rain capacity. The street sweeper he bombarded with questions acted sullen, unwilling or unable to answer, indeed, had probably never considered such questions until Jenret inquired. Pushing his head between the grates, Rawn wedged his head inside the drain.

Eyes bright with longing, Jacobia had dawdled at every shop window displaying fabrics, laces, ribbons, or jewelry, darting from one to another as she matched colors and textures for an imaginary outfit. Doyce had let herself be enmeshed in the fantasy for a time, but had finally broken free to rejoin Muscadeine, embarrassed by the delays. Now Jacobia had drawn Aelbert and Nakum into her beguiling orbit, Nakum more wide-eyed than Aelbert, each torn by his own interests, but quick-dashing to Jacobia's side when the other investigated something new. The ornate corner-post carvings on some of the oldest houses and shops fascinated Nakum, while Aelbert's practiced eye assessed which shops prospered, what goods created the most demand and what attracted few purchasers. Saam prowled the streets and side alleys, alert to new sounds and smells and sights, while N'oor made timid little forays, jettisoned as soon as Aelbert drew too far from her.

"Come on, everyone, let's pick up the pace, the Chevalier Capitain's waiting!" She pitched her call to carry over the street sounds. "Well, I've tried." She pulled a wry face at Muscadeine, his black, polished boot jittering with impatience. Reluctantly, Jenret and Rawn abandoned the wonders of the drain, Jenret dusting his hands on his pantaloons as he sauntered toward them, all too clear from his stride that he'd not rush but would let them wait, cool their heels. Just as well, she decided. Neither wanted to meet the other's eye this morning. Easier to pretend last night had never happened, dismiss her tangled emotions, fretting that somehow she bore responsibility for what had nearly happened. Had she led him on? She didn't think so, not when the intimacy of friendship still seemed too strong to bear after her recent emotional isolation. What had become clear on their arrival in Sidonie was Jenret's and Muscadeine's rivalry, their words and actions constantly competing for her unstinting attention and approbation. Why did it matter so much to them? Should she care? *"Why are men so egotistical?"* she asked Khar, but the ghatta shared a commiserating look and refused to answer.

Aelbert and Nakum swept up Jacobia, hustling her along, protesting at the treats and treasures foregone. The three swung around Jenret, laughing and chattering, Jenret solemn and quiet as a judge. But Aelbert dropped back, started lecturing Jenret about the seven distinct and separate woolen weave patternings he'd counted, expression absorbed as he ticked them off on his fingers.

"We're not here to buy trinkets, souvenirs," Jenret snapped, but Doyce had the sneaking suspicion his remark was really aimed at Muscadeine.

Aelbert's condescending response wasn't lost on Jenret. "No, we're not. But if you truly fancy yourself a merchanter, a trader, you just might notice which goods command a premium here, and whether you're capable of supplying it. Or corner the trade on something to buy cheap and sell dear at home, if making a profit interests you. I've noted a few things with future investment potential, if you haven't. So has Jacobia, for that matter. Her instincts are good." They had pulled level with the others now.

Although she shrank from his presence, Jenret took Doyce's arm and turned her along a new street just as Muscadeine hooked her other elbow and started in the opposite direction, stretching her between them like a wishbone. "Stop it!" she yelped, breaking loose, struggling to resettle her tabard. "I can't go two ways at once. Cracking me in half doesn't get you your wish!" Their faces reflected shock at her testiness, although Jacobia's wore a look of shrewd awareness she couldn't fathom. "Well, come on," she urged and pioneered a new direction, not caring if they followed or not. It took them a moment to gather their wits and follow, though Jacobia seemed to be having a problem making her feet obey. Indeed, the commotion made Doyce cast a glance behind her.

Deeply engrossed by the shop window to her left, Jacobia trotted rightward without charting her path, and the man exiting the shop she crossed in front of was moving swiftly. He was tall with a whip-cord strength emphasized by his well-cut doublet, the lace at his sleeves giving emphasis to his hands, scarred hands, livid with long white and red scars, pucker spots from long-gone sutures. Even at that distance the hands gave him away, made Doyce notice him even with he white lab coat missing. The Public Weal Lord had politely excused himself from most of her meetings, attended only one—understandable, his job had little to do with trade. From her slightly higher vantage point two blocks up, it struck her that Jules Jampolis acted fully prepared for what followed, one hand prodding his sword sheath behind Jacobia's leg as she stumbled, already off-balanced from their collision.

Tumbling backward into the mouth of a small alley between two shops, Jacobia landed with a crash and a tinkle on something that sounded extremely breakable, hence, costly. Doyce started to run after Jampolis, but he'd disappeared. A wail of pain and chagrin overrode the final crash and discordant sound of strings twanging and snapping. By the blessed Lady, a luthier's shop, Doyce winced as she skidded to a halt to see if Jacobia were hurt.

Aelbert had already plunged into the alley, trying to haul Jacobia upright, while Nakum disentangled her feet from splintered frames and snapped strings. Easing him aside to survey the damage, a sound filled Doyce's ears, a deadly, thrumming hiss that cleaved the air in two. Her whole body jerked forward, out of control, her chest and face slamming against the rough wood of the outer wall. It stung, splintered her cheekbone, her bewilderment growing. Was she really tacked against a wall? She brushed fingers along her side, unable to see. A what . . . a spike? Something pierced her tabard and the jacket beneath, nestling against her ribs, a fraction short of impaling her. A crossbow quarrel?

Shouts, screams, running feet—she could hear but not see. Nakum ran his hands over her side, whispered she wasn't wounded and ran off, feet pounding, knife drawn, Saam springing by his side. Bellowing a command, Muscadeine hailed some off-duty soldiers, sent them pouring down the streets, weapons at the ready. Abandoned, neglected, she spread her arms, embraced the wall for support, praying for release. She wanted to cry as Aelbert disentangled himself from Jacobia and the crushed lutes and began to scream at the top of his lungs, "Assassins! They're trying to assassinate the Special Envoy!"

"Steady!" Jenret instructed, hands on her shoulders again, so unlike the other night. "Stand straight, don't sag!" His hands left her as he braced his foot against the wall and tugged the quarrel free; with that, she regained her freedom as well, sliding down to collapse on the ground. Khar bounded into her lap, pink nose stress-paled, shoved her head underneath the tabard to inspect her side. Even her feather touch hurt—the quarrel may not have speared her, but it had bruised, scraped along her ribs. **"Are you all right, beloved?"** The ghatta tested with all her senses. Then, relieved but not fully satisfied, she pulled free, stretched to lick Doyce's sweat-slicked face, blurted, **"I'm glad we decided against the skewered meat for a midmorning snack."**

The thought made her shiver, clutch at the ghatta for comfort. But Khar stepped across her lap, tail caressing her ear. **"I should help the others hunt."** Her mindvoice pulsed with frustration. **"This isn't good, not good at all. I felt no sense of anger, no sense of danger, none of the emotions that would herald an attack. How could I warn you? A cold-blooded act."**

Cold-blooded was right, she decided as Jenret and Muscadeine helped her to her feet. Her blood ran even colder at the thought that she'd pushed Nakum aside only at the last moment. Had the quarrel been intended for him? Or even for Aelbert, standing just behind and above him? She tried to focus her thoughts. "Arras, Jules Jampolis rushed out of the shop and tripped Jacobia on purpose, I'd say." A confirming hiccough and sob from Jacobia, overlooked, still entangled.

He gave yet another urgent order as additional soldiers flooded the alley, almost cross at her interruption, as if it were irrelevant. "No. No, it couldn't have been." He listened to a report, came back to her. "He never leaves the castle. Hasn't since Maurice brought him in a few years ago as his personal eumedico. Out of pity, if you ask me, the same with his appointment as Ministration Lord. Besides, he didn't fire the quarrel."

Jenret thrust the quarrel under Muscadeine's nose. "And isn't it made of your precious arborfer?"

"So? Many things are made of arborfer." Cool, Muscadeine barely acknowledged it.

"But not as new as this one appears to be," Jenret persisted. "Not if it's true about the scarcity of arborfer these days."

Head spinning, side and face smarting, she kept worrying it through. Jampolis, not Jampolis? Arborfer, not arborfer?

But what she did know for sure was that someone was displeased with their presence in Marchmont. Highly displeased.

✿

Jules Jampolis slapped the curtain with the side of his hand, cursed the loss of fine motor skills slashed to ribbons with the rest of his dreams, his loves. Unable to pick up the merest edge of the lace curtain between thumb and forefinger, or tease a loose thread from the weaving. Gone, long gone. Still, he could see through the gauzy curtain, hoped he couldn't be seen from below. The thought made him shiver, made him yearn for the safety of the castle and his research. That was all that remained, his skill as surgeon destroyed, along with his wife and daughter. But at least Maurice had tried to give him something in return for sharing his research, but something wasn't always better than nothing, and he avoided his duties as Public Weal Lord as much as possible.

The retired apothecaire had been overjoyed to see him, whisking him up to his second-story living quarters, more than amenable to rushing to the nearest tavern for a bottle of brandy, Jampolis's coins in hand and the promise of a long chat afterward. That left Jampolis in the second-story room, able to spy on the activity below, his handiwork, or at least partially his. The young woman, dark-haired with violet eyes, showed such beauty, reminded him so achingly of Germaine. But Maurice had solemnly sworn she wasn't the one to be hurt, and so he'd acquiesced, gathered his courage and abandoned the castle for the first time in two years, face a rigid, foreboding mask, daring anyone to greet him, comment on the hands thrust before him like two useless slabs, capable of chopping and sawing only air.

Maurice had been right about the pain and fear radiating from across the street. It *was* enlivening, *was* enhancing, buoying even his own meager skills, making him feel alive, catching whole sentences of unarticulated speech floating on the air. Not as powerful or as seductive, though, as the night Germaine and his tiny daughter Rhea had died. . . .

Childhood fevers were not uncommon, he still held to that, a tenet of eumedico knowledge, even though children weren't his specialty. But Rhea's had soared higher and higher, the toddler burning in Germaine's arms, and whatever it was, he suspected Germaine had caught it as well when he stroked her cheek, trying to break her concentration away from the baby to tell her he was going for help. Oh, yes, galling to admit he didn't know what to do, but he didn't. All he knew was that it was beyond his skills, not the neat surgical incision, the probing for a diseased organ, the tedious, minute resectioning of severed muscles, the perfectly placed sutures. At that he was king, none better.

He'd rushed to locate another eumedico, someone who knew pediatrics, running through the list in his mind, weighing proximity against talent as he whipped the horse through the dark, rainy streets that night. Three were out on calls, and he left messages with each, ranging farther through the city, tears streaming down his face, the rain and the cold numbing him. In the middle of stitching up a man slashed in a tavern brawl, the fourth eumedico promised to come when he finished. So Jampolis had wheeled and ridden for home, already in terror at having been gone so long. His baby, his precious Rhea, and Germaine, high-strung, never quite the same since the baby'd been born, now sick as well.

He'd led the horse into the lean-to, not bothering to unsaddle him, and rushed into the house, calling Germaine's name. No answer. Calling again as he rushed up the stairs to the nursery, he'd grabbed at the door, discovered it locked. "Germaine, open up, darling, it's me, Jules!" He rattled the door, slammed his shoulder against it. "Metropol's on his way!"

No sound, nothing all from inside, and then finally, the creak of floorboards, an unceasing, metronomic tread that made him cringe with dread each time he knew she approached the bad floorboard, the one that creaked no matter what he'd done to it. "Germaine, open the door!" He coaxed, crooned, commanded, but nothing reached her, until at length he was pounding, hammering on the door, tearing at the grill work. And all through the lullaby running through his mind, as crystal clear as if he stood beside her, both of them bending over Rhea's crib as she drifted off to sleep. But there was nothing to hear inside, and the certainty that he'd heard it in his mind, he who had become a surgeon because he had no mindgifts at all, was driving him mad.

Hands bloody, swollen, he'd raced back down the stairs, outside, slipping and sliding on the wet grass, the mud, hoisting himself onto the porch roof that ran beneath Rhea's room. He peered in the glass, breath fogging it, swiped at it with his arm, rapped on it with his knuckles. At the far end one candle lit the room, enough for him to make out Germaine's dark shape, pacing, pacing, Rhea limp in her arms, head thrown back and dangling. "Germaine!" he screamed it again and again, but she never hesitated or faltered in her pace, the child half-sliding from her increasingly limp arms. Pounding on the glass, fighting it as if it were his enemy, he punched through it, shards cutting and slashing at his hands, his livelihood, soft palms, sensitive fingers, knowledgeable hands.

He pounded, grabbed splinters, heaved them free of the caulking until at last he'd cleared a space big enough to step through. He knew it then for the first time, the sense of sweet, supreme ecstasy and supreme denial as he beat against the glass, hands and forearms bloody and beribboned with flesh, tendons slashed, the sense of communion that came without words. Germaine's last fevered thoughts, incoherent, swelling through his brain, touching him in a way she'd never touched him in life. Oh, she'd wanted to, but it was he who was too mentally blind to feel the touch. Germaine stared at him, soaked with rain and blood, dripping with it, looked through him and wilted to the floor, Rhea slipping from her arms, baby head slamming against the floor with a thud.

As soon as he touched the baby, he knew she was dead, had been for some time, body feeling cool and natural for the first time in days except where it had been warmed against Germaine's breast. The streaks of blood against the child's white flesh struck him as unseemly, and he wiped at her with a corner of his drenched cloak before he touched Germaine's throat, trying to feel a pulse through the vitality of his own pain, the blood throbbing out his wounds. Gone. Everything gone now, his loves, his life, his career, and the only thing he retained was something he hadn't even known he'd possessed, a tiny shard of mindpower and the knowledge that pain augmented it. . . .

Jampolis stepped away from the curtain as he heard his old friend reenter the room, breathless with excitement and perhaps a private taste of brandy. "Trouble outside," he chirped, all innocent excitement. "Somebody tried to murder that Special Envoy from Canderis."

Well, he'd done his job, and the fact that Maurice's man
Gregor hadn't wasn't his fault. He settled in the chair, listened with grave concern, holding his glass between the
palms of his hands, unable to flex his fingers. Would
Maurice let him have the dark-haired girl, he wondered? Not
that she was Germaine, but the similarity was there. Better
a living simulacrum than a dead reality.

❖

Not, not, *not* in *my* kingdom! thought Constant fiercely
from the safety of the solarium that night as he paced from
window to window, ceaselessly tracking the constellations.
Sunlight, moonlight, starlight, they all poured on the polished collection panels at the domed top, had fed him their
energy for so many years, octads upon octads. Enhanced
photovoltaic cells charged from direct sunlight or any other
natural light source, no noxious emissions alerting the citi-
zenry to his illegal technology. Oh, how noble to abjure
technology and all it entailed, but he'd not been foolish
enough to set out to establish his kingdom without scaveng-
ing the best of the Spacer equipment left behind. Other than
a straight chair and a plain wooden table, their joints dried
and loose, the room was sparsely furnished. Its centerpiece,
if one could call it that, an anodized aluminum rectangle,
coffin-sized, took pride of place in the room's center, cables
snaking from it, slithering toward the roof panels.

Practically no one alive today recollected the solarium's
existence above the library, presumed the dome a decorative
but empty shell, long curved window slits divided by shiny
panels, a treat for the eye when the dome reflected sunlight.
He no longer thought of it as a solarium, but as his hibernaculum, where he'd lain for near two hundred years, neither
living nor dead, suspended between two worlds. All that
pomp and ceremony, that weighted but empty coffin respectfully carried to the mausoleum, enough to make him smile.
No doubt they still laid wreaths there to commemorate his
birth, his "death," and the founding of Marchmont. And no
one except the new ruler and each succeeding ruler learned
Constant's secret, that he reposed here, waiting for word
from the stars, word from Carrick.

Hoping that one star might appear that wasn't a star, the
afterburn of a spaceship entering the atmosphere, Constant

returned to the present at last. An old man's fancy ... or folly, he wasn't sure which as he patted the anodized aluminum. But Carrick sailed through space somewhere out there while he remained here, earthbound, still hearing ghost echoes of Carrick's mindvoice in space. It just grew fainter, more distant through the years, though none of the conversation was ever lost, like the mathematical conundrum about going halfway to a door, then half the remaining distance, and half and half and half again to infinity. Technically one never crossed the threshold, although in reality he had stepped through the door, heard it slam shut on Carrick's voice so long ago. The pain of his twin's last cries never diminished ... or ended. But memories distracted him from the problem at hand.

His metabolism raced, he knew, but even a normal pulse felt rapid after years of solitude. Not, not, *not* in *my* kingdom! He tested the words again, beating his hands to punctuate each word, the old skin soft and pale, calluses gone but reforming. By the blessed virgin, how he missed Wilhelmina's calm reporting: fifty well-chosen words night after night, increment upon increment, the rhythm of punctuation—when absolutely necessary—breaking in at the cost of a word each—clap for a period, foot stamp for a comma, table rap for a query. As each succeeding king or queen ascended the throne, they inherited the nightly reporting duties. A few had believed; his son—Marchmont's second ruler—had known Constant too stubborn to give in to death, not while a technological "half-life" existed to let him pursue his quest for Carrick. Well, the others, he suspected, had considered the reporting an empty, embarrassing ritual— worse than talking to one's self. But Wilhelmina's ability to compress events without losing their flavor or savor, inject a little gossip, had been so succinct, so far superior to her ancestors. Clap, stamp, rap, he ran through the litany for old time's sake.

Well, Wilhelmina was dead and gone now, as were all the rest of his nightly reporters, and only he remained, awake again at last. Now, what to do about the situation? Didn't he have enough to worry about? Assassins in Marchmont? All too true—he'd heard the evidence, seen the Special Envoy's involuntary shaking, that little Marbon woman, as she'd delineated the events, amplified upon and sometimes contradicted by her colleagues and Arras Muscadeine.

Still, what choice had he had but the one he'd taken? The secret message he'd entrusted to Aaron Rossmeer must have been delivered, must have brought them, else why would they be here? Clever to use his trade embargo as the impetus for their visit. Even in times long past he'd been politic enough to know it wasn't wise to burn all his bridges with Canderis. The Seekers Veritas had been formed well after he'd left for Marchmont, but reports of them had intrigued him, made him wonder if he'd inadvertently omitted some part of his equation for founding a kingdom.

Tonight Maurice had been right, without knowing why. Arras Muscadeine had failed to protect them, and these Canderisians and their ghatti were too precious to waste. Palace confinement under armed guard for their safety's sake until they determined responsibility for the assassination attempt. Perhaps a lone lunatic, perhaps not. Had events passed him by all these long years despite the reports? When had the changes come? Changes that shivered the castle's very air, literal pain in those changes, but formless, its source obscured. Who had learned the secret that pain augments and expands mindpowers? He worried fretfully at a hangnail with his teeth, enjoying the sensation even as his consciousness denied the act, still wrestled with the problem. Small pleasures, yes.

It had to be settled soon, it must be. Every extra heart throb, every additional lungful of air extracted its price; the sluggish pumping of blood through veins and arteries was an extravagance he couldn't afford. And he couldn't escape up here as often as he'd like to recharge the portable battery pack that regulated these functions, enveloped him in a subtle energy field that supported his ancient body, kept him from desiccation and dust. Damn, where was Eadwin! He hadn't planned to take a direct hand in this, hadn't planned to come awake at all. The low-grade cryogenics, suspended animation, had been meant to preserve him until Carrick returned, not for this. Bare life enough to scan the stars for a signal, still inquisitive enough for fifty words a night to connect him to the life bypassing him. Would he never be called to the stars? Wrenching mortality while his identical twin remained immortal in space?

Eadwin's disappearance had confounded everything, left him balancing worse than a child on a totter-board. And damn Wilhelmina for believing she could manipulate

Maurice, bypass him and have Eadwin declared heir before she died! Hubris, hubris! He knew it all too well, had had more time for hubris than all his successors combined—how else could he recognize it so easily in others? Frightened by Eadwin's vanishing and the knowledge that her own death approached more rapidly than anticipated, Wilhelmina had shared her secret with Fabienne, brought her here, instructed her in the reporting procedure, the necessity of training Eadwin to it when he took the throne.

If it hadn't been for Fabienne, hysterical over Wilhelmina's death and Eadwin's continued disappearance, pouring out her heart, would he have even bothered awakening? How many times in ages past . . . twice?. . . or was it three times?. . . had something stirred him, made him laboriously move his thumb toward the latch, sluggish, only to let it fall from the lock mechanism. It hadn't been time then, but it was time now, or was it just hubris again? There was no ruler, so he must rule, buy time until Eadwin could be found. Actually, truth to tell, he was enjoying it! The machinations and manipulations, a subtle beglamourment to convince castle dwellers and the various Domain and Ministration Lords that they'd seen him around for years, vaguely tottering about the library, puff-proud with his distant, distant relationship to Constant I. Ignacio might suspect, for chamberlains had their own legends as well, handed down through the years.

With a sigh he adjusted the belt pack under his robes, fiddled with the settings until his pounding heart slowed and steadied. He limped to the old table, pulled a pencil and a yellowed sheet of paper from the small drawer. Make a list. Always helps, always soothes. The cramped handwriting looked as old-fashioned as he, the letter shapes bent and twisted, just as he was, nothing modern or comely about them, but legible.

1) Keep Special Envoy and her colleagues out of
   harm's way.
2) Find Eadwin.

He knew all too well that his innermost heart's desire would never come to pass if he failed at these tasks. More likely he'd run down, slowly fade away, never to have another chance to hear Carrick's voice. That was what duty meant, and it was his duty to preserve Marchmont. He was the only one who viewed it that way, he was sure. But then, years of hindsight did have their value. Now, if he could just keep Maurice and Arras from each other's throats. He chuckled at the thought. Frankly, he didn't care if he succeeded at that or not. Still, for Wilhelmina's sake, for Fabienne's sake, he'd try.

PART
FIVE

PART

FIVE

"We must leave! Return to Canderis before another madman
decides to finish us off! Our lives are jeopardized and our
country insulted!" Bashing with a poker at the glowing logs,
Venret wheeled to face the others, truculent, his poker extended like a sword. "Bad enough before to be confined to
the city, but now we're further restricted," a broad sweep
around the suite with the poker, "virtual prisoners, truly
under guard. And pent up like this, it's even easier to attack
."

They'd argued it time and again since they'd been escorted to this high tower suite to ensure their safety, they'd
been informed. Doyce sat, face buried in her hands, Jacobia
with a protective arm around her shoulders. Khar had draped
herself across Doyce's lap, ever-watchful.

"The four of us finally raised T'ss." The recollected effort made Rawn wince at the strain. **"He and Sarrett have
advanced close enough to receive. They'll alert the others
of our predicament."** Rawn had captured everyone's attention except Jacobia's. **"They need to know the truth of the
matter."** Khar's amber eyes widened with approval, then
closed as she concentrated on her Bond. Fine but frightened
after the attempt on her life, Doyce now quivered like the final ivy leaf being buffeted from its stem by a winter's storm.
Delayed shock, Khar judged, but Doyce had been chary
about revealing her innermost thoughts, wrapping them
tightly around herself, not exactly isolating the ghatta, but
not accepting her strength either. Humans wasted their ener-
gies in the wrong causes, so prodigal. It was over, done.
Why wouldn't Doyce let her heal the damage?

Nakum sat cross-legged on the floor, Saam crouched beside him. "I agree, Jenret, but how do we," he paused, surveyed their suite, "escape this tower, avoid the guards? And
leaving's only our first obstacle."

Aelbert claimed the center of the floor. "Escape? Absolutely not! A greater danger and an unspeakable breach of faith with the Marchmontians. We'll never attain our goals if we leave!" Jenret confronted him, tapping the poker's tip against Aelbert's top uniform button, right at the base of his throat. N'oor squeaked in alarm and came rushing, only to have Rawn shoulder her away, blocking her, sidestepping in front of each frantic move. Face red, Aelbert continued, volume unabated, "May I remind you, our mission is to determine the cause of these incidents and find a solution!"

"You can't find a solution if you're dead!" Jenret stood nose-to-nose with him now. "Or do you think that if something happens to Doyce, you'll negotiate for Canderis, you little. . . ." The final word unuttered, Jenret stabbed the poker into the floor, just short of Aelbert's foot.

Never taking his eyes from Jenret's face, Aelbert edged the poker aside and entreated, "Don't you see? This is our chance to negotiate a favorable treaty, while they're embarrassed and shamed by this incident. I couldn't have planned it better if I'd tried. It enhances our bargaining position." He rubbed his hands with glee, oblivious to Jenret's scowl, his expression indicating an open-handed blow was all too likely to follow.

But instead Jenret broke away with visible effort, poured himself another drink, glass unsteady. Stung by his forgetfulness, he queried, "Doyce? Some brandy? It might help."

Her head jerked at his voice and her haunted look struck him dumb. Please, blessed Lady, don't let her slip backward again. First last night, now this, and he wouldn't blame her for withdrawing. How much of it did he bear responsibility for? He thought she nodded in agreement, but he wasn't sure; she still shook too hard. Taking it for assent, he poured. Even if she didn't want it, it wouldn't go to waste, he'd see to that. At least they were comfortably quartered, though no comfort came from imprisonment. He silently laughed at the thought, wondering how long she'd imprisoned his heart? After last night she'd paroled him, the last thing he wanted. Bringing the drink, he wrapped her hands around the glass, risked cupping them with his own, steadying, patient, ignoring his sister's startled understanding, as if she at last appreciated the depth of his involvement.

"I agree with Jenret. Returning to Canderis would be prudent." The vote of support came from Saam, who had stalked to Doyce's side, gray bulk comforting against her legs, nose stretched to touch Khar's, testing the ghatta's reaction.

"But there's no way to leave without being seen—the door's guarded. Do we fly out of a fourth floor window, wing our way home?" Aelbert protested. "We simply have to sit tight, have patience." How was he supposed to report to Maurice, locked up like this? And why had someone tried to kill Doyce? That wasn't part of the plan, not as he knew it. At least N'oor realized he'd had nothing to do with that, that he could have been killed himself. Or was that Maurice's plan?

Rawn stepped aside from the trembling N'oor, letting her run to Aelbert's side. He didn't understand the little ghatta, but he admired her loyalty. **"There are always ways to leave, and ghatti have always found them. We simply haven't looked yet, but look we shall. But where do we run after we escape? Won't they search for us at the borders?"**

"So, we work the puzzle a piece at a time," Nakum clutched his earth-bond to still its clamor, enthusiastic at the thought of an adventure, of being free, of being in charge again. "Can we escape and regain our horses? If not, everything will take longer. You can't move with the speed and stealth of an Erakwan." Knowing his final statement an incontrovertible fact, he surveyed them, relieved that Doyce held herself steady, heeding his counsel. She believed in him, trusted him, and he wouldn't fail her.

Hand on Jacobia's shoulder, she stood, the movement capturing everyone's attention. "We should leave, not only because of the physical danger, but also to personally report to the Monitor and the High Council." She rubbed her temples as if trying to force the words free. "The stakes are too high and our negotiation powers limited. If we have to go to ground before we can safely reach Canderis, so be it. I . . . I can't bear . . . being cooped up like this, no matter what dangers loom outside. Khar, love, can you and the ghatti find a way out for us?"

Khar's expression turned grave, thoughtful. **"Won't know until we've tried. Rawn, Saam,"** and the final name came with a certain reticence, if not outright distaste, **"N'oor, let's see what we can discover. The Marchmontians don't really comprehend our ways—or our abilities. They may** let us out—indeed, have to let us out." Her whiskers ruffled and spread as she side-glanced the others.

Saam rubbed a paw across a ghatti smirk, erased it. **"Yes, I didn't notice any ... ghatti 'facilities' ... should I say? And I, for one, have been seized by a powerful urge to answer a call of nature. Haven't you?"** Rawn nodded in excited agreement, and even N'oor appeared in thrall to the power of suggestion, ready to scratch at the door.

Of the humans, Nakum, grinning, was the first to understand, and rapped at the door, held whispered colloquy with the guards outside, their mutters rising, disconcerted. "And the smell," he elaborated, "if they don't get outside in time. Impossible to remove, permeates everything." With a straight face he pushed the door open and waved the ghatti through, tails erect, marching in single file, Saam, followed by Khar and N'oor, Rawn as rear guard. N'oor cast an anxious look over her shoulder as they exited, but that was all.

Jenret poured himself another drink. "Well, now we wait."

The waiting encompassed several days as the ghatti roved at will, wary guards gradually growing complacent about their excursions at any time of the day or night. The ghatti made brief forays, wandered through corridors, explored rooftop routes, wall-walked, drain-checked, charted the shift changes, the movements of meals and visitors, all with green and gold-eyed innocence, purring greetings at the guards, rubbing an unsuspecting leg. Jenret paced in a lather of impatience, while Aelbert merely hummed and smiled with long-suffering patience. His time spent in carving intricate shapes into a smoothed piece of kindling, Nakum's brow creased with concentration as he worked a tiny obsidian crescent that no one had identified as a knife of sorts. Otherwise it would have been removed with the rest of their weapons. Pale, edgy with lack of sleep, Doyce immersed herself in a tattered romance, an escape—if not from this guarded suite, then from everyone around her. Jacobia alternated reading with whining, wheedling each in turn to play cards, complaining under her breath about Jenret's continued drinking, or constructing card houses with Aelbert's help.

Yanking yet another bottle from Jenret's hands and tossing it into the fire hard enough to break the bottle, Nakum finally broke the impasse regarding Jenret's drinking. The flames danced and flared as they swallowed the alcohol. "Enough," he announced, wiping his hands on his leggings, half-stunned by the enormity of what he'd done, confronting someone so much older than he. "We can't carry you when we escape, not if you're drunk. Uncloud your mind."

Jenret went slack with drunken shock, but the anger helped clear his head. "All right, all right, I'm in control!"

Jacobia scuttled to the fireplace, swung the crane to hang the heavy iron kettle, ready to boil water for cha. "Jenner, please," her voice sounded lost and afraid. "Please be good. Listen to Nakum and don't be angry at him."

With as much steadiness as he could muster, he kissed his sister on the forehead. "Sorry, love. Brew me some cha and I'll be right as rain." A boldfaced lie, but how could he explain? He'd survive without the liquor, conquer the mind-voices on his own, refuse to listen as he had before. He'd sensed their distant taunts through their days of imprisonment, words at the very verge of hearing. Locks and keys, always something about locking in or locking out, cruel irony given their situation. Once he'd sworn he'd heard Constant Minor's testy, *"Oh, bosh! Listen, you blockhead!"* Rawn had tried to comfort him, remind him of his over vivid imagination. How susceptible was he? He'd go insane if they didn't escape soon!

A scratching in the hallway, one of the ghatti waiting for entrance. Aelbert waited for the sound of the key, opened the door a crack to let N'oor slide through. **"Others'll be back soon."** The little ghatta twitched her skin, hectic with eagerness. **"Others'll be back soon, but said I could bring the news. Sarrett and T'ss and Bard and M'wa are within the city walls, working on a plan!"**

A tiny muscle twitched by Aelbert's left eye. "Well, good. How clever of you all," and he muffled his sarcasm, muffled his despair, and hid his shaking hands beneath his tabard. It wasn't N'oor's fault he couldn't share her enthusiasm. What should he tell Maurice? And did he want to? He'd done as he'd been told, hadn't he? Perhaps he could find a way to let the others escape without him; they weren't really necessary to his plan.

♣

Syndar Saffron hoisted the beer stein and toasted Boersma. "Lysenko, you old bastard! Thought you'd failed me for sure. Oh, Giselle Goelet oozed sympathy, but had to admit that justice smiled on the Internal Affairs Lord, what . . .?" he groped for the name as he drained his beer.

"Emeril Alighieri, and don't shout about it," Boersma implored as he hunched over the table. "Syndar, you've *got* to understand the situation here . . ." A whoop and a roar drowned him out as an arm-wrestling match reached an unanticipated conclusion, delighting a minority of wagerers. He checked around him, drew closer, "Syndar, you've got to listen. It took me three days away from Sidonie to straighten this out, and by rights I should have let them whip you and dump you back across the border. I don't know what's gone on in my absence; alliances shift overnight. Even Giselle didn't act as cordial as before." He chewed at his lip, eyes somber and watchful under sandy, bushy brows.

But Saffron was engrossed in the next arm-wrestling match. "Remember when we used to do that?" He turned serious, pivoted toward his friend. "Blessed Lady, the beer's fine, but I could do without. Why waste time here? I want to see her so much, Lysenko, see that she's safe." The skin on his bullet-shaped, hairless head clenched and rolled in fleshy folds, his amethyst eyes suspiciously damp. "You don't know what it's like, can't begin to imagine," he choked, "and I can't even claim her as my own, not without dishonoring the memory of my best friend and shaming his wife! Can't we go now?"

Boersma hardened himself to the plea; too much was at stake to have Saffron bulling into the middle of the situation. "Just listen to what I'm trying to tell you! It's probably safer to talk here, not back at the castle."

The tavern door swung open, bringing in a gust of night air and a host of new arrivals, all well dressed, mannerly, surrounding a man wearing violet and white satin stretched across what had once been a magnificent chest, now slack muscles and fat sinking toward gut. For some reason Syndar Saffron noted the legs, pipestem thin in comparison to the rest of the man, hose accentuating well-turned calves. Popinjay, he snorted, too old and too fat to parade around like that. Suspicious, he sniffed the air—perfumed and pomaded, too, although he could use a touch of that himself: three nights in a jail cell hadn't done much for his cleanliness. He smiled as the man put finger to his lips, tiptoed behind Boersma, still striving to make Syndar listen.

"Lysenko, as I live and breathe!" the man roared, a ringed hand slapping Boersma's back, driving the smaller man's chest into the table at the unexpectedness of it. "More ale, over here, quickly!" He waved and tavern boys ran for the bar. "What happened to your friend here? Looks as if he's had a bad thrashing, but undoubtedly took a few down with him." Pumping Saffron's hand with enthusiasm, "I'm Prince Maurice, Lord of the Nord and Defense Lord."

Tired as he was, Saffron caught the triple titles, rose respectfully. "Syndar Saffron, Merchanter." No fool, he left off from where, watched Lysenko right himself with something approaching relief. "Fool goddaughter's run off and I've been searching for her for days, scared heartsick."

Maurice edged Boersma along the bench until he'd gained enough space for comfort. "Oh, I know, I *know*." Deep sorrow tinged his voice, the pathetic bravado of a man putting on a brave front. "Has there been any sign, any word?"

"I thought she was likely to be here, and Lysenko's confirmed it." He leaned back, feeling suddenly expansive in his relief, delighted to find someone to share it.

Maurice's eyes closed, he bowed over clasped hands. "The Lady bless your endeavors. I know, I know what it's like, truly I do." He choked, patted at his chest. "My ... Eadwin, my son, only child. Missing for near a year now. At least there's one happy ending." Suddenly he sat straight, a smile almost cracking the makeup on his face. "But what are you doing dawdling here? Go, go! Let's ride to the city together and find her!"

❧

Although well into the time of night when the first true sleep hits heavy and hard, not a person in the suite slept. All stood ready, gear winnowed to bare necessities, strapped for carrying if they couldn't reach the horses. The absence of weapons galled them, had from the beginning, but they'd have to do without. All lamps extinguished, the room was dense with darkness, comforting and close, the final fireplace coals charring themselves to ashes.

"We need a distraction," Nakum whispered, the sound foreign in the silence. "A surprise, but not overly alarming."

"I can manage that," Khar mindwalked, smug.

Rawn growled back. **"No, let me. I'll give them a surprise they won't soon forget."** Most of Jenret's pent-up frustration had been transferred to the ghatt, invisible in the dark.

Saam chuckled, turned two tight circles. **"No, Rawn, let Khar. Her plan has a simple, economical ghatti elegance you'll relish. Wait and see."**

Blindly reaching in the dark, Doyce hugged the ghatta. *"Khar, what are you up to?"* No response except for a purr, but the ghatta's whole body twitched with amusement. *"Well, be careful, then,"* she chided as the ghatta slid free.

"Ready?" And Khar began to scratch at the door insistently, harder than usual, claws scraping its polished finish.

"Damn cats never know which side of the door they want to be on," the guard complained from the hallway, followed by a sound of sleepy stretching as he unbolted the door to let the ghatta out.

Khar came at a brisk trot, stopped dead just over the threshold, hunkering on the carpet and looking with plaintive entreaty at the guards. "AYE-wah-wah!" A cry of pain split the air as she began to cough and heave, sides rippling as she stretched her neck and grimaced. "AYE-wah-wah! WAH!" Retches of dry heaving followed by a vomiting gurgle filled the air.

"Sweet Lady, what's wrong with the cat!" exclaimed one of the guards. "Do ye think it's been poisoned?"

Khar heaved again, panting, as if trying to turn her stomach inside out. "I don't know," replied the other, "but we're in deep trouble if she sickens and dies on us! The Prince said to keep them as safe as the people."

"Well, I'm going for help!" cried the first guard, and a nervous clatter reverberated from the stairs.

With that Jenret and Nakum slammed their shoulders to the door, cannoning the guard into the wall, silenced and disarmed before he could shout for aid. Nakum snatched his sword and dagger.

Doyce pelted behind them. "Khar, Khar, love, are you all right?" she crooned as she gathered the limp ghatta to her. When she spotted the pile of what looked like soggy gray matted felt on the carpet she began to chuckle under her breath.

The ghatta washed her face, gave a lingering stretch as

she inspected the deposit. **"Fur ball,"** she confirmed. **"Felt it building for days."** She looked around pointedly. **"I do think it might be wise if we left as speedily as possible. Unless we have time for a snack?"** Her hopeful hint disregarded, she watched Jacobia and Aelbert come out, laden with bundles and packs, Aelbert protesting vehemently but quietly, Jacobia shushing him as she pushed him along. **"No, I guess not. Rawn, lead the way."**

"No, wait!" Rawn cuffed Jenret's leg, snagging him back. **"This way! Now!"** Jenret ducked behind the corridor's bend just in time to avoid a pair of guards at the head of the stairs.

By the eight Disciples! If only he had his sword or staff, he'd show them! But he didn't; they'd confiscated all their weapons, and that—as much as the assassination attempt—had convinced him of their vulnerability, helplessly dependent on the guards. And the Household Guards obeyed Maurice. To disallow them the means to protect themselves meant only one thing—that they truly were prisoners. Doyce was now armed with the guard's confiscated sword—he'd insisted despite her heated, whispered protests, refused to see her defenseless again—and Jacobia held the dagger in a death grip. Resettling his grip on the piece of firewood, he wished now that he'd brought a bottle, not a full one, but an empty to serve as club, or to slash with its jagged, broken neck. Raising his makeshift club, he began to creep forward.

Rawn cuffed harder, halted him. **"No need, no need. Back up and take the turning at the left."** He retreated and gestured Nakum to him. Far better than having Aelbert at his side, and better yet that he didn't have to call on Doyce to second him. To have her so damnably close to danger again, but acting as a team . . . he let the thought fade.

A change in the silence surrounding him, the most minute movement of air, as Nakum ghosted to his side. **"Where does leftward take us?"** He pressed his mouth to Nakum's ear, confessed, **"I'm so blasted turned around that I don't know where we are."** With any luck, Nakum's days of tagging after Ezequiel might have taught him the castle's layout.

Nakum considered, body spring-coiled, ready but conserving his energy until needed. **"Through private chambers, I** think, and toward the rear of the palace," he mouthed back. "Saam says there's one more guard to pass."

Saam chimed in **"But he'll have a surprise from a different direction. A little welcome from Bard. M'wa says he's moving into position now."** They crept with aching slowness through the dim hallways, not pitch-dark but the kind of heavy darkness that shifted and moved, palpably alive with their shallow breathing; shadows assumed the false weight and quality of solid, immovable objects, and immovable objects stood concealed, ready to trip the unwary and betray their presence. **"A bit farther, just a bit,"** Saam guided Nakum even with Jenret and Rawn, Jacobia in the middle, Aelbert and Doyce with their ghatti in the rear.

Suddenly aware of an unexpected shaft of light behind him, Jenret heard Jacobia's choked-off gasp. Everyone froze as a guard exited a privy chamber, head bent while he fumbled at trouser buttons. Materializing from behind Jacobia, Aelbert floored the unsuspecting man with a wicked blow to his neck, chopping as if he had a chicken on the block. Doyce caught the man as he fell, Jacobia moving to help as if she'd done it all her life. The guard was trussed with scarves, handkerchiefs, and belts before he knew what had hit him. Aelbert slipped the dagger, the guard's only weapon, into his belt, ignoring Jenret's outstretched hand.

"Nice of you to mention we had company," Doyce hissed at Khar.

"Thought he was going to be occupied longer with that disgusting picture pamphlet," Khar responded, dignity injured. **"Besides, N'oor and I were ready when he came out."** N'oor squeaked a hurried agreement as she bounded over the guard and spat at him.

Overeager, they rushed now, crowding and bumping each other until common sense and stealth took hold, causing them to slow and drop back, mimic the exaggerated silence surrounding them. Only the ghatti and Nakum traveled as if darkness were second nature. Finally, the weak light of a wall sconce reflected around the next junction, wavered in the air currents from a stone stairwell. With deliberation Saam advanced, each paw pad caressing the carpeting, avoiding the stone flooring at the carpet's margins so his half-extended claws didn't click. At the bend in the hallway he sat, ears twitching in impatience.

"**Ready**," came M'wa's mindvoice, prosaic, matter-of-fact.

Saam craned around at the humans. "**Don't panic if you hear a little scuffle**," he instructed. "**Tell Bard 'now.'**"

It sounded like the plumping of a pillow by a zealous housemaid; two quick, practiced thumps, then the rustling sound of a pile of blankets and dirty linens efficiently tossed to the floor. Without waiting for instructions, Nakum and Jenret eased forward, flat against the wall but poised to charge to Bard's aid. From his kneeling position on the floor, Bard caught their eye, warning them ahead softly. He still cradled the guard's prone form, laying him comfortably on the floor, gagging the unconscious man's jaws as the two helped bind the figure.

Rather than risk any further noise, Bard let M'wa do the talking. "**Greetings from Bard**," M'wa transferred the thought with ghatti politeness. "**Nice weather, health good, so forth.**" The black ghatt with the high white stocking on his left front leg dipped his head in greeting, white whiskers electric with amusement. "**This way, please.**" Bard was already descending the stairs, hand signals guiding the others who followed. "**Sarrett and T'ss are in the stables. All we have to do is cross the side yard unseen and we'll be there.**"

Doyce stayed at Jacobia's elbow, realizing that she alone had no idea of what instructions M'wa transmitted. She cursed herself for over-anticipating but couldn't help it as she mindspoke the ghatt in the lead. *"And how do we leave the stables unseen?"*

M'wa's tail lashed one question mark through the air, stilled. "**Don't know—yet**," he confessed. "**Khar, could you produce another fur ball?**"

Khar sounded miffed. "**I saved that one for days! You don't manufacture them on command, you know!**" Despite the tension, Doyce grinned. She'd often wondered if the ghatti considered them a sort of sacred deposit, meant to adorn the most costly carpet, never the bare floor.

"I don't think a fur ball will distract everyone from six mounted strangers with five ghatti asking for the gates to be opened during the dead of night, do you?" Fur ball or no, their predicament didn't seem very humorous. No one answered her plaintive mindthought as they crept, huddled against the buildings, ducking beneath windows, lighted or

not, pausing at each closed door before gliding past in urgent silence until one by one they gained the half-open stable door. Aelbert bumped into it, making the old hinges creak, and choked down a curse.

Two dusty, glass-globed lanterns lighted the stables and highlighted Sarrett, slumped on a bale of hay. When she moved, they saw the unsheathed sword hidden by her cloak. A cluttered trestle table showed a sticky scattering of cards and dice, empty ale flagons and stoneware rum bottles, one on its side still dripping. Muffled snores and the smell of vomit mingled with the smell of oats, hay, horse liniment, leather. Two stable hands, one young, barely to shaving, the other gray-thatched and with a wooden leg, were gagged and bound to a support pillar; neither wore much in the way of clothing, the older man dressed in a tatty gray undervest, trousers, and one stocking, the younger with vomit-stained pants only. They slept undisturbed, chins propped on chests, snorting and groaning.

Khar trotted to the younger of the two as T'ss materialized from a stall. **"Fur ball, I think,"** said the white ghatt with the black stripings, nodding at the younger man and crinkling his nose.

Sarrett unsteadily greeted them, and for the first time Doyce noticed her hair, her beautiful silver-gilt hair, reflected dun brown in the light. Still lovely, but on an entirely different, almost approachable plane of beauty. Bard took her arm, his usually soft speech rough with disapproval. "Are you all right?"

Swallowing a belch, Sarrett threw them a sickly smile. "Fine," she whispered with exaggerated caution. "Went according to plan, ekshept," she pulled herself straight, clenched her lips against another burp, "except I had to drink more than I intended to keep the game going. Poured out as much as I could, downed the rest."

"Well, you went a bit overboard on verisimilitude, I'd say." Bard surveyed the table and benches, scanned the floor and retrieved a belt and a weskit, a neck scarf. "Anything else you're missing?" Loath to check beneath her cloak, he stood dangling the offending articles of clothing in his hand.

"Course not! Parse taught me a few sleight of hand tricks, how to palm cards, lead them on."

Jenret blocked Jacobia's view of the scene, his disapprovng voice starting to rise. "You mean you strip-wagered at 'ally-Ho?"

Doyce peeled Sarrett's cloak back, discreet about what the younger woman wore underneath. Helping Sarrett into her veskit, buttoning it, cinching the belt around her waist, Doyce loosely tied the scarf in place while Sarrett stood like a doll being dressed, arms propped on Doyce's shoulders. "I've wigured a fay out of here," she confided breathily, too close for comfort, given the blast of rum that greeted Doyce's nose. Then her complexion drained to a fish-belly white, she burped again, and staggered to a stall where sounds of retching could be heard.

Torn between admiration and pity, Aelbert shook his head. "My, what a wretched experience?" he punned as he located a bucket of water and a clean dipper and went to Sarrett's aid. "No matter," he said as Doyce tried to help, "I've dealt with this sort of thing since I was old enough to walk. Earned a ha'penny for each drunk I cleaned and sobered enough to drink some more. But I never expected it of Miss Perfect here."

Wondering at Aelbert's revelation, Doyce joined the others as they began saddling their horses, stowing their gear, offering Sarrett as much privacy as they could, given the need for speed and silence. "I don't know what Sarrett planned, don't know if she knows at the moment," Bard brought his gelding around, brows furrowed, "but I think it involves the postern gate through the ring wall. We discussed that earlier as the most likely exit, but we'll have to figure how to pass through without causing too much of a stir."

Aelbert rejoined them, wiping his hands on an old piece of sacking. "I can cause a diversion. I don't plan to go with you, so there's no problem at all if I'm captured."

His furtive anxiety took Doyce aback. "You came with us, and you're going with us, Aelbert. As Special Envoy, I'm ordering you. Is that clear?"

"No, *you* don't understand! It's crucial I remain!" A strange glitter of suppressed relief flashed in his middling brown eyes, but he wasn't looking at her, she realized as the shadows moved, reshaped themselves to reveal four men, each armed with a heavy crossbow, cocked and drawn.

"I think we should discuss precisely where you plan to go." Arras Muscadeine stepped into view with a jaunty arro-

gance that matched the small, superior smile lurking unde
his mustache. "Please be so kind as to drop your weapons.'

❖

The Monitor knuckled his brow as if to embed a new ide.
in his weary brain. Too much on his mind and now this
"Perhaps within the realm of possibility, but not very prob
able." Even granting that much bothered him, and his reluc
tance shown all too clear. Hadn't he known the lad, boy t
man? "Mahafny really believes A.O. is Aelbert Orsborne?'
Saying it aloud did little to convince him.

Refusing to say more, Swan Maclough let him wrestle
with the idea. She trailed a hand on Koom's shoulder
blessed his warm solidity. **"Have you accepted it your**
self?" Koom gave her hand a rough lick.

"I don't know," she confessed. *"Mahafny's not prone t*
jumping to conclusions without supporting evidence. The ev
idence isn't as strong as we might like, but it's there. Do yo
believe?"

The ghatt considered. **"I don't know. Strange, but I'v**
only the haziest memory of N'oor's and Aelbert's train
ing, and I don't think I'm becoming forgetful in my ol
age ... or you in yours."

"Exactly," she skimmed the files in her lap. *"Even review*
ing the records doesn't help much, as if things have bee
erased from my mind." She finally spoke aloud. "I don't lik
it, Kyril."

Elbows on the desk, fingers splayed across his face, th
Monitor mumbled from behind them, "But why woul
Aelbert have been at the Hospice?"

"What do you really know about him?" she countered
"Try to tell me, fill in as many details as you can."

He rocked, eyes screwed shut in concentration. "Funny
he's been with me so long, always at my side, that it's har
to remember the details. I guess," he hesitated, "that I'v
taken him for granted, the way you do any useful object un
til it breaks down on you. Not exactly a complimentar
thing to say about another human being, is it?"

The ruddy ghatt planted front paws on the Monitor's kne
poking his head under his arm for attention. Van Beiever
obliged by tickling his ears. "N'oor was always too bashfu
to let me do that."

Slowly now, Maclough counseled herself, it's not a pleasant suggestion, but it's necessary. Koom knew what she was contemplating, agreed with it himself without actually saying so. "Kyril, would you consider letting Koom Truth-Seek your thoughts? At least verify them as you tell me what you remember about Aelbert? We have to know more. I dislike judging him when he isn't here to defend himself, but if there's something . . ." she chose and discarded words, couldn't find a one she wanted, "unstable about him, he may be putting the others in jeopardy, whether he realizes it or not."

Kyril van Beieven jerked his hand from Koom's head as if the ghatt had burned him. "Blessed Lady, Swan! I *am* the Monitor, you know! Truth-Seek the Monitor?" he snorted.

"Are you pulling rank on me?" Swan inquired with all the sweet reasonability she could muster. "Or are you claiming the Monitor is beyond reproach, beyond human frailties, all-knowing, all-seeing, all-powerful? Never tired and irritable and sometimes forgetful, like a certain Seeker General I know?" She slapped the file folder on her lap, and the papers fanned and fell loose to the floor. "Oh, flu-flar and fardle!"

The exclamation brought a smile to the Monitor's lips, albeit a small one, more rueful than anything else. "Compared notes with my wife about my forgetfulness, have you?"

Scrambling to retrieve the papers, Swan stretched under the desk for the last one. "Damn it, Kyril, *I* can't recall much about them, and neither can Koom, and that scares me. Let's put the pieces together between us, let Koom judge if we're remembering accurately." Her head popped above his desk, her face flushed, "And you ought to have this place dusted more often."

He came out from behind the desk, helped Swan into her seat again, remained standing. "Fine, I'll tell you both what I know about Aelbert." A hand gesture invited Koom to perch on his desk, and the ghatt sprang up, head turning from one to the other.

Shifting his weight from foot to foot, van Beieven began. "Ten, no, eleven years ago I found Aelbert hiding in the barn when I went to do the milking. The lad looked frightened to death and twice as hungry and cold, no jacket, just a tattered sweater about two sizes too big for him. Took him to be about ten, but it turned out he was twelve, or so I learned later."

He shrugged. "What could I do? I brought him inside and had Marie feed him. Seemed polite enough, well-spoken, but edgy, scared. I reached for a slice of bread when he wasn't expecting it and he pulled back as if I were going to swat him, dodged and rolled out of that chair faster than anything I'd ever seen. Thought Marie was going to break into tears, it was so pitiful.

"Couldn't get much out of him, got the sense he'd been on his own for some time, making do the best he could, odd jobs, petty thievery if necessary. Didn't volunteer much of anything, though I got the impression he'd been sick recently, had been in a Hospice ..." the Monitor shook his head, shocked by the word he'd dredged out of the depths of his mind. "Hospice?" he repeated, and Koom's green eyes glinted.

"At any rate, I kept him on, gave him odd jobs about the farm, and before I knew it, he was indispensable, couldn't imagine trying to run the place without him. I was considering running for Monitor in the next election, testing the waters, doing some politicking, and more and more of the work fell on his shoulders. Figured that if I won, I could leave him in charge of the farm while I served my term. But it didn't quite happen that way."

Despite herself, Swan interrupted, over-eager, knowing the question in her mind and in Koom's. "When did he Bond with N'oor?"

"That's what I was coming to," the Monitor complained. "I swear all you Seekers want to know about is yourselves and your precious ghatti. Perish the thought the rest of the world exists!"

Humor it was, but a little too heavy-handed for Swan's liking. **"Because it comes too near the truth,"** Koom muttered, abashed, as Swan winced an apology in the Monitor's direction, not quite trusting her voice. **"We're a bit ... self-centered sometimes."**

As if sensing he'd gained the moral upper hand, the Monitor patted Koom, magnanimous in victory. "It's all right, you know, but we lesser mortals can feel a tinge of jealousy. At any rate, Marie sent Aelbert into town one day for supplies," he caught Swan's eyebrow query and amended, "right before the elections, it was. He was trotting down the road, barefoot, said he moved faster that way, boots in a sack. He always pulled them on before he got to town, concerned about his appearance, always painfully neat and tidy now that he had the chance. Did his own laundry, borrowed the pressing irons so as not to burden Marie." Realizing he digressed, the Monitor pulled himself back on track. "There he was, trotting along, when the next thing he knew a little ghatten latched herself around his ankle, sank her teeth into his big toe when he tried to peel her off. She was the skinniest little thing, biggest feet I've ever seen, all those extra toes. You know," he appealed to Swan and Koom, "the funny thing is that I didn't know there were any ghatti within leagues of us. Still don't know where that little mite came from, seemed just as lost and scared as Aelbert when I found him. But they certainly seemed to need each other.

"The rest you know. I hated to lose him, but I sent Aelbert and N'oor to you for training. I came to Gaernett when I won the election, asked for him back as aide as soon as you could spare him. We've always had a Seeker serving the Monitor, more ceremonial than anything else these days. Good to have him back, I'd forgotten how much I depended on him until he was gone for that year of training. And when he came back, it felt as if he'd never been away."

"That *year* of training?" Swan pounced on the word. "A year? Kyril, you know full well Seekers train for two years."

"Well, of course. But you told me then they were such apt pupils that you could accelerate their training. Don't you remember? I didn't until just now."

But Swan barely listened, studying her files intently, traced her finger under one line. The dates were there in black and white and she hadn't noticed.

"But it makes no sense," she protested. "I can't believe I'd have allowed that unless you twisted my arm. They'd need a full two years of training to ride circuit after your term as Monitor is done. What guarantee would they have the next Monitor would keep them on, wouldn't choose another Seeker pair? A year just isn't enough—you could learn everything, but you wouldn't have the practice you'd need to be fully proficient."

Koom's underjaw worked back and forth, nervous little shiftings. **"One year, not two. What they think they know and what they know from practical experience are two different things. Bonds could falter or fail, misunderstandings arise. Not a good thought."** The ghatt's worry was clear. **"So, what we've gained are two little nuggets:**

first, that Aelbert did go to a Hospice at least once; second, their training was abbreviated, and there's nothing in the report other than the date that would indicate you thought them so exceptional.

"Other than that, the Monitor's memories were too concise, don't you think? He's not blocking, but every time I try to read him, I feel as if I'm mirror-gazing, me reflecting back at me, absolutely dizzy-making. He's not fighting the Seeking, but something is. An impulsion of some sort, the same that we have when we strive to remember Aelbert." The ghatt left the desktop with a bound, pressed himself against Swan, daunted by the confusion surging inside him. Failed, he'd failed, when so much more needed to be understood. A half-truth was not the truth.

Clutching at straws, Swan grasped for one final question, any question whose answer might shed light on the riddle of Aelbert. "And he's been with you ever since?" What was she searching for? If Koom couldn't find it, how could she? Still, common sense never hurt, and she had that in abundance, plus a plucky stubbornness from her years as Seeker General.

"Swan," the Monitor grumbled, "I've *told* you that. Yes, yes, yes!"

"Yes, but I *assume* he eats, sleeps, everyday things of that sort?"

Gauging the acidity lacing her comment, the Monitor strove to be serious. "Of course, but in moderation, just as he does everything else."

"So, no friends, no romantic interludes? Hasn't he ever taken some time off, a few days here or there to relax?"

"No, he's always at my side." The strain was beginning to tell on van Beieven and he fought a desire to laugh, anything to release the building tension. The Seeker General'd worry him like a dog a bone! "Marie grumbles she's surprised she hasn't woken up and found him sleeping between us so he'd be fresh to start work as soon as I arose. That's why Marie felt so relieved when he ..." van Beieven struck his brow, discomfited at the unforeseen direction his conversation was heading, ". . . when he took three days off a year ago last fall. Said he'd run into a childhood friend, wanted to attend his wedding in the bride's northern village. I . . . I honestly didn't remember until now," he appealed to Swan. "Almost didn't feel as if he were gone, he left N'oor with me for company, to keep me out of trouble, he teased."

And had no idea why Koom suddenly leaped with excitement. **"That's when Mahafny said Yulyn and Davvy told her Bert visited, apparently not for the first time, but for the only time in years, and the only time the two of them met him. Oh, well done, my Bondmate!"**

❧

The smell of steam, wet wood, waterproofing compound, and tar hung in the long pontoon shed, enclosed on its sides, but open at each end. Eight men, Faeralleyn Thomas amongst them, worked at sets of sawhorses, each supporting a pontoon under construction.

Faertom held the rib against the frame and lashed it in place with a long strip of dampened cedar bark. Some preferred rivets or staples, but they didn't have the give that bark did—allowing the frame to subtly shift and compromise with the water's force. Rivets and staples pierced the wood, stressed each piece because the metal wouldn't yield gracefully. That he'd learned from his boat-building days with his father and brothers. And he was as fast with his lashing as the others were with their methods. With the spring surveying completed, he'd been assigned here at the pontoon sheds, preparing for the spring floods that might wash out bridges or leave them underwater. While he preferred being out and in the open, wondered what Twink was doing without him, he didn't mind this. Easy enough to lose himself in the work and forget his fellow Transitors existed under the same shed roof with him.

Finished with the last rib, he went to the stack for one of canvas jackets used to cover the pontoons, two jackets to each, stitched together at the middle and then waterproofed, seams sealed with tar. The canvas was awkward and Faertom struggled to align it with the pontoon tip so he could pull it snug and smooth from nose to middle. Just the way his mother so carefully pulled her stockings on each morning by the kitchen fire. And that memory made him lonely, aware he labored in the midst of this bustle with no relatives near and no close friends either.

But in the midst of his sorrow, he jerked his head up, dropped the canvas so its seams fell askew and raced to

Nick's side almost before the shout rang out, "Faertom! Lend a hand over here, lad!"

He placed his strong hands beside Nick's to press the long curve of one of the horizontal frames back to meet the ribs. "Not cured long enough," Nick grumbled. "Just let me pop a rivet in and it won't snap at me again like my old dad's hickory whip." He held on, obedient, while Nick jammed the rivet through, pounded until its head spread and held. The various lengths of frame and ribs were steamed to bend them into their appropriate shapes in the long curing boxes, stones propping the ends, weighing down their middles. The ribs fit into special molds, curved to conform a bit at a time over several octs. "I swear, boy, you've eyes in the back of your head," Nick complimented. "You was here practically afore I called."

He hated it when they said things like that—a little too near to the truth. And in truth he'd gleaned Nick's desperation, the strain on his aging muscles before he'd even sung out for help. With a straight face he turned away from Nick, thrust his hands through his thick mane of tawny hair until his index fingers popped out the back, wiggled them. "Yup, Nick, eyes in the back of my head, see?" Deflect any comments that strike too close to home with humor, his father had lectured, make them laugh at you, never laugh at them. That way they'll be well satisfied you're one of them, nothing frightening or unexplainable about you. Nick slapped his knee in appreciation and guffawed, yelled for the others to look. "Eyes in the back of his head, he has!"

"Well, well," the shop foreman commented. "Just when we have visitors, we decide on a little entertainment, do we?" Dropping his hands, Faertom moved to Nick's side. "Gentlemen Transitors, two new High Conciliators who've never had the pleasure of visiting one of our pontoon works. May I present Roxana Mowbridge and Darl Allgood?"

Lady help him! What was he going to do? Faertom lurched into Nick, stepped on his foot. Wonderful, make himself noticeable, why didn't he? What was he going to do? Absolutely nothing if he valued his own life, Allgood's as well, and stared at his shoes as if his existence depended on it. Perhaps it did.

The tour progressed uneventfully, the men showing off their skills to the visitors, trying to outdo one another, while Faertom concentrated on straightening his tangled canvas

cover, sliding it into place. Allgood stopped to watch, helped
hold the two pieces together while Faertom plied the heavy
curved needle to stitch them together. "You look young for
such responsibility. Far from home, lad?" Allgood asked.

"Aye." Faertom worked the curved needle around and
around, strove to keep his stitches tight and even.

"Must be lonely. I'm far from home as well and I know
it is for me. Not always sure the natives of a new town like
me." Their eyes met at last, Allgood cool, Faertom flustered.
"It's not always easy to get up the courage to speak with
strangers. Hard to reveal your heart to someone new."

*"Don't be afraid, lad, your secret's safe with me, as I hope
mine is with you. You must be Thomas-kin. I recognize the
lashing style. Ordered one of their boats years back, had it
carted all the way west to Leger Lake. That's where I'm
from, Wexler, wine-growing country."*

Faertom gulped at the revelation, anchored himself to the
words now spoken aloud. "If you're in Gaernett sometime,
stop by. Maybe I'll be free for a chat. Always like to meet
someone new with such special talents."

"Aye, I'd like that." And Faertom felt a broad smile flooding his face and his heart. Acknowledgment!

Without warning Jenret threw himself at Muscadeine,
wrestling with him for the crossbow, but Muscadeine jerked
free and clouted him under the chin with the stock. Jenret
reeled, dazed, fighting to clear his head. A low growl issuing
from his throat, Rawn snapped his tail once, green eyes
warning Muscadeine not to pursue his advantage. All four
crossbows were again trained unwaveringly on the group.

"Arras, not you!" The betrayal left Doyce heartsick. He'd
pledged his friendship, revealed secrets, taken her into his
confidence. She'd trusted her instincts, judged him worthy,
and she'd been deluded in her trust, betrayed herself and her
friends. Let them all be manipulated like pawns. The proof
stared her in the face that she still wasn't well, wasn't
whole, not if she could make an error of that magnitude.

"Don't judge so harshly or so quickly," Khar admon-
ished.

A smile flashed white beneath the luxuriant mustache,
then his face went somber, solemn again, as if harking to an

inner voice. His conscience, she hoped. At a terse nod, his men obediently released the tension on the crossbows, pointed them groundward. "No, not me, truly. But we haven't much time." His words held an invitation that she didn't know what to make of. Risking a tentative step in his direction, she found she couldn't force herself any further; she would not abandon her friends. Part of her heard Sarrett moan and cough, then swallow hard—no more retching at least.

Muscadeine cocked his head at the sound. "Can she sit her horse? Or will she be decorating our fair country far and wide?"

"With a dose of medication she should be able to stay in the saddle and regret every jounce and hoofbeat enough to make her wish she were dead. But that's a moot point, isn't it?" What was he up to, what did he want? The danger seemed less, but still there, as foreign as Muscadeine and his soldiers.

"And will that one," he nodded in Aelbert's direction, "accompany us willingly or do we bind him to his horse?"

"Ask him yourself and judge. I'm not sure what control I have over him, and I'd like to clarify his loyalties."

Aelbert faced her, body at attention, expression unfathomable. Please! Not now, not when he was so close to his goal! "I think it best to remain, keep lines of communication open with Marchmont. That's what I've been trained for, devoted my life to doing. Complete withdrawal doesn't seem wise, despite the situation we face, but if I'm overruled ... I'll obey."

"Do you trust him?" Arras snapped, brows knitted together. "Do the ghatti trust him?"

The question took her aback, that a Marchmontian would value the ghatti's views. More facets to him than she could easily judge, no way to compartmentalize him—or Aelbert for that matter. "Khar, what do you and the others think about Aelbert and N'oor?"

Conspicuously excluding N'oor, the five ghatti clustered nose-to-nose, deliberating, whiskers flickering, ears twisting as they conversed in falanese, beyond her skill to interpret. **"Something isn't right, but not entirely wrong either. We've warned N'oor of her responsibility."**

At ease against a pillar, Jacobia hovering at his side,

Nakum commented, "Should we ask them your intentions toward us?"

Dropping his jaw, rolling his eyes in mock incredulity, Muscadeine's smile flashed generously wide. "You mean you haven't already?"

So fast and smooth as to almost defy the eyes, Nakum was at his side in one easy movement, his slight build exaggerated by Muscadeine's bulk. "Of course I have. Why else do you think you've lived this long?" A tiny obsidian crescent, nearly lost between his fingers, caressed Muscadeine's throat, drawing a thin line of blood, before he removed the blade.

Eyes never straying from Nakum's, Muscadeine touched a finger to his throat, raised it to his lips for confirmation. He gave a crow of laughter, then quieted, realizing the sound could carry. "Ah, and I wondered about that myself, my Erakwan friend! But then I trusted your judgment from the start. Now, if you don't mind an escort," he paused while his three men joined their circle, "I think it's time to depart."

"Depart where?" Doyce gathered Lokka's reins.

"Where you wish to go, of course, to Canderis. But it will take longer than you anticipated; if you wish to reach there alive, the route must be indirect, I think. Now, let us make ready."

❖

Stripped of all identifying colors and insignia that would mark them as Muscadeine's men, the three soldiers tossed loose turnips and potatoes over the burlap sacks covering Doyce and the others in the wagon-bed. Sarrett groaned, burrowed deeper, death grip on the bucket the youngest guard had thrust, not ungently, into her hands. Doyce sneaked a quick look at the harnessed horses—Lokka and Ophar, the geldings Aelbert and Rolf had ridden—a less than likely looking team, and then sighed, ducking her head under the canvas. Muscadeine's mount was tied to the tail gate.

Throwing a loose tarp over the load, Muscadeine motioned for the ghatti to slide underneath. Then he whistled, calling Felix to him out of the darkness and the dog sprang into the wagon-bed and settled, nose sniffing wetly, eyes bright with doggy excitement. The ghatti hissed and muttered, withdrew farther, bristling at the intrusion. "Sorry, ghatti, but my Felix is too noticeable at my side. Nor would I leave him behind, just as you wouldn't want to be parted from your Bonds."

"Hardly an apt comparison," huffed Rawn, squirming from the dog, who'd extended his long muzzle to sniff a rather personal spot. **"If he licks me, I cannot guarantee my self-control."**

Jenret snarled at the ghatt to be quiet, then continued aloud, "Muscadeine, you'd better know what you're doing." The return of their weapons, including their original ones, had mollified him, Muscadeine decided.

Unable to resist a hearty slap to the canvas bulge he full-well knew to be Jenret, Muscadeine resettled his farmer's smock and clambered onto the wagon seat, tilted his dilapidated straw hat so the wide brim shadowed his face. "Ready," he warned and slapped the reins on the horses' backs. His three soldiers rode the remaining Canderisian horses—flanking the wagon and one following in the rear.

The city streets were darkly quiet, nothing stirring as they reached the postern gate and its guards. "Yo! Load coming through!" shouted the lefthand rider as he rousted the two duty guards. They sprang from the gatehouse, wide awake and capable despite the late—or more aptly—early hour. "Supplies comin' through for the East Troop! Let us through, let us pass! If ye demand a writ for taters 'n turnips we're in sorry shape!" he joked.

The guards surveyed the odd procession, the mismatched team more suited to riding than drayage, the handsome war steed tied to the wagon gate. "That be the Chevalier Capitain's horse," remarked one, envious eyes traveling the length of the procession. A thumping resounded from beneath the tarp and Doyce flinched, unable to see what was happening, but furiously aware of Felix wagging his tail hard, banging back and forth, clearly delighted at recognizing an old friend's voice.

"Course it is," responded the second rider. "Trust you, Corporal, not to forget the Capitain's horse. Kin tell by your badges that you've seen service with the Capitain—only wish I had. Mayhap he'll take me on when we arrive. Beast needed reshoeing. Lord knows I'd love to ride'm stead of this old nag, but 'twouldn't be proper, bringing him tired to the Capitain."

A plumed tail sprouted beyond the canvas, wagging stren-
usly, but hurriedly withdrew at the sound of a hiss. The
:ond watch guard exclaimed, grabbing the Corporal's arm
make him notice and comment. The Corporal refused to
pond, instead shoving his mate toward the gate to open it.
est let ye be on your way then, with your load."

Muscadeine raised a foot to release the wheel brake and
ided the team through, head slumped on his chest as if
lf-dozing. The three riders followed and they rolled out-
le the city walls.

As the watchmen closed the gate, the Corporal com-
nted to his mate, "Notice anything odd 'bout the farmer?"

"No, not particularly."

The Corporal smiled to himself. "Nice boots for a farmer,
il nice boots."

The second watchman may have been slow, but he wasn't
pid, not by a long shot. He squinted, replaying the scene
his mind. "Riding boots, they was. Nice and shining-like,
th spurs. Lord have mercy, ye don't suppose . . . ?" He left
e thought unfinished.

"I don't suppose nothin', and neither do you. Not our
ice to suppose. And if ye should decide to 'suppose' to
meone who'll carry word to that old fart of a Defense
rd, I'll guaran-damn-tee you'll be spitting teeth."

"Did that once after a fight—wasn't a pleasant feeling,
r one I'd like to have again, I guess. 'Suppose' any wise
in wouldn't."

"Fine, just so we're understood on that."

The jouncing went on and on, the air close and dank with
rth, root smell, tarriness from the canvas, and . . . Doyce
iffed, decided once was enough. Khar gave a constricted
eeze. **"Wet dog, phew!"** The ghatta rested her chin on a
rnip with stoic resignation. **"Thank heaven we don't
nell like that when we get wet,"** her superior tone unmis-
kable.

T'ss's voice echoed beneath the canvas. **"I knew a nice
g once, but I was very young."**

"Must have been just yesterday," Rawn snapped. **"Or
e day before at the most."**

The bickering continued as they rolled and bumped along,

silent bickering to human ears, but bickering all the sam
Still, the driver, the Chevalier Capitain, had the oddest fee
ing that he had his back turned to full-scale grumbling. T
ghatti fascinated him, but not for the first time did he that
the Lady that he preferred dogs. Pushing his hat up on h
brow, he cast around to check the lonely road as the s
rose-tinted the rolling hills and meadowlands. Soon he'd
riding again, the Marbon woman at his side, trying to e
plain to her what was happening, what he hoped for, what
feared. And maybe, just maybe, she could help. If not,
would still enjoy the ride and bask in the jealous looks ca
at him by the merchanter, his scowl as black as his clothe

❖

Slicing a turnip with her pocket knife, Doyce hande
pieces to the horses, the velvet softness of Lokka's lips tic
ling her palm as she nibbled at the treat. The mare shook h
head, dismayed, chewing, but not very happily. Her ey
rolled and a dribble of saliva and turnip juice threatene
Doyce's boot. "Not your favorite, eh?" she sympathize
"At least you can leave them behind—bad enough to have
drag a wagon load of them without having to eat them."
Muscadeine snagged the remainder of the turnip from h
and ate it like an apple as he mounted his horse. "They'
not bad—mild, juicy, with a peppery aftertaste. Some wh
aren't so fortunate would be pleased to have these to eat.
Swinging onto Lokka's back without disturbing Kha
Doyce kneed the mare at right angles to Muscadeine. "The
let's leave them for those in need. And what I need to kno
is precisely what you think you're doing. I don't care for b
ing the expendable piece in whatever game you're playing
Are we your prisoners? Escapees? What? Why should yo
so blithely assume we need your assistance or will acce
it?"
"You have already," he stated reasonably and clicke
heels to his horse's sides, whistling Felix after him.
Lokka followed, bringing Doyce even with the Capitain'
steed. "Accepted it, yes—with four crossbows pointed
you, it seemed the prudent choice. Whether we needed it
another matter."
His eyes were constantly scanning the surrounding cou
tryside, with no time to spare for her indignation. With

negligent swing of his arm, he sent his three soldiers, now mounted on their own horses that had been left tied out of sight and waiting, to the sides and the lead while her own group bunched behind her, uneasy at their new-found freedom. They trusted her, and she had to make sure she deserved it, could discharge her duty. "You needed it as well." His words snapped her back to herself with an abruptness that reminded her she had no idea where on earth they were.

They began to wind their way into a stand of long-pin pines, each similar in size and spaced with precise regularity. The lower branches had been pruned, piles of brush were waiting to be removed, and the ground beneath the horses' feet showed a rusty-orange tinge of faded, fallen needles. Any way she looked she traced a straight line, tree after tree serving as connection points, as if they journeyed across a giant grid pattern, a chess board, and he, Arras Muscadeine, was the Chevalier Capitain, the knight, capable of moving in all directions on the board.

"Watershed area. Pioneered and planted by the late Prince Maarten. I remember when he planted them." He eyed her, brusque and assessing, as if to peel through the layers of her thoughts. "I did what I did because you needed help—and I, in turn, require yours. You should understand, I have disobeyed my sacred oath, my orders, to do so. To some, perhaps many, I'll be seen as a seditionist, a turncoat, someone who consorts with the enemy. Except I don't think you are the enemy—the enemy is amongst us, within us, not outside us, and so it has been with our battles on the Northern front. For doing this, my position will be forfeit, and very possibly, my life, if Maurice has his way."

She rode in silence, pondering his confession, the way he held himself eager yet supremely confident in the saddle, awaiting her answer. Dressed much as he'd been when first they'd met, the vivid colors, slashed, flowing sleeves, his strange, barbaric splendor made her heart beat faster in anticipation. "I can't determine if I, if we, can help, until I know precisely what it is you require. All I hear from every Marchmontian, you included, is pleasant words and indirection. And the occasional arrow." She paused, thought further. "Are you asking for my personal favor or a favor from me as Special Envoy?"

"I think," and his hand grasped hers on the reins, "that the favor I ask is for all Marchmont, not me personally, but it must come personally from you and your friends. The end result will be beneficial to both our lands. You have potentials within you that you don't even begin to apprehend."

How she hated those words! Always someone presuming to understand her better than she could understand herself! She jerked her hand free, swatting Khar, Lokka veering at her changed grip on the reins. Khar looked down her nose at the knuckles planted in her rib section. **"Fixate on the first part of his statement, not the last. I think,"** she nosed Doyce's knuckles out of her ribs, **"he wants us to find Marchmont's proper ruler."**

"And how do we do that? Ride across the length and breadth of Marchmont crying 'Come out, come out, wherever you are'?"

The ghatti ignored Doyce's exasperation. **"He wants *us*— not just you—to locate the blood royale. We ghatti might be useful."**

With an incredulous stare at Muscadeine, she blurted, "You want us, I mean the ghatti, to discover the rightful ruler? You think one of Ludo's offspring can be found after all this time?"

Exhaling a pent-up sigh of relief, Muscadeine moved closer, his thigh and knee rubbing intimately against hers. "Any bastard offspring has to be superior to Maurice. Yes, could you, could they? I'll see you're returned safely to Canderis as soon as possible, though the route may be indirect, but if the ghatti could bend their minds toward a solution as we travel . . ." he left the thought unfinished. "I don't know precisely what they do, how they do it, but I'll pin my hopes on anything that might help. After all, our beloved Wilhelmina begged us to wait for the ghatti. Perhaps it's their verdict for which we wait. The truth as they find it."

She glanced at the other ghatti, M'wa, Rawn, T'ss, Saam, N'oor, all alert on their pommel platforms, all twitchily inquisitive and eager. Just the sort of puzzle to delight them, a solution to assuage their curiosity. "But without a formal Seeking, I don't know what they can accomplish. They don't simply read minds for the sake of reading minds," she protested. "And you're assuming someone holds the key to the solution in his or her mind, witting or not."

T'ss's voice danced. **"Too bad Parse isn't here, he loves puzzles. Wait till I tell Per'la about this!"**

With a diffident cough and gentle nudge, Bard announced

his presence, politely intruding, his skin a matte honey gold in the diffused light of the watershed. "M'wa thinks it possible. He says this land boasts enough random thoughts, enough flavors in the very air itself to provide information if they can be deciphered."

M'wa licked the length of the long white stocking on his left leg, examining it as if nothing concerned him except his proper ablutions. **"P'wa would say why not try? As do I. Marvelous reverberations to be heard here, as if thoughts never die, just float fainter and more distant. We have the patience to listen, even if you don't."**

"Chevalier Capitain?" Bard, insistent but reserved, polite but implacable. "It might help if you permit the ghatti to read you as we go along. Would you agree? And would you be kind enough to tell us precisely where we're going? As far as Nakum and I can determine, we're heading north and west, and that's hardly the direction of the border."

"To answer the last first, I think it best we take cover for a time. The border crossings will be the first places patrolled. When they find you haven't crossed, they'll fan out to search for you—most likely to the south and east, the next closest border areas. They assume no one seeking safety would willing venture toward trouble and uncivilized land in the mountain north."

"And that's where we're heading?" Bard asked.

"No, not precisely that far, but to a way station on the edge of the troubles, so to speak, our arborfer nursery. We'll leave a trail as far as the river, then have my men lay a false trail to lure them. And you'll see a sight that few foreigners have been privileged to see."

Nakum rode practically on their heels, face suffused with excitement. Abashed, he dropped back, ashamed of eavesdropping.

"You see, your young friend finds the idea of merit," Muscadeine added. "And," he fingered his mustache, tugged at it, "As to your ghatti inside my mind, I will permit it, though one at a time. I don't relish the idea, but I'll trust to their decorum and their solemn promise to leave my poor Felix in peace!"

❖

Ignacio Lauzon stood erect and proud, shoulders back, eyes straight ahead. If he glanced leftward, he'd see Maurice pacing, ranting and raving, and hearing it was punishment enough without watching it. A glance to his right would reveal his grandson, Ezequiel, exquisitely still except for an imperceptible shuddering Ignacio could sense as surely as if his hand rested on the boy's shoulder. And that he would not dare, not if they stood any chance of emerging unscathed from Maurice's frenzy. A hand on Ezequiel's shoulder would betray the boy's weakness to Maurice like the scent of blood. The best he could manage was a surreptitious brush of his knuckles against the back of the boy's hand. His old eyes watered, exhaustion, he told himself, the stress from being rudely awakened, hauled down here like a common criminal caught in the act. Why couldn't Constant Minor have chosen tonight to be sleepless?

The steady pacing sound, the swish, swish, of soft-soled shoes behind him told him that Jules Jampolis still lurked there, gathering every nuance from his self-imposed outpost. Near Maurice's wrath, but not too near, a wise decision to Ignacio's mind. Maurice barked an order, and the third guard backed away from the Prince and into Ignacio's line of sight. Sweaty and pale, and not just from the wound on his head where he'd been hit. The fourth and final guard now endured Maurice's scrutiny, questions soft and lulling, then rabid, shrieking anger, canny quizzing and challenges that left their victim reeling, off balance. No answer ever seemed right, never turned Maurice's wrath elsewhere. It was coming closer now, all too close, Ignacio knew that with a sick dread.

"Tell me again how it happened! Don't misplace a single detail; you *do* know what a detail is, don't you?" Maurice's scorn burned and scourged, humiliated a proud guard.

"As I told your majesty. . . ."

"And I told you to tell me again, assuming you can recall the same paltry lies you conjured before. Such face-saving whining and whimpering I've never heard in my entire life! You and your fellows the butt of every joke in the household guards for such craven dereliction of duty! What I am supposed to do? Whip you? Send you North to serve—except they don't take cowards there, do they?" His voice dropped, intimate and seductive, "Nor do I succor them here."

Despite himself Ignacio risked a glance at Ezequiel,

wrapped in a fragile composure he hadn't given him credit for, eyes calm, a slight movement of his lower lip indicating he worried at the inner flesh with his teeth.

The guard attempted to justify himself yet again. "If it please your majesty, you instructed us yourself to take special care of those large catti ... er, ghatti. Thus, sir, when the bold striped one exited the premises and began to show signs of severe illness, fearful moaning and vomiting, sir, practically turning herself inside out, sir, I rushed for help."

"Leaving Tycho alone?"

"Yes, sir. He was armed, they weren't. And they haven't made a move to escape since they've been there."

Maurice flung himself into a chair, the very heaviness of his landing revealing his disdain. "And then what?" A growling sigh as if in pain at allowing this charade to continue.

"What, sir?" The man was jittering, losing his ability to string words together.

"Did you find help, you fool?"

The guard nodded, nodded harder and harder with conviction. "I got Mimms from the kitchen, sir. A bit simple-minded, but loves his cats, sir, never a one do we find in our stew when old Mimms is cooking. Fast, he's not, but he scrambled along as best he could. As we headed back we run into Ezequiel Dunay, there, the Chamberlain's grandson, so he came along, too."

"And?" Light, lilting, as if he could care less, Maurice let the word hover.

The guard licked his lips, prayed he neared the end of the interrogation, deliverance in sight. "That's when we found Tycho, sir, all bound up like an old parcel. Got the gag out and he sputtered and swore bloody hell, excusing myself, sir. Said they'd escaped. That's when Ezequiel said I should alert the Chevalier Capitain, and that's what I did."

"Why the Chevalier Capitain?"

"Well, begging your pardon, sir. The middle of the night and all, that's what he's trained to do, in'it?"

Maurice reared clear of his chair now, advancing on the guard until they both came into Ignacio's line of sight, Maurice's face thrust close to the guard's, the poor man bending backward, wilting. Ignacio blinked, could feel the spittal spattering the guard's face as surely as the guard himself did. "Just get out of my sight! Now! You'd take orders from a toadstool, wouldn't you!" To his credit, the guard managed a limp salute as he left the room, ignoring his fellow guards still lined in a row.

Swish! Swish! With little ice-skating sounds, Jules Jampolis appeared at Maurice's side, and Ignacio shivered. It didn't do to forget Jampolis hovering near one's vulnerable back. He wore his long white coat, a sham of a eumedico, and a sham as Public Weal Lord. Was this what Marchmont had sunk to, that the person chosen to protect the public good—mind, body, and soul—was in thrall not to the people's needs, but to Maurice's? But his voice soothed, and Maurice did seem to calm, and with that, Ignacio did as well, praying the storm had passed.

"Well, Ezequiel, what do you have to say for yourself?" The contrived tenderness of the tone told Ignacio that the storm hadn't abated, but was about to buffet his grandson in its midst. He began to pray as he had never prayed before. All his life he'd tried to do right by the throne, making the royal family his first family rather than his own flesh and blood. No wonder his daughter had fought him, done as she'd pleased, looking for love as she found it, but at the end he'd gotten her back, long enough to beg her forgiveness and be given the little grandbaby to raise. He hoped he'd done better by Ezequiel, but it was so hard to abandon his allegiance to Wilhelmina and his private allegiance to Fabienne, Maurice's wife, knowing what he knew, though it wasn't public knowledge.

Ezequiel stepped forward. "Prince Maurice." He bowed, perfect position, the exact degree of obsequiousness. "When I arrived, the prisoners ..." he stopped in bewilderment. "No, prisoners wouldn't be correct. After all, they remained there under your own gracious protection, your concern for their well-being." A smile of innocent approbation lighted his face. "Of course foreigners may not always know what's best for them, and they grew impatient at their constraints."

Maurice nodded, basking in the genteel language, and for the first time Ignacio wondered if possibly, just possibly the boy might pull it off. Striving for control, he fisted his right hand, away from everyone's vision, and pressed his thumb against knuckles, cracking them.

"When I realized what had happened, I immediately ordered the alarm sounded, hoping we might find the Canderisians before they fled too far and did themselves irretrievable harm. It seemed only logical to alert the Chevalier Capitain; after all, you've often said he's your strong right arm, your buckler and shield, and who better than he to rescue them without disturbing your slumbers?"

Easy on the butter, easy on the butter, Ignacio tried to convey the thought to Ezequiel, though he possessed limited skill in that direction. Worst of all, Maurice might overhear, and all he could hope was that the man would have no idea what he meant. And at that moment he felt compelled to turn his head, found himself looking straight into Maurice's eyes. One eye gave him a slow, considering wink.

Maurice cleared his throat, made a rapid, huff-huff-huffing sound that might have been strangulated laughter, becoming louder at Jampolis's scandalized gasp. "Yes, lad. Well, tonight you showed what proper training can do, no hesitations, an informed knowledge of protocol, efficient management. Now, off with you, and take your grandfather with you."

With synchronized bows, Ignacio and Ezequiel backed out of the room. He chivvied Ezequiel through the door ahead of him, made one final obeisance to the man at the far end of the carpet. Rising with all the grace his storklike body could muster, he thought they had gotten away with it, until the words slithered and hissed their way to his feet, writhed around his legs, up his body to his mind. *"Oh, Ignacio. We'll . . . talk about this . . . another time . . . won't we? Before any other mistakes in judgment are made? And by the way, we've a new visitor from Canderis, one Syndar Saffron. Treat him very nicely because his mood is going to be even worse than mine about what happened tonight."*

Ignacio strenuously doubted that.

Every sense pitched to detect danger, they rode all that day and into the night, Muscadeine punctuating their journey with precisely calibrated rest stops before relentlessly pushing them forward. No more than a brief allocation of sleep, poised to flee at any hint of pursuit. Pursuit might have been preferable, something tangible to evade, rather than the phantom fears that left them all mentally and physically frayed. The horses were tired as well, would need time to recover, but Doyce had to respect the fact they'd not been ridden into the ground. Indeed, the one she felt most sorry for was Felix, running at Muscadeine's side.

When she remonstrated with him, he merely cocked an eyebrow. "Felix and his kind are bred to run an elk from dawn to dusk and bring it down when it tires or turns at bay. If anything, this journey bores him with no hunt in sight." Snuffling and snapping at a flea, the dog sprawled at his feet during one of their infrequent stopovers, perking up at the sound of his name.

At dawn they reached an outcropping of land shaped like a giant thumb, a high bluff at the convergence of two rivers that melded into one, bending and looping in the distance between the forest. The rising sun reflected off it like strips of copper bossing, polished to shimmering brilliance. "I've no wish to linger long in such a visible spot, but I could not resist sharing the view with you." Muscadeine waved his arm expansively as if he alone were responsible for the beauty of the scene.

A reflexive shiver rippled up Doyce's spine, one that she tried to quell but failed to master. The height, the reflecting sunlight—dawn, not dusk this time—catapulted her back to Rolf's and Chak's final exit, Oriel's death as well, forced over a cliff top. Did the others feel it as well, huddled at the bluff's center? Jenret appeared particularly pensive, flashed the Lady's eight pointed star when he thought no one saw him. An overpowering roaring flooded her ears, eery mimicry of the great falls, but the sounds lodged inside her head, waves of vertigo sweeping over her, making her doubt her solid footing. As blackness swamped her vision, she wavered on her feet, made a little mewling sound of panic. When the world stabilized, she found herself harbored by Muscadeine's arms, cradled against his solid chest. Without thought, she turned into that broad, comforting chest like a weary child, clutching at his leather vest for stability, oblivious to the wrath suffusing Jenret's face as he chaffed nearby, helpless and shut out.

Teeth chattering, she felt the spout of a wineskin thrust between her lips, a trickle of wine on her tongue. She swallowed, swallowed again, managed to grasp the wineskin and redirect its flow, squeezed before it was pried from her greedy grip. Cracking open her eyes, she dared the world to spin again, but it held solid, steady, and bright, despite her cowardice. With effort, she scrambled to her feet, shaking off hands eager to help, Jenret's the most insistent and intrusive, proprietary. Always he was too near, too eager, unable to leave her in peace.

"Where do we go from here?" The thought nagged, why waste time for a scenic view in the midst of their flight?

Muscadeine stoppered the wineskin, hung it on his saddle. "Ah, now the journey varies, for isn't variety the spice of life—not to mention love?" His raillery flowed just beneath the surface. "Some will indulge in a brief nature hike while others will ride a bit more. Take a small bag of necessities, each of you, something easily slung on your shoulder to leave your hands free. My men will herd our horses back the way we came and lay a false trail, should anyone be tracking us. After they've rested, the horses will be returned to us by another route."

"And where do we go after our 'nature hike,' as you so charmingly call it?" Motions jerky with fatigue and anger, Jenret's gentian blue eyes blazed like semiprecious stones in a face chalky with dust and fatigue. He stifled an exclamation, ready to defend himself as Nakum's head popped above the bluff's edge like a disembodied apparition. With a leap, he scrambled to join the group, dusting his hands together as he came.

A grin split Nakum's face. "There's a boat! A boat down below, the biggest I've ever seen! Are we going to ride in it?"

"Sail in it, you mean," Muscadeine corrected. "Let the wind do the work while we rest. The river's swifter and surer than horses to reach our destination, and the boatmen serve Roland, so we're safe."

Khar gulped, front feet shifting in place. **"I hope it's smoother than the raft-run across the Greenvald River!"**

Saam slithered over the cliff edge, blue-gray body dappled with ocher dust. **"Oh, I think so! It looks, it looks,"** he strove for words, **"swallow-trim, gliding smooth. Not as big as the Sunderlies trade ships, but big enough. It skims the water, doesn't plow through it like that raft. Oh, remember poor Harrap and Parm!"**

Jenret stalked to the cliff edge, squatted to stare downward and finally outward. "There's a trail, not much of one, but I've seen worse. Bard, what do you think?" Joining him, Bard examined the proposed route, Jacobia and Sarrett crowding behind their restraining shoulders, peering over, exclaiming. Sarrett's heartfelt moan was overridden by Jacobia's enthusiastic, "Oh, what fun! I can hardly wait!"

Sucking at an abraded knuckle, Doyce leaned against the gunwales of the boat, thankful to be at rest. Her legs still trembled from the stress of the descent, leaning backward to foil her body's forward momentum until she'd firmly planted each foot. The ghatti had rollicked and frolicked, investigating crevasses and caves, playing pounce-tag, skittering out at each other from around blind turns. She picked at the oozing scrape, used a fingernail to dislodge a piece of gravel, souvenir from where she'd skidded and tumbled, hands blindly outthrust to break her fall.

Sarrett sat beside her, fruitlessly tugging at a three-cornered tear in the knee of her pantaloons. "Don't suppose you have a sewing kit with you?" Doyce shook her head in the negative and closed her eyes, the water plashing along the boat's sides, canvas cracking and snapping in the breeze.

T'ss, eyes saucer-wide, stretched across the rail, head dangling over the edge as he cheerfully chattered, **"Look, N'oor! A fish! I think I saw a fish! It's so big!"** Clearly mingled with his excitement was the subtext of dinner, of eating that fish.

"Don't want to see the fish!" N'oor wailed. **"Want to be on dry land again!"** She crouched in the deck's center, claws extended to combat the rhythmic slide and roll the other ghatti took for granted, until at last Aelbert took pity and pulled her onto his lap for comfort.

But Rawn had made his way to T'ss, lithe black body stretched bowlike beside the white and black younger ghatt, T'ss's eyes sparkling bluer than the waves as he nosed Rawn. **"Yes, it's big,"** the black ghatt allowed. **"But see there, very scaly, like armor. Too much effort for eating. When we land, I'll find us a shallow eddy beneath some tree roots where the water swirls round the rocks, and then I'll teach you to fish."** T'ss's whiskers bristled with anticipation as he stretched farther, one hind foot digging into the gunwale to lever himself higher.

With a sigh, Sarrett half-turned and dragged him down. "If you fall overboard, I can't swim out to save you," she chided.

"**Why not?**" T'ss groomed himself from the handling.

"Because I'd wash the dye out of my hair!"

T'ss made a taunting dive for the rail. "**For such an im-
rovement I'd willingly go overboard!**"

Despite her tiredness, Doyce laughed at their exchange.
arrett aimed a good-natured cuff at the ghatt but gave
oyce a look of utter seriousness that made her older than
er years. "Is what we're doing wise? Bard and I took a
hance by crossing after you, but the farther we go into the
terior, the greater the distance from Byrta and P'wa and
arse and Per'la. Rawn and the others had trouble reaching
s when you were in Sidonie."

Biting the corner of her lip, Doyce reflected, "With a
indnet, a mindmeld of six, especially with M'wa, it should
e possible. I don't want the others crossing the border to try
rescue us."

"Not to mention Syndar Saffron rushing to our aid."
arrett jutted her chin at Jacobia, flirting with the young
an at the boat's long, sweeping rudder. "I hope Byrta and
arse tracked him down, read him the riot act, but if he in-
sts on bulling on alone in his quest. . . . " She left the
ought unfinished.

"You don't know what kind of china he may break."
oyce finished the thought. "And Parse and Byrta didn't
atch up with him; he's already here somewhere. Jenret and
haven't said anything to the others about it; it got pushed
ut of our minds by our other problems. Lady Bright, I'd
ke to sleep for an oct and awake with this behind me, and
e snug in my nice, narrow little bed back at Headquarters.
ut it doesn't look as if that's going to happen. And I won-
er what—if anything—the ghatti can discover about the
entity of Marchmont's legitimate ruler."

Sarrett turned her head leftward, toward the prow of the
oat where Arras Muscadeine and his dog jutted forward
ke figureheads, the dog's ears streaming in the breeze. "I
on't know why, but I suspect he usually gets his way. He's
very compelling man."

"Oh, I wouldn't know about that." And the guarded de-
nsiveness of her response made Sarrett look at her friend
little more closely, only to glance to where Jenret
ycherley stood, arm around the mast, scowling at anything
d everything in his path.

❦

Wishing the mast were Arras Muscadeine's neck, Jenret clenched it tighter, overtaken by a fantasy of conquering the Chevalier Capitain, forcing him to his knees to beg for mercy. All in all, it was highly satisfying. Of course, how could he beg for mercy while Jenret increased the strangle hold around his neck? Since it was *his* daydream and he directed it, he decided to be magnanimous, release the pressure enough to listen to his pleas, but continued the chilling scowl that had quelled Muscadeine's spirit.

But what came was not Muscadeine's abject capitulation his sniveling admission of Jenret's superiority, his cry for mercy, but a cacophony of voices pinwheeling through his brain, a tinnitus of sounds tolling inside him. He rubbed at his head, but the ringing voices remained. Well, at least they weren't trying to communicate with him this time; it was more like being just beyond earshot of a conversation involving him.

"Do you hear that?" he blurted to Rawn. *"Can you hear it? Don't listen to me, listen through me!"*

Rawn strained to drink in the resonances floating on the horizon of Jenret's mindspeech, and at last nodded, somber his ear hoop swinging in cadence to the inner calls. The exact words eluded him, but the timbre of voices remained, the rising and falling intonations of a conversation . . . no, an . . .

"Argument?" he ventured.

"Exactly!"

Concentrating with every fiber of his being, Rawn worked to unravel an underlying pattern. Argument was close, but not right, unless one person could be said to argue with himself. **"No, it's more like ... "** he groped, **"what's the expression you use when you talk to yourself? Thinking out loud? It's as if someone's thinking is so agitated that it is out loud."**

With a shushing sound, Jenret lingered by the mast, back to Arras Muscadeine and the dog, too distant to overhear but focusing hard.

"What right have I ... ?" *"But what other choice do you have, fool?"* *" ... the petite Marbon, so sweet ... wish .. potential ... love to ..."* *" ... potential ... passive? No, latent ... possible Wycherley, that foppish pretty boy ... "* *"Unfair, so unfair! Danger everywhere ... how can I ... ?"*

" . . . *harm Wycherley?*" "*Too much trauma for one mind to bear.* . . ."

The anguish in Muscadeine's thoughts astonished Jenret, but the arrogance didn't. Of course he assumed Doyce would be his! And "foppish pretty boy" to describe him? Didn't think he could take the trauma of losing Doyce, did he? Well, he might have misjudged Muscadeine's intentions that night when he'd been goaded into assaulting Doyce, but didn't this mental conversation provide incontrovertible evidence of Muscadeine's designs?

Unless . . . unless? Impetuous he might be, and jealous as well, but Jenret Wycherley didn't count himself a fool. And when he could bear to admit it, even retained a certain grudging regard for the man's skills. And what about Jared's voice and the others he'd heard one night, or the time he'd sworn he'd heard Constant Minor say, "Oh, bosh! Listen, you blockhead!" Perhaps listening was exactly what he should continue doing until he had an answer of some sort, a solution to the puzzle the various voices presented. Not fair to damn a man over half an overheard conversation. But he still didn't have to like him or trust him around Doyce, and he'd make sure Muscadeine had no chance to harm her in any way. Not even bruise her spirit, he promised himself. He could be her guardian, if nothing else. Sliding down the mast, he sat on the deck, thinking, scowling.

Rawn chewed on his knuckles, brought him back to the present so he no longer considered Muscadeine's thoughts and the roles he and Doyce played in them. But that's what he desired above all: in what part had Jenret Wycherley been cast and did he choose to act it?

"It's not polite to listen to something not meant for your ears. You know that. We ghatti take care never to cross that line. Did Muscadeine say to you, 'Mindwalk if you will'? No, he did not, so in future, don't."

"*But how can I be hearing him inside my head? Is it me or is it him that's responsible?*" A headache was beginning to knot right behind his eyes, working its way upward to engulf his entire brain.

"I don't know who's responsible . . . yet." But Rawn had some very interesting speculations. What was it M'wa had said about there being enough random thoughts, enough flavors in the very air itself if they could only be deciphered? And the black ghatt hoped he deciphered them soon, because he, too, was acquiring a resounding headache.

Stiff and weary, they climbed the overgrown path from the riverbank, bushes slapping, snagging at clothes and their puny sacks and totes of belongings. At the top of the bank old flagstones paved the path, bleached-straw remains of tall grasses and last season's wildflowers poking between stones, no well-tended, well-manicured lawn here for some time. Picking her way along, Doyce heard Sarrett's low cry of delight at the two-story house of pale gray, irregular stonework looming ahead of them like something from a fairy tale. Bits of mica sparkled in the late afternoon sun, made it seem homey and gentle, waiting to embrace weary travelers. A closer, more accurate appraisal revealed sagging, banging shutters, grimy windows with old leaves lodged in sill corners, curling roof shingles, the lack of welcoming chimney smoke.

"Roland should be here shortly." Cheerful, Muscadeine hooked his hand under Doyce's elbow to hurry her along. When had he been able to contact him? How had Roland known to send the boat? Amazing how things fell so neatly into place for him. And would that she knew how he did it! "He's been playing caretaker since Eadwin disappeared, but he needs to spend most of his time at the out-camp, nearer the nursery."

Jacobia skipped from flag to flag for all the world as if she played hopscotch. T'ss imitated her, face wrinkled in concentration, though it was absurdly simple for a ghatt. "Then this is Eadwin's house?" she shouted after them. "And who's Eadwin and where is he?" Both feet centered on a reddish flag, she viewed her options, chose two green flags as her next goal and jumped, one leg stretching to land on the farther green stone.

"The Lady Fabienne's and Prince Maurice's son," Muscadeine responded with practically no hesitation, and Doyce suspected only she'd noted the brief pause before he uttered Maurice's name. She shifted her bag to her other shoulder, momentarily lost in the irony of the situation—Jacobia, unaware of her real father, asking about an unknown man who was not, she strongly suspected, Maurice's son. And wondered what information, said or unsaid, had drawn her to that conclusion? Brief snatches of conversation always wafted on her mind's periphery, drifted just beyond conscious hearing, making her head ache with the strain of grasping them. Now that she thought on it, Jenret also looked as if he'd suffered a perpetual, low-grade headache since they'd come to Marchmont, although she'd laid it to his drinking.

They reached the entryway and Muscadeine dug into his pocket for a small key ring, fumbled through the keys, cursed and started the count again until, closing his eyes, his fingers reached for the proper one. "'Tisn't really Eadwin's house, 'twas built by Prince Maarten, Wilhelmina's brother. He gave me my own key when I was a lad." He swung open the door and Doyce almost tripped across the threshold, propelled from behind by Jacobia's and Nakum's eagerness to see inside.

She regained her footing, nose crinkling at the scent of musty disuse, mouse droppings and stale, old fires. Shelter, and far better than some she'd had in the past. No doubt the house boasted its own long-ago charm, though how well a bachelor like Maarten and his successor, Eadwin, had taken care of it remained to be seen. A cobweb dangled in her hair, and as she twitched away, she brushed against an old sideboard, made a strangled sound of disgust at the dust now coating hip and sleeve. Wiping away the cobweb, she smudged her cheek with the dirt coating the palm of her hand.

Nakum and Muscadeine both whirled, as instantly aware as only hunters can be of any tiny suppressed noise that indicates the whereabouts of the hunted—or of something stalking them. At their movement, Bard and Jenret pressed forward, cramming everyone together in the confined entryway, only Aelbert outside, hands in pockets, whistling.

With a practiced flourish Muscadeine whipped a snowy white handkerchief from a pocket. "Stick out your tongue," he commanded, and Doyce did without thinking. He briefly touched the handkerchief to her tongue, then rubbed along her cheekbone and down the line of her chin, lingering while his index finger raised her chin, turned her face this way and that as he examined his work. "A bit dirty here," he conceded, as if to her alone. "You know, I've an idea," and now his glance encompassed the others. "You ladies must be tired after your journey, and I know just the thing to refresh you while we men put this place in rough order.

"What this estate boasts is a hot spring, a lovely, bubbling spring flowing into a natural rock pool large enough for three ladies of your delicate size to free yourself from clothes and cares, soak and linger while we engage in spring cleaning." His look was intimate, direct. "And it's sheltered, protected from prying eyes so you may linger as long as you like. We men can bathe after you've refreshed yourselves to your heart's content."

Sarrett moaned in heartfelt appreciation. "I'll willingly relinquish housecleaning in return for cooking dinner tonight."

Jacobia's violet eyes eloquently implored Jenret's permission, despite his knowledge of the likely worth of her dinner contributions. At his reluctant nod of assent, she spun and capered, pulling Doyce with her. "And where do we find this marvelous hot spring, Chevalier Capitain?" she cried as she and Sarrett pushed Doyce out the door with no time to think or refuse.

"Follow the path along the west side of the house and through the orchard. You'll finally see a dip with a stand of drooping willows, greener than the rest at this time of year. Within its heart, you'll find your hot spring."

Such intimacy, such luxury, such blessed warmth ... almost sinful! She rested her head against a small rock outcrop that served as a natural pillow, and let her toes float pinkly to the surface, buoyed by the bubbling water, then drew one foot toward her, judging its wrinkling. Lady Bless, so what if she turned into a prune, it felt so good! She applied a sliver of precious soap between her toes, followed by a handful of fine bottom sand to scrub her sole—good for the calluses—before subsiding back underwater.

The three fit comfortably without crowding, except when Jacobia became overenthusiastic. As if reading her thoughts, Sarrett bobbed beside her, their shoulders rubbing. Errant wisps of steam rose from the pool, mist streamers spiraling against the cooler spring air, shrouding everything with placid unreality. Impossible to be hunted while they soaked like this. Jacobia's foot blundered against her thigh like a nibbling fish, and Doyce grasped it, eased it aside. Facing them from the other end of the pool, Jacobia opened dreamy eyes. "Sorry, didn't mean to poke. Just dancing to the water music in my mind."

All growing things around the pool flourished with the rich verdure of late spring, not the early, more tentative colors of the rest of the land. No doubt the warmth, water, and shelter served as a sort of forcing house for plant life. Close by stood an abandoned greenhouse frame with a few unbroken glass panels, fragments of red clay pots scattered among minute spring violets. Mineraled overtones scented the air, the hot spring's legacy, and she identified the mineral deposits in the soft green and lilac tints of the pool's rocky sides.

Measuring the sun's decline, Sarrett retwisted her hair, tucking up the loose ends before tugging Jacobia's foot. "Come on, minnow, out of the pool. The men will be wanting their baths soon. Let's dry off and head back." Jacobia rose obediently, though with obvious reluctance as the cooler air hit her skin. Sarrett gave Doyce a little shake, bringing her out of her reverie. "Come along."

With a mock growl, Doyce sank even lower, chin pointed at the skies, tilting her head into the water, her hair floating and fanning free around her ears. "Don't want to!" With a lazy roll she flipped onto her stomach and sculled a few strokes, able to indulge in motion with more room in the pool. Hands patting the sandy bottom she floated along, crawfish-pretending. Jacobia started to splash her, but Sarrett made a sharp, cutting gesture, and Jacobia subsided.

Doyce craved the luxury of privacy as much or more than the indulgence of the water, Sarrett suspected. Well, that she could gift her with for a time. Wading from the pool's center, she sat on the bank, grabbed at her dirty shirt to dry her feet. "All right, Doyce, stay a bit, but be aware your penance will be all the dinner dishes, and any other chore I can think of that's suitably dirty, finicky, and annoying."

Blowing bubbles at them, Doyce waved a languid hand, loving the way her arm sliced through water into air, the hairs on her arm rising at the chill, the slow descent of her arm sinking underwater. The last words she paid any attention to came from Jacobia, one leg raised to step into her pantaloons. "I thought *I* was assigned all the dirty, finicky, and annoying chores. Don't tell Jenret I've been given a reprieve!"

♣

Floating, hands steepled behind her neck, she shoved feet against the bank of the pool, on a mini-voyage to the farther shore. Finally, at the shallows, she curled on her side, bent elbow and hand supporting her head, the water bearing most of her weight. Something had thawed within herself in that hot pool. An early violet drifted beside her and she contemplated it, flinched as a small pebble arced through the air and splashed beside her nose. At that she sat up straight in the water. "*Khar! Stop that!*"

The boldly striped ghatta curled her paw beside another pebble, ready to loft it into the pool. **"I'd suggest you get out and get dressed. Jenret's coming down the path, ready for his bath, and he's cranky, out of sorts."**

"*Hardly unusual lately. I wish he could just let it go, accept that I can't love him,*" she complained. "*But why didn't you warn me sooner? What have you been up to all this time?*"

"Well, *I* didn't need a bath. Besides, I wanted to watch Rawn teach T'ss to fish. The young one's enthusiastic— and about as wet as you are." Her fur rippled with obvious distaste at the idea. **"Thought you'd hear Jenret crashing along or I would've hurried more. He's been cursing and whacking at branches all the way."**

Scrambling out of the pool while Khar talked, Doyce looked for her pile of clothes, then searched again more wildly. Right here? They'd been right beside everyone else's, hadn't they? Only her boots remained, upright sentinels, but obviously poor ones, revealing nothing as to the whereabouts of her missing clothes. "*Khar, quick! Can you find my clothes? Anything, even a shirt?*" The ghatta began quartering the ground, sniffing, as Doyce pulled at her boots, tugging them on, her wet legs dragging against the leather.

Blessed Lady! Where to hide? What to do? The abandoned greenhouse offered scant shelter, no hiding behind a pane of glass, regardless of its dirt and milky aging. Jenret's brusque footsteps rattled on the path's graveled turning. With unceremonious haste she dove into a scratchy stand of hackleberries, cursing as they lashed sensitive skin but thankful for their dense cover.

Jenret marched poolward, stripping off his tabard and throwing it on the bank. He stood, one foot in hand, struggling with his boot, anger resurfacing at something concrete to rail against. Rawn, legs wet, belly fur clumped, but the rest of him dry, sat beside the tabard and began to lick himself dry.

"Psst! Jenret! Toss me your tabard, quick!"

Perplexed, Jenret gave up the struggle with his boot and swung toward the sound. "Jenret! No, turn back! Don't look this way, please! Just toss your tabard behind you."

He froze as he recognized the voice. "A talking hackleberry bush?" he queried no one in particular.

Rawn watched Khar march to his side. **"No, I think it's a talking Doyce bush."** Utterly ignoring him, Khar attempted to drag the tabard toward the bushes, finally slipping inside it, trying to drape it so that its shoulder served as a chestband to strain against. **"And as I remember,"** Rawn continued sternly, **"Doyce bushes have very sharp thorns and bitter berries and expect instant obedience. One should never peel the berries, I'm told."**

"What are you talking about, ghatt?" Jenret turned from the bushes to the ghatt, but his eyes immediately wandered back, drawn by the leaves' shaking. "Doyce, what's going on? Why are you crashing around back there?"

"Jenret, dammit! Throw the damn tabard! It's cold back here! Throw it and leave or I swear you'll be sorry!"

He untangled Khar from the tabard and tossed it high toward the berry bushes, rewarded by the flash of a bare white arm and shoulder rising to snatch it. He whistled with surprise. Doyce naked? That's what she'd meant, that's why she'd wanted his tabard! But where were her clothes? He circled, wildly checking in all directions. To have her naked and alone like this ... he let the thought drop, fury igniting as he channeled it to *who* had left her naked, alone and vulnerable like this. Had that damn Muscadeine been dallying with her here this afternoon, taking advantage of her under the pretext of leaving to find Roland?

With a crash and a clatter, Doyce burst through the bushes, tabard draped over her like a skimpy shift, one shoulder protruding from the too-large neckhole, the hem barely covering her. A final frontward tug resettled it so it hung reasonably straight—and almost to her bare knees. The draft from behind told her what it wasn't covering.

The sight of her in the oversized tabard plus a pair of boots, dripping wet, hair in rat tails, face and neck scarlet with vexation, made him feel incredibly protective as he stepped forward, eager to console. Then he noticed the marks on her neck and her upper chest and went rigid. Love scratches, love bites? Following the direction of his eyes, she fingered them, a little self-conscious smile playing on her lips. All the proof he needed! Damn it all, he'd been right!

"I'm going to thrash that Muscadeine, that Chevalier Capitain! Beat him senseless!" he roared as he dashed toward the house. After a stunned pause, Rawn sprang after him.

"Jenret? Jenret, what?" The man was making no sense. She pinned the tabard sides tight around her, clutching them with both hands as she hunted for the sash. It dawned on her what he was thinking. "Jenret! It wasn't Arras! He didn't take my clothes! I think Jacobia's playing a joke! Jenret, come back!"

Boots odd and clumsy from the wetness of her feet, the absence of stockings, she lumbered after him. *"Khar, what are we going to do? Have Rawn stop him, warn the others he's coming! Do something!"*

"And why do you always expect me to solve your predicaments?" Khar reproached as she shot ahead. And Doyce was relieved that Khar didn't wait for an answer.

Pell-melling around the corner of the house, frantically gripping the oversized tabard at each side, Doyce skidded to a halt, stunned by the scene in front of her. No frozen tableau of acrimonious recriminations, but a brawl of epic dimensions. Jenret's arms swung like a windmill in a gale, thrashing the air, and—when lucky—Arras Muscadeine, who blocked and parried, clearly mystified by the situation. At length Jenret steadied, settled like a dancer discerning his partner's rhythm, and more blows crashed on Muscadeine's face and chest.

Rawn flung himself at his Bond, slamming his chest, his shoulder to drive him back, Saam attempting the same maneuver as well, while Khar and M'wa jointly edged Muscadeine away. **"There's no reasoning with him,"** Rawn panted. Aelbert and Nakum struggled to restrain Felix, barking, baying and lunging, tossing them from side to side as he lunged. N'oor danced and hissed, blocking the dog with swats to his snout, threatening claws making him lurch back.

Dodging blows and airborne ghatti, Bard wove and ducked, sought for an opening to separate the two without favoring one or the other.

Avoiding a stinging right to the jaw, Muscadeine still felt the blow connect, a solid thump to the head. "But what's wrong? What have I done? How have I wronged your Special Envoy?" Seeing his chance, he landed a solid return blow to Jenret's ribs, no longer bothering to pull his punches. The man acted crazed, closed off to all reason.

"Dis ..." Jenret railed, "dishonored her! T ... took advantage of her! Not right!" One arm flailed crazily, swept Bard aside, exposing Jenret to the exploding black missile that was Rawn crashing into his chest.

But M'wa had overshot Muscadeine, and the Captain drove forward, fists pumping in short, precise blows. "How?" he asked in deep concern. Tangled together now, they grappled at each other, locked together more in a fumbling wrestling bout than a boxing match.

Hurtling out of the house, oaken water bucket slopping at her side, Sarrett hurled the contents at the two combatants, catching them full in the face. Dropping their arms simultaneously, they both swiveled toward the unexpected baptismal source, water streaming off them. "That's how you separate brawling, lovesick tom cats!" she shouted, eyes bright with anger. "Have you two no sense, no rationality? Haven't we trouble enough without turning on each other for no reason?"

Sidling around the door, clutching a bundle of clothes, Jacobia hid behind Sarrett, tear-stained face peeking out. "Jen, Jenner, he didn't *do* anything. I took Doyce's clothes for a joke, a silly joke, a silly, *stupid* joke," she sobbed. "I didn't know you'd react like that, I thought ..." but her thought remained unfinished as she saw Doyce standing by the corner of the house, silent, seething, and highly mortified by the whole situation. Head bent over the bundle of clothes, she marched toward Doyce, thrusting the bundle at her and galloping away, shaking with tears.

"Then you mean ..." Jenret wiped the water from his face, scrubbed his hair back, "you mean, nothing happened?"

"No, nothing happened, as you so circumspectly put it," Doyce snapped with a fury burning so harsh she wasn't sure she could contain it. "And if it had, Jenret Wycherley, it

would be absolutely *none* of your business, just as it would
be none of Arras Muscadeine's were the situation reversed!"
She stood locked in place, unwilling to advance or retreat,
acutely conscious of her near-nakedness, and not about to
start dressing in front of an audience. Wisdom of the eight
disciples, had they no sense? What was she, a raree show for
their entertainment? Or a prize to be fought over as if she
had no say or right in the matter? Men!

Arras Muscadeine saluted her predicament with a slow,
solemn wink, nothing flirtatious to it, but somehow commiserating, as if he could read her churning thoughts. With a
cautious hand on Jenret's shoulder, poised to withdraw
should it provoke, he attracted the younger man's attention.
"I'm not sure what I'm apologizing for, but I do so, most
sincerely, and suggest we all retire so your Special Envoy
may dress with dignity and decorum."

Jenret's mouth hung agape and he at last managed to firm
up his jaw. "My apologies as well," he said curtly and
pushed past Muscadeine toward the house, the rest following
without a backward glance in Doyce's direction.

❖

Thrusting his glasses up his nose, Constant peered through
the amber lenses, grumped at the fingerprints on them. He
took them off, made a show of polishing them, holding them
to the light, knowing they hung on his every move, stretched
the delay as long as he could, letting their uneasiness build.

And that it already had, he could see in some of the faces
in the crescent facing him, some uneasy, others concerned, a
few with a downright jubilant smirk they tried to erase but
which crept back in the little, self-satisfied curves of their
mouths. The old tradition was Domain Lords to his left,
Ministration Lords to his right, but within those clusters, order had broken down.

Quaintance Mercilot, Lord of the Sud, sat at his far left,
alternating glares at Prosper Napier's dapper form with eye-
rolling encouragement at Auguste Vannevar, the Lord of the
Levant shrinking in his chair, hemmed between the Lord of
the Ouest and Maurice, Lord of the Nord and Lord of Defense. Pity such a weak specimen as Vannevar had inherited
the Domain. He searched his mind through Wilhelmina's
years of nightly reports, collected the tidbits of information

'd stored away. Vannevar had been a good, solid Domain
ord, supporting his Quadrant and his people, easy to work
ith, always willing to seek common ground. Wife? Some-
ing about his wife? Brainsick? Worse since the Bannerjees
ad left and now totally in thrall to Public Weal Lord
ampolis? Something not right about that, not at all, but he
ad no time to explore further.

A throat-clearing jerked them to attention, and he made a
roduction of fumbling his glasses into place as he surveyed
e rest of the room, Ministration Lords to his right. To
Iaurice's left, Jules Jampolis, his scarred hands thrust under
e table. Maurice laughed, leaned against Jampolis to whis-
er, but immediately sobered his expression. Next after
ampolis, Justice Lord Giselle Goelet, and Commerce Lord
ysenko Boersma, both grave and anxious, clearly unhappy
ver something. Beside Boersma, Exchequer Lord Faribault
eSaulniers to the right of Valeria Condorcet, Lord of Exter-
al Affairs, and to her left, Emeril Alighieri, Lord of Internal
ffairs. Condorcet looked especially unhappy about where
e sat, ignoring the men on either side of her. Don't blame
er, not a bit. Nasty souls, DeSaulniers and Alighieri.
Vilhelmina had respected their expertise but doubted their
edication to Marchmont. And right she'd been.

He snorted, have to be blind not to read their allegiances;
e colored cockades made it glaringly clear. Two neutrals,
e dithering Vannevar and the uneasy Condorcet conspicu-
usly bare of any badge or declaration of intent. Quaintance
Iercilot, Boersma, Giselle Goelet, with Wilhelmina's laven-
er and white enclosed by the black mourning edging.

And those with the lavender and white trimmed by the
eep royal purple, their silent way of saying Maurice should
ile: Maurice, Jampolis, dapper Napier, money-hungry
eSaulniers, and Emeril Alighieri. If the two neutrals cast
eir lot with Mercilot and the others, it would be tied, five
 five, except for one problem: as Lord of the Nord and
ord of Defense, Maurice held two votes, breaking the dead-
ock.

So it's come to this, Constant thought, that a man can con-
ive, promote himself to the throne . . . but that wasn't why
e'd gathered them here. "Maurice." Constant snapped his
ame more harshly than intended, glad it no longer inhabited
is mouth. "I understand the Special Envoy and her people

misinterpreted our efforts to protect them from harm. Too
it upon themselves to reject our hospitality. Is that correct?"

Maurice rose, sagging torso overhanging the table. "Un
fortunately, that's correct, Steward. Worst of all we still hav
no real leads to the person or persons who attempted to as
sassinate the Special Envoy. By eluding our protection
they've made themselves even more vulnerable to attack,
fear."

Pious platitudes, was that all the man was capable of? Pi
ous, pompous platitudes, he amended. "I understand th
Chevalier Captain Arras Muscadine has gone in search o
them, will perhaps be able to convince them to return? If he
can locate them, they'll be in good hands. Do you have any
thing to report on that?"

A piece of paper traveled down the table from Internal Af
fairs Lord Alighieri toward Maurice, Jampolis wedging i
between two fingers and handing it to him. Unfolding it
Maurice made a show of reading it, manufactured a look o
shock in Alighieri's direction. "Most esteemed Steward, I've
dire news, heinous news. We have proof that Muscadeine
has been consorting with outsiders for some time, trading
gold for information before the borders were closed, be
traying our problems and our weaknesses to Canderis, insin
uating we were ripe to fall into their hands."

"Impossible!" Valeria Condorcet shouted, struggling to
rise, fighting off DeSaulniers's and Alighieri's calming
hands that employed more force than necessary to keep her
seated. "As Lord of External Affairs, I'd know if that were
true! That is *my* Ministration ward, not Alighieri's. The
Chevalier Captain has always been true to Marchmont!"
Well, well, Condorcet was hardly neutral when it came to
Arras Muscadeine. And while Muscadeine owed his position
with the army to Maurice, he hardly supported him as
Marchmont's new ruler.

"Well, Valeria," Alighieri spoke with a slippery smooth
condescension. "Just because you've been lax in your Min
istration is no reason for our country to suffer. We've evi
dence of Muscadeine's complicity, and very possibly your
own complicity as well."

An eruption of shouting, exclamations, defenses and
countercharges. Quaintance Mercilot had gained her feet,
imposing body striving to reach Valeria's side, hampered by
Auguste Vannevar's clinging, begging her to retake her seat.

She reminded Constant of Wilhelmina, the family resemblance definitely there, and she looked ready to box her
cousin Maurice's ears. He wished she would. What was it
he'd caught in the little Marbon woman's mind?: "Mercilot
and Clairvaux are relatives but act like foe."

He shouted for order, frail voice exuding an unexpected
power and persuasiveness, a shaming quality that made them
all feel like unruly schoolchildren caught misbehaving when
the teacher leaves the room. With grumblings and muttered
complaints they sat. "We'll deal with the evidence later.
Thoroughly, carefully, and extensively, to make sure no one
is unjustly accused." Valeria Condorcet sighed, dark eyes
closing as her head dropped, weak with relief. "But in the
meantime, what steps, if any, have you taken, Lord of Defense, to gather up our wandering Canderisian neighbors, as
well as the Chevalier Captain Muscadeine?"

"And haven't I been asking him the exact same thing for
days now?" A massive, bald-headed man stormed into the
chambers, Ignacio and Ezequiel each hanging onto an arm
but unable to do more than fractionally slow him. Constant
hid a smile behind his hand, remembered a particularly frac-
tious bull with a feisty terrier attached to its lip, being
shaken like a limp rag. The chamberlain and his grandson
acted as if they were going through the same mental process
the dog had—hang on or let go, and neither choice very
good.

Violet eyes raked the Domain and Ministration Lords before coming to rest on Constant. "My goddaughter's
amongst the missing Canderisians and I want her found—
NOW!"

"My, my, goddaughter, you say?" Taking pity on Ignacio
and Ezequiel, he waved them aside, left the man unfettered.
What an interesting development, and one he hadn't been
aware of until now.

"I followed her all the way here when she ran away, and
I won't be balked now!" Hands on hips, the man continued
to glare at the room at large.

Leaving the Ministration Lords' table, Lysenko Boersma
bowed once to Constant. "May I present Syndar Saffron,
Merchanter, sire? A rather unanticipated visitor from
Canderis, as both Giselle Goelet and Emeril Alighieri can at-
test. An unfortunate misunderstanding about the previous

ownership of a horse." He gave Saffron a surreptitious kick
and hissed, "Bow, you fool!"

Constant saw the man wrestle his emotions under control,
drop briefly to one knee, as if realizing at last that there
might be more important concerns than his missing goddaughter. "I apologize for the intrusion, but I've been sick
with worry. And he . . ." he pointed an accusatory finger at
Maurice, and Constant enjoyed his discomfiture, "assured
me, promised me, he'd have her and the others back in no
time at all. I was so close to catching up with her!" Anguish
twisted his ugly face worse than a scowl would have.

Feeling sorry for Saffron, Constant followed his pointing
finger. "So what do you have to say about that, Maurice, not
to mention my previous question?"

"Troops have been sent to scour the country for them, the
borders watched and reinforcements moved in. We're sending another search party north; if Saffron would like to ride
along, he's welcome." Maurice pinched the flesh of his upper arm, and Constant felt Syndar Saffron's problems dwin-
dle in importance, suddenly sick at heart at the magnitude of
the malignancy radiating from Maurice, the sick power he'd
sensed before but hadn't sourced. Not, not that! he prayed to
himself. Let it not be that. Coercion? Did Maurice hold that
kind of mindgift? And beside him, Public Weal Lord Jules
Jampolis, holding the position where a minute amount of coercion had always been allowed for the people's good.

But compelling the masses to avoid foreigners or coercing
them to employ proper drainage to control diseases, rather
than lecturing unwilling ears was hardly the same as what he
detected before him. Maurice pinched the soft flesh of his
inner arm again, twisted it, and Constant wanted to reel
back. Pain as an enhancer, the power augmentation? Ah,
he'd slept too long, too innocently, but who could have foreseen that? Too, too old to go through this again, and too
afraid . . . his energy drained, mind and body blowing away
like ash and dust, never to listen to the stars again!

❧

Scattered about the kitchen, some lounged on the well-
worn brick floor, others on the few rickety chairs still capable of bearing their weight, creaking in protest. Roland
d'Arnot cranked the spit, listened to the sizzle of juices and

fat dripping on the fire. "I think I've brought enough." Dubious, he counted the spitted chukkars. "Didn't have much time for hunting after I received your word. Still, we've other things to eat, even if they may not be fancy, they're filling." Although he was pleased to see Nakum, he wasn't sure about the others' company. What was Arras Muscadeine doing allying himself with these outsiders, foreigners? Made his flesh crawl worse than that night of the formal dinner, it did.

Bard and Jacobia laid the table, hunting for mismatched serving crockery. Using a damp cloth to wipe a mug, Bard inspected it, passed it to Jacobia. "I think Roland has saved a secret for us—or he doesn't want to share it. Found a keg of ale in the basement, nearly full. We can toast our escape and our adventures."

Flat on his stomach on the floor, chin propped on hands, Muscadeine broke off his mutual staring match with M'wa, hunkered into a tight loaf-shape, eyes hooded but capaciously aware and equally occupied. "Eh, bien," he said to no one in particular, stretched to find Bard. "Is he reading me now? Sometimes I sense a tickling, but perhaps I'm only imagining that, eh?"

Bard stifled laughter as M'wa struck a meditative pose, nose bowed over inturned paws, and mindspoke, **"I suppose it would be rude to inform him that I've been reading him ever since he gave permission and he didn't seem to notice. Frankly, all I'm doing now is enjoying the fire's warmth, the cooking smells, the rest."**

"I don't mean to disillusion you, Chevalier Capitain, but M'wa wishes to note that he's merely resting."

"But how can that be?" Muscadeine clamored to his knees. "Not with those eyes staring at me, staring through me. Roland, have you ever seen their like in your life? Look at them!" Dutifully, Roland scrunched on hands and knees, lowered his head. "For heaven's sake, Roland, now you look as if you make obeisance to the beast! More dignity, please!"

Unnerved by Muscadeine's enamorment with the ghatti and their Bonds, Roland sprang up to check the spit again, hiding his dismay. "At least I didn't grovel on my belly before it as you did!" he protested "What will poor Felix think seeing his master brought so low?"

And so the evening continued with more bantering, eating, the pouring of ale and the sharing of a few bottles of wine Roland had brought. Finally tiredness overtook them, yawns breaking out, sometimes politely suppressed, sometimes not when the urge became so overpowering there was no gainsaying it. One by one they drifted off to the two sleeping chambers that been dusted and aired until only Doyce, Nakum, and Roland remained.

Still shrouded by embarrassment although fully dressed and dried now, the afternoon's misunderstandings weighed on Doyce's mind. The dinner chatter held no appeal, and she'd eased herself clear to lounge against the lidded kindling box, plate of food pushed away half-eaten, including most of her share of the chukkar, succulent, juicy, skin crisped. She'd nibbled the leg, some bread and cheese, and found it sufficient. Now she began collecting empty plates, tidying while the two young men helped in a desultory fashion, joking and chatting with each other under their breath. Roland appeared relieved and at ease with Nakum, had shed the rigid politeness he'd employed all evening with them. She caught bits of conversation about the arborfer nursery, guard watch for the night, but let it slide over her.

At last the two young men left, Roland going outside but giving Khar and Saam a wide berth as they followed him, while Nakum mounted two flights to keep watch from a tiny windowed room at the top of the building, the kind of place called a "widow's walk" in sea-faring towns. Relieved to be alone, half-blind with an exhaustion of the nerves as much as of the body, she sat, poured the last of the wine into her mug, and stared at the dying fire, embers squeaking and hissing to themselves, the final log settling. Ought to build it up again, and she would, as soon as she'd rested a little. She put the mug on the table, rested her head against her hand. Damn, that was her plate over there in the shadows, wasn't it? Retrieve it later, when she did the fire. Might as well wait until Khar finished exploring for the evening and came in to bed. Her head wavered, and she shoved back the bench a bit, pillowed her head on now-folded arms, stared at the fire as if it contained a message about herself that she must decipher, until suddenly the deciphering didn't seem as important as ... sleep.

PART
SIX

Hungry! So, so hungry! He swallowed hard, saliva filling his mouth, clenching, gut-empty agony at the food smell, tantalizing, just beyond reach. Chukkar, small, juicy ... portable. He could imagine his teeth biting into it, nose delirious with the scent, inhaling until it swamped his senses. Ah, patience, patience, just beyond reach but not for long if he judged rightly. And patience and time he had in plenty, had had for longer than he cared to remember. Soon, soon, he could seize the chukkar and run, carry it as fast and far as he could, deliver it where it rightfully belonged. He settled, silent in the claustrophobic space between wood box and wall. No crude snatch and bolt to alert them to his presence, he couldn't afford that.

The woman stretched her legs beneath the table, her sleep light and troubled, restless. Each shift left him tense, poised to flee, but he argued his muscles into calmness, listened for sounds of discovery, struggled to ignore the meat smell so achingly near. Think! he commanded, think of the here and now, the need for caution and stealth, not of the food so close, not of how long it had been since he'd eaten anything like that. Oh, not that he hadn't subsisted on squeakers and flutterers, grubs and finnies, but it had been slim hunting all winter. Everything he'd caught he'd shared with scrupulous precision and sometimes total generosity, simply dropping the meager catch through the slotted window and fleeing before the "thank you" could reach him, fleeing not from the thought, the love, but from the hunger he had to outrun, outrun and hope to assuage with another hunt, often fruitless. He'd had no one to teach him the hunt, and often, at first, he'd miss, only a feather or clump of fur his portion.

How he'd slipped in undetected tonight amazed him, for he'd detected their presence almost too late. No trouble avoiding the tree-man on his occasional visits to the house, but these newcomers, well, they were a different story. Too many of them out there, too many and too much like him, sensing and scenting for danger on all sides. But they were soft with easy living; these were his woods and forest, his trails and hiding spots, his narrow tunnel into the cellar that he'd so painstakingly enlarged. How often had he slipped in and out undetected, stealing the little comforts, things he could easily carry? Leather gloves lined with rolapin fur, dragged out one at a time. A handkerchief, delicate and snagging in the brush. The leather notebook that meant so much to his loved one, though he'd despised the oiled taste, the awkward, protuberant corners. The silver-cased lead pencil on its chain. He knew what he brought wasn't always useful, but he'd done the best he could, small pleasures, things to ease boredom.

Patience, he counseled himself again, patience. Soon, soon, yes, so soon, and he swallowed spasmodically with anticipation. Sleep more deeply, stranger. He crooned the thought of sleep to himself, his own eyes sliding shut in sympathy, and jerked them open, pupils wide in the dark. Yes, soon, he propelled himself forward ever so slightly, ever so silently. Yes, yes, almost within reach. He could not, would not fail. He had promised himself that and he hadn't failed yet.

Sleep, whoever you may be, sleep and let the mighty Hru'rul hunt! That chukkar is mine!

❖

Dawn-streaked brilliance through dirty windows, sunlight undulating on the wall, moving with life, some strange light-dazzled beast's skin rippling. Oh, late, too late! he lamented. Had dozed despite his hunger and now he was too late! Fool!

He sensed around him, trolling for unseen presences, danger, minute sigh of relief. No, maybe time, time enough if he moved sleek-smooth as fur. The woman still slept, uncomfortable against the table's hard surface, close to waking, stirring and moaning as if bad dreams haunted her sleep. He slithered between wall and kindling wood box, footing sure and automatic, then reached, stretched farther, farther, fumbling at the rim of the plate. Risk the noise of snagging it near or hope that one quick snatch at the congealed chukkar carcass would suffice? He debated, paw still outstretched, hovering.

And then, abruptly, no time for debate but only for action as he shivered with the sensation of a new "other" entering the room, an "other" so much like him he wanted to cry out in recognition . . . and in fear. Claws splayed wide he hooked the chukkar breast, clamped it in his mouth as he spun within the confined space, ready to dash down his bolt-hole. But the cold, stiffened chukkar wing snagged the hole's edge and anxiety screamed through his mind, evinced itself in a muffled growl of frustration. Drop it and run! part of him howled while the other half savored the taste, vowed he'd never let go until he'd honored the one he'd promised his heart to, who needed him so desperately now.

For the briefest heartbeat Khar froze, paw raised. Mind reeling with the impact of the "other" in the same room as her beloved Bondmate, she exploded, yowling defiance in falanese and a warning mindshout of **"Beware! Danger, Doyce! Feral ghatt on the prowl!"** She sprang on the wood box to launch an aerial attack on the intruder. Low, menacing growls rumbled through her body, her fur spiking along her spine. **"Show yourself, sneak thief! Who are you? What do you want?"**

The strange ghatt spat a curse in rusty mindspeech, almost archaic to her, furiously jerked his head to rip the chukkar wing free as he threaded himself down his bolt-hole and ran.

In a panic, Doyce rushed to Khar's side. Tail lashing with rage, the ghatta tried to wedge herself into the crack between the lid's overhang and the wall. **"Wood box! Move it away from the wall! Quick, so I can follow!"** Sleepers from the other rooms came tumbling into the kitchen, half-dressed, half-asleep but alarmed and armed. Ignoring the commotion, Doyce levered her foot against the wall and grappled with both hands at a corner of the wood box. It was full and heavy, nor, she suspected, had it ever been shifted from this spot, years of seeping mop water welding it to the bricks. Straining, hands slipping, splinters sliding under her skin, she concentrated on her braced leg to help, and the box yielded—not much but enough, she hoped.

Khar dove into the space, thrust her head into the tunnel mouth, whiskers extended to their fullest to judge its width **"I'm going after him!"** Khar's mindvoice ordered all those present who could understand. **"Saam, rooftop! See where** he pops out! Rawn, guard the tunnel exit we found last night. T'ss, N'oor, M'wa—outside! Flush him out, stay on his tail at all costs!" And she was gone, her tail disappearing with a snakelike wriggle.

The thought of Khar underground in a winding tunnel, unsure of what she followed, unable to turn and flee, terrified Doyce. What if they battled underground in tight, cramped quarters? Who else, what else, might lurk in ambush? Roland, Muscadeine, and Jenret joined her beside the wood box as she continued trying to pull it farther from the wall. They grabbed with a will, heaved it into the room's center, the old box splintering, cracked, and half-demolished by its unceremonious journey.

"What in the name of Lady Light is going on here?" Muscadeine winced, sucked at a splinter. "Have we had a prowler or what? And hiding behind the wood box? Hardly enough space, I'd think."

But Nakum and Roland crouched, examining the hole, whispering and nudging each other. "Large enough?" Roland queried, face dubious. "I've only glimpsed it twice and it's very large." But Nakum concentrated on the tuft of fur caught on the bolt-hole's rough edge. "Large enough, perhaps. I think much of its size is illusion, a very heavy, thick pelt from winter's cold."

"What? A ghatt, not a human?" Muscadeine snatched the tuft from Roland, inspected it in the light, Doyce at his elbow.

Sarrett voiced their confusion. "What's a stray ghatt doing here? Is he wild? Does he have a Bondmate? What could he have wanted with us?"

"What the poor beast wanted was dinner, I suspect," offered Nakum, showing them the chukkar's torn-off wing. "Poor ghatt, to be so hungry he'd resort to stealing."

Now Roland slapped his leg with sudden enlightenment. "I think, my friend, that if we wish to see the denouement we should not be muddling here but rushing to the old badger set at the west edge of the field. Perhaps we'll find our answer there."

But Doyce was already out the door, Khar mindspeaking in occasional bursts when she remembered, sometimes projecting only a stray grumbling sound as the ghatta advanced through the twists and turns, sneezed at the dark and dust,

e falling dirt, working her way along unknown, untrodden
derground paths.

Faster! Faster! His breath screamed in his ears, thundered
rough his lungs, leaving him panting, choking, not daring
lay down his prize to rest, ease the ache in his jaws. He'd
toured through a little used, pinch-tight shaft, hoping his
evious scent in the main tunnel would lure the "other" the
ng way, give him brief respite. The air pressed close and
sty in his nostrils, filled with old badger stink and the
oming scent of the "other." He could hear her mind-
eaking in jumbled bits and pieces, striving to damp her an-
r, bury it in reassurance, but he didn't think he trusted her.
ster! Faster! She'd soon be nipping his tail, his very heels
he didn't hurry! The strain from his wide-spread jaws,
nched tight around the meat, made his eyes water.

Did he dare sprint toward the tower as his heart pulled
m? Or better to dash a crazy pattern of deceit and delu-
n, go to ground and hide? So afraid, so afraid! Others of
s own kind? A seductive "familiarity" to their voices, but
long, long since he'd heard them. But he could elude
em, run like the wind and reach his goal, present his offer-
g to his loved one before fading away to distract them. He
ust not take risks, knew he must not, for without him his
loved had no one.

He burst into sunlight, fresh air. Yes! He could make it!
d then with a frightened sob he saw the black bulk of one
the "others" looming in front of him, back arched and
ittery-toed, ears back, mouth a red snarl of disapproval.
rror! Sharp white fangs, scythelike claws flashing against
e black fur! He lowered his head, dug in his paws and ran
he had never run before, bowling over the black "other,"
mpling his face, springing with both hind feet planted
re and hard on his opponent's vulnerable belly, driving the
eath from him in a surprised, prolonged whoosh. Free!
w faster, faster! He was Hru'rul, magnificent Hru'rul and
thing could stop him now!

Rawn sprawled on his back about two meters from th
tunnel mouth as Khar hurtled out in hot pursuit, just manag
ing to spring over his supine form. She skidded to a stop an
reversed. **"What happened? Are you all right?"**

With a wheezy inhalation mimicking a whistling kettl
trying to inhale its own steam, the coal black ghatt rolled t
his side, managed a little whoof of misery, mindspeec
equally shaky. **"By the Elders, ox-stomped! What was tha
thing that stormed at me like that? Incredible sidechop
and tufted ears and a contorted, snarling face."** He licke
his belly, winced as he smoothed the fur straight. **"Feet th
size of saucers and planted right in my gut. Haven't bee
snookered so badly since ghattenhood!"**

"Shall we chase him?" Khar roved back and forth, co
cerned for Rawn, but equally clear her curiosity about wha
she pursued.

Rawn experimentally unkinked each leg and stretche
mask wrinkling in a grimace. **"Ouch, my ribs!"** He grun
bled and began a ragged trot, Khar at his side. **"The othe
are on his trail, let them catch up with him first. Whe
they bring him to bay, I plan to box his ears, bite his tai
and then do whatever else I can think of to what's i
between!"**

Wounded dignity, Khar thought—not unlike his Bondma
in that regard. Still, for a ghatt to have caught Rawn unpr
pared, to have bowled him over like that bespoke an incre
ibly powerful beast. And not a one of them had truly reache
him with their mindvoices—he seemed to hear, comprehen
some of the sharing, but distrusted the many voices insid
his head. Her pink tongue tip protruded as she pondered i
somehow his mindvoice wasn't fully formed. Injury,
strange immaturity? But throughout her torturous journe
underground she'd absorbed two clear mind-images: a tal
foreboding pinnacle, and the face of a man, framed by
window slit, a window so narrow she couldn't view all h
face at once, but must wait for it to shift to view each sid
He'd tried to shield his thoughts, but they'd burned to
strongly in the ghatt's brain for him to bury them, hide the
from her keen mind.

"We should wait for Doyce and the others," she pr
tested, eyeing Rawn's stiff-legged gait, gentling her pac
"I've said we're fine, but they're still worried."

He stopped, pretending offense, but secretly relieved, sh

spected, and touched her nose with his. **"Is he one of us?"** e poked again, a little harder, impatient. **"Does he have a ondmate?"**

As if to outrun her answer, she trotted ahead, not waiting see if he followed, she knew he would, curiosity stronger an his pain. **"I don't know, but I think—yes. Will you ally hurt him when we catch up with him?"**

Rawn began a deep chuckling, stopped abruptly as if the brations hurt his ribs. **"Probably not, not unless he derves it. But I could threaten to feed him to Felix if he esn't behave!"**

❖

Others had picked up the trail, tracking through the ods, listening and swerving at ghatti directions and admotions. But Nakum and Saam followed closest, most swift d sure, their movements so attuned that no words, verbal mental, were needed.

Nakum clutched his pouch, his earth-bond, let it drop and ing against his chest as he broad-jumped a small ravine, ccasins scarcely denting the ground as he landed. Saam d chosen to sprint along a supple tree trunk, a blow-down at spanned the ravine, roots still anchored in the earth. It nt, flexing beneath his weight with a vibrating rhythm, un-it began to resemble a bow-string ready to fling the ghatt e an arrow.

Momentarily in the lead, Nakum glanced to see Saam rled into the air with the tree trunk's final protest at its ugh use. Faintly bemused by the take-off, Saam sailed yward like a glider-squirrel coasting the breeze, before he lled himself tight and prepared to land. He did so and ertook Nakum. They both listened to the noises behind m—Muscadeine, Felix's single bay of excitement at the ase, Jenret, Bard, Sarrett, Roland, as well as the more si-t sounds and muffled commentary of the ghatti. Along th Jacobia, Aelbert and N'oor had reluctantly remained at house to guard against other intruders, other potential nger.

The strange ghatt was leading them a merry chase, though kum for the life of him couldn't figure out why. Though desperately wanted to ask Saam, he didn't want to in-de. The ghatt didn't feel evil, no wrongness to him the

way there'd been with that perverted white ghatt, Clou
who'd Bonded with Doyce's long-lost stepson Vesey, t
Gleaner. Besides, his earth-bond would have warned. Th
he was sure of deep in his heart. But why the obvious fea
the running, the reluctance to meld his mindvoice with t
others'?

They skirted a marshy sedge now, dense with last year
growth of rice grass and cattails, tough, sharp blades slas
ing at arms and legs; the new growth hampered as well, b
yielded more easily. The ghatt had spun them through ever
compass point, changing direction as aimlessly as a cape
ing, berry-drunk bear. Twice he'd glimpsed it, so similar y
dissimilar to Saam—the ghatt, if ghatt it truly was, boaste
a short, stubby tail, high hindquarters with powerfu
bunched legs, and huge paws. The way was clearer no
woods thinning as if they'd once been cared for, not pr
cisely groomed, but rough tamed. Remnants of overgrow
lawn were dotted with stumps, not the jagged stumps of na
ural windfalls, but clean-cut from trees felled long ago. Iv
the kind he'd seen winding up the sides of houses, twine
round them and engulfed the remains of a half-fallen stru
ture with latticed sides.

His breath lodged in his throat as he looked ahead, h
eyes drawn upward, shock almost driving him to his knee
This, *this* was what had been drawing him on all along
He'd fought the tugs wanting to pull him this way despi
the ghatt's jarring detours. Had sensed it deep within h
earth-bond's core that *this* was where he was meant to com
A tower, tall and sere in the early morning sun, the pale gra
of dead ashes lancing toward the sky at least ten times h
height. And spiraling around it, a carven band of som
darker material that extended beyond the tower's surface b
about two hands'-width.

Heart pounding, he halted at its base, pouch shudderin
against his chest, tilting back to see the top. And as he stare
upward, the strange ghatt scrambled around the spiral's la
turn, still clutching the chukkar in his mouth. At a tiny wir
dow ledge, if the recessed slit could rightly be called a wir
dow, the ghatt reverently placed his burden down. A han
reached out to retrieve it. Resolutely the ghatt spun fro
the beseeching hand and began his descent, charging dow
the spiral. He spat defiance as he sprang off the carve
walkway, the elm tree incredibly distant to Nakum's eye

and he opened his mouth wide to scream a warning, knew he was too late. No creature could jump that far. But the ghatt landed and clung in the outermost tender branches quaking and bending under the impact, the thrashing motion gradually moving deeper into the heart of the tree, and then he was gone.

"Follow?" Saam asked, hopeful of continuing the chase.

With a regretful shake of his head, Nakum laid a restraining hand on the steel-gray ghatt. "I think we should see what we've found here first. There's someone in that tower."

"True," Saam muttered. **"But from the looks of the door and the windows, he isn't going anywhere. But the ghatt can."** Saam was perfectly correct. The door to the tower had been boarded and nailed shut from the outside.

❖

Creeping along the spiral tracery, feet outturned, chest brushing the sleek surface, Nakum paused, pressed his cheek tight and closed his eyes. He did it, not because he was afraid of heights, but because it allowed him to sense more intensely, become one with what he touched. Shouts, instructions, floated up, hollow thumping and banging. The others had arrived, pounded at the boarded and nailed door, testing for weak points. They wouldn't get very far. The arborfer planking had been pegged in place while still fresh and flexible; now, having hardened, only diamond-tipped saws could cut it.

It had taken time to comprehend what he'd instinctively grasped: the tower was both natural and man-made. It had grown almost since time began, setting its roots deep into the soil, anchored from winter winds and gales, soaring skyward, a mighty arborfer, one of the progenitors of them all. And yet, most strangely, it had been sacrificed, topped while still alive, domed over and hollowed, bark peeled clean except for the spiraling, carved strip he now trod. The tree whispered of past times, past lives, chanting its history and its end; nor did it sound an ignoble one, despite the fact that its heartwood had been cored from it while it still lived. Eyes shut, he edged higher, higher, heeding the voices below, the voice of the tree itself, and—almost as if the tree enhanced his own abilities, the muffled beat of a heart up above.

Strange, more than passing strange his people had created this; he doubted it not, and it awed him. His people wandered, hunted, grew a few necessities during the long sun season, but they weren't builders, architects, artificers of this magnitude—or so he'd thought. Nor had his grandmother Addawanna ever mentioned it in her tales. Had their skills been lost over the years? Had they once been far different from what he'd assumed? Or had this been one special, incredible effort, a rising to a challenge above and beyond their normal ways, a homage so spectacular and hallowed that he couldn't begin to conceive it? With the arborfer fled from Canderis so many years ago, of course none of his people retained such skills.

His heel touched an irregular boss that extended from the spiral, his roadway to the top. Moccasined toes groping, he patted the shape, explored the new form it had been given, a carved face, mouth wide in grimace or shout. A branch had once grown here, its lopped stub transformed into this. An owl shape and a flower-shape grew lower down, petals frozen in arborfer, unfading, unchanging with the seasons.

More calls, more activity below, and then a rhythmic, steady screech-screeching that set his teeth on edge. Roland and Bard had returned with diamond-tipped saws, coarse, heavy-duty equipment to clear dead-falls where trees had died and hardened in place; not the delicate tools used for carving decorations, jewelry. When the tree was fresh— alive, or just felled—conventional tools sliced through it with ease before its implacable hardening.

All this time he'd been curving upward, feet seeking their path regardless of his thoughts. Though he'd never been this high before, the height didn't bother him, but the turnings did, or perhaps he dizzied simply from the enormity of what he saw and felt all around him. Almost there, nearly to the narrow slit window where the strange ghatt had stopped, deposited his burden. Who was up here? Why? And not from choice, not from the barricaded door below.

His fingers stretched to the window ledge, reached for the side casing when the touch come, exploratory, feather-soft on his hand. He started to jerk away reflexively, but the hand withdrew and he heard a startled intake of breath, almost a sobbing sound. Waggling his fingers in what he hoped was a friendly manner, he took the last few steps, pressed his face against the slit, trying to peer inside, beyond and through the shallow darkness.

"Hello?" he spoke hesitantly. "Hello, who's there?"

Rustlings and thumpings, a muffled shush-shush sound of reluctant feet dragging across the floor, a forced advance, as though stealth and retreat were more greatly desired. "Hello? Don't be alarmed, I won't hurt you. We're trying to free you."

"Oh, by the Lady's Apostles!" cried the voice, "Oh, Lady, let this be real! Don't let me be imagining this yet again! Please, please! Are you real?"

Nakum twisted back and forth, staring with first one eye and then the other, the slit too cramped for him to look head-on. "Yes, I'm real." He made the words as unthreatening as he could.

A fierce laugh, a prideful one, almost. "Prove it! Prove it, or I'll know my mind has finally snapped! Harry's real, I know that, but he's the only other real thing in this circumscribed world!"

Easing himself sideways, removing his face from the slot, Nakum thrust his arm in as far as he could reach, felt his hand seized, examined, flexed and bent. He squeezed back, fingers running up and down his arm, tugging as if they'd yank him inside. "My name is Nakum" he began as the fingers slowed their frantic testing, "and I can't come in any further, much as I'd like to. I won't fit. Could I have my arm back, please?"

"Nakum, Nakum, that's a nice name." A wild chuckle. "But then any new name on my lips has the savor and strength of heady wine. Who are you, Erakwa? What are you doing here? Are you here to rescue me or merely taunt me?"

"Rescue you." Nakum pressed his face against the window again, his eyes adjusting to the semi-darkness, bars of light from the other window slits like gold-barred scepters, the rest in darkness. Loud chewing sounds, the man cramming the chukkar in his mouth, Nakum could smell it. "Do you have a name?"

The voice backed away, seemed to realize the difficulty of seeing, and a figure positioned itself in one of the light shafts. Nakum glimpsed a thin face surrounded by long, shaggy hair, a bearded face with a sensitive, quirky mouth. The figure smiled, struck a pose, mouth quivering as if at the absurdity of what it was doing. "Yes. Eadwin Clairvaux, at your service."

"No, Eadwin Clairvaux, we are at *your* service. I must descend to help if you'd leave this tower. Can't you hear them working below?"

The man rushed back to Nakum's window slit, hand thrusting blindly outward. "Shake on it," he insisted. "Shake on your honor that you'll not abandon me here!"

"Done." And Nakum did just that. The gesture was foreign to him but the emotion wasn't—reassurance. He craved it himself after this strange meeting, this even stranger journey toward the skies.

Arras Muscadeine trimmed the lantern wick with raw, bleeding fingers, angled the light where it would do the most good. Shoulders and arms aching, he wearily picked up the saw, guided it into the groove he'd worn and began the repetitious back and forth motion.

Jenret shouldered him aside, forced himself into place. A wiry lock of dark hair hung over his sweaty brow. "No, rest for a while, eat something. Turn and turn about's the best way, and it's my turn now."

"But it's my cousin in there, my Eadwin!" Muscadeine protested as he slumped next to Bard, who passed him a mug of cha with blistered, puffy hands. Roland squirted a shot of liquor into the mug.

They'd been sawing all day, and now into the night—through the boarded ground-floor door, through the timber barricades on two more doors, working their way from level to level to this final door. He could hear Eadwin on the other side, catch some of his words, some not, balked by the thick timbers. Soon, soon, he consoled himself, but was fresh out of patience. To be so near, so close to Eadwin, missing so long, and not to be able to reach him!

The merchanter-Seeker, the "pretty boy," had the right of it, though. He watched the inexorable rhythm of Jenret's arms, wanted to yell at him to go faster, to bear down harder. But Wycherley had learned from painful experience that too much speed, too much force did nothing but jam the blade. Or worse, snap it. A pile of fragments bore mute testimony to that. Let the saw do its own work, that was the way. And momentarily, he dozed, head lolling against the wall, until a movement by his side told him that Roland had relieved Jenret. Turn and turn about, he told himself hazily, turn and turn about, and slept again.

"Through! We've cut through!" Bard yelled and joined Roland, prying at cracks, at the hole where the door ring once hung. "Push from your side! Push!" Staggering to his feet, Muscadeine grabbed for what handholds he could find and the door crept forward, hinges creaking. A distant pounding of running feet on the other side of the door, and he realized their import just as the door smashed open, Eadwin cannonading against it with all his might.

And his cousin, Eadwin Clairvaux, his Tantie Fabienne's son, stumbled into the room, into his arms. He stared at the face, saw what he'd never noticed before. The Lady and Her Disciples be praised for the answer to his prayers! Or more accurately, praise the ghatt, that strange wild beast who had led them here! Tantie Fabienne's son, and son of the man he had worshiped as a small boy, the late Prince Maarten.

"They require permission to speak?" Possessively clutching his soup bowl, sopping up the last drops with a piece of bread, Eadwin polished its interior and gobbled the final morsel, eyes riveted on the ghatti gathered at his feet. He thrust a tentative hand toward N'oor, who squeaked in surprise and sniffed at it gingerly. T'ss had no reservations and shoved his head under the outstretched hand. "How do I give them permission?" Still clinging to the bowl, he awaited enlightenment, a youngish man with a premature streak of gray at his left temple, angular with hunger, beaky nose jutting over a quirky mouth, sensitive, kind, and puzzled. "Do they truly speak? Harry and I hold converse of sorts—after being alone that long I'd have talked with anything and believed it answered." The humor was forced. "But for us it is more emotions than actual words, shared sensory contacts." With a noisy sigh he wiped his eyes with his sleeve. "I wish he'd come back. He's hungry, too, I can feel it, could feel it when he left me the chukkar. Oh, that was good!"

A childlike wonder suffused his voice; not that he was slow or childlike, Doyce decided, but that the long solitude made his thoughts come haltingly and simply. She put a hand on his forearm, attracted his attention. "Perhaps if you speak with the ghatti, you'll learn how to speak with Harry." Odd to give the ghatt a human name—hadn't he chosen one of his own? Each ghatten spoke its name aloud for the first time at the moment of its Bonding. Hadn't Eadwin heard it?

Khar gave a dainty-priss sniff at Eadwin's feet. **"He's not over-clean but not over-dirty, either. He had at least some washing facilities there."** She tagged his shin with a paw, expectant amber eyes gleaming. **"Tell him to hurry up, give us permission to 'speak him."**

"Eadwin," Doyce instructed, "what you have to say, not only aloud, but in your mind—and you have to mean it—is 'Mindwalk if ye will.' The ghatti converse only with their Bondmates unless granted permission to mindspeak someone else. And if you don't wish to give permission, they'll respect that."

"Mindwalk ... if ye will," he muttered, testing the flavor of the phrase, invocation, incantation, he wasn't sure. But not so unlike what Resonants did, or so he'd been told. And his deficiency at that, given his heritage, sorely shamed him. Still, fewer and fewer had it these days, but its lack handicapped, made him feel inferior to people like his cousin, or his parents. Perhaps conversing with the ghatti would be a substitute of sorts. "Have they spoken with you, cousin?" he asked Muscadeine.

Straddling the bench, Muscadeine shook his head. "I've permitted them to read me, but they haven't spoken, nor have I asked them to. I think they generally prefer to speak with other Seekers, those like their Bondmates." He scratched M'wa's chin and the ghatt winked at him. "Though in an emergency, I think they would, or tickle me with their tails until they captured my attention. But they seem convinced you're one of their own, so this is an experience not to be missed. Try it."

"Perhaps since I've no other talents, I have this?" Eadwin concentrated, forming the phrase in his mind, lower lip tremulous. Just another way to fail, prove his uselessness to his father. His expression clouded, then cleared, a wide smile splitting his face, beard wagging with delight. "So many names to remember, but politely, one after the other." He roll called left to right, "Rawn, so midnight-hued, Saam, bashful N'oor, T'ss, Khar—no, Khar'pern—and M'wa." A fretful query to Doyce. "Why do they want to know what Harry's real name is?" Before she could respond, dawning comprehension flooded him. "But not on purpose—he never told me! I swear it!"

Perched on the remains of the kindling box, Aelbert looked less than his usual natty self, uniform trousers wrinkled and dirty, jacket discarded in favor of the old, patched sweater, his other change of clothes, the one he'd loaned to Chak. The sweater barely fit, short and tight of sleeve, its hem too short as well, riding up his midriff. Rubbing his fingers over a darned spot on the elbow, picking at it while he studied Eadwin, "Do you think you could convince 'Harry'," he pronounced the name with distaste, "to join us? We won't harm him, and you'd probably both feel better if he were here."

"Rawn might hurt him," N'oor piped up. **"He said he might."**

The black ghatt scolded her in falanese, unsettled by her tattling to everyone present. **"I said I might, but then again I might not."** He sauntered in Eadwin's direction, leaped on the table and tapped his shoulder with a paw. **"But tell him he's welcome, that I welcome him as well, so long as he doesn't crush my middle again. He's big, but he acts like a frightened ghatten, not fully wise in our ways."**

"He's full grown," Eadwin protested. "Except perhaps for a little more weight. He was born about a year ago, he's almost nine octants old. Had him tucked in my pocket, found him practically new-born, the day I was imprisoned. Didn't think I could keep him alive, but I did."

"More of the story later," M'wa interjected, **"but try calling him to you now. We'll convey our welcome, while you reassure him we mean well by him and by you."**

"It's hard, you know," Eadwin admitted. "The best I can do is send him thoughts of safety, contentment. I have to picture it, not just say it, paint a scene in my mind. And so much depends on how far distant he is."

"As Khar would say, 'Think food, it always helps!'" M'wa's eyes twinkled as he rolled on the floor, digging in his shoulder to scratch an itch. **"Remind him of the juicy chukkar and promise him a piece for his very own, without sharing!"**

And Eadwin obediently concentrated, mouth pursed, forehead wrinkled, while the ghatti sat semi-circled, faces up-turned toward his, helping him send reassurance.

Would the ghatt dare approach, make an appearance? The waiting grew difficult, would have left them poised on the edge of their chairs if they hadn't busied themselves with routine tasks, anything to pass the time. Jacobia fussed and fiddled, giving Eadwin little pokes to retilt his head as she snipped his hair and clipped his beard short. Jenret worked at a bit of leather mending while Aelbert, Sarrett, Roland, and Bard played Tally-Ho with a greasy, tattered deck of cards, Aelbert sputtering when he miscounted and lost a hand. Nakum lounged by the fire, Saam carpeting his lap, while Muscadeine helped Doyce clear the table, all the while peppering his cousin with questions.

Caught between the exigencies of mentally coaxing Harry near and responding to Muscadeine, Eadwin yipped as Jacobia's scissors nicked the nape of his neck. She planted hands on hips in exasperation. "Well, I'm sorry, but you twitched, tossing your head back and forth like a squeaker dashing between two barn cats." Brandishing the scissors, she snipped a lock just as he nodded to acknowledge the truth of her statement. "Hold still! Now this piece is too short and I'll have to even the rest until it matches."

"Better hold still," Jenret advised without stopping his mending. "Another mistake and she'll have to even that, and then another, and before you know it, you'll be clipped short as a convict shipped to the Sunderlies."

Eadwin fingered the empty space where hair had been and almost bobbed his head in agreement, thought better of it. "I think he's coming. The images are stronger, clearer, and that means he's closer. But he's coming very cautiously." He lifted his palms, made a show of manipulating empty air. "You know, it's like juggling, carrying on one conversation in your mind and a totally different one out loud."

Doyce wrapped his hand around a fresh mug of cha and went to kibitz on the card game. "Don't try it so consciously. Let your mindvoice be a homing beacon, flashing the proper safety signals. Pretend you're keeping a steady beat with one hand while the other picks out a melody."

But Muscadeine had had enough talk about ghatti

mindspeech. He'd burst, explode with suppressed questions, if he had to allow his cousin any more space and time to absorb the idea of his freedom again. Encouraging Eadwin to relax and talk, he'd forced himself to keep his previous queries superficial. No way to soften it now, he had to know, had to ask, and he barked it out as if it were a command. "How were you imprisoned there? *Who* imprisoned you?" The words darkened the mood, shattered the pretence of a friendly, companionable reunion. Uneasily, Roland tossed in his hand, came to stand by Muscadeine as the Chevalier Capitain sat heavily beside his cousin, unwinding the impromptu barber's apron from around his neck. "You look like a buffoon," he grumbled.

The room divided—outsiders on one side, three Marchmontians on the other. Jacobia quick-scurried to her side of the boundary to avoid trespassing.

"I . . . it . . ." Eadwin, elbows on knees and hands clasped behind head as if ready to curl into a ball, protect himself, tried to speak, failed. "They . . . so sudden, so unexpected!" He buried his head in his hands, shielding himself from the memories.

Appalled, Muscadeine crushed him against his chest, but Eadwin pulled away, squared his shoulders. "I'd left the tree nursery to come here and write some reports. I've always liked it here, felt comfortable somehow, as if it were an extension of me. The Queen said I was doing such good work at the nursery that she gave me her own key to the house, said that it hadn't been used for years, but I might enjoy it. Father knew about it, he was there when she gave it to me, though not Mother. Father and the Queen had been arguing before I came, I could tell from his face, and in a funny way I think she gave me the key to spite him, not just to reward me.

"Anyway, I decided to keep my records here, growth reports, cutting reports, sales records, whatever," he waved a hand to indicate the paperwork, the time involved. "Accommodations aren't as rustic here as they are at camp. And I get along better alone. Roland and I work fine together, but some of the older men still resent me, try to bully me as they bully the Erakwa help behind my back. They think I'm worse than Maarten was with my pottering and planning to increase yield. All they want to do is clear-cut and pocket the profit. That's what Father's done in the North Domain, and now he has practically nothing left. The nursery contains almost all the arborfer that exist now." His indignation soared. "Well, there'll be nothing to pocket if they wipe it out because we still can't figure how to speed propagation or fight the blight." Roland nodded his head in somber agreement at the assessment.

"Hardly a secret I came here twice an oct, usually Third-Day and Fifth-Day, to work on the reports. Sometimes I'd come late the night before and stay over.

"I rescued Harry on my way in that day, found a goshawk struggling to get airborne with his prey, knew I should have left him with it, that's nature's way, but I could hear whatever it was squeaking in terror, knew it was alive. I scared the goshawk off and discovered an infant wildcat, so tiny I couldn't believe it. Figured I'd made a mistake by saving it, it was too young to survive without its mother and I had no idea where it'd come from."

"Leave the beast out of it and get on with the story," Muscadeine growled.

"But I can't!" Eadwin shouted back. "They're a part of each other, a part of why I'm alive!"

Folding his arms across his chest, Muscadeine jerked his chin in a savage bob to indicate he should continue.

"Slipped him into a pocket to warm him and came rushing inside to find an eyedropper, something to feed him with. Lady knows where I thought I'd get milk, but I decided I'd figure out something. Didn't really notice the horses tied just off the path, though I smelled them, realized that later, didn't realize I had visitors.

"Visitors is hardly the proper word." He managed a hollow laugh at his innocence. "I burst in and they came bursting out of the other rooms. Six of them. All roughly dressed, no badges or markings to indicate whom they served, if anyone at all. I thought one looked faintly familiar, someone Father'd recently hired to supervise the guards for the Nord estate. But he shifted so I couldn't see his face.

"There wasn't even time to struggle, I was in such shock. They bound me and dragged me out to the horses, threw me across one." He took a deep breath. "But they hadn't been quite as careful as they should have, one of the horses wore Father's colors on a bridle streamer. It didn't make sense, still doesn't for that matter. I can't believe Father would have anything to do with this, and Mother must be frantic."

Muscadeine grunted a noncommittal sound, mouth stiff under his mustache. "She has been, but she won't be much longer. My word on that." A look passed between them, Eadwin hopeful until his cousin gave a shamed head shake, muttered, "I'll explain later. Now go on."

Baffled, Eadwin shrugged but continued. "They led the horse to blessed Founder Constant's old observatory. I don't think anyone's visited, been up there since Maarten died, even the Erakwa avoid it, and their people built it." Nakum stifled an exclamation, lifted Saam off his lap as if he'd leap up but subsided, clutched his earth-bond. "I'd never been in it myself, though the keys the Queen gave me included an old-fashioned one for the padlock on the door. Father always swore there were bad memories inside, and the Erakwa nursery-workers always seemed to feel that way as well. As if they'd crafted a perfect setting to highlight one man's mysteries, the person they revered as a holy one in communion with the stars, and now that he was long-gone, the setting was no longer needed.

"I screamed my throat raw, fought each flight of stairs until we reached the observatory level and they thrust me inside. Heard the door slam shut, heard them hammering and pounding, the hammering fainter at each landing. I was screaming out the windows, throwing myself at the door. I knew they were using arborfer planks and pegs, though I don't know where they found so much fresh and workable—it's so scarce, strictly accounted for. We've inherited most of the little that's left. Only Father has enough. . . ." He stopped, struck by the implication of his words, changed his conclusion. "Stolen, obviously."

He was pacing now, face·contorted by memories. "It . . . it wasn't all that bad at first. You remember, Arras, that Maarten had tapped into the hot spring, piped the water up and into the tower for warmth against the winter snows and winds, so I had heat and water. They'd left some supplies, blankets and food. And for a while, every oct they'd send someone to leave a supply package—they'd left a note instructing me to lower a rope every Acht-Night. That's how the food came . . . at first." A hand fisted his belly to quell the remembered gnawing emptiness.

"I don't know how I managed to keep Harry alive—he was so tiny and frail, little nipped tail-stub, sides lacerated where the goshawk had pincered him, his eyes not even open. No milk for him. I'd mix the thinnest gruel I could, or chew and chew at shreds of meat, force the pulp into his mouth. He was my only entertainment, my only companion, the *only* friend I had." The next sentence came almost as an afterthought. "And then they started missing visits with the food packets."

"Could you ever see who delivered them?" Roland asked.

He shook his head. "No, not a chance. Think about it, Roland. It was dark, night, and the windows no more than slits. You can look out and up through their top curve, but you can't look straight down."

"But we never saw strangers around!" Roland protested. "We've been looking, searching all over . . ." he stuttered to a halt. "But we never thought of the King's old tower, passed it by a million times. No one lives in a monument!"

"I know," Eadwin agreed, wistful. "I saw you once in the far distance, shouted, screamed myself sick, cried."

"Birds, we thought it was birds nesting in the tower. And any time we searched too near, the Erakwa always shied away, as if it were haunted. Maybe they thought old Constant had come back, I don't know." The mounting horror of his omission strained Roland's whole body.

"I know, Roland, I know. No one thinks to look under his own nose." Eadwin slapped Roland on the back.

"You said they stopped delivering the food packages?" reminded Muscadeine.

"Yes. At first they varied the schedule, skipped dates, came at odd times, as if they were taunting me to put the rope down and find nothing at the end. Then the waits became longer and longer, nothing you dared count on. Harry and I were gradually starving, as if they'd finally decided my fate. Imprisonment and isolation weren't enough! Harry was about half-grown, so I knew I had a chance to save him, or at least to give him a chance to live. He could still fit through the window slit, and I had to release him while he could squeeze through, before he grew any bigger. I dropped him out on the spiral trim, prayed he could maneuver himself down, and told him to go, run free. How I dreamed of joining him!

"But he kept returning day after day, dragging what tidbits he could hunt in the woods—voles, birds, grubs, salamanders. I've eaten them all and been thankful for his bounty. He didn't really know how to hunt at first—what could he catch in the tower? I could sense his frustration, envision the things that had escaped. I think sometimes he gave me what he'd caught without worrying whether he'd eaten. After a time I realized he could sense pictures in my mind, like the house here, small objects I wanted, and he'd sneak in, retrieve what he thought might please me. He was my only contact with the outside world, and each day I was terrified he'd leave for good, wander off or be hunted and killed. And if he had, I knew I'd lose my mind. Simple as that." Tears streamed down his face, seeped into his newly cropped beard. "I want him here so badly, pray that he hasn't been frightened away. Humans scare him."

Wiping his cousin's face with his old handkerchief, Muscadeine held him in a hard embrace, face livid with anger. "Eadwin, do you have *any* idea why you were imprisoned, whether your father actually had a hand in it? Think, lad, think, you must have had plenty of time for that, if nothing else."

"I've thought and I've thought. Father and I've never been particularly close, he hated it when the Queen put me in charge at the tree-nursery, said it wasn't suitable, demeaning to work like some farmer, but . . ." he hiccoughed, sides heaving as he battled for self-control, begged for reassurance. "But there's no reason. Everything's just a coincidence, isn't it? Oh, true, some dislike Father—he's not an easy man to get along with—but not badly enough to hurt his son. Everyone worships Mother, and if the Queen ever found out someone had hurt me, they'd be in jeopardy."

"Wilhelmina is dead, has been dead for some time, Eadwin." The words came out flat and final.

Eadwin flashed the eight-pointed star of their faith. "Then who? Is it Father?" Pushing away, he tried to scry the answer in his cousin's eye. "Father's not first in line, but he is in line for the throne, unless the Queen named an heir. Who rules us now?"

"That's an excellent question, Eadwin, for which I've no answer yet." Muscadeine's eyes sought out Doyce's over Eadwin's shoulder.

Silent, silent, yes, yes, yes! That was right, oh, so silent. Think only of muscles that must move, make them flow, set

each paw just so, hesitate, hesitate, a little more weight, now
more, safe. Not even a bristly whisker shadow to betray.
Keep thoughts clamped down, oh so tight, oh so silent, no
betrayal from body or mind. I will not accept that. A few
grains of dried sand slithered and roared in his ears. Be-
trayer! he cursed and muffled the slide with the coarse outer
hairs of his coat. I am Hru'rul, and I am coming, my friend.

Dangerous to use the same trail, the trail he had taken
earlier for escape? Perhaps . . . perhaps not. Most squeakers
avoided, at least for a few suns, any trail where he'd caught
one, and no doubt humans thought the same way. They
would look for him elsewhere—if he came at all. But the
"others" still worried him. They weren't so easily tricked.

He slid forward, hind legs bellying him along, slipped into
a low crouch where the tunnel roof rose. Silence, silence. He
choked down a laugh as a mindbeam from the black "other"
sailed by, harmless. How silly he'd looked, gawping expression on his face as he'd stormed over him! Easier to appreciate the expression with terror subsided, had seen it then
but hadn't enjoyed it until now.

Silence, yes. But was it necessary? Enough noise, enough
loose, rowdy thoughts and gabbling voices to hide his passage sounds. Still, no chances. Not while he who had saved
him, he to whom he owed his life, remained in danger.
Hru'rul had repaid his debt a hundred-fold with each morsel
so painstakingly retrieved, ignoring the hunger in his own
gut. But it was beyond repayment, beyond measuring what
was owed, for he was loved, the only love he'd ever known.
Something lacking about that love, at a level he didn't understand, that seemed to exist with those "others." If he
could rescue his friend, perhaps he could discover it, something deeper and richer to share.

Slow, yes, easy now. Closer. A difference of darkness, no
light, but a lessening of dark. Their odors played around
him, caressed his muzzle and whiskers, made him want to
sneeze. No! Damper that! He took several shallow mouth
breaths and eased ahead.

Saam's left ear swiveled toward the wood box and he extended the claws on his right paw, waited until Khar caught
his signal. Better to speak falanese, no mind vibrations to

veal their awareness. Khar passed on the signal to M'wa
d Rawn, who acted miffed by the news but remained
tue-still, pose alert. She hesitated at T'ss and N'oor,
oked to Saam for confirmation. He folded his ears for-
rd, mouth prim and knew she took it as a "no." They'd
alize soon enough the game was afoot, but he didn't quite
ust them not to mindsqueak their excitement. Lucky for all
at Felix slept by the fire, already engaged in an imaginary
nt, whining, legs jerking. He extended his tongue, brush-
ked his shoulder, signaling Khar to advance.

The tiger-striped ghatta did, her padding footsteps obvious
any of the ghatti, just as intended, as she strolled across
e room. M'wa joined her, step matched to step, both con-
ntrating on lightening their padding to sound as if only
e nonchalant ghatt traveled. Khar froze, while M'wa
lked more heavily now. Rawn's eyes swept the room but
 made no other move.

They all heard the tiny sounds now, Saam could tell. His
ysical senses were more acute than the others', had been
er since Oriel's death and his temporary loss of mind-
eech. Even with its return, the "otherness" remained, a
fference that kinned him with the strange ghatt crawling
th such deliberate patience and stealth through the tunnel.
e could feel Nakum's eyes on him, presumed the Erakwan
d deduced something amiss, though he had no idea what.
uch as he wished to reassure him, now was not the time,
d he apologized in his heart. He loved the Erakwan, but
akum's constant unvoiced need to understand all wore at
m. Even Mahafny's total denial was preferable at times.
e forced himself not to think about that.

The stranger, Eadwin, told his tale of imprisonment, the
hers reacting with horror and shock, oblivious to the ghatti
ound them, waiting for a different tale to unfold, a tale that
uld tell them where and how this strange ghatt fit into the
st and present pattern of their lives. Or was he a foretaste
 the future? The beginnings of a Major Tale to be told and
told, woven into the threads of ghatti history now and for-
er?

Yes, nearly there, he judged. Even a whisker could cast a
adow, and it had, there behind the remains of the kindling
ox. Not close enough yet, but almost, almost. Eyes the
lor of ancient bronze widened and his eye whiskers
cked directions.

"Yes! Now, now, now, now!" he mindspoke, deployi the ghatti, spurring T'ss and N'oor to guard tasks they did even realize they had. Khar dove behind the wood bo spooking the strange ghatt into the open, rushing at his hee while M'wa jammed himself across the tunnel mouth, bloc ing retreat by that exit. And the ghatt, large, chunky wi heavy winter coat, face broadened with cheek whiskers th merged into his ruff, dashed clear, racing for the safety Eadwin.

The humans froze at his command, or the Seekers did, a Saam trusted them to hold the others in place, to let t ghatti finish their task. Even the dog, exploding from slee paused.

But halfway across the floor, Rawn materialized in th ghatt's path of flight, midnight challenge, and Saam snapp his teeth in dismay. Damn the ghatt! Stranger and defend stared at each other, neither moving, neither yielding, Raw delving deep into tawny eyes flecked with darker chestn brown, speaking in a chest-deep rumble as well as shapir the words in mindspeech. **"Peace. No harm. Peace. N harm. Friends, same-sort creatures, friends."**

Eadwin was screaming "Harry, Harry! Don't go, it's right, it's safe! Stay!" stretching his arms in welcome. Th strange ghatt lowered his eyes first, shifted to look behir him, only to find Khar still in place. His bobbed tail gave nervous flick, then was still, the tension in his body margir ally easing as he made a nervous "merowing" inquiry Eadwin's direction.

Deserting his post by the door, impetuous, T'ss pranced sideways skitters, gaining and retreating, until forward m mentum overcame his fears. **"Hello!"** he chirupped, stretcl ing to greet-sniff the newcomer.

It was too much for the strange ghatt, and a lightning pa wide and thickly furred between toe pads, slammed down c T'ss' neck, pinning him to the floor. He made a little gu gling sound and held perfectly still.

"Let him go!" Rawn commanded. **"Do you not kno proper greeting etiquette?"**

A jumbled response, smothered, images and randor words flashing in and out of the ghatti's minds. **"Prop(greet? Sniffy greet? No, no, no! Greet scratchy-ea chinny-rub."** He startled, mystified to discover T'ss benea his paw, a reflexive action he'd not even been aware of. R leasing his paw pressure with exaggerated courtesy, he wiggled his toes in clumsy parody of a human hand, claws retracted, scratching behind T'ss's ear. T'ss attempted to purr, managed a breathless trill.

Khar insinuated herself around Rawn. **"Ear lick good, too."** She demonstrated, and the ghatt's eyes blinked in momentary bliss. Stepping over T'ss, she stretched for the other ear and did that.

"Raspy nice, so, so, so, so long ago!"

"Yes," Khar crooned, **"Raspy nice, so long ago, little ghatten, too young to think, to speak, but not to feel. Feels nice, feels good, nest safe, all warm."**

"Nest safe, all warm! Loved one safe!" The ghatt hunkered down, chin draped over T'ss, curling beside him, throwing a possessive leg over him as if T'ss were his littermate. **"All safe, all warm together!"**

There was work to be done here, Saam knew, but it would be done.

❖

Damn! He'd known he'd burned certain bridges by throwing in his lot with the Canderisians, but he hadn't anticipated how many would be burnt beyond salvage, never to be crossed again. Politicking against Maurice's desire for the throne was one thing, but to start an internal war over succession was something he hadn't intended. Now it seemed all too likely. Maurice had conspired against the rightful heir to the throne, been willing to sacrifice his putative son for his own ends. How could he have assumed Maurice was just a vain, fat fool obsessed with his lineage? This was a conniving, evil man, and far more powerful than he'd given him credit for. He'd suspected without clear evidence that Maurice boasted more mental powers than he laid claim to, and now he was sure, and because of that he didn't dare let his mind range free, transmit the joyous news of Eadwin's rescue back to Fabienne. Who else might be listening? Who else might hear?

"I must go back, return to Sidonie. You know that, don't you? You understand why?" Muscadeine hooked one foot behind the other, struggling to slip his foot free from his boot. It loosened and he bent to grasp it, one hand at his heel, the other at the boot's throat, his face obscured.

He and Doyce sat alone in the kitchen, the night late, everyone else asleep. Setting down a chipped mug with perhaps a finger's worth of wine in it, Doyce grabbed Muscadeine's ankle and straddled his leg, tugging until the boot slipped off. Back still turned, she reached for the other foot, grasped and pulled. "Because of Eadwin, I assume. There's more to it than the simple fact he's been found, isn't there?"

He massaged a tired foot, swung round and divided the last of the wine between them. She wondered when he'd be able to face her. "Yes. How much have you figured out? How much do the ghatti know?"

"Enough, I think, though confirmation is needed. You know that, don't you?"

Handing her the mug, he met her eyes at last. "Eadwin is Maarten's son. It was clear to me when we broke through the last door and I saw him, thinner, aged by the experience. He's nearly the age Maarten was when he died, and he looks so much like him now it's impossible not to be struck by the resemblance. Oh, his coloring's his mother's, but the rest is definitely Maarten, even his habits and interests. Of course there's a superficial resemblance to Maurice—they *are* related, after all, but not as father and son. First cousin once-removed, I think."

He raised his hands in surrender, begging her understanding. "I didn't know, I never guessed, though I think a part of me always knew deep inside, but I was too young to read the clues. Maarten and Fabienne were always close, and it was clear she wasn't eager to marry Maurice. I remember that when she decided to marry Maurice, it was sudden, the wedding subdued so soon after Maarten's death. Not a joyous event—even a child notices things like that."

"So what do you plan to do?" She turned her mug, the handle retreating, returning. All a matter of control, of degree, as were so many things. You could choose to retreat, you could choose to return to life. "You'll need more evidence than his looks and the ghatti's word, surely you realize that? I'm not sure your people are ready to accept the fact that the ghatti are incapable of lying. And there's danger involved as well—or Eadwin wouldn't have been imprisoned, would he?"

Dark eyes opaque, mouth shielded by the mug, he was impossible to read. Always closed to her, perhaps it was his foreignness, while she suspected he could read her like a book if he chose, but too polite to trim the pages without permission. A strange potential there, different from her communion with Khar, and one that she wasn't sure she wanted to initiate because even she didn't know the end of her "book." Only his extravagant mustache seemed familiar, and even that drooped with sorrow. She pressed home another point, "And you don't know for sure who imprisoned him, who all your enemies are. Though you may suspect, don't discount what you don't know—that's where the real danger lies."

"I know, I know. And Wilhelmina's dying words to consider as well—about waiting for the ghatti. Strange, isn't it? As if she perceived something in advance of us all." He thumped the mug down. "My men will be back by the morning. Eadwin and I will return with them to Sidonie after we set you on your path to Canderis. We'll try to slip into the city without anyone seeing us. My troops are loyal to me, and we'll rally them as fast as we can. Others will join our cause as soon as they hear the news—we Marchmontians are romantics, and the thought of Eadwin as Maarten's son will bring them flocking to our cause."

She cut through his false optimism, refused to let him feign how easy it would be. "And others will view him as a pretender, do anything in their power to stop him from ascending the throne. Are you sure that Fabienne will acknowledge the truth, after living so long with this lie? Think about Maurice—publicly revealed as a cuckold. And what about Constant Minor, your Steward? Who and what is he? He seems to relish the power of ruling. I swear I still don't understand how he became Steward to begin with! Anyone I've asked never explains it very clearly, but seems perfectly satisfied by the explanation, bemused, befuddled, bespelled!"

He crashed the mug from the table with a backhanded blow, face suffused with anger. "I don't know! I don't know about Constant Minor, I don't know about Maurice, I don't know what I know about anything since your arrival! And what would you have me do? Nothing? I am Chevalier Capitain, sworn to uphold the throne, with fealty to our ruler, and Eadwin is the rightful ruler—I know that! I can't ignore that no matter the danger!"

"What would I have you do?" She thought about the question, the implications, had no choice. Why couldn't she leave well enough alone? Why insist on making everything her responsibility? "What would I have you do? First, I'd suggest we accompany you to Sidonie, help substantiate Eadwin's claim." She hoisted her mug in a brief salute. "And it might be wise, though painful, if you broke it to Eadwin that he's Marchmont's new King. Remember, he has no idea, no inkling that he's anything other than what he thinks he is. Not to mention the minor problem of Harry that we Seekers and Bondmates need to work on. He is and isn't fully developed, and we need to figure out why, and what—if anything—we can do about that."

"I don't want to tell him until Fabienne's there, has seen him first. I owe them both that much," he apologized. "But you are saying, in effect, 'Do not rush off stupidly until you have all your knowledge at your disposal.' And beyond that, what is this problem to you, why involve yourself? Your life was in danger in Sidonie, why throw yourself in harm's way again?"

"Because the ghatti love puzzles. And because my task as Special Envoy isn't done, our problems never were resolved."

He saluted her, kissing both cheeks. "You are a special woman, Doyce Marbon, Special Envoy."

"No, Arras, not special, but stubborn, very definitely stubborn." It involved paying back what was owed, no outstanding debts to eat up her credit—emotionally or ethically. And it involved what she owed herself as well, the chance to control and conquer her fears, feel whole again, work through this strange attraction so close to seducing her mind.

The four old friends—Khar, Rawn, Saam, and M'wa—gathered in the night's solitude beneath starry skies. No invitation had been offered to T'ss to join them; fond as they might be of him, he was still juvenile at times, and besides, his presence comforted Harry. Much to Khar's relief, N'oor was standing guard duty with Aelbert, no need to include her, indeed, it might distract her from her task.

"**I've had absolutely enough!**" Tail switching, she stalked back and forth, aggravation palpable. "**She agreed to help Muscadeine without even asking me!**"

"**Jealous, are we?**" Rawn couldn't resist it. He stretched and rolled. "**You don't act jealous about the possibility that someday Jenret and Doyce might have a relationship.**"

"**That's entirely different!**" She refused to dignify the rest of Rawn's comment with a reply.

Saam tilted his head, regarded her out of one yellow eye, then the other. "**How so?**"

"**Because ... because Jenret's a Seeker, and while he'd try the patience of the Elders themselves,**" Rawn shrugged his agreement as Khar continued, "**he's basically a good person.**"

"**And Muscadeine isn't?**" M'wa queried.

Khar's tail lashed again, forced M'wa back to avoid the sting. "**Of course he is! I'd sense it if he weren't! It's just that ... that ...**" she trailed off helplessly, amber eyes sad.

"**I told you! Jealous!**" Rawn couldn't restrain his triumph. He knew it! She'd been jealous because he'd expressed genteel interest in N'oor and now she was jealous of Muscadeine! "**Ghattas!**" He ear-flicked the final word to Saam in falanese. If she caught him, she'd nip his ears.

But Khar ignored Rawn's words, turned to M'wa, almost beseeching him to explain. "**What's he truly like? You've been reading his thoughts, he gave you permission.**"

M'wa found himself unready to comment. It was too soon. What he'd found there had been a surprise, a revelation of such magnitude that he hadn't been prepared for it. Nor, he suspected, were the others yet. Rawn had asked some pointed questions, but he'd remained mute, appreciating that Arras Muscadeine respected people's privacy as stringently as the ghatti did. A good sign, a promising one. "**There is a potential in him we've never before imagined.**" That was the most he dared say.

"**Somehow I feel I'm losing her to Muscadeine in a way I can't understand or share, not the way I'd share her with Jenret.**" Khar's confession touched M'wa, but he had to doubt the accuracy of her comment about Jenret. Rawn, too, acted as if uncomfortable doubts remained.

Saam strove to comfort, licked the side of her face. "**You're trying too hard, wanting too much. Don't push. Nothing can break your Bond unless you let it. Talk with her, share with her.**"

"**I don't want to intrude any more than I have. After**

having nothing for those octants before, I'm blessed by what I do have." And Saam knew exactly what she meant. "I feel as if this journey is pulling us farther apart instead of bringing us closer together."

"You let her go before and she came back. She will again. Trust in her." Whether they realized it or not, M'wa sensed that for some the journey had only commenced. In the morning they'd begin another part of it. He stretched, rose. "From the sounds outside I'd say Muscadeine's men have returned with the horses. Tomorrow will be a long day. Best sleep while we can."

They padded away to their Bonds. Only Khar remained, gazing at the stars, wistful. For no reason she could imagine, she thought of Constant Minor, the Steward, and wondered if he felt equally lonely when he stared at the stars.

The horses and Muscadeine's three men had slipped in during the night, the men exhausted but full of news about tightening security in Sidonie, rumors running riot, including the proposed arrest of External Affairs Lord Valeria Condorcet for complicity in Arras Muscadeine's supposed plot to throw Marchmont to the Canderisians. Maurice's loyalists crisscrossed the country in search of Muscadeine and the Envoy. As Muscadeine had expected, the borders showed the greatest increase in activity, Maurice's men overstepping their bounds, taking advantage of Condorcet's tenuous position. In the early morning debate over why they should return to Sidonie with Muscadeine and Eadwin, Doyce had a nagging suspicion she'd overlooked something, but couldn't think of it for the life of her.

Everyone busy with watering and saddling the horses, Doyce fussed with Lokka's girth, the tongue of the buckle catching in the wrong notch as she grumbled, "Where're Aelbert and N'oor—still sleeping?" At least one member of her party would be thrilled by the news of their return. She gasped. How had she missed Aelbert's absence this morning?

Khar's head snapped up. **"No, don't you remember? Muscadeine assigned them guard duty outside."**

"Well, then, why aren't they around?" she asked, unreasonably edgy, "and who spent the night watching from the widow's walk?"

"I . . . don't know," Khar admitted as she began furiously questioning the other ghatti, none of whom knew where Aelbert and N'oor were, either.

A pod from last season's milkweed plant gave a dry death rattle that rasped on her nerves just as Felix bolted from the barn, charging into the woods as if to flush something. Distracted, Doyce wondered what the dog had scented. Yet Harry, close by Eadwin's side, acted the most perturbed by the dog's rocketing exit, venting a yowl of piercing anger and disquiet. Nakum and Muscadeine were the first to react, Arras springing in front of Eadwin and drawing his sword, scanning the woods as the wild ghatt rowled with rage, claws extended to ward off an invisible foe. Hidden in the shadows of the trees, armed men silently ringed the house and barn, crossbows cranked ready, began moving inward, inexorable as the tightening of a noose, coming at them from all directions. At Jenret's shouted warning, Nakum seized Doyce by the wrist, dragging her backward, away from the group's exposed front.

At a signal, crossbows swept against shoulders, were cocked and aimed as a man wearing Maurice's lavender and white with its wide purple trim marched forward from the soldiers. "Halt where you are!" he shouted. "In the name of our ruler, King Maurice, you are our prisoners. You have broken the laws and covenants of Marchmont, betrayed our land and our King, and must be remanded to the capital to await his judgment." As he spoke, three horses pressed close behind the circle of armed men, one ridden by Syndar Saffron, and the second by Jules Jampolis, reins looped around his palm. The third, most-rearward horse was mounted by Aelbert Orsborne, hands tied loosely in front of him, expression a mixture of vexation and smugness as N'oor made lighting paw jabs at the soldier holding the horse's bridle, trying to scratch his hands.

"Jacobia!" roared Saffron, and spurred his horse forward, oblivious to the circle's disruption, intent only on seeking his daughter. He threw himself from the horse, leaving the reins dragging, the horse sidling and twitchy with nerves as his rider shoved by him. Trying to decide whether to track their previously assigned target or focus on a new one, the bowmen wavered in their aim as people shifted within the circle's center.

Mortified at having been chased all the way to Marchmont yet relieved to spy a familiar face in the midst of danger, Jacobia wailed and rushed for his outstretched arms. With the distraction she caused providing a cover Roland sprang beside her, diving for the saddle of Saffron's vacated horse. He landed, jammed heels into the horse's sides as he hauled the reins short, and the panicked horse reared on hind legs, forelegs pawing the air, threatening close guards, before Roland drove him through the throng. Quarrels sliced the air, over-eager bowmen endangering everyone, sowing more confusion as soldiers dodged arrows from their own ranks. The man in charge cursed, tried to enforce order, while Jules Jampolis watched with a supercilious expression of contempt.

Making the most of the commotion, Muscadeine pulled Eadwin back, shushing his protests, shouldering him toward Nakum and Doyce. Harry followed, silent at last, broad mask still contorted with spitting rage, ready to strike anyone near. Arras pushed Eadwin between Nakum and Doyce. "Get clear!" he ordered hoarsely. "Get him out of here, keep him safe! I'll provide the opening."

"Where?" Doyce bit back further questions, exchanged a shrug with Nakum. The Erakwan lad nodded at Muscadeine as he seized Eadwin by the wrist, motioned Doyce to take the other. Reassured, Muscadeine sprang forward, sword weaving as he feinted at a guard's wavering crossbow.

"For the true King, for the blood royale!" he jeered as he slashed the guard down, spun on the next one close enough to threaten them. Felix's long, tapering form shot through the press, gleaming canines hamstringing a third guard. With a shout of encouragement in her direction, Jenret raced to guard Muscadeine's back, while Bard and Sarrett lunged at other enemies, the ghatti attacking, clawing, springing to dislodge crossbows. But the final disruption was again Jacobia's doing as she pulled free from Syndar Saffron's embrace and ran, screaming Jenret's name, Saffron in hot pursuit. Her random, harried dash played havoc with order, and in the milling confusion, Nakum sprinted clear, towing white-faced, openmouthed Eadwin while Doyce tagged along. She heard Muscadeine bellow an order. "Felix! Go! Guard! Guard Eadwin!" With a moaning howl of protest the dog loped away, long-eared, long-snouted head turned in farewell before he gashed the throat of the only guard in their path.

Nakum followed quick and close behind Felix's opening, Saam and Khar behind them, Harry now in the lead. Hand locked on Eadwin's wrist, Doyce pulled abreast of Nakum, Eadwin a pace behind, arms strained as they hauled him along. "Where, Nakum?" she gasped, heart pounding to match the pounding of her feet.

She sensed the current of his strength pouring all the way through Eadwin to her, could see him being fueled by it as well. "Follow Harry for now," Nakum instructed, hazel eyes darting, checking for concealed enemies, gauging the trail, the cover. "He has to know somewhere safe, it's his territory."

"Down a badger hole, most likely," muttered Khar.

Nakum's lips twitched as he signaled Felix to the rear-guard position, Khar and Saam moving beside them. "First we hide, then we head for the mountains, as high as we can." And left unsaid that this was his secret desire as well as their necessary course. Into the mountains, to the arborfer, toward his people, however distantly related they might be. Like with like at last! Horns blasted in the distance, a raucous rally to victory.

Saam growled, spun back. **"They've been taken prisoners,"** he snarled. **"We must help!"** Yellow eyes pleaded with Nakum.

"No, Saam," he chided. "Freedom first. Then we can decide how to help. Being captured with them does no good."

Eadwin finally found his voice. "I hope Roland broke clear. He'll ride for help!" But neither had the heart to ask Eadwin whom he thought Roland could rally. Nothing was certain any more.

❧

Arms pinioned by two guards, Constant's head whirled as he stood in front of the dais, glaring up at the throne, up at Maurice. It burned, burned in his craw, made his heart race in fury, bleeding away too much precious energy, energy he might not be able to recoup if he were cast into the lightless dungeons. Fabienne hovered halfway up the steps, staring from one to the other, elbows cupped in her hands. Other

than that gesture, she appeared calm, or as composed as
could be expected under the circumstances, Constant judged
and mentally signaled his approval. *"All we can do is play
along with him for now,"* he reminded her silently. He
counted on Maurice not bothering to monitor his wife or any
other paltry being in the room.

And Maurice wasn't concentrating on them for the moment, hand on his brow, a blood-stained bandage encircling
his forearm. He brightened, crowed with triumph. "They've
captured Muscadeine and the Seekers!" Then his lip curled
as he spat out, "But Eadwin got away, Eadwin, that damned
Special Envoy, and the Erakwan boy. No matter, we'll have
them all soon. Don't worry, my dear," the last brisk comment addressed to Fabienne. "We'll have him safe in no
time at all." He dipped his chin, regarded Constant again.
"Don't you see, old man? Your time is past, long past. Best
go quietly into confinement, give me your pledge that you'll
obey my orders. My time has come, yours has faded. You
could be useful if you choose, but if not, it's no matter to
me."

If truth be known, he was long past his time, but Maurice
had no idea of that. Now was the time to set a lure, Constant
decided, let that fat, smirking fool believe in his supreme
control. He wouldn't, couldn't bring himself to do what he
had to do, not yet, not after so many years. He'd learned the
hard way what the control of other human beings meant,
what it did to the controller, and the taste left a bitterness in
his mouth. Why, why had he ever decided to awaken, come
back to a world he no longer knew? But until they had
Eadwin safe, he had no choice but to work from the outside,
manipulate as best he could, avoiding the final pitfall until
absolutely necessary.

He drew himself up between the two guards, confident he
looked foolish and fragile, old and quivering. Part of it was
an act, part of it was not, and sometimes he wondered which
was which. "No. Absolutely not. I will not aid you, you
usurper! You're naught but a rotten limb in the family tree,
ready to snap and break at the first good storm. And you've
yet to feel that storm as you will when Arras Muscadeine
has a chance at you!"

"But Muscadeine is captured," Maurice reminded him
silkily, looking to his courtiers for approbation, for the nods
and smiles, some outright, some complicitous, that fawned

on his power. He wished that Fabienne's face wore a similar expression, but she still worried about Eadwin. And would be more worried still when she discovered what he truly planned for Eadwin. But until then she had considerable value, if all unwitting: her devoted service to Wilhelmina, her long marriage to him making her beyond reproach, able to give her approbation to his noble decision to take on the burden of ruling. "Now, old man, are you sure you don't want to reconsider?"

"Never!" raged Constant, and sucked at his cheeks, his dry tongue to work up a little spittal, send it wavering toward the bottom step. Had he goaded him enough? If so, could Fabienne shelter him from the worst of Maurice's wrath? Ah, if only the ghatti were here to strip the truth bare, strip this man bare in front of his believers, those that were innocent puppets, at least, and he felt convinced there were many of those. Maurice had worked his wiles on them with far greater ingenuity than Constant himself had used to convince them of his existence, the tired old man always faint in the background, but willing to serve, do his part.

Retying the saturated bandage more tightly around his arm until blood oozed, Maurice leaned forward. "Then feel *my* power, little man, little dusty library grubber, weak little worm who hadn't seen the light of day for so many years! The Lady only knows how you came to be Steward, but you're not Steward now, not with me as King!" And his eyes bored into Constant's faded blue ones. The old man trembled, sank to his knees, tears leaking at the mental pain. Yes, pain he'd expected, pain he could easily withstand if he so chose, when he so chose, but the greatest anguish of all came from seeing mental powers abused like this to control, coerce another human being. Never, not ever, had the "enhancement" been meant for this perversion! He wailed, a high keening sound, and managed an obeisance, groveling on the floor, white robe tremulously shaking. "I . . . I . . ." the words lodged in his throat.

Smug gratification puffed Maurice even further. "You're no threat to me, old man. I've proved that. Still, a few days in the dungeon might prove salutary to remind you of your loyalty, your overwhelming loyalty to me." He motioned the guards to drag Constant to his feet, where the old man hung between their arms, weak and helpless, hands scrubbing tears from withered cheeks.

With swift steps Fabienne rushed to his side, releasing one of Constant's arms from the guards and draping it across her shoulder. "Oh, Maurice, please," she beseeched. "He's too old and and weak for that. Would you have the man's death on your conscience? He may have served wrongly, but he served as well as he was able. Lock him in his old, familiar library, if you must. Leave him guarded there, but not in the dungeons. This isn't how you want to begin your rule, by killing a harmless old man? All power should be leavened with clemency and mercy."

Maurice rubbed at his upper lip with his thumb. "And of course I will need someone to crown me," he mused. "You're right, my dear. Mercy, it is. Guards, take him to the library. Make sure he has food and water, see that he's locked in and guarded day and night. No one to pass without exception. Except, of course, the Lady . . . or rather, Queen Fabienne." A smirk of exquisite pleasure at the title's ring.

As gently as they could, the guards took Constant's arms, clutching him a little too high, his feet vainly treading air. As they exited, Constant cast a supplicating look over his shoulder toward the high throne. Maurice nodded regally, never noticing when Constant's head drooped and he winked at Fabienne.

❖

About three paces behind Byrta, Parse cursed himself for having frozen there, unable to read her face when she stopped dead, arm out from her side, halting him in his tracks. Lady knew she was already mad enough at him. Abandoning his assigned post, he'd stealthily ridden to join her, conning the trail with swiveling, guilty glances for anyone who might notice he didn't belong there. He'd been proud of his stealth, though he acknowledged he owed most of his luck to Per'la's quick instincts and hissed instructions. Byrta had grumbled mightily about this unauthorized contact, but he'd be damned if he'd let her displeasure quell his aching need for physical companionship, someone to directly share his fears and his worries, not be content with listening to the ghatti's secondhand descriptions of how the other Seekers fared. Oh, she'd accepted his presence, mayhap even secretly glad, though she might not admit it, and now this—this peremptory command, the being ignored.

Per'la leaned against his leg, frozen as well, head cocked. "Hush," she emphasized. "Don't disturb her, there's word from Bard and M'wa. Direct word from Bard." And Parse's mouth dropped, the hair on his head rising and tingling at the roots until he wanted to stroke it down, control it, if nothing else. Hard to believe the twins could communicate directly, without the aid of their Bonds, but it was true. And the distance they communicated was astounding. Or he assumed it was, since no one had heard from Sarrett or Bard or Doyce and the others in too long.

Byrta's head with its close-cropped hair, maple sugar curls as tight as tiny wood shavings, swayed back and forth. Once he almost caught her profile as she strained to focus on the distant mindspeech. "Can you hear what they're saying?" he whispered to Per'la, "Has P'wa given you any clue?"

Peridot eyes rolled in a long-suffering look as eloquent as any reproach and more eloquent than Bryta's order to stand and be patient. Biting his tongue until he thought he might burst at the silence, the immobility, the strain, he obeyed but fretted all the same.

With a suddenness that sent him stumbling backward, P'wa leaped into Byrta's arms, her black head with its white star flashing over her Bondmate's shoulder. Her right paw with the long white stocking crept up, followed by the left with its short white boot, front feet kneading the fleece tabard, digging deep for contact and comfort. "It's bad. Very bad," she confided, tongue quick-licking lips and whiskers as if she were going to be sick. "They're captured, really and truly this time, though Doyce, Nakum, and one of the Marchmontians are free. Bard is in great pain, his thoughts jumbled, but he thinks a revolution is in progress and he can't judge their safety or what will happen next. Ah, no!" the ghatta grimaced. "They just pulled the quarrel free! The pain! Nothing more to hear!"

Byrta spun abruptly on a booted heel, almost looking through them, thoughts far distant. He reached to comfort her, but Byrta shrugged him off, finally seemed to notice him for the first time. Her face looked set in stone, eroded by the tears streaming down her cheeks. Parse tried again, and this time she permitted his hand to remain, the hammering heat of his fears burning against her ice cold dread.

Her mouth moved, though no sound came out, then moved again as if she finally realized that with Parse it was truly necessary to articulate the words, not depend on mindspeech alone. "We must go after them," she declared with a painfully polite emphasis she might have used to say "you must try a piece of this fruit cake" when she served cha. Not that he could fathom Byrta in a cozy, domestic scene, guests gathered for cha and sweets, demure hostess insisting no bashful guest ignore the treasure trove of treats.

"We will, Byrta, we will," he soothed, "but we have things to do first." And gulped as smoky-colored eyes darkened, glared at him. Relentless, she pushed by, heading for her horse, P'wa still in her arms, staring in mute appeal at Parse and Per'la.

Byrta snarled a one-word response to Parse's inanity. *"Now!"* Trailing in her wake, Parse managed to catch up, thrust himself ahead and, running backward, tried to force her to focus on him.

"Dammit, Byrta, we will! May Per'la leave me if I lie!" He hoped the oath sank in, a phrase no Seeker Veritas would use lightly. He blocked her path, nervous about the consequences. But she continued walking, prepared to clamber over him, no more inconvenient than a downed log in her path. Desperate, he grabbed her upper arms and braced against her forward momentum. Hampered by her grip on P'wa, she hesitated, shifting the ghatta in her arms.

"Go ahead," P'wa instructed, constricted by her grasp. **"Hit her! Slap her out of it!"** Wincing at his temerity, Parse hauled off and slapped her, hard, the sting and tingle racing all the way to his elbow. Lacking further guidance, he shook her, and prayed Bard never learned what he'd just done to his sister.

Shoulders cocked earward, hands ready to slap her blows away, prepared to duck and dodge, he caught a semblance of sanity in Byrta's face. "I . . . I'm sorry," he stammered, then stopped, drawing himself as tall as he could, though he lacked Byrta's height. "No," he corrected himself, "I'm *not* sorry. You *have* to listen, Byrta. There's more at stake than just Bard's safety. I promised on my honor and on Per'la's honor that I'd help, and I will, but we can't just charge into Marchmont without a plan. And most of all, we have to alert the Monitor to what's happening. The Guardians must be mustered, put on alert."

She was nodding, nodding slowly and musingly at him. Bending, she released P'wa beside Per'la, and straightened, hand cradling her cheek. "I am sorry about that," he gestured toward her face."

"I ... know. You're ... right." She managed an almost-smile over the welling pain. "You must hurt as well. They've caught Sarrett, too."

He had known it but hadn't wanted to admit it, hadn't let himself dwell on it until now. And he wouldn't think about it yet, couldn't, or he'd be racing Byrta for the border, raving like a madman. "Now," he consoled, drawing Byrta along with him, settling her down. "Now, tell us everything Bard and M'wa told you, word for word. We have to plan, send a message back. *Then* we can rescue them and damn anyone who stands in our way!" And he had no idea how incongruous those menacing words sounded coming from him.

❖

PART
SEVEN

❖

Labored breathing behind him alerted Nakum to slow down. Balancing on the edge of the outcrop he'd swarmed over without a thought, he stretched to point out the easiest hand-holds, knowing the others had been concentrating on planting their feet without slipping. Saam bounded to their level, offering encouragement, retracing the path. While he waited, Nakum tossed his head back to stare up the incredible mountain range with its single, lofty snow peak, their goal since fleeing Maurice's forces.

The dog Felix struggled beside him, panting, sides heaving. The dog had kept pace, though he'd had to search out zigzag routes, unable to spring high and land surefooted on a wafer-thin ledge or level spot the way the ghatti could. Nakum patted him, and the dog plopped at his feet, glad of the respite.

Boosting Eadwin toward Nakum, Doyce stretched for Nakum's welcoming, extended hand and levered herself up. Impatient, Harry had plunged beyond them with springing leaps, twisting and descending to meet Eadwin, throwing himself across his lap as he collapsed on the ledge, face scarlet, open mouth sucking in great lungfuls of air. His constricted life in the tower had left Eadwin unfit for the harried escape and punishing climb. "How much farther?" he gasped and lay back, hand pressed against a stitch in his side.

From her position as rearguard, Khar caught up, swirled past Felix, offered a grazing lick at a scrape on Felix's leg. The dog gave a gentle whoofle of thanks that ruffled her fur. **"We have to rest,"** Khar implored Nakum. **"I haven't heard any pursuit for some time now. Have you, Saam?"** The gray ghatt dipped his head in agreement. **"I don't know how high we have to climb, but Eadwin needs to rest. We all need to rest."**

Ashamed, Nakum sank cross-legged, hid his head in his hands. How could he have forgotten? Blessed with his earth-bond, he could summon strength and power from the very earth he traversed, while the others could not. And the worst of it was forcing himself to admit that there was more to this headlong flight than their pressing need to escape. His bond was drawing him into the mountains more strongly the farther they climbed, just as the tower had lured him before. He grasped his pouch, felt the thrumming power swell through him, call him higher and higher. Why? What awaited him there?

He took a trembling breath, brushed loose hair from his forehead, only to realize they regarded him expectantly, waiting for him to answer. Propped on his elbows, Eadwin waited, an anxious smile on his lips, his face paling from pulsing scarlet to rose. "We should climb higher to avoid pursuit, but I don't know precisely where," Nakum conceded. "This isn't my land and I don't know where we are, what lies above us, if we'll find shelter or not. We've nearly reached the timberline."

Doyce passed a waterskin, their one waterskin, and each took a sparing sip. "Shouldn't we go sideways, so to speak, rather than straight up? Eventually we'll have to climb down, and we shouldn't descend at the exact spot we started from. Too obvious." She brushed needles and twigs from a bowllike dip in the granite, squirted some water so the ghatti and the dog could drink as well.

"You're right." It galled him to admit it, made him hedge, "but I still think we should climb higher first." Nakum knew he was being stubborn, caught by his own ulterior motive, the strange dragging presence the mountain exerted over him. Higher, higher! Exultation coursed through him. What other wonders awaited?

"Would you abandon your companions, leave them on their own in the midst of danger?" He had soared, but now Saam's words had dragged him back.

"I don't know," he responded almost sulkily. *"If they can't keep up."* And shame flooded him, not his own, but Saam's shame at his behavior. *"Sorry."*

"You know what's up there?" Eadwin pressed to share his knowledge. "I've heard that at peak-top you'll find the remains, the branchless trunk of a dead arborfer, the biggest ever, far bigger than the one the tower was carved from. The

Erakwa nursery workers said it rears straight toward the sky as if it could reach up and touch it, pierce it. The granddaddy of them all."

The words struck Nakum breathless. Was it possible the old legends were true? He scrambled up without thinking, began to climb again. "Just a little farther, please!" he begged and the others wearily followed.

♣

Riding at the fringes of the guard, Syndar Saffron on her right, Aelbert on her left, Jacobia had spent most of her time staring at her reins, confused, mind working furiously, shooting an occasional furtive query in Syndar Saffron's direction. She'd never really considered whether or not she liked the merchant; he simply *was,* a part of her existence, her world, in and out of the offices and around the house so often that she simply expected him there. Always brusquely kind, sweets stashed in his pocket when she was a child; now that she was older, an occasional gift, inexpensive and often ineptly chosen, as if he had no idea what a young woman would desire. And what she desired now, she didn't dare ask for because the world as she knew it would irrevocably change.

Clearly Mother hadn't received her note, or if she had, Saffron had departed before it had been delivered. But how had he come to be a part of this group, seemingly accepted, trusted? She worried at the thought, brow furled, eyebrows scrunched. He wasn't bound nor was she, as if he stood surety for her behavior. Which obligated her not to disgrace him, betray his trust. And what was she supposed to think when Aelbert's hands had been unbound while Jenret, Sarrett, Bard, and that devilishly handsome Arras Muscadeine were tied, riding clustered in the center, closely guarded? Bard had had a quarrel shaft roughly removed from his shoulder; the shaft had snapped his collarbone. The others bore bruises and sword wounds aplenty, most minor, but some were going to require stitches. Assuming prisoners were allowed medical care, she found herself wondering. After all, what had the man with the scarred hands said? "Not really all of you concern us, but a touch of prison might curb your meddlesome instincts." He'd been looking right at her when he'd said that, and the way he'd licked his lower lip as he continued to stare had twisted her stomach. It was the same stare that merchanter had given her when he'd told her about Mother and Syndar Saffron.

She realized that Saffron had said something and she had no idea what. Startled at his violet eyes on her, she made a weak gesture to indicate bewilderment. He smiled, repeated himself. "I said that I'm sorry, but I can't convince them to untie Jenret. He's too volatile to their way of thinking."

She pitched her voice low, head turned in his direction, and whispered, "But why is *he* untied?" Her eyebrows winged in Aelbert's direction.

"I'd like to know that as well. He didn't put up much of a fight when we caught him, seemed relieved. Why don't you ask? He seems concerned about you. He's riding with us, not chatting with Jampolis or the guards."

With a toss of her hair, Jacobia eased her horse toward Aelbert, flung a smile in his direction. He showed a wary brightening and reciprocated, nudging N'oor to indicate they'd been noticed. "I'm sorry," he said. "I suspect this is all rather confusing and frightening, but things will be fine shortly, I'm sure. They know you're an innocent bystander and have nothing to do with what's been going on. This isn't your battle, after all."

"Is it yours? Whose side are you on, Aelbert? You're the Special Envoy's aide, you're aide de camp to the Monitor. As a loyal Canderisian citizen, shouldn't you be bound with the rest? Are you some sort of turncoat?" Despite herself, Jacobia almost spat the last words, frustrated beyond endurance by the bland expression on his face. Lady Bright, what did it take to shake the man, make him show some emotion, some honest emotion, no matter what it was? She couldn't live with bottling herself up like that, she'd burst!

And for a brief moment she did glimpse an honest emotion—hurt, humiliation dulled his eyes, but he quickly smothered it, while N'oor touched his hand with one of her absurdly large paws. He rubbed his cheek against the ghatta's head before turning in her direction. "No, not that, but my . . . agenda . . . is different from yours. You don't understand. None of you understand." He said it matter-of-factly, as if it were all he expected.

"Well, then, explain it to me!" Jacobia shot back, but found she was shouting at his receding back as he pulled ahead, now riding separate from everyone.

❖

They'd stopped for the night at the tree line. She'd put her foot down about that, glad she'd insisted. Still, they'd continued their vertical hike until the halt, some strange obsession luring Nakum along while they trailed wearily in his wake. Puzzling. Convincing him to stop had been like trying to shake a sleeper awake, make him conscious of the world around him instead of the dream within. She shook her head again speculatively, but found no answer. Still, once she'd regained his attention he'd been apologetic, agreeable about finding shelter for the night. What tomorrow would bring, she had no idea, but suspected she'd best keep a close watch on the Erakwan lad. Even Saam acted perturbed by his actions.

Taking his bow and arrows and actually dragging reluctant feet downward to hunt, Nakum had cautioned that game might be scarce at this altitude. At least she'd found water, an icy, milky-white run-off from the snows still covering the very top of the mountain. The thought of the snow made her shiver, huddle closer to Felix.

After arranging branches for a small fire, Eadwin slapped his head with his hand. "How are we going to light it?" he moaned. "I don't have flint and tinder, do you?"

He looked for a moment as if this were the worst thing that could befall him, had reached the end of his endurance; to him this was the last straw, the final indignity after the shocks of the past two days, the betraying weaknesses of his body, and the aching admission that his father had ordered his capture. Rummaging in her pockets, trying first one, then another, she fished out the little bronze cylinder. "No, no flint and tinder, but I do have . . ." she unscrewed the cap, shook the contents into her hand, "seven lucifers. Will that do? Unless you have the energy to rub two sticks together." Make it seem ordinary, everyday, give him something to hang onto, pull himself toward self-control.

He found the grace to laugh, more in relief than in amusement, but she appreciated his effort and what it had cost. "I think you'd better try, then. Can't afford to waste any, and my hands are shaking too hard. I'd snuff it before I'd light anything." Kneeling beside him as he cupped his hands around hers to shelter the flame, she struck the lucifer, holding her breath. She wasn't that steady herself. She held it, resolute, until the stick burned all the way to her fingertips, ignoring the heat, the singeing, wanting to be sure it caught. At last she had no choice but to drop it, relieved that a tiny flame fingered through the kindling, catching slowly, not over-eager but growing.

"I'm no good for anything. I can't help," Eadwin muttered, still crouched protectively against a breeze that threatened the flame. She started to protest, then stopped at his expression. He waved a dismissive hand. "I didn't mean just starting fires." He wore a distant, searching look, almost yearning, as if he sought to hear and was troubled by the silence.

Rocking back off her knees, she sat, toying with a twig, forcing it to burn and dropping it into another spot that hadn't yet caught. "So what *do* you mean?" Did she want to know?—no, but he needed to talk, his hunger reached out to her, made her put aside her own exhaustion. He'd been so long without talking to anyone.

"I should know what's going on, be able to grasp their thoughts, let you know if we're in danger and why! I used to be able to, at least a little, in fact Mother said I showed talent for it—and early, too! We don't usually gain our full range until adolescence or later. But oh, no, not me, not me! I got my growth spurt and that was about all." His words were bitter. "My powers just stopped, evaporated." He snapped his fingers to indicate the suddenness. "No, that's not right. I can feel them dormant inside—I can't project and I can't receive—but they're locked away as if I can't find the key, just as I was imprisoned inside that tower."

"What are you talking about? What do you mean?" Doyce asked with careful precision, the hairs along her arms rising in goose bumps. She didn't at all like the direction this conversation, this confidence was taking.

Taken aback, Eadwin asked, "Didn't Arras explain? You mindspeak as well, don't you? I mean, you must if you can converse with Khar, with the other ghatti. Lady's mercy, I'm *such* a failure! I can't mindspeak, I can't even manage to properly mindspeak Harry! Father's right, I'm a full-grown man and a failure, good for nothing but pottering around with arborfer!"

Her tongue cleft to the roof of her mouth, but she willed the word out at last, despite praying not to ever say it. "You

mean you're a Gleaner?" To have come so far only to meet
with them again! No escape, never any escape from their
powers. Caught in their web forever, as surely as Vesey had
trapped her.

"Gleaner? Is that what you call us in your country? Why?
Everyone knows the proper name is Resonant."

"*Everyone* . . . knows?" she choked. "You mean it's commonplace here to be a . . ." she stumbled on the word, "Resonant? Is . . . Arras one?"

Surprised, off-put by her obvious distaste, Eadwin looked
puzzled. "Well, of course. He's one of the more talented
ones. The Bannerjees are the best all-around—that was why
it was such a blow when they left Ministration Service. Being a Resonant is nothing unusual, any more than being left-
handed is. I guess about one in ten people possess some
level of Resonant powers. It all goes back to our first King,
Constant, being a communications officer on the starships
that brought our ancestors here."

"Communications officer?" Her voice hit a higher register
than she was used to. "Starships?" And had the roiling, sick
sensation that an old, familiar tale was suddenly about to
transform itself into a horror story. Her face, she knew, already mirrored her mounting revulsion.

"You didn't know? You and Arras weren't sharing
thoughts? You seemed so intimate, so attuned. I'm sorry.
I've put my foot in it, haven't I?" He reached a hand toward
her knee for comfort, only to have her flinch before holding
steady. He admired her willpower. So, the old stories were
true, the Canderisians didn't have the gifts of old, or if they
did, they didn't know how to use them. Yet how could that
be if Seekers Veritas, so very close to being Resonants, were
held in such respect? And Gleaners? What were they? Her
quiet bitterness and fear hadn't escaped him. "I don't know
what your Gleaners are, but Resonants are honored members
of our society."

She nodded, swallowed hard. "I think you're going to
have to begin at the very beginning and assume that I know
nothing, because that's absolutely true."

"Would you rather wait until Nakum returns, so that he
can judge the truth of my story as well?"

Her relief was palpable. "Yes, I think that might be wise.
Neither Nakum or I can judge the truth, but the ghatti can,
if you'll allow it. If you'll permit Khar and Saam access to

your mind, your thoughts just as they would at a Truth-Seeking. It's far deeper than the conversations you've had with them."

He rumpled Harry's fur, tickled behind the tufted ears. "I wish Harry had real access to my mind, the way you have with Khar. As I said, I can't manage to do anything right."

That, at least, was something to talk about that she could accept, would keep her other anxious thoughts and suppositions at bay. She tried to gather her wits, think through the situation logically and search for the missing puzzle piece. What had gone wrong with their Bonding? "You can share emotions, correct?" She ticked it off on her finger as he nodded agreement. "You can think about, visualize, objects and make him comprehend?" She ticked off the next finger. "But you can't really converse?" She worried the thought around from different angles. "Every Seeker says the rush of communication at Bonding is instantaneous, often an incredible, overwhelming babble. It does tend to be babble at first because the ghatten are so young—it's like hearing a child chattering relentlessly in your head. But they soon settle down." She smiled reminiscently. "Once those sharp little teeth puncture your finger and draw blood, you're Bonded well and true, sharing your innermost thoughts."

"Puncture your finger? You mean you *let* them bite you?" Eadwin recoiled in shock. "I've never let Harry bite me, let alone draw blood. The Heavens know he tried often enough when he was little, but I'd rap my finger on his nose. You have to teach them some sort of discipline. Besides," embarrassment flooded him, "I can't stand to be nipped. Almost phobic about it," he confessed. "One of our farm tenants on the manor had a sheepdog when I was little, maybe four. I was running across the meadow, dashing back and forth, playing my own private games, shouting at the top of my lungs, when the dog saw me. He came rushing after me, barking and nipping at my ankles and calfs, sending me dodging to escape those snapping teeth. I think he was playing, pretending to herd me like a stray sheep, but all I knew then was that it hurt. And he wouldn't stop and he wouldn't stop, a nip here, a nip there, and my father and the farmer standing at the fence laughing, doing nothing to help me! I was bruised, even bloody in a few spots because I'd jerked away. I just can't stand to be nipped," he finished, shaking his head at the memory.

Khar's knowing amber eyes found Doyce's. **"Well, that certainly explains a great deal. Harry has never tasted Eadwin's blood to complete the Bonding. At most it's been a shadow-bonding. And when Eadwin didn't accept the ultimate sharing, remember that they were in the tower. Who else could Harry Choose? A snap on the nose, indeed, when the poor ghatten tried to do what was right."** Khar sniffed in disgust.

Heartened by Khar's comment, Doyce still feared raising Eadwin's hopes. *"Do you think it's possible for them to Bond? And if they do, will it affect Eadwin's missing Resonant abilities?"*

The ghatta limbered her shoulders as if considering, and indeed she was. How much to say, how much to reveal? Was this why she was afraid of Arras, because he could communicate in a way she'd believed hers alone with Doyce? She could not lie, but she could be indirect. **"Oh, they can Bond, I think. Tell Eadwin he's a late bloomer. I'll explain to Harry, hope that Eadwin's discipline hasn't inhibited him after all this time."** And refused to mention there might be other late bloomers as well, tried to conquer her jealousy.

After explaining what was required for Eadwin to truly Bond with Harry, Doyce sat back as Khar escorted Harry toward Eadwin. Khar chin-rubbed the large, furred shoulder, and Harry purred with barely suppressed nervousness. The ghatt sat, staring at the young man, waiting, expectant. Sinking to his knees, Eadwin extended a badly shaking hand toward the ghatt. Harry stretched toward it gingerly and Eadwin's hand jerked back, then he thrust it out again. "Just don't *look!*" he commanded himself and buried his head in the crook of his arm.

Eyes squinched shut, frantic with anticipation, the ghatt lunged, lips curled back, teeth bared as he nipped Eadwin's index finger, one long fang puncturing the tip like a lancet. He scrambled back, scrubbing his face with a paw before anxiously side-glancing at his loved one. "Oh, oh, oh!" was all Eadwin could manage, wonderment flooding his face. Harry looked equally startled. "Not Harry, not Harry, but Hru'rul! All this time I never knew!" He pressed his hands against his temples. "He's inside my head! I can hear him, he can hear me! We're talking!"

"Now all we have to do is teach them what we know,"

Khar grumbled. **"Not as if we have nothing else to do, I suppose you've noticed."**

"Yes, well, all in a day's work. Gleaners, Resonants, Seekers, whatever."

Stiflingly hot inside the casque, his own exhalations reflected against the steel, panting breaths beading face and mustache with moisture, trickling down his neck with scant room to seep beneath the padlocked metal collar securing the casque. Lady above, how he hated being encaged like this, abhorred it with a rising claustrophobic panic. No way to see, although narrow slits allowed the illusion of light and the passage of air. He flexed bound hands convulsively, aching to attack the steel helmet, wrench it free. But it was no good, they held the key, not him. Something velvet soft prodded at his hands and he startled, back rigid, head swiveling, unable to see, unable to imagine what touched him.

An interrogative throat clearing sound, as if someone were trying to attract his attention, and the sound came inside his head, not a muffled, outside distortion. It struck him. *"M'wa?"* he queried, but allowed no sound to escape his lips, simply concentrated on the name. *"Do you wish to speak with me?"*

He'd forgotten he rode Bard's horse, the black-and-white ghatt on the pommel platform in front of him. Bard was lashed to Arras's own steed, unconscious from the pain of his shoulder wound and the removal of the quarrel. The guards had been unsure what to do about the ghatti, but had finally decided they should ride with their Bonds. But with Bard slumped forward and lashed to the horse, there had been no room for M'wa.

The little throat-clearing sound came again, more insistent, as well as a harder prod at his hands. *"What, my friend?"* And it dawned on him, while he had previously given permission for M'wa to read his mind, he had never given permission for the ghatt to 'speak him directly. What were the words Doyce had taught Eadwin? *"Mindwalk if ye will?"*

"Thank you," M'wa responded and confided, **"I'm worried."**

Muscadeine forced his thoughts into order, still shocked to

find himself communicating with a ghatt. Somehow he'd expected the voice to be high-pitched, a little eerie, rather foreign-sounding, but it was not. And how much of a conversation could one have with a ghatt? Best keep it simple at first. *"You're worried about Bard, of course."*

The answer surprised him. **"No, not really. A bit, naturally. It's best for him like this, so he won't feel the jouncing and pain of the ride. The wound is clean and will heal nicely, I think."** The ghatt shifted on the platform and Arras could feel the shift and sway. **"Why have they locked that thing on you? Isn't it uncomfortable? What does it do? Where are we going? What will happen to us? I must know to pass word to the others."**

Never had he been bombarded with quite so many questions. *"This 'thing,' "* he tossed his head, felt the band of metal catch and drag at his throat, chafe at his adam's apple, *"this 'thing' is called a Mute. They believe it baffles my Resonant skills, that my thoughts cannot pass through this barrier into another's mind. Thus they think I cannot seduce their minds, change their wills."*

"But it doesn't work, does it? Or we wouldn't be able to 'speak, correct?" The ghatt continued more urgently. **"Would they Mute us, the ghatti, if they understood our gift? We ghatti don't seduce minds, change people's wills. Do you?"**

"I don't know if they would or not," Arras confessed. *"I don't think they comprehend the scope of your powers, indeed, I'm not sure I do, though I'm learning. Learning very rapidly."* M'wa's chuckle tickled his mind. *"As to the Mute working, it does to a certain extent; it limits the range and scope of my thoughts. On those with lesser powers, it can be quite effective, trapping all mind communication, even driving some mad when the Resonant ability is reflected back upon itself."*

The ghatt persisted, **"But *do* you seduce minds?"**

The question angered him, the pressing curiosity, the rudeness of the words, but he had to admit M'wa only reiterated his own words. *"No, no, of course not. That's not a Resonant's way, to twist and mold another's mind, no, the gift isn't meant for that."* Yet he knew with an all-too-great clarity why the question made him so uncomfortable, guilt-ridden. Because someone, someone obviously was coercing people's minds, remolding them to his wants and needs.

Maurice, damn him! Maurice and that damn pet eumedico of his! Damn, he'd had no idea such subtle, warped power lurked in Maurice! How had he gained it?

The ghatt followed his train of thought with no trouble at all. **"Then we'll confront him when we return to the castle. We *are* going there, aren't we?"**

"I believe so, though it's possible we might be imprisoned elsewhere or killed along the way. I've brought you all into deep trouble, my friend."

"No, if they planned to kill us, we wouldn't have survived the attack. Besides, I think your Maurice enjoys toying with his prey before he kills it. Best he remember that toys have sharp claws and teeth as well as other powers." The ghatt's evident relish reached him through the helmet.

But there were still a few hidden pieces or players in this game, Arras reminded himself, and hoped for the best. Eadwin had escaped, and he trusted him with Doyce and the Erakwan lad. And Felix was there to guard him too. If only Eadwin had matured into his powers. The thought wrenched at his gut. Playing the game at this mental level left Eadwin vulnerable, unable to protect himself.

"Don't worry." M'wa consoled. **"He'll flower when he's ready. It can't be forced. They're fine for now, safe according to Khar."** Then he became totally pragmatic. **"What shall I tell the others?"**

"I think as little as possible for now, if you would be so kind. I know you haven't shared my secrets with the others, and for that I thank you. Doyce wouldn't have been as comfortable with me if she'd realized my skills, though I think a suspicion lurks in the back of her mind. And possibly an inherent talent in her and the other Seekers. I would prefer to tell them on my own terms."

"Before all I had were suspicions, but I can't continue keeping secrets from my ghatti brethren, especially my sib! I'll tell them, but ask they not yet share the knowledge with their Bonds. It isn't right, but it's necessary." He sounded more cheerful. **"And the layerings of your Resonances are a puzzle we would love to piece together!"**

❖

With a gleeful whoop, Nakum danced into the circle of firelight, Saam prancing at his heels. "I heard him loud and clear all the way below! What happened? How did you do it?" He pounded Eadwin on the shoulder, embraced him. "Isn't it wonderful beyond imagining to hear him speak?" Eadwin wore a dazed, beatific expression, eyes far-staring as if he concentrated elsewhere, and Nakum knew he did. He surfaced momentarily, squeezed Nakum in return as Hru'rul swatted a large paw against the fringe of Nakum's leggings, insistent for attention.

"Hel-lo? Hel-lo? That is right? Hello? I can speak ... form things walled inside my head! Eadwin free from tower, my head free, too!" The ghatt's mental rapture almost bowled Nakum over.

He scratched the ghatt's tufted ears. "Yes, but you don't have to do it quite so fast or we'll all have headaches. Saam, help Khar, show him how it's done." He turned to Doyce. "How did you do it?"

She slumped by the fire, gave Eadwin an indulgent look that he never noticed, and turned back to Nakum, her fixed half-smile totally at odds with the wariness clenching the rest of her face. "Simple, really. So obvious once we understood. Harry ... I mean, Hru'rul had never blood-bonded with Eadwin."

He hunkered beside her, forgetful of the three squirrels tied to his belt. "Blood-bonded?" His hand brushed the carcasses and he remembered. "Here, come along while I gut and skin these, and tell me about it."

"Is that all we're going to have for dinner? Three pathetic little squirrels for three people, three ghatti and one very large, let me repeat *very* large and *very* hungry dog?" she gave a little sniff of pretend dismay as she followed.

Setting to work with his knife, Nakum glanced at her, worried at her tiredness and buried trepidation. "I don't know how Seekers and ghatti join their minds, what does it? Does this mean Eadwin will become a Seeker?" Jealousy twinged at him; no one had suggested *he* become a Seeker when Saam had decided to stay with him. But then, did he want to exchange his life for theirs? With Saam or without Saam, he was something special, he was Erakwa, and he thumped his chest to remind himself of that.

"What it takes is a blood-bonding to set things in motion. Ghatten do it instinctively when they're ready to Bond with the person they've Chosen." She sighed, pulled a squirrel to her, and reluctantly began skinning it, trying to touch it as little as possible. "They nip the Chosen hard enough to draw blood and that opens the floodgates of shared mindspeech. But Eadwin never let Hru'rul nip him—he was near phobic about it. Any time Hru'rul tried, he'd discipline him, and Hru'rul trained himself to fight off the urge."

He concentrated on the squirrels again, chewing at his lip, puzzled by the contradiction. "But Saam's never bitten me. How does he mindspeak me?"

She sounded impatient, as if she had other, bigger things on her mind, but it was important to him, very important. "The same way that Koom and Swan Maclough do. Once a ghatten has Bonded, tasted blood, he can communicate with anyone—if he so chooses."

"But you told me Parm nipped Harrap?" he persisted.

"Well, you know Parm. Overzealous to a fault." She laughed, half-helplessly but immediately sobered. "I'd guess he wanted to erase what was left of his Bond to Georges Barbet. He wasn't sure it would work, but he had to try. Neither Koom nor Saam wish to erase the memory of their previous Bonds from their thoughts." Pushing the squirrel aside with her foot she began pacing, as if summoning the courage to reveal the rest of her thoughts. "Nakum. Nakum, there's more." She wheeled back to him. "I think . . . I think Eadwin is a Gleaner, or has the potential to be one. Though he doesn't call it Gleaner, he calls it Resonant. I don't know if I can trust myself so close to one again! It frightens me to the furthest hells!"

Nakum found a long, supple branch, stripped it of even finer twigs, and strung the squirrels on it. "But do you know these Resonants always bode evil?" He strove to sound reasonable, reassuring, make her think it through instead of reacting with blind panic. "I sense nothing bad about Eadwin, not as I did with Vesey and Evelien. Not every mind branches the same. You don't know for sure he has the power or how he will use it, so you must wait and your judgment must wait. Khar and Saam and I won't let anything happen to you. We'll protect you."

She heaved a pent-up sigh. "Nothing is the same anymore, nothing that I can count on. I'm so afraid, and tired of being afraid. It stunts me. Sometimes I think I'll never heal."

He felt very protective and prayed for the wisdom to

guide her rightly. She was older than he and wiser in different ways, but she needed him and that made him swell with pride. Taking her elbow, he escorted her to the fire. "I've had an adventure today, too."

She angled her head to look up at him, and he realized he was at last taller than she. "In addition to the day-long one we've had—and are still having?"

"Yes, I found a cave not far below. It's very deep, safe and clean, no sign of habitation. We can spend the night there after we've eaten."

"Lady bless! Shelter? And downhill, not up? Hurrah!"

He'd made her happy under false pretenses and fought back the explanation that his pouch had urged him toward it as strongly as it had driven him upward earlier. All he could do was follow. Saam was the only one who knew, but the ghatt had kept his silence on the subject since his earlier scolding.

"I wonder where it leads!" Eadwin crawled around the boulder partially blocking a passage that led away from the cave's depths and farther into the mountain's heart. He grunted with effort, wedging his makeshift torch into a wall crevice, his body and Felix's casting absurdly long, wavering shadows. Indeed, he looked a bit shadowy himself, hands and face sooty from the smoky pitch of the torch, clothes streaked. Guilty as a schoolboy, he tried to brush it off. "It's not all from the torch," he temporized. "The walls were sooty in spots, it rubbed off where it was narrow. I'd say others have passed through here before."

"Not recently, I hope!" Doyce jerked sharply, mouth a pinched line of nerves, but Nakum's face lit with interest until he gauged her reaction. So close! The pounding of his heart told him that, gaining on it, the mystery to be revealed! Saam fixed Nakum with a steady, commanding stare he couldn't elude. **"So what will you do about it?"** he asked. **"Where does your responsibility lie?"**

To gain time, Nakum whittled another branch stub, peeling thin shavings on the gnarled joint. Like making little feathers, he decided, feathers to flare and catch when they were lit. *"I must do what my honor and my responsibility permit me to do,"* he 'spoke back to Saam. *"My duty is to*

*guide, you know that. I know that. That means guiding them
to and from Marchmont, but now I think it also means guiding Doyce wherever she needs to go.*" Satisfied with his response and his future torch, he laid it aside and started on another.

"**Yes, but does your desire determine where we should
go? What if her needs aren't yours? Can you put her
needs above your own wants?**" Saam wandered, fretful, no
pattern to his steps, always returning to Nakum's side.
"**When I'm near you I can sense the power as well. It
calls to me through you.**" Sullen denial in his pose, Nakum
refused to listen further, pretended interest in the torch.

Hru'rul engaged in mock battle with Felix, the dog
crouching and springing, long muzzle darting in harmless,
noisy snaps, the ghatt springing up and over him, swatting
a paw as he passed. At a frantic yip of delight from Felix,
Doyce clapped hands over her ears, the piercing barks rebounding off the cave walls. "Enough!" she shouted.
"Eadwin, please, make Hru'rul stop tormenting Felix. I can't
stand it!" Tears squeezed from her tightly closed eyes.

Collaring Felix, Eadwin hauled him across his lap, called
Hru'rul to him, cuddling them both, unsure why it was *his*
fault, why he was to blame. The cave was better than shivering outside in the cold, trapped in conifer density that blotted out night stars, the wind laughing and mocking through
their branches. After being locked in the tower so long, it
surprised him to reject the forest's freedom, the fresh air, the
ability to move at will when and where he chose. But something about this mountain left him prickling with a supreme
uneasiness—and Doyce as well, he suspected—although not
Nakum. All in all, the cave's containment felt secure, perhaps ten meters long and six at its widest, the ceiling thrusting higher than he'd expected. No trace of animal habitation
except for a few bat droppings at the entrance.

Their paltry fire in the center burned yellow-bright but
couldn't begin to illuminate the ceiling's height. Strange to
feel safe yet want to be moving, not mewed up again, and
the cave and the passage he'd discovered did offer the possibility of diversion, activity. Besides, the small portion of
squirrel they'd shared before sheltering here had barely
dented his hunger, and he didn't want to fixate on it. He'd
done too much of that lately, had trained himself to think beyond his stomach or risk madness. Would Doyce approve of

his exploration? Did it matter? No, he was near thirty, capable of taking the lead despite what his father might think, and nearly her equal now that he could mindspeak Hru'rul. Although he didn't know her well, he had no desire to hurt or worry her; Arras liked and trusted her, and that was good enough for him. Strange she'd turned so edgy since he'd explained his lack of Resonant skills. He pondered it, both hands busy, one rubbing Hru'rul's chin, feeling the purr vibrations, the other tickling Felix until his hind leg jerked. Why did she act as if such skills were dangerous? It bore discussing, but that wasn't what he wanted to do now. Nakum would follow his lead.

He listened to the rattle-sounds of pebbles being kicked across the cave, ducked as one sailed by him. She'd been doing that with increasing intensity since their arrival, shoulders hunched, head bowed, clenched hands jammed into pockets. Edging a stone with the side of her foot, scooping it here and there, and finally, losing patience and lofting it away. Frankly, the randomness of the sounds irritated him just as much as Felix's barking had irritated her. "I'm going exploring," he announced. "Anyone want to come?" At his words Hru'rul dashed to the mouth of the tunnel, and Felix, not to be outdone, followed hot on his heels.

Doyce stopped short, one foot poised to kick another stone. "Let it wait until morning. Assuming it's really necessary. We should get some sleep now." Waspish with nerves, she slammed her toe against the final pebble. "Come morning we have to return, see if we can help your cousin Arras and my countrymen, who have been captured—might I remind you—by your father's men." She fired the words in a jerky, uneven pattern, the same way she had kicked at the pebbles.

"I know. I know too well." He groaned at the thought of his mother's long anguish, shuddered with the memory of his own uncertain waiting, not knowing if he'd ever be rescued. It was his duty to return. He'd been a dutiful, obedient son for almost thirty years, but he had a premonition that he'd eluded his true duties for too long. Nothing was the same any more! Was it only last night that Arras had given him a token from his mother? A ring that suggested a smaller version of the Queen's ruling ring. And what had Arras shouted in the midst of the struggle? "For the true king, for the blood royale!" Almost as if Arras were proclaiming him King! On what grounds could he proclaim himself king? He was too old to indulge in silly fantasies. He had to consider his obligations, duties, not fantasies.

And what was he to do, turn against Maurice, support someone else as king, serve as a pawn in something he didn't understand? Why had Maurice had him imprisoned? And why did he always think of him as Maurice, rather than Father? Without noticing, his hands fisted as if to fend off the pain of his admissions. Because in all his years of growing up, Maurice hadn't really cared about his existence at all, ignoring him most of the time, chivvying and bullying him the rest. He'd become a man, excelled at a vocation he took pride in, yet still let Maurice cow him. Was being imprisoned another way of showing him his true worth or was there a deeper significance he hadn't recognized? He took a deep breath to clear his head. Well, all this groping and pondering wasn't getting him anywhere tonight, guaranteed to leave him sleepless. He wouldn't run from his fears, his suppositions, but he could leave them behind for a time. Resolved, he grabbed his torch from the wall, hefted one of Nakum's new ones, and started off. Whether they followed or not was up to them.

Nakum already waited beside the large guardian boulder while Saam pressed close to Khar, restive, yellow eyes uneasy. "Doyce?" Nakum entreated. Her head snapped up at the sound of her name; she looked as if she had been staring into another world beyond the walls of the cave, and whether it was the outer world or an interior one only she was sure. "Doyce," he cajoled again, and the reassurance in his voice drew her as nectar draws a butterfly.

Rueful, she spoke out loud to Khar, "Khar, I'm going to regret this, aren't I? But anything's better than sitting and thinking." She wedged two torch-branches into her belt, and took a final torch, crossed it against Eadwin's until it caught.

"Well, better than booting stones and thinking, at least," Khar replied. **"I'll take the rear."**

Maurice toyed with the goblet, turned it to make the light prism against the jewels embedded in the gold lattice basket that nestled the glass cup. All his now, rightfully his, heirlooms of the first rulers, his ancestors, now in the just hand of their legitimate successor, himself. His glow came not from the wine, but from the suitability of it all. It had been so long a wait, that old cow Wilhelmina not proclaiming him heir when it was obvious there was no one more suited to the throne, no surviving offspring of either Maarten or Ludo. Or rather, the one surviving wouldn't survive long, he'd see to that. And now he'd have to deal with this little toady who'd thrust himself on his attention so long ago, and been totally useless up until now, his reports circumspect, devoid of substance.

Well, now he'd have a chance to rectify that. Maurice snapped his fingers. "Gregor, bring him in now." And his giant servant hauled Aelbert in by the scruff of his neck, his normally pristine uniform ruckled and twisted, nearly garotting him, the ghatta following closely at his heels. "Gregor, I hope you made it suitably authentic when you removed him from the cell with the others. Wouldn't do to have his cover blown now, would it?"

An ice-slashed grin was Gregor's only response as he dumped Aelbert into a chair opposite Maurice's, pulled a glass of wine in the aide's direction, then bowed and left. Maurice waved off-handedly, more concerned with the malevolent expression in the beast's green eyes. Good to see that Aelbert didn't share the same expression.

"Well, Aelbert? We have to arrange tomorrow's ceremonies. I have Constant under control. But I need you and that cat," he corrected himself, "that ghatta, whatever her name is, to legitimize my ascension. Some sort of ritual mumbo jumbo, the ghatta communing with you, with some of the others, planting the thought that this is the truth. You'll confirm that Wilhelmina's dying words were correct, to wait for the ghatti to name me as king. After all, modesty precludes me from doing it myself." His tinted lips simpered.

After all, there was nothing to indicate a Seeker Veritas couldn't lie, it was only the stupid animal that couldn't, or at least that was what he'd derived from the stories that garrulous old fool Rossmeer had spouted. The Canderisian Consul had been absolutely verbose on the subject. And if the threats of thievery and traitorousness weren't enough, Maurice still had one additional snare to set to ensure Aelbert was firmly bound to his cause.

Aelbert shifted in his chair, acting neither ill-at-ease nor easeful against the cushions. Tilting his glass for a sip, he spoke before completely lowering it, obscuring his expression although not his words. N'oor sat at his feet, glaring and fidgeting. "But I'm not the Special Envoy, Doyce Marbon is," he reminded Maurice. Yes, closer now, if he could just continue playing everyone off against each other! He deserved it, and with vigilance it was within his grasp!

"True, but you will be by tomorrow. My men are combing the mountains to flush out Eadwin and your two compatriots—although far be it for me to say that that Erakwan is your compatriot, that would be too insulting. They'll all be dead shortly. Taken care of one way or the other just as you so conveniently disposed of that first Envoy the Monitor appointed—what did you say his name was, Rolf Cardamon?" He lifted his glass in a toast.

"But I . . .!" Aelbert's chair rocked back, he brought it steady, evened his voice. "That was completely unforeseen, the culmination of a chain of events I inadvertently began." He watched N'oor's pupils dilate with terror at the import of his words, her mind flooding his with a string of questions, doubts, entreaties. How could Maurice have possibly known? Had N'oor's shielding slipped at some point? And with her here listening, wondering yet again if he were truly blameless! Even he wasn't confident in his innermost heart. Lady bright, how it stung to be so misjudged, but then hadn't he been all his life? He 'spoke her with all the sincerity, all the honesty he could muster, wanting to make it right, wanting to explain. *"Later, trust me, please, just trust me! I haven't failed you, haven't failed us yet! Believe in me and we're this close to attaining what we so richly deserve!"*

"Oh, poor Chak!" she wailed, tail lashing. **"What have you done to our Bond? Maybe all we deserve is each other!"**

He'd missed what Maurice had been saying, prayed that it hadn't been important and that he could pick up the thread of the conversation again. Maurice poured more wine, wine he didn't want, didn't think he could swallow. All the stealing, all the lying to survive during those early years before he had Bonded with N'oor, was it all coming back to haunt him, couldn't he ever evade it, if not rid himself of it? He slipped his hand inside his cuff and touched the too-short sleeve of the old, darned sweater he wore underneath, too tight, much too hot, unnecessary but needed all the same for its consolation. Oh, Mother, they denied us too long, but I'll make it right, I swear. He blindly nodded in Maurice's direction and tried to concentrate. If Maurice only knew, if N'oor only knew. Well, if he could continue the juggling act a few more days, soon they all would. Justice at last.

"Fine, we'll be ready." And didn't care what he was agreeing to, anything to conclude this meeting, try to right things with N'oor. He rose and bowed. "I assume Gregor will escort me back in the same inimitable fashion he brought me here?"

"Of course." Faintly quizzical at the abruptness of the departure, Maurice looked at Aelbert more closely. Ah, excellent, he'd instilled fear. "I'm glad you enjoyed that little charade, though there's no need for you to stay with them any longer."

"No, I'd rather," he protested. "N'oor would rather." They, after all disliked him less, he hoped, even though Maurice needed him more. And with Doyce not there, he wouldn't have to feel he'd betrayed her again. He'd used her, yes, but he hadn't meant to betray her or any of them, still wasn't convinced he had. He'd make them understand when it came time for explanations.

"But I didn't have any choice! You saw him drag—"

"You little bastard!" Aelbert felt himself being picked up and thrown bodily against the door that had just been closed and locked behind him. "You conniving, lying, twisted little bastard! I don't think you're playing straight with anyone! Doubt that you can! Consorting with that pretender up there who'll have all our heads before he's done!"

"But I couldn't! He insisted—" Particolored stars wheeled around his vision, cheerful and bright in their impunity to the stabbing pain as the back of his head slammed against the door. He saw hands, Jenret's, swarming around his face, slapping him until his head rolled helplessly. "N'oor," he begged, "stop them, make them understand!"

"No," the ghatta responded. "I can't explain what I don't understand. What do we truly deserve? You've never even told me, your Bond! Explain it yourself. I can't physically leave because we are trapped in this room, but I can leave you alone in your mind." She stalked to the far side of the cell without looking back.

And that was the unkindest, the cruelest denial of all. Aelbert's eyes flooded with tears and his body sagged against Jenret, now grasping the front of his uniform, holding him upright while he continued raining open-handed blows against his head. Nowhere to turn to evade them, just as there had been no escape from the innkeeper's blows, sure the child was holding back more than his share of what he'd stolen from drunken customers. The innkeeper had been right, but he'd needed the coins.

Propped on his good side on the makeshift pallet, Bard watched without comment, Sarrett pausing in redressing his wound while she surveyed the drama playing in front of her. Jacobia pressed one hand over her mouth, moaning in sympathy with each slap, but did nothing to stop her brother. Sarrett wished she could measure Arras Muscadeine's expression, but his head was still encased in that strange steel casque, completely shielding his face, hands manacled and chained to the cell wall, aware of trouble but unable to see or stop it. Fists thrumming against thigh muscles, then finally stilling, Syndar Saffron at last heaved himself from the damp rushes on the floor and strode to Jenret, roughly grabbing his arm. Jenret shook free, landed another blow. "You bloody, cowardly traitor! You didn't want to come with us. You wanted to stay. You've sold us out, haven't you? For what, that's what I'd like to know!"

"And so would I, Jenret, if it's true," interposed Saffron as he wrapped his arms around Jenret's chest from behind, pinning him and lifting him off the floor. "Something's not right, but we don't know what. Give him the benefit of the doubt till we find out for sure." It's going to turn into a full-scale brawl, Sarrett decided, Saffron has the build for it, but Jenret's anger is almost incandescent. His grasp on Aelbert broken, the Monitor's aide de camp slumped to the floor. "And we'll get nothing from him if you beat him senseless." He shook Jenret in his arms, gave him another squeeze for good measure.

Jacobia rushed to Aelbert, tried to roll him onto his back, but he stayed facedown on the floor, face buried in his arms. He was weeping, hysterical sobs beyond all rhyme or reason and beyond all hope of eliciting information for some time. N'oor sat hushed, unmoving, making no effort to intervene, despite Rawn's assessing looks in her direction.

The voice was suppressed and indistinct, but they heard,

nonetheless. "Leave the boy be. You'll get nothing from him now—unless you indulge in torture. And that I absolutely forbid."

Jenret found the floor under his feet again, Syndar's arms releasing him. Guardedly inhaling to check his ribs, he turned, relieved the mocking face was masked from him. "Seems to me you aren't able to forbid anything, Chevalier Capitain."

"No, I'm not. But infighting will get us nowhere." Muscadeine's faceless mask was unnerving. "There are questions to be answered and they will be answered, perhaps sooner than we'd like. Now I would appreciate it, Wycherley, if you'd come here and tell me what you see, describe where we are. Perhaps I can judge our location."

Tugging his tabard straight, Jenret strode to Muscadeine's side, fought an urge to rap the helmet with his knuckles. *"I wouldn't do that, if I were you,"* the disembodied voice warned, and he let his hand drop. The voice had sounded inside his mind. Rawn shook his head in negation to indicate that he hadn't spoken. He raised a surreptitious hand, and again the voice cautioned, *"Don't."*

The exact same voice he'd overheard on the boat, but without the self-doubts, the arguments. Aimed into his very brain, not an emotional spill-over! "As to where we are . . ." he wished his sight could penetrate the helmet, penetrate deeper, let him know if his fears were true, "we're in a cell, and I would assume," he let his voice drip acid to cloak the fear, "that that means a dungeon. Just how many dungeons do you happen to have here? More than one?"

They all heard the laugh, debonair despite the indignity of the helmet. "Just one," Muscadeine acknowledged. But only Jenret heard the final words, *"Except for the one barred with your own fears, the fears that imprison you within your own mind. You don't know the gift you've walled yourself away from."* Nor was he sure he wished to know.

"There! Halfway across! Hurry, they can't know the current picks up around that bend!" Muffled oars dipped, and the dory shot forward, propelled by two sets of strong arms. Ahead Roland could just pick out two human heads and two wet, slicked-back ghatti heads, a V-shaped eddy behind each; the horses were easier to spot, swimming strongly, heads and necks surging, strong legs churning the water white. Roland bent his back into the oars and the boat responded.

Lady above! Now he was afloat after all that riding and hiding, dodging anyone with Maurice's colors. He'd ridden hellbent for the small barracks just north of the city where some of Arras's reserves rested before reassignment. Arras had brought Eadwin and him there once for a tour, introduced them to the one-legged staff sergeant who served as Resident Resonant. It hadn't been easy, he'd acknowledged, but Arras had managed to plant a Resonant in almost every one of his troops to facilitate communications. "Makes Maurice think I know more than I do," he'd joked, "so let's not disabuse of him of the idea."

He'd sought out the one-legged Octavian Florenz, convinced him of Muscadeine's peril and the danger to the true king, Eadwin, if Maurice seized the throne. Florenz had agreed to search out those soldiers nearby whose loyalty to Muscadeine was unquestioned, gather them, assemble more as quickly as they could. Encamped with the first hastily assembled squad at a secluded spot farther down the river, Roland had been panicked when Octavian's brother, Michel, came rowing along with the news that two foreigners were fording the river. If these impulsive foreigners attracted the wrong attention, his own forces were likely to be discovered as well. Damn them for barging into the middle of his problems like this!

"Do ye dare hail them?" Michel, the old fisherman, rowed with a rhythmic prowess that Roland, a landsman, could barely match.

He didn't have breath for the words, managed to gasp between strokes. "Don't want ... to scare them.... Can't chance ... the sound ... carrying ... causing a rumpus." He skipped a beat, oars held clear to not impede Michel's stroke, compensating for both of them. "They don't know who we are." Timing himself, he dipped his oars, stroked again.

"Well, if they breast the current, they be more surprised by the men mustering down below," the old man stated reasonably. "Still think it best ye hail'em."

"I *told* you why not!" he gasped, pain stitching his side. Why was the old man arguing? They were gaining, he could see their heads more clearly in the moonlight, though they hadn't yet noticed they were being followed, intent on their swimming.

The old man gave a snort of disgust, spat overboard. "I dinn't say hail'em out loud, ye young ninny! Ye be a Resonant, a Sender-level, be ye not? Give those pur, wet chittychats a mindcall. Let them be a judging the truth of what you're calling."

Well, of course he could Send and Receive, that was why he'd been seconded to help Eadwin at the nursery. Still, it stung to be reminded another way existed to reach them. Shipping his oars, Roland gathered his nerve, wondered what it was like to touch a ghatti mind: was it possible, or entirely different from what he'd been taught? Arras had said the ghatti hadn't spoken with him, and Eadwin and the strange wild ghatt didn't fully communicate. What was he supposed to say, how to introduce himself? *"Hal-lo? Hallo, ghatti friends of Khar and Rawn and Saam and the rest. We've come to help. There are rapids ahead. Tread water, if you please, until we come."*

"Well, it's about time!" The mindvoice was feminine and cranky enough to make him wince. **"I am *so* wet and bedraggled!"**

Roland stood cautiously in time to see a flurry of water splashes and an angry, commanding hiss. One bedraggled head momentarily vanished as the other beast slapped a restraining paw on it, and dunked it underwater.

"P'wa here. How dare you? Who are you? *What* are you to speak us so?" The head had turned, ears pasted back, straining higher for a better view, large, round eyes almost reflecting moonlight. A white forehead star did. Roland could feel the eyes boring into him even at this distance. **"We are *not* defenseless,"** the mindvoice warned.

"I am Roland d'Arnot, friend and supporter of Arras Muscadeine." He thought hard, desperate to be believed. It mattered to him, he'd known as soon as the eyes perused him. *"I have met your compatriot Doyce Marbon and the others. They have helped me and now I would help you. Read me, read my truth, see if I am not right."*

Far different than communicating with another Resonant. It pierced deeper within him, not harming, altering nothing that he could judge, but not missing a fraction of his thoughts, conscious or unconscious, examining them from all angles, all facets. He felt faintly lacking, but not bad, not as if he had anything to hide. **"Well, you wouldn't be able to even if you did,"** the voice informed him matter-of-factly. **"Can you take us aboard? My Bondmate's leg hurts in this cold. The horses can swim to shore if they're not dragging our Bondmates."**

Roland nodded to Michel and sat, grabbing the oars in blistering palms, and set out rowing once more.

At first they clustered, bumping shoulders, stumbling over each other's heels in anticipation and suspense, thrusting the torches high to illuminate their path, low to gauge their footing. The brilliance dazzled, reflected off glistening stalactites, the choppy angles of quartz seams catching and refracting the light. Wide enough to accommodate three across, the passageway occasionally constricted, though to Doyce's great relief never enough to make her feel like a cork being forced into the neck of a jug. Saam and Hru'rul scouted ahead, first one, then the other disappearing beyond the torchlight, the other's glowing eyes pausing until the humans caught up. Khar's occasional quiet comments floated from the rear where Felix ambled with her. All in all, Doyce wasn't as nervous as she'd expected, but she still wasn't happy at leaving the cave behind.

Nakum and Eadwin exclaimed and peered at everything, waving the torches as if they were giant sparklers. Nakum's boyish wonder hardly surprised her, but Eadwin was equally entranced, as if he'd cast a heavy burden aside and was at last enjoying himself. Hand clutched tight to his waist pouch, Nakum spun suddenly to his left, into the shadows, free hand gesturing for her torch. Pounding back to his side, Eadwin obliged with a theatrical swoop of flame, only to stop short, holding the torch steady about halfway up the wall. Despite her black humor, her nerves, Doyce crowded closer to look, shut out by their shoulders.

Glyphs, strange incised marks inlaid with something foreign. Nakum ran his fingertips over them reverently, marveling, while Eadwin scrutinized them, flicked at them with a fingernail. "Arborfer!" He gave a high-pitched yell of delight that rang off the walls and dinned in her ears. "Are they decorations or do they mean something? Do you know? Can you tell?" And then, consideringly, "I wonder who made them."

"My people did, but I can't read them all. It's been too long since we used this script for me to read it clearly." Tracing each symbol, Nakum studied them, brow furrowed. "Some symbols are the same as the ones carved on your old buildings, but I couldn't puzzle them out either, only a few," he confessed. "This one means *mountain,* and that," he pointed as if instructing, "means *arborfer.* Here is *top,* I think, or *summit,* but I've never seen it used with *cloud.* Or, I don't know, maybe it's *sky.*"

"Well, that's all very interesting," Doyce edged back, tired of straining to see, anxious about the torches' closeness to her hair. "Don't you think we should go back now? I've lost all track of time, but I think we've explored long enough. How many fresh torches do we have left?" She started to trudge the way they'd come when, sharp and anxious, Khar's mindvoice shouted, **" 'Ware! Beware, there's some-one in the cave now!"**

Nakum and Eadwin sprang from their crouches, Eadwin paling despite the ruddy cast of the torch on his hair and beard. Instead of sprinting toward her, Nakum ran in the opposite direction, waving them after him. Panicky at being closest to the cave, Doyce started to run, too, until Nakum violently gestured her to a walk. Saam 'spoke from ahead. **"Shh! Nakum says walk quietly, watch where you put your feet. If you must speak, whisper close or let us transmit your words."**

With exaggerated care, she strode forward, noticing for the first time that the path was blanketed with pale, spar-kling sand and small, tumbled stones, as if deposited by a stream. Each footstep made a squeaking, scrunching protest, abnormally loud in the stillness. Glancing back down the passage way toward the darkness behind them, she nearly jumped out of her skin as Felix ghosted by, his nose an icy, damp shock to her dangling hand. She wiped it against her tabard without thinking. **"Yes, I know, soggy,"** Khar com-mented. **"I sent him ahead. He'd make a lovely rearguard surprise, but he's too exited and likely to bark. He's promised not to, but I'd prefer not to tempt him."**

Doyce answered back, *"Is it safe to keep the torches lit?"*

The thought of being lost in the darkness, despite the acuity of the ghatti's vision, made her chest tight.

"I think so, for the moment. They haven't left the cave yet, and we've rounded enough bends to hide the light. Sound carries more than light. Now go ahead, beloved. All of you, go!"

And so they moved ahead, heeding each step, trying not to scuff. Several times the trail branched and each time Saam and Hru'rul selected the branch winding upward, never downward. Precious moments dissolved when Nakum would spy another set of glyphs, pause to examine them. Hand clenched on her sword hilt, she scurried along, listening for Khar or the other ghatti, listening for sounds of pursuit.

Up and still upward they went, Nakum lighting a fresh torch from the one stub still burning. "Don't leave the stub behind," Eadwin warned, commandeering the fresh torch, but Nakum had already tossed the stub aside. His recklessness baffled her, it was automatic for the Erakwa never to leave evidence of a trail.

Her leg muscles complained at the steepness of the climb, made her wish desperately for a pause, a rest. *"Are they behind us, love?"* she ventured, jittery from the enforced silence, yearning for Khar's voice and most of all, for her physical presence, the need to touch the silky, striped fur.

"Faster!" Her urgent cry spurred her on, shredded her hope of solace. **"They're closing the gap! Running now! They're gaining. Move!"**

And they all began to run, unmindful of the noise, the two ghatti and the dog leading. An indistinct growl from Felix, who had stopped short, hackles rising, just as Eadwin bowled into him and tripped, dropping the torch. He slid on his stomach, tried to recapture it, but Nakum pulled him upright, pushed him ahead. "Never mind! Hurry, it's not much farther! Run!"

Not much farther to what? she wondered and prayed her eyes would adjust to the shrouding dark. The walls, the ceiling, her fears, everything closed in on her like a hand at her throat, throttling her breath. By the Lady, she must be losing her mind, slipping under just as a drowning victim does, glimpsing a faint brightness, unattainably far away, just as sun and air hover so tantalizingly above the strangling water pulling its victim down.

"Yes, is light. Is nice light!" Hru'rul comforted. **"Come hurry, scurry. Safe soon, Saam think so, me know so. Very cold, though. Oh so snowy-icy."**

The lightness, the brightness increased as she fled toward it, Khar at her heels, encouraging her onward. And then it glowed above her, a bright, beckoning wash of light—except it shone too high to reach. She halted, head thrown back, staring at the opening, panting, impossible to reach it. Shouts bounced off the walls behind her, loud with glee at finding the evidence of the fallen torch. Dark shadows bending over the hole, Nakum's and Eadwin's arms stretching to clasp hers, haul her to the surface. She scrambled onto an outcropping of rock, raised her arms, felt Eadwin lock onto her wrist, comfort and hurt all at the same time. She flailed and found Nakum's hand, let her feet search out any toeholds she could find. For a sickening breath or two, she dangled, feet thrashing the air, dancing on nothingness.

She dug an elbow over the lip of the hole, Nakum's free hand shifting to her tabard sash as he heaved her sideways until her hip found purchase. Another heave and she burst clear, rolling like a log. Too bright, entirely, too bright, and she scrambled back to peer down. *"Khar, are you all right? Can you get clear?"* How could she have been so terrified that she forgot Khar, not passed her first to those welcoming hands? Horrified, she swung her legs into the opening, ready to drop back inside.

"If you land on top of me, I will *not* be pleased," Khar warned. **"Just be patient. They boosted Felix out because he couldn't get a running start, but we ghatti have left worse places behind."** Flopping back with a sigh of relief, she searched for her bearings as Khar came springing out.

It soared like an iron spear flung from the mountain peak into the sky, the skeleton of a tree surrounded by snow that never entirely melted this high up, white, compact and pure, distilled upon itself season after season. Nakum and Eadwin stood transfixed, ghatti and dog at their sides. And against the whiteness of the snow, a movement, a distant, disembodied speck of coppery-brown for a face, two more minute specks for hands, the rest as white as the snow around it. She saw Nakum's mouth open in disbelief, words evaporating, breath condensing.

"Na'lesh vriecom," the distant figure hailed them, "or as

you tend to say, Welcome, strangers." Tears of awe trickled down Nakum's cheeks as he saluted, made a low obeisance.

Fabienne angled the embroidery tambour on her lap, needle darting silver dolphinlike through the fabric. How much longer could she go on, pretending, pretending, endlessly false—to Maurice whom she had once respected though never loved, to herself, and to Eadwin, most of all to Eadwin, if he still lived, still existed? She believed he did, for it was something a mother would sense, death's final intangible severing. Any mother would know, even one who was not a Resonant, and much good being one had done her in locating Eadwin. She'd thought she'd discerned the briefest whisper of reassurance from Arras's mind a few days ago, but had decided she was dreaming. She didn't even know where Arras was, if he were safe. But any place away from Maurice was safer than this—had to be. Look where it had gotten Constant, and she had trusted, despite herself, in his powers.

Extraordinary that Wilhelmina had divulged her secret shortly before her death, invited her along on that short visit she made every night without fail. Prayers, she'd always said, but Fabienne had never thought the Queen that devout a woman, enmeshed in the trappings of religion. Didn't she, Fabienne, have to remind her sometimes when a high holy day was approaching, or which of the eight Apostle moons waxed or waned, and when?

So she'd followed along meekly enough that night, determined that if the Queen wished her to pray, she'd oblige. Prayers never hurt anyone and sometimes, though rarely, they helped. Simply because her own never were answered was no reason to stop hoping. Surprising then, that they'd gone not to the Queen's private chapel but to the library, so rarely used, but prayers could be said anywhere. The Lady always heard.

Fabienne had gasped as they'd entered the dim library, bookcases close and cluttered, tilting with age, had sworn she'd glimpsed a shadowy figure look up from its book, raise its glasses to the top of its head, and stare back at them. "Oh, don't worry, that's only Constant Minor as we call him. Father used to see him, as have all of us at one

time or another. Sort of the leftover emanations of our beloved founder, Constant I. He started collecting this library,
probably the only one who truly cared about it. I think he
gets a bit lonely sometimes until I report."

"Emanations?" she'd quavered, casting the eight-pointed
star at it.

"Oh, not really. The human mind is infinitely suggestible
and Constant always made the most of that while he
reigned," Wilhelmina chuckled, paid no attention to the apparition, and with her solid sanity, Fabienne acknowledged
that her imagination was running wild. "He's such a strong
personality that it's hard to think of him resting quietly,
waiting."

Waiting? If not in this life, perhaps another, as the Lady
promised? The Queen was becoming older, true enough, but
she'd always made sense before. But now Fabienne was beginning to seriously wonder what sort of strange night per-
ambulation they took. Wasn't it enough that there'd been no
word from Eadwin in two octs and she seemed the only one
concerned? To have to deal with this, the maunderings of a
woman she'd respected and served almost all her life?

Wilhelmina leaned heavily on her arm as she started up a
narrow stairway secluded behind the final bookcase. "Ah,
easier with you here to help. I remember how the stairs tired
Father at the end. Now push," she ordered, and Fabienne
did, helping shove the trap door clear to reveal a night sky
vision of beauty.

Exclaiming, Fabienne had rushed from window to window, staring up at the stars in all their glorious brightness, so
close she could nearly number them, name them if she
chose. They were, she deduced, inside the castle's dome, had
never known it possible to enter, had never been so high before. She turned back, embarrassed at her distraction, only to
find Wilhelmina sitting on a rickety old chair, breathing
heavily, but with a reminiscent smile on her face. And beside her, something large, ominously like a giant coffin of
a sleek material she didn't recognize.

"This is the hibernaculum, and this," Wilhelmina stroked
the coffinlike object, "is Constant I."

"He's buried here?" At least she hadn't shrieked.

Wilhelmina sighed, her years, her regrets and pain
abruptly lined her beloved face. "It's not as simple as that,
Fabienne. You must believe, you must!" she implored.

"Constant lives on inside this, listening for the stars, listening for his twin brother Carrick. But he cares about what happens here. What I'm revealing to you tonight is told only to each succeeding ruler. You *must* believe what I tell you, memorize everything, because it's up to you to reveal it to Eadwin if I can't." The Queen registered the shock and shame on her face. "Yes, of course I've known. You must pretend to know nothing of this! Not even tell Maurice, least of all him."

And she wouldn't have believed, would have assumed the Queen was in her dotage, if she hadn't fled to the hibernaculum for solace after the Queen's death, carefully rehearsed her fifty word message, and choked it out through her tears that night. Of course there was no one to hear, to care, but what a relief to pour out her heartaches without being overheard. A sigh and hiss of compressed air escaping, the almost imperceptible movement of the heavy lid rising, slowly blocking the stars at the window, a head suddenly popping up, eyes bewildered at first, then kind and compassionate.... Believe but make believe, dissemble, feign, pretend, and between them they'd done it, given "life" to Constant Minor to disguise Constant's identity. After all, the human mind *was* infinitely suggestible. And Constant was simply another thing she couldn't reveal, just as she couldn't reveal Eadwin's parentage.

Pretend, pretend, pretend—pretend to be engrossed in this damnable embroidery. She focused on it the first time, dismayed that she'd continued too far with the coral floss, destroyed her careful pattern. Worse than that; when she tried to shift the tambour from her lap to the table so she could reach her sewing box, she saw she'd stitched through the panel and into her skirt. She balanced the scissors in her hand, ready to sever the threads when Maurice walked into the room without knocking. And for once it was all she could do not to rise and plunge the tiny sewing scissors into his throat, end instead of pretend. Instead, she cowered over her work, prayed that he wouldn't notice her stupidity. Something like this, her inattention, her carelessness was enough to set him off in a flash of unreasoning anger, cause him to lash out at her verbally—or even worse—physically.

But no, not today. With a self-satisfied smile on his face he walked past her to the credenza and poured himself a glass of wine. A tiny compressed pout of satisfaction, she noted, as if he hoarded it to himself, warmed himself on it. It meant that he wouldn't hurt her today. But if not her, then whom? She might be safe, but others weren't, because he thrived on pain from somewhere, someone, the pain that augmented his rather paltry powers as a Resonant. How long had it taken her to admit what he was doing, that he had broken the constraints? Too long to realize that she didn't deserve the blows and abuse he rained on her at random intervals, leaving her beholden for grace periods, sure her unworthiness merited the bad times.

He carried a glass of wine in each hand, one for him and one for her, presented it with a courtly gesture. Those gestures had become as natural as breathing or eating, and she remembered with an almost forgotten fondness how he'd struggled with them at first, youngest son of a younger son of royalty, fully due a place at court but ignorant, untutored in its graces the way she was. He raised his glass toward hers for a toast, and pulled back his sleeve, brandished the bloodied scrap of bandage around his forearm. "My own pain for my own gain, my own power—for the moment, at least," he confided. His breath was heavy with wine; he'd already been drinking. "It brings quite a rush, a different flavor to the experience."

She held her own glass stock-still, couldn't raise it to chime against his, his words so shocking to her. Had Jampolis revealed that secret to him? He didn't seem to notice, tapped his glass against her frozen one, and took a small sip, set his glass on the sewing stand. "Of course, the flavor—and the savor—will be Augmented at the investiture. I'm quite looking forward to it."

She tipped her head in acknowledgment, not trusting her voice. Now he bent over her and took her free hand, as if to kiss it. Too late she saw his fingers dart toward her embroidery, pluck the needle free and jab her finger, then raise the bloody finger to his lips. "Just a memento," he crooned through lips stained red with wine. "And a reminder. You will see the old fool toes the line tomorrow, won't you? And don't forget Wilhelmina's ring. I know you've been hiding it from me."

She nodded once more, short and sharp, and prayed hard that if she had pretended this long, she could continue the pretense, for this lie was necessary for preservation, perhaps not her own preservation, but for Eadwin's and the kingdom's. Not a lie to herself as so many of the others had been.

❖

"But I'm a forester, a graduate of our agricultural collegium, not a military tactician!" Roland expostulated, running his hands through his hair. How had he ever gotten himself into this? And on top of everything else to be saddled with these two outsiders, foreigners! Yet despite his agitation, his aggravation, the uneasy repugnance his two guests engendered in him, he couldn't help noticing they still shook with cold. He fished another blanket from the shelf behind him, draped it over their quaking shoulders. "How are the ghatti?"

"You might ask us directly, you know. Would you care to be talked about as if you didn't exist?" P'wa murmured as Michel, the old fisherman, fussed over her, rubbing her dry. Per'la sat vigorously grooming, intent on untangling and fluffing her long tail fur.

"I apologize. I forgot." he said out loud. The ghatti fascinated him, but he lacked time to consider them now. How, precisely, did this odd pair, this long, lithe, unreadable woman with the strange golden skin, and her scrawny partner with the aureole of red hair and an unpromising tendency to sneeze at the most inopportune moments, expect him to be a commander, stage a rescue? By the Lady's Disciples, he was no Chevalier Capitain Arras Muscadeine. There was a man to be respected, who could lead! He wanted to show them a rush of word pictures, but he could not do that, did not have permission to enter their minds, though the ghatti didn't object to his wary converse with them.

As if on cue, Parse sneezed. "Well, someone has to lead, at least initially. You seem to have done an excellent job gathering as many supporters as you can, deploying them. There must be other commanders of that Muscadeine fellow's ability, how do you contact them, where are they located?"

"Aye, and even if we rally them, double-march them in from the outlying troubles, we can't be sure how many are loyal to Maurice, how many he's compulsed. Octavian's trying to sort that out now. We don't know how many behind the castle walls are loyal, wittingly or unwittingly." Michel looked up from his work on P'wa, hawked and spat at the fireplace in disgust. "We need an ally, that's what we need. Me, I'd contact the Bannerjee girls, sharp as whips, they are."

But Roland had no choice but to ignore his advice as Byrta began staring straight ahead at nothing, disregarding the conversation around her. Suddenly she leaped to her feet, tossing the blankets aside. "I've got him! I've contacted Bard! So close, yet so far away, blocked by those walls!" She spun around, clapped her hands in excitement, then her expression faltered. "They're imprisoned, they don't know where Doyce and Nakum are, or that young man you mentioned, Eadwin, was it?" P'wa was beside her now, neck elongated, staring into her, willing her mindpowers through her Bondmate's.

"Bard insists we contact the Monitor, have him send a Guardian sally into Marchmont. Rumor has it that there's troop activity on both sides of the border." Roland flinched at her words. Had Maurice already discovered his small group?

"But whom can we contact to pass the message on?" Parse seized handfuls of carroty hair, ready to pluck it at the roots. "We sent one paltry message back. Now we're out of position, out of range, and you know it, Byrta. We pretended to do our duty so we could rush here like fools, jeopardize everyone!" The realization left him weak and cold—and humbled. Damn his impetuosity, though he doubted he could have kept Byrta away if he'd tried. Damn him for being a flippant fool as usual, frivolously haring after whatever struck his fancy.

But Byrta paid him no heed. "If they've already started gathering, then there must be some Seekers assigned to the Guardians for transmitting messages, orders back and forth. Swan Maclough wouldn't have ignored that." She grasped Parse's hands, drew him to his feet. "We've got P'wa and Per'la together. Perhaps I can channel some of my twin-speech into them."

Now it was Roland's turn to look flabbergasted. "You mean you can speak directly with this Bard? Without the aid of the ghatti?" Foreigners could do that? He'd never heard of them having Resonant ability.

"Of course," she snapped, impatient at the interruption.

"We're twins, we've always been able to share between ourselves."

"Just like the Bannerjees. Like Venable and Carrick Constant." He shook his head, still lost in amazement. "Then perhaps you are more than you know, than you realize." Roland chose his words carefully. "Let me try to reach the Bannerjees first. If I link with you and you link with the ghatti, perhaps we can reach that Hospice of yours to the south."

"The Hospice? With the Gleaners?" Parse nearly shrieked. "Byrta! Never! Don't touch them, don't tangle with them! Remember what they did to Doyce!"

"And I remember that Bard and I were unable to help Doyce because of them. We've no choice, Parse. I'll reach for anyone who can help us save our friends."

Ezequiel stuffed his market basket behind a rain barrel, flattened against the shadows on the whitewashed wall, checking all around before he dashed across the street and into the next shadow. He'd done his ostensible errands as conspicuously as possible, making a great show of ordering for the castle and the forthcoming ceremony. "See and be seen, but not where you shouldn't be," his grandfather Ignacio had advised under his breath. "And get back as soon as you can." He glanced around, started for the next sheltered spot, pulled back, trembling, as raucous laughter and the screech of shutters above his head warned of someone who might see. Water poured down just beyond his feet, spattered, muddied his livery, but the window banged closed and all was silent again.

Into the recessed doorway and wait, then take the corner—no one near—and over the fence. He allowed himself to rest, arms crossed and hands tucked in, as if he could compress his noisy breathing back into his lungs. He loitered, tried to look innocent, an average young man incapable of arousing suspicion, nudged at the cellar door latch with his toe, then bent quickly and lifted one side and slipped down the stairs in the dark. At the bottom step he sat and waited, composing himself, inventing explanations for his presence if someone discovered him. Common thief was the most likely tag he'd receive.

The dark of the Hospice storeroom was perfumed with medicinal herbs, the bracing smell of alcohol, vinegar, and fragrant oils. The bobbing light of a candle floated like phosphorescent marsh gas in the distance, accompanied by the sound of humming, the light rising and dropping for its bearer to read labels. He held his breath, suppressed a sneeze, and caught a glimpse of white broken by a red and green striped scarf. Good, Eumedico Bannerjee. Safe in his identification, Ezequiel had no idea which one, though he'd grown up in their presence.

She moved, swung the candle in his direction, aware of his presence before she had any right to be, except for who she was. Pressing his finger under his nose to stop the sneeze, he rose, respectful, waiting for her to come closer. "Grandfather's sent me. The Lady Fabienne wanted you to know there's trouble."

Holding the flame against some candle wax already on the end of the shelf, she waited for it to warm, and twisted her candle into the makeshift stand. "I know. Roland d'Arnot contacted us. Even without that, we suspected." The candle glinted in her aquamarine eyes. "Not to mention Quaintance Mercilot's nonspecific mindtrumpeting, enough to wake the dead. Little talent, less technique, but incredible volume." The next question came from another direction, "Did anyone see you?" as the other Bannerjee twin came into view. "Maurice has imprisoned Muscadeine," she mused.

He was aware with them of just how unaware he truly was, working in the shallows of Resonant skills, able to Receive and Send a little, nothing more. His family had always shown some minor knack, necessary for anyone serving the royal family, able to receive and relay orders silently, instruct the under servants. "But Eadwin, the Special Envoy, and the Erakwan are still free. Grandfather overheard Maurice and Jules Jampolis when they brought Muscadeine and the others in. They've Muted Muscadeine." It made him shiver. "Can you contact him? Eadwin, I mean?" Nervous, he brushed one polished slipper against the back of his calf, repeated the gesture with the other.

The Bannerjee twins continued their mirror-image stares, and the ring hands told him who was who. "Break the compulsion Maurice laid on him?" Wyn frowned, magnificent dark eyebrows pinched together. "It's too dangerous, too revealing from this distance. Besides, it's not our role to re-mold human minds."

Dwyna rounded on her, ignoring Ezequiel. "It is if it means righting a grave wrong."

"We'd have to employ the same coercive force Maurice used. Do two wrongs make a right? Break our trust after all these years?"

Openmouthed, Ezequiel listened to them argue. Never in all his years had he heard them disagree, their thoughts as one, a united front.

"We always have, in little ways, at least," Dwyna argued. "We knew the price when we became Lord of the Public Weal. It wasn't a thing to be taken lightly, but we respected coercion for the common good. The health of our people came first. Mentally inoculating them, convincing them to improve their diets, take sanitary precautions."

"Stop beating their spouses and children, learn to distrust foreigners," Wyn taunted. "Clever little constraints by clever little people, sanctioned by the precepts Constant laid forth."

As if abruptly aware Ezequiel was privy to their dissen-sion, the twins focused on him, spoke as one. "We'll think on it," their faces implacable, closed. Dwyna relented, smil-ing, "Don't try to contact Muscadeine in the castle. You don't have the skill, and you're liable to trip and crash in the commotion. The air hasn't been silent lately."

He knew, had sensed too many different voices, near and distant in the air, overhearing things not meant to be heard, not hearing things he should.

With a rippling, chiming giggle they glanced at each other as if sharing a private joke. "Have the trees talked yet?" They elbowed each other, instantly sober. "It's a legend. You were always too fanciful, Dwyna."

"Well, there *have* been other voices. Not just the ghatti, and you know it." Dwyna paused, thinking. "Voices on the riverbanks, and not just Roland and his people."

Totally lost, Ezequiel tried to regain control, fearful of the time, knowing he had to retrieve his market basket, saunter back to the castle, careful to be seen, as if nothing had hap-pened. "Please, the Lady Fabienne and my grandfather ask if you'll come to the ceremony? Ignacio will endeavor to sneak you in, let you watch unobserved."

"We'll try. And we'll try to help. At least stay in contact

with Roland and his group, let it be their decision. That's all we can promise for now."

He bowed, felt his way back up the stairs. It was all he could hope for. No one coerced a eumedico about anything.

She saw him from the third floor infirmary window—running full-tilt, face flushed, tonsure flying, robe billowing. She let herself smile, enjoying the sight of the Shepherd dashing through the rock garden—wheaten white of his habit flashing against the blacks and grays of the ragged stone with its tiny tiny spots of pink, fuchsia, yellows, oranges of greenhoused flowers just transplanted into saucered indentations. Parm ranged a full six strides ahead of Harrap, running low, fast . . . and urgent.

Mahafny's smile clouded into a frown. She'd thought it play at first—Parm in the aftermath of a prank and Harrap in hot, indignant pursuit of the miscreant. But an entirely different emotion colored the scene, it slowly permeated through her, chilling her more than the stone sill she leaned her forearms against. The same feeling she'd experienced each time she'd awakened several times during the past few nights, heart racing, hand reaching to soothe the blue-gray ghatt who seemed close enough to touch—Saam, pacing back and forth, mouth open in a silent mew of entreaty, begging her to do . . . what? And she had no idea, felt as hopeless about this as she so often felt during her waking hours, trying to comprehend the Gleaners. Was he trying to help her understand, or was there something else he wanted to share?

With an abrupt move she stepped back, pulled in the window panels and latched them as if they could hold back her frisson of fear. Starting down the spiral stair, she cursed her need for a painstaking, cautious descent. She swore she'd been hearing windchimes in her head ever since lunch—auditory hallucinations? Davvy up to one of his tricks? Perfect to take her mind off the shooting, cramping pains in hands and feet.

She burst out the door and into the garden as Harrap ran to meet her. Tears streamed from his eyes and he wiped them heedlessly with his sleeve as he collapsed on a wooden slatted bench, chest heaving. Parm flopped by his feet, exhausted but twitching as if he'd fly out of his skin.

"What is it? What's wrong?" The words seemed so banal. Harrap dropped his head, scrubbed hard at his face with his sleeve, then faced her abruptly.

"Get every eumedico and assistant you can spare ready to travel," his voice rasped and he swallowed hard. "Full supplies, especially surgical, bandages, drugs."

She was already ticking off the priorities as she repeated, "What is it? A disaster of some sort? An epidemic?"

Parm paced from one to another, usual ebullience gone. Harrap aimed an abstracted pat at his head but the ghatt had already turned toward Mahafny.

"War!" The word fell hard, with the strength to jar petals from carefree spring flowers. "War. Doyce's negotiations broke down. They were forcibly detained, tried to escape, were captured. Armies are massing on both sides of the border at Islebridge. A partial message came down from the north, through the ghatti—distance distorted them. The Monitor is marching, leading a force of Guardians, more to follow as they muster. The High Council's asking for volunteers, not just the Guardians."

"Oh, dear Lady, what went wrong?" She didn't expect an answer but she received one.

"Don't know. There's been no word from Doyce or the others for days. Nor from Sarrett or Bard. Byrta and Parse turned in the first alarum. And the message we just received, though there's something about it that Parm's loath to explain to me." Parm paid guilty attention to the travels of an ant, ignoring Harrap's comment.

The door to the garden slammed against the wall and Yulyn burst through, gawky with fear, angular limbs flying in all directions. She skidded to a stop in front of Mahafny, trying to catch her breath, face taut with terror. "I heard it, too—war! But . . . but," she swallowed, forced the words out as if entrusting them to the eumedico and the Shepherd, "not through the ghatti so much as through . . . other sources. I intercepted a message. The voices were searching for you, Eumedico Annendahl. Someone called Dwynwyn? They broke off when they realized I wasn't you. It was hard to understand . . . the strangest chiming in the background." She closed her eyes tight, her face screwed up so as not to see the impact of her words on Mahafny, then she lifted her head. "There are Gleaners in Marchmont, except they're different from us, they're trained, called Resonants. Factions are battling for the throne, and one faction is very much like Vesey. We have to help the others, we must. They mean us no harm, but the others may!"

"What?" Mahafny could find nothing more to say, tried to still her palsied hand with her good one, clutching it tight. Dwyna and Wyn Bannerjee from so long ago? Impossible! Impossible that they could, that they'd think *she* could. Preposterous! But the twins always did wear those damn chinkle-chiming bracelets.

With a flurry of crumpling skirts Yulyn had knelt in front of Parm, hand under his chin. "Tell him," she instructed with a fierce intensity, "have him vouch to her that I speak truly." Copper-red hair swung across her back as she tossed her head over her shoulder to stare at Mahafny. "Oh, I'm used to it by now, the doubts, the fears, the wondering if we're to be trusted. But it still hurts. What do *I* have to do—what do *we* have to do—to prove ourselves to you?"

Harrap laid a gentle hand on her head, and Yulyn leaned into the beneficent touch. But his words were directed toward Mahafny. "She speaks the truth, Parm concurs." For a moment the Shepherd felt daring, ready to dare much to promote the unity and trust so sorely needed. "I think Yulyn and a few other Gleaners should accompany us. They may be needed more than we can possibly imagine. You wouldn't even try to 'speak Saam. You can't expect anyone else to be able to contact you. But they can Yulyn."

Which road to take? Or were there many roads one could travel in search of trust? How many detours, how many lost ways? With trust was truth of a sort, though not necessarily the truth of the ghatti. But this was the best she could manage, and prayed that listening to her heart rather than her brain would prove right. So much to lose, so much more to gain. She had denied Saam once; could she deny Yulyn? Mahafny reached for the supplicating hands and guided Yulyn to her feet, shifted her grip to Yulyn's angular wrist and felt Yulyn do the same, each linked to the other's heartbeats through the palms of their hands. "Whom else do you intend to bring?"

Yulyn named Davvy, and old Mr. Farnham, a good distance Receiver and docile. Expressionless, Mahafny concurred. And with that, Yulyn dared one more name. "Towbin, of course."

"And Towbin, of course," Mahafny said solemnly at the mention of Yulyn's husband's name, just the slightest quirk to her mouth. "Out of the frying pan, into the fire."

"A poor choice of words," Yulyn shot back. "Especially after what we've all already suffered." And with that, she left to gather her friends and husband.

Mahafny winced. For once the poor girl certainly had been right. The fires, Vesey, Evelien. The fires had already been faced, but what faced them now she didn't know.

PART
EIGHT

PART
EIGHT

This had to be the oldest woman she'd ever seen in her life, Doyce decided as the woman in white walked forward, a flash of bare coppery feet against the white of the snow giving her a mothlike disembodied look, extremities floating against the whiteness. As the woman passed Nakum, she touched his shoulder and murmured, but he still remained crouched in reverence.

As Eadwin edged toward her, seeking to shelter her behind him, she watched the ghatti advance at a slow, stately pace, Hru'rul flanked by Khar and Saam, Felix following a step behind, tail wagging in propulsive swoops, scattering snow crystals. But she felt frozen in place, unable to move, unable to return Eadwin's reassuring squeeze as they blindly locked hands. The animals didn't so much block the old woman's path as flow around her and reverse themselves to become part of her procession. The whiteness of her clothes, Doyce determined at last, was the whiteness of bleached doeskin, a cloak of fluffed white feathers mantling her shoulders.

"*Khar! What? Who?*" she pleaded in desperation as the woman made her inexorable way toward her and Eadwin. Nakum had turned to watch but still knelt in the snow, hands over his heart, elated.

"**Hush! Don't worry,**" Khar murmured and her amber eyes glowed warm with trust.

The woman stopped in front of them, reached out her hands, palms uppermost. Against her better judgment, against her mental command to control her body, Doyce placed her own palm against the woman's left hand, while Eadwin did the same with her right. A jolt of power shot up her arm and down through her body, grounding itself in the earth. No pain to it, but a new energy and strength flowed through her, an exhilaration.

"Greetings, Doyce, Eadwin. You both looked a little peaked. I hope you didn't mind a sharing of the earth-bond. Now, if the three of you would come with me, we have much to discuss." She moved to lead the way, Doyce knew not where. The woman pivoted back for a moment, as smoothly as if she floated above the ground on a turntable. "By the way, since Nakum is too overawed to do his duty, and the ghatti are remarkably silent despite the fact that I've satisfied their curiosity, my name is Doncallis, Callis for short. Actually, the full name's a bit of a joke in your language, or used to be a long, long time ago, so I was once told—Don't call us, we'll call you. I never grasped the significance myself—or cared. But stranger sayings exist, don't you agree?"

❧

They reclined on low, fur-strewn platforms carved into the smooth-walled grotto, curved just below the ground's surface like the inside of an egg, even to the diaphanous membrane hangings on the walls. It looked as if a giant bubble of air had been sealed by hot, extrusive rock eons ago to form the grotto. From the direction of the tunnel mouth they'd exited, they could hear anguished cries, abruptly throttled by a rushing flood of water, then overwhelming silence. Someone had paid a price for this peace. Their pursuers in the caverns? She suppressed a shiver, shaking hands extended toward the brazier burning cheekily in the grotto's center. Eadwin flinched at the shouts, gathered himself as if ready to fight or flee, but finally resettled himself. Nakum noticed nothing, raptly observing the woman in white who fussed with a battered cha kettle heating over the brazier.

Callis lifted the lid, crumbled and scattered cha leaves into boiling water, shifted the kettle away from the direct heat. "Yes, your followers have been removed." Her tone placid, unconcerned, she stated it as if she'd made a passing comment on the weather. "It seemed advisable to entice them along and make their disappearance more difficult to trace, should anyone be foolhardy enough to do so. I start my spring housekeeping with plenty of fresh, running water to wash away . . . impurities." The whole scene seemed incongruous to Doyce: the mundane homeyness of a woman who appeared to be Erakwa and far more ancient than

Nakum's grandmother Addawanna looked, but equally hearty.

"Yes, cha is an acquired taste to our people, but now I don't know what I'd do without it. And how is dear Constant?" Callis enquired, passing Eadwin's filled mug; he nearly dropped it, the words scalding as much as the heat from the mug. A tiny shocked whimper lodged deep in his throat, a question, a plea.

"Constant Minor, the Steward?" Doyce asked, since Eadwin acted incapable of speech. But how would the old woman know about Constant Minor? She wasn't even sure that Eadwin knew, or completely grasped that Constant Minor ruled Marchmont as Steward—or had until Maurice had seized the throne.

Callis's laugh had the silvery, whispery texture of an errant breeze ruffling pond rushes. "Oh, that trickster! Is that what he's calling himself now? Dear old Venny! Sleeping the sleep of the just—or so he hoped—while he listened for Carrick but poised to save his land if it should ever be needed. Venable Constant, so gifted yet so unaware in many ways! Yet he grew less impetuous, less headstrong as he aged. Has he mellowed and matured at last?" She passed mugs to Doyce and to Nakum, who accepted it as reverently as manna from the gods.

Doyce's head whirled. How could Callis talk about Constant Minor and Venable Constant, first ruler of Marchmont, in one breath, as if they were one and the same?

"Pity save us. Ghatti seized your tongues, have they?" Callis beamed at the ghatti, though her gaze rested longest on Khar, who evinced a keen interest in the smooth domed ceiling. "Ah, keeping secrets, are we? Was that wise?"

"Perhaps not wise, but prudent. Saam and I wondered if he could be, but weren't sure. A mechanical truth beyond the scope of our truth at first," Khar allowed after a huffy pause. Shocked, Doyce realized that Callis had understood her directly.

"Khar!" she reproved. *"You haven't permission from Callis to 'speak her. How dare you be rude, forget your training like a ghatten? Hru'rul I could excuse, but you?"* Khar made a little mouth movement, prissily reproachful.

Flourishing a willow basket, Callis invitingly waved a piece of smoked fish in Khar's direction, offered pieces to the other ghatti and the dog. Felix gave it a suspicious sniff before gulping it down, while Khar's purr resounded throughout the chamber. "Ah, but conversation can carry in other ways. Don't blame Khar for ill manners when I listened through the earth-sounds. We," she made a gesture to encompass Nakum and herself, "draw our strength from the earth, its heart and core. So have I heard for many years, have known your paltry goings-on. Oh, paltry only in that they're so current, so fixed to the moment, with no sense of past or future. Time enough for others to absorb all the languages of the earth and those who walk it. Your feet have trod enough of our paths to leave more than a trace of your tongue."

"Then it is true?" Nakum spoke at last. "My grandmother was right?"

She fixed hands on hips in mock exasperation. "And when has my granddaughter, your grandmother, *not* been right? Now, we have much to discuss, things more serious than this sociable, shallow cha-chatter. Eadwin, your people have been hurting my trees, my arborfer. Even my regeneration has been hindered by your carelessness. If only your father, Maarten, had lived to set it right, but I've had to wait for you instead."

Eadwin bolted upright, panic flooding his face as he crumpled to the floor in a dead faint. "You'll need some stiffening for sure, young man," Callis reproved as Doyce struggled to loosen his collar. "I hope you've the same mettle as your father and your fifth-greatgrandfather."

Shouts, curses, the staccato chunk-thunks of axes and the repetitious, rocking whine of cross-cut saws, bodies dashing and distracting the eye, until one examined the scene and determined a pattern to the seemingly aimless busyness. Kyril van Beieven, the Monitor, rotated in the saddle, semaphored an arm to direct the loaded wagons and crew, finished by scouring his stubbly face with a gloved hand. Too long without sleep, too much hard riding, too much organizing and plotting and planning. He hadn't convinced the High Conciliators as much as overridden them; their cautiousness rankled, but he respected it—as long as he got his way. At least Darl Allgood and the other stalwart, sensible ones were firmly on his side. Allgood was here somewhere, he'd lost track of him, too much to do, but he suspected the man was pulling his own weight as if his life depended on it. Another chain of wagons rolled up, brimming with pontoon sections chained in precarious place. Lady's mercy, best not to be riding behind one of those overloaded wagons up a steep grade . . . if that chain snapped and a pontoon spun off, he'd be eating it for breakfast!

"Take over," he told the Guardian Captain at his side. "You know where they're supposed to go. Probably know better than I do." The Captain's salute was respectful but acknowledged the statement's truth. Van Beieven grabbed the man's forearm, both in thanks and to momentarily stay him. "Have you seen the Seeker General?" he asked.

"About a half-league back, sir!" Attention diverted by a wandering wagon with no apparent idea of its destination, the Captain stood in his stirrups, cupped his mouth with both hands and hallo-ed them in the proper direction. "Stationed at the temporary infirmary the eumedicos have set up. Funny," he added, concentration split between the conversation and his duties, "I thought there was little love lost between the two."

"All depends on whom you ask, Vlad." And the Monitor wheeled around and rode toward the rear lines. More Guardian squadrons marched in from different directions as he rode, working their way against their flow, most of them shouting a greeting, throwing a good-natured salute without breaking stride. Mustering as fast as they could, but whether it was fast enough, he had no idea. Mayhap he'd know more when he spoke with Swan Maclough. Then the farmers and laborers, displaced merchants, the Transitors he'd pressed into service to gather the pontoons from their various warehouses and storage points could be released, sent behind the lines.

Pontoons? He must be out of his mind. The thought made him snort. Aelbert would say so if he were here. He missed the aide de camp's careful, methodical ways, his ability to play the devil's advocate, not to mention serve as lightning rod to attract van Beieven's anger from others to smash harmlessly against himself. Would Aelbert have balked at the idea of pontoons or would he have suggested it first? Did he even know anymore what Aelbert would do or had become? The loss, the uncertainty hurt. He shrugged his cloak back as he rode, warming a little as the sun tracked higher.

Well, they'd try the bridges, make a feint at a forced crossing at Islebridge and mayhap they'd succeed, but all the bridges up and down would be heavily guarded, no doubt of that. So, too, the few fording places. Even if they seized the bridges, only so many troops and supplies could roll across during a limited time—six to eight abreast at best for foot troops, two wagons at the most, especially given their size. And who knew if they'd be hammered at as they crossed the bridge, vulnerable in that tight, small formation or if they'd be able to advance on Sidonie before fighting?

No, with the pontoons they could span The Spray with multiple bridges as they chose, wherever the enemy might not expect them, stretching them thin guarding a third of the river's length against such an incursion. Thank the Lady his predecessors had had the foresight to stockpile pontoons for bridge repair work and for flood seasons when the waters inundated the bridges. And thank the Lady Allgood had mentioned visiting the pontoon shed.

He spotted the blue flag with its three white four-pointed stars snapping in the breeze ahead of him, and he hurried his horse. Maybe Swan would have news. Mayhap it wouldn't be necessary, perhaps it was all a gigantic misunderstanding. He was only a farmer, had been for years before his election to Monitor. Why not negotiate? Did you turn bellicose and invade a country because they've captured six of your citizens? Eight, if the rumors were true about Jacobia Wycherley and Syndar Saffron. But if you backed down, when did you stop backing down? Like a cat who'd shot up a tree with no trouble, but now was faced with climbing down again. And that, he'd seen from experience, was a difficult trick. He wondered what the ghatti would say to that analogy, and almost smiled.

Send his people to war, to die . . . for what? An ideal of honor? Or the actual danger of invasion? But dead was dead. A lamb died just as surely whether it went to the slaughter or had its throat wolf-slashed on a rolling, green-grassed hill. And now was a perfect time for people's fears of Gleaners to explode out of control as he pulled Guardians out of towns and villages, mustered them here. They'd believe he'd left them exposed, defenseless, though what a Guardian could do against a Gleaner, damned if he knew. Were his countrymen so sheeplike, so easily led by their fears that they thought the Guardians would protect them like sheepdogs guarding their flocks? Depressed, he wove his horse through the white tents, searching for Swan Maclough and—if not answers to his questions—information at least.

❧

Day? Night? How much or how little time had passed within this snug, ovoid chamber? It seemed to have stopped for all Doyce knew, as if the currents of her mind and body flowed in new, even-deeper channels of consciousness than she had ever been aware existed.

Callis neatened, swept with a twig broom, sketching patterns in the sand floor, extending her sweeping motions outward, poking at Nakum's thigh where he lay, dozy and content on the floor, Saam curled against his chest. Eadwin perched, taut and withdrawn, on the platform beside Hru'rul, worrying things over in his mind, things he'd known or subconsciously suspected but never accepted. Puzzle pieces locking into place, the forming picture not at all to his liking. Doyce empathized with his sorrow for the ache and pain of self-discovery, better late than not at all.

Prodding Nakum's ribs with the broom, Callis teased at the ghatt with the twig-ends. Saam slapped his paw, pinioned a twiglet, snapping it free from the compacted body and tossed it into the air, swatting it from paw to paw, keeping it aloft. "I would wish to hear a story," Nakum remarked, voice sleepy and contented, dragging himself upright and pummeling Felix from a pillow into a backrest as the long, questing tongue licked his ear.

Fixing her sparkling dark eyes on Eadwin, the old woman spoke. "And do you wish to hear one as well? Something to explain one tiny piece of the quandary in which you find yourself?"

"I . . ." he struggled for words, still buried in his own thoughts and startled at surfacing again. "I . . . if you wish." An unwilling politeness at this wrench to the present.

"Well, I certainly would." Doyce surprised herself by the eagerness in her voice.

Laying the broom aside, Callis resumed her place by the fire, shrugging off her robe until the white feathers pooled around her in drifts, an eaglet in its well-feathered nest.

"The story I have in mind is one of our people's oldest legends, so old that few now know it, though they honor its spirit whether they realize it or not. This is the tale of Hatachawa and how our arborfers came to be descended from him."

"But I know that legend!" Nakum interrupted, hands outthrust in triumph. "Addawanna made me learn it before we came to Marchmont, though I don't know why she thought I needed this dose of past lore."

"You? How came my granddaughter to break the strictures and initiate a male as legend-bearer?" Callis's face screwed tight, enclosed upon itself as she pondered the implications. "It is not . . . wrong." She groped for an explanation, as if past and future and present had broken free from one another, fracturing her wholeness. "Men in the past have told these tales, but were too quick to forget them and their meanings. Thus it was decided that women should be their rightful bearers. Ah, but your grandmother is old," and there was no self-consciousness to her statement, no sense of incongruity that she was far older than Addawanna, "and you are all she has left since her daughter's death. It's so hard to keep track of the present, sometimes."

And Doyce found herself skeptical how Nakum's mother's death when he was still an infant could be considered the present, but Callis seemed enmeshed in a different reality than her own, living wholly in the timelessness that she herself was experiencing within this chamber. It made sense, not sense as she'd normally know it, but sense given the flow of powers.

"So, do you wish to tell this tale or shall I?" Callis grumbled, and Nakum looked crestfallen. Relenting, she continued. "So, let us hear the legend. Let me judge if you have it whole and true, and if so, you may have the makings of a true Erakwan in you, despite your mixed blood." She reached inside her pouch and pulled out a pair of shell finger cymbals, slipped them on. She snapped middle finger and thumb together once, and their pure, high sound froze the passage of time even further. "Begin."

Eyes closed as if to better see within, Nakum launched into the legend, guttural and high-pitched with anticipation, then steadying into a full-voiced invocation.

"Once, long, long ago, long before time was time as we know it and the Erakwa had not yet been created, animals and birds and trees, mountains and streams and lakes walked, talked, and lived in this world as friends and brothers, some greater, some lesser, but all aware and a part of the world.

"Of all these creatures and things, trees were perhaps the best loved for their slow and sturdy ways and their generosity—they sheltered small animals in their branches and hollows, they provided sustenance with their leaves and bark, nuts and cones, tender buds and fruit. They shaded creatures from the sun, and the many leaves not eaten fell crisp-colored to blanket against the winter's chill. They uttered joyous laughter and warning with their rustling leaves, and they walked with lithesome grace, boughs dancing over the animals, caressing the lakes and streams, root toes dabbling the waters. They were thoughtful, not quick to anger, though they could be roused if the need were great.

"Bear loved the trees for their acorns and for the honey bees they harbored, their patience with his unwieldy climbing to reach the combs. Crow appreciated the trees for the nests they let him build in their crowns, as did Squirrel, who constructed his home in the crutch of their branches and who also buried their seeds, both for future meals and to help propagate their kind. Raccoon slept in their hollowed hearts while Badger burrowed his entrance at their feet, though he grumbled when he discovered one of them had wandered off. Then the tree would toss its crown in apology and point Badger on his way. Woodpecker tickled the trees with his beak as he tapped and drilled to remove the insects that made them itch and scale.

"Of all the trees, perhaps the most revered was Hatachawa, so straight and tall that animals spent days looking up to his crown. Only Eagle had ever stared him in the eye, hovering on an air draft, for try as he might, Hatachawa simply could not bend low enough to see the ground animals. When Hatachawa was young, he had been as supple and flexible as his brother Birch and his sister Willow, but as the seasons passed he stood lofty and firm, a sentinel watching over the land to protect its peoples.

"Now it came to pass that the Heavens grew jealous of the comfortable life on the world below and wished to claim it for their own Sky People. But they were wily and cunning and knew a direct attack would fail. So slowly, slowly, Sky pressed lower and lower as the seasons changed, forcing Sun to travel a declining arc, the days turning faster and the seasons spinning more quickly. The birds and animals, the hills and streams, felt oppressed, but they knew not why. At last Wind whispered in their ears, 'I have no room to blow, no space to frolic. What is happening?'

"So a Council was called and much discussion ensued. Eagle was sent to spy on the Heavens, lofted into the air by Wind. Eagle flew up and up, though not as high as he had soared before, because he hit a cloud bank, discovered he could not pass through it as in the past and descended in defeat.

" 'I heard them laughing up there,' he complained, ruffling his neck feathers, preening a flight feather to hide his irritation. 'They think us foolish creatures who will never notice our world has been crowded out, flattened to make room for the constellations. And as our space grows tighter and we cannot move as freely, they plan to attack.'

"A mighty clamor rose from the council members, each proposing plans, discarding another's, and no one could agree. Finally the Northern mountains spoke. "My brethren and I can stop them from crushing the life from us, but we cannot push them back. We had done with growing long ago, and the constant pressure will wear us down. What if you shoot your arrows into the Heavens while we hold them steady?'

"They readied their bows and arrows, Eagle giving some of his feathers for the fletchings to help the arrows fly high. And some of the smallest birds perched on the arrows so that their keen eyes might guide them. And so they shot, wave after wave of arrows, into the Heavens. And the Heavens laughed as the arrows bounced back, maiming and wounding those below.

" 'This won't do!' growled Bear, plucking a spent arrow from the hump on his back. Robin's breast glowed red with blood from an arrow's nick, and Chipmunk's long, plumy tail was now a stub. 'If only we could attack from above, we would surprise them and make them retreat.'

"Eagle, mourning the loss of some of his wing feathers to no avail, clattered his beak. 'A good idea, but how can we rise to those heights without ropes or ladders?' And everyone sat and thought and thought.

"At last, Hatachawa, who had been silent all this time, spoke. 'I would prefer to be at peace with our neighbors, but they are forcing themselves on us, and that is not just. I am not yet done growing, and perhaps if I reach up and up, I can touch the Heavens, or reach close enough for you to jump into them. Climb up me, one by one.'

"Bear sprang up. 'Yes! Some of us will climb up and pull from above while you push from below, and we will shove the Heavens back where they belong.'

"And so they climbed, or flew from branch to branch, or crawled and slithered. They gave Snake a head-start since he had the farthest to travel, coiling round and round and round Hatachawa's trunk. He started first, but arrived nearly last.

"Bear and Eagle and fleet-footed Squirrel reached the Heavens first and they gave them a mighty yank from above. The Heavens wept in shock and rage at the sudden pain, and Rain fell, released from bondage, nurturing the land and swelling the strength of the rivers and streams. Crow passed through, followed by Deer and Badger and others, and added their strength to the effort. And the Heavens set lightning bolts of rage free, bolts that crashed and created Fire, and Hatachawa and all the other trees welcomed him into their hearts for safekeeping, hiding him from the Heavens.

"And still Hatachawa heaved upward, striving not to harm the Heavens but only to return them to their proper sphere. He sank his toe roots deep into earth until they reached down and down to anchor him. He pressed his arms straight up to Sky, pressing harder and harder as he felt him yield. Beads of sweat formed and congealed into droplets all over his body, rigid with effort. He would not retreat, would not fail his friends, would not let the Heavens crush his resolve or his body.

"At last the Great Spirit decided to see what caused such commotion and gave a mighty roar of disapproval. 'You, Heavens, return to your home. You have a perfectly good place above Sky and no need to usurp another's territory. And you, birds and animals, back down to your world. You all have your places, and you do not belong here.' And feigning reluctance, but with secret relief, everyone withdrew to their proper locations, except for Hatachawa.

" 'I do not purposefully disobey your words, Great Spirit, but I cannot seem to move,' said Hatachawa, fingers still reaching toward the Heavens. 'I have pushed so long and so hard that I cannot move away. I do not think I will ever be free like my sister and brother trees again. My feet are sunk deep into Earth and my arms arch up against Sky.' And he wept pale, honey-colored tears of resin.

"The Great Spirit looked and saw that Hatachawa spoke true. Never more would Hatachawa roam the world. 'Ah, ever-faithful, ever-green Hatachawa, know this. You will be everlasting, the pillar separating the world from the Heavens, surveying all for safety. Your children shall grow strong and tall as you have, for they are needed to help my children, the Erakwa, when I bring them forth on this world. All of your children shall be everlasting, even beyond death. You are blended of Earth and Wind and Water and Fire now, and even when death overtakes you and yours, your bodies shall be impervious to decay, hard as metal forged in Fire, tempered by Water, cooled by Wind, and lasting as Earth. Your fragrant tears of pitch shall be cherished as jewels. With such endurance, you will be few in number, but all will respect and honor your children wherever they are found, guarding and protecting each generation, knowing that you must not be felled like other trees unless the need is dire.' "

Nakum exhaled a pleasurable sigh, still lost in the tale's telling. "Your fragrant tears of pitch shall be cherished as jewels," Eadwin repeated the words, pensive. "You know," he continued, turning to Doyce, "our Queen always wore a ring like that, a pale, smooth, honey-colored stone that smelled faintly like the forests, like pine. Said it's been passed down for generations as the Ruler's Ring. It looks much like this one." Digging into his pocket, he pulled out a ring, displayed it on the palm of his hand. "Arras brought me this from Mother as a token of her love; she prized it dearly, but she never wore it often, said Father disliked seeing her wear it. I knew the setting was arborfer, but I didn't realize the stone was as well."

"I gave Constant three rings," Callis recalled. "One for himself, one for his wife and one for his eldest, his heir."

"I wonder how Mother came by it, then, why it didn't stay in the family?" He shrugged, "No matter, though, it's a good tale, Nakum."

But Nakum's hazel eyes grew sharp with dismay that deepened into the pain of recognition. "How dare you flaunt the twin of my earth-bond!" With shaking hands he jerked his pouch free from his waist, fumbling with the drawstring until at last a ring twin to Eadwin's glowed in his hand before he almost greedily stuffed it back. "How dare you claim that after what you and your kind have done! You've no right! I never knew! We never knew!" he gasped in Callis's direction. "We've been so far removed from the rest of our peoples that we called it legend, never knew! Why didn't you send word?" he appealed. "Why didn't you tell us the arborfer was dying, fading away! And all because of those who stole the land from itself!" He spun around, slammed Eadwin with an openhanded blow, "Your fault! Yours and all your kind! Wasters! Destroyers!"

Features frozen, stunned, Eadwin clutched his chest, hunched and cowering to avoid another blow. But Callis flowed between them before Doyce could move, soothing Hru'rul, abristle from the unwarranted, unexpected attack on his Bond. She cupped Nakum's face in both hands and he shivered and trembled at the power flowing through them, through him, cycling up and around from the earth and through the earth, cleansing his mind. "Ah! And my kind as well!" he faltered and stood up straight, planted his hands on Callis's shoulders. "Always I was drawn to this, even as a baby, to this ring my foreign grandfather left with my grand-mother to show his faith and love. Always I feared being drawn toward his people, not ours, but the ring is both!"

Callis released her grip and Nakum reluctantly drew back, clutching his earth-bond, fingering the contents through the leather pouch. "So, you know much of the legend, much of the tale, but you jump to conclusions without knowing how you arrived at them." Her chiding was intimate and warm, caressing the air around them. "Some have hurt, some have helped, like people anywhere, good and bad, innocent and evil." He nodded, ducked his head to knuckle a tear from his eye. "So what are we to do, do you think?"

"I do not ... know," he confessed. "I thought I knew, it seemed so clear to me as I unfolded the tale. And now ... now it's gone. Is there any rightness, any wrongness, or is it all as it is, too late to be more or less? Can we still honor and believe in the tale without doing anything? Am I too much of one, not enough of the other to help? You know," he reddened with shame, "that I am not full Erakwa."

Crowing with laughter, Callis hugged him. "Silly one. Is a stew less worthy because meats and vegetables mingle, or is it more complex because of the melding and blending of different flavors?"

Despite himself, Nakum began to grin. "So now I am a stew, revered one?"

"Truly, but with need of proper seasoning and long simmering over slow heat. Now, will you take out your problems and pains on Eadwin, or will you direct them elsewhere and perhaps change things for the better?"

A dimple flashed on Nakum's cheek. "I am sure I could stew on the problem for some time, but hope to hear you answer. Your wisdom far exceeds mine."

"Then I think we should visit your cousin's home and see how things fare."

"Cousin?" Eadwin blurted. "Just because we've similar rings doesn't make us kin."

Callis's smile was small, pleasantly secretive. "Well, in like interests if not in like blood, but even that bears your thinking about with an unclouded mind."

And without knowing how she knew, Doyce suspected that the rings had been inherited by Wilhelmina, and her brothers Maarten and Ludo. She interrupted, "But returning could be dangerous. They want us—and especially Eadwin—captured, perhaps dead. Can we succeed?"

"Who knows? The only certainty I know is that each winter the snow falls. As to the danger, while I am here to direct the flows, it shall be minimal. Trust you must have, in me and in yourselves."

♣

Sweat sheening her strained face, coppery hair damp and tangled, Yulyn squeezed her eyes shut, arched against Towbin's supportive hands clasping her upper waist. A breeze teased at her gray dress, patchy with perspiration, her own and the damp stripings imprinted by her husband's anxious fingers. Kyril van Beieven stood to one side, clutching a moistened cloth and waterskin, ready to swab her face, while Swan Maclough stood opposite, arms folded across her paunch, mouth a grim line of protest. Koom sat at her feet, tail twitching and alert.

"And again," Mahafny directed from her camp stool in front of Yulyn, her back to the escarpment overlooking the river. Yulyn's chin dipped in acknowledgment as she clenched her teeth, concentrated. Her eyes rolled until only the whites showed beneath fluttering lids. "I cannot, I *must* not intrude—I'm being flung away! There's laughter, little chiming sounds, but they don't have time to notice me. I'm less a distraction than a buzzing fly!" Without warning she staggered, almost crumpled and fell if it hadn't been for Towbin's bracing hands.

"Enough!" he snarled at Mahafny. "She can't take any more of this! She's trying as hard as she can, what more can you ask?" He squatted, cradling her limp form against him. Embarrassed to intrude, the Monitor extended the damp cloth, pulled a flash of brandy from his pocket, caught Towbin's eye, and offered it.

Yulyn opened her eyes, waved the flask away. "Almost," she rasped, her voice as tired as the rest of her. "It's the distance combined with the fact that I don't have a key."

Swan relieved van Beieven of the flask, took a long, thirsty swig. "Key?" she queried, wiping her mouth on her wrist.

Towbin, as bereft of Gleaner potential as his wife was rife with it, answered for her. "'Cording to Yulyn, those Marchmontian mindwalkers seem to key their mental signatures at a very early age. Without the key, it's almost impossible to reach into another mind uninvited. Or more like," he worried at his lip, striving for a comparison, "rapping a special, coded knock to identify yourself before you're invited to enter another mind."

"It's nothing we've ever had here," Yulyn added, and shivered in remembrance. "Vesey never bothered with a key if he wanted to enter any of our minds, and none of us could stop him." A hint of color had crept across her face, but the circles under her eyes looked as dark and deep as a gravedigger's nightmares. "It's strange. I've even tried the Seeker you call Byrta, I think, but she's even more peculiar, attuned only to her twin, her rapport more narrowly focused than any I've ever seen, as if she and her brother don't even realize what they have."

Mahafny rose, ungainly, hips aching with the damp and the taut compression of the canvas seat-sling. "We have to keep trying." Her words had the flat brittleness of slate. She ignored the unvoiced protests radiating from Towbin and van Beieven, didn't bother to gauge her cousin's expression, knew already what she'd read. "We're desperate for information, Kyril, you know that," she appealed to the Monitor, confident she'd scored a direct hit. "Being soft now won't help later. We *must* find out what's happening across the river! The knowledge may save lives."

Weary but game, Yulyn attempted to shrug off her husband's enveloping arms, but Swan broke her silence. "Well, if you can't enter by the front door, isn't there another entrance? Or at least another mind to try?" She bent, stroked the ruddy ghatt's head. "Koom's reminded me that we've enough ghatti to mindlink, reach P'wa or Per'la, ask them to connect us with someone there. If that doesn't work, don't they have some sort of distress call, a plea for help that would open any mind nearby? If someone were injured, in danger, wouldn't they broadcast a plea for aid without knowing who might receive it?"

"No!" The Monitor snapped. "That would be a false luring. I won't have that. We'll fight as honorably as we can, if fight we must."

Extending her hand, Mahafny pulled Yulyn to her feet and answered the Monitor without looking at him. "It's not false if our plea is peace." She rounded on him, "And we do want peace, do we not?"

"If it is at all possible," he agreed. "But not peace at any cost. Some costs are too high to bear."

But Mahafny was walking Yulyn down the narrow path from the top of the escarpment, and it was unclear precisely who was helping whom. "Have Koom try the mindnet first. Yulyn needs to rest. Then we'll see."

As the Monitor and Swan left, pensive and perturbed, they ran into Darl Allgood. "Looking for me, Darl?"

"No, no," Allgood stammered, and van Beieven thought he looked as strained and exhausted as Yulyn. "Just on my way to help out wherever I can. Let me know if you need me."

❖

Allgood dodged through the double-line of laden wagons pulling up to unload, almost stumbled where wheels had churned ruts in the dirt. Easiest to give a mindcry, but that he didn't dare, not here and not now. Darting from wagon to wagon, he scanned the Transitors and Guardians hoisting down pontoons, stacking some, reloading others onto larger flatbeds. At last he spotted Faertom atop a load, tying them into place.

"Get down here! Fast!" he hissed. Eyebrows knotted, Faertom checked the last rope, slipped a pad beneath it so it wouldn't chafe the canvas pontoon covering if the ride were rough.

He jumped down, swiped at the sweat that beaded his hairline, matted his tawny mane dark. "What? What's the matter?"

Too many people nearby for Allgood's comfort, but sometimes the more noise and distraction the better for confidentiality. "Did you hear what that young woman was casting through the air?" Never had he heard one of his own kind employ her talents with such profligate disregard for who else might hear or suspect. Hard to remember the distinction between them: she'd already been revealed for what she was, while he had not been—nor had Faertom.

Faertom's eyes reflected eager wariness. The wariness reassured Allgood, but the eagerness didn't bode well. Youth. "There are others across the river like us, but we're like country bumpkins compared to them. I wish we could help her connect. Mayhap if we all concentrated together we could determine what they use as a key ..." his suggestion shaded into a plea. "You're older, you *must* know more than she does, than I certainly do."

"Don't even think it!" Darl snapped. He'd known he'd sensed nonspecific empathy in the air, feared Yulyn had drawn on it as well. "Whatever you do, don't get overzealous on me now, Faertom. Don't get all 'heady' on me!"

"But if we can help ...?"

"And the biggest help we can tender is to keep ourselves to ourselves just as we've always done unless there's a crisis. Yulyn has the eumedicos and the Seekers to protect her. Whom do we have if we reveal ourselves?"

Faertom swiped at his brow with his sleeve. "But you're a High Conciliator, friends with the Monitor," he objected.

How had he come to be so innocent? He supposed the island had been constraining but safe. "It's not enough, Faertom. He's not ready for a revelation of this sort now. What if word leaks back about us, exposes our families, our loved ones for what they are? Most of the Guardians are here as well as many of the Seekers. Who's going to prevent the general populace from going for their throats if they're discovered?" He pressed the point home. "Do you think your fellow Transitors are eager to share a tent with a Gleaner, let alone their thoughts?"

Reluctant, Faertom nodded, acquiesced. "Still a secret, always a secret."

"Mayhap not someday—at least for your children, or your children's children—if we're lucky. A time to be proud of what we are, of what we could be."

A giggle, childish laughter floated from behind the wagon wheel, and a boy of about twelve with dark hair that looked as if it'd been trimmed around the edge of a bowl, dashed away, mischievous grin splitting his face. "Don't worry, that's only Davvy. Don't know why someone would bring a boy here, not with what we're facing. Still, he's a good lad," Faertom opined from his lofty vantage of seven additional years.

Allgood went tight with anger, fought the rising rage. "You absolute fool! He's one of us, *and* one of them, one of the Hospicers! What if he tells the others we're here?"

And Faertom swung back to his work without waiting to be told, tried to pretend everything was normal, and how could it be when he was an oddity in a normal world? He prayed Davvy had been trained about strict self-control and common sense when it came to naming his fellows, but he couldn't be sure. After all, at twelve he'd never have dared run free and playful in a crowd of "normals."

With a slap on the shoulder Allgood left him to his work, took a meandering course designed to bring him near the eumedico tents, and wondered what it would take to put that youngster Davvy over his mental knee as a warning. But the thought of abusing, even punishing anyone for his Lady-given talents was more than he could bear. He hadn't sunk that low yet, hoped he never would.

The distant plinking of water met his ears. Drip, drip, then a pause, drip, a longer pause until he thought he couldn't hold his breath any longer anticipating the next one. Of course, what good is a cell without dripping water? Better to be driven mad by relentless, constant dripping or by their irregular soundings, trying to form their pattern? And if dripping water accompanied imprisonment, weren't rats de rigueur as well? Jenret snarled. As if on cue, a rustling in the straw, and he convulsively threw himself against Sarrett, who jerked and moaned but didn't waken.

"Not likely to be rats while we're here," Rawn muttered as he curled into a ball, tucked tail over nose. **"That's just N'oor. She can't help herself, even asleep her tail's been thrashing like a headless snake. She nailed poor T'ss's nose right while he was in the midst of a yawn. Almost bit his tongue before he realized what was happening. I'm going back to sleep now, you should do the same."**

Trying to shift without disturbing Sarrett, Jenret stretched just as Sarrett rolled over. This bump joggled her awake, sleep and fear warring for control of her body. "Shh, it's just me, sorry!" he whispered. But Sarrett was already struggling into a sitting position, knees hunched to her chest for protection.

"'Sall right," she mumbled, and her unbound hair engulfed her face as she leaned closer, a strand tickling his ear. Once it had been as soft and golden white as new corn silk, but now he could feel its harshness from the dye, dark and rough as the tassel at the end of a matured ear of corn. "Was having . . . bad dream." She buried a yawn in the crook of her elbow. "Glad you . . . woke me."

"Go back to sleep. Dreams can't be any worse than the nightmare we're in."

Her asperity stung like a slap. "You don't have a monopoly on nightmares, Jenret. All of us have something haunting us."

"So what are your nightmares about?" He was curious, but she rolled away. He thought she wasn't going to answer, fretting he'd been condescending, but she merely checked on Bard, sliding a hand under his tunic to adjust the dressing. She came back slowly, almost reluctantly, and the remembrance of her gilded beauty invisibly haloed her to his eyes. Always so untouchable, so cool, as he'd learned to his dismay one evening a few years ago. And now, while he still recollected that beauty and lauded it, she was as physically remote, untouchable, for an entirely different reason. What he wanted, craved with mind and soul—and body, if honesty were served—was Doyce. He had no idea where she was, and even if she were here beside him in place of Sarrett, he feared that she, too, was equally distant. And for that he was to blame as well.

She groped for his hand and patted it. "Confidences in the dark? Supposed to be easier that way, but I'm not sure. It's the here-and-now that's got me skittish. I don't want . . . to die like this."

He gathered her in his lap the way he used to scoop up Jacobia when she'd skinned a knee, but this was far more serious. Sarrett regained her poise almost immediately. "I just wish I knew what Aelbert's game was. I just wish I knew where Doyce and Nakum were, if they're all right. I keep having the strangest dreams about them . . . and Parse, too."

"I'm sure he's fine," he responded automatically, but his answer sounded lame even to him. For a moment Jenret was convinced their minds had melded, her worry and love for Parse flooding his senses, shaming him for his intrusion. Something uncanny about this country, damnably uncanny, thoughts constantly floating through the air, there to read if he but knew how. Enough vibrations to leave him with a constant, low-grade headache and a resounding temper. And that one, mocking in his mind! He flung a look at Arras, helmeted, propped against the wall like a hooded hawk, perhaps asleep, perhaps awake. "At least Parse isn't in Marchmont in the midst of all this."

"You wouldn't want to wager on that, would you?" She pushed away from his chest, tilted her face toward his. "He's never missed the 'fun,' as he put it, if he can possibly help it. And he's with Byrta. Can you believe, can you possibly believe that Byrta isn't on her way, or already here after learning Bard was wounded? She told me once their hearts beat as one and she meant that literally—she showed me, I felt their pulses. The same rhythm, in tandem like a matched pair of carriage horses."

He made a little clucking sound of dismay and comprehension. "Of course Byrta will be here, with Parse beside her, if not enthusiastically leading the way. Thank the Lady you don't take money from fools."

"Nor candy from babies." And with that she separated from him and laid down to sleep. He imitated her, though he knew that neither of them would sleep much more tonight. Too much thinking to do. He was over his fury with Aelbert, but an abiding distrust remained. If he were up to something for his own advantage, Jenret felt clueless as to his goal or what it would take to stop him. And if thinking weren't enough, there were always regrets to count and recount as a miser fondles his gold.

❖

As they exited the oval chamber into the bright cold outside, Doyce hesitated, hands clutching the sides of the circular door that had manifested itself from nothing, a sinkhole swallowing her sanctuary. What was out there? What day was it? How much time had passed inside? Out of nowhere her mind crowded with fears, tangible and intangible; her body shaking in reaction, arms and legs trembling, quivering until she lost control. How long had she been fighting against learning more, coming to grips with what she already knew? Except that new things always intruded, painful as a nail poking through a shoe. Felix's considerable canine bulk pressed against her legs, almost toppling her in his eagerness to leave, but she couldn't budge, neither forward nor backward. Without volition, she collapsed, doubled over, hands to mouth to stifle the little moaning sounds leaking out. Felix nosed her neck in concern, and Khar looked at her anxiously from outside.

She felt her ankles grasped, and her whole body straightened as she was plucked through the doorway, sliding clear without a hitch. Raising her head, blinking in the sunlight, she wanted to howl her fears, her dismay at being forced to reenter this world. Callis pulled her a little further, and then let her go. "So, you do not like being reborn? No one meets the first birth or any other with gladness." She made a tsking sound, motioned for Doyce to rise. "You can fight to remain or go out into the world, out of your shell."

She struggled to sit up, gain her bearings. Hiding her face by reaching to tug her boots, dragged half-off from Callis' pulling, she managed to mutter, "And a breech birth at that. My apologies. It's just that I'm so tired, so afraid of the unknown."

"Ah, but the 'known' isn't always pleasant, either. At least with the 'unknown,' you have the potential for betterment. So do not fear."

Scrambling to her feet, Doyce trailed in Callis's wake, the snow crunching and squeaking beneath her booted feet, although Callis's footsteps made no sound. And no mark, she realized, looking more closely. Khar rubbed against her leg, purring and sending two thin jets of steam from her nostrils into the clear air. **"Ah, beloved, will you truly let me in**

now? We 'speak but you've allotted me only a portion of
your thoughts, left me begging at the door to your mind."

"Reborn together, you mean?" She cast a tremulous grin
in the ghatta's direction. *"Every time I struggle to protect
myself I leave you vulnerable. Can we begin anew together?"*

"Always," the ghatta crooned, and they both unselfconsciously shared in the absurdity of the dog's actions, his
delight at his release. Felix frolicked, barking and rolling
in the snow, running in crazy circles at the sheer joy of being outside. He started to raise a leg to christen a snowbank, and Callis sent one sharp word his way. Dropping his
leg, head drooping in shame, he glanced back at the
Erakwan woman for permission to run ahead and leave the
snowcap. She nodded, and he zoomed away, christening a
rock before going about the more serious business of sniffing and stopping, marking and dashing to the next outpost.
At length, satisfied, he returned. Callis, Doyce and Khar
judged with a chuckle, hadn't wanted the permanence of
yellow stains on her beloved snow since they'd never fade
but remain for eternity, just as the snow did.

Callis was removing snow blocks from a small, domed
mound nearly invisible to the casual eye. Eadwin and
Nakum joined her labors, lifting the solid blocks, haphaz-
ardly stacking them to the side. Doyce watched with wonder
as a low, sleek shape, ashy white against snow white, took
form, about three meters long, and perhaps two-thirds of a
meter wide with a hooded, sloped front like a needled,
questing nose. She approached warily, trying to discern its
purpose.

But Nakum had no qualms about it and whooped with
glee. "It's a slaithe! Look at it, just look! I've never seen
one so large, so crafted for speed." He dragged Doyce
closer, pointing out the runners she'd failed to notice, long
white curves of bone on each side. A shorter front pair
looked as if they might pivot, then the longer, solidly anchored back runners. On closer inspection, the slaithe was
not pure white, but flecked, striations of black and gray to it.
"Bark," Nakum informed her and Eadwin with proprietary
delight, "from Hatachawa's sister, Birch."

With a sinking sensation she decided she examined some
sort of giant sled or sleigh. Was that how Callis planned on

descending the mountain? And what in the name of the heavens did she expect to do when the snow ran out?

But Callis was muttering to herself as she dragged a curved, transparent piece from storage in the hollow nose cone of the slaithe. Humming and grumbling, paying no heed to the others, she fiddled with it, fitting it into the rear edge of the nose, in front of the open space where riders would sit. With shock Doyce identified it as a plexi-shield, a windscreen. Where had Callis found plexi-materials? Practically none existed any more, the little remaining zealously hoarded, incredibly priceless relics of their spacer ancestors' inoperable ships. With a sharp snap, the plexi-shield locked into place, and Callis flicked imaginary dust with her feathered cape. "Constant was always kind about sharing little offerings that might 'improve' my life. He couldn't fathom that most were unnecessary, though this one I have enjoyed." She winked. "This, and the cha."

"And we're riding down the mountain in that?" Doyce's voice cracked, and, worst of all, Nakum and Eadwin appeared delighted with the idea, tugging and poking at each other like overgrown boys discussing the merits of a new toy. "What happens when we run out of snow? Do we stop and climb down from there?"

"Of course not." Busy unrolling a white pad that had been crammed inside the slaithe, Callis spread it the length of the vehicle. "We simply keep going. The runners are very strong and supple. And arborfer, not bone, Nakum," she corrected.

"But arborfer does not stay white," he protested. "It hardens and darkens after it's been cut from the tree."

"Ah, but this was freely given long ago, not forcibly removed." Finger tapping against lips, she measured the dimensions with her eyes, looking at first one and then the other, deciding how to position them in the slaithe. "A tight fit, I think, especially with the ghatti and the dog to consider."

She lifted her head, suddenly alert, then looked down at her feet planted in the snow. "Ah, they come. How bothersome. More would trespass, hurt, not heal. Nakum," she clapped her hands once, "come along. It appears my spring washing wasn't enough. Now for a good dusting. Time you learned." She grabbed Nakum's hand, let her power range through them and down into the earth. In the distance, on the mountain's far side, a faint rumble, snow particles rising and flinging themselves into the air.

"Avalanche," Nakum whispered.

Oblivious to the brief distraction around her, Doyce considered the puzzle of four people, three ghatti, and a dog not sheering off this delicate, soaring slab of birch bark. Already recovered from the momentary drain of energy, Nakum now was poking and prying, under and over and around the slaithe. "If we stow two ghatti in the nose, they won't impede the steering ropes as much as Felix's bulk would."

Callis nodded agreement. "And I will steer. Doyce behind me hugging Khar in her lap. Then Eadwin as the biggest, holding Felix tightly between his legs. And you, Nakum, last of all, to push us off and then jump in, and operate the brake lever if necessary."

And so, aghast, heart rising in her throat, Doyce crawled into the slaithe, wrapped her legs around Callis's waist, Khar squeezing into her lap. Feet and knees poked, Eadwin settled behind her, Nakum coaxing a perplexed Felix into the limited space between Eadwin's legs, shoving and shifting so the dog's long limbs didn't hang over. "For pity sakes, Eadwin, don't let him pinch his tail under a runner," Nakum advised as he took his position at the slaithe's rear.

A shift to the left and an ear-splitting crack, a shift to the right and another crack as Nakum broke the runners free from the frost, the motion jarring in its anticipation. **"Will we soar like a hawk?"** Khar asked with jittery interest, **"or crash like a booby bird?"**

"Don't even think it," she warned, trembling. And then slowly, haltingly, they began to slide, faster and faster as Nakum found his footing and put his whole being into the effort, drawing strength from the earth below into each straining leg, returning the power to the earth. Eyes clenched, refusing to look, Doyce buried her head against Callis's back, sensed the breeze tearing at her hair, her clothing, and tried to think of nothing at all. The world was mad and so was she.

❧

Amazed at how effortlessly Octavian Florenz glided over the cobbles despite his wooden leg, Roland tried to emulate him, but couldn't manage even half as well as the two soldiers accompanying them. He skidded, sank one boot into a puddle, and cringed as the water seeped through. They were pretending to be just a band of late-night revelers who'd been sampling some of the more disreputable taverns, oh, not exactly disreputable, but ones known for their hard-bitten clientele, soldiers on leave. Dressed soberly in work clothes, their gaudy, slashed uniforms regretfully laid aside, neither Staff Sergeant Octavian nor the two soldiers, Denys and Benoit, looked like what they were, a precaution this far into the city.

Benoit lagged a bit to the rear, watching but not watching who came along behind them, out of alleyways and side streets, anyone who appeared to move too quickly or too purposefully. Denys and Benoit had served under Muscadeine in the attritions against the North Domain, chasing what seemed like will-o-the-wisps through mountainous terrain and at other times turned out to be grizzled mercenaries who attacked with every cunning, underhanded trick in the book. The two had lost too many friends to the depredations and blamed not Muscadeine, their leader, but Maurice for his strangely hampering orders and counterorders. "As if he wanted us to run in circles, give the mercs a chance. Suspect he even hired them to supposedly plague himself and preoccupy us," had scoffed Benoit on pledging himself to Octavian in support of Muscadeine. And Denys had countered, "Aye, preoccupying's fine, but dying ain't, see. Not without a reason, and Muscadeine was honest enough to admit he couldn't find the reason behind the attacks."

A relief to have them with him for this brief reconnoiter of the city, a chance to visit a few taverns, judge who else might prove disaffected, loyal to Muscadeine and willing to lend support. Octavian had done his best with his Resonant skills, contacting as many troop Resonants as he could to pass the word, but many men still needed to weigh the honesty of a face, the firmness of a handclasp before deciding to throw in their lot with theirs. And with good reason—loyalty to Muscadeine meant disloyalty to Maurice, being adjudged traitors to their land with the Chevalier Capitain imprisoned.

If their luck held tonight, they'd garner perhaps another dozen to the cause as they could slip away. And if their luck held further, he and the others would slip back through the defense walls without being recognized. *"Worst of it is we niver get to drink enough ale,"* Octavian grouched.

"I know. I've wished for at least another mug, if not a half-cask. But I'm afraid Benoit and Denys would beat me to it." Drinking in moderation was prudent if they wanted to keep their wits clear, avoid any spies from Maurice's household guard.

Almost clear, almost through the gates if no one recognized any of them, asked Staff Sergeant Octavian what brought him into town on this rainy, drizzly night, and where was his pass, if you please? He turned his collar up for protection from the rain.

A flash of sky-blue livery highlighted by a misted halo of lamp light caught Roland's eye before he realized its significance, had feared the household guards, as he heard a cry of "Ro—" abruptly shuttered. Denys had efficiently clamped his hand over the mouth of Ezequiel Dunay, the chamberlain's grandson. At Roland's sharp mental command, Octavian signaled Denys to release him.

"A bit late to be out," Roland whispered, shielding Ezequiel's too obvious livery from casual passersby.

"Well, of course it is, but Grandfather and I figured it was the best time to find you."

Octavian gave the lad an assessing look. "Hope you hadn't planned on tavern crawling prinked out like that. Very pretty legs in those hosen. Shame they're all damp and clammy."

But Ezequiel held his own against the old soldier. "Don't be foolish. As a hard-working assistant chamberlain I've been assigned to check ale quality and prices for the forthcoming coronation feast. As long as I promise Grandfather not to sample too much." For a moment he looked as thirsty as Roland felt. "Here!" He furtively thrust a waxed packet at Roland. "Grandfather managed to borrow copies of at least some of the old castle plans. There are all sorts of passageways and tunnels if you know where to look. I've traveled some of them, and Grandfather knows even more. When you've had a chance to study this, mayhap you can slip in and rescue Muscadeine and the others!"

"I thought you and Ignacio were loyal to the throne." It wasn't that he distrusted the lad, but that he had always thought of him and the chamberlain as integral parts of the society they oversaw, their loyalty unquestioned.

"We *are* loyal to the throne, to what it represents—the hopes and aspirations of our country. Does Maurice embody those hopes? Not a petty tyrant like that!" He rushed on passionately, "Is it really true about Eadwin? Grandfather suspected, but it wasn't his place to say. Is he safe? Can we win the throne for him?"

Thrusting the packet into his cloak, Roland heard Benoit's whistle that a party approached. Time to leave as quickly and unobtrusively as possible. "How can we contact you? Do either of you Receive that strongly?"

Ezequiel shook his head, glum. "No, except at night when we're resting. At least Grandfather's getting more rest these nights now that Constant Minor's been locked in the library." He saw Roland's face, realized he hadn't known or hadn't paid attention, so concerned was he about Muscadeine and Eadwin. "Don't worry, he's fine. Fabienne's watching out for him," he reassured with such vigor that raindrops flew from his dark red hair "No, as I said, we don't Receive all that well. During the day the strain of organizing and directing the servants is too great. If you truly need us, try late at night. Or contact the Bannerjees. I'll try to find another excuse to visit them whenever I can get away."

And with that he was off, long legs striding, an officious air about him as if all the castle responsibilities rested on his slim shoulders, a young man on the rise, and not to be bothered in the night streets by anyone wise in the ways in which power is conferred.

"Yaaaaa!" Nakum exulted as the slaithe built up speed. The left front runner swooped halfway up a snow covered boulder and the whole slaithe tilted rightward before landing back on the trail of dense snow. In front of her Doyce could feel Callis shifting, hauling on the steering ropes as if she sawed at the reins of a headstrong horse. Without warning they were airborne, soaring, glistening whiteness below, blue sky above as they shot over a ledge and sliced through the air. Sure that her stomach lofted ten meters above her, Doyce groaned as they began to plummet, landing with a jarring crash and careening on their way.

Felix poked his muzzle over her shoulder, wind streaming

his floppy ears against her face like ribbons in the breeze, a hot blast of doggy breath, panting delight. **"The dog is drooling on me,"** Khar announced unnecessarily since Doyce could feel the moisture herself. **"He's mad for speed."** The ghatta wedged her head under Doyce's elbow, stole a peek to the side. The runners threw a dusting of ice crystals on her nose and whiskers, frosted Doyce's arms and legs.

Felix was sandwiched tighter against her, Eadwin bending close to shout something into her ear. Despite a constricted woof of protest, she leaned back to listen and gained her first unobstructed view over Callis's hunched body. The sight made her oblivious to Eadwin's words. The whiteness gone, left behind—green, green loomed ahead, greens and browns and grays and blacks. The timberline, demarcation between the high snow peaks and the lower mountain loomed with the finality of a stone wall. She opened her mouth in a soundless cry of warning and feverishly began to pray, "Oh, Lady, blest above all, who watches the infinite change of the world never-ending. Only You are immune from change, only we and Your disciples wax and wane, guide us now in this time of transition."

And still they coasted, no sign of slackening speed, no yell to abandon the slaithe. What she wanted above all was to close her eyes, not see the crash, but her eyes were locked open. For the briefest moment she had a crazy vision of the old china doll she'd loved as a child, with its white porcelain skin and vivid, painted blue eyes. She'd ached with fright one night when she had awakened and seen the doll in the dim light of her mother's one sewing candle. Its eyes were still wide open, and she'd cried out, "She won't sleep, Mama, why won't she sleep?" Her mother had laid down her mending with a weary gesture and tucked both her and the doll back under the covers. "She only closes her eyes when you do, and when you open yours, so does she." She had disbelieved, but had fallen asleep despite her determination to test her mother's words.

The forest-line rushed at them, Callis bodily heaving on the lines to send them skidding around a gnarled tree, blind limbs poised to grab them. They jounced skyward again and the runners struck sparks on the rocks as they landed, then settled in as Callis guided the slaithe through hairpin turns between tight-packed trees. **"I wish someone would tell us** what's going on, warn us of bumps," Saam's voice echoed peevish in her brain. "Hru'rul and I can't see, cramped in the nose like this. It's worse when you can't see. I think Hru'rul's sick. He's gulping and he's starting to drool."

With Nakum too intent on riding and releasing the drag brake—all seemingly without signal from Callis—to converse with Saam, she promised, managed to 'speak "Hard landing ahead!" as Callis pointed them toward another ravine and they sailed into nothingness. The front runners bit into the ravine's far edge and lurched forward, but the very rear of the slaithe hung suspended in air. In scrambling, wordless unison they threw their weight forward, not daring to breathe. The slaithe teetered and balanced, then the nose sank and they sped off. Khar gulped once, and a shiver rippled from her ears through her tail. "Saam, you don't want to know, truly."

"Short-cut!" Callis sang out merrily. "Haven't had this much fun in, oh, at least a hundred and fifty winters!"

And after a time Doyce didn't care, she simply clutched Khar in a death-grip and tried to pretend she was part of the slaithe, at one with it, until at last they reached the mountain's base and braked in a wide, flourishing circle that cast up a spray of dirt and fir needles.

"Now let's visit the castle," Callis encouraged as she popped free of the slaithe, but Doyce prayed she'd never have to move again.

♣

"And why hasn't my son been found, reunited with me?" Maurice made no effort to hide the twist to his lip, the sneering emphasis on "my son."

Jules Jampolis made a small, quieting gesture, not of appeasement but as if to remind Maurice to take care. Maurice nodded, made a rueful expression he didn't feel. Let Jampolis think he still maintained control, no need to let him know otherwise. "I had Alighieri send another six men as high as the timberline, but there was no sign of Eadwin or the two with him. Nor, for that matter of either party of men sent to bring him back." Jampolis announced, unsure how Maurice would react. Indeed, he still wasn't sure whether he believed the report, though he'd teased and contorted the men's minds for every scrap of information they contained.

They'd be good for nothing for some time now, if they'd ever be good for anything again. Still, they were expendable, they had others.

"Avalanche, you say?" Maurice leaned his bulk forward in his chair, elated, breathing coming fast and pleasurable. "They were all wiped out by an avalanche, you say?" The melting snows, frost easing from the ground, runnels of water seeking and wearing new courses, the land was bound to be fragile, ready to shift, a scarp peeling itself free. So easy, so right, to let nature take its course. So what if they'd sacrificed a few men if the avalanche had swept Eadwin along with it? Interred under tons of snow. Surely he was dead! And it left his hands clean.

Jampolis answered too quickly for his liking. Have to teach the man not to be so self-assured, so confident that only he knew the answers. "Yes, sire. Alighieri's men said everything seemed natural wherever they dared search, as if not a living being before them had passed through. Nothing could have survived that power. Every mark of their passage erased so cleanly none could read them. Just flickering, writhing, white shadow-shapes hovering over the mountain, like ground fog." What he didn't add was that the men were convinced the white shadow-shapes had laughed and mocked at them, followed at their heels, tweaking hair and clothes. He'd read it in their minds but didn't deem it true, a mass hallucination brought on by the thinness of air, perhaps. "All of Alighieri's men were experienced trackers. And the dogs caught not a whiff of any scent, not even of that whelp of Muscadeine's. They're buried deep beneath the shifting snows."

Why wasn't the man taking more obvious delight in breaking the news to him? Why be dazzled by nature's power when it was Maurice's powers Jampolis should stand in awe of? Well, there'd be time enough to rectify that, and a pleasure to do so. For a moment he considered enjoying that pleasure here and now. Having Jampolis stripped, setting the honed crescent nail-sheaths onto his own fingers, tracing a pattern across sensitive, thin belly skin, razor-edged blades writing their blood message—a message of power to enhance his Resonance, augment his power until he could reach out and crush Eadwin, twist the mind to his. Ah, but no need for that now if Eadwin were dead.

He licked his lips at the thought, oblivious of Jampolis'

assessing look, twisted his hands into the deep purple silks he'd taken to wearing. The renegade eumedico had taught him well. But no, if he reached out to see if Eadwin lived, he'd be forced to release the compulsion that had rendered him mindblank, ignorant of his potential and of his true position. He couldn't afford the chance that Fabienne was still reaching for Eadwin, searching for him. She'd be aware of the least little signaling if he released the compulsion and Eadwin still lived. Her mindskills were paltry compared to his own, but he suspected a mother's desperate love might reach farther than even his own enhanced abilities.

Ah, to find and lay that body at Fabienne's feet would pay for all! And she'd never know, never suspect that he'd made sure of the sacrifice himself.

Jampolis made a throat-clearing sound to catch his attention, awaiting his command, and Maurice came back to himself, frowned as the pleasure thoughts dissipated. "Now that I don't have to worry about Eadwin being brought in, we'll have the ceremony tomorrow at high noon. Warn that old fool, Constant, to be ready. And see that our friends in the dungeon are cleaned up and made presentable, especially Aelbert Orsborne."

"What about Muscadeine, my lord?"

"See that he's presentable as well. And that includes," he rubbed a rosy pomade on his lips, glanced in his hand mirror, "making sure his manacles are polished. Poor Auguste Vannevar's wife was such a weakling, don't you agree? Brain-crazed after the first day in the helmet. Too bad we couldn't experiment further. Muscadeine will have the strength to survive until I'm ready for him. Be sure to leave the casque on him at all times, though. That's one hawk I won't fly until I've imposed my training on him." The metaphor pleased him, Muscadeine as a hooded hawk, jesses binding him to his perch. And best of all, the thought of flying him, controlling his mind and mentally sharing in the swoop and kill, the warm, bleeding carcasses of his enemies. . . .

"But, sire, I don't think he's had food or drink since his capture." Jampolis was not a compassionate man, hadn't been since his wife's and daughter's deaths, but even he could imagine the hot closeness of the helmet, the dark broken only by hair-thin stripings of light, the dry mouth, the itching ear unable to be scratched. For an instant he experienced the oppression as if it were his own and it surprised him, because he was hardly empathic, nothing like the Bannerjees when they so chose. Thought currents, subtle, tenuous, delicate, swarmed inside his head, fluttered from without. He shrugged them off, no one could manipulate him like that, no one else was powerful enough—except Maurice.

What had he wrought by aiding Maurice's discoveries, helping teach him these enhancements of power? The enhancement was so haphazard, unpredictable at times. Would additional training control it or was Maurice's mind already warped in a way he hadn't foreseen? And why was he rambling like this in the middle of a conversation with Maurice? He'd risen beyond guilt long ago. Besides, who'd dare charge him with malpractice? What had come over him just now?

"Well, surely you can feed him broth through a straw. And perhaps, just perhaps, if he swears fealty, he'll join in the feast after my coronation. Yes, I'm sure the Chevalier Capitain could be welcomed at one of the lowest tables, if nowhere else."

Bowing, Jampolis departed, and locked his thoughts tightly inside himself until he was well away from the throne room. The fluttering sensation struck again; he could hear distant giggles and the jangle of bracelets, this time clearer, more assured. He almost fell to his knees in shock. They wouldn't dare! They couldn't have! Too cowardly, too moralistic and priggishly self-righteous to attempt this—after all, he'd known them most of his life, trained with them. The Bannerjees, the Bannerjee twins were out there somewhere, mentally tweaking and tickling his mind, prying at it, just as those strange white shadow-shapes had harassed the searchers on the mountain. He banished the thought, cursed his suggestibility. Stress, nothing but stress, and with Eadwin safely out of the way, the stress had been dramatically halved. Maurice was right—the coronation could proceed with no fear of trouble. With Eadwin dead, even the Seeker Pairs other than Aelbert would have to acknowledge the truth of Maurice's right.

❖

Roland stood, holding a bowl of soup, staring into it as if to scry his fortunes there within. His belly clenched and rumbled with hunger and he salivated. His body knew, even if his mind did not, that it needed food. But his mind whirled, full of plans, details, the pressure of command and, worst of all, the sick knowledge of what he'd just learned from the Bannerjees' brief return message. Arras, his idol, his ideal, imprisoned like that, his very essence, his Resonance trapped like that!

Parse and Michel took his elbows, guided him until the backs of his knees encountered a low bench, forced him to sit. "Now eat," Michel growled, "or ye'll mindwipe when we need ye most." One gnarled hand clenched painfully tight around his wrist, guided the bowl to Roland's lips. The soup was hot and thin, more a broth, really, for which he gave thanks, easier to swallow.

The two ghatti materialized at his feet, the creamy-colored one with the long, fluffy fur and plumed tail—Per'la, he believed her name was—and the black and white one, so like the housecats he'd played with as a child, but so much larger. P'wa, the one he'd first conversed with in the middle of the river. "H . . . hun . . . hungry?" he stuttered and started to set the bowl in front of them. He'd had enough, and enough to share.

Per'la's nostrils dilated and flexed, keen interest in her peridot eyes until she demurely looked elsewhere. But P'wa claimed a knee with her paw and for just a moment he sensed the claws, a pinprick warning that brought him back to himself. **"Drink it,"** she commanded, **"and eat the bread Parse brought."**

He started to refuse. How could he eat when Arras had nothing? Holy Lady, the Bannerjees said he sounded like a man shouting from inside a well, bleak echoes that barely penetrated. Arras apparently held no illusions about their survival at Maurice's hands. He stuffed a heel of bread into his mouth and chewed, mechanically pulping it until he could bear to swallow. Evidently Arras suspected that Maurice would attempt to use the ghatti to legitimize his claim to the throne. The Bannerjees had relayed the information, refused to interpret it. How could the ghatti do that? Bewildered, he registered that only a crust remained, the rest mysteriously consumed although he didn't recollect it. P'wa acted secretly amused by his discovery.

Now the stranger, Byrta, interrupted his thoughts, the nameless dreads and fears. She limped from an old injury, a badly broken leg, she'd explained, but had refused to say why she favored her left shoulder, occasionally wincing in pain, though no bandage covered a wound. "I know you're tired, we all are, and you most of all, but there's one left who would speak with you, if you'll grant leave."

"But of course." Odd that someone needed to be granted leave. In this upheaval, he'd left his mind open to receive as many sharings as possible from trusted Resonants who knew his key signature, given them leave to interrupt him sleeping or awake if there were news. The two ghatti sat statue-still, wrapped in a web of concentration. "Who desires . . .?"

"**No one you know,**" P'wa interjected, "**as yet. She'll be introduced through us by Koom, one of our kind. She's been knocking at mind doors in vain, too reticent to enter without permission. Grant her that and you may commune directly.**"

Whom could he have overlooked? A woman, they said. He'd avoided Fabienne, fearful of opening some fissure Maurice could read through, trace back. But Fabienne knew his mental signature, had often contacted him to pass messages to Eadwin. A mellow ghatti voice slipped into his mind, male, he judged, polite but authoritative. "**Greetings, mindwalk if ye will. I am Koom, lofted high in our thoughts by my brethren across the river.**" Across the river? Roland shivered. The Canderisian side? And through Koom's mind he saw images of men and women laboring, chaining pontoons into position, others marching in tight formations, armed and ready. Oh, help us, Blessed Lady! War within and war without! he concluded and choked at the thought. Would he have to fight Maurice or the Canderisians first?

"**We can discuss where you'll strike your first blow later,**" Koom informed him, "**but for now, I ask you 'speak with Yulyn Biddlecomb. She's one of you, one of yours, those you honor as Resonants and we too often fear as Gleaners. She's unskilled, untutored in your ways, but she would help. Please impart your mindpattern.**"

A trick? Some backhanded, double-dealing trick devised by foreigners to make him reveal himself, reveal the plans he'd struggled to lay? Little good they were likely to achieve, but they were all he had, his only forlorn hope of toppling Maurice, freeing Arras, seeing Eadwin on the throne, if he returned alive. But outsiders? How could he consort with Canderisians to attain his goals? The mere idea galled him. No one in Marchmont had much use for foreigners, but he needed all the help he could find or make, unpalatable though it might be.

For the first time in his twenty-five years, Roland was convinced he'd had a revelation, although he detected a subtle nudge and flutish laughter sounding almost sheepish in his mind, embarrassed by the intrusion. The Bannerjees tended to be indirect, but even indirection was preferable to his own stymied thinking. *Why* did he despise outsiders without rhyme or reason? He'd liked those he'd met, valued their unstinting efforts to free Eadwin. But overall, the dread of sharing with foreigners constricted his throat, made his heart race fast with an unnamed dread, stomach churning as if he'd eaten tainted meat. Why such aversion?

Unaware, he traced his mental signature in the forefront of his mind, not the full key that disclosed all, but enough for at least a superficial converse. *"Hello? Hello?"* The sound blasted at his brain, cracked and exploded like a fire-heated rock. Retching, groaning, he dropped to his knees, cradling his head to muffle the din, only to discover that only he, of the humans at least, had reacted.

"Quickly! Explain how to modulate—she doesn't know how, she doesn't mean to hurt!" P'wa's words balmed his throbbing mind, channeled off the worst of the vibrations. Eyes involuntarily tearing, head still pounding, he gasped a few simple instructions, commands, drew on the memory-rhymes of childhood training. How could anyone be so undisciplined, so naively extravagant with her power? How fast could she learn? Quick enough to let him survive, he hoped, with or without the headache throbbing in his mind.

The voice reached again, hesitant now. *"I am so . . . sorry!"* And the "sorry" resounded with full-force anguish, rocking him on his heels until he could shoot back a terse reminder. *"Never have I consciously hurt another; but I do not know, we do not know our own strength or how best to use it."* A mind image of a copper-haired young woman, plainly dressed as if she wished to avoid notice, floated in his mind's eye, permeating the signature barricade he'd originally set. Somehow she'd unconsciously evaded his blockade, and with apprehension Roland granted her full access to his mind, tensed for the buffeting he expected. He wondered yet again, why him, why not the Bannerjees, someone, anyone more capable? But he was the closest one with even this much skill.

"Are you going to attack us?" he persisted, haunted by the images, the soldiers drilling, pontoons being dragged into place. It hit him; they wouldn't need the bridges to invade!

"We don't want to, but you've unlawfully imprisoned our people. If they were released unharmed, it might not be necessary." Still tremulous at her temerity, Yulyn's mindvoice faltered but retained a basic, instinctive control. What natural power, what a gift! He could sense the strain it caused her, strain and a hint of delight at the discovery.

"Maurice holds some of our people hostage as well as yours, and I don't think there's much chance he'll release them," he confessed. *"We've our own reasons to challenge Maurice, the filthy, usurping thief, though we've little chance of winning."*

"Then mightn't we . . .?" she hesitated, as if listening between levels, and he judged her concentration stretched to the snapping point between mental converse and outside speech. Dangerous for the uninitiated, a major risk, but she straddled the two worlds without faltering. *"The Monitor, Kyril van Beieven, bids me say he'd consider joining forces with you, if it would benefit both our causes."*

He considered, rudely chivvied her to the forefront of his mind to preserve his privacy, the deeper text of his thoughts, and she yielded without balking. No reason to fully trust her yet, regardless. Consort with outsiders, join forces with them? It clashed, warred against every fiber of his being and his heritage. But was his visceral dislike, his hatred, baseless? He gasped; she was ensconced within him again without so much as a "by your leave," when he had walled her out, compelled her to wait. *"It's a compulsion, isn't it?"* she asked diffidently. *"So deeply set you didn't even realize it had been triggered, though now that you know you can release it."*

A compulsion? Was that what the Bannerjees had prodded him to see? His head swam. Had they all been head-locked without even knowing it? But who had done it? How? And for so long, generation upon generation. It would explain so much, why no one in Marchmont really approved of foreigners, though they appreciated their trade. Commerce was one thing, friendship, equality, unity, another. How to cope with this revelation in the midst of the disaster around him? And how could she know such a thing? Compulsions were strictly forbidden, invoked only by the monarch under the most dire necessity. Constant the First had been clear about that, and of the burden they entailed.

"Perhaps it was necessary for outsiders not to know that your land boasts so many Resonants, so many skilled in mindspeech when we have so few in Canderis. And so feared and misunderstood," she offered as an afterthought.

Feared? How much more could he absorb? Steeling himself, Roland returned to the matter at hand. *"I would think on this and what your Monitor offers. But I must have time to decide."* It wasn't his decision to make, was it? If only he could reach Arras. *"The choice could change our land as we know it."*

"So could not choosing," she responded with pity. *"But better to choose for yourself than let others control you, whipsaw you back and forth as they may. That I know all too well."*

Spine prickling, he knew that she did, and in a way he didn't even like to imagine. *"Give me your signature so I can reach you."* And had to help her create one they could both identify, because she had no inkling as to who and what she really was. Helped her write it in her mind as shaky as a child scratching her first letters on a slate.

He sat silent after that, drained. Could the Bannerjees release the compulsion that engendered his hatred of outsiders? Or more important, would they? They loathed tampering with things beyond their sphere of influence, but Marchmont's survival was at stake.

Constant roamed from window to window, peering upward at the sky, ignoring the commotion in the courtyard below. Overcast, overcast, overcast! He needed sunlight, damn it all! He'd slipped upstairs from the library to the hibernaculum last night to drain the solar collectors and precious little recharging they'd had today. Consuming power like a wanton, a profligate—how Carrick would have laughed,

Carrick so rock-solid stable, unflappable, while he was impetuous. Yes, identical in everything but personality. Well, what choice did he have? The strain would be too much if he weren't frugal. But by the gods he'd drain every drop of energy he had to halt Maurice! Muttering, he shifted the drapings of his robe, fiddled with the dials of the energy pack strapped around his waist. Lower, yes, one more notch, hoard it for when it was necessary.

He resumed his walking, pace slower now, his feet dragging, breathing slowing. He hated the loginess, but best his heart slowed, his circulation, all his physical processes. He readjusted the dial yet again. Not his brain, he couldn't afford slowing there, but it drank so much energy. He reached a feather-light mental touch to the dungeons, found Arras asleep and let him sleep. That travesty of an iron mask! Did they really think it would completely stop Constant from reaching in or Arras from reaching out? Oh, it hindered all right, enough to make him cautious about reaching for Arras until the time was right. Maurice was an old-fashioned, ill-trained fool, enamored by the myths of what Resonants could and could not do! Except he had discovered the value of pain as a mind-enhancer, had trusted the legends and half-forgotten lore and made them work when he, Constant, had deemed them safely buried.

A rapping on the door and he turned, with effort. A good sign if someone knocked, it meant they wanted to alert him to their presence. Otherwise the guards flung open the door as they chose, with or without warning, a continual reminder of his powerlessness, that he was at their beck and call. The rapping let the guards think everything was normal; he'd already heard Fabienne's mindvoice outside. The guards had no Resonant ability, he'd tested that to his satisfaction. And that meant Maurice had no fears of him in that area. He sucked in his breath with a certain delight. The fool, to so badly underestimate him!

Fabienne entered with a tray of food. "I can't stay long, but I wanted to make sure you had nourishment." She spoke aloud, ensuring the guards would hear, but her mind bombarded his with her questions and fears.

"Thank you, my dear," he responded and despite himself, viewed the tray with interest. Food and drink meant little to him now, indeed, were basically unnecessary, probably hurtful as they made his body work harder, burn energy to digest them. But after so many long years in limbo, he couldn't avoid the desire for food, though the mental taste and savor of memory sometimes seemed superior to the actual meal. The aroma of the apple in his hand—when had he snatched it up?—assaulted his nose with the memory of the crisp, juicy flesh, the feel of the juice running down his chin. His jaws convulsed and he took one bite, and this time, this once, reality surpassed memory. Yes, fear could increase the savor of some things.

Reluctant, he put the rest of the apple back, listened to Fabienne's chitchat about the coronation, the disguise to their mental conversation. *"There's still no sign of Eadwin,"* Fabienne confessed, and her heart's pain caused his own to spasm.

"Perhaps that's just as well," he consoled. *"What Maurice doesn't have, he can't damage. And while there's still time, there's still hope."*

"The ceremony is for tomorrow at high noon. *He wants the ring, somehow he's guessed I have it."*

"I know, and I shall be ready for Maurice and his followers. Don't give up hope yet, my dear. Can't you sense the discontinuities, the changes? It's all around us if you read it rightly. I'm not the only one to have shaken off my shackles."

She shook her head. *"I've never been that adept. But I've heard rumors that an army has massed on the other side of the Spray, that the Canderisians are on the move. And so are Maurice's forces because he fears insurgency, though he won't admit it. Would that it were—and for Eadwin. What does it all mean, Constant?"*

"Potential, my dear, potential. Mayhap not what I would've liked, would've chosen, but we'll make do with what we have. It may be time for us to enjoy closer relations with our southern neighbors. Indeed, there's another kind of potential in some of those Canderisians, especially those Seekers. I still pray that Wilhelmina and I were right in believing what Rossmeer told us about the ghatti—that it wasn't a pipe-dream. Who would have ever thought it after all those years? I may have brought the best and brightest with me to Marchmont, but their strain is strong—and wild."

Fabienne didn't look much comforted but bowed, started to exit with the tray. "I can't stay much longer, there's so much to do for tomorrow." Despite himself, his hands grabbed for the tray, snatched it back toward him.

"I could have, I could have the rest of the apple, couldn't I?" His voice wheedled out loud, cajoling, begging not her, but himself for permission. He snatched at the apple. At least he could look at it. He licked the spot where he had bitten into it, the tartness, the sweetness, ecstasy!

But Fabienne regarded him strangely, perplexed by his behavior, holding the tray between them like a shield to fend him off. "Just the whims of an old man, my dear." And he set the apple back, tore himself away and went to gaze out the widow. Was anyone his own age left? No, of course not! Small wonder he thought of everyone as a lad or lass, generations removed regardless of their age. A vain hope that Callis still existed, the only one who could possibly understand the strange passage of time that had left him changed yet unchanged. He'd almost given up wishing for Carrick.

"I'll be in touch with Arras a bit later. If I learn anything of interest, I'll contrive to get word to you. Especially if it's anything to do with Eadwin."

She curtseyed, the deep, old-fashioned sweeping curtsey that he'd not seen in so many years. These young ones dipped and bobbed like awkward cranes. At least someone remembered some of the old ways. He sketched a hasty blessing in her direction without looking and knew she was out the door now, gone on her way, leaving him to his work.

When she contemplated the length of time they'd ridden and then traveled by boat to reach Arras's hideaway, not to mention their day's climb into the mountains, Doyce was amazed at how fast they traveled toward Sidonie. After patting the slaithe as if it were a living creature, Callis had gathered them together and informed them they would march.

In a way, she'd rather expected Callis would entice some secretive forest creatures from their glades, elk or deer, and they would ride triumphantly toward Sidonie. But Callis had read her unspoken daydream and said with great seriousness, "No, they don't enjoy being ridden unless I find it absolutely necessary."

"They who?" Eadwin queried but gave up, flustered by Nakum's giggles.

Callis joined Nakum's hand with Eadwin's, both reluctant at the bonding. "You are cousins, now learn to share." And with that she took Doyce's hand and led the way, their feet fleeter than the rising sun. And Doyce felt no tiredness as their feet flew along, or perhaps they stood still and the land flowed beneath them, anything seemed possible given the strength Callis derived from the earth.

"Are you tired, love?" she'd asked Khar once in concern. According to Muscadeine, Felix enjoyed this sort of jaunt, but she wasn't sure the ghatti did. *"Can you keep up?"*

Khar pranced about her feet. **"Amazingly enough, yes. I feel springy as a ghatten. As long as I stay close to you, the earth energy tingles up through my paw pads."**

"And you must always stay close in my mind and beside me, no matter what I've done to you in the past." And with that she stretched to caress the ghatta's head, let her fingers trail along the forehead stripes as if to imprint her very own mark.

Callis tugged her straight, swung their joined arms companionably. "See what you've been missing in your hurried quest to own the world?" And she did, every living thing emerged vivid and luminous in her gaze, as if she'd never truly plumbed the inner essence of anything before today. And so must the blind feel on recovering their vision, she decided. A world of wonders beyond possession.

A moment of breathless panic seized her as a farm cart came trundling down the road toward them. "They'll see us!" she exclaimed.

"No they won't, as long as we don't stand in the middle of the road. It upsets the horses." Before Doyce could fret any more, Callis pulled her to one shoulder, while Nakum took Eadwin to the other side, and the cart rolled by as if they were invisible.

"No, not invisible, but so much a part of the land that we belong to it, can remain unnoticed if we choose." On they went, covering more ground than Doyce could conceive possible, never once feeling hunger, thirst, or tiredness, until they approached the very walls of Sidonie. But this time no trumpets heralded their arrival. And a part of her would have been relieved to have seen Ignacio trotting down the stairs, stumping and grumping, muttonchops flexing as he screwed up his face in dismay at the late arrivals.

"Now what?" For once she held her curiosity at bay, because every recent experience had become more and more curious. Callis would know, just as she had everything else.

But Callis turned in little circles, propelling Doyce along with her. Nakum, obedient but unsure, spun Eadwin, while the three ghatti and Felix sat and watched. "Just don't let go of him," Callis commanded her grandson, "no matter how much he struggles to free himself." She continued her circular survey. Finally, a bit aggrievedly, "Well, I can't know everything . . . immediately. The earth has been much altered here since my time, but the power still resides, if only I can find a reference point. Build, build, build! That's all your people know how to do," she scolded Doyce and Eadwin. "Destroy and build, destroy and build—and who are you to say that what's built is superior to what the earth held before? Even Constant couldn't understand that, much as I argued with him."

Despite what she knew, Doyce still retained the uneasy feeling that they must be presenting an interesting spectacle to the guards on watch on the walls, but again no one noticed their presence.

Eadwin struggled to break Nakum's grip. "We're here! I can't wait any longer! I must go see Mother, tell her that I'm alive. She can't bear much more and neither can I!"

"You will not," Callis informed him, implacable. "The time is not yet ripe." He subsided, but resentment showed clearly in his stance.

"Ah!" Callis pointed her free hand. A small outbuilding, half decayed and falling down with age, huddled against the outer ring wall. What it had once been used for, Doyce had no idea, but clearly no one had bothered with it for years. "Now this at least is returning to the way it should be," Callis sounded relieved. "It was well-built, but the earth's power is stronger, drawing it back to its beginnings.

"And its beginnings," she continued triumphantly, "were when Constant had it built as a gardener's shed. At last I know exactly where we are and how we can enter!"

And inside among the dry rot and dust of generations, Callis rooted around until she found the trapdoor cunningly hidden in the floor. "Silly old Constant," she said lovingly, "perhaps I should have given you more credit. But you did promise I'd never have to use the back door while you were King! Oh, well, needs must."

✤

Fur brushed his knuckles and he stiffened, his breath hot and fetid, thrown back at him from the restraining face plate of the helmet. He pushed rigid against the wall, every muscle tensed. Rats! Wycherley had been right. How he hated them! When he could see, he could tolerate them, but not now, not like this. Ignacio had sworn that no rats inhabited "his" castle while he was chamberlain. Well, old friend, how often have you had the dungeons turned out recently? Ah, have mercy! The thing was crawling on his lap! He readied himself to buck it off.

"Oh, please don't," a voice begged in his mind. **"So lonely, so confused."**

"Who?" he gasped, shrinking back, spine digging against the stone wall, manacles drawing him up short.

"Ah, I am not myself." Contrition in the tone. **"May I mindwalk? You're not one of us, but I've no one else to turn to."**

The ghatta N'oor, he realized, not a rat, and his heart steadied, his muscles relaxed.

"Rat? Oh, dear, dear me! So sorry, so very sorry." And the furred form started to pour from his lap until he managed to stretch his chained hand to its furthest extension, give a choppy but reassuring stroke to the fur.

Turning twice, she resettled herself, and he continued stroking, sensed a snag, his cuff caught on her earring, the hoop, he decided. He disentangled himself as politely as possible and resumed stroking, the purring vibrations, reluctant at first, tingling his fingers. The warmth on his thighs felt good.

"Is it day or night, little one?"

"Oh, night, still," she assured him, **"though there's never enough light for you to tell. We know, though."**

"Well, with this helmet on, I've even less chance of being able to tell," he snapped. *"I take it everyone's asleep."*

A gentle affirmative, a scene of dozing figures spilled across the cell, sleep-felled despite the discomfort of cold, damp stone, aged straw. *"Why aren't you cuddled with Aelbert, little one?"*

The purring stopped and she gathered herself to spring away. **"Because I don't know, I just don't know anymore!"** she wailed and he could share the sense of betrayal and shame washing over her. **"He's tightroped between Truth and Not Truth. He is not bad,** *not* **bad,"** she emphasized, as much to reassure herself as him, **"but the slightest breeze could topple him, and I don't know if he can resist! I've tried so hard to guide him, but something gnaws deeper than I can reach. A wanting, a yearning I can't satisfy no matter how hard I try! I'm not enough for him, not sufficient."** Agitated claws punctured his thigh, and he grunted in pain, shifting to ease them.

"You see! All I do is hurt, not help! Even you!" And the claws retracted one by one.

"Have faith, little one. What would happen if you didn't help, ceased trying?" He managed, by touch, to scratch under her chin with one finger. *"All I can do is try, and it may not be enough, but I would hate myself as a coward if I didn't."*

"Ah, but must I break faith with my breed or with my Bond? Betray one or the other?" Anguish made her body shiver.

A cruel quandary. And he had no answer for that because he knew how it felt to be accused of betrayal, justly or unjustly. Perhaps another question would guide her or at least inform him. *"Do you have any idea what Aelbert will do during the coronation ceremony? I know Maurice has assigned him a role to play—and you as well, I suspect."*

She spoke with reluctance. **"He wants Aelbert to use me to Truth-Seek, say that Maurice is rightful heir to the throne. And I can't do that! That's lying and ghatti cannot lie! But Maurice doesn't suspect what Aelbert really plans to say—and while what he plans is truth, it still is not the whole Truth. I don't know if I can convince him to see because he wants it so badly."**

"So what is it he believes, this truth that is at least some of the truth?" He was genuinely curious, and any foreshadowing of what would happen tomorrow might give him an edge.

"I can't tell. It isn't meant to be shared."

His hands fisted and he wanted to shake the knowledge out of her, but he could never ill-treat an animal like that, not any animal, and most especially a thinking, speaking being such as herself. Tantamount to hurting one of his own kind. He mentally apologized because he knew the thought had reached her. **"I know,"** she sighed. **"We aren't always easy to live with—or without. Aelbert says I'm always on the wrong side of his mind—wanting in when I am out, and out when I am in."**

"There's a favor you might grant me, if you would?" The idea had come to him of a sudden, but he wouldn't hope too much. *"Could you reach your mind and check if Harry is anywhere near? If he is, then I may hope that Eadwin is as well."* Was it possible to have a ruler, a rightful ruler of the blood royale who did not possess the abilities of a Resonant? Still, better one without than one with twisted, perverted skills.

"I can try. This new one is hard to 'speak, but he projects strongly. If he's anywhere near, I should be able to reach him." She sat straight in his lap, her spine flexing like a serpent's under his fingers, every hair on her body alert.

"Ah, he is!" And then, more excitedly, **"And Saam and Khar as well! All of them near, as well as someone, something I've never sensed before. What would you have me say?"**

A risk to communicate, but he surmised neither Maurice nor Jampolis were listening for ghatti voices. *"Have Doyce contact the Bannerjees. Find out what's afoot."* And at the end, Arras appealed, *"I hope you're not too burdened, my sweet N'oor, with all this information? Some of it Aelbert should not have, you know."*

"I know. But what shall I do about Aelbert?"

He was at a loss, because he couldn't determine how Aelbert fit into the puzzle, but he knew that Aelbert held the key. Whether Aelbert was cognizant of what lurked—for better or for worse—behind the door his key would unlock was another puzzle. He regained his voice at last. *"Love him, N'oor. Love him, support him as much as you can, counterbalance his fears, the yearnings in him. Just try as best you can. Have faith."*

Where they wandered beneath the city since entering the tunnel at the gardener's hut, she had no idea, but she sensed they gravitated toward the heart, the castle proper. After

their previous joyous progress above ground, Callis moved
with slow prudence, almost vacillating as if her memories of
these paths were ancient, loath to surface in her mind.

"No, I haven't forgotten the way, but the memories are
hard to bear sometimes."

At that moment Hru'rul slammed Eadwin with a large,
furry paw. **"Arras! Arras sending word. Little ghatta
N'oor reaching out to me!"**

Khar broke in. **"N'oor says he wants us to contact the
Bannerjees."**

"Wonderful!" she exploded. "How does he expect us to
do that? Eadwin has no Resonant abilities. Are we supposed
to just stroll up out of the depths and inquire about directions?" Her palpable frustration reflected her sense of im-
pending danger, the idyll with Callis impossibly distant.

Callis scratched Hru'rul's ears, taming his excitement.
"No, it's easier than that. We'll have a guide shortly, I can
sense his nearness." As if her good spirits had been restored, Callis picked up her pace. "I sense he's a nice
young man, organized, resolute, and knowledgeable about
these tunnels, at least in part. Come along." Doyce,
Nakum, Eadwin, and the animals followed after, Eadwin
exclaiming under his breath as he realized their location.

Nakum gave a start of delight. "The wine cellars!" he announced as if he were a tour guide.

Racks of green wine bottles slanted downward to keep
corks moist, the temperature cool but comfortable, neither
too humid nor too dry. Barrels of ale pyramided along one
wall. And in the circle of lantern light ahead, Ezequiel de-
canted a bottle of red wine, mouth screwed up in concentration, eyes fixed on the candle shining through the bottle to
judge when the sediment would shift.

Callis nudged Nakum. "Go, ask his aid." But mischievous, he shooed Saam ahead, waiting expectantly for the
ghatt to reveal himself.

"Saam!" Ezequiel exclaimed with gladness. "Nakum?"
And Felix bounded out, tail wagging, thumping the table leg,
threatening to upset everything. Listening gravely while
Nakum explained the situation, Ezequiel grabbed the lantern
and led them through tunnels, then slipped them out a side
door and through the night streets to the Bannerjees and the
Hospice.

Once they'd halted, hidden, barely breathing as twelve of

he House Guards marched by. "Looking for deserters," Ezequiel had explained once they'd passed. "Each day more soldiers and common folk slip outside the gates to join Eadwin's cause." With shy pride in that statement, and an inability to look Eadwin in the eye, the young man was clearly oo overawed to face his new hero.

Once inside the Hospice, Doyce was shocked by the coolness of the Bannerjees' reception, or at least by Wyn's coolness. Yes, the emerald on the left hand, it must be Wyn, the solemn, serious one, while Dwyna cooed with excitement over Khar, the new ghatti, and the handsome dog. How much help she could expect, she wasn't sure; both were overly punctilious about the extent of their involvement.

"We've already promised Ignacio we'll be there at the coronation tomorrow," Wyn admitted begrudgingly. "I'd prefer to ignore the whole thing, but if you can spirit Arras and the others out, we'll divert Jampolis. He's earned our enmity. Eumedico indeed!"

Dwyna giggled, "Tweak him a bit more soundly than before?" And her twin gave her a withering glance. "What about Maurice?"

"That's their problem. He is of the blood royale after all. I can't bring myself . . ." she let the words nearly die, shivered, "to fight fire with fire."

Dwyna tucked a protective arm around Eadwin. "You can stay in the balcony, watch with us. Let the others proclaim you King, but it's too early for you to make an appearance, not with Maurice there. Who knows what else he might do to you? Unless . . ." she pleaded to Wyn.

"No, absolutely not. Dwyna, I forbid it!" A stamping foot emphasized Wyn's point. "It's not right to tamper with the compulsion Maurice laid on him. We agreed not to tamper with the general compulsion regarding foreigners, didn't we? It's possible for them to break those bonds themselves without us meddling."

"But it's our duty to mend that which has been broken, to heal the crippled." Dwyna pressed home her advantage. "Our humiliation is that we allowed this to happen, refused to see it for what it was. If we do nothing to save Eadwin, we're as guilty of misusing our powers as Maurice!"

Browbeaten, stymied, Wyn rounded on Callis. "Why didn't you release him? You possess the power, I can sense ."

"It is not my role," Callis responded without elaborating. "That's not what my power is meant for. It's your decision."

Wyn helplessly regarded her twin. "Mayhap I overreacted. Can we do it? Dare we? Would you at least lend us your strength?" she appealed to Callis.

While each twin placed a free hand on Eadwin's temple, the Erakwan woman joined her hands to theirs, creating an unbroken circle. Eyes shut tight, faces taut, little sweat beads blossomed along their hairlines. Without warning, Eadwin jerked free, contact broken, eyes alight. "Yes!" he exclaimed, "Yes! It's not just Hru'rul I can hear inside my head, I can hear you, know what you're saying! Never have I been so blessed, so doubly-blessed by this and by Hru'rul! Thank you!" He fell to his knees, kissed their hands.

"Whatever you do, *don't* contact Fabienne," Wyn warned. "Don't try to contact anyone until you've had practice. We can't afford to give the game away now. We'll contact Roland and Arras, let them know what to expect."

And with that they went back to rehearsing their plans to disrupt the ceremony on the morrow. For better or worse, Doyce decided, the Bannerjee twins had shifted from neutrality to involvement whether they admitted it or not.

They'd been given leave to wash and change into their dress uniforms, and the unexpected courtesy surprised Jenret. He mulled it over as he and Syndar Saffron eased Bard into the dark green jacket, restrapping his arm, and settled the dress tunic over his head and sashed it. Sarrett and Jacobia sorted and matched uniform pieces from the pile the guards had tossed on the floor.

"Jenret, I'm afraid you may have to do with only one boot," Sarrett teased as she retrieved a polished boot and set it aside. "Aelbert, I think all of your dress uniform as Monitor's representative is here." Aelbert sat slumped in the corner, unresponsive.

Jacobia waved a flounced and ruched overskirt in the air, semaphoring her delight. "Ooh, I think this must be for me!" Then, contrite, she offered it to Sarrett, "Unless you'd like to wear it?"

"No, dear, I belong in Seeker garb. It's a gem, though,"

arrett considered it, holding it this way and that, "but I
ink it's more Syndar's color, don't you?"

"Mine as well, with that violet trim, I'd say," Jacobia re-
orted as Syndar growled an inarticulate comment, the sound
f any man aware he's being harried, plagued by women.
After all, our eyes are exactly the same shade . . ." and she
opped short as Syndar whirled around, shock and longing
lain on his ugly, scarred face. Jacobia burst into tears.

With more compassion than he thought he could muster,
enret clasped Syndar's upper arm, restraining him, muscles
unching under his hand. Syndar didn't move, stood riveted
o the floor. "This isn't the time or the place for it. Our very
ves are at stake."

"And if not now, there may not be a *then*!" Syndar jerked
imself away, and began to walk stiffly in Jacobia's direc-
on. He shot back over his shoulder, "For your mother's
ake, I'm sorry, Jenret, more sorry than you can imagine.
nd for Jadrian's as well, but what's done is done. I can't
ce dying without Jacobia knowing the truth! It's all I have
ft to bequeath her. Maybe it's selfish of me, but I have to
y to make it right."

The voice came muffled to Jenret's ear, at about knee-
vel, he'd forgotten Arras Muscadeine sitting there, chained
id patient. He was thankful it was out loud instead of in-
de his head. "Let it be, Wycherley. He needs it for his
ul's sake, and Jacobia for hers as well, though she may not
alize it yet. This won't be the first or the last by-blow ac-
owledged today, I fear."

With a stiff nod of dispensation, Jenret indicated the far
orner of the cell to Syndar. "The most privacy I can pro-
de." As hesitant as if he handled fine china, Syndar slipped
s arm around Jacobia's shoulders and drew her to him as
ey stepped away, but she balked, holding out her hand in
earning for Jenret.

Jacobia's upper lip trembled as she fought back tears. "If
ou'd claim a daughter, you'd best prepare for a stepson as
ell. We come as a package, and you can't split the set."

"Nor did I ever intend to," Syndar responded, although he
id Jenret traded wary looks, sizing each other up, judging
e bounds of a possible new relationship. "For what it's
orth, this many years too late, I apologize to you both.
our mother and I aren't ashamed of what we did," he
ared at them, defying them to contradict his words, "nor of

what came of it—Jacobia. We loved each other and needed each other because our losses were so great. If you'd accept me as your father," he managed a jerky bow to Jacobia, "I'd be honored. And if you," he included Jenret, "would accept me in addition to your own father, share the burdens that men share with men, I'd hold that trust in high esteem."

Wordlessly, Jacobia took Syndar's hand, staring with hopeful longing at Jenret. The pause lengthened, Jenret unmoving, emotions masked. "I won't lose a brother to gain a father, Jenner. Please!" And at last Jenret placed his hand on theirs.

Aelbert rocked himself back and forth in the corner, ignored. Not the first or the last by-blow acknowledged today—not the first, not the last. *"Oh, N'oor, I need you so much! Help me have faith in myself and what I must do!"*

Horns, those damnable horns! The blast bored through Nakum's ears, a torment, torture. Letting the curtain fall, he drew deeper into the darkness and clapped hands over ears. **"Not musically inclined?"** Saam's ears flattened in sympathy. **"Sounds like something Felix would want to out-howl."**

Doyce took his place at the drapings' overlap and peered out. He hissed a warning. "Not too close, don't slide your toe under the drape!" The tapestries hung out from the wall only about thirty centimeters, marginal space at best. Dressed again in Rolf's uniform, she jerked her foot clear but gave no other indication she'd heard, still pondering how they'd managed to get inside. After Ezequiel had returned them to the castle, they had rested for the night, Eadwin in an agony of rising expectations. But come late morning they'd discovered it was taking them too long to move stealthily through the back hallways, avoiding servants on a thousand-and-one harried errands for the ceremonies. Their random patterns had been difficult to outguess and yet had served to their advantage, everyone so glassy-eyed intent on errands they barely registered anything beyond the tasks they'd been assigned to perform.

Or so she'd thought until she spotted Ezequiel in an alcove, face drenched with sweat, hand pressed to his temples. "Hurry, go, go!" he'd implored. "They're trained to obey mind commands, but I can redirect them just so long before they realize I'm not Ignacio. He'll take over downstairs, ease your passage through, but he's juggling all Maurice's needs as well. Roland's somewhere about, but he's gotten lost in the tunnels again."

Callis had ghosted to Ezequiel's side, put a palm on his brow. Eyes clearing, the strain evaporating from his face, Ezequiel whispered, "Thank you!" and the servants had glided about their tasks even more efficiently, any haunting reminder of their unorthodox passage completely obliterated from their thoughts.

"I'm going to see how Eadwin's doing," Nakum interrupted her musings and slipped the length of the rear wall, the drapery never shivering or billowing as he eeled along. Doyce looked out again, almost jumping out of her skin as the feathers of Callis's overrobe stroked the back of her neck, her ear.

"The hall is filling." A statement, not a question, although Callis hadn't bothered looking. Eye at the chink, Doyce watched swirls of people flowing through the main rear entrance, others entering through the two sets of side doors. Knots of color and activity, low-pitched buzzing, heads turning, evaluating. A few arguments over precedence, who would sit where, who outranked whom were settled by stony-faced guards armed not with decorative ceremonial weaponry, but with swords that had seen hard use, comfortable to grip, the hand's logical extension. Their uniforms were those of the House Guards, but they appeared to be true soldiers, and she feared Maurice had compulsed at least some of Arras's troops into serving him. Callis made a disgruntled tsk-ing sound. Few of the guests boasted arms; those who were appeared high ranking and reluctant to be parted from their weapons. The ribbon rosettes ostentatiously displayed determined who claimed prime positions close to the empty throne and who sat farther distant, who kept their weapons and who surrendered them.

Additional liveried guards ringed the room's perimeter, all armed with halberds. **"Excellent for keeping unruly people at arm's length,"** Khar noted. **"Just as we use our claws."**

The balcony that ran around the walls was unguarded, deserted for the moment. Strange; she was no strategist, but she would have mounted guards there, armed with bows and arrows or the crossbows the Marchmontians favored. Again,

Callis picked up her thought without glimpsing what she saw. "Time enough to station them there. Why make the guests any more uneasy. Though guests may not be the word for them, whether they realize it or not."

Once more the trumpets blared a crescendo, and the crowd shifted and whispered, shushed itself, and settled with uneasy rustlings and creakings. All faces turned expectantly toward the empty throne, some studiously neutral, others excited, some suffused with smoldering anger.

Bewildered, white hair and beard in wispy disarray, Constant wavered and tottered into the hall, Fabienne on his arm. Doyce wondered who escorted the other. Fabienne's head was high, her carriage regal, but her poise revealed nothing. Patting the old man's hand, she allowed him to conduct her to an elaborately decorated chair positioned a step lower than the throne. After seating her and kissing her hand, he laboriously descended to ground level, paused to bow once to the empty throne, and assumed his place, easing into a humbler chair a step below Fabienne's, the traditional Steward's seat that he'd spurned before.

Now, down the center aisle marched the seven Ministration Lords, led by Internal Affairs Lord Emeril Alighieri escorting a frightened Valeria Condorcet in a cruel grip, DeSaulniers with Giselle Goelet, Boersma paired with Jules Jampolis. Separate as befitting his dual status as Lord of Defense and Lord of the North Domain, Maurice walked at a regal, dignified pace, bejeweled and begemmed, clothed in lush velvets and satins, but head bare, shoulders naked of a robe of office. The tight little smile on his face, the way he cast his head from side to side, the acknowledging tilt, sometimes with eye contact, sometimes with bare politeness, more an assessment, really, chilled Doyce. How many would meet Maurice's standards, how many not, and what would befall those who didn't?

Behind Maurice followed the other Domain Lords, the wide shape of Quaintance Mercilot unescorted, glaring left and right but most of all at Maurice's unprotected back, then Prosper Napier supporting a week-kneed Auguste Vannevar. The three pairs of Ministration Lords split, forming wings, Maurice at their apex. With a deep genuflection, Alighieri bowed to Maurice, then rose and returned to his position so that Maurice might ascend the steps to the throne. To Doyce's ears each quiet but purposeful step sounded a note of doom. He bowed to the throne, turned his back to it, and greedily surveyed his audience. Ignacio and Ezequiel appeared from behind the throne, one bearing royal purple robes, the other the crown on a velvet pillow. Another trumpet blast peeled forth.

"We Lords are assembled here today to witness the coronation of a king, a king of the blood royale worthy of the throne." Alighieri's voice rang out, overriding the great hall's heavy silence. "It is fitting that Maurice Louvois Diederick Clairvaux rule us, not only because of his direct descent from our revered Venable Constant, his great-great-great grandfather, but also because we are persuaded beyond doubt that his ascension nobly fulfills our late Queen Wilhelmina's dying admonition: 'Wait for the ghatti. The ghatti will show you the truth.'

"And so the ghatti shall, wondrous strange as it may seem," Alighieri continued smoothly. "Our 'beloved,' " as he put a sneering twist to "beloved," "Steward Constant Minor, who has so dutifully held the reins of governance during this time of transition, is prepared to reveal the mechanism of truth to you, as it is his obligation to tend the throne until a true successor is named and crowned. Let us now hear Constant Minor's words of wisdom regarding the ghatti." And with that Alighieri took up a position near Fabienne, who recoiled and then sat straight, unmoving.

Doyce's breath caught in her throat as Constant pressed against the arms of the chair and painstakingly levered himself to his feet, standing as if lost. No longer was this the bouncy, cheeky little man who had so intrigued her on their first meeting, a man who had nourished himself with the crowd's adoration. This man was frail, a wisp of hoarded strength holding him upright, the blue eyes dim, the walk the shaky caution of old, fragile bones, wasted muscles. Callis was by her side, finally straining to gaze between the draperies. "Ah, poor, poor Venny," she sighed. "Was it worth it, love? Well, only you can be the judge of that." And for a moment his head rose, his eyes sparkled, as if he sensed someone hidden from him, someone hidden not just in the literal sense but lost to him by time and distance. Then, just as abruptly, his head dropped and he shuffled forward, feet making a sad, distant whisper against the floor.

"Bring forth our visitors from our sister-land Canderis. Though we have branched and grown in different directions,

our common beginnings give them a stake in seeing justice
impartially served," he quavered, making a jerky, halting
motion like a broken-winged bird. Guards swung open the
door to Constant's right and in paraded Aelbert Orsborne
and N'oor, followed by Jenret and Rawn, Jacobia and
Syndar Saffron, Sarrett and T'ss, Bard and M'wa. Last, and
restrained by a guard on either side, each holding his man-
acle chains, Arras Muscadeine, still helmeted, still stepping
blindly, head ceaselessly moving like a cobra testing the
very air for scents. Someone had affixed a plume of jaunty
purple feathers to the helmet, the feathers swaying, then
stilling, as he lifted his head to the balcony.

All eyes following them, Aelbert and N'oor approached
while the others were herded to the side, aligned as if at attention. "Further, let it be attested that the traitor Arras
Muscadeine, stripped of his rank of Chevalier Capitain,
masked to protect the innocent from the warped use of his
Resonant ability, has been summoned to bear witness to our
clemency and justice, and to be formally discredited before
his peers and betters. His punishment shall be meted out
later." Constant stared straight ahead as he concluded his little speech, the words rolling by rote off his tongue.

"Now, will the Canderisian Special Envoy please declare
himself?" Aelbert strode stiffly beside Constant, his whey-
colored face bruised, hair slicked back, still indented by the
marks of the comb. For once his expression revealed a definition and character so often deferentially absent, a sense of
deep privation, not of food, of sleep, but of something
deeper, more immeasurably private. N'oor walked at his
side, a calculated distance from him as if to denote her inde-
pendence. Her fur looked ill-groomed, tail drooping almost
to the floor, yet her eyes shone with resolve as if she'd
warred within herself and won.

Aelbert bowed toward Maurice, a deep, sweeping gesture
with far more humility than the one he'd rehearsed for that
first formal meeting with Constant. He'd positioned himself
sideways, able to gaze up at Maurice and equally able to address the crowd without rudely turning his back to the
throne. "I intro . . ." he started to speak, but paused, mouth
open, then shut it hard. Constant's bony arm poked out and
his fingers rapped Aelbert in the ribs. Somehow his whisper
encompassed the furthest reaches of the room. "What's the
matter, lad, cat got your tongue?" A sprinkling of laughter,

sharply stifled, broke out in various parts of the room, including the balcony, where a red and green striped shawl flashed in momentary view, like a familiar wave from a friend. It made Doyce want to giggle with relief; the Bannerjees had come as promised!

With a look of pure hatred crimsoning him from neck to crown, Aelbert jerked clear and compulsively straightened his tabard, dissociating himself from the intrusion. "I introduce myself to you as Aelbert Orsborne, Seeker Veritas, Bondmate of N'oor, and aide-de-camp to the Canderisian Monitor Kyril van Beieven. In the absence of Doyce Marbon, who violated protective custody to consort with your traitor Arras Muscadeine, I assume her place and authority as Special Envoy."

Livid with anger, Doyce started to part the drapes. Callis restrained her with a whispered "Not yet."

He had found his voice now, a voice that surpassed his unprepossessing appearance, an orator's voice that soared and fell, intimately bound his listeners to him, left them hanging on his words. "But it is as a Seeker Veritas that I have been asked to confirm Maurice Louvois Diederick Clairvaux as your King. Those of you gifted as Resonants are intimately familiar with mind skills, but you may be unaware that Seekers Veritas boast a similar power—and perhaps a greater one." He paused, let it sink in. "We cannot read minds as you do, but our Bondmates offer us the insight to explore the human mind and—more than that—they are infallible in judging the truth, in knowing whether a person thinks one thing but speaks another, lies to others or to himself. No one, *no one* can escape the ghatti's righteous assessment of the truth. No escape," he emphasized. "No lies can prevail when a ghatt or ghatta reads the truth."

Could he compel poor N'oor to lie? The poor little beast with her multi-toed paws and wistful yearning. *"Khar, we've got to stop him, we've got to stop Aelbert and N'oor! What are we going to do?"*

"First, trust in N'oor a bit more. She is ghatti." Khar responded with slow dignity. **"And give Aelbert what trust you can, for he still truly does not know which way to turn, although he believes he does. He's hidden from himself too long."**

Aelbert beckoned the guards to lead Muscadeine forward. "If a man with the very power to alter your minds, convince others to treason, can be made to admit the truth, will you not believe?" he beseeched the crowd. Jules Jampolis positioned himself on Muscadeine's other side, ostensibly offering assistance in unlocking the helmet, but fixated on the balcony above him.

Khar nudged her leg, and Callis pressed the flat of her hand against her back, the other hand parting the drapes as she pushed her through. Just as they'd rehearsed in the scanty time available—the Bannerjees would attempt to neutralize Jules Jampolis, not let him hurt Muscadeine, while she caused a diversion. If they could only free Arras, he could rally additional support for Eadwin's cause.

At first no one noticed her abrupt entry, but the metronomic clicking of her boot heels as she marched across the floor finally attracted everyone's attention. Center stage, make it yours or someone will steal it from you. "Aelbert Orsborne, I thank you for your assistance, but not for your attempt to attain a position you've no right to claim, just as Maurice has no right to claim the throne." She swung to face the audience. "As you can see, I am not missing, nor have I consorted with any traitor, only listened to the truths that all sides spoke. Even the condemned can speak truth while the innocent attempt to lie. How innocent Maurice may be remains for you to judge, because judgment, not punishment, is the Seekers Veritas way.

"I am Doyce Marbon, Aelbert Orsborne's superior in both Seeker Veritas ranking and as Special Envoy. If you would hear the truth, you must hear it from me and my Bond, the ghatta Khar'pern. Yet confirmation must come from you." She wished she could gauge Maurice's expression, but she couldn't spare the distraction.

Khar had no such compunction. **"Shading toward plum purple, I'd say. The fruit kind and the explosive kind."**

With a clenched jaw she ground her snicker into bits. "Before Khar and I ask Arras Muscadeine to publicly identify the rightful heir, we would ask one who retains the respect and love of all. She faithfully served your late Queen and shared nearly thirty years of her life as the wife of Maurice Louvois Diederick Clairvaux. Fabienne Marie Elizalde Clairvaux, name for us the rightful ruler of Marchmont. Understand clearly that the ghatta Khar'pern and the other ghatti here assembled will determine if you speak truth or falsehood."

Without a look to either side, Fabienne rose, hope dancing in her eyes. "Let the ghatti and the Blessed Lady be my witnesses. The true and rightful heir to Marchmont is my son, Eadwin, fathered by Prince Maarten shortly before his untimely death. Had he lived, we would have married, and Eadwin been declared his legitimate heir."

"But Eadwin is dead, dead, dead! He has to be! The last searchers utterly disappeared without a trace. Whatever powers that mountain may have, Eadwin is too weak to withstand them and live!" Maurice roared. "And you lie to stab me in the heart, humiliate me in front of everyone!"

A voice rang out from above. "She does not lie, nor am I dead! And I won't allow you to dishonor Mother with your venomous lies, your plots, your schemes, or any more of your wanton killings!" Eadwin sprang down the spiral steps from the balcony two at a time, Nakum, Saam, and Hru'rul pounding in his wake. Hru'rul stalked Jampolis, hissing, the Ministration Lord shrinking clear of Muscadeine, helmet still clamped in place. Ignoring the cowering Jampolis, the wild ghatt advanced on the throne, speckled yellow eyes measuring Maurice from head to toe.

"You've tortured Mother and me too long to enhance the warped strength you use to mold the minds of others. The Bannerjees have pierced the veil you used to shroud my Resonant skills for so many years. What you accuse an innocent man, Arras Muscadeine, of is only what you've done yourself to further your own ends. It will stop now!"

Those closest to the throne heard Muscadeine's urgent prompt, "The ring, Eadwin, show them the ring!"

Eadwin thrust his hand high, the light reflecting, warming against the glowing ambered gem in his ring. "Know now that I am Maarten's son. See this his ring that he gave my mother to pledge his troth, though death overtook him before they could wed. You all know the history of these rings, how three were crafted from the tears of the arborfer by ancient Erakwa, and given to our first ruler, Constant, as a token of amity and our promise to protect the land and the arborfers. Venable Constant wore one, his consort the second, and his heir the third. And so they were venerated, handed down from generation to generation, until finally our beloved Wilhelmina wore the largest one, and bequeathed the others to her brothers, Maarten and Ludo. And Ludo's has at last been found as well, safely secured by his grandson—and my younger cousin—the Erakwan Nakum. I pray that you'll grant me the ruler's ring to pair with the one I have by right of blood!"

"By my faith, that *is* Maarten's ring!" Quaintance Mercilot boomed out. "Clever lads to protect them so!" She grabbed Eadwin's hand and held it aloft in victory. "Now for the ruler's ring!" shouted Boersma, and other hardy souls took up the cry.

Hiding first behind Ignacio, then Ezequiel to avoid Hru'rul's stalking wrath, Maurice shouted, "Bastard he is, but not Maarten's!" but few heard.

Aelbert's eyes glistened with avidity. "Thief! By rights that ring should have been mine!" He pushed to Nakum's side, striving to rip Nakum's earth-bond free, but he held it firm, pushed Aelbert back with a melancholy comprehension of his pain, his longing. "That ring should have been mine by right, it's my heritage! Mama told me, described it time and time again, how she'd played with it on her father's hand when he came to visit. Ludo left her mother unwed, with a bastard daughter, disowned, dishonored, a daughter who became a tavern slut, sleeping with anyone who'd pay and drinking up most of the money. What does a child know of hope with a mother like that, but I always believed I'd find where I rightfully belonged! Or would make it happen, no matter what, no matter who I hurt! Now I'm nothing again. Someone else always comes first! When will I ever be good enough?" Breathless, he shoved between Nakum and Eadwin and disappeared, N'oor scampering at his heels, looking strangely relieved.

"Well, we've found Ludo's grandsons, or they've found us," Arras Muscadeine muttered inside his helmet.

This wasn't going the way they'd rehearsed. Struggling to reattract the crowd's attention back to her and conclude what was fast becoming a farce, Doyce desperately shouted, "The ghatti know the truth in the hearts of Eadwin and Fabienne and the truth that Maurice connived to disinherit the rightful heir." Hopeless!

The crowd had surged to its feet, some ripping rosettes of Maurice's colors from their clothes, others arguing and fighting. Quaintance Mercilot's booming laugh mingled with the Bannerjees' high-pitched giggles as they hung over the balcony, waving. Maurice's loyalist guards swooped in, struggling to maintain order as fighting began to erupt. Bursting through the closed main doors at the rear of the hall, a sentry rushed down the aisle, shouting "Invasion! The Canderisians are massing on our side of the river! They march toward Sidonie!" The distraction the Bannerjees had promised, no invasion yet but a subtle insinuation into susceptible human brains, already prone to dislike and distrust foreigners. Or, Doyce felt a chill ripple through her, had Roland succeeded in an alliance with the Monitor?

People dashed this way and that, trying to break through the guarded doors; men and women screamed, shouted, cursed. A tugging at her arm and Doyce at last noted that Constant was beseeching her attention. "Now," he mentioned politely, "might be an excellent time for an exit. Especially if you'd like to stop the invasion. The real one that's coming."

"What about Maurice?"

"He hasn't won yet, and Eadwin and Arras and I don't intend to let him. But it's time to regroup and survey our options. Too many innocent people could be hurt." And he was herding them toward the draperies behind the throne, Maurice apoplectic in the middle of a tangled throng, feebly fending off Hru'rul with his unworn royal robe. Jampolis and Alighieri shouted orders, countermanding each other, Jampolis nervously peering at the balcony for further signs of activity, trying to make sense out of chaos. Boersma and Goelet danced an insolent jig of premature triumph, elbows linked, spinning each other round, while Quaintance clapped the beat. "Little exit I had made for myself some years ago," Constant gave a deprecative wave of his hand, but continued more eagerly, "Is Callis truly with you? I sensed her, but I couldn't believe it, near as improbable as reaching Carrick again. Oh, where is she? Has she finally left her sanctuary for me? Or is it for Eadwin? No matter—she's here!"

Old he might be and indignant at resorting to physical force for the first time in sixty-odd years, but Ignacio'd be Lady-damned if he'd let this one off the hook! Let him try to wriggle away! Actually, he reflected, force wasn't all that necessary, but he couldn't help venting his frustrations as he tightened Aelbert's arm behind his back and frog-marched the sobbing man up the enclosed back staircase to the balcony.

He'd marked Aelbert's veering flight from the audience chamber and as soon as he'd been able to tear himself free for a few moments—ostensibly to find some wine to blunt Maurice's seething rage at the debacle of the investiture—he'd sought out Aelbert. The aide-de-camp hadn't run far; he'd found him weeping, slumped in a back hallway corner, rocking his ghatta in his arms. The ghatta had sprung free, rubbed around his ankles at his approach.

Let the Bannerjees deal with him, he'd thought fiercely at first, yet found himself sorrowing over the young man's plight, his shattered dreams. Destroyed hopes were something he was intimately familiar with, his own shattered dreams over his late daughter, Ezequiel's mother. He'd been transformed into a different man after that, picked up the pieces and moved on with his life, more cognizant than ever that merely wanting wasn't enough, even if you might justly deserve it. Whether Aelbert would have the strength to grow beyond the hurt, he wasn't about to judge.

"Please don't hurt him!" a voice begged in his mind. It wasn't one of the Bannerjees, that he was sure of, and then he saw the ghatta trailing up the stairs behind them. So, they did speak! Deciding actions spoke louder than words, he let Aelbert's wrist drop lower behind his back, relieving the pressure on the shoulder joint. **"Thank you!"** Odd little voice, it was.

Checking to see if anyone watched from below, he dragged Aelbert with him through the cramped door, hoping the Bannerjees hadn't left. Let them decide what was to be done with him; he was too old for life or death decisions.

Twin pairs of aquamarine eyes regarded him. "Ah, Ignacio," Dwyna's merry banter floated up from where they sat on the floor of the balcony, unseen by casual passersby. "Gentlemen callers usually knock, and they generally bring flowers. This is an unusual token of affection."

He wasn't in the mood for her teasing. "Do what you will with him," he said more brusquely than he'd intended, tugging at his muttonchop to conceal his embarrassment. He'd stolen a kiss from one of them once when they were all younger and more daring, but he'd never known which one he'd kissed. Now he thought he had the answer. He thrust Aelbert to his knees in front of them as if to let him confess.

"I'd best return before Maurice misses me." Making a production of dusting his hands to denote the end of his involvement, he left. It was a warning of what forces still remained to haunt, possibly hurt himself, and he wasn't sure where Ezequiel was right now. He hoped the boy was safe.

"Fine. We'll deal with Seeker Veritas Orsborne." Aelbert shrank away, but N'oor pressed closer to the Bannerjees, her ear hoop jangling against Wyn's bracelets.

Dwyna touched his forehead, let her fingers stray to his temple. "Feverish," she reported.

"Anticipation often causes a fever, thwarted ambition an even higher one, the body burning with longing," Wyn replied, touching his other temple.

And for the first time in his life Aelbert Orsborne poured out his fears, his hungers, obsessions and aspirations into nonjudgmental, nay, almost sympathetic ears, while N'oor listened in mingled relief and envy. Not enough for him, she'd never been enough for him, but if they could cure the cravings it would be all worthwhile. At length Aelbert wound down, shuddering with relief, his soul cleansed. "You know what you must do, don't you?" Dwyna probed tenderly.

He stroked N'oor's head, and the beloved contact made her tremble at the solace of his touch. Protect him, love him, trust him, and she had, perhaps not well enough, but with all her heart at least.

"Expiation. I don't know what it entails, but I'll try. First, though, I have to return to Maurice."

"Is that wise?" Wyn queried, eyebrows meshing in distaste.

"No, but it's just. He'll void some of his anger on me and that will be a distraction for the others. And besides, he still thinks I'm trapped in his own little web. He'll think I kicked too hard before, but have settled in now, ready to be bound by his desires."

Strength seemingly restored, Constant bustled through cobwebbed passages, up and down hidden stairways behind walls, often with a finger to his lips to denote the need for silence. They stumbled after, a ragtag crew breathless with haste and fear. Powder-soft dust floated and settled, coating with a fine gray film that melded to everything it touched, lodged in the folds of their clothes, filmed their faces and hands, making them look like clay figurines, figurines that walked and spoke. Occluded beams of light shone a paler gray, disrupted their eyes, and disappeared before they could count on them. Constant's robe whipped a powdery cloud that trailed like a comet's tail, spreading after him. Hru'rul sneezed, an abrupt explosion; a giant paw swiped at his nose, his whole muzzle scrunched in tickling dismay.

Without warning, Constant careened to a halt and Doyce nearly crashed into him, muttering under her breath as she threw herself sideways. Others behind her weren't so lucky at the precipitous halt; she could tell from the muffled oaths, the soft thuds of flesh colliding against flesh. Constant nibbled at the end of his beard, sputtered "Phah! Dusty!" under his breath, mouth working in faint spitting sounds.

"Acts as if his mind is light-years distant, and when we can least afford it," she grumbled. *"How old is he, truly?"*

"You know. After everything else you've accepted, why not this?" Khar chided, Hru'rul chuckling as if they shared a secret.

"Because I don't think my sanity can take it." Why had they all followed so blindly? As promised, the Bannerjees were wreaking minor havoc up above, tweaking minds, granting them the time they needed. Despite their fears of falling into the same trap of power and pain that had snared Maurice and Jampolis, the Bannerjee twins were having fun doing what they were doing, she had no doubt of that, like school children nagging their Edifier when his back was turned. The harsh reality was that they had no other choice but to rejoin Roland and his forces. If they couldn't gather additional support, and quickly, Maurice still retained enough supporters to thwart their plans. Arras had hit his casque against a low beam, despite guidance by Jenret and Syndar Saffron. No time or leisure to try to extricate him from it; anyway, Jampolis still held the key.

Callis swirled by. She'd almost forgotten the ancient Erakwan woman followed in the rear escorted by Ezequiel, unperturbed by the fighting, oblivious to their strange journey. Constant greeted her, catching both of her hands in his, raising them to his lips, a curious, courtly gesture from a long-ago era. Freeing a hand with gentle persistence, Callis pretend-scowled, stamped her foot for attention, and gesured along the way they'd come. Brightening, Constant urged back, hustling between Eadwin and Jacobia, stopping to tug at a piece of molding that ran along the wall, midway between ceiling and floor. He pushed his palms against it, heaving upward with all his might. "Overshot!" he chirruped to no one in particular. "Taking longer strides than I thought, counted right but paced too long!" What he was talking about, she couldn't fathom, nor could any of the others, she guessed.

A wall segment began to split in half, the top rising, the bottom sinking, until she could smell the dankness and dampness of a more natural corridor, not as artificially constructed as the ones within the walls. It loomed, dark and ominous, engulfing with its coolness, beckoning with a potency that reminded her of Nakum's reaction to the tunnels they'd traversed through the mountain to the peak. With a crow of delight, Constant stepped inside, fumbling above his head, the rusty rattle of a disused chain, the screech of old metal hinges shivering up her spine. Sparks spangled the darkness and the dim light of a lantern expanded and glowed, forcing her to shield her eyes against the surprise of seeing faces materializing out of shadows, too close and almost menacing after the clinging dark.

"Well, come on, come on." Constant did a little hopping dance as if to entice them to enter. Surprisingly, Eadwin was the first to step through, followed by his newly acknowledged cousin, Nakum. The rest came after. Another light winked in the distance, two flashes, then disappeared. Constant's lantern flashed back. "Good!" His voice indicated real satisfaction. "They're here." And the distant light slowly grew to reveal Parse and Roland, Felix straining and whimpering at their sides to reach Muscadeine, Per'la gamboling in front of them.

Despite her ardent desire to leave everything behind, escape from these confines, Doyce grabbed Parse in a rough hug, but he broke free without a second glance and rushed to Sarrett. He mumbled something, staring at his feet, then squatted to shake T'ss's tail. "Er, nice to see you all," he puttered, and Doyce couldn't decide if the back of his neck was ruddy simply because of the lantern light or from some powerful emotion.

Sarrett shoved by, one hand brushing his flyaway carroty hair. "Couldn't stay put, could you?" she reprimanded, but the gleam on her cheek betrayed her. T'ss bounded after her, eyes huge with mute appeal as he regarded the still-crouched figure.

But Bard had other concerns. Arm still in a sling, he sank the fingers of his good hand into Parse's tabard, hauling him upright. "Byrta?" he hissed. "How is she, how fares my twin?" A look of naked anguish, naked appeal on his face.

Caught by utter surprise, Parse stammered "F . . . fine. Of course. Why? Haven't you communed?"

Roland, sunk on one knee in silent homage to Eadwin, had the grace to apologize. "I begged her not to," he explained, "for fear it might reveal us. Your abilities are too wild, erratic, coded in your private language, but they can be sensed by others of my ilk. To sense an unexpected, unexplained voice so near might give them something to track us by."

Raised up by a no-nonsense tug from Eadwin, Roland was unable to restrain himself as he ran his fingers over Arras's helmet. "We've got to get this off, I can't stand seeing him like this!" Parse moved to help, glad as usual of a puzzle to solve, and they struggled with the padlock, Arras helpless under their hands, trying to hold still. The hilt of Parse's knife slammed the helmet, caused a ringing clang far more clear and carrying than when Arras's head had connected with the beam. Arras reared back, moaning, and the sounds of distant footsteps reached their ears as the gonglike sound faded away.

"Quick! Scamper along, no time to lose!" Constant began driving them down the passage. "They're coming, and closer than I expected!"

Constant checked to verify the secret door panels had meshed, the wall seemingly solid again. "Can't do anything about the disrupted dust on the other side," he whispered to Jenret and Parse. "Still, they may not realize we've detoured, just think we stopped to rest and scuffled it worse than just passing through. Depends on how thorough a job Ezequiel did when he went ahead." Parse gave a distracted nod, eyes never straying from the counterweights and balances that had allowed Constant to separate the wall with such ease. He wore the look of a puzzle-lover mentally cal-

ulating solutions, fingers twitching to explore the intricate
mechanisms. After the episode with the helmet, it was best
o make him jam his hands in his pockets.

"If they don't know the spot to push, the only way in is
o blast," Constant encouraged them. "I don't think Maurice
ver bothered to study the castle plans the way Ignacio and
Ezequiel did, but I used to hear Jampolis sniffing around the
ibrary. When I worked there, of course," he added hastily.

"Now remember, don't make a sound, just listen for any-
ne passing, whether they continue on or backtrack. When
ou're sure we've shaken them off, join us. The first bend to
our right takes you directly to the old barns right next to
he ring wall. It's farther away than you'd think so make
aste. We'll be waiting. Someone's got to let Roland's forces
n, can't have them all tramping through the tunnels. If you
o straight, you'll eventually end there, but you'll have
ourneyed by way of the chapel, and that entry's been bricked
ver for years. You could wander forever. The Shepherds always meant well, but I just didn't like them having access,
whether they knew it or not, to my tunnels." He sounded
ossessive and proudly so.

"Yours?" Mystified, Jenret scratched his head. These
amned tunnels were as ancient as the castle itself, not some
ecent addition built to satisfy Constant Minor's busy, rab-
iting ways. They'd been constructed when the castle wall
ose, part and parcel of it. And from the looks of them, no
ne had used them for ten octads or more.

"Well of course, mine." Asperity tinged Constant's voice.
Do you think I'd have built all this without bolt-holes? Par-
noia ill-becomes a ruler—witness Maurice—but prudence
equires alternate means of entrance and egress. What if a
lumb had exploded, leveled the castle? What if the Erakwa
ad attacked, though once I knew Callis, that was remote.
till, plan ahead, I always said, and I still do say." Then,
athering himself together into the present, Constant patted
ach man on the shoulder. "Remember, first branch to your
ght."

❖

Plumbs? Was the old man daft? Well, no time to think
bout that, nor to translate the distant voices playing in his
ead, their good-will messages as remote as he and Parse

were from the others. Jenret leaned against the closed entrance, cheek flat against the panel, listening, sword held at the ready. He didn't like this sword, missed his own, but cold steel was comfort of sorts, and he gave brief thanks for Roland's and Parse's foresight in bringing them. Like a matching bookend, Parse mirrored his pose, head cocked intently to discern any noise.

Rawn's head turned back and forth, eyes glittering. **"Fascinating—like a mouse at its hole, wondering if it's safe to venture forth."**

Per'la curved her plumed tail around her toes, sniffing at the wavy marks it had carved in the dust. **"Let's just hope the predators are too big to venture in.... Though if they do—"** and she raised one front paw, claws outstretched, suggestively shredding air.

Jenret smiled despite himself and whispered, "When did Per'la become so bloodthirsty?" But Parse had gone rigid with foreboding, every sense straining as he mimicked the breath-holding ghatti posture. A creaking complaint, more overhead than anywhere else, as close as Jenret could judge, and he rolled his eyes ceilingward at the old beams, trying to judge where the straining sounds emanated. A stream of dirt, a quick release of pebbles and rubble cascading into his face, his shoulders, and with a sick certainty he conceded that more than one way into the mousehole existed. They wouldn't dare blast, bring down the castle on their own heads, would they? He was already sprinting down the tunnel, hissing at Parse to follow when an overwhelming roar baffled his eardrums, swept over him like a tidal wave, and the weight of what felt like a giant breaker surged over him, swept him off his feet, spun him this way and that and, senses overcome, he knew no more.

"This isn't sane! Trust these foreigners?" Octavian thumped his peg leg as added emphasis to his mindspeech, made a concealed but contemptuous gesture to where Byrta and P'wa perched on a log near the water's edge, as far away from the fifty soldiers as possible. Other soldiers were ranged out of sight in case of an ambush.

Roland continued staring across the river at the shadowy advancing figures, long white ghost shapes of pontoons floating through the dark on the almost invisible shoulders of the workers, then being lowered into the river and lashed into position. Secluded here, almost too secluded for his liking, but the narrow river bend had been scoured for interlopers, whether Maurice's men or spying Canderisians. He could hear the soldiers shifting behind him, restive and uneasy as the chain of pontoons elongated, stretching closer and closer.

"Because we have to trust them. How else can we put Eadwin on the throne and avoid full-scale war with Canderis? Arras agrees with me. The Bannerjees agree, you heard them yourself. Look, Octavian, I know it's perverse after all these years to consider them as possible friends, allies. Remember, it's a compulsion so deeply ingrained that it's not easy to be rational about it. Think about it, Octavian," he smote his thigh, desperate for a comparison the older soldier would grasp.

"Ever dislike, absolutely hate a certain food forever? Wouldn't even let it on your plate? Avoided it with a passion?"

Octavian pursed his lips and nodded. *"Them salty black olives from the Sunderlies."* They both winced at the sound of another pontoon slapping the water, the figures and pontoons advancing as inexorably as a creeping night mist.

"What if I served you a dish, a casserole, say, with so many things in it that you didn't immediately taste the olives? How would you react when I told you you'd eaten them, even asked for seconds?" He waited, expectant but not daring to expect too much. The Bannerjees had been adamant that what had begun as a compulsion years ago was now inherent historical attitude, capable of being challenged by rational minds. And that it was up to him to do it. If he could influence Octavian's mind-set, he could rely on the Staff Sergeant to convince his troops to change as well. A truce between old and new beliefs was all he asked for, a way to hold the old beliefs in abeyance at least for a time. Arras Muscadeine could have convinced them, but he was no Arras Muscadeine.

Octavian spat into the water, dragged forth the words as if he were loath to admit them. *"I get your point. But it's going to be a lot harder than olives to get me to like those Canderisians. Look at her sitting so smug and self-contained with that big cat."*

"You don't have to like them, just don't dislike them quite so strongly. Arras cares about them, likes them. If he's open enough to do so, can you do less?"

He saw matting being unrolled over the pontoons to offer a firm footing. Another eight pontoons, he estimated, and the two countries would be connected by this fragile bridge, as fragile as the trust they strove to construct. It had been agreed through Yulyn that they'd meet in the middle of the river—the Monitor and a few trusted advisors and Roland with Octavian and Byrta. Nothing to do now but wait.

The last pontoon floated into place and a young man jumped ashore with a heavy mallet and stakes, pounded them into the ground, and used them to secure the ropes. Finished, he gave a half-salute. "Transitor Faeralleyn Thomas at your service, sirs."

His avid curiosity made Roland feel as if he were being devoured and without thinking, he mentally snapped, *"Don't push me, Transitor whoever you are. I'm not a milk cow up for auction."*

Startlement exploded across the younger man's face, mouth half-open in shock before he gathered his wits. *"Never said you were, sir. But you're my first, see? And please, the others don't know about me. Trust you with the secret, sir."* Octavian growled and started after him, the Transitor backing away rapidly. "If you're ready, I'll return, pass the word for the Monitor to advance to the middle, and wait for you." Roland gave a terse nod of agreement as the figure walked with springy, almost bobbing steps across the river, the pontoons sinking and rising as he passed over each one.

"Come on." He slapped Octavian's back to hearten the man, to enbolden himself. "Byrta, are you ready?"

As she and P'wa joined them, he began to walk ahead, each footfall rustling the woven matting. The bridge felt elastic under his feet, resilient as a living thing. They, too, had to bend but not break, plot their passage into the different world he was attempting to create. Lady help him if he were wrong! The figures from the opposite shore were closing in on him now. He'd have to rely on the scant moonlight to read their faces, their intentions.

P'wa broke into his thoughts. **"You're about to meet the Monitor, Kyril van Beieven, Seeker General Swan Maclough and her Bondmate Koom, and Yulyn**

Biddlecomb. **You've heard her voice before, but now you'll meet her face-to-face."**

Squaring his shoulders and holding his head high, Roland reminded himself that for better or worse, he had charge of their destiny. Under his authority they'd remake their world or die in the attempt. He reached out and shook van Beieven's hand, gripping more forcefully than he'd intended as the pontoon swayed and shifted under their weight. Pressure was returned, and he wondered who would dominate whom? As if van Beieven had arrived at a similar realization, they simultaneously released their grip, equals for the time being.

"So, do we cooperate?" The Monitor's heartiness sounded forced, and Roland could sense the fear lurking underneath.

"What do you want from us?"

"I want my people released, our trade resumed." And a heartfelt, "I want things to be the way they were before."

But things would never be the same as they were before, and the enormity of that truth hit Roland, making him waver on his feet, leery of the tentative bridge supporting them. "Why should you fight for us?"

The Monitor scraped a hand through his hair, striving for an answer. "I don't know what impulses, what fears have somehow coalesced, brought us to this stage, but I think battle is inevitable. And," he hesitated, "there's a hoary saying: The enemy of my enemy is my friend."

Roland weighed his suspicions, tossing out an accusation like a gauntlet. "How do I know you won't turn against us, overrun us once we've allowed you a foothold in Marchmont." Out of the corner of his eye he could see Octavian nodding somber agreement, poised to defend Roland if necessary. *"Olives,"* he muttered. *"Don't think I like olives either."*

Yulyn gave him a puzzled look as the Monitor laughed without understanding what had generated his relief. "Because, believe me, I've all I can do to govern Canderis most of the time. I'm not an empire builder, just a plain farmer trying his best to guide his country." He gestured toward Byrta and P'wa. "If you trust them enough to have them present, ask P'wa to judge the truth of my words."

But both P'wa and Octavian had stiffened, eyes searching behind the Monitor and his group. Twisting for a clear view beyond the Monitor's bulk, Roland spied a figure creeping along the bridge. Treachery!

A boyish voice piped up loud and clear. "Are you really a Resonant?" And a stocky twelve-year-old boy raised himself to hands and knees for a better look. "Bet I can Send farther than you! Are you really a soldier? You don't look like one, not like he does," and he pointed toward Octavian. "Are you going to fight us? All sorts of glorious battles and heroic feats of derring-do and honor! Or are you going to hurt and cripple with your mindvoices like Vesey?"

Yulyn and Swan dragged Davvy forward, the boy's emotions precariously balanced between awe and delicious fear. He reminded Roland of his little brother, and he knew instinctively that anyone who brought a boy into danger of this sort had faith enough to believe it could be avoided. How could he dislike someone who reminded him of his little brother?

With wary, cautious tones he began to outline his plans.

Covered, shrouded, eyes, ears, nose, mouth swathed in what felt like clinging-wet black velvet, smothering him, clasped implacably close, breathless, heart poundings magnified by the closeness, like being buried, but alive, so achingly alive. Weight pressing him front and back, pinning each limb, and beyond the soft, inexorable pressure, a solid, unyielding density thrusting down on his right leg until he felt it would cleave straight through flesh and bone, no impediment in its path.

"Sit, dammit!" He recognized the voice in his mind, struggled to obey as a sleeper forces himself to sit up in the middle of a nightmare, bursting the bonds of sleep tethered to the roiling fears of the mind, physical action reuniting the sleeper with the waking world. He opened his mouth to protest that he couldn't, and dirt poured in the way sand rushes into the bottom of a timer-glass. Terrified, he surged upward and managed to sit, arms tossing, shaking his head, spitting, gasping, coughing, retching. Runnels of dirt trickled off him, still lodged in his hair, his ears, jammed into his nostrils, caked his eyelids shut. The pressure on his chest and lungs, his windpipe eased, but there was no escaping the knife-sharp pressure on his leg, pain flailing like ineffectual wings.

"Dig free! Hurry! We've got to dig Parse out!" Rawn, gruff with fear, winded and harried, but Per'la's terror roiled through his mind. **"Parse, please, love! Please!"** And then an actual high-pitched wail of anguish. **"He's unconscious! His breathing slows!"**

The lantern had rolled to the far wall, but at last he made out its lopsided, dim light casting crooked, flurried shadows of two ghatti tenaciously digging at a mound of dirt. Wiping gritted, dirty hands against his eyes, tears streaming at the irritation, Jenret pulled himself further upright and shoveled dirt off his lower limbs. Damn! His right leg still throbbed, feeling as if it were still trapped by the jaws of a giant animal. He rolled back and forth, trying to loosen it, aware that precious time was slipping away. The pile of dirt covering his legs blocked the lantern light, so he reached down cautiously, tracing his hands along his leg until he hit the solid, squared outline of a beam, a splinter jamming under his nail. The minor hurt after such worse pain galvanized him, and he dug, furious, slammed his left foot against the beam and tried to lever it free. Nothing! He kicked it again and again. Parse was smothering, suffocating, and he couldn't help, couldn't even rescue himself!

Agitated, he scooped with his hands, digging beneath his leg, shifting loose dirt until he hit hard-packed floor. Space—some, but not much—enough to maneuver? He grabbed just below the knee and pulled, felt the boot freeze in place and his calf and foot begin to slide loose. Hurt! Hurt like the very devil himself, protesting redemption. The jut of his anklebone lodged and he ignored the pain, bracing and pulling, tears slicing mud tracks down his cheeks. His foot popped free, and he wallowed and rolled in the direction of the ghatti, still digging, grim, intent.

"Where's . . . his . . . head?" Jenret gasped, crabbing along with his good leg, arms sweeping over the soft, shifting dirt.

"Here, this way," Rawn instructed, and Jenret crawled closer, swinging his arms back and forth, hands cupping, paddling, pushing back dirt, wrestling stones free, splintering on beam fragments.

How long, how long had it been? He didn't dare ask the ghatti, didn't want to know the answer, know it was futile, that all his labors would unveil a corpse. A steady stream of dirt shot from beneath Per'la's paws, driving like pistons, her beautiful fur bedraggled with dirt, ears pinned flat with dread. He dug, shoveled with his bare hands, and at last felt a cool, yielding touch beneath his fingers, the angle of a jaw, the ear above it. He uncovered Parse's face, dug into the packed nostrils, scooped bleeding fingers into the clogged mouth. In agony, he dove lower, working to free the chest, leaving the ghatti to rough lick and cleanse Parse's face. He worked like an automaton, prayed that Parse wasn't beam-pinned as he'd been. Fought himself not to go back and feel for a pulse, to do what he had to do first, lighten, if not completely remove, the debris crushing Parse in its embrace.

If he were lucky, he could do it, pluck him clean from the earth the way one pulls a carrot. The idea left him giddy, a hysterical thought of Parse as a carrot. Oh, Lady, Lady! Let me free him! And he pushed the ghatti aside, scrambled on his knees behind Parse and propped head and shoulders, crouched and slipped his hands under his arms, locked them around the still chest. One foot booted, the other bare, ankle swelling, he planted and heaved, ignoring the protest in his battered leg, dragging Parse with him as if he raised him out of his grave, out of the netherworlds.

Parse hung limp and Jenret squeezed him in a bear hug, freed him long enough to hammer between the shoulder blades again and again to dislodge anything in his throat. Per'la moaned, paced, desperate to reach her beloved, rearing on hind legs and balancing for a better view. Oh, Lady, no, it was like desperately hugging a limp rag doll! All for nothing! A laugh of hysteria trembled on his lips.

"Breathe for him," Rawn commanded, and for a moment it was beyond Jenret to comprehend. Then he knew and for a moment quivered in revulsion—never, never had he kissed another man full on the mouth. **"Breathe for him, don't let him drown in dirt!"** But nothing mattered now, except Parse, Parse whom he'd never realized he was so fond of, and most of all whom Sarrett was fond of, loved. And he flipped the body flat on its back and tilted the chin, old training returning, check the passage ways for clogging— what a joke under these circumstances!—and clamped his mouth over Parse's cold, muddy lips, heaved a breath into the chest, listened for it to whistle back. And again, and again, and again, he forced aching lungs to work for two until at last he encountered resistance, breathing battling against his own labored attempts. He pulled away just in time and rolled Parse on his side as he began to vomit.

How long he sat cradling the man he couldn't guess, but felt Per'la pressed against Parse's side, a ragged purr shuddering her entire body. He searched his pockets mechanically, surprised himself by finding a reasonably clean handkerchief. With shaking hands he wiped Parse's mouth, his face, fingered the heartbeat that pulsed in his neck. And incredibly weary, stretched beside Parse and drifted asleep.

A sour, damp smell against his face, a brush of air current, and the labored rasp of breathing made him rear back, eyes wide in the dark, seeing nothing, fearing everything. "Jen ... ret," the voice at his ear burned hot, insistent, the sound shadowy, fragile as memory. Again, it came, "Jen ... J ... en ... ret!" More imploring this time, straining to make contact, communicate. And abruptly he knew where he was, whom he was with, and why he was here. The lantern had extinguished itself, entombing them in inky blackness. The comforting bulk of Rawn shifted beside him, invisible but present.

"Yes, Parse, I'm here," he crooned, and a hand reached, halting, to his cheek. A sigh as fingers touched, traced his features, then the hand fell on his chest, spent.

"So ... long. No air," the voice whispered. "Per'la dis ... appearing from my thoughts." A heavy swallowing sound. "And that ... was worse ... than dying ... though death was close behind." A long pause. "Do you ... under ... stand?"

He clutched at Parse's hand, tried to will whatever strength he possessed into the frail, battered body. "Yes, I do."

"Oh, Per'la ... love." And he felt Parse pulling away, groping for the ghatta.

Rawn bounded across Jenret's lap, rubbing against him, brushing under his chin, the hard head butting him. **"Too close, too close for comfort, that one was,"** he murmured. He began a meditative chew on Jenret's knuckles, stopped. **"Dirty."**

"Well, what did you expect?" And real laughter bubbled out of Jenret as he clutched the ghatt to his chest, rocked them both back and forth. A tongue scraped across the stubble of his jaw. *"Lick me clean?"* he suggested.

"Too much work," Rawn countered. **"My tongue's too**

small and too tired. Besides, let's save grooming until we've rejoined the others. If we can," he reflected solemnly. **"It's already night."**

Parse broke in as if haunted by the same worry. "Think I can walk ... a little. Must meet the others at the barns. If we're lucky, Maurice's men will think they destroyed us all in the landslide. They blew a hole somewhere ... hope it's drafty ... but they didn't do it in the right place."

Jenret heaved himself up, held a hand to Parse, and dragged him to his feet, the slimmer man swaying and rocking. He slung Parse's arm over his shoulder. "Any idea of the way?"

"First bend to the right, direct to the barns."

And they began, limping, stumbling over fallen debris, toes searching out hidden rocks and stones, weaving and wobbling like two drunkards secure in each other's arms, bosom friends while the liquor held.

❖

Existence was bounded by what his bruised hands could touch, tattered knees and shins could feel. Nothing to see ahead, nothing behind him, no change in the air currents against his fevered skin, no sound except the ragged groans of the man on his back and his own harsh sobs for breath as he crawled along, his own hisses of pain sharp against his ears as his knee sliced a rock's jagged edge. He pawed ahead, searching for a smooth spot. None. Forward, always forward. Not going to die like this, not now. Not going to let Parse die.

Jenret stopped long enough to check the lashing holding Parse on his back, the unconscious man's legs bouncing behind him. They'd traveled halfway down the righthand bend toward the barns when the ghatti reported the tunnel ahead was blocked by fallen beams and debris, a weak spot had shifted in sympathy to the earlier explosion. They'd traced their way back, safety even farther distant now by the chapel route and then to the barns. Amazing to think they traversed the city underground, while people walked free and unfettered above. With an apologetic sound, Parse had collapsed shortly thereafter, unable to be roused even after rest, so Jenret had slung him on his back, staggering through the darkness, the ghatti's keener night vision charting their path

Occasional scurrying sounds and distant thumps from beyond the tunnel walls caused them to freeze, then advance, the ghatti leary about projecting mindspeech too far. Who knew what waited out there, friend or foe?

But Jenret's beam-injured leg had faltered under Parse's dead weight, swollen ankle rolling under him, his bare foot abused by the rough passage. A stocking gave no protection, no support without the abandoned boot. And finally, Jenret had no option but to crawl like an insect with a burden on its back, dragging himself sluglike over each impediment, ignoring them, ignoring the pain that chewed at raw knees and shins, lacerated palms, stubbed fingers, everything sticky with sweat and seeping wound fluids.

Rawn ranged ahead, scouting, Per'la pacing at his side where there was room, lagging when there was not, fearful of straying from her Bond's side. She stretched to nose Parse periodically, the touch reassuring her, reassuring him that the dead weight lived. **"So sorry, so very sorry,"** Per'la's mindvoice warbled with sorrow. **"You are so kind, so good to my beloved. Never will I forget."** He paused and she rubbed against him, leaning into him, twining herself against his aching arm, sharing the strength of her determined passion.

Rawn's mindvoice drifted back, detailing the last of the route, encouraging. **"Close. Very close. Contacted M'wa. I'm not sure how to say this."** An apologetic cough, a pause. **"Roland led the others out by a different route and slipped back to the barns by a side shaft. Constant's forgotten where our doorway is. Says we can't miss it on our side, but too many additions and changes have altered the barns since his day. He's trying."**

Gritting his teeth, Jenret dragged himself ahead, drenched with sweat, mouth so dry he thought he might die. Damned if he would! And damn Constant for not remembering how to rescue them! He nursed the anger, husbanded it and lurched forward, hauled himself and his burden along, a trail of seeping blood behind him, a blood signature, penance for his arrogant, self-centered ways, stubborn selfishness. But he'd fan that stubbornness flame-bright to see them through.

Sounds and chatter from unknown people, nonexistent people concatenated in his head, and he denied them as he had since coming to Marchmont; it blurred his concentration, concentration reduced to moving one hand forward, then the opposite knee, and repeat on the other side, his gait was sprung, and so was his back. *"They've been wandering in there a full day! Can't you do something?"* *"Arras and Callis and I are trying to draw him with our voices, but he won't listen, won't follow."* *"Don't quit, my darling!"* he imagined he heard a voice beg and it was cruel, because it mimicked Doyce, and that was the cruelest trick of all, to believe he heard her here beside him. But it would suffice to goad him, pull him along step by step, just as a magnet draws its load.

❧

Dark, still so dark! Where? Where was Parse? Where was he? Strangled by terror, Jenret reared up, chest heaving, propped himself on raw elbows and shuddered at the pain that mill-raced through them. Wrong way, wrong! Can't drag Parse if I'm on my back! "Parse?" he whispered, uncertain, alone. "Rawn? Per'la? Where?"

An arm fell soft across his chest, pressing him flat against his will, but he was too spent to fight it. His knees and shins oozed and swelled like bloating, putrefying meat, his right ankle ached, each heartbeat a gong of pain, a new pitch to each throb, then subsiding to the unremitting pain of hot metal plates searing his skin.

"Hush, Jenret. Hush, darling," the voice soothed, and a damp cloth stroked his brow, caressing the lock of dark hair off his forehead. A muzzy awareness that his lower legs, forearms and hands were encased in bandages, binding the pain, swathing him in it. If he could only sit up, strip off the bandages, let the pain escape. The arm restrained him as easily as if he were a baby. "Hush, Jenner. You're here, here with us. Parse is fine. We found you both, brought you into the barns, you're safe with us."

"Doyce?" He couldn't keep the strained eagerness from his voice. Please, not a dream, not a phantom voice like the others, that would be cruel, too cruel after all he'd suffered. A monumental jest at his expense, and what had he ever been guilty of to deserve that, ever done except hopelessly and longingly love someone who didn't care, someone he couldn't reach? Yet despite the darkness, he could smell her, smell the indefinable scent that was hers alone, and he couldn't make that up, imagine it, could he? Nor, now that he came to think of it, the odors of grain, manure, leather, horseflesh, hay—and the prickly stabs through a blanket, stiff pokes and prods, but ultimately, blessed softness. Not the unyielding rockiness of the tunnel floor. He swept one arm in an arc, sensed even through the bandages yielding straw as opposed to dirt and stone. "Doyce? Out of the tunnel? Truly?" He croaked like a crow, testing his voice, and felt his head lifted, a tin mug of water chilling burning lips. He started to swallow, greedy at the cold sweetness, then stopped, swished the water in his mouth, dirt rising and churning, and spat. Then he drank greedily.

"Yes. Safe for now. Rest, now, love. Nothing can harm you while I'm here." Relieved, Jenret slept.

When he woke again he endured the pressure against chest and shoulder, pulled his arm tight and sensed Doyce slept curled against him. He nuzzled his lips against her hair, filled with a sense of well-being ascending beyond pain. And despite that pain, an overwhelming need to make love to the woman he held. Why was that? Making love in the midst of danger, possible death, as an affirmation of life? It struck him as funny, but true. What faced them outside this barn, outside this place, he dared not fathom, but he knew he feared for his life, and most of all for hers. So fragile yet so strong, and he desired her with a longing that he'd never encountered before, not just the urges of his body, but with the most profound needs of his heart and mind and soul. His need for her ran so deep that without it he would die.

With a soundless sob of yearning and hope, he pulled her to him and began to kiss her face, her lips. And with mingled wonder and dawning joy felt her respond, feverish as he with the craving. His hands, clumsy in the bandages, fumbled at her clothes and he could feel her helping, prayed she wasn't still half-asleep, thinking herself dreaming, allowing the dream to continue, riding out the waves of passion. That would be the most infinitely bitter irony of all, to merge with her, become one with only her body physically present. Yet he didn't dare utter a word, destroy the spell. One part of him heard Khar and Rawn rise and jump from the loft, granting them privacy.

And then, without volition, he felt himself sliding into her mind. With ragged sobs he tried to tear himself free, mentally and physically, but she grasped him tighter yet. He rolled on top of her and gasped at the pain in his knees—hot

coals pressing into his flesh, reality. He rolled back, knew
that he couldn't complete the act like this, mind warring
with body, and her body open, vulnerable to the results of
his lust. "No, don't!" he choked out. "No protection!
Mustn't!"

But she was snatching at his clothes, mounting him, murmuring words of endearment, slipping him within her with
the same sure swiftness his mind had entered hers. And they
were bound together in every way known to man and
woman, and in a way he didn't understand but for which he
was profoundly grateful and frightened. This, *this* was what
it was meant to be, he decided, not the other times, not the
urgent press and sticky slap of flesh, the climaxing release
and ebb, but this towering culmination that brought an explosion of radiant joy bursting behind his closed eyelids.
"Doyce!" His exultation never reached his lips but lodged in
her mind with the consummate sharing.

❖

When he awoke again, he lay alone, eyes adjusting to the
gray light that sifted through the roof peaks' vents. He made
out Rawn's darker form reposing beside a basin of water.
Had it been a dream? He cast around the loft, caught the soft
drift of voices below. **"You smell a bit niffy. Could do with
a wash,"** Rawn wrinkled his nose. **"How are you feeling?"**
Concerned, the ghatt moved closer, sniffing at the bandages
on his legs. **"Not much skin left in spots,"** he commented.
"I saw when they bandaged you."

With slow, awkward movements, Jenret fought to skin his
tunic over his head, bit his lip to stifle a cry when he flexed
his elbows. How he was going to stand didn't bear thinking
about; there was no sense imagining the agony. *"What's
been happening?"* Grasping the basin between his palms
and dragging it toward him, he dipped one hand into the water to retrieve the wash rag, exhaled through clenched teeth
as warm, soapy water soaked bandages, sought out the lac-
erations and raw bruises. Bending his head, he swabbed the
back of his neck and his face with the wash rag. Rinsing it,
he began to scrub under arms, down chest and belly. *"Well?
Better?"* he prodded as he sloshed and rubbed, shivered at
errant trickles of water.

"Parse is very, very sore," Rawn confided. **"Cracked**

bs, bruises all over, yellow and green and purple and
d. Looks like someone cranked him in a clothes press."

While the news about Parse lightened his heart, it wasn't
hat he wanted to hear, and he wondered if Rawn were
voiding the issue. The ghatt was too much the discreet gen-
eman to mention Doyce, or had last night been a fantasy?
*I take it we're trapped in this barn, or are we simply hid-
g, and Maurice and his crew have no idea we're here?
ow long has it been? I've lost track of everything."*

Rawn shifted his weight on his front paws, bent to exam-
e the soap scum ringing the basin's rim. He gave a little
huffle, watched part of it eddy and drift. **"Second after-**
on since we botched Maurice's coronation," he said at
st. **"Frankly, we're in the middle of something bigger**
an that." Reluctantly, **"Truth seems secondary. The**
onitor and the Guardians are attacking Sidonie."

"Why!" Jenret wrenched out the word.

"Because of the fact that they've captured us, because
the broken trade agreements, because of the instability
governance here." Rawn ticked off the points, gave a
wn of nervousness. **"And because, whether the Monitor**
lly realizes it or not, because of the Resonants. He's
ined forces with Eadwin's supporters. Roland's agreed
ey should work together to defeat Maurice. Our troops
ill be crossing the river shortly. The city's in turmoil,
aurice's and Eadwin's factions clashing amongst them-
lves."**

Jenret began the arduous task of putting his tunic back on.
*But we're not captured, at least not now. And what the
lls are Resonants? Aelbert mentioned them in his pretty
tle speech, but I didn't know what in the Lady-starred skies
was talking about."*

"Gleaners. Trained Gleaners are Resonants in
archmont. Arras Muscadeine is one. Roland has some
ills, and Eadwin's have just been liberated. They're a
rt of the very social fabric here, respected, honored.
hether we fight for Marchmont or against it, who
ows what we'll loose on our own land."** Rawn sighed.
'ruth is so muddled now. Never in all my days have I
en it tossed aside like this. They have the gift of
indspeech, but they cannot read Truth, and innocent
ople will suffer and die because of that."**

"Not if we can help it, eh, Rawn?" And concentrating on

what had to be done, Jenret lurched to his feet, ignoring the
pain, and walked stiff-legged toward the trap door of the
loft. *"Where are the others? It's time we had a little talk
and decided what to do."*

❧

"Fascinating." Constant rubbed a meditative finger
against his lip. "I'd suspected I'd left some behind, though
I attempted to gather all the psychics I could—latent, reces-
sive, or active—bring them here to safety, away from the
Plumbs. Our only hope for surviving, so I thought then, lay
in continuing to broadcast for rescue, reach the stars with
our mind signals. And we've survived over two hundred
years with no response. Arrogant, wasn't I? But everything
was intertwined with my desire to reach Carrick.

"There were more of us than you might have expected in
that original Spacer complement: communications officers,
doctors, psycho-linguists for dealing with any intelligent in-
digenous life forms." He hmm-hawed to himself. "Amazing
how we missed the ghatti. Amazing oversight. At any rate,
Resonant powers were always viewed as invasive, faintly
suspect, even by those who depended on us and should have
appreciated our powers. Thought I'd muddied the last link to
our existence when I destroyed every copy of old Tavistock's *Journey to Marchmont* that I could beg, borrow, or
steal. One of my last acts, and I felt sorry for the poor, meddling fool, but his curiosity and his lists could have been the
death of us. I didn't know what it might reveal in the wrong
hands."

Doyce nodded, numb. Once you accepted that Constant
Minor truly was Venable Constant, and well over two hundred years old, surviving on illicit Olde Earth technology,
anything was possible. Callis's words had been an abstrac-
tion, he was the reality. Her fumbling attempts to explain the
Gleaners had been instantly understood and expanded upon.

Vesey's medallion as a talisman for his Gleaner powers
had made Constant scoff, then soften. "Poor, misguided
child. Not really necessary for Resonants. We use such
things as a childhood training aid or mental crutch on occasion. Might be suitable to bring Eadwin up to snuff if the
Bannerjees let me have a hand in his training. But what as-
tounds me," and he swallowed hard, "was how he learned to

aster pain, use it as an enhancement to augment his powers
 such an early age. It should have killed him by all rights.
Ve were taught it after years of training as a last-ditch
urvival effort, not to be taken lightly, toyed with, or
erverted."

He patted her shoulder. "You fed off Vesey's pain—
advertently—in his final funeral pyre. Your own psychic
ain as well. I saw the explosion of power, the faces of peo-
e known and unknown bursting across the skies like fire-
orks. I sensed it all the way here, wondering what power
d woken. You don't exhibit the trait now, but if it's still
ithin you, best unlearn it. It should have burned your brain
ean or launched you as a full-fledged Resonant, no half-
easures."

"Khar and the ghatti saved me, reminded me what Truth
as, what Vesey wasn't." She clasped her hands, staring
own at them, ashamed. "I would have failed, died, without
em, but the psychic wounds were deep, some still not
aled."

"You may be one of us yet. You're fallow ground, waiting
 be seeded." He beamed, pleased with his metaphor until he
w her cringing reaction. Callis internally chided him. *"Im-
rtinent old man! You know full well what went on up there
st night. It's closer than she thinks in many ways."*

Melodramatic, but he couldn't resist: the quickest, least
inful way to descend from the loft was with the rope and
lley that hauled up the hay bales. Making sure the end was
cured, he fitted his foot into the hook like a stirrup,
rapped his arms around the rope, and swooped down, giv-
g a yell of triumph and warning as he swung by, pendu-
ming back and forth until the rope lost momentum and he
mped free.

Parse applauded his entrance, eyes shining in his pale,
raped face. But Doyce wheeled away from a private con-
rsation with Constant. She looked as if she'd gone too
ng sleepless, face drawn, eyes puffy and bruised-looking,
most as she had when she'd been sick of life, cowering in
r room at his mother's. The memories of those days still
hed, but after last night they'd faded, a bad dream dis-

pelled once and for all. Joy in his heart and mind, union
partaking of each other at last!

"How are you feeling?" One finger pressed the bandage
on his arm, the rest of her remote. Then, impatiently, "I
there trouble? What do you want?"

"You!" He couldn't help himself, kissed her full on the
mouth, drawing her to him. No response in her body, or in
her eyes, but Khar threw him an annoyed look, mirroring
Rawn's whispered warning not to press. He'd blown it, one
word and he'd been deluded, overwhelmed by himself, not
reading her emotions, her needs. And, he sensed, no leeway
no chance to make amends, though he could try. "Doyce
I'm sorry. Like a fool I assumed after last night ..." Bes
stop there, not dig himself in deeper.

"It was what you wanted, wasn't it? What you yearned
for, another conquest?" The words took his breath away, a
blatant injustice after such intimate sharing. Then, defiant
"It was what I wanted, too, so don't become swell-headed
about it."

Stumbling, reeling from the blows her words inflicted, he
reached for her mind to openly reveal how he felt, touched
only adamant blockage. Where had the communion gone
where was it when he needed it? In despair he caught a wave
of sympathy from Arras, *"It's not you, but the hurt is still
lodged within her. She's taking out her fears on you."*

She marched toward him, close enough to whisper. "Now
forget it, pretend it never happened, or those bonds may kill
us and everyone else we care for!"

Disconsolate, weary beyond belief, he slumped beside
Parse and Sarrett, envious of their intimacy, their clasped
hands. Jacobia brought him bread and cheese, a mug of wa
ter, and he ate, ate because he was starving, both for food
and compassion.

At length Muscadeine helped him limp up into the loft
"Rest. I'll send Nakum up to keep watch from above. When
you can, spell him. Try to take your mind off her. She can'
cope with the potential inside her, the potential inside you
And now her daylight fears are worse than any nightmares."

After a wearing morning and afternoon of inaction, the
sounds of battle resounded outside, moving closer throug

the narrow streets. Horses neighing and stamping, frenzied galloping, and the few horses remaining in the barns preoccupied by their brethrens' exaltations and fears, restless in their stalls, eyes rolling. The clash of swords and pikes, the swish and thunk of misdirected quarrels, screams, hoarse shouts and growls, a whiff of burning, the scent of blood all filtered through the thick walls of the barn, leaving Doyce in limbo, trapped in the still center of chaos.

Sidonie besieged itself, fighting having spread from the castle all the way through the city to the defending walls. What forces awaited them outside remained another threat. How much more could she stand? Jenret hugging his hurts to him, cast away after revealing himself to her, she'd ruthlessly excised him to save them both. Constant's implicit promise—threat?—that she could be a Resonant. No escape from those or from the barn itself.

She stepped back from the shutter peephole where she'd been monitoring the action and motioned Arras to take her place. He pressed close, jostling her, and she flinched at the contact as if it burned. His mustache tickled her temple as he spoke, "It's only a matter of time. Sometimes things build of their own momentum, carried by the weight of events, and woe to anyone who tries to stop it. It doesn't matter if you're talking about your own life or about war." The mixture of personal with outside events caught her off-guard.

"One side or the other will explore the barns, claim them as a rallying point or for a defensive stand. Let's just hope it's Roland and his troops. Blessed Lady, would that I were at his side, not cooped up here!" This close she could see the bruises and chaffed flesh ringing his neck, the scab on his forehead where the helmet had rubbed its implacable steel against his skin. How had he been able to bear being imprisoned in it, cut off from the world? He smiled. "There are ways and ways to be cut off."

She ignored his comment, knew it cut too close to home. "Do we have any idea who's winning?" So far Marchmontian fought against Marchmontian, Maurice's supporters against Roland's hastily rallied troops, many from Muscadeine's old command, and folk supporting Eadwin. They fought with a crazed desperation, ignoring the Canderisian forces slowly forming outside the city, waiting for Roland to capture the gates and admit them. And when they did, would the Marchmontians lay aside their grievances and unite against their common foe?

He stood, silent, concentrating, before he answered; she'd gotten used to that, knew he sought for silent voices, voices that might tell him who prevailed. Still, it rocked her to the very core of her knowledge to accept it as a function as natural as breathing. Because that was what Jenret had entrusted her with last night when they'd made love, his mind searching hers, interweaving with hers as generously and as passionately as their bodies had woven together. And now in the light of day, she confessed to her irrational fear of that ultimate union, despite its transcendent perfection of the night before. How else to explain her inability to look Jenret in the face this morning?

Arras smiled again, as if he'd read her mind, though she knew he'd set himself the task of not doing that without permission, his previous remark no more than an empathic guess. "Touch and go. I can advise, and I have. To be out there, sword in hand, shouting orders to my troops! But my paramount duty is to protect Eadwin. What mockery to win a throne if Eadwin is killed before he can sit on it? So I must bear my burden, and Roland his, as ill-suited as we both may be for our tasks. He's set up a wedge to drive through for the gates, but a maneuver like that makes some think he's ready to flee the city, that Maurice has prevailed. The tide turns every little while, them, then us, them again."

She backed a few steps, his frustration at being penned in striking a responsive chord within her, frustrated by everything that ran through her in contradictory patterns of hope and fear, longing and dread. "Don't you think finding Eadwin and us safe and sound might reassure your people and mine? Instead, we're dependent on Maurice's tender mercies if his side discovers us! Have Roland rescue us before he seizes the gates!" At the sharp tone of rising panic in Doyce's voice, Sarrett turned from where she knelt by her window watch-post, looked hurriedly away, feigning disinterest. Suddenly she had a feeling that everyone was watching her, scrutinizing her and Arras to deduce their fate from their actions.

"Well, then, feel free to go out and meet them. Tender my regards to Roland if you feel safer visible than invisible." The bow he swept her mimicked the irony of his words as another wave of fighting exploded outside the barred door.

Not trusting herself to answer, she spun on her heel and walked away.

She roamed purposelessly through the dimly lit barn, as directionless as her spinning emotions. After having been the focus of all eyes moments earlier, she realized now that the others took great pains to ignore her agitation, kept to their posts to watch for attack or rescue from any direction. Jenret slept in the loft, while Nakum traded watches with him. She waved to Nakum, bow strung, arrow laid in loose position, ready if necessary. Perched on a barrel, Bard sat a little farther on, face glued to a knothole, good hand incessantly picking at his sling, unraveling a thread, while his twin stood calm, observing from a window at the opposite side. Syndar Saffron hovered over Jacobia as they both guarded a rear window. How they'd reconciled themselves, she had yet to ask. And Eadwin sat with Constant and Callis in the open center of the barn floor, intently discussing Resonant skills, diplomacy, the mantle of leadership. A thousand and one things she didn't want to know or even consider. Futile, everything was so futile! The ghatti prowled, here then there, restless, listening for word from outside.

And then she heard it, the muffled roar of a crowd, everyone stiffening at the sound. The roar separated into individual shouts and curses, yells of anger, and a steady, monotonous chant. "Outsiders! Kill the foreigners! Kill the ghatti!" Another voice, deep and bellowing, vibrated the very beams of the barn. "Death to all foreigners! In here, boys! Only place we haven't searched!"

The ram boomed against the door, the crowd giving an echoing growl like a lower gut rumbling until elbow slams against abdomen to quell the sound. Hungry for blood. Rhythmic pounding against the double doors of the barn, dull clangings of doom. Too late for Roland or the Guardians now! She threw her minor weight on the door, holding the bar from bouncing clear of its rickety braces, straining beside Syndar Saffron and Arras, who'd both rushed to the door. The battering ran swung again, its blows transmitted to her own body. "How many!" she gasped.

Syndar leaned his back and shoulders against the door, dug heels into the dirt and settled himself. "Nearly twenty on the ram, crushed so tight it's a wonder they can find a grip. More behind them, eager as well." His bald, bullet-shaped head glistened, forehead wrinkling with stress as he absorbed the next blow, heels gouging deep.

Arras caught his eye, made a gesture at the bar. "Shall we invite them in for sociability's sake, then?"

What he was talking about? Was he mad? But comprehension and calculation sparked Syndar's violet eyes. "Odds are in their favor if they all pour through. Doors counterweighted, are they?"

"We open just as they swing the ram, let momentum do the rest. Nakum can hold the others at bay with his arrows until we can slam the doors shut and welcome our guests."

"A risk," Syndar allowed, "but a controlled risk. We fight the whole pack at once, so twenty sounds reasonable. Wager on who scores higher—Marchmont or Canderis?" He spat on his palm, shook Arras's hand to seal the bet. "Let's do it!" And Arras and Syndar began to slide the bar free from its brackets.

❧

Swan's horse reared, forelegs desperately pawing air as the gelding tried to win through the four soldiers hemming it in, grabbing at its reins. Koom spun on the pommel platform, striking at anyone within reach, fending off one, then another as Swan's sword darted. She harbored no illusions; she was fighting for her life and for Koom's, and the thought ravaged her soul. To kill was not the Seeker way. And despite herself, despite her danger, what occupied her mind was Doyce, Doyce accusing her of forcing her to kill her stepson Vesey.

"Survive first! Moralize later!" Koom snarled and raked a hand groping for the bridle. **"On your right!"**

She reacted without thinking, smashed the basket of her sword into the nose of the soldier nearest her, a satisfying geyser of blood erupting, then backhanded her sword butt into the bloody mess. The soldier staggered back. How in the hells had she gotten separated from the others? Seekers Veritas were serving only as message senders, stationed at strategic posts, the ghatti as well as Yulyn, Davvy, and old Farnham relaying instructions about troop deployment, Roland's efforts to secure the gates. And under strict orders, her orders, to be precise, not to be caught up in the battle, retreat from danger, fight only to save one's life.

When the gates had swung open, fighting had spilled outside the walls, Roland's outnumbered soldiers battling with a fierce exultation as they lured their foes toward the Guardians. Their heroic foolhardiness had spurred the Canderisians into action before the Monitor could even give the order to advance, and for long moments, no one was in command.

He'd sat his horse, dumbfounded before finding his voice. "Swan, if they fight that passionately, pray they never overcome their differences and decide to unite against us." The Guardians had reacted with much the same awe and trepidation; all their training a paltry imitation of the reality of war that the Marchmontians had already experienced.

A ragged cheer grew sustained and full as the Canderisian banners were unfurled, each staff tied with lavender and white streamers to commemorate the late Queen and the future King Eadwin; Roland had been insistent on that. Drums rattled, trumpets skirled, overpowering in their excitement.

It was then that the Gleaner Davvy had caused her predicament. Unable to contain his fervor, he'd ripped a banner from where it had been planted and had pell-melled into the shifting battle zone, waving his flag, an exuberant cry falling from childish lips. The battle had swallowed him whole before her eyes.

Goading her horse toward the roiling bodies, she'd discovered Darl Allgood, the High Conciliator, in possession of a war steed and riding double, a young Transitor perched behind him. "Go back!" he'd yelled. "You can't find him in this press. We can!"

That struck her as doubtful. "Two can cover twice as much ground," she'd shouted back, wasn't sure if he'd heard. For a moment she thought she spied a wobbling banner, lower than its mates, pointed it out.

"Now, Faertom! Call him back!" Completely baffled by Darl's command, she'd seen the young Transitor take on the same intent, farseeing expression she'd viewed on Yulyn's face when she'd tried to make contact with the Marchmontians. Before she could determine what it all meant, the Transitor slid free of the saddle and dove into the tail end of the struggle, and emerged with Davvy kicking in his arms as he tossed him up in front of Allgood. Holding the stirrup, the Transitor ran beside the horse as they sped off. And now she was stranded out here, alone.

She could see reinforcements running to join the soldiers attacking her, at least five more. And they, she judged with sick precision, were a great deal closer than Transitor Faertom, if that was his name, now astride another horse and pounding back in her direction. Allgood followed in his wake, apparently having deposited Davvy behind the lines. Likely she'd be pulled from her horse, captured or killed long before they could break through to her.

"Duck pins, Koom!" Inspiration overtook her, or perhaps insanity; she'd decide later if there was one, and trusted the ghatt to read her mind. Without hesitation the ruddy ghatt launched himself, a seething mass of fur with four sets of lethal claws splayed and lashing the air. He landed like a bladed nightmare on the face and chest of the nearest soldier, claws ripping against armor and unprotected flesh. Shrieking in demented terror the soldier stumbled into the arms of the man tight behind him, and they both crashed in a tangle of arms and legs. Swan used the space to wheel her horse and dispatch the remaining soldier with her sword. Then, holding her gelding in place for a moment, she 'spoke Koom to her and began to race like a demon for her own lines. She never saw the pike that took her from behind, pinning her to the pommel platform and pushing Koom aside.

The doors swung inward, the battering ram's momentum carrying the rioters halfway into the barn before they could halt. Nakum's bow twanged and thrummed, forcing the rest to duck out of arrow-range while Syndar and Arras slammed the doors shut.

Nine to a side, the interlopers dropped the ram, and in practiced unison drew swords that shrieked like ripped silk from their sheaths. The first sword thrust revealed that this was no untrained, ignorant rabble, but some disguised, elite troop prepared for their mission. Jockeying for position, they double-teamed Doyce, Arras, Syndar and Byrta, while only a single swordsman each bothered to engage the wounded Bard and Parse, Sarrett, and a badly frightened Jacobia. Other swordsmen herded the unarmed Eadwin, Constant, and Callis to the barn's center, Eadwin shielding Constant's body with his own, interjecting himself between the sword's point and Constant. Nakum's bow sang, and Sarrett's attacker dropped, arrow feathering his neck.

Wasting no time, Sarrett spun and dispatched Parse's attacker with a stab to his chest, and then paired herself with Doyce. Reassured that their Bonds were protected, T'ss and Khar raced clear to create havoc where they could. She'd never credited Sarrett as a skilled swordswoman, an almost textbook perfection and precision enhanced by a ferocious, driving anger. She strove to emulate that skill, meld it into a flawless teamwork that let her rise above her own usual utilitarian parry and thrust. A double duet of steel singing in her ears, they rallied to beat off Jacobia's attacker, sent her scrambling up the loft ladder.

A shrill whistle pierced her concentration as a figure sailed across her line of vision, spooking her so badly she nearly dropped her sword. Like black terror incarnate it swept past, sword flashing, the most beautiful sight she'd ever seen—Jenret swinging clear from the loft on the lift rope, Rawn perched on his shoulders, launching into a penultimate arc that sent the howling ghatt into a knot of stunned combatants. Jenret swung back, still slashing as he went.

But one flaw to Jenret's dramatic entrance revealed itself with stark clarity as she dodged her distracted opponent and waded into the thick of things. Jenret's swooping journey had catapulted Bard and Parse into a cluster of the enemy, one of them armed with a sword she'd never seen the like of before. Near as long as she was tall, the flat, double-edged blade a good palm-width wide, and the man welding it was equally imposing. Gregor, the giant, ice-cold man in Maurice's entourage that first day. He made a little salute of acknowledgment in her direction. The blade riveted her, she could envision it slicing through a side of beef—or a man—with one powerfully casual stroke. The blade began a deceptively low, lazy curve, scattering everyone from its path, except for Parse and Per'la, frozen in disbelief. The sword sliced through Per'la's beautiful, plumed tail and thwacked into Parse's thigh with meaty greed.

With a negligent twist of thick, corded wrists, Gregor backed the blade clear, sending it on a reverse plane to carve Bard's side just below the rib cage. Sick with fear, knowing she was too late, she fought toward them alone, Sarrett abandoning her to rush to Parse.

But Byrta arrived before her, berserker scream curdling the air, and three men in her path never heard another sound. With a desperate twist Bard evaded the broadsword, beat it off course with his own before the sword scythed through his blade like a flower stem. The twins stood firm, Byrta flanked just ahead of Bard, identical death's-head grins splitting their faces. P'wa and M'wa jumped for Gregor's sword hand and with a flick of the wrist almost too fast to see, he slammed the weighted hilt into P'wa's head, crushing it, batting M'wa aside with the back of his hand. Teeth bared in a snarl, Byrta lunged for the kill to avenge her Bond, regardless of her own safety, and the sword glissaded to caress her neck, slashed off her head.

Bard dove to catch the severed head, cradled it as he murmured and crooned to it, kissing the lips. It was the most bizarrely strange yet touching gesture Doyce had ever encountered. Two pairs of twins, severed, bereft. One Bond that remained. Hearts that would never beat in tandem again. M'wa let out a high-pitched scream of anguish and Khar joined in.

"Hold! Or the old fool dies!" Sick, overwhelmed by loss, appalled at the carnage, she heard but scarcely comprehended, everything alien and extraneous to her emotions. Casting a dazed look over her shoulder, she saw Maurice, backed by Aelbert, Jampolis, and a squad of soldiers had burst into the barn from the hidden tunnel. Maurice poised his sword at Constant's throat, the old man's chin held high, straining to avoid the point. Three men restrained Eadwin and two others guarded the unmoving Callis. Unwilling, Doyce let her sword sag, the others doing the same one by one as it sank home that they were outnumbered. "I hope you enjoyed my little distraction."

Her sword jerked ungently from her hand, she paid it bare heed as she registered the frozen tableau. A burst of anger rocketed through her; she'd forfeit life and soul to destroy Aelbert for his final betrayal, even if it meant summoning up the wild mindpowers Vesey had exploited. She strained for them, but it was not to be; despite herself, a surge of pity for Aelbert washed over her. Sick with uneasiness, part and yet not part of the group, he remained at the fringes. To never belong anywhere, never claimed, never acknowledged. Constant stood nearly on tiptoe now, the sword blade whisking strands of snow-white beard from one side to the other. A severed strand floated downward. The corners of Constant's mouth curved in a taunting smile. "So I'm to be clean-shaven again? Like my portrait, no doubt."

"Oh, I don't think that's really necessary." Maurice's voice was as caressing as his sword, and as lethally invasive. "I'm more curious about what you have in your naked brain than what your naked face might reveal. I want to know who—and what—you are."

"All you had to do was ask, but then you've never asked, have you, Maurice? Only taken, taken without permission, taken with pain, proving once again that the blood of Venable Constant runs thin in your veins, perverted." Constant's eyes strayed to the high-beamed ceiling, flickered down as he tried to focus on the man in front of him, stare down the length of the sword. "Hardly fit to wear the crown." He sneered the last words, soft and intimate, as if only the two were present.

"And what would you do with it, old man? Constant Minor, what a fitting name, but the name alone doesn't give you the right to the throne. You held it vacant, kept it free, then oh-so-insinuatingly thrust yourself to the forefront. Where did you come from, old man? Who do you think you are? Until Wilhelmina died, I'd never even seen you around the castle, regardless of what Fabienne insists. Perhaps you were deposited on the doorstep in a basket? An antique foundling." The sword lowered, hovered over Constant's heart, and the old man viewed its circling pattern with as much interest as one would watch an insect deciding where to light—and sting. He brushed at it absently, then examined the thin tracery of blood on the palm of his hand. He licked at it, and Maurice swallowed convulsively, avid.

"I was waiting for you to regain your senses, rein in your pride,. and acknowledge Eadwin as the rightful ruler."

"And acknowledge that I'd been cuckolded? Shamed, humiliated, betrayed by my wife, that my son was not my son at all, but a royal by-blow? That the blood of Venable Constant runs so thin, as you put it, that it can only produce cuckolds and bastards?"

"Blame your failings on your warped mind, not my blood. You've corrupted everything I stood for, and you still don't understand, do you?" Constant smiled, dreamy and far away. "You never even had the sense to take the old Resonant lore, the old histories literally. What did you think it meant when they said that 'One day Venable Constant shall awake, cry out to the stars, and smite those who pervert their talents'?"

Incredulous, Maurice glared, the sword now making little jabbing feints along the old man's body, at last tracking back and forth across his paunch. "I'm not that credulous, not with a kingdom at stake." Aelbert moaned, struck by the words. "Whether you're Constant Minor or Venable Constant, legends can die either way. I've no time for more of this—the Canderisians are through the gates. Your pain will augment my powers, drive them back." He appeared to notice Eadwin for the first time. "Watch all your followers die," he jeered, "and you'll have a hint of an idea of what awaits you."

In the barn loft, Doyce heard a rustling no louder than a mouse, and she strained not to glance toward it, betray her discovery, because she suspected he'd run out of arrows. Nakum surreptiously worked his way around to Jacobia's refuge. She surmised Constant, too, had identified the sound but was ignoring it. Indeed, his expression went blank and distant as if he fixated on something hard to reach. Callis nodded her head. At length he came back to himself, "Eh?" he asked. "What were we saying?"

The apparent forgetfulness drove Maurice to the brink of frenzy, sword point jabbing and retreating, poking and prodding around Constant's plump belly. Constant tracked the moving sword's point and began to giggle, as if it tickled. "Oh, I'll see Eadwin king and you in the furthest reaches of the starry hells for warping your Resonant's gift!"

"Well, if it's perversion you want, I'm sure I can afford you that pleasure—and myself as well." Face flushed, Maurice panted with excitement, arm shaking from holding the sword. "I'd planned to be kind, a gentleman as befits one of my stature—"

"Not so much stature, as girth, wouldn't you say?" Constant interrupted, giggling again, taunting and goading, almost leaning into the sword. "Are you really sure you want to do this?"

"That does it!" Maurice exploded. "Jampolis! Map the cuts for maximum pain! If it's pain you want, it's pain you'll have, pain that I'll love, bathe myself in, enhance my mindforce to twist everyone to my will! Even that puerile army of Canderisians at the gates with their few bush-colt Resonants! Marchmont and Canderis will be a magnificent prize for me, ruler, emperor of all!" The sword point froze at Constant's midsection, poised and ready.

Jampolis's scarred hand pointed to the first spot. "The cries enrich as much as the actual wounds, you know. How many gut stabs can you stand, how many can you suffer before you beg Maurice to kill you?"

"Only way to find out is to try and see." Constant beamed, arms outspread, waiting.

Face twisted with hatred, Maurice slammed the sword into Constant's gut, and a surge of electricity dashed up the blade, enveloped him in a halo of blue light, until he looked as if he'd been struck by lightning. Maurice danced and jerked convulsively in the arc of light, and the smell of charring flesh seeped through the air.

Constant smiled, but his outline contracted, his whole body beginning to shrink and collapse in on itself. "Knew I had enough charge left to do it," he said to no one in particular as his skin turned leathery, everything about him dessicating, almost petrifying before their eyes as he shriveled and died. Maurice jerked once more and dropped to the floor.

As Eadwin screamed and tried to break free, Aelbert dove for Jampolis, slammed a knife between his ribs. With the last of his strength Jampolis clamped his scarred hands on Aelbert's head, beginning to wipe his mind clean and empty. N'oor rowled with shared agony as she tried to claw Jampolis's hands free, but the infusion of pain only empowered him. Hands locked on Jampolis's wrists, Aelbert managed to pry him loose long enough to shout an anguished plea toward the loft. "Cousin! Set us free, I beseech you!"

Mouth gaping, Nakum came upright in the loft, bow dangling from lax hands. A scream of renewed agony galvanized him and he clutched his earth-bond, drawing on its power. Still he hesitated, then wrenched open his pouch and slipped the arborfer ring over the shaft of his arrow, sent it soaring to find the middle of Aelbert's back, his final arrow following fast after, releasing N'oor from her misery. "Thank you, cousin!" Aelbert murmured as his eyes went blank.

❖

PART
NINE

❖

Mahafny conferred with Wyn Bannerjee, amplified on a possible surgical technique, then reseated herself beside Swan's cot. She eyed the pile of dirty bandages and the basin of bloody water with distaste, and an orderly swooped to remove the offending objects. Even three days after the battle it was still impossible to impose order on the impromptu tent hospices. The fighting had been intense but short, Maurice's and Jampolis's deaths had taken the heart out of their supporters, some of whom looked like sleepwalkers awakened as Maurice's compulsion over them faded with his demise.

More than enough wounded and dying to go around, a waste of life, of human potential, but less waste than there might have been, she decided. But she couldn't cope with the needless waste of Swan. She shared a worried glance with Koom, huddled at the foot of the bed. They'd managed to reinflate Swan's lung, but she harbored few hopes. The wound was nasty, already infected despite their best efforts, and Swan was too weak to travel to better facilities for a long time.

With a start she realized Saam sat at her feet, near but aloof. "Where's Nakum? Did you misplace him?" She strove to make it a joke, but sensed she'd failed miserably as yellow eyes regarded her, unblinking. Despite her better judgment she trace a finger down his spine, longed to press him against her legs for the wordless consolation he projected.

Swan opened her eyes slowly at the sound of her cousin's voice, focused on Saam. "Don't deny him again, Mahafny," she rasped. Mahafny tried to shush her, busied herself by taking her pulse, unwilling to meet the imploring eyes. Her hands shook so much nowadays that she could barely manage that, hadn't chanced any surgery during this crisis, had contented herself with supervising.

Harsher than intended to quell her traitorous yearning, she

answered back, "He has Nakum. He doesn't need me." Found she couldn't bring herself to utter the ghatt's name, though she whispered it in her heart.

A coughing fit seized Swan, white face turning scarlet with stress. "He does. Are you too busy to know what happens around you?" Mahafny raised her head, tilted the water glass to Swan's lips, saw she drank thirstily. "Nakum's returned to the mountains with Callis to tend the arborfers, find new ways to make them thrive again. Aelbert's death finished making a man out of him." She paused, took another swallow of water. "Saam didn't choose to go with them."

"Why not?" She swiveled to stare at the ghatt and found herself being consumed by the yellow stare, mesmerized.

"If you'll pardon the intrusion, because it's very cold up there." Not at all what she'd expected, more like trading confidences with an old and valued friend. Why her? Why not someone else? Could she reject this second generous offering of companionship, be strong enough to refuse the lure?

Swan made a fist, thumped her cousin's back. "Don't be a fool this time! You may not get another chance, you pigheaded mule of a eumedico!"

Despite herself she laughed at her cousin's irritation, wiped tears from her eyes. "My, you do concoct strange beasts!"

Swan smiled thinly. "You won't have me to annoy you much longer," and waved away her cousin's protests. "I'm no fool. Who else but Saam could put up with your arrogant, stubborn ways? Tell you the truth about yourself that you'd never listen to from me."

An act of faith, like stepping off a cliff into thin air, waiting to see what would support her, rescue her from her downward plunge. "Mindwalk if ye will," she choked the words out, and meant them with every fiber of her being.

❖

The negotiations between Canderis and Marchmont had progressed in slow increments, treaties being hammered out over three octs and with more to come. Kyril van Beieven represented Canderis, and Eadwin, soon to be crowned king of Marchmont, aided by Arras Muscadeine, newly appointed

Lord of Defense. With the Seeker General critically wounded, Doyce had found herself pressed into service against her better instincts. It was all too achingly familiar from her short tenure as Special Envoy. How things were ever accomplished she still wasn't sure—perhaps the least exhausted won in this war of words.

Walking into the tent that morning, she made a wide detour around the breakfast buffet spread at the tent's far side as she called a hello to Ignacio. The smell set her stomach churning, as it had for days. She swallowed hard, but it was no use and she exited the tent at an indecorous run, hand clutched over her mouth. Past tents she couldn't bother to identify, snaking her way between them, tripping over guy ropes, not sure how much farther she could distance herself. At last, dignity cast to the winds, she bent, retching, bile rising in her throat, sides heaving, heaving again until nothing remained, though there'd been precious little to begin with. Lady bless, what had gotten into her—or more precisely, out of her?

She knelt, exhausted and trembling, tears streaming from the force of the explosion within her. Handkerchief—she knew she had one somewhere, where? She fumbled until someone thrust a damp cloth into her hand. Grateful, she wiped her mouth, refolded the cloth, wiped the rest of her face, still bent double, not bothering to look up.

"So, how long has this been going on?" Mahafny inquired, helping her to a bench she hadn't even noticed. Legs splayed, she rested forearms on her knees, still spent. She swallowed, winced at the taste in her mouth, and found a beaker of water thrust into her hand. "Rinse and spit first. You've already decorated the landscape, so I doubt they'll notice a mite more." Mahafny kicked dirt over the spot where she'd spewed. "Small sips, don't gulp. Give it a rest, see if it settles."

"I know." She tried to rise, avoiding Mahafny's face. "I have to get back now, they're about ready to begin. We're discussing sharing Resonant training knowledge. You should be there as well." The water sloshed over her hand, and she rubbed it dry against her tabard. She could feel the coolness of Mahafny's restraining hand through her sleeve, knew she wasn't going to get away this easily.

"Doyce, what is it? How long has this been happening?"

The eumedico waited for her to describe the symptoms, head cocked to one side, understanding, concerned. "I have to know. What if it's illness, some sort of disease running rampant through the wounded, the weak after the battle?"

She managed as much of a smile as she was able. "It's hardly an illness, Mahafny. At least you never indicated during my training years that pregnancy was an illness, simply a natural occurrence, you indicated."

"Pregnant?" Mahafny neutralized her voice. "Arras Muscadeine's child? I've noticed the way he looks at you, how solicitous he acts."

She sat again, the older woman sitting heavily beside her. "It's more complicated than that, Mahafny."

And now the older woman's face drained of color, her worst fears racing to the fore. "Not Jenret? You know his heredity! What are you going to do about it! He's just come into his own powers as a Resonant. I'm still striving to figure out how to train them, to channel their powers productively, for their own good, for everyone's good. Do you want to bring a child with that potential into the world?"

"I don't know. I just don't know." She looked up sharply at Mahafny. "And Jenret doesn't know about this. It's not up to you to tell him. Not until I've decided."

The day-long meetings had anodyned the anguish of the decision she faced. She'd been utterly truthful this morning in confessing to Mahafny that she didn't know what she was going to do. And still didn't know. The canvas walls of the tent closed in on her, even Sarrett's light sleep-breaths a distraction. Pulling the covers higher over Sarrett, exhausted from nursing Parse, she tickled T'ss's flank and abruptly left the tent.

"**Would a walk by the river help?**" Khar shadow-swirled at her side. Interestingly, the ghatta and Saam had been conspicuously absent at this morning's meeting with Mahafny.

"I'm not sure anything will help." She kicked at a stone, morose. *"Khar, what am I going to do? What should I do? Help me know what's right, what's best!"*

Khar's heart tore with the agony of Doyce's plea. **"Take**

a step," she insisted, ever practical. **"Any journey, whether to the river or the unknown, begins with a single step."**

Stooping, she pretended to box the ghatta's ears, cupped the pointed face instead. "Such philosophy! Well, I think I can put one foot in front of the other and at least arrive at the river, if not a decision." Concerned about being noticed, she avoided the trampled paths, slipped through the make-shift tent city toward the beckoning river, glinting pale dapples in the moonlight. The scene promised peace. Whether insight thrived there remained to be seen.

Khar kept pace with her until they were clear of the tents, then darted ahead and turned to face Doyce, eyes glowing. **"Do you want the child?"** and prayed to the Elders her Bond's answer would be yes. Selfish, perhaps, but she yearned for a ghatten-child to watch over, play with, guide—especially this ghatten-child.

"I . . . yes." The response jolted out of her, took her by surprise. *"Yes, I do."* And admitted for the first time that she truly did want this unique being tucked inside her. More unique than she dared anticipate, truth be known, but she didn't care.

Unsure whether to press her luck, Khar continued gingerly, **"Do you want Jenret?"**

Doyce paused, ready to clamber over a stone to reach the shelf of the bank. *"And that, love, is what I don't know. I'm so afraid of what he's becoming, of what he could become."* Sitting, she began to strip off boots and stockings, dangled her feet in the water. *"There's so much potential for evil, for such misuse of Gleaner . . ."* she corrected herself, impatient, *"Resonant power. I panic when I think about Vesey and Evelien, about Maurice and Jampolis. About Jenret's brother Jared. Jenret's so intense, so quick to let emotion sway him. Does he have the willpower, the strength to control this gift or will it control him? What is his destiny?"* She shrugged. *"What's mine, for that matter?"*

Settling herself against Doyce's side, Khar sensed the bitterness behind the words, bitterness and wistfulness. But for a moment all she could do was sigh with pleasure as Doyce's hand rested on her back. **"Jenret is himself, no one else. You humans do take a very long time to grow up. You could grow up together."**

"Take our first steps together on that unknown journey, you mean?" She sighed, knuckled one tear that had trickled

free. *"Frankly, after this I thought I was pretty well traveled."*

"Ah, toe dabbling, are we?" Doyce started at Arras's voice behind her shoulder, noticed that Khar didn't act the least perturbed by his sudden appearance. Keener hearing, obviously. "May I join you lovely ladies? I heard Khar calling for me, saying you craved my advice." Rich laughter, "Rarely does anyone crave my advice. An opportunity not to be missed!"

"Khar, why did you 'speak him? Why are you dragging him into this? I thought this was private between the two of us!" She gave the ghatta a little shake and Khar went limp in injured innocence.

"Because I want to share you with him, have him convince you of the goodness that resides in Jenret, within most Resonants."

"Come, tell Uncle Arras what the problem is," he coaxed.

"I'm pregnant and I'm afraid."

Astonishment, but he covered it well. "Afraid of what?"

"Of the unknown, the unknown within myself, and the unknown within Jenret. What will he be like when his Resonant powers are truly developed? What if it transforms him beyond my ken?"

Sinking onto the bank beside her, he hooked his heels over the edge, lazily tossed a pebble into the river. "Afraid of the ripples, are you? Afraid they might rock your safe little boat, capsize you?" He tossed another pebble, harder this time, as if to express a concealed anger. "Did I change in your eyes when you discovered I was a Resonant?"

Stung, she quickly shook her head. "A little, perhaps, another facet added to you, but basically, no. I guess because I already knew you, or thought I knew you." She plunked a pebble in the direction Arras had thrown his.

"Come, that won't work. Let me show you something else." Exasperated, he jumped up, pulled her to her feet, began hunting on the bank.

"What?" she exclaimed, "Did you lose something?"

"No, you've lost something, obviously your sanity. You know Jenret far better than you know me." He displayed a flat stone in the palm of his hand, grasped it between thumb and first two fingers, cocked his arm. The stone skimmed across the water, hit once, hit twice, skittered on to strike five more times. "Only seven," he feigned disappointment.

"I usually manage eight, but you've distracted me. Perhaps it was eight, but the moonlight's weak."

"So?"

He grasped her shoulders, forced her to face him. "So, it rebounded, and rebounded, and rebounded. Don't you think you and Jenret can rebound just as well? You don't have to sink like a pebble just because someone tosses you into new surroundings."

She groped for a stone, tried to duplicate his feat. It hit twice and sank.

"Practice is everything. Along with faith and hope and love." He kissed her cheek, his mustache tickling. "Good night. Think on what I've said, but I don't want to hear you shying stones all night. The river's rocky enough." He pressed one into her hand. "Keep this one as a memento."

"He's a wise man—and a handsome one." Khar teased.

"Don't try to distract me, love. You've both connived to prod me into some serious thinking tonight and for the next few nights."

♣

"Doyce!" He caught up with her that night after supper, the sky already dark, just one faint streak of crimson still in the air. It seemed important to her to watch that last streak fade, as if when it were gone, she'd known what to do. She'd promised herself that. She tossed a flat stone into the air, caught it, and put it away safe. No heads or tails to it. What was she, what wasn't she? And did it matter as long as she tried her best? Not Resonant yet, perhaps never, perhaps someday. Time to live in the present, not crippled by fears of the past or the future. "Doyce!" A hand on her arm eased her around, but she twisted in the direction of the west. "Are you all right? Mahafny said you haven't been well. You haven't looked yourself lately."

The crimson streak faded and she knew. A rightness, a symmetry to it she couldn't deny, not as she'd denied so many things before. She began to walk and he followed, still linking her arm, trying to turn her toward him, trying to read her expression in the growing darkness. "How's Parse doing?" she asked absently. What the enemy broadsword hadn't accomplished, the eumedicos had, amputating the leg. While his own injuries healed, Jenret had been spending time helping Mahafny with the wounded, helping Bard and M'wa grieve for the loss of their twins, relearn life as a single Bond-pair. His gait was still stiff, as if bending his knees hurt incredibly.

"Languishing in Sarrett's arms, at the moment," he joked and then immediately sobered. "I wish you'd languish in my arms sometimes."

She rounded on him, hands on hips and he waited for the sharp retort he sensed coming. Instead, a small, serious voice demanded, "Jenret, will you marry me?"

"Doyce, I . . . I . . ." he stuttered, shock numbing his mouth. So much he wanted, so much he'd never dared hope for, but he hadn't expected this. Learning to understand each other was gift enough to ask at first. "D . . . d . . . don't you think you're rushing a bit? I know you've reservations about me, reservations about yourself. There's time, love. Just give us time and we'll work the doubts through."

"Then you don't want to marry me?"

He stumbled and rushed again. Even if he were to read her mind, he suspected he'd never be able to second-guess her. "I didn't say that. I'd do it in the blink of an eye. But are you sure? And why the rush? I promise not to escape." The thought of being with this woman for the rest of his life, the rest of their lives, took his breath away. "Besides, I want you to be sure you know what you're getting into. I don't know what it means to be a Resonant, and it may be more than either of us can live with, given our past histories, our past fears."

More than he knew, more than she knew right now, but there was time enough for them both to learn. Her fingers meshed with his, and she raised their hands between their chests, leaned into him. "We're already linked together, already meshed, whether we will it or not. Jenret, I want my child to have a father. But if you're not ready, the child and I can make a life for ourselves elsewhere, leave you free to pursue what you must, find who you are."

A thousand fears, large and small, real and unreal, swept over him, and hesitantly, he mentally reached to stroke her mind, willing her to invite him to enter without impediment. What he read there convinced him, told him that she would be his safe harbor if he would be hers, no matter what storms of fear or mistrust swept through and tried to wreck them.

He freed one hand, dug into his pocket, his fingers closing on the ring he'd knotted into the end of his handkerchief, Rolf's family heirloom. They'd found it in Aelbert's pocket, still wrapped in a screw of paper with Rolf's final message: "Marry her, you fool! Don't let her get away, she's worth the effort." And beneath that, Aelbert's hastily scrawled note: "He's right. I'm sorry for everything, but I'll try to redeem myself."

With his other hand he raised hers to his lips, formally kissed it. "Wilt thou, Doyce Marbon, do me the honor of marrying me?" He slipped the ring on her finger, conscious that the handkerchief still billowed below like a white flag. *"I surrender, heart, mind, and soul to you if you will share yours with me."*

Rawn glanced at Khar from where they crouched in the bushes. **"One step at a time,"** she murmured. **"And now I know what sharing truly means."** Restraining himself, Rawn gave her ear a rough lick of encouragement.

In Memoriam
TULIP
7 November 1973—17 November 1993

May you see with eyes of light in everdark, may your mind walk free and unfettered amongst all, touching wisely and well, may you go in peace. But wait for me, beloved.

GAYLE GREENO

☐ **THE GHATTI'S TALE:**
  Book 1—Finders, Seekers   UE2550—$5.50
The Seekers Veritas, an organization of truth-finders composed of Bondmate pairs—one human, one a telepathic, cat-like ghatti—is under attack. And the key to defeating this deadly foe is locked in one human's mind behind barriers even her ghatta has never been able to break.

☐ **MINDSPEAKER'S CALL**
  The Ghatti's Tale: Book 2   UE2579—$5.99
Someone seems bent on creating dissension between Cand-eris and the neighboring kingdom of Marchmont. And even the truth-reading skill of the Seekers Veritas may not be enough to unravel the twisted threads of a conspiracy that could see the two lands caught in a devastating war . . .

☐ **EXILES' RETURN**
  The Ghatti's Tale: Book 3   UE2655—$5.99
Seeker Doyce is about to embark on a far different path—a ghatti-led journey into the past. For as a new vigilante-led reign of terror threatens the lives of Seekers and Resonants alike, the secrets of that long-ago time when the first Seeker-ghatti Bond was formed may hold the only hope for their future . . .
